LEGACY OF THE CURSE

By Deborah Grace White

The Kyona Chronicles Book Four

Copyright © 2020 by Deborah Grace White

First edition (v1.0) published in 2020
by Luminant Publications

The characters and events portrayed in this book are fictitious. Any similarity to real persons, living or dead, is coincidental and not intended by the author.

ISBN: 978-1-925898-34-7

Luminant Publications
PO Box 201
Burnside, South Australia 5066

http://www.deborahgracewhite.com

Cover Design by Karri Klawiter
Map illustration by Rebecca E. Paavo

For Cressida
You've never been afraid to use your voice.
I hope that never changes.

Kynton

Forest of Rune

Dragon Realm

VAS

Kerr

Montego

Pravat

KYONA

GREAT RIVER

Nerita

Argath

Alezae

MARSHLAND

NORTH L

SOUTH L

BALENOL

BASE TREE

North Wilds
ELISA
VALORIA
DRAGONCAVE
LOCH ARINE
Arinton
Basal Headlands
Wyvern Islands
Bryford
ANDS
ANDS
Razad's Bastion
Nohl
Jeweled Peaks
Thirl
THORANIA
Logging Camp
SPICE FIELDS

CHAPTER ONE

"I don't like it, Elnora, and I don't understand why you're so positive about the idea."

Jocelyn paused outside her mother's private receiving room, her hand on the doorknob. She was surprised by her father's tone of voice. It was highly unusual to hear her parents arguing. Whether because they never fought, or because they had the discretion to only do so in private, she'd never figured out.

Of course, as a princess, she'd been drilled in all matters of good etiquette, including the impoliteness of eavesdropping. But still...it was a tantalizingly rare opportunity.

"Jocelyn can handle this, Cal. You don't need to be so worried for her."

They were arguing about *her*? Now there was no way she was going to resist the temptation to eavesdrop.

"It's not about being worried," returned her father, obstinately. "You read the missive. Do I really have to explain to you why I'm not eager for either of my children to be pushed—or even prompted—into a marriage alliance? Or have you forgotten how hard *we* had to fight? I don't want her to go through the same—"

"Of course I haven't forgotten," interrupted the queen, calmly. "But no one has proposed a marriage alliance."

In spite of her raging curiosity, Jocelyn couldn't help but smile at her father's snort. It wasn't a very kingly sound.

"Are we reading the same letter?"

Jocelyn heard a rustling of paper, then her father spoke again, clearly reading aloud. "We would be delighted for Her Royal Highness Princess Jocelyn to have the opportunity to become acquainted with our son and heir, His Royal Highness Crown Prince Ormond." There was a pointed silence. "Tell me again that they're not thinking of a marriage alliance?"

"I didn't say they're not thinking of it," her mother said patiently. "Of course they are. But they haven't said as much. My point is that it's not a formal proposal of any kind, and if she goes on this visit, it won't commit us—or her—to anything."

"The whole thing is outrageous." Her father clearly wasn't listening. "She's far too young to be a marriage prospect. Isn't their crown prince twenty-five or twenty-six?"

"I'll admit, she's a little young," said her mother, and Jocelyn could picture just the way her forehead was creasing.

"A little young?" her father repeated. "She's seventeen!"

"And I was barely eighteen when we were married." The queen sounded amused now.

"But that's—"

"Let me guess, that's different?" Jocelyn's mother was definitely amused.

"It *is* different," persisted the king stubbornly. "Because we chose each other."

"Tut, tut, listening at keyholes, are we? That's not very princessly."

The whisper made Jocelyn start, the speaker unexpectedly

close to her ear. But she didn't feel embarrassed to be caught eavesdropping. She knew that voice as well as her own, and there wasn't much she'd be ashamed for him to know about her. She'd caught him in plenty of worse exploits, after all.

"Quiet, Eamon," she shushed, gesturing for her twin to drop his voice still lower. "They're arguing." His eyes lit with interest, and she pushed on. "About me."

"I see," he whispered back. "Fair game, then." And he placed his ear against the door.

"It's not just that she's young," their father was saying. "She's not ready for something like this. She'd be all alone over there... if this alliance happened, she'd be their queen eventually, and...I don't know, I just don't like it."

Eamon raised his eyebrows at Jocelyn, his expression saying as clearly as words, "What have I missed?"

She just grimaced, her heart sinking inexplicably at her father's words. It was no surprise that he didn't think her up to the job of being anyone's queen, given her detachment from everything of substance in their own court. And he wasn't wrong —she would bring disaster on anyone under her care, more likely than not. But still, it stung that he had so little faith in her.

"I don't want her to be far away, either, Cal," her mother was saying, so quietly that Jocelyn had to resort to pressing her ear against the door, like her brother. "But I think that this could be a good opportunity for her to stretch her wings, explore something outside of Kynton. She's not happy here. You know I'm right."

"Yes, I know." The king sounded subdued. "But I don't know why."

"Neither do I, to be honest," his wife admitted. "But she gets more withdrawn with every year that passes. And I don't know how to help her. Maybe a change of scenery—just a temporary one—will bring her out of herself."

"I don't understand it." King Calinnae sounded frustrated again. "She used to be so energetic as a child, so witty and funny and...now it's hard to get her to say two words in front of anyone outside the family. I feel like I'm failing her somehow, but I don't know what to do."

Jocelyn lowered her gaze and stepped back slightly, suddenly not wanting to hear any more. She had heard it all before, from others as well as her parents. Eamon sent her a look that was so full of sympathetic understanding that she was tempted to lean her head against his shoulder for comfort. But for all they were closer than most siblings, Eamon was still a seventeen year old boy—even he didn't want to have his shoulder cried on by his sister. If it had been Luciana looking for his affection on the other hand...

Jocelyn sighed, thoughts of her best friend just making her feel more lonely. Even Lucy didn't know the cause of Jocelyn's reserve. Maybe they had been too cautious—maybe they should have confided in their parents at least. But somehow it had been too intimate—and too frightening—a thing to share with anyone but her twin.

"Don't be too hard on her," came her mother's voice. "Or too hard on yourself, Cal. Like you said, she's young, and she's facing all kinds of pressures we don't really understand. You were raised in a tiny fishing village, and I was raised in a street gang. Neither one of us has any idea what it would be like to actually grow up royal. We're both out of our depth, if we're honest."

Come on, Eamon mouthed, clearly having heard enough. Jocelyn nodded, in total agreement. Once their mother started being hard on herself, it was time to steer the conversation in a new direction.

"Why do you think they wanted us to meet them before the meal?" Eamon asked at full volume, sending her a wink as he rattled the door handle unnecessarily loudly in the process of turning it.

She just rolled her eyes as she followed him in. Somehow, while she was willing to eavesdrop on her parents, it seemed beneath her dignity to participate in her brother's show of covering their indiscretion.

"Come in and you'll find out," said their father placidly, regarding his son with a fond eye.

Jocelyn suppressed another sigh. She knew her father loved her, but he never looked at her with such pride. He spoke to her just as warmly, but it was impossible to miss the underlying concern in his expression whenever he watched her.

"Joss," he said now, greeting her with a hug, a rare indulgence reserved for the privacy of the family.

"I'm glad you're here," said their mother, gesturing to the paper still held in her husband's hand. "We wanted to tell you about a communication we've just received from the king and queen of Valoria." Her eyes settled on her daughter as she named the kingdom that neighbored Kyona to the east. "It's about you, Jocelyn."

Jocelyn looked an inquiry, but said nothing. It was Eamon who spoke up, once again more willing to feign ignorance.

"About Joss? What do they say?"

"You may be aware that we are sending a delegation to Bryford to renegotiate our trade agreement," said the queen, her eyes still lingering on Jocelyn. "It's a routine visit. But the royal family has issued a formal invitation for Jocelyn to accompany the delegation, and to spend the summer at their castle."

"A state visit?" asked Jocelyn, her forehead slightly creased.

"Yes," cut in King Calinnae, before his wife could answer. "It would be a formal state visit."

"For what purpose?" Jocelyn pursued.

"For no specified purpose," said the queen. Jocelyn didn't

miss her father's pointed look, and her mother added, "But it seems likely that they have a marriage alliance in mind, with their oldest son, Prince Ormond. Nothing official, of course. You wouldn't be agreeing to anything. Just an opportunity to meet him, and to see something of Valoria."

Jocelyn nodded slowly, turning it over in her mind. As unexpected as the sudden invitation was, the concept that as Kyona's only princess she might be sought after by other kingdoms for a marriage alliance was not exactly new to her. She had no idea what Valoria was like, other than that they were at peace with Kyona. She could feel curiosity building alongside her nerves. Would life in the Valorian capital of Bryford be significantly different from life in Kynton?

"Do you wish me to go?" she asked at last.

"No," said her father.

Her mother answered at the same time. "I want you to consider it." Queen Elnora frowned slightly at her husband. "I want to know what *you* think—what you want."

"I wouldn't go, Joss," said Eamon, lounging comfortably against a reclining couch. "You'll miss our birthday if you're gone all summer! Plus, they're probably stiff over there, like real royals."

Even their normally serious father smiled at the family joke. Kyona's sovereigns made no apologies for some of the unorthodox notions their unusual background had introduced into life at the castle. The king's smile disappeared in an instant at his son's next words, however.

"*They're* probably not in the habit of asking princesses what they want. Once you're there, they might just order you to marry him, and then you'd be stuck."

"They certainly will not," said their father emphatically. "Jocelyn is a princess of Kyona—not to mention my daughter—

and no Valorian, royal or not, has any right to order her to do anything."

"It's all right, Father," said Jocelyn, restraining a smile. "Eamon was joking." Her father's protective streak was one of his most predictable qualities, and she and Eamon had often been unable to resist using it to get a reaction out of the normally difficult-to-ruffle king. Not that he had any idea of that, of course.

"I was only sort of joking, Joss," said her brother, his expression unusually serious. "They might push you around."

His eyes held an extra layer of meaning meant only for her, and she knew what he was leaving unsaid. She would be hampered, as always, from asserting herself the way she might want to.

"As admirable as it is that both of you boys are looking out for her," cut in Queen Elnora dryly, giving her husband and her son a look, "the whole point was to find out what Jocelyn thinks. How she's supposed to speak for herself with the two of you in the room is beyond me."

Three pairs of eyes turned expectantly toward Jocelyn, and she barely refrained from sighing. How she hated being asked her opinion. Almost as much as she frequently wished she *could* express the many very decided opinions with which her frustrated mind was crammed.

Eamon at least knew all this, and his look was once again sympathetic. She felt a little bad for him all of a sudden. He very heroically took their mother's criticism on a regular basis for his supposed tendency to speak for her instead of letting her speak for herself. The queen could have no idea that he did so because she begged him to, for everyone else's sake.

But she pushed her self-imposed reticence aside. With her family she could afford to speak her mind, at least to an extent.

"I'm not sure what I think," she said slowly, staring at the back of the letter in her father's hand as if she could read the words through the paper. "I mean, if I'm honest, I'm not exactly in a hurry to be married off for an alliance." She saw the meaningful look her father directed at her mother. "But I suppose it could be interesting to see what Valoria is like." She met the queen's eye. "Do you really think that I could go without committing to marrying their prince?"

"Absolutely," said Queen Elnora with conviction. "There would be no obligation."

"It wouldn't cause tension if they offered and we didn't accept?"

"That's not an issue, Jocelyn," said the king quickly. "We can handle tension. The question is, do you really want to find yourself away from home for the entire summer, with no support?"

She raised her eyebrows. "I thought you said they couldn't order me to do anything, Father. And surely I wouldn't be going all alone."

"Not literally alone," he conceded. "But none of us would be there." He frowned. "I would feel better about the whole idea if I could accompany you. It's been years since I've been to Bryford —not since King Gresham died, and I attended King Malcolm's coronation. It's probably time I paid another visit to our neighbors. But I can't leave while the conflict over the freedmen is unresolved."

"Conflict?" repeated Jocelyn quickly. "That's a strong word. Has it become as bad as that, Father?"

"I'm afraid so," he answered seriously. "There have even been a number of violent clashes." He took a deep breath, his expression troubled. "If things progress on their current course, I don't think it's too strong to say we're headed for a crisis."

Jocelyn exchanged a look with Eamon, alarmed. Things were much worse than she had realized.

Their father shook his head, seeming to speak almost to himself. "I just wish I knew where it was coming from."

"It does seem to have come from nowhere," said Eamon, frowning. "Was there no tension when the freedmen originally sailed here from Balenol, Father?"

"Of course there was," said King Calinnae. "The process of integrating such a large number of Kyonans, some of whom had never even set foot in the kingdom, most of whom were traumatized from being either sold or born into slavery, was never going to be straightforward. There were some who didn't want to see homes, and jobs and farmland go to the freedmen, and I won't deny that some of the former slaves were not able to put their anger and trauma behind them sufficiently to live honest lives. For the first few years we had our work cut out for us."

He shook his head. "But that was almost twenty years ago. At the time we spent a great deal of energy convincing the freedmen that they needed to engage with the rest of the country, that they weren't going to be allowed to live in isolated communities of their own. We were trying to avoid exactly what's happening now—ongoing division and suspicion. And we thought we had succeeded. In time they did integrate—the complaints died down on both sides, and everyone seemed to prosper, more or less."

"So what's changed?" Jocelyn asked.

She knew she was betraying an unusual interest in such a weighty matter of state, but she thought it was worth the risk. Her unease had been growing ever since her father used the word "crisis", and she needed to find out just how bad things were. If her kingdom was in trouble, she wanted to help. And, depressing as it was, the best way to do that would be to disappear completely. Suddenly a summer in Valoria was looking like her most responsible option.

"I don't know," answered her father simply, looking defeated.

"Even Jonan doesn't seem to understand it at all, and he's closer to the issue than anyone."

Jocelyn nodded at the mention of her father's oldest and closest friend. He and his wife were the leaders of the community of Raldon in the nearby Forest of Rune. The settlement had been formed to provide a home for a significant number of the freedmen, along with some of the former rebels who had helped her father reclaim his ancestors' throne before she was born. It was now a thriving forest town.

"Not quite closer than anyone," she said absently, speaking aloud before she thought it through. "He was never a slave, was he?"

Her father hadn't seemed to be listening, still lost in his thoughts, but his forehead suddenly creased in a frown. "I wonder if Jo *is* missing something," he said to himself. "Maybe the freedmen don't have as much faith in him as I thought."

Jocelyn shot a frightened look at Eamon. He shook his head slightly, his expression reassuring, but she decided she had pushed her luck too far, and it was time to change the topic.

"Speaking of the foresters," she said lightly, "if I do go to Valoria, do you think I could go via Raldon? It would be nice to visit Lucy. I haven't seen her in weeks, and if I'm going to be away all summer..."

"So you'd like to go?" the queen asked, giving her daughter the piercing look that had so often made Jocelyn wonder how her mother hadn't read her secret on her face before now.

She shrugged. Wanting didn't have much to do with it, but she wasn't about to tell her mother her real reason for leaving Kyona. "I suppose so."

"Jocelyn, you don't have to go just because they invited you," said the king quickly. "I could write back and suggest that you go next summer. After all, you are very young to be going so far alone. I'm sure King Malcolm would not take offense."

"Well, she doesn't have to go alone, Father," said Eamon brightly. "I'll go with her."

"No you won't," said their father flatly.

"Why not?" Eamon was clearly aggrieved. "You don't want her to go alone, and I don't see why I can't—"

"Because you weren't invited, for one thing," said Queen Elnora dryly. "And Joss won't be alone. She'll be perfectly safe, so everyone can stop worrying."

"Well, I'll at least start the journey with you, Jocelyn," said Eamon, with dignity. "You'll feel lonely starting out all by yourself, and it will be more pleasant if I see you through the forest."

"An excellent idea, Eamon," said the queen, exchanging an amused smile with her husband that Eamon loftily pretended not to see. "Now we'd better go, or we'll delay the meal, and have a horde of angry courtiers down on our heads." She made for the door, stopping to lay a hand briefly on Jocelyn's cheek on her way past. "We'll miss you, Joss, but I'm proud of you for taking the opportunity."

Jocelyn smiled but said nothing, waiting for her parents to disappear through the doorway before turning on her brother. "I'll feel lonely, will I?" she scoffed. "How considerate you are. As if we don't all know you couldn't care less about coming with me. You just want the excuse to see Lucy."

But apparently Eamon was not in the mood to be baited. "Forget about my love life, Joss, apparently you've got your own to worry about. Do you really want to be married off to some dull Valorian prince?"

"Of course I don't," she snapped.

"Then why were you so quick to take up this offer?"

She shrugged. "Honestly, there's probably not much risk of a marriage alliance. Once they realize how dull *I* am, they'll probably lose interest."

"You're not dull," said Eamon firmly, but she just shrugged again.

"You know what I mean. Did you hear what Father said about the freedmen not trusting Uncle Jonan?"

"Yes, I did, and you're reading too much into it. It's a natural thing for him to wonder. He had probably already had the thought, you probably had nothing to do with it. Mother and Father aren't usually affected, you know that."

She shook her head. "It's getting stronger, Eamon, don't tell me you haven't noticed."

He was silent for a moment too long, and she raised her eyebrows pointedly.

"Fine, I have noticed," he admitted.

Jocelyn gave him a curious look. "What about yours? I haven't noticed a difference."

He shrugged. "Neither have I. And if mine isn't getting stronger, I have no idea why yours would be." He gave her an appraising look. "But that's all the more reason I don't like the idea of you far away in Valoria all summer."

Jocelyn smiled to herself. Eamon could chuckle at their father's protectiveness all he liked, but it wasn't lost on her that he had inherited the trait in abundance.

"That's the very reason I'm going," she said aloud. "You heard Father—the tension over the freedmen is getting worse, and the country is already divided enough. The last thing anyone needs is me hanging around the castle, spreading confusion and chaos every time I open my mouth."

"That's ridiculous, Joss," said Eamon sharply. "You're not a danger to anyone as long as—"

"As long as I keep my mouth shut," she finished dully. "I know."

He frowned. "That's not what I was going to say. You know I

think you restrict yourself much more harshly than you need to. I was going to say as long as we're careful."

"We?" Jocelyn asked, a bite in her voice that she couldn't quite restrain. "I don't see you having to be careful what you say. Everyone loves it when you speak."

Eamon looked guilty, and immediately Jocelyn felt remorse. It wasn't his fault that he had been the arbitrary winner of their particular coin toss.

"We should go to dinner," she said quickly, to cover her ill-humored remark. "Mother and Father will wonder what's keeping us."

"Joss." His voice was unusually gentle. "I really will miss you while you're gone."

"Thanks Brother," she said, punching his arm as if they were still thirteen. She dodged out of the way of his retaliatory elbow as she led the way out of the room and toward the royal banquet hall. "I'll miss you too."

She grinned. "Unless of course I'm having too much of an adventure to think of you at all."

CHAPTER TWO

J ocelyn had assumed that a state visit would take a long time to organize, but everything came together alarmingly quickly. In only a few short weeks, she found herself on the point of departure. She wouldn't admit it to her parents, especially as her father looked at her with more concern in his eyes than ever these days, but she felt nervous at the prospect of such a prolonged absence from home.

As promised, Eamon was to accompany her to the Forest of Rune, where she would stay for a few days before going on toward the mountains that separated Kyona from Valoria. After that she would be on her own, which in royal language meant that she would be stifled under the weight of a chaperone, two maidservants, a group of diplomatic officials with their servants and assistants, and an entire squadron of royal guards.

She had always been an early riser, and on the morning of her departure, she was mounted and waiting before the rest of the group had appeared. As she walked her horse up and down the practice yard, she found herself wishing she had risen still earlier so that she might have had time for a last gallop across the hills surrounding Kynton. It would be months before she would have the chance to indulge in one of her favorite pastimes. She supposed the Valorian royals enjoyed riding as well, but it wouldn't be the same as her own familiar vista.

"Ah, I heard that you had arrived last night. Yes, the council will convene in a couple of hours."

The lazy voice made her sigh. She had never much liked this particular nobleman. Sir Sanctimonious, Eamon had called him once, and Jocelyn had to agree. He had a loud voice, and a blissful belief that women either couldn't hear or couldn't understand anything he didn't intend for them to know.

She didn't recognize the nobleman striding across the courtyard with him, but that wasn't a great surprise. Her father had called a council of nobles to discuss the tension over the freedmen, and lesser nobles had been filtering in from the countryside for the last week. Another reason to get out of Kynton for a while.

She kept her mount steady as the men passed her, hoping to avoid notice. But the stranger glanced over as they walked past, and his companion followed his gaze and saw her.

"Your Highness."

He gave a stiff half-bow, which his companion mirrored. Jocelyn inclined her head politely.

"Good morning, My Lord. I trust you are well."

"Indeed," he replied awkwardly, and Jocelyn groaned inwardly at the man's obvious discomfort. Even his companion, to whom she hadn't actually spoken, seemed to be ill-at-ease.

"Don't let me keep you from your business, My Lords," she prompted, and the two men gratefully took their leave.

She let out her own relieved breath. She was no stranger to the fact that people tended to feel uncomfortable in her presence, but she didn't need the reminder. Not now when she was trying to assure herself that her visit to Valoria wouldn't be an unmitigated disaster.

"That's the princess, of course," came the local nobleman's carrying voice. "Pretty enough, I grant, but sullen. The prince on the other hand, is a fine youth. Very confident, very intelligent."

Sullen. Stupid. Vapid.

She could list a dozen other uncomplimentary words that she had heard used to describe her habitual silence. She ground her teeth, imagining what she would say to Sir Sanctimonious if she decided to pay no heed to the consequences. How satisfying it would be. It was tempting to do it out of spite, just to watch the man self-destruct as she could surely make him.

But no. She sighed. A princess should be above such a petty sentiment as spite.

"Jocelyn!"

She started guiltily at her mother's voice, hoping her face didn't betray her thoughts too clearly.

"Good morning, Mother."

"You're early, Joss. So eager to be gone from us?" The queen's voice was slightly wistful, and Jocelyn dismounted to give her mother an embrace.

"Of course not. To be honest, I was trying to ride out my nerves."

"You don't have to go, Joss," said her mother quickly. "It's not too late to change your mind if this isn't really what you want. If I pushed too hard—"

"Of course you didn't," said Jocelyn, trying to restrain her irritation. "I chose to go, and I'm not regretting it. Just a little nervous."

"That's perfectly understandable," said her mother. "But I'm sure you'll be glad you went, once you have a chance to settle in. You will write, won't you?"

"Of course I will," said Jocelyn, with a smile. "Just promise me you'll write back, because we both know neither Father nor Eamon will."

The queen acknowledged it with a laugh just as the culprits themselves strolled into the courtyard together, deep in conversation. Eamon was leaning his head toward his father attentively, a richly embroidered traveling cloak around his shoulders. His expression was grave, but Jocelyn thought that his step had an eager spring to it.

There was no opportunity to hear the topic of their discussion, however, because as soon as they approached, the king turned his full attention on his daughter.

"So you're really leaving, Jocelyn," he said. She couldn't help but be warmed by his melancholy expression, as much as his anxiety exasperated her.

"Only for the summer, Father."

"We'll miss you around here. Don't grow too fond of Valoria."

Jocelyn smiled. "To please you Father, I will aim to dislike everything and everyone I see."

Her father chuckled at her joke as he gave her a quick squeeze, despite the public setting. He must really be feeling sentimental. Perhaps the memory of his own battle to avoid having a marriage arranged for him had brought out this fierce affection. Stepping back, he held her at arm's length, examining her face as if trying to read her thoughts.

"You know, it's not too late if you want to—"

"No need, Father," she said, stopping him with an upraised hand. "Mother and I have already done this. I'll be fine."

"Fine?" Eamon chimed in, swinging himself up into the saddle of the horse that a servant had led across the practice yard at his appearance. "You'll be much better than fine. Look at you, the picture of grace and poise—fair enough to snag any prince, wise enough to be a desirable queen for any kingdom, noble enough to—"

"We get the idea, thank you Eamon," Queen Elnora cut in.

Eamon grinned at his family, unperturbed by the glares his flippant words had incurred from all three of them.

"Feeling full of spirit at the thought of seeing your sweet Luciana today, are you Eamon?" returned Jocelyn maliciously, trying to turn the conversation. Their father looked like he was reconsidering the whole idea ever since Eamon's mention of her snagging a prince.

"I don't know what you mean," said Eamon loftily, apparently as unconcerned by his family's amusement as he had been by their disapproval.

The rest of their entourage had arrived by this time, and they all took a more formal leave. The start of the Forest of Rune lay only a few minutes' ride from the city gate, and it took a matter of about four hours to reach Raldon on horseback.

The journey was uneventful, the route being familiar to both Jocelyn and Eamon, who had traveled it more times than they could count. It seemed like half their childhood had been spent either visiting their second family in the forest, or receiving them at the capital. The dappled light of the trees was soothing and restful, and as they pressed deeper into the hush of their shade, Jocelyn found herself wishing she was staying longer with Lucy before leaving for Valoria.

Despite the pomp and ceremony of all the extra bodies, the group made good time and, having set out early, reached their destination comfortably before noon. Jocelyn had learned to ride when she was a small child and was an excellent horsewoman. But it had been a while since she had ridden for as long as four hours without a break, and she was very happy to slide out of the saddle by the time they arrived.

"Jocelyn!"

She had hardly gotten her bearings before she was engulfed by the enthusiastic embrace of her best friend.

"You're finally here. How has it been so many weeks since

you've come? And now you're leaving me for the whole summer! No Benjy, let her breathe!"

"Let's not talk about that yet, Lucy," Jocelyn complained, extricating herself with difficulty from a boisterous hug from Benjamin, Luciana's youngest brother. "We've got three days, let's just enjoy that. Hello, Benjy, let me look at you! What's this? I thought you were ten!"

"I am ten!" said Benjamin, his eyes wide.

"Then how is that you look so grown up?"

Benjy puffed out his chest, beaming, but he was quickly brought down to size by a new voice.

"She's just saying that to make you feel good, Benjy, don't get conceited. You're as much a runt as ever. Hi Joss."

"Hello Miles," said Jocelyn, torn between amusement and exasperation at the lofty air assumed by the next brother up. He evidently felt that at twelve he had the world figured out enough to lord it over his little brother. But he had already lost interest in her, turning to the true object of his devotion.

"Hi Eamon! I'm glad you've come! I got a new charger, you should see him. And Father has been teaching me to use a bow and arrow!"

"Charger?" scoffed the final piece of this energetic puzzle. "You're calling that slug of a pony a charger? Hello Joss."

"Matheus," greeted Jocelyn. She restrained a chuckle at the fourteen-year-old's assumed air of nonchalance as he leaned against a tree, eating an apple and clearly trying hard not to look like he was vying for Eamon's attention.

"Polo is not a slug!" Miles cried, firing up immediately in defense of his mount.

"Well, clearly I'll have to see him to judge for myself," said Eamon diplomatically, looking like he was holding back a smile of his own.

"Ugh, brothers," complained Luciana as an aside to Jocelyn. "You're very lucky you only have one, and that he's older."

"I'm not sure that a difference of eight minutes really counts as 'older'," countered Jocelyn, watching Eamon with long-suffering amusement as he turned his attention to her best friend.

"How are you, Lucy? You look well."

He spoke with a studied carelessness, but his eyes shone eagerly. Jocelyn privately thought his expression made him look much like the younger boys who hero-worshiped him.

"I'm very well, thanks, Eamon. And have you been in good health? It's so kind of you to accompany Jocelyn for the start of her journey."

Jocelyn rolled her eyes openly at Lucy's suddenly demure demeanor, and she exchanged a look of disgust with Matheus, the oldest of Lucy's brothers. There was no need for words—the two of them had a sporadic but recurring alliance through which they attempted to keep their older siblings from monopolizing each other's attention.

"Run along now, Eamon," she said, shooing her twin energetically with her hands. "The question of Polo sounds pressing, and don't think I'm going to share Lucy with you. I only have three days, then I'll be gone all summer. And you needn't think I don't know that you've arranged to stay on for longer on your way back through the forest."

"You see how I'm spied on, Lucy," said Eamon in a tone of mock hurt. Lucy laughed, but had no opportunity to respond, Miles cutting in before she could do so.

"You'll probably be gone longer than the summer, Joss. You'll probably be gone forever! Aren't you going to have to marry the Valorian prince and stay over there?"

"Nonsense, Miles, don't talk about things you don't understand," snapped Lucy, but Jocelyn could already feel her face growing hot. Had everyone already decided her fate? If she came back without having formed this alliance, would the whole kingdom assume she had been found wanting by the Valorians?

"Jossie, Eamon, you made it!"

"Hello, Uncle Jo."

Jocelyn turned with relief to the dark-haired man who had chosen that propitious moment to approach them. He greeted Eamon with the traditional Kyonan clasping of arms, then pulled Jocelyn into an affectionate hug. She returned the embrace warmly. She and Eamon were both extremely fond of "Uncle Jonan"—who was no actual blood relation—although there was no denying that it was Aunt Scarlett they adored most.

Uncle Jonan pulled back from the hug and held Jocelyn at arm's length to study her, much as her father had done that morning, but with a twinkle in his eye instead of the anxious expression that had become so familiar over the past few weeks.

"How are you, sweetheart? I hear you're off on your own adventure. It's about time you had some excitement! Look at you —you're all grown up!"

"Tell that to Father," said Jocelyn with dry humor.

Uncle Jonan laughed delightedly. "Don't take it to heart, Jossie. Cal was always a worrier, even when he was as young as you."

Jocelyn smiled. Uncle Jonan's characteristic cheerfulness always set her at ease. To one brought up in the sometimes stifling confines of the court, his irrepressible impudence was a balm. Despite the fact that her father had now been king for almost two decades, she had never heard his oldest friend use his title outside of formal state occasions. And Lucy confided in her that he only did so then because Aunt Scarlett made him. The strangest thing about it was that her father didn't seem to mind in the least.

"Why is it that Jocelyn is all grown up, but I'm still a child anytime I want to do anything you don't like, Father?" quipped Luciana, raising an eyebrow.

"Well, you're younger than Jocelyn, Lucy," reasoned Uncle Jonan, attempting to draw his daughter into a hug, which she did not welcome as Jocelyn had done.

"By one year," she protested as she danced out of reach.

"You say that like it's nothing!" countered her father winningly. "But one year is an age. One year can change your life. In one year I went from a nobody in a fishing town, to an almost king bandying about with dragons, back to a nobody, to an adventurer in a foreign land where I became a rebel and a spy, to a well-respected leader and a—"

"And a husband, which was the best adventure of all, yes, yes, we know," muttered Matheus, unimpressed.

"Well, I have to say that when your mother is around," said Uncle Jonan, winking confidentially at Jocelyn, "but to tell you the truth, the dragons were also pretty exciting."

"I heard that," said a musical voice, and Jocelyn and Eamon both turned eagerly to greet its owner.

"How are you, Jocelyn?" Aunt Scarlett asked after embracing both twins warmly.

The question was accompanied by a piercing look that was entirely absent from her greeting to Eamon. Jocelyn held back a sigh. Clearly everyone was well informed as to the fraught nature of her venture into Valoria.

"I'm well, Aunt Scarlett," she said aloud. "How are you? Other than as beautiful as ever." The last part came out almost involuntarily—no matter how many times she saw her, she was always a bit dazzled by Aunt Scarlett's stunning appearance.

"Tut, tut, Joss, you'll get yourself in trouble," chided Uncle Jonan jokingly. "Don't you know Scarlett doesn't like being told she's beautiful? Much better to point out her flaws. If you look closely, you'll find that one eyebrow is slightly higher than the other."

"Thank you, darling," said Aunt Scarlett dryly. "You are as chivalrous as ever."

"I'm just trying to endear you to the youngsters," Uncle Jonan explained helpfully. "The girls don't want you outshining them now they're all grown up."

Luciana of course pounced on her father's admission that she was grown up after all, and the scene descended once more into chaos. Jocelyn couldn't hold back her smile as she watched on. She had always felt jealous of Lucy for how free her family was to argue and joke and just generally carry on, and she always enjoyed her time with them immensely.

Jocelyn wasn't fooled by the banter, and not just because the sparkle in Uncle Jonan's eyes as they rested on his wife said more clearly than words that she still outshone everyone as far as he was concerned.

And he wasn't wrong. Aunt Scarlett was as gorgeous as she had been from Jocelyn's earliest memories. Her caramel skin, so unusual in Kyona, where Balenans were rarely to be found, seemed to reflect the warmth of her personality. It always made Jocelyn feel pale and sickly by comparison. Her face was set in perfect lines, and the chestnut hair, perfectly matched to the color of her eyes, was as thick as ever, with no hint of gray. It was pinned up in a braid at present, but on Aunt Scarlett the style was as attractive as it was practical.

It was no wonder that, underneath his joking words, Uncle Jonan was clearly still as smitten as a love-struck youth. Jocelyn had never seen any couple look at one another the way Lucy's parents still did, with the exception of her own parents in rare private moments. Having been raised in court, she understood perfectly that the difference was simply that Uncle Jonan and

Aunt Scarlett had the luxury of less exalted positions, and could therefore afford to show affection more openly.

But still, while she would never admit it to Eamon for fear of being teased, she had always found both their story and their manner terribly romantic. Much more romantic than having a marriage arranged by foreign royalty, she reflected glumly.

"You must both be tired after your ride," Aunt Scarlett was saying, ignoring the ongoing banter of her husband and children and smiling warmly at the visitors. "Don't let my brood carry you off for shenanigans until you've had something to eat and gotten settled in."

"You'll be staying in my room, of course, Joss," said Lucy quickly, stepping up and claiming Jocelyn's arm in a proprietary way. "I want to keep you to myself as much as possible before you escape over the mountains."

"More likely she'll be trying to escape back across the mountains by the end of the summer," chimed in the incorrigible Miles. "I bet the prince is boring and old."

"That's enough, Miles," said Aunt Scarlett, frowning at her middle son. "No one is going to need to escape from anywhere."

"We'll see," Miles muttered, but at a sharp glance from his father he desisted.

Jocelyn once again felt a flush on her face, and she could only be grateful when Lucy carried her off without further delay. Glancing back, she saw Eamon being instantly mobbed by the boys, their mother attempting to ward them off. He was watching the girls leave with a disconsolate expression that had nothing to do with his sister's departure. She rolled her eyes at him. Speaking of love-struck youths...

Not that she could really blame him. As well as being the sweetest person Jocelyn had ever met, Luciana was as lovely as her mother. Her skin was a shade lighter, somewhere between her parents' two tones, and she had inherited her father's dark hair. But she had her mother's huge brown eyes and perfect features. She was striking, as much for her unusual coloring as for her beauty. Her foreign heritage might have made an unattractive girl an outcast. It earned Luciana recognition as an exotic beauty.

Lucy chatted away as they wended between the buildings that dotted the large clearing at the hub of the forest community. The family lived in an enormous wooden house at one edge of the open space. It was raised up on stilts, and children from the community were playing underneath, their laughter wafting contentedly through the air. Lucy's room was on the second story, at the back of the house. Jocelyn had always loved being able to look out her friend's window and feel like she was high up among the trees of the forest.

Lucy raised her eyebrows at the way two of the royal guards followed them and then stationed themselves underneath the house, causing the children to hastily remove themselves and find somewhere else to play. But she waited until the girls were ensconced in her room before commenting.

Jocelyn grimaced. "I'm sorry about that. It's not that anyone doesn't trust the people who live here. I think it's more in case there's any unpleasantness directed at the community from outside as a result of the royal visit." She gave her friend a searching look. "Have you been caught up in this sudden prejudice against the freedmen?"

Lucy shrugged, busily unpacking her friend's things with a fine disregard for Jocelyn's privacy.

"Not really. I mean, I know my parents have been concerned about it all, and some of the freedmen who live here are a bit offended. But no one in the forest is siding with the ones complaining, obviously, so everyone just mutters a bit then gets over it." Looking up, she saw Jocelyn's expression of concern and stopped, clearly surprised. "What?"

"Nothing, it's just...it's getting worse apparently. My father thinks we're on the point of a crisis. I don't want you to be caught up in it, and I know your family is sort of at the heart of the issue."

Lucy frowned, a small measure of alarm making its way onto her previously cheerful face. "Maybe I *should* be worried," she said slowly.

"No, no," said Jocelyn quickly, her own alarm growing at the look of confusion that, while it was most familiar, she had rarely seen on her best friend's face. It really was getting stronger. "No use in worrying. No one has a grudge against you, I'm sure."

Lucy still looked uncertain, so Jocelyn tried a different approach. "Your family aren't really freedmen, after all."

"That's true," said Luciana with a smile. "Father was never actually a slave, and Mother is, you know—"

"Balenan," supplied Jocelyn with a grin. "Which means that you're not a freedman. Just a half-breed like me."

Lucy laughed musically at the reference to their private mockery of the fastidious subset of the court that still took issue with Queen Elnora's common blood. Lucy's mother, who came from nobility herself, had very scathing views on nobles who looked down on commoners. And Jocelyn's mother had taught her when she was very young that if she could brush off the criticisms of such people instead of taking them to heart, she would find that she could use their low expectations to her advantage.

"Do you think the Valorian prince really will be old and boring?" Lucy asked, the sudden change in topic catching Jocelyn off-guard.

"Probably," she answered, her tone instantly subdued. "I overheard Father saying he's at least twenty-five."

"Oh. Well, that's not too old," said Lucy hesitantly. Jocelyn just shrugged, so her friend pushed on. "Maybe he'll be great. Maybe you'll fall in love with him on sight."

Jocelyn snorted. "No thanks. He's their crown prince—he's sure to be serious and responsible, with no sense of humor. Not at all love-at-first-sight-worthy."

"You don't know that," argued Luciana. "I mean," she paused, her cheeks tinging with color, "Eamon is our crown prince, and he's not at all like that."

Jocelyn gave her friend a pointed look, but kept her mouth firmly shut. Lucy sighed and dropped the subject, resigned from long habit to Jocelyn's perpetual unwillingness to discuss the budding romance between her brother and her best friend.

Jocelyn hoped Lucy didn't think she disapproved—nothing could be further from the truth. And as much as she didn't particularly want to discuss her twin's romantic appeal, Jocelyn would have been willing to do it anyway, for Lucy's sake. But Eamon had flatly forbidden it. Too dangerous, he said. Too risky.

"It doesn't really matter what Prince Ormond is like," Jocelyn hurried on. "There's no formal offer, you know, Lucy. My mother is convinced that there will be no obligation just because I've visited. Honestly, my hope is that they'll show me a pleasant summer and give me a chance to see a little of Valoria, then send me home unattached with polite greetings for my parents. They just need to get to know me enough to see that I'm not queen material."

"Not much chance of that," said Luciana loyally, if counter-productively. She turned Jocelyn toward the tall looking glass that stood in the corner of the room. "Any kingdom would be lucky to have you as queen. I'm sure they'll be eager to snap you up."

"I think you're looking at the wrong reflection," said Jocelyn dryly, her eyes drawn to her friend's lovely image next to hers.

Had she been allowed to do so, this was where she would

have made a quip about Lucy being unavailable to be Valoria's future queen because she would be too busy being Kyona's.

But Lucy wasn't interested in either Jocelyn's compliments or her self-deprecation. She glowered at her friend in the mirror.

"Don't pretend to think you're ugly, Joss, I won't believe you. You're lovely, and the Valorians will be sure to see your grace and poise and charm. I wish they wouldn't, because I don't want to lose you to them!"

"Grace and poise and charm?" protested Jocelyn. "Now I know you're describing yourself instead of me. In fact," she said accusingly, "I'm pretty sure I've heard those exact words in court, after your last visit." Her tone turned aggrieved.

"Why is it that when you're quiet through a state dinner, you get described as graceful and elegant, but when I don't have anything to say I get called sullen?"

"What?" said Lucy, outraged. "Who dared to call you that?"

"Sir Sanctimonious," grumbled Jocelyn. "Just this morning."

"Oh him." Lucy waved a dismissive hand. "He's a sour old complainer, don't listen to what he says."

"I don't, usually," said Jocelyn. "But...well, I know I said I don't want a marriage alliance, and it's true. But if I'm honest Lucy, I still want to make a good impression. I know my father thinks I don't have what it takes, and I don't want the Valorians to think I'm an empty-headed peahen."

"Your father," said Luciana firmly, "thinks you're wonderful. And so do I. And so will any Valorian worth your notice."

Jocelyn smiled sadly. She was more relaxed around Lucy than anyone else, except Eamon, and Lucy didn't realize just how insipid her friend came across to most people. But as she turned from the glass with a lingering look, Jocelyn at least acknowledged to herself that Lucy was right about one thing. She didn't think she was ugly. She couldn't hold a candle to Lucy of course, but then who could?

It might have been nice to have a little more height, but she didn't begrudge her mother the inherited short stature, not when it came with the same slim figure. Her hair was darker than her mother's golden waves, more like her father's, the color of ripe wheat. With her pale coloring and blue eyes, she presented a sharp contrast to Lucy beside her, but neither girl's appeal suffered from the juxtaposition.

On the whole Jocelyn didn't think that her appearance would disgrace the Kyonan royal house in the sight of the Valorians. If only her manner could be as fitting for a princess as her face.

CHAPTER THREE

The time with Luciana and her boisterous family flew by much too quickly, and Jocelyn found herself back in the saddle before she felt fully unpacked. This second farewell was more relaxed but just as momentous to Jocelyn. She had begun to wonder if she had undertaken this state visit too lightly. Somehow she had the feeling that her life would never be the same again.

She became more withdrawn as they journeyed the remaining two days to reach the other side of the forest, where she would part ways with her twin. She was so quiet even with Eamon, that he drew her aside just before they quitted the trees.

"Are you all right, Joss? What's happening in that mind of yours?"

She looked away, back into the forest where the rest of the group had stopped for a break some time before. They were all starting to prepare for their journey toward the mountains, with the exception of the few guards who would travel back with Eamon.

"What am I doing, Eamon? I don't want to be married off to some Valorian."

"You won't be! You're not signing up for anything, remember?"

"I'm starting to wonder if that's really true," Jocelyn muttered, still not meeting her brother's eye.

"Of course it is." Eamon spoke firmly. "This is just a chance to make new friends."

"How can I make friends if I can't open my mouth?" grumbled Jocelyn.

"Approachable body language?" Eamon's winning smile did nothing to dispel Jocelyn's gathering gloom.

"I'll be voiceless as well as friendless," she said, her voice dropping almost to a whisper. "For the rest of my life, if I do have to marry Prince Ormond. You won't even be there to speak for me."

"No I won't, and I think that's why Mother wanted you to go, to be honest," said Eamon, clearly trying to lighten the mood.

"If only she knew how much I would like to speak for myself if I could," said Jocelyn dryly. "But yes, there's no way she was going to let you come."

"There's another reason they wanted me to stay, actually," said Eamon, and she caught the note of pride underneath his casual words.

"What do you mean?"

"Father has invited me to sit in on the council when I get back. He's increasing my responsibilities. He wants me to help find a solution to this crisis."

"That's wonderful, Eamon," said Jocelyn, trying to hide the inexplicable sinking in her heart. It was an obvious fact, but somehow she had forgotten that while she was off having experiences that didn't involve her twin, he would be doing the same. A gulf seemed to be stretching out between them, and she had never felt lonelier.

"Don't worry about Valoria, Joss," said Eamon cheerfully,

apparently not sharing her gloomy reflections. "If worst comes to worst, just endure it for the summer and then you'll be home again, and everything will be back to normal."

Jocelyn decided not to comment on how much less appealing her normal was than his.

"At least there's Montego to look forward to," she said instead, brightening a little at the thought of the mountain town, which was her next destination. "I've wanted to go there ever since hearing Mother and Father describe their visit when they were young."

"I know you have, and I'm glad you get to check out the famous mountain people," said Eamon. "But I'll admit I was surprised that Father agreed to it. From what I hear, they're not exactly staunch supporters of the whole royalty concept, and I would have thought that marching a squadron of royal guards through Montego would create tension that we don't need right now."

"But that's the best part!" said Jocelyn quickly. "Didn't you hear? Of course they wouldn't like the royal guards throwing their weight around, and Father doesn't want to offend them when he already has his hands full. So the guards will go around by the highway and meet me on the other side of Montego."

"What? You get to ditch your babysitters?" demanded Eamon, sounding both impressed and annoyed. "How did you argue that?"

Jocelyn shrugged. "It wasn't that hard."

Eamon raised an eyebrow, and Jocelyn laughed in spite of herself.

"What? I did it without cheating!"

"Joss."

Eamon's tone was unimpressed, and Jocelyn couldn't help chuckling again.

"Well, mostly without cheating."

Eamon opened his mouth again, but she cut in before he could speak.

"Don't tell me off, Eamon. It's getting more potent and less predictable. Honestly, I'm not sure how to be completely confident I'm not using it, unless I don't speak at all." Eamon was frowning thoughtfully, so she hurried on.

"But truly, Father wasn't hard to convince. Apparently the same chief is still around from all those years ago, and Father trusts him. I just told Father that I desperately want to visit Montego. You know what he's been like around me since it was decided that I was going."

"Like you're a lamb off to be slaughtered," nodded Eamon. "Of course he would want to say yes. But still, he had guards following you around even at Lucy's house. It's hard to believe he's going to let you stay in Montego alone."

"Oh, well, you know what 'alone' means," said Jocelyn dismissively. "One of the maids will come with me, and two of the guards in plain clothes."

Eamon laughed. "That sounds more like it. Well, you've apparently gone to a lot of effort to visit Montego. I hope the reclusive mountain folk are as interesting as you expect."

"It's not just them," said Jocelyn quickly. "There's dragon magic in the mountains, you know that. That's why the mountain people are so unusual. Because they live on the doorstep of the Dragon Realm."

"Yes," said Eamon dryly, "everyone knows that, thanks to Father's dramatic ascension to the throne. But I can't see what good you think it will do you. No one's so much as seen a dragon since Elddreki helped stop the coup right before the freedmen came back. People have been roaming the mountains trying to get into the Dragon Realm for twenty years, and I've yet to hear of anyone succeeding."

"But we're not like most people, are we?" said Jocelyn,

glancing around to make sure no one was within hearing as she gave her twin a significant look.

Eamon frowned back at her. "What are you saying, Joss? Please tell me you're not going to wander off into the mountains looking for dragons."

"Of course not," scoffed Jocelyn. "But half the reason I wanted to go to Montego was to look for answers. I don't know if you'd call our...situation...magic exactly, but it's not natural."

Eamon shrugged, looking uncomfortable. "I know it's unusual, but it's just part of who we are, Jocelyn."

"That's easy for you to say," said Jocelyn with a snap in her voice. "You don't have to spend your life with your mouth clamped shut to avoid ruining everything in your path." She took a deep breath, willing herself to swallow her frustration the way she so often swallowed her words. "My point is, the mountains are where the dragons are, and I've never heard of magic that has any other source than dragons, have you? Think about it, Eamon! If anyone has answers, it'll be the mountain people."

"I don't know, Joss." Eamon sounded more uneasy than ever. "You need to be careful. Asking about dragons won't win you any favor in Montego. Word is the mountain people are so sick of all the mania that they drive any questers off themselves these days, by force if necessary."

"Eamon," said Jocelyn, compelling her brother to look at her. "Are you seriously telling *me* to be careful what I say? Do you really think I need that warning?"

He laughed reluctantly. "I suppose not. Just...don't get yourself into trouble, all right, Joss? I know I give you a hard time—it's a brother's primary responsibility after all—but it really would kill me if anything happened to you."

"I never knew you could be so sentimental, Eamon," chuckled Jocelyn. She gave him a quick hug. "But thank you. I'll do my best to stay out of mischief, and with a bit of luck, the mountain people will refrain from expelling me violently from their town."

IT WAS A GOOD THING, Jocelyn reflected to herself a few days later, that she had set her expectations so low. Because while the mountain people showed no sign of wanting to forcefully eject her, her welcome to Montego was not exactly warm.

They reached the mountain town not long before nightfall, and Jocelyn was weary. After traveling south alongside the mountain range, she and her small cohort had said goodbye to the rest of the group when the road turned east and began to wind up into the peaks. They had sent their horses on with the others to cross the border further south, and had continued on foot all day, climbing steadily and drawing their traveling cloaks closer as the air become cool in the higher altitude. Jocelyn was fit and managed the continuous slope without too much difficulty, but the maidservant who had come with them looked utterly miserable.

Even the two guards looked uneasy as they approached the opening to the town, which as the travelers had been warned, wasn't visible until they were almost upon it. But Jocelyn suspected that their discomfort was less to do with the physical exertion and more with the reputation that generations of superstition had given to the inhabitants of this mountainous region.

To her own surprise, Jocelyn didn't feel nervous at all. She felt excited. As the landscape had changed from the green grasses of the plains below to the unvarying aspect of hour upon hour of gray rock, she had felt the telltale tingle in her spine for which she had been waiting.

As a child she had listened, spellbound, to her father's description of how his royal blood had inexplicably allowed him to feel the magic of the mountains, even before he knew his own ancestry. She had hoped that her share in that bloodline would give her the same ability, and she could feel the elation building inside her as she found that it had.

The feeling was new and exhilarating, but in another way it was utterly familiar. She had felt it since her earliest memories, in a different form, but one that she somehow recognized as akin to the power that hummed through the very air of these mountains. She had felt it almost every time she opened her mouth to speak.

Surely the similarity of the sensation was a good sign that she might be able to find here the answers she so desperately wanted.

As soon as they passed between the stone gateposts marking the entrance to Montego, a silent escort appeared alongside them as they made their way into the central space. The mountain men were just as Jocelyn's father had described them to her, dark-haired and dressed in varying shades of gray, the style of their clothes unlike any she had seen before.

They looked wild and dangerous, but at the same time, their movements seemed controlled. It was as if they were all synchronized to a rhythm that might be unfamiliar to outsiders, but that would be perfectly predictable and consistent to everyone within the community.

Jocelyn felt the maid draw nervously closer to her as they walked toward the large fire burning in the middle of the flat central area. One of Jocelyn's guards greeted the man closest to him with the information that their group was expected. Jocelyn wondered if the local man could hear the unease behind the guard's gruff words as clearly as she could. The mountain man spoke not a word in reply, his face as inexpressive as the stone around them.

Glancing around the village, she could see a number of

other people also watching them, their faces neither hostile nor friendly. Strangely, the silence comforted Jocelyn. It didn't seem to indicate unhappiness, and at least here she could keep her thoughts to herself as much as she chose without standing out.

Before the guards could get too nervous, one of the villagers slipped away and disappeared into one of the stone houses that were spread all over the level ground. Some of these buildings were built from cut stones, not unlike the stone houses that could be found in many Kyonan towns. But others, like the one the man had entered, were cut into the rock of the mountain itself.

In a moment, the man reemerged, now following in the wake of a tall confident figure whom Jocelyn could tell at a glance must be the mountain chief, Darius. He was an elderly man, probably in his seventies, but his frame was still straight and strong, and his gray hair flowed thickly around his shoulders. An unpolished wooden circlet rested on his forehead, but it was the unmistakable air of authority that identified him to Jocelyn as the leader of the community.

She was used to being around powerful people—the court was full of men of genuine influence, as well as those who were simply self-important. But this chief was nothing like any leader she had ever encountered. Not being a fool, she could see that he wasn't someone to be taken lightly. But still, for reasons she couldn't articulate, she found she liked him instantly.

Jocelyn stepped forward, navigating around the guards who had instinctively placed themselves in front of her. Holding back a rueful chuckle, she thought of Eamon's flippant advice about approachable body language as she met the chief's eye confidently. His eyes lingered on her as he spoke to them all.

"Welcome, travelers, to Montego. You are expected."

"Thank you for graciously receiving us," she said quietly, then barely refrained from jumping in surprise.

She had not spoken all day—there had been no need to, and her companions hadn't questioned the restraint, well-used to her habitual silence. These were the first words she had spoken since entering the mountains, and the feeling of that familiar yet novel power swirled more intensely around her than ever. It was as if her words disappeared into the invisible web that seemed to fill the air here, adding her own signature to the interwoven mass of power that swallowed them up.

The chief looked at her closely for a moment, but it was difficult to tell whether he had noticed anything. The mountain people, like the royal line, were supposed to be attuned to the magic of the dragons, but perhaps he was so inured to it from living in the mountains that he wouldn't notice her small contribution.

But Jocelyn, who knew that she had both mountain and royal blood in her, had never experienced anything like it before, and the feeling was overpowering.

"I am Darius, the chief of this region," he said, "and you are welcome here." He gave her an appraising look. "I met your father and mother many years ago. They and their friend left our town searching for something—and succeeded, I understand, where no others have before or after them. It was an achievement indeed."

"If they were present, sir," said Jocelyn evenly, "I think they would say they cannot claim achievement when those they sought chose to be found." Remembering Eamon's warning, she avoided actually using the word dragon, but it was clear that Darius understood her meaning perfectly, and he seemed pleased with the answer.

"And I would reply that they had spoken well." He smiled as he met her eye. "And taught their daughter well, in a matter that is much misunderstood." He nodded, the gesture encompassing all four of the travelers. "Lodgings have been prepared for you—

please make yourselves comfortable. Our custom is to eat communally, and we would be pleased for you to join us for the evening meal." He gestured toward the large fire, and Jocelyn could see that people were already beginning to prepare food.

The maidservant still looked nervous as she followed Jocelyn to their appointed dwelling, and even the burly guards continued to cast cautious looks around them as they entered a building nearby. Jocelyn suspected that she would be the only one to fulfill Darius's request that they make themselves comfortable in the mountain town.

When they joined the rest of the community around the central fire, twilight had fully descended, and the gray-clad figures of the villagers seemed to flit like shadows through the increasing gloom. There was an eeriness to the scene, intensified by the continual hum of power that Jocelyn could feel pulsing through the air. But it was also peaceful. She wished they were staying more than two nights.

The meal was eaten in near silence, despite the number of people clustered around the fire. The maid clearly wanted to hover near the safety of the guards, but Jocelyn surreptitiously placed herself on a large flat rock a reasonable distance away. Her escorts behaved too formally toward her for comfort, and she wanted to observe the curious mountain people in peace. They seemed wonderfully uninterested in their royal visitor, and Jocelyn found herself relishing the fact that neither her status nor her silence was attracting any attention in this unusual community.

Most of those who were chatting quietly were young people like herself, the elders apparently content to focus on their food. Just as Jocelyn was finishing her meal, a girl of about her own age approached her, her face open and friendly.

"I don't wish to disturb you," the girl said. "I just wanted to say that you are very welcome. We don't get many visitors in

Montego." She wrinkled her nose, a squat little feature. "Except for questers, and they don't count."

"Thank you," said Jocelyn quietly, returning the smile.

The girl hesitated for a moment, glancing back at a group of other youths who were watching her eagerly. "I know it's not our way to make a fuss, even over important people, but we," she gestured toward her young friends, "think it's great that you wanted to come through Montego instead of going around by the highway. We heard that it was at your own request. We hope you'll like it here."

"Thank you," said Jocelyn again, surprised but gratified. She would normally leave it there, but the graceful stillness of the mountain town had her feeling relaxed, and she pushed on recklessly. "I like it here already. It feels like I've stepped through a portal into a timeless world. Like nothing has changed here for generations, and nothing will change for generations more."

The girl, who had looked enthusiastic at the start of Jocelyn's uncharacteristic outburst, was undergoing a rapid change in expression. Her friendly smile faltered, replaced by an all-too-familiar look of confusion.

"It is like that, isn't it?" she said slowly, her tone suddenly uneasy as she looked around the village. "Maybe we're too stuck in the past. Maybe it's time things changed around here."

"No! I didn't mean—" Jocelyn bit her tongue, holding back the words clamoring for release, to clarify, to undo the damage. She knew from long experience that more words would just make it worse.

The girl didn't meet her eye, still looking confused. "Well, welcome, anyway," she said, wandering back to her friends, whose eager faces now looked concerned.

Jocelyn turned away, hoping desperately that none of them had seen the tears springing to her eyes. She blinked rapidly in an attempt to keep them at bay. Why had she opened her mouth? She knew better. What damage might she do to this wonderful place? They should never have let her come. She should go to the chief right now, and tell him that she would leave first thing in the morning, before she could wreak havoc in the peaceful community.

She looked around wistfully, her eyes still stinging with the tears she was trying not to shed. She had thought, foolishly, that this place was a haven, where she could be silent and still, and no one would think less of her. But she should have realized that, on the contrary, she was more dangerous here than anywhere. She should have known it the moment she felt the strange power of her words mingling with the unquantifiable essence of the mountains, that indescribable energy that some people called magic.

She took a deep breath, trying to master herself. She couldn't unsay what had already been said. But she could keep her mouth clamped firmly shut on any more unnecessary reflections. She chanced a glance at the young people. One young man, sitting a little apart from the others, was watching her with a creased brow, but the rest were no longer looking her way. No one else seemed inclined to approach her. She would just keep to herself.

"Friends and brothers."

The clear voice made Jocelyn start. She hadn't realized that Darius had stood to address them all. The assembled group was already too quiet to be gripped by the hush that usually heralded a speech. But now that she looked around, she saw that everyone in the circle had turned their eyes to the chief, and she did the same.

"It is through our stories that we know who we are."

"May our stories never be forgotten," chimed the listeners.

CHAPTER FOUR

Jocelyn's distress was momentarily forgotten in sudden excitement. She knew what was happening—the mountain people were famous for their storytelling. She found herself leaning forward.

"We have special visitors among us this evening, travelers passing through from one side of our mountains to the other," continued Darius calmly. His eyes passed around the circle, skating over the nearby young people and pausing on Jocelyn for only a moment before moving on. "In honor of them I will tell a tale of others who made Montego a resting place to break their journey from one kingdom to the other."

A few other people's eyes flicked to Jocelyn, then back to Darius as the mountain chief continued.

"Generations ago, there was a king in Kynton, the ancestor of the king who now sits on the throne. He was a strong king, and not unconnected to our people. His queen was the daughter of our mountain chief, and through her our blood mingles even now with that of Kyona's royal line."

Again Darius looked at Jocelyn, and she held his gaze steadily. His keen glance as well as his words held her in thrall in the flickering firelight. She knew without doubt which of her ancestors he was describing. Her father had inherited the gift for storytelling that characterized the royal bloodline, and she had grown up on tales of the past. Only one sovereign—King Cael, the last king before the corruption in which the throne was usurped—had married a woman from the mountains.

Queen Jacqueline had been beloved, and for a short time it had seemed that the mutual distrust between the mountain people and the rest of Kyona might begin to fade. But after her grief over her daughter's death and the events surrounding it had driven her to an early grave, public opinion had turned against her, and the royals by association. The mountain people had become embittered, more aloof and less loyal to the crown than ever.

Jocelyn knew all this, and she felt trepidation along with curiosity as she waited. What aspect of King Cael and Queen Jacqueline's story would Darius focus on?

"The queen visited her mountain home many times after her marriage," Darius continued. "Sometimes she was accompanied by the king, often she brought her children. But it is not her visits that I find in my mind tonight. Their eldest daughter, save one who died in childhood, made a journey of her own through our mountains. The Kyonan princess was on her way to Bryford, to begin preparations for her marriage to the Valorian crown prince."

Jocelyn had been leaning forward, listening intently, but as Darius's eyes bored into hers, she suddenly sat up straighter, a flush rising up her neck as she registered the ambiguity of his last sentence. A number of the villagers were again looking at her, and she resisted the urge to tug nervously at her skirts.

She knew that he was talking about Princess Sarai, the daughter of King Cael and Queen Jacqueline. She had married the Valorian crown prince some few hundred years ago, the countries being then on good terms with one another, as they were now. But it was impossible to miss the extra layer of meaning in the chief's words, his omission of names suddenly seeming significant. Jocelyn wondered why she hadn't thought of Princess Sarai before now, given the similarity of their situations. She searched her mind, but she couldn't remember that her father had ever told stories concerning the long-deceased princess, other than the bare fact of her marriage into Valoria's royal house.

"According to the stories of our ancestors, the princess was ill-at-ease when she passed through our town," Darius went on. "Much like our own people, it is not the custom of royalty to show emotion freely."

Jocelyn thought there was humor in the chief's eyes at his reference to the famed reticence of his people. She felt a grim amusement herself. He certainly wasn't wrong about the expectation placed on royalty to be unimpassioned.

"But in Montego, the princess was among friends. She was, as I have said, the granddaughter of our chief. To her more distant kin she communicated what both duty and affection prevented her from displaying to her nearest family in Kynton. She did not wish to leave Kyona. She did not know the man to whom she was betrothed, and she was apprehensive at the prospect of becoming Valorian."

Jocelyn felt a chill at the man's words, even as her curiosity flared. She had never heard any of this before—she supposed that the royal family in Kynton may never have known of Princess Sarai's interactions with her mountain cousins. But the phrase "becoming Valorian" sent a shard of ice through Jocelyn's heart. She supposed that if she were to marry the crown prince, as Princess Sarai had done long ago, it would mean becoming Valorian.

I'm Kyonan! she wanted to shout. *I will always be Kyonan.* It was somehow even harder than usual to bottle her words inside her, but she held them in firmly. The magical quality of this place swirled so strongly around her, that she almost thought that if she were to say the words aloud, even she would become confused as to whether they were true.

"The princess found comfort with her relations in Montego," Darius was continuing. "She stayed some time with them. She found strength from their ways and their identity. She saw that they belonged neither to Kyona nor to Valoria."

Jocelyn raised her eyebrows at the openness with which the chief disclaimed his people's allegiance to the kingdom in which the mountain region was technically situated. It was a good thing Eamon wasn't here. He wouldn't like that.

"They belonged to the mountains, and the mountains to them," said Darius simply. "She found that she need not lose herself to her new homeland. Neither must she hold herself back from her new life out of loyalty to her old kingdom."

Again Darius's eyes swept around the circle as he continued to speak. "She also took great interest in our tales of dragons. At that time, neither those of Kyona nor those of Valoria gave credence to the legends of our interactions with dragons. They believed the mighty creatures to be nothing more than a myth."

A disgruntled rustling went around the group at his words. "If only that were still true," Jocelyn heard a nearby man mutter. She winced slightly, remembering her twin's comment about how irritated the mountain people had become by the regular invasions into their secluded region of questers seeking dragons.

"But the princess took the stories to heart," Darius continued calmly, giving no indication that he had noticed his listeners' reaction. "In keeping with her mountain blood, she felt the magic of this place, and she was eager for knowledge of its source. She asked many questions, but her time in Montego was short. She spoke of returning, of bringing her children to visit the mountains, as her mother had brought her. But once she crossed into Valoria, she did not return. Soon after her marriage, the Kyonan royal house from which she came fell into disarray, and there was no more interchange between the two kingdoms."

The chief's eyes lingered once more on Jocelyn. "The princess departed from Kyona long ago, and never again entered their stories. But here in the mountains, where she found a temporary haven between her two kingdoms, her story is remembered. The tale of the princess of Kyona is our story."

"May our stories never be forgotten," the villagers answered in unison.

It was clear that these words signified the end of the story-telling. People stood, casting furtive looks in Jocelyn's direction as they stretched and began to clear the remains of the meal or make their way toward their homes.

Jocelyn remained frozen in place, hardly knowing what to think. The chief had clearly told the story because of its relevance to her—he had said as much. But what was his purpose in doing so? Did he intend to encourage her or warn her? If he had intended encouragement, he certainly hadn't succeeded. The thought of being ripped from her beloved homeland and forgotten by its history was heart-rending, and the possibility that her visit to Montego would live on in mountain legend provided no comfort at all.

She wished she could contradict the chief's words. But as far as she knew, he was right, and Princess Sarai had never returned to her home kingdom. When the throne was usurped, she had remained in Valoria, and almost certainly had never seen any of her family again. Jocelyn knew that her own situation was not equivalent—even if she did marry Prince Ormond, there would be no violent uprising to prevent regular communication between her and her home.

But still...it was a distressing thought. Kyona wouldn't be her home at all. She would become part of the story of the Valorians instead. She wondered why she had never before questioned what became of Princess Sarai. The rest of King Cael and Queen Jacqueline's children had either been killed or had gone into hiding within Kyona, their descendants traceable even to this day. She herself was the descendant of one of those children, Prince Jonathon. But what had been Princess Sarai's fate? Surely she had not been unconcerned by the plight of her parents and siblings? She would have become Valoria's queen. Would there be records in Bryford about the rest of her life? Perhaps Jocelyn would be able to search for them during her stay there.

She was still deep in thought, staring unseeingly into the fire in front of her, when she was startled by a voice right next to her.

"Good evening."

She jumped slightly, looking up at the speaker. She recognized him as the young man who had sat apart from the other people her age. The only one who had continued to look at her after the disastrous attempt of the friendly villager to speak with her.

Remembering her resolve not to engage in any unnecessary speech for the remainder of her time in Montego, Jocelyn stayed silent, acknowledging his greeting only with an incline of her head.

"May I join you?" the young man asked, nodding meaningfully at the space next to her.

Jocelyn hesitated. She should have chosen a rock with no room for an extra person. But she hadn't thought it necessary. She was so used to the fact that her presence made most people uncomfortable, that it hadn't occurred to her that someone might want to sit with her. She couldn't refuse now without seeming excessively impolite.

She gave a tight nod, and the man seated himself readily, apparently undeterred by her less than encouraging expression.

"That was an unusual story, wasn't it?" he opened cheerfully. "Not so much a story as a reflection. The other tales I've heard were more eventful." He paused for a moment, but when Jocelyn didn't respond, he pushed on. "My name is Kincaid, by the way. What about you?"

She looked up at him in surprise. She hadn't been publicly greeted or honored as royalty on her arrival—and she hadn't expected to be, knowing what she did about mountain culture—but she had been under the impression that everyone in Montego knew who she was and why she was here. Did he really not know her identity?

Her confusion must have shown on her face, because Kincaid added apologetically, "I'm not from Montego. I'm Valorian. I come from Bryford."

She blinked, more surprised than ever. It hadn't occurred to her that he might not be a local, but it certainly explained why he was the only one seeking conversation with the outsider. Now that she was paying attention, she could hear the slight difference in accent that should have told her he was Valorian.

He was still watching her, an expectant expression on his face, and she realized that she had never responded to his question as to her name. She cleared her throat, unable to see a way to avoid this small amount of speech.

"Jocelyn," she said, again inclining her head graciously, in the hope that it would make her concise answer seem less rude. But he was still waiting, and after a moment she added, "I'm from Kynton."

If he really didn't know she was a princess, there was no need to enlighten him. Not being a mountain person, he might feel the need to use her title and show deference in other ways that would just be uncomfortably out of place in the setting.

"I'm pleased to meet you, Jocelyn," he said, his eyes alight with interest as they rested on her. It took all of Jocelyn's royal restraint not to fidget nervously under his scrutiny. "So you're on your way to Valoria, are you?"

Jocelyn nodded tightly.

"To Bryford?" Kincaid persisted.

Jocelyn nodded again, not meeting his eyes. She was aware that he was still watching her closely, and it was a strange and unfamiliar sensation. People tended to look away when in such close proximity with her. Kincaid certainly didn't look uncomfortable, though. And he didn't wear that well-known look of confusion—although that would be because she wasn't really speaking to him. Still, it was remarkable how at ease he seemed, and how eager he was to engage with her. It was a sensation that was novel and, Jocelyn suddenly realized, strangely exciting.

She snuck a look at him, and their eyes locked briefly. She looked away quickly, not wanting to see the friendly openness in his gaze turn into uncertainty, as had happened with the local girl. But as unwilling as she was to look into his eyes, she couldn't help another surreptitious examination of the rest of him.

He was young, probably a few years older than her, but if he was over twenty it couldn't be by much. She should have realized without being told that he wasn't from the mountains. When she had glimpsed him earlier in the evening, his features hadn't been clear in the gloom of twilight. But sitting right next to him, she could see that his hair, while not as light as hers, was still not dark enough to match that of the villagers. At first glance she had thought it was brown, but as the firelight danced across it, illuminating glints of red, she realized that it was actually auburn.

And it wasn't long like the mountain people's hair—men's and women's—which tended to reach down their backs, either in braids or flowing free. It wasn't cropped closely like Eamon's either. Kincaid's hair bounced around his head in a casual way that Eamon, as prince, could never have gotten away with. But it was still undeniably stylish, Jocelyn admitted to herself. And Kincaid's features were good, his face well formed and attractive, and not just because of its pleasantly open expression. Involuntarily, she met his eyes again, and felt a small flush rising up her neck at being caught examining him.

But he had clearly been examining her as well, and there was no hint of embarrassment on his face. His eyes, which she noted were a warm brown, were still bright with interest, and his smile remained casually friendly. She returned her gaze to the fire, trying to puzzle him out. As incredible as it seemed, he still showed no hint of discomfort. Her blank silence should have deterred him by now, if nothing else, but instead he looked intrigued.

She felt a sudden powerful longing rise within her, a desperate wish that she could make a good impression. It was a familiar feeling, but somehow much more potent than usual. How she would love to say something interesting, to make this friendly young man assess her as something other than sullen. And she knew just what she would say if she could. He was clearly a good-humored person—he seemed to have a permanent twinkle in his eyes. She was sure she could make him laugh if she could just...but she pushed the feeling down. She had long ago learned to accept her limitations, and there was no use rebelling against them now.

"So you're from Kynton, and you're heading for Bryford," Kincaid mused, breaking the silence at last. "That's funny."

He chuckled, inviting her to share the joke, but Jocelyn just looked at him blankly.

"Just because I'm doing the same in reverse," he explained. "Stopping in Montego on my way from Bryford to Kynton. Well, not Kynton necessarily, but Kyona at least. I've never been there before, and I thought I'd explore a little."

She gave a perfunctory smile, wondering what it would be like to have that kind of freedom. She suspected that being a regular girl would be restricting enough, but being a royal one was a death sentence for any dreams of adventuring. This heavily scheduled and escorted state visit was the closest she was ever likely to come.

"How long are you staying in Montego?" Kincaid asked, his tone as friendly as ever, as though his listener was not sitting in unresponsive silence for the whole conversation.

"Two nights," said Jocelyn, barely restraining a sigh. She didn't mind listening to him talk, but she wished he would stop asking her questions.

"Two nights? That's not long. Hardly worth it."

Jocelyn just shrugged. If he only knew what a process it had been to achieve even that! Between the royal family sending her, and the one receiving her, Jocelyn's time had never been less her own.

"I've been here for three weeks," Kincaid continued, and Jocelyn looked at him in surprise. She had assumed he was also a recent arrival. "And I had planned to stay several more. It's a fascinating place, and the people here are so unlike anyone I've met before. I'm afraid they won't engage with you much in only two days. It was at least a week before anyone spoke more than two words to me. I think it took that long for them to be convinced that I wasn't a quester looking for dragons, to be honest. They wouldn't have had the time of day for me if I had been."

He chuckled to himself as he spoke, and Jocelyn shot him a furtive look. She had wondered herself if he might have been a quester, but hearing that he wasn't made her instantly respect him more. She wondered if she dared ask him what Bryford was like. Better to play it safe. No unnecessary speech.

The sound of approaching footsteps made her look up

quickly. The maid was approaching, clearly to chivy her mistress toward bed. The appreciative lift of her brows as she took in the princess's companion told Jocelyn that she had not been the only one to notice Kincaid's attractive features. Jocelyn stood abruptly, hoping to forestall conversation that might unnecessarily draw attention to her rank.

"It looks like your friend is coming to collect you," observed Kincaid. "I'd better head for bed, too. They rise with the sun here."

He spoke pleasantly, giving the maid a friendly nod. But his words were directed to Jocelyn, and his eyes once again searched her face with that keen interest as he took his leave of her.

"It was nice to meet you, Jocelyn. I imagine I'll see you in the morning."

The maid had caught his casual farewell, and she turned to her mistress with wide eyes as Kincaid strolled confidently away around the ring of firelight.

"Doesn't he know who you are, Your Highness?"

Jocelyn just shrugged, and the maid let it drop, well used to receiving non-verbal replies from the quiet princess. As she followed the maid back to their lodgings, Jocelyn found herself hoping that no one in her entourage would give her away the next day.

She had very little pride in her status, and she liked the undemonstrative manner of the reserved mountain people. If she was honest with herself, she liked Kincaid's casual friendliness even more, and it was too much to hope that he would be comfortable to maintain it if he knew who she was.

She didn't even entertain the idea of actually asking the maid or the guards to keep her identity secret from the Valorian traveler. Even Jocelyn couldn't imagine what chaos would eventuate from her vocalizing such a desire. Besides, Kincaid was altogether too interested in speaking with her. And as flattering as that might be, it wasn't compatible with her determination to keep speech to a minimum while in Montego. She would be wisest to avoid him altogether tomorrow.

And yet, that very sensible and responsible thought didn't stop her from pausing and turning in the doorway of her dwelling to watch Kincaid's confident figure disappear into the gloom outside the circle of flickering light.

CHAPTER FIVE

"Let me help you with that."

The voice, pleasant as it was, made Jocelyn sigh. Kincaid was a difficult man to evade. She felt like she'd been trying to get away from him all day. To her bewilderment, he not only continued to show no sign of discomfort in her presence, but he seemed not to be in the least deterred by her increasing aloofness. She had spoken maybe five words to him during the entire course of the day.

She relinquished the bucket she was carrying without protest. Uninterested in spending a day sitting around doing nothing, she had joined in with community activities wherever possible. None of the villagers had objected, or even seemed to find anything notable in the princess assisting them with menial labor.

At present she was helping carry water from a nearby spring toward the central fire in preparation for the evening meal. She didn't particularly want Kincaid's help to carry her bucket, but refusing would be much more difficult to achieve than agreeing if she wanted to avoid both speech and rudeness.

"I looked for you after lunch, but you'd disappeared," said

Kincaid cheerfully, hoisting the bucket up with one hand and starting toward the fire. Jocelyn followed silently, admitting to herself that he was encountering much less difficulty carrying the load with one hand than she had when using both of hers.

Apparently Kincaid had stopped expecting a response, because he pushed on without waiting for one. "There's a small meadow nearby, which I discovered a week or so ago. I wanted to show it to you. There are still a few spring blooms left there, and even some of the elusive dianmons."

Jocelyn looked up in spite of herself at this mention of the beautiful white flower that was Kyona's emblem, and that grew only in the mountains. Kincaid, seeming encouraged by her interest, continued enthusiastically.

"From what I understand, the villagers sometimes gather them to decorate on special occasions. I was going to ask you if you wanted to help me find some for tonight, but I suppose there isn't time now before the evening meal."

He spoke lightly, and Jocelyn frowned in confusion. What was the special occasion that night? She didn't ask, of course.

"It doesn't matter, though," Kincaid finished cheerfully. "I'm probably of more use helping you here anyway."

Jocelyn held back another sigh. She was clearly not going to get rid of him easily. Maybe it was time for her to be a little more active in deterring him.

"It's probably for the best that I wasn't available to go with you," she said, and Kincaid came to a stop, turning so quickly toward her that he slopped water out of the bucket in his evident astonishment at her prolonged speech. "Aren't you trying to make a good impression on the locals? It might put them off if you want to spend all your time with the only other outsider."

Kincaid's look of amazement slowly changed into a deeply thoughtful expression. Jocelyn waited for it to progress to the inevitable confusion, her heart contrarily sinking at the success of her efforts. But she was the one to feel confusion at Kincaid's reaction.

"*Would* it make them push me out again?" he asked, apparently speaking to himself. A moment later, he shook his head, as if clearing the thought away. "No, I don't think so. You seem to be welcome here." He smiled easily at her. "And I wouldn't let that stop me anyway. I'm sorry if you've had the impression that your company was somehow going to be a hindrance to me. Is that why you've been avoiding me? That must have been uncomfortable, not to mention lonely."

She stared at him, nonplussed. Of course he had no idea how true his words were, or how incredibly lonely her life was, but it was still unnerving how well he seemed to have read her. And so much for the mountains increasing her power—her attempt to change his mind about sticking by her side had been completely unsuccessful. Perhaps she had been too direct with her comments. She had figured out over the years that the power of suggestion was often much stronger than direct statements.

"Some people prefer to be alone, maybe to everyone's satisfaction," she tried again.

Kincaid laughed in real amusement, hefting the bucket up and beginning to walk again. "If you're trying to convince me that you want to spend all your time alone, or that there's something wrong with you that makes you somehow unfit to be included with other people, I don't believe you on either count."

"Why not?" asked Jocelyn, without thinking. The words had come out involuntarily in her amazement at the unexpected response. What was happening? Were her words having less impact, or was he strangely immune? Or not immune, exactly. After all, she had planted her suggestion effectively enough. But his reaction to it had been entirely unpredictable.

Kincaid stopped again, turning to her with astonishment

written all over his face. "You *were* trying to convince me of that! Why in the kingdom would you want me to think that about you? Surely you don't believe it yourself?"

She just stared blankly back at him, for once not even tempted to speak. She honestly had no idea what she would say. By this time the others whom Jocelyn had been assisting to fetch water had emptied their buckets, returned to the spring, and were on their way back past again. Jocelyn saw some of them frowning in displeasure at Kincaid's dawdling, but he didn't seem to notice.

"You are a most unusual girl, Jocelyn of Kynton," he said slowly, his expression uncomfortably searching as he examined her face. "To answer your question, I don't believe that you want to be alone because I've been watching you, and I can see how you look at everyone around you. It's just the way my little sister watches the older, more fortunate girls all dressed up in their finery, on their way to a dance. It's the look of someone who's desperate to join in, but knows that she can't."

He paused, as if waiting to see if Jocelyn would deny or explain. But she just stood frozen, all her focus required just to prevent her mouth from hanging open. No one had ever said such things to her. Realizing that she was not going to speak, Kincaid pressed on.

"And I don't believe that there's anything wrong with you that would justify you being alone, because such a suggestion is simply absurd." His eyes swept calmly up and down her person, as though reading a signpost. "There's nothing whatsoever wrong with you that I can see."

"Not everything can be seen," Jocelyn shot back before she could stop herself. She had been rattled by his scrutiny, betrayed into hasty speech, but she instantly wished she could take the words back. He was looking at her more searchingly than ever, and she had no idea what was in his mind.

She felt a prickle of fear, and this time it was for herself. All her concern before had been for what damage she might do to this community, but for the first time in her life, she felt at risk of someone figuring out her secret. What the consequences of that might be for her—or even for Eamon—she couldn't begin to imagine.

"Excuse me," she said quickly, deciding that the only thing to do was to extricate herself before she made it worse. "I need to prepare for the meal."

"Wait!" said Kincaid, so loudly that a number of nearby people turned and stared. Jocelyn ignored him, her face heating as she hurried toward the safety of her lodgings.

She closed the door and leaned back against it, her eyes squeezed shut. How had she let her guard down so drastically? She felt desperately alone as she wondered what, if anything, she should do about her careless words. Her heart ached with longing for her twin. If only Eamon were here, he would fix it in a heartbeat. He would smooth over the uncomfortable moment and put everyone at their ease. With a few well-chosen words, he would have even Kincaid feeling certain that nothing was amiss.

She straightened her back. But Eamon wasn't here, and that was the whole point of this trip. Well, at least as far as her mother was concerned. She opened her eyes, and barely refrained from jumping. She wasn't alone after all—the maid was here, staring in surprise at the princess's unusual behavior.

"Are you all right, Your Highness?" she asked tentatively.

Jocelyn did her best to muster up a gracious smile as she nodded.

The maid approached the door, peering out a small window set alongside it. "Is it that Valorian traveler, Your Highness? Did he say something impertinent? I didn't think it was appropriate the way he spoke to you last night, and I've noticed that he's been following you today. He's staring at this building right now. Do you want me to ask one of the guards to speak with him?"

"Of course not!" Jocelyn said in alarm. She couldn't help the words—the maid was still looking cautiously out the window, and hadn't seen the princess frantically shaking her head.

"I suppose that would be an overreaction, wouldn't it, Your Highness?" the maid said quickly, turning to look at her mistress with a little too much eagerness. "I could always speak with him if you wish."

Jocelyn raised an eyebrow, her mouth curving into an involuntary smile, and the maid giggled.

"Forgive my jesting, Your Highness," she said. "It's just that he's very handsome, isn't he?"

"Is he?" asked Jocelyn dryly. "I hadn't noticed."

She had intended the words to be obviously humorous—surely Kincaid's appeal was evident to any female observer—but a familiar and wearisome expression of confusion came over the maid's face.

"Yes, he is—that is, he seemed attractive to me last night. But now that I think about it..." The girl peered out the window again. "Perhaps he's fairly ordinary after all." She frowned. "I'm not sure why I thought he was...oh well," she gave her head a little shake. "You can stay in here to avoid him until the meal, Your Highness, and I can sit with you this time, to make sure he keeps a proper distance."

Jocelyn couldn't pretend to herself that she was excited about the prospect of an evening in close proximity with the girl, who was good-hearted but had the sense of a peahen. But on reflection she realized that she probably did need some assistance to keep Kincaid at bay, given the evident strength of his curiosity. She only had to avoid him for the evening and she would be safe, because her party was due to depart early the next morning.

She felt a pang at the idea of leaving without any further conversation with the young Valorian. She would love the chance to puzzle out the mystery behind his unpredictable reactions. But he was clearly trying to do the same with her, and that was dangerous. Not to mention the way his unusually searching scrutiny made her feel exposed in all sorts of ways.

So she submitted to the chaperonage, and true to her word, the maid stuck to her mistress's side like a plaster for the entire meal. Kincaid, seated halfway around the fire, made no attempt to approach them, but Jocelyn could feel his eyes on her as she ate. Everything about the evening seemed the same as the one before, and Jocelyn wondered what Kincaid had meant about gathering flowers for that night.

But once the food had been cleared away, it became suddenly obvious that everyone else knew something that Jocelyn didn't. A faint air of excitement was rippling around the circle, and a number of the locals disappeared into their homes only to return with instruments made of wood. Jocelyn had never seen any instruments like them before, but she could tell that they were used for making music.

The villagers carrying the instruments resumed their seats, and without fanfare or explanation, began to play. The sound was much louder than Jocelyn would have guessed from looking at the instruments, but even in the usually quiet community, it wasn't out of place. The music was smooth, the melody otherworldly. It was as though the shadows that ebbed and flowed with the light of the flames had somehow been turned into sound.

Some of the villagers who weren't playing instruments began to sing, their voices swelling the music seamlessly. Jocelyn was mesmerized, the wordless melody somehow penetrating straight to her heart. It wasn't a happy sound, exactly. But it was more genuine than any music she had ever heard. She felt tears standing in her eyes as it wove around her, communicating more strongly than words the connection of this strange people to their mountain home. It was a love so intense it savored of longing, and it spoke to the depth of her own yearning.

She was tempted to join the song, sure that her own much weaker voice would be lost in the chorus and not cause any embarrassment. But the powerful energy of the mountains had never felt stronger than it did with this music swirling through it. Even though there were no words to the melody, it seemed like much too dangerous a risk.

After a few minutes, villagers began to rise from their seats and drift forward into the firelight. Those who were singing or playing instruments stayed where they were, but the ring of light still seemed suddenly full of moving figures. Jocelyn watched in amazement as they began to dance, the movements graceful and fluid, like water coursing down a rock face. Both men and women twirled and swayed, and somehow still looked fearsome rather than absurd.

As Jocelyn watched, spellbound, a rhythm seemed to emerge. She realized that everyone was not moving randomly, as she had thought. The dance was coordinated, the movements consistent. She was fascinated, trying to copy the gestures in her mind, wondering if she would be able to mimic the choreography if she were to dare to join the dance. Not that she intended to do any such thing, of course. She wasn't sure if outsiders were even allowed to join in, and either way she didn't want to make a fool of herself.

But just as she had the thought, her eyes flicked away from the dancers, caught by a movement on the edge of the circle. Kincaid had stood up, and was beginning to make his way toward her. She gulped. She was certain from the look on his face that he was determined to get to the bottom of their strange conversation that afternoon, and was not above using the cover of the communal dance to corner her when it would be rude for her to slip away.

She couldn't risk speaking with him again—she simply couldn't. Her eyes flicked to her maid, but the girl was watching the dancing with wide eyes, her expression more unnerved than admiring. With the best will in the world, Jocelyn didn't think the maid would be a match for Kincaid, anyway.

The Valorian was halfway toward her when she made her impulsive decision. She was sure her actions would shock her escorts, who knew her as reserved and retiring, but she was convinced that it was actually the more responsible course. No speaking was required, after all. And the inexplicable yearning she felt to join the villagers and let out her pent up emotions through expressive movement had nothing to do with it.

As predicted, the maid gasped audibly as Jocelyn rose to her feet and slid forward into the throng of dancers. In her peripherals, she saw Kincaid come to an abrupt halt, his amazement clear in the lines of his figure. But to her relief, the villagers showed neither disapproval nor surprise as she approached. The movement of the dance flowed around her, seeming to draw her into the mass without a check, so that she was instantly enveloped by swirling, twisting figures.

They didn't even look at her directly, acting as if it was natural for her to want to join in, and their disinterest helped Jocelyn swallow any self-consciousness. Putting both Kincaid and her companions from her mind, she closed her eyes and focused on the music. It was incredible how everything else instantly fell away. Almost involuntarily, she began to move, trying to mimic the gliding spins and rolling turns she had been watching. She didn't open her eyes to check, but she thought she was doing all right for a total novice.

She realized she was scrunching her face slightly in her effort to remember the moves, and suddenly she wanted to laugh at the absurdity of it. The mountain people were clearly not focusing on their steps—that was the beauty of the whole dance. They were lost in the music. The dance, probably built through generations of musical expression, was surely learned by observation from earliest childhood and flowed out naturally without effort.

It was an expression of their love and longing, and Jocelyn didn't need anyone to teach her how to feel those things. They were inextricably linked together for her, as they were for her mountain hosts. Her love of her brother interwoven with her longing to be free of the weakness that, through no fault of his own, was the price she paid for his strength. Her love of her country, so strong that the thought of leaving forever, like Princess Sarai had done, pierced her heart. How could she separate that love from her longing to be what a Kyonan princess should be? And how could she think of her love for the people close to her without longing hopelessly for them to really know her?

She knew perfectly well how to feel, but she was so often denied the chance to express what she felt. She was trapped as surely as she so often trapped her words inside her throat. But no words were needed here. She stopped trying to copy the mountain people's choreography and simply poured her own heart into her movements. She felt graceful in a way she never had before as she flowed across the space. She kept her eyes closed, not wanting to know if her departure from the locals' example had created any displeasure.

How exactly it happened, she couldn't be sure. She just knew that she was channeling all her unspoken words—all her frustration and uncertainty and hope and confusion—into her dance, her movements getting stronger and faster with each passing second. She could feel the invisible web of interwoven power in the air around her more strongly than ever, as if it was being fed by the music, the singing, the movement of the dancers, even her own silent heart-song. Then, all of a sudden, she felt a surge of the indefinable energy burst out from her in all directions. It was like the familiar sensation she felt when she spoke, but so much more potent. She felt as though she had unintentionally thrown a net out all around her, and everyone else in the vicinity had been caught under it.

The music didn't stop, and neither did the dancing, but Jocelyn heard the dip in sound that suggested the musicians had faltered for a moment, and she felt the subtle change in the dancers around her. It was hard to define, but it was like the mood of the group was suddenly akin to the expression of confusion with which she was so familiar.

She came to a halt right in the middle of the still-dancing throng, and her eyes sprang open, searching the space frantically. For a moment she couldn't understand what she was seeing. The dancers continued to move, but their gestures were no longer fluid, and their faces looked confused. And it wasn't just that they were less confident—something else was off about their movements. It took several long heartbeats for Jocelyn to realize what it was, and when she did she stepped blindly back, almost stumbling into the fire in her horror and confusion.

The dance had changed. The steps she had observed so closely from her seat were nowhere to be seen. Instead the villagers were attempting new movements, swaying and revolving in a dance that Jocelyn recognized with an icy thrill to be her own. She was sure no one was intentionally trying to mimic her. They moved almost as clumsily as she had done when she first attempted to copy their steps, and they all looked confused, as if they didn't know how or why they had changed their familiar choreography.

Jocelyn's eyes slid across the circle of seated villagers, noting that many of them were looking around uncertainly, trying to understand what was happening. Her maid and the two guards sitting nearby seemed oblivious to the anomaly, their vaguely uneasy expressions unchanged from how they had been for the whole duration of the group's time in Montego.

Jocelyn continued her visual progress around the circle, and she took another involuntary step back as she encountered Darius. The mountain chief's gaze was fixed unblinkingly on her, his expression piercing. He at least seemed to have realized the source of the mysterious surge of power. She looked away quickly, her heart pounding, but her eyes fell instantly on an equally unnerving sight.

Kincaid was right where she had last seen him, halfway across the circle. At some point in the dance he had evidently sat down on an unoccupied stone. Unlike the Kyonan outsiders who had traveled to Montego with Jocelyn, the Valorian man had obviously realized that something strange was going on.

He was looking around at the dancers, his forehead creased in concentration. As Jocelyn looked his way, his eyes suddenly slid to her, and a look of amazement transformed his features. His gaze was far too shrewd as he held her eyes steadily, and she felt panic rising within her.

Forcing her feet to move, she stumbled forward, pushing her way out from among the dancers. She tried not to look at Kincaid, but she had somehow become far too aware of him in the short space of their acquaintance, and she knew that he had jumped rapidly to his feet and was moving to intercept her. She was sure that she didn't have the capacity to evade his questions through subtle means. She would have to evade him more literally.

She abandoned any attempt to be inconspicuous and ran blindly toward the stone hut where she was being accommodated. She could sense Kincaid not far behind her, but she pushed on, almost throwing herself through the door and slamming it shut. She leaned against it as she had done that afternoon, breathing hard.

"Jocelyn!" Kincaid's knock as well as his shout made Jocelyn jump. She had somehow thought that the closed door would be enough to end his pursuit.

She remained silent, her heart racing so frantically she felt like it might burst out of her chest.

"Jocelyn," he tried again, his voice dropping in volume but not in intensity. "Are you all right?"

She stilled, surprised by the question, but didn't respond.

"Jocelyn, I don't mean you any harm," Kincaid said, and the sincerity in his voice brought a lump to her throat. "Please...I just want to talk to you."

She bit back a hysterical laugh at his words. Talking with her was exactly what he should not be doing.

She could feel Kincaid's presence as he waited hopefully outside the door. But after a few minutes, during which she remained unresponsive, he evidently gave up, because she could hear his retreating footsteps.

She let out a long breath, banishing him from her mind. She couldn't imagine that she would be called upon to answer his questions now. She was leaving first thing in the morning—unless Darius expelled her before then after witnessing whatever had just happened—and she was unlikely to ever see the young Valorian again.

There was plenty else to occupy her racing thoughts, after all. What in the kingdom had just happened? She wished she could convince herself that the strange change in the villagers had some other cause, but there was no doubt in her mind that she had been the source. She had felt the power leave her, stronger than it had ever been.

But how was such a thing possible? She hadn't opened her mouth—she had just been dancing. Were her movements going to start having the same impact as her words? She felt a numb terror racing over her skin at the thought. She would have to lock herself in a lonely tower like some princess from legend if so.

If only Eamon was here to help her make sense of it, but she was more alone than she had ever been in her life. And more afraid.

The uncertainty about what had just happened was bad enough, as was the fear for her future. But there was something even worse. She couldn't shake the memory of how it had felt to release such power, even though it had been unintentional. To her shame, underneath the horror and confusion and shock, she felt an intoxicating thrill at the way she had, with a single motion, compelled so many people to bend themselves to her will.

And that terrified her more than all the rest.

CHAPTER SIX

Given the disturbing events of the evening, Jocelyn was not surprised that she had great difficulty falling asleep. The very air of her hut seemed to hum with power, and she couldn't turn it off any more than she could stop the constant litany of unanswerable questions from running through her mind.

But just as she was accepting the idea of a wakeful night, she most unexpectedly felt herself slipping toward unconsciousness. It was a strange feeling—she was sure it wasn't normal to feel that transition from waking to sleeping, but that's how it was. One moment she was awake but drifting, the next she was asleep, and instantly dreaming.

The dream was lifelike, realistic. She was lying on her pallet in the same stone dwelling, but instead of moonlight, the light of late afternoon slanted through the small window. She knew it wasn't real, and not just because there was no way she could have slept that long. She could just tell.

As she lay there, wondering what the point of such a mundane dream would be, she felt an urgent compulsion to rise. For a moment she struggled with it, instinctively resisting the concept of an external force interfering with her will, but it would not be denied. All at once she realized there was no reason not to follow the inclination. It was a dream, after all, and she therefore had nothing either to fear or to lose.

She stood and pulled on her clothes, her movements unhurried. Making her way out of the hut, she entered the central space with confident steps. She was unsurprised to find that no one else was in sight. After all, this dreamworld belonged to her, didn't it? Why should anyone else be present? The fire was still smoldering, no longer properly burning, but not fully out either, ready to be stoked for the day's activities.

But she didn't head toward it. Still prompted by an unidentifiable urge, she turned instead toward the northern edge of the village. She hadn't strayed to this side of Montego during the previous day, but she somehow knew exactly where she was going. She walked calmly between dwellings until she reached the end of the flat area that marked the mountain capital. There was an opening in the rocks, out of which a small track emerged, winding up toward higher ground. It was not the way east toward Valoria, but she took the track without hesitation. It didn't matter where she went—it was only a dream.

As she followed the track, something strange began to happen. The light, so strong when she had left Montego, began to fade. The shadows lengthened, just as one would expect, but much too quickly, as though the transition of twilight had been condensed from hours to minutes. Likewise, she became confused about how long she had been traveling. One part of her mind was dimly conscious of having walked for some time, but the greater part of her perception suggested that the journey had occupied only a few short minutes. Before she knew it, she was walking in the darkness of total night, only a clear moon illuminating the mountain track.

Incredibly, she still seemed to know exactly where she was

going, the strange compulsion pulling her forward. And she still followed her route without reluctance. She was curious to see where the dream path would lead, and more intrigued than ever by the strange anomaly that was allowing her mind to understand that she was dreaming even while she remained in the dream. Perhaps most surprising of all was that she was not in the least afraid, despite the fact that she was walking alone through unfamiliar mountain terrain in deep darkness.

Only once did she feel a small stirring of fear, when a sudden sound, like falling rock, broke the stillness of the summer night. She stopped for the first time since leaving Montego, looking behind her in an attempt to locate the source of the noise. But there was nothing there, and after a moment she continued, unable to deny the persistent pull that still gripped her mind.

The walk had so far been monotonous, one rocky outcrop looking much like another. But just as she was starting to become aware of being both cold and tired, she rounded a bend in the path and came to an abrupt halt, her mouth falling open.

This dream had just become interesting.

Because there, eerie and enormous in the gleaming moonlight, stood a dragon. It was as tall as five men, and although its wings were currently folded against its sides, she could tell that if they were spread, their span would be monstrous. The creature was looking steadily at her, eyes alight with a studied interest that brought Kincaid and his scrutiny irrelevantly to her mind. The vast reptilian head of the dragon, its bearded ridges framing the temples, swayed slightly toward her, as if taking in every detail of the human visitor. The clear summer moonlight glinted off its enormous scales, their color lost in the cold light.

"Well," said Jocelyn, speaking her thoughts aloud to the beast in a way she never would have outside of a dream. "I didn't expect you."

"Didn't you?" the dragon responded amiably. "But I've been expecting you."

She just blinked, her eyes roaming over the beast's vast form, from the triangular plates running from its neck down its back to the tip of its enormous tail, to the muscular strength of its back legs. It leaned back on its haunches, its front legs resting on the ground in front of it. Jocelyn tried not to stare at the dagger-length talons that sprouted from the ends of its legs. It was probably best to be polite to a dragon, even a dream one.

She frowned, something niggling at the back of her mind. Her father had described dragons to her on more than one occasion, so it shouldn't be a surprise that her unconscious mind could conjure up such an image of one. But she felt unnerved—the beast seemed altogether too real. The dragon magic it emitted in a constant ebb and flow was so strong that she felt like she was at risk of losing consciousness as it washed over her. But such a feeling shouldn't be possible in a dream, should it?

"This is a strange dream," she muttered.

The dragon had seemed content to let her look it over in silence, but it made a strange guttural sound in its throat at her words. After a moment of alarm, Jocelyn realized that the creature was chuckling.

"You are not dreaming, daughter of kings."

Jocelyn raised her eyebrows at the strange salutation. "I must be."

The dragon shook its head. "No."

"But..." Jocelyn trailed off. As enjoyable as it was to speak so freely, what was the point of arguing with a creation of her own consciousness about whether it was real? But still...again she felt a stirring of unease. Looking at the mighty form of the creature in front of her, it felt somehow presumptuous to conclude that it depended on her mind for its existence.

"I am very real, young one," said the dragon, as if it could read her thoughts. "And you are in truth here with me in the mountains. I called you from your sleep and led you out of Montego to meet me here. You should have known it was not practical for me to come to the village to meet you there."

"I don't understand," said Jocelyn, again frowning. It must be a dream, but she had no idea what her mind was getting at. Why would she expect the dragon to meet her in Montego?

The dragon did not immediately respond, instead narrowing its eyes and leaning its mighty head closer to her. She resisted the urge to pull back.

"Hmm," was all it said.

"Who are you?" Jocelyn asked tentatively, for the first time entertaining the thought that all this could be real. But surely not—no one had seen a dragon in almost two decades.

"You don't recognize me?" the dragon asked, surprised. "I am Elddreki. I did not think you would forget our previous meetings so quickly."

"Our..." Jocelyn stopped herself, feeling more unnerved than ever.

The dragon was certainly behaving consistently with what she had been told about the beasts. Her father had explained to her that, perhaps due to their immense lifespan, it was the way of dragonkind to think of a human bloodline almost as though it was one person rather than a long series of separate individuals.

Many times she had heard her father talk about Elddreki, the dragon who had twice helped him to protect his throne, the only dragon to leave the Dragon Realm in centuries. She knew that to Elddreki, any interaction with her would be considered a continuation of his friendship with her father.

She swallowed.

"I'm glad you came," Elddreki continued, conversationally. "I wondered if you would forget our agreement—human memory is so frail."

Agreement? Jocelyn blinked, but didn't say the word aloud. It was finally breaking on her that this was really happening. Somehow, impossibly, she had walked in that trance-like state from Montego to this meeting place, and was actually speaking with the famed Elddreki. Her heart raced frantically inside her chest as she tried to figure out when dream had ended and wakeful reality had begun. Or had she been awake all that time? But certainly the sunshine that had illuminated her path at the start of the journey had not been consistent with the reality of this moonlit night.

The strangest thing was that she still didn't feel afraid. Elddreki was awe-inspiring, no question. But she knew innately that she didn't need to fear him.

"I'm...I'm Jocelyn," she said when the silence had stretched to its limit.

"I know who you are, young one," said Elddreki indulgently. He gave her a hard look. "Do you know who I am?"

She nodded, her eyes again traveling over the dragon's impressive form in the moonlight. He was just as her father had described him and yet, somehow, not at all what she would have expected. He spoke to her as if they were...well, friends. And she could feel it, too—an undefinable kinship. Elddreki's magic was overwhelming as it rolled off him, but at the same time, it was familiar. It woke an answering whisper within herself, as though her own power—which she had never understood—was a trickle to its raging torrent. No comparison in its magnitude, but identical in its substance.

"I'm sorry," she said, her voice coming out more confidently this time, "but I don't know what agreement you mean. I suppose it was made between you and my father, but I'm afraid he never mentioned it to me. What did he agree to do?"

Despite the tension of the situation, her words brought the same release that Jocelyn always felt from prolonged speech.

The energy of the mountains swirled around her as she spoke, weaving past the dragon and settling over Jocelyn like a net even as her own words seemed to add to it. Instead of answering her question, Elddreki stared hard at her through his snakelike eyes, which were once again narrowed.

"There it was again," he mused, apparently to himself.

"What?" asked Jocelyn nervously, although she was pretty sure she knew. She could feel the power coming out with her words just as surely—and just as inexplicably—as she could sense that it was having no hint of its usual impact on her most unusual hearer.

"There's something surprising about your words," said the dragon patiently. "And it takes a great deal to surprise a dragon." He gave her a searching look, and she tried not to fidget. "It's almost as though they have magic. But that can't be the case."

Jocelyn remained silent.

"Say something," prompted Elddreki, the moonlight bouncing off his scales as he shifted slightly, as if making himself comfortable for a fascinating show.

"I...what do you want me to say?"

"It doesn't matter," said Elddreki calmly. "Say anything you want to say. Just speak."

For a moment Jocelyn just blinked. The invitation was such a contradiction to the one inflexible rule by which she lived. Say anything she wanted to say? She felt a sudden urge to laugh, followed instantly by a rush of the agonizing loneliness that was her constant companion.

"Anything I want," she repeated, her voice not quite steady as she looked away from Elddreki, staring out into the darkness.

"All right. The tension about the freedmen can't be coming from nowhere. It must have a source, and we should be trying harder to find what that source is. Calling together a council of nobles isn't a bad idea, exactly, but it's not a very complete solution. It could make the freedmen feel like they're being talked about without giving them the chance to have their own say. People get very frustrated when they can't have their say, and I should know. What Father should do is identify the main complainers—it seems strange and sinister to me that it's so hard to identify who is really voicing these complaints. Then he should get them in a room with some of the key leaders from the freedmen. Do it without the audience of the whole court, and let them argue it out, with him there to mediate. It would be a good place to start."

She took a deep breath, changing topics abruptly and disregarding how the energy of her words was building as she barreled on, speaking much too quickly.

"Eamon and Luciana are perfect for each other, and everyone can see it. It's not as though I want her to start mooning over him every time we're together, but of course I want her to become my sister, and I don't mind talking to her about him. And Eamon is being an idiot. He should have more faith in her than to think her interest in him is at risk from me speaking to her about it. As if it's not bad enough that I can't even tease my best friend about her love life, it stings that *he* of all people is muzzling me. How could he do it? He's supposed to be the one person who I don't have to explain anything to, who doesn't put any restrictions on me."

Her voice was growing stronger and even faster, throbbing with the intensity of the torrent now that the dam had burst.

"And why does that Kincaid have to make small talk all day? Can't he use his imagination and figure out that I'm desperate to know what Bryford is like? All that wasted opportunity to give me some useful information, to prepare me for whatever I'm walking into. He says he can tell I don't want to be alone."

She snorted at no one in particular. "How perceptive! Of course I don't want to be alone! What am I, a hermit crab? Who would want to spend their life alone?! It's all right for him to be so cheerful and unconcerned, wandering across the kingdoms with no responsibilities. He wants to talk to me, does he? Befriend me? Acting like we can relate to one another because we're both outsiders here. As if he could ever imagine how far apart our lives are. It must be nice to be so free—I couldn't be less free if I was locked in a cage!"

The last word burst from her with unnecessary force. She could feel the energy behind her words racing out and away, but the dragon was clearly unaffected. She fell abruptly silent, breathing hard, torn between embarrassment at her unprovoked complaints and overwhelming relief at the release of tension. Such an outburst was unprecedented for her, at least since childhood.

Elddreki had listened in silence to her tirade, his fascination clear in his eyes even in the darkness.

"What a curious combination of thoughts to voice," he observed. "It felt as though you had been trying to hold back an avalanche with your bare hands, and were relieved to finally give up and be swept away."

Jocelyn laughed weakly. "Yes, it did feel a bit like that."

She glanced up at the beast, intrigued. Perhaps there was something in the generational friendship philosophy of the dragons. Because she could find no other explanation for how comfortable she felt around Elddreki, a creature who logically should terrify her. Perhaps it was because she had just shared her thoughts with him more than she had with anyone but Eamon for years, but it really did feel as though he was a friend, despite the fact that they had just met.

Elddreki was still regarding her unblinkingly. "There's definitely something strange about your words, young Jocelyn. I thought I knew all there was to know about humans, but I do not have any idea what it is."

Jocelyn felt herself deflating. She hadn't dreamed that she would actually encounter a dragon on her way through the mountains, so it wasn't exactly that she had built up hopes that had now been disappointed. But it was still discouraging to discover that even an actual dragon couldn't tell her the secret of her words.

"If you figure it out," she said heavily, "please let me know."

"Well, I will certainly try to figure it out," said Elddreki comfortably.

"You will?" Jocelyn asked, her head snapping up in surprise. "Truly?"

"Of course," said Elddreki, his eyes widening slightly. "You are a fascinating mystery."

Jocelyn wasn't sure how to respond to being described in such terms by a magical creature out of legend, but she was spared the necessity to reply because Elddreki pushed calmly on.

"I imagine there will be ample opportunity for me to contemplate the question as we travel together."

"Travel together?" repeated Jocelyn, startled.

"Yes, we will need to travel." The dragon seemed to sense her confusion, because he paused. "Presumably you are here to fulfill our agreement?"

"I...well, no," said Jocelyn lamely, not liking to remind him that she had already told him that she didn't know about the supposed agreement.

Elddreki gave her an incredulous look. "Then why are you in the mountains?"

"I'm just passing through," Jocelyn explained quickly. "On my way to Bryford, in Valoria."

"But surely you humans generally prefer to cross the border further south, using your highway," said Elddreki mildly.

"Well, yes," Jocelyn admitted. "But I requested to come through the mountains. I wanted to visit Montego."

"Why?" Elddreki probed patiently.

"Because...I suppose because it's in the mountain region, which is supposed to have, you know..."

"Magic?" suggested Elddreki, and she nodded. "By which you mean dragon magic?"

"Well, of course," said Jocelyn cautiously.

"So you specifically chose to come through the mountains, now, because of the region's proximity to dragons?"

"I suppose so," said Jocelyn, and the dragon gave a satisfied nod.

"Like I said, you're here to fulfill our agreement."

"But..."

"Your father said he would be glad to assist me in whatever way he could, and I suggested that he come and find me in twenty of your years. And here you are, right on time. Well," Elddreki cocked his head to one side, thinking. "Perhaps a year or so early, even. But it was not an exact arrangement."

Jocelyn frowned. "It does seem a strange coincidence," she began, but she stopped as Elddreki once again made the unnerving laughing sound.

"Humans are so fond of that word," he chuckled. "It is a purely human concept, I assure you." He smiled down at her, his expression slightly indulgent. "Having established that it falls to you to fulfill the agreement, are you ready to begin? Will you join me?"

Jocelyn hesitated for only a moment, staring up at the vast reptilian form in the moonlight. Did she dare? Did she have a choice?

"Yes," she said steadily. "I will."

CHAPTER SEVEN

Jocelyn looked out over the vista before her, a frown creasing her forehead. It was a pleasant enough view, with the rocky slopes descending rapidly from where she stood to the level ground far below where the broad waters of the Great River glittered in the morning sun. The pastureland on the other side of the river looked unremarkable, much like the approach to the mountains on the western side—the Kyonan side. But Jocelyn knew that the similarity was deceptive. The land she could see on the other side of the river was not her familiar homeland.

It was Valoria.

The neighboring kingdom had occupied her thoughts almost constantly over the last several weeks, the topic creating a bewildering array of emotions. But since hearing Darius's unsettling fireside tale about Princess Sarai, who so unwillingly became a Valorian, Jocelyn had felt nothing but apprehension at the name.

Still, that wasn't what brought the frown to her face now. Her uncertainty about her future was not the most pressing of Jocelyn's concerns.

"You look troubled, young princess."

Elddreki's voice made her jump. She had not realized the dragon was so close behind her. He moved with astonishing stealth for a creature of his size. Jocelyn was silent for a prolonged moment, weighing her words, before suddenly remembering that she didn't need to be careful what she said around her new companion.

"Yes," she acknowledged. "I do feel troubled."

"By what?"

"Well..." she hesitated. "I don't mean to suggest that I'm not pleased to be traveling with you. But I'm concerned about my family. I've been thinking about just how alarmed they'll be when it's reported to them that I went missing from Montego. Let alone what the Valorians will think. They'll probably assume I ran away rather than follow through with my visit to their castle. How could they not be offended? I just hope I'm not creating a crisis between the two kingdoms."

The matter had indeed been weighing heavily on her ever since she had set out with Elddreki. It had been more than a day since her surreal meeting with the dragon the night she left Montego. She had discovered from Elddreki that in her trance-like state she had walked several hours, meaning that only a couple of hours remained before dawn. The dragon had solicitously found her a sheltered place to sleep for those remaining hours, but they had set off not long after the sun had risen, and walked all the next day.

Jocelyn had been so tired by that following night that she had slept deeply even on the hard rocky shelf where they stopped to rest. And now that the sun had risen, she could see that the day of hard walking had paid off. They were almost at the edge of the mountains.

But the further she traveled from the original route of her

cavalcade, the more uneasy she became. Conversation had been surprisingly lacking, Elddreki seeming as quiet by habit as Jocelyn herself. He had asked her a number of questions throughout the day, all aimed at trying to understand the mysterious power of her speech. Accordingly he seemed more interested in listening to her voice than in the words she spoke. But other than setting their course northeast, he volunteered no information about the nature of their quest, and Jocelyn hadn't liked to ask.

Which had given her far too much time to reflect on the consequences of her hasty decision to abandon her companions and join Elddreki.

"Will your family really be so worried?" asked Elddreki, apparently fascinated. "What will they be worried about?"

"Well, that...that something has happened to me, I suppose," said Jocelyn haltingly.

Elddreki seemed to be waiting for more, but she wasn't sure how to explain something that she found so obvious to a creature who she believed to be infinitely superior to her in understanding.

"Something? Like what?" the dragon prompted. "That you got injured? But most injuries heal, don't they?"

"Well...well, yes," admitted Jocelyn. "If they're not too severe. But they might not think I got injured. They might think I got lost, or abducted by someone, or even, you know..."

"No I don't," said Elddreki placidly when she trailed off.

"Died," Jocelyn supplied, and Elddreki looked more fascinated than ever.

"Would they really think, just because they don't know where you are, that you had died? How interesting."

Jocelyn shrugged, uncomfortable. The whole thing might be a curious study in human nature to Elddreki, but her conscience was pricking her at the very idea of her parents and brother being afraid that she had met an untimely end in the mountains.

"I'm not saying they'll assume the worst, but my father is something of a worrier."

"Yes, I remember observing that," said Elddreki reminiscently. "But then, humans are always worrying about something." He turned his penetrating gaze on her. "But I still don't entirely understand. If the worst thing they might imagine is that you're dead, is that really such a catastrophe?"

"Uhh..." Jocelyn blinked.

"What I mean is," Elddreki clarified kindly, apparently taking pity on her confusion, "aren't you going to die anyway, in only a few short decades? I thought humans invariably did."

"Well, yes," said Jocelyn, fighting a sudden urge to laugh at the absurdity of this conversation. "We do all eventually die. But that doesn't mean we're in a hurry to get there."

"Really?" said Elddreki, still sounding fascinated. "But humans are always in such a hurry to do everything else."

"Are...are we?" asked Jocelyn, and Elddreki nodded wisely. "Well..." Jocelyn considered the point. "I suppose we are often in a hurry to get to things we think are good. But we tend to think of death as a bad thing."

"Hmm," said Elddreki, as he thought this over. "Yes. I suppose I can understand that. Many dragons feel the same way, after all."

"Do they?" asked Jocelyn, surprised. "I thought you couldn't die. Or is that myth?"

"No, no," said Elddreki vaguely. "It's not myth. I can't die, or at least, it's almost impossible." He returned his attention to his companion. "But you have to die, as you said. And at best you can hope for what, fifty more years? Sixty perhaps? It seems a short time to me. Would the loss of those years truly be such a disaster in the eyes of your family?"

"Yes," said Jocelyn firmly. "It would. A huge disaster. My parents see me as little more than a child, and they would be devastated if something terrible were to happen to me."

"Because humans have an extra instinct of protection when it comes to children," said Elddreki, nodding as if pleased with his inside information. "I've observed that."

Jocelyn looked up at him curiously. He had settled on a rocky ridge next to her, his tail curled around his feet and his head bent low to facilitate their conversation. His form looked altogether too fierce to be real, but his expression was benign. She shook her head to clear it.

"Don't dragons feel the same way about their young?" she asked, and was surprised by the look of sadness that passed over Elddreki's features.

"I don't know," he said simply. "I've never seen a dragonling. No one has in a long time."

Jocelyn was tempted to ask more, but something in Elddreki's expression discouraged her. The dragon was silent for a long minute, then he shook himself out abruptly. The motion, which was accompanied by a continuous rattling sound, started at his head and passed over his shoulders and down his back, all the way to the tip of his tail.

"Well, daughter of kings," he said lightly. "If you wish to allay your family's alarms, it seems to me that it can be easily achieved if I just tell your father that you're with me. Then he will know that you're not lost, or injured, or dead, and he can tell the rest of your family. Will that reassure them, do you think?"

"Yes," said Jocelyn, surprised. "I think that would reassure them. But how will you get a message to my father? Are you suggesting that we go to Kynton before continuing on our journey?"

"Of course not," said Elddreki calmly. "We don't need to go to Kynton to talk to your father. I could visit his dreams, as I did yours, but I think it is unnecessary to do so. He has a way to communicate with me."

"He—he does?" asked Jocelyn, startled.

"Certainly," said Elddreki. "It has been some time since I have spoken with him, but if he is as worried as you anticipate by the news that you disappeared in my mountains, I think he will contact me. I can then reassure him with the information that you are with me, fulfilling his agreement." Elddreki's expression suddenly became stern. "If he had not forgotten our arrangement, he could have anticipated this outcome, and saved himself unnecessary concern."

Jocelyn didn't quite agree that any such recollection would have made Elddreki's interception of her journey predictable to her father, but she didn't say so.

"What's his way to communicate with you?" she asked instead.

Elddreki considered her for a long moment. "If he has not chosen to tell you about it, young princess, then I think I will not take it upon myself to do so."

Jocelyn nodded, disappointed but not really surprised. "Well, at least he won't be afraid that I'm dead," she reflected. How long would it take her companions to get an urgent message to her father about her disappearance? Was someone riding hard for Kynton even now? Had they already arrived? "And he won't blame the guards who were with me in Montego for letting me get away," she added as an afterthought. "And I suppose he can send a message to the Valorians."

"So that your absence won't create a 'crisis', as you called it?" Elddreki gave a slight chuckle, as though he found Jocelyn's application of the word humorous.

"I wonder if he'll tell them that I'm on a quest with a drag-on," mused Jocelyn, a hint of humor in her own voice. "Or if he'll just make up a diplomatic excuse. The mountain people would know my disappearance was mysterious, but I can't imagine them carrying any tales to King Malcolm." She grimaced. "I don't think my poor maid will recover quickly, though. She was terrified enough of the mountains before I vanished in the night, let alone the state the poor thing must be in now."

Elddreki shook his head. "Every word you say is fascinating, daughter of kings," he said wonderingly.

Jocelyn looked up quickly. "Do you have any more ideas as to what it is that makes my words so strange?"

For a moment Elddreki looked confused, then his expression cleared. "Ah, you are referring to the magic in your words. No, no, I didn't mean that. I meant the words themselves. It has been too long since I spent time with humans. Everything you say gives birth to more questions in my mind. Why would your father make up an excuse instead of telling the Valorians that you are with me? Why would your maid be afraid of the mountains, so far from the Dragon Realm?"

He shook his head. "But I won't ask you for answers, because no doubt your replies would just create more questions. As to your magic, I don't have any answers to give you." He smiled. "And you seemed surprised when I said that humans are in a hurry! I have been considering the question for less than two days. Did you think I would have reached a conclusion so quickly?"

"No, of course not," said Jocelyn. She frowned. "You're calling it magic, though. Are you sure that's what it is?"

"Very sure," said Elddreki placidly. "There can be no question. You have some kind of magical property about you."

Jocelyn blinked. If only Eamon was here to hear the certainty in the dragon's voice. "But I thought only dragons had magic," she said eventually.

"That's right," mused Elddreki. "Which is what makes you so

fascinating. It is certainly dragon magic that hangs about you. But no." He frowned, as if in concentration. "It doesn't hang about you exactly. It emanates from you." He shook his head slightly. "Such a thing shouldn't be possible. I believe it to be unprecedented. But it must be dragon magic. What else could it be? Besides, it is familiar. So familiar in fact, that..." He trailed off, apparently not inclined to voice the rest of his thoughts.

"You are sure this is your first visit to the mountains?" he asked at last. "I cannot imagine how you could possibly have done so without me being aware of it, but you haven't entered the Dragon Realm, have you?"

Jocelyn shook her head. "I'd never even been to the mountains before. I certainly haven't been to the Dragon Realm."

"No," mused Elddreki. "I knew you could not have. It has hardly ever occurred, after all, with any human. Only once in my lifetime." He stared thoughtfully at Jocelyn. "I wonder..."

Jocelyn fidgeted nervously as he once again trailed off.

"I will think on it," said Elddreki placidly. "But now, young princess—"

Jocelyn cleared her throat involuntarily, and Elddreki looked at her, surprised. "Is something amiss, daughter of kings?"

"Oh," she said, flustered. "Sorry. It's just—you can call me by my name if you like. It might be easier."

For a moment she was afraid that the dragon would be offended, but Elddreki took the request in his stride.

"Very well, if you prefer it. Jocelyn." He seemed to roll the name around inside his mouth. "I like its sound."

"Thank you," said Jocelyn politely, hiding her relief. She didn't think she could take days or even weeks of being called "daughter of kings" every time she exchanged speech with her sole companion.

"As I was saying," Elddreki continued, stretching out his

wings, "the morning is wearing away, and we should continue if we hope to cross the river before noon."

"So we are going into Valoria, then?" asked Jocelyn quickly. Elddreki had begun to climb down the rocks. He moved at a pace that must have been excruciatingly slow for him, but Jocelyn still had to scramble to keep up.

"Of course," said Elddreki, turning to crane his neck back in her direction. "Did I not say so?"

Jocelyn shook her head, her eyes on her feet as she navigated a steep portion of the slope.

"Actually," she said apologetically, "you haven't told me anything about where we're going or what we're doing. If I'm honest, I'm having a hard time imagining what it is that my father—or me, now—could help you with that you couldn't do much more effectively yourself."

"I have clearly been distracted indeed," said Elddreki. "Your fascinating magic has occupied my thoughts too completely." He spread his wings for a moment, balancing himself. "You are limited of course, as a human, but I think you could be of great assistance in my search."

"Your search for what?" Jocelyn asked.

Elddreki's eyes seemed to light up. "Dragons."

CHAPTER EIGHT

"Dragons?" Jocelyn repeated, startled. "You think there might be dragons other than the ones in the Dragon Realm?"

"That's right." Elddreki leaped nimbly from one rock to another. "I have long wondered whether there might be other dragons within the land you call Valoria. We do not have contact with any other dragons, but there were once more, many centuries ago."

"What happened to them?" Jocelyn asked.

"That's what I would like to ascertain."

"But how can I help with that?" demanded Jocelyn. "Surely another dragon would be a better companion on your search."

"It was not another dragon who made the offer to help me," said Elddreki, a hint of sternness in his voice. "It was you."

Jocelyn opened her mouth but closed it again. There was no use arguing. It was clear that to Elddreki, a promise made by her father was a promise made by her.

"Besides," Elddreki continued. "None of my dragon companions have any interest in accompanying me. They are not willing to leave the mountains."

Jocelyn nodded. She was already aware from her father's stories that with the exception of Elddreki, who had twice left the mountains to come to her father's aid, no dragon had left the Dragon Realm in centuries.

"Why Valoria?" she asked.

She looked up at the dragon as she spoke, her attention momentarily diverted from the shaley slope beneath her. Her feet slipped alarmingly, and she only managed to avoid tumbling unceremoniously down by reaching out a hand and grasping a rocky outcrop nearby. She winced at the sting on her hand where the sharp rocks slashed at her skin.

"Hm?" Elddreki had been looking behind them, but at her question he returned his attention to Jocelyn. If he had noticed her near disaster, he gave no sign of it.

"Why Valoria?" he repeated. "I have heard of a place across the river, not far from here, that the local humans refer to as 'Dragoncave'. I wondered if dragons may have had some history with the place, long ago, to create such an association."

Jocelyn frowned, but kept her eyes on the slope this time. "If it's not far from here, wouldn't any history with dragons be with your dragons?"

Elddreki shook his reptilian head. "I do not think so. My colony has no history whatsoever with Valoria. These mountains are our home—they have always been our home. And the friendship that has stood for generations between our kind and the Kyonan royal family has solidified our connection to the land. We do not have much interest in other places, or the doings of other humans. But long ago, many generations beyond any history you know, some of our kind left Vasilisa, our Dragon Nest, and never returned."

"Why did they leave?" asked Jocelyn curiously.

"There was a rift," said Elddreki. "We do not speak of it."

Jocelyn chanced a glance up at the mighty beast. His expression remained placid, but somehow she knew with absolute certainty that the topic was closed.

"So," she said instead, "you think that those other dragons might have spent time at this Dragoncave, and that it became known by that name as a result?"

"It is possible," said Elddreki, inclining his head. "It is perhaps optimistic to hope for a clue within the cave as to their eventual destination, but it seems like a sensible place to start. Which is where I hope you will assist me. I have reason to believe that I cannot enter the cave, but I hope that you can."

"Me?" asked Jocelyn, surprised and a little bit alarmed at the idea of being sent somewhere a dragon couldn't go. "Surely I can't do anything that's not possible for you. Why do you think you can't enter?"

"I'm too big."

Jocelyn blinked at the unexpectedly simple reply.

"Too big?"

"Yes," said Elddreki conversationally. "I am the smallest dragon in my colony, but you have surely noticed that relative to humans I am large."

Jocelyn craned her neck back to take in Elddreki's full girth as he moved fluidly from rock to rock, his wings spread for balance. From one tip to the other the wingspan was about twice the size of the building she had slept in that fateful night in Montego.

"Yes. I had noticed."

"We can fold ourselves into smaller spaces than you might imagine. But there are limits."

"So any human would be able to help you," said Jocelyn, trying not to feel deflated by the realization. "And yet you waited twenty years for my father to be ready."

"You say that as though it's a long time to wait," chuckled Elddreki. "I had already been interested to explore the matter for decades before I met your father. What was twenty more years? I am not in a hurry."

"Evidently," muttered Jocelyn, as she glanced up to see Elddreki seated in a relaxed posture on a nearby rock, watching her struggle down the last of the slope. In order to move at a pace with which she could keep up, the dragon spent more than half the time sitting immobile, waiting.

But there was no sign of impatience or frustration in the fluid motion with which he descended to stand beside her on the level ground. The river stretched before them, looking wider from up close than it had from the height of the mountains.

"So how far away is this Dragoncave?" asked Jocelyn. "Will we go there today?"

"I think as the man travels, one day will not be sufficient to reach it," said Elddreki placidly. "Perhaps tomorrow. Depending on how long it takes you to swim across the river."

"Swim?" repeated Jocelyn nervously. "You want me to swim across?"

Elddreki looked surprised. "What a strange question. I hadn't thought about whether I *want* you to swim."

"I mean," corrected Jocelyn hastily, "do you expect me to swim?"

"Oh," said Elddreki, his expression clearing. "Yes, of course. Did you expect something different?"

"Well..." Jocelyn hesitated.

She knew that had she continued with her original entourage, they would have followed the track due east from Montego, and crossed the border into Valoria by means of a small but well-maintained road. One that included a bridge across the river. But the point where she and Elddreki now stood was significantly further north than that road, and she could see neither bridge nor ford in either direction.

"It's just that...I'm not a very strong swimmer," she finally admitted. "And the river is wide."

"Are you saying that it might take you a long time to get across?" asked Elddreki, his voice reassuring. "Don't let that concern you on my account. It makes no difference to me whether we reach Dragoncave tomorrow or a week from tomorrow."

Jocelyn sighed. She was fast realizing that for all the superior intelligence of dragonkind, with this dragon at least, if she wanted to be understood, she needed to be explicit.

"No, Elddreki, I'm not saying it will take a long time. I'm saying I'm not sure I can swim that distance at all. If I tried to swim across, I might very well not make it to the other side before I drowned."

"Hm," said Elddreki, with a small chuckle. "Well, you certainly wouldn't make it to the other side after you drowned." He tilted his head to the side. "How interesting. You have been walking for a day and a half, with no ill effects, but swimming for a fraction of that time would probably kill you. How frail humans are! I begin to despair of you living long enough to complete our quest together."

Jocelyn was starting to have the same doubt in light of her companion's cavalier attitude toward her survival, but she kept her reflections to herself.

"I'd like to do my best to remain alive until the task is done, however," she said instead.

"Your resolve does you credit," said Elddreki gravely. It was hard to tell whether the dragon had appreciated the irony in her comment. "That being the case, perhaps we should find another way for you to cross the river. I can fly as easily as swim. Would you object to me carrying you?"

"No, of course not!" said Jocelyn. "But I thought maybe you didn't like the idea."

"Why would you think that?" frowned Elddreki.

Jocelyn's aching muscles seemed to scream in frustration as she thought of the day and a half of grueling—and apparently unnecessary—trekking through the peaks. It was fortunate, she reflected, that she was practiced at keeping her thoughts to herself.

"Never mind," she said, her voice a bit short. "If you're willing, I definitely think that's the best way for us to cross the river."

"Excellent," said Elddreki brightly, and before she knew what was happening, the dragon had launched himself forward and seized her shoulders with his taloned feet.

The ride was short—her startled squeak had barely left her mouth when she found herself being placed gently on the ground on the far side of the Great River. But she suspected that no length of time would be sufficient to accustom her to the sensation of flying.

For several moments she gasped frantically, struggling to take in enough air to fill her lungs. At least Elddreki's claws had, surprisingly, not punctured her shoulders. But she had the uncomfortable feeling that she had left her stomach behind in Kyona.

In Kyona! Her head snapped up at the realization that she was in Valoria. She looked back over the river toward her homeland, then quickly around her in an attempt to take in the new environment. It looked similar in landscape, so it must have been nothing more than a foolish fancy that made her think that the very air felt foreign.

But it was foreign. It was a kingdom she had never been to before, one that had occupied her thoughts almost obsessively for weeks past. All of a sudden, without warning, she started to laugh. The sound bubbled from her hysterically for a full minute, and she didn't try to hold it back. The release of the torrent was even greater than the normal effect of prolonged speech.

When she finally subsided, she looked up to find her companion watching her with surprise and the by now familiar expression of interest.

"Sorry," she said weakly, wiping tears from her eyes. "It just suddenly struck me how funny it all is."

"What?"

"This!" Jocelyn made a broad gesture that encompassed the mountains, the river, the Valorian countryside, and her strange companion. "All of it. It's just so…unexpected. I've been thinking about my visit to Valoria incessantly for weeks. In all my speculation, I never imagined arriving by means of flying across the river in the middle of nowhere, carried by a dragon."

Elddreki chuckled responsively. "I daresay you didn't. Sometime I will have to carry you on a true flight. I think you would find the experience even more remarkable if I were to show you just how much higher and faster I can fly. I believe your father found it invigorating when I carried him."

"I'm sure I would," said Jocelyn. "Why don't you show me now? You could carry me to Dragoncave, and save us some time."

"Save it for what?" asked Elddreki. "What would you do with it? I thought we established that you don't get many years to your lifespan. Don't you want to fully spend the few you have? Besides," he glanced back across the river, "it just seems like it would be a mean-spirited thing to do."

Jocelyn paused, her mouth open. She had been about to point out that her idea of "fully spending" her time was not to use it in interminable walking, but the dragon's last words had distracted her.

"We should keep going, don't you think?" continued Elddreki. Before she had a chance to ask him what he had meant, the dragon was moving again, and she had to hurry to keep abreast of him.

They walked north for several hours through rough hills. This part of Valoria seemed to be as sparsely populated as the corresponding Kyonan area on the other side of the mountains, and they didn't pass a single soul.

While Elddreki was content to move at a pace that Jocelyn could sustain, it didn't seem to occur to him that she might want to stop to rest more often than he did. By the time evening began to fall, she was beyond hungry and tired.

"Elddreki," she tried, her voice coming out croaky. "I'm going to need to stop soon. I need water, and I need to eat something."

"Again?" asked Elddreki, his tone surprised rather than irritated. "I must bear in mind how often humans need to eat."

"Multiple times a day, usually," said Jocelyn dryly.

"But surely you haven't eaten since this morning," said Elddreki. "Why didn't you have some food before now?"

"Because I don't have any left," said Jocelyn shortly. The food in the pack she had brought—which she didn't even remember collecting in her dream-state—had run out that morning.

"We must get you more," said Elddreki promptly. "Would you like me to catch you a goat?"

"Uhh..." Jocelyn blinked. "I have to admit I've never actually slaughtered and prepared a goat. And I suspect that any goats around here," she gestured to the farmland to which the hilly crags had recently given way, "belong to people who would resent us eating them."

"Good point," said Elddreki thoughtfully. He peered ahead through the fading light. "Is that a town? Perhaps you can purchase some food there?"

Jocelyn followed the dragon's gaze. "I don't see anything."

"It's there, all the same," said Elddreki comfortably. "Humans have weak eyesight, that's all."

Jocelyn had by now become sufficiently comfortable around her formidable companion to roll her eyes at this slight on her kind, but she didn't otherwise reply. They walked on for another half an hour, by which time even Jocelyn could see the small town up ahead, despite the fact that twilight had truly set in. They had until now followed the course of the river rather than a road, but up ahead Jocelyn could see a path winding in from the east and curving up to meet the little hamlet.

"Will there be food for you in there, do you think?" Elddreki asked as they approached this path.

"I hope so," said Jocelyn, as her stomach grumbled on cue. She was pretty sure she was tougher than most princesses. But she had never gone so long without food on an inactive day, let alone one where she had been walking from sunup until sundown.

"Hold on," said Elddreki suddenly, and looking up Jocelyn saw that he had cocked his head to one side and was wearing a look of great concentration.

"Is something wrong?" she asked nervously, looking around for an approaching figure.

"No, nothing's wrong," said Elddreki, sounding absent. "But you go on ahead without me. I'll meet you back out here once you've gotten yourself some food." And without further warning, he shot up into the air, the accompanying gust of wind so strong that it whipped Jocelyn's hair and skirts around her.

"But—!" Her startled protest was swallowed up in the darkness. Elddreki was already out of sight. He had disappeared so quickly she hadn't even seen what direction he took.

Jocelyn turned around, suddenly realizing just how dark it had become. She swallowed, momentarily overwhelmed by her vulnerability, all alone in the night in this unfamiliar kingdom. Then she squared her shoulders and pushed on toward the village, her hunger overcoming her fear.

She walked with a falsely confident step as she passed between the first buildings. It was probably best that Elddreki didn't go with her, she tried to reason to herself. She was aiming to be inconspicuous, and that would be impossible with a dragon in tow. News of the strange duo would be all over the kingdom within a week if Elddreki showed himself to other humans, even in this sleepy hamlet.

But the further she pressed into the village, the more it became evident that she was anything but inconspicuous. It was clearly an isolated area, and everyone she passed stared unashamedly at the outsider.

Even keeping her head down, she quickly got the measure of the town. Having been raised amid the maneuverings of court, Jocelyn was skilled in observation. Clearly, the people of this village were neither prosperous nor contented. Everyone she passed watched her sharply, and she was disconcerted to see a calculating gleam in many eyes. She had been wrong to think that this hamlet was sleepy. It might be isolated, but it was clearly awake.

Darkness had fully fallen by now, and she knew that there was little likelihood of finding any market stalls open for business. As unpalatable as the idea might be, the only option she could think of was to look for a tavern, in the hope that they might sell food as well as ale. She contemplated asking one of the watching villagers for assistance, but she was deterred as much by her reluctance to speak unnecessarily as by their unfriendly demeanor.

Pausing to listen, she thought she heard sounds of merriment, and she steered toward the source. Her heart pounded uncomfortably in her throat as her steps led her off the main path and down a side street. Maybe she should leave and try again in daylight. But her stomach drove her on.

"You're a pretty young thing to be out all alone."

The coarse voice made Jocelyn jump. She hadn't seen the man lounging in a doorway until she was alongside it.

"Where you goin', sweetheart?"

Jocelyn quickly looked forward again, intending to hurry past without answering. But the man stepped onto the path and grabbed her arm, moving with a swiftness that belied his previous lazy posture.

"Now, now, don' be rude, darlin'. Didn' you hear me ask you a question?"

Jocelyn hesitated for a moment, thinking. "My apologies, sir," she said in her soft voice, and instantly she saw the man hesitate.

Confusion creased his forehead at the unexpected title, as though he was contemplating whether he was a gentleman after all, and what such a circumstance might mean for his next move. Jocelyn restrained a smile. Good—an easy one to manipulate, then.

"I didn't mean to offend you," she continued. "I was just concerned that my brother will be angry if I'm late."

The man let go of her arm, stepping back. Jocelyn saw that well-known expression of confusion overtake his features, as her suggestion took root and he tried to decide what to do about it.

She didn't wait for him to figure it out, hurrying on as soon as he released her. A quick glance back showed that the man wasn't pursuing her, and she let out a relieved breath. A surge of fear raced belatedly through her at the memory of the man's uncomfortably strong grip, and the way his eyes had gleamed as he leered at her. But even as she shuddered, she felt a tiny thrill of satisfaction at having successfully extricated herself without assistance.

The tavern was close, judging by the raucous laughter she could hear. Jocelyn had just rounded the last corner, wondering whether they would take Kyonan coins, when she was hit by an unfortunate realization, and her steps faltered.

She had no coins. It was true that she had grabbed her pack during her strange trance, but princesses didn't travel with coins on them, especially when being escorted by a diplomatic retinue.

She barely restrained a groan as her stomach once again grumbled angrily. What could she barter? She remembered that she was wearing a bracelet. Her heart sank at the thought of forfeiting it—she was very fond of it—but it wasn't an heirloom, and after all, she had to eat.

She pulled up the sleeve of her gown, examining the delicate silver chain wistfully. She had just reached up her other hand to unclasp it when she was suddenly grabbed from behind. Before she could even shout, a hand was clapped roughly over her mouth, and she felt herself being dragged backward into the shadow of a nearby alleyway.

Fear raced through her frantically. Whoever had seized her kept his hand over her mouth, and she knew her unnatural words would not be able to save her this time.

"That's a *very* nice bracelet you have there," drawled a hoarse voice, and a shudder ran through Jocelyn at how close the man's mouth was to her ear. "Not at all safe for a pretty young thing like you to be carrying such a valuable trinket around. I'd better take care of it for you, I reckon."

Jocelyn tried to ignore her racing heart, willing her mind to think clearly. If the man really did just want the bracelet, perhaps she should let him take it without a fight. But something about the possessive way he clutched her gave her a nasty feeling that he wasn't going to just let her go so easily.

And, she thought, with a spurt of determination in defiance of her fear, if she was going to have to attempt to fight him anyway, she may as well do it straight away, on the slim chance that she could hold on to the bracelet.

The man had wrapped an arm around her, holding one of her arms pinned to her side, but her other arm was free. Jocelyn had been using her free hand to grab fruitlessly at the hand over her mouth, but with her sudden decision, she redirected its efforts, hiking up her skirt in a practiced motion.

The man's delighted guffaw was instantly silenced, but not by anything Jocelyn did. She had succeeded in retrieving what she was reaching for, but she almost dropped it in her shock at the sound of a furious voice that was somehow much more familiar than it had any right to be.

"Let her go immediately! How dare you accost a defenseless traveler!"

CHAPTER NINE

Kincaid must have been twenty years younger than the man he was challenging, but he held himself with a self-assurance that seemed to give extra years to his lean, strong figure, and his voice rang with authority.

He had been glaring at Jocelyn's attacker with murder in his eyes, but his gaze flicked momentarily to Jocelyn, his eyes traveling quickly up and down her person as though checking she was unharmed. When he took in the dagger now clasped firmly in her free hand, he started visibly, and his eyes flew to hers in a look of astonishment.

The man who still held Jocelyn clasped against him didn't appear to have noticed her weapon, however, and Kincaid's lapse in attention apparently gave him new confidence.

"What gives you the right to challenge me, whelp? I saw her first, go find your own wench." He grinned unpleasantly, revealing several missing teeth. "The bracelet looks like real silver, and this dress should fetch a pretty sum." He gave Jocelyn a shake, the hand that was still wrapped around her torso tugging suggestively at the fabric of her dress.

Jocelyn narrowed her eyes angrily, dimly aware that Kincaid

had let out a growl at the man's words. She registered the ring of steel only belatedly, as she brought her own already exposed blade around to make contact with the restraining arm still around her middle.

She only slashed the man shallowly, but he still let out a yelp and released her, clutching at the injury. He stared in astonishment from her weapon to her face, his shock quickly giving way to anger as he started toward her.

"Why you little—"

He halted his advance abruptly, a much bigger blade suddenly against his throat.

"What were you saying?" Kincaid's voice was a deadly purr, reminding Jocelyn of Aunt Scarlett's stories of the graceful jaguars that haunted her jungle home, always ready to pounce on unwary travelers.

The man stared down at Kincaid's sword as though hypnotized, looking like he wanted to gulp but didn't dare with the point so close to his throat.

"I think you should apologize to the lady," Kincaid was continuing smoothly. "For the insult you've offered her."

The man let out a frustrated growl and spat on the ground. He was evidently reluctant to debase himself to someone he clearly considered should be an easy target.

"If she don't know no better than to come parading around here in her finery, then it's her own fault if—"

"Or," Kincaid interrupted pleasantly, "I could just run you through and leave your body behind that horse shed over there. I doubt anyone would miss you."

The man struggled with himself for another moment, but he seemed to read in Kincaid's eyes that the younger man meant what he said.

"I apologize, wench," he spat at Jocelyn. "My mistake."

Kincaid's arm tightened rather than withdrew at the man's

insulting form of address, but Jocelyn wasn't interested in prolonging the encounter. She just shrugged as she turned away to re-sheath her concealed dagger. Then she went silently to stand beside Kincaid, content to let him continue to do the talking.

Her heart had leaped strangely at the handsome Valorian's timely arrival—in a manner that a niggling voice in the back of her mind told her was not entirely explained by her relief at being rescued—but it had sunk right back down at the realization that she once again had to watch her words.

"Get out of my sight, then," Kincaid was dismissing the local man, his expression still hard. He watched the man slink away into the shadows, then turned to Jocelyn.

"Jocelyn," he started, then paused, suddenly hesitant. "Are you all right?"

Jocelyn nodded, but an involuntary shudder ran over her at the sudden memory of the man's hand over her mouth. She could still feel its pressure, and the foul taste of his skin lingered on her lips. At the movement, Kincaid took an impulsive step toward her, but stopped abruptly.

"I'm sorry I didn't get here sooner," he said quickly, and she frowned up at him in confusion. How had he gotten here at all? But of course she didn't ask.

"Come on," said Kincaid, seeming more thrown by her continued silence than he had been in any of their interactions in Montego. "We should get out of here. That man might come back with some friends."

He turned to go, but Jocelyn didn't move, looking longingly toward the nearby tavern. Her hunger had been momentarily forgotten during the recent crisis, but it was reasserting itself with a vengeance now that things had settled down.

"Jocelyn?" Kincaid repeated, seeing that she wasn't following him. "What is it? Surely you don't want to stay here."

He looked around uneasily. "Why did you come here, anyway?"

Jocelyn sighed. Unless she wanted to start miming—and she had no desire to make such a fool of herself—she would have to speak.

"To buy food."

"Oh," said Kincaid, his expression clearing slightly. But following her gaze he took in the tavern, and his forehead instantly creased again. "You were going to try to buy some in there?"

Jocelyn nodded. Seeing Kincaid's alarm, she felt an inexplicable need to justify her actions.

"I knew it was dangerous, but I've been walking all day, and in all that time I haven't seen anywhere else that might sell food."

Kincaid's face softened at her words. "You're hungry," he said. "Starving, I'm guessing."

Jocelyn restrained a sigh. She hadn't intended him to know how desperate her situation was, but of course the suggestion behind her words had come through more powerfully than the simple statement she had articulated. Kincaid might have shown his responses to it to be unexpected, but he wasn't immune to her strange ability.

"And I know you've been walking all day," Kincaid continued, with a dry chuckle. "So have I. And I'm hungry too." He looked at her in silence for a moment, his concern evident. "But this is not a good place for you to be. Don't you know where you are?"

"Uh...Valoria?"

"Yes, Valoria," said Kincaid, with a touch of impatience. "One of the most dangerous parts of Valoria. Haven't you heard of the North Wilds?"

Jocelyn shook her head, and Kincaid sighed.

"Well, that's where we are, and it's not the safest place for lonely travelers to explore."

"Evidently," said Jocelyn. She grimaced, and again found herself trying to justify her actions before she even realized she had decided to speak. "I was foolish, I suppose. I should have waited until I was inside to take off my bracelet. That man must have seen it."

"You were going to barter that?" asked Kincaid, gesturing with his head at the bracelet Jocelyn had been fingering while she spoke. His eyes were wide with alarm again, and Jocelyn felt more foolish than ever. "That would have ended badly," said Kincaid firmly. He glanced around. "In fact, you should hide it now."

Jocelyn pulled her sleeve over her wrist nervously. "But I really do have to get some food," she said. "And I don't have any coins—Kyonan or Valorian."

"Don't worry about that," said Kincaid quickly. "I have coins, Valorian ones. I'll buy us some food."

"But—" Jocelyn went pink. "You shouldn't have to pay for my food."

"Nonsense," said Kincaid dismissively. He flashed her a sudden cheerful grin, which she had to admit to herself was irresistible. "Truth be told, I'm starving myself. I'll buy something, and we can share it."

Jocelyn wavered for only a moment before giving a curt nod.

Kincaid gave her a searching look, and she felt her cheeks go pink again under his scrutiny. She was certain she must look as disheveled as she felt, and it was somehow both impressive and maddening that Kincaid didn't.

He had the rough look of someone who had been traveling, certainly. But although he claimed to be starving himself, he was just as tall and strong and alert as ever. She had thought about him more than once since leaving Montego, but she had forgotten just how handsome he was. Or perhaps he had been made more attractive by her gratitude at his intervention.

"Well, then," said Kincaid at last. "I suppose we'd better get it over with."

Jocelyn came out of her thoughts with a start, embarrassed by how long she had been staring at him.

"Stay close," Kincaid muttered as they passed through the doorway, and Jocelyn was only too happy to comply.

The tavern was small, as she had expected from the size of the hamlet. But it was the rowdiest and dirtiest place she had ever been. Unless her estimation of the population of the village was way off, almost every man who lived there seemed to be gathered in the dingy room. And despite how early in the evening it was, more than half of them were already fully intoxicated.

Jocelyn made no attempt to involve herself in the bartering for their food. She just stood nearby while Kincaid argued with the man behind the bar, watching the crowd warily. As volatile as the situation clearly was, Jocelyn couldn't help but feel a spark of interest as she took in the crowded room. As a princess, her life was necessarily sheltered, and the unfamiliar setting was fascinating.

It wasn't long before she realized that she was being watched with every bit as much interest as she was watching those around her. Many pairs of eyes had followed the newcomers on their path from the door to the bar, and it was clear that Jocelyn was much more conspicuous than Kincaid. She suspected this would have been the case even without her expensive clothes, since the only other women in the tavern were the serving maids.

Jocelyn's heart went out to these girls as she watched them, taking in how they were dressed, and the way the men interacted with them. She couldn't imagine what it would be like to live her life in such conditions. She felt a twinge of guilt as she remembered all the times she had complained about her father's restrictive rules. She had thought him overprotective, but she felt a surge of gratitude at the reminder that not every girl had someone so dedicated to keeping her safe.

And caring as much as he did about her safety, what was her poor father thinking now? Even her usually level headed mother must be sick with anxiety. And Eamon...well, Jocelyn suspected that if her twin wasn't currently riding for the mountains to look for her, it was only because he was still at Raldon, in the forest, and hadn't yet heard of her disappearance.

The sound of smashing glass brought Jocelyn out of her thoughts. Someone in the corner had clearly taken offense at a neighbor's comment, and a tussle was breaking out. Kincaid looked around quickly, his eyes skating over the room and pausing for a moment on Jocelyn, their expression tense.

And Jocelyn could see why. Even the growing altercation had drawn very little attention away from her. Brawls were presumably a familiar occurrence, because no one seemed to think it worth their notice when compared to the presence of an unknown young woman. At least half the men were staring now, and while some of the drunken ones were leering at her, more concerning were the ones who were looking her up and down in a calculating manner, shrewdly taking in the signs of wealth on her person.

"Let's go," said Kincaid tersely.

Jocelyn looked around, startled. "Did you get the—?" But she cut herself off as she saw him putting a large bundle into his rucksack.

Without another word, the two of them made quickly for the door. The many pairs of eyes following them gave Jocelyn the unpleasant sensation of being pursued, even though no one moved from their seats.

The cool night air was a welcome relief after the stench of the close room, but they didn't pause, pushing on without stopping until they were clear of the town. Kincaid set a fast pace, and Jocelyn had to hurry to keep up, her stomach protesting as it demanded the food that it somehow knew to be close by.

Kincaid was leading them south, back the way Jocelyn and Elddreki had come. The lights of the village quickly faded, but with a clear sky and a bright moon, Jocelyn had no difficulty seeing where they were going. After a short while Kincaid veered right, toward the river, coming to a stop behind a rocky outcrop which hid the village from view.

"Let's stop here," he said, and Jocelyn nodded.

Kincaid pulled the parcel out of his pack immediately, unwrapping it to reveal a few loaves of bread, a skin of wine, some cheese, some apples, and some dried meat. No food had ever looked so good to Jocelyn.

"Here," said Kincaid, handing her an apple.

"Thank you," said Jocelyn, trying not to look too eager as she took it. She hesitated before taking a bite, however, noting that Kincaid was once again standing, looking around like a sentry.

She cleared her throat, and Kincaid looked down at her inquiringly. When Jocelyn gestured toward the food, Kincaid shook his head.

"No, it's all right, you go ahead, and I'll keep a lookout. I can eat later."

"No," said Jocelyn, putting the apple down with decision. "You said you were starving. And you said if I let you buy the food, we'd share it." Her stomach rebelled furiously, but she ignored it.

Kincaid looked from her to the apple and sighed. He seemed to understand her silent message, that she wouldn't eat unless he did.

With a final look around into the dark night, he threw

himself down on the grass and reached for one of the loaves of bread. After satisfying herself that he was really going to eat it, Jocelyn retrieved her apple. It took all her court training to eat slowly and gracefully, instead of shoveling the food into her mouth.

"So you *let* me buy the food, did you?"

Jocelyn looked up quickly to find Kincaid's eyes on her. He was once again giving her that irresistible grin.

"Of course," she said with dignity. "I could see that you were dying to display your chivalry, so I graciously humored you." She might speak regally, but she couldn't keep the twinkle from her eyes, and Kincaid's eyes sparkled responsively.

"That was generous."

"But I really am grateful," said Jocelyn softly, feeling emboldened by the relative darkness. "And not just for the food."

Kincaid's face instantly became serious. "And I really am sorry that I didn't get there sooner," he said. "I would have pushed myself harder if I'd had any inkling you were going to wander into a town alone, and at night."

Jocelyn frowned, but before she could speak, Kincaid pushed on, apparently determined to get his apologies out of the way.

"And I'm sorry I called you a defenseless traveler when I was talking to that lowlife. That was my mistake, evidently."

Jocelyn laughed. "I'm not offended."

Kincaid smiled. "Well, I'm glad you're not annoyed with me," he said lightly. "I was trying to help, but when I saw your blade, I wondered if maybe you had the situation under control, and might resent my interference."

Jocelyn shook her head. "Of course I don't resent your help. I was certainly going to try my best to escape, but I think 'under control' is generous."

Kincaid didn't respond, and Jocelyn studied him curiously for a moment.

"Did you seriously just apologize for rescuing me?" she asked at last. "Why would you think I would be angry?"

To her surprise, he chuckled. "I was just thinking how mad my little sister would be at the suggestion that she needed me or anyone else to rescue her. She's fourteen, and..." he smiled indulgently, "precocious."

Jocelyn smiled as well. She could easily imagine her fourteen-year-old self holding such an opinion. How many times had she insisted that she was as capable as Eamon? But that was before her power had grown so much stronger. She had become practiced at standing in the background now.

"Well, your sister might not need anyone's help, but perhaps she's never been grabbed by a foul-smelling stranger and dragged down a dark alleyway."

She had spoken jestingly, but Kincaid's brow immediately darkened again.

"No, I'm happy to say she hasn't," he said, looking at Jocelyn with distress in his face. "And I'm more sorry than I can say that you had such an experience."

"You and your apologies," said Jocelyn lightly, uncomfortable with the intensity of Kincaid's scrutiny. Her eyes narrowed. "If you should be apologizing for anything, it's for following me all the way from Montego, which I'm starting to suspect you must have done."

"Yes, I did," said Kincaid unashamedly, "and that I'm not sorry for. I just wish I'd been following more closely. But it took me ages to find a safe place to swim across the river. I didn't have the benefit of the...uh...shortcut you used."

Jocelyn looked at him sharply. So he had seen her with Elddreki. She noted for the first time that his hair and clothes did indeed look damp, as though they had gotten saturated much earlier in the day and hadn't fully dried. Her heart raced as she thought of the various conversations she'd had with the dragon. How much had Kincaid heard?

"I must say," he continued, in a casual tone belied by his keen glance, "I wouldn't have picked you as a quester. Where is your...companion, anyway?" He looked up at the sky, as if expecting that the mention of the dragon would cause the beast himself to descend upon them.

"I don't know," said Jocelyn shortly. "He had to go somewhere, but he didn't tell me where. And I'm not a quester. Why did you follow me?"

Kincaid shrugged. "Plain curiosity. You would have done the same probably, if you'd seen what I saw. I couldn't sleep that night, and I was sitting by the communal fire after everyone else was in bed, when out you walk, all alone and dressed for travel." He gave her a curious look. "Did you see me there, watching you?"

Jocelyn shook her head.

"No, I didn't think so," Kincaid continued. "You seemed unaware of your surroundings, almost like you were in a trance or something. I'd never seen anything like it. You walked straight out of town, clearly in no hurry, and clearly perfectly sure of where you were going. Well," he shrugged again, "what else could I do but grab my things and follow you? I wanted to find out where you were going, and I wanted to make sure you didn't get yourself into trouble."

"But that was two days ago," protested Jocelyn. "You could've revealed yourself long before now."

"I could have, I suppose," said Kincaid, giving her a look. "But in case you've forgotten, you were traveling with a *dragon*. I wasn't entirely sure whether it would eat me if I made myself known."

"He," said Jocelyn absently. "Not it. His name is Elddreki."

"Well, he sounds lovely," said Kincaid conversationally. "I'm sure he's a friendly fellow, very nice to travel with if you just try not to look too closely at the foot long talons, or the razor sharp teeth. But for those of us not on speaking terms with him, he looks like death on wings."

Jocelyn couldn't help but chuckle. "So did you follow us to try to get on the inside with the first dragon anyone's seen in two decades, or to rescue me from being eaten by him?"

"Honestly?" Kincaid flashed his dangerously attractive grin. "I'm still making up my mind."

"But seriously," Jocelyn persisted, trying not to show her anxiety. "If you've been following us for two days, you must have seen and heard enough to know that I'm not in danger from Elddreki."

Kincaid's smile suddenly seemed faintly indulgent, as though he could tell what information Jocelyn was trying to dig for. But she couldn't see how he would be able to—as always, she had chosen her words carefully.

"Well, I could see that he wasn't aggressive toward you, but I was never close enough to hear any conversation."

So he hadn't heard about her secret. Jocelyn let out a tiny exhale, but she surprised herself with the realization that there was a small measure of disappointment amidst the relief. Somewhere in the back of her mind she had felt freed by the idea that it might be too late to keep it from him, that there might be no point in being careful. Already she had been allowing herself to speak too freely.

But, she argued with herself, it didn't seem to be doing any harm. She felt strangely at ease in Kincaid's presence, and she was hardly feeling any power leave her. She had figured out long ago that some people were much more affected by her words than others. Perhaps Kincaid was simply difficult to manipulate, and wouldn't be greatly impacted. The more honest part of her mind knew she was justifying her irresponsible desire to keep talking with him, but she ignored this voice of reproach.

"And," Kincaid was continuing, oblivious to her inner wrestle, "while he may not harm you directly, he seems to have no idea of how to keep you safe. Not if he's sending you off to wander around the North Wilds alone at night."

"Keeping me safe isn't really a priority to Elddreki," acknowledged Jocelyn ruefully. "I don't think he sees my well-being as his responsibility, and he has a very incomplete grasp of how vitally important the whole life and death issue is to humans."

Kincaid once again looked alarmed. "Good thing you're not as helpless as you look, then," he said. "I mean," he corrected himself hastily, "that sounded very rude. I don't mean that there's anything wrong with how you look, just that...you don't seem like...oh dear." He grinned sheepishly, the expression still somehow unreasonably attractive. "I'm making a mess of it, but I'm trying to compliment you on being more prepared than I would have guessed. I have to admit, I didn't expect a princess either to be wearing a dagger or to have any idea how to use one."

"Yes, well." Jocelyn's tone was dry. "I'm not exactly an ordinary princess."

"Evidently not," said Kincaid, sounding impressed.

"It's because of my mother actually," Jocelyn began, but she cut herself off abruptly as the full meaning of Kincaid's words belatedly hit her. "Hang on!" She glared at him in the moonlight. "You little sneak!"

CHAPTER TEN

"What?"

Kincaid looked startled at the form of address, and for a moment Jocelyn was embarrassed. She had spoken to him like she would speak to Eamon if she caught him tricking her, but of course it was a liberty with someone she knew so little.

Still, it didn't stop her from continuing to glare at him.

"You know who I am, don't you?"

"Oh, that," said Kincaid in sudden understanding. "Yes, I do."

"Have you known it the whole time?" Jocelyn demanded.

"Well, yes." Kincaid's tone was apologetic. "I'd been in Montego for weeks, remember? I know they didn't make a big show of your arrival, but surely you realized that a visit from their kingdom's one and only princess was going to create a fair bit of interest. The matter was the main focus of the town for at least a week before you got there. Even as an outsider, I could hardly help hearing about it. And if I didn't already know, I would've figured it out from the whole dragon thing."

"What do you mean?"

"Well," said Kincaid reasonably, "who else would be wandering around the mountains with a dragon except the daughter of King Calinnae Dragonfriend?"

Jocelyn lifted an eyebrow at the title. She knew that it was what many of the Kyonan common people called their king, but she hadn't realized that the epithet was used beyond their borders.

"So why did you pretend you didn't know who I was?" she asked, nonplussed.

Kincaid shrugged. "Well, I didn't set out to pretend, as such. I just came over to introduce myself, but it seemed like you didn't want your identity to be known. I didn't see any benefit in bringing it up, to be honest." He looked at her curiously. "Why didn't you want me to know who you were?"

Jocelyn sighed. "I don't know," she said wearily. "I didn't plan to pretend, either. But I liked the mountain people's understated ways, and I liked not being bombarded with my title all the time. I liked blending in, I suppose." She smiled crookedly. "And I figured if you knew who I was, you'd become formal with me, and to tell you the truth, unrelenting formality is exhausting."

Kincaid grinned. "Well, I'm happy to continue to be impertinently casual if it helps, *Jocelyn*."

Jocelyn returned the smile uncertainly. In all honestly, if he really had known from the start that she was royalty, she was surprised by Kincaid's readiness to dispense with her title and the respectful deference she was used to. It wasn't that she disliked the informality. She just wasn't sure what it said about how seriously Kincaid took life.

But he had been serious enough about keeping her safe, even though he had no reason to care what became of her. The thought warmed her.

"Have you eaten enough?" Kincaid asked. "I know you must be tired, but I think we should keep moving. Unless I'm very much mistaken, half the people in the tavern were intending to follow us and take everything of value the moment we're asleep. Some of them will be too drunk to follow through, but I think if we stay so close to town, we'll be guaranteed at least a few unwelcome visitors."

Jocelyn nodded in agreement, hurrying to return the remaining food to Kincaid's pack. Hopefully the movement would hide the sudden flush that had risen to her cheeks at the way Kincaid spoke, as though they were traveling together. Which she supposed they were now.

But before they could move away from their hiding place, a sudden rush of wind made them both look up.

Elddreki approached so quickly that he seemed to appear by magic. One moment the sky was empty, the next he was landing next to them, his mighty wings folded back into his sides before Jocelyn could blink.

"Ah," he said brightly, looking between them. "The Valorian has caught up to us, I see." He lowered his enormous head to peer interestedly at Kincaid, who seemed to be frozen. "Greetings, Valorian."

"G-greetings," said Kincaid, and Jocelyn hid a smile at the confident young man's sudden drop in self-possession. Then she realized what Elddreki had said.

"Wait a minute." She frowned up at the dragon. "You knew he was following us?"

Elddreki nodded serenely. "Didn't you?"

Jocelyn shook her head, feeling disgruntled. "You could have said something."

Elddreki looked surprised. "Yes, I could have. Did you want me to?" He paused, frowning. "But that doesn't make sense. If you didn't know he was following us, how can you have wanted me to say something about it?"

Jocelyn rubbed a hand across her eyes in a long-suffering

gesture. She was too weary for the mental effort required to comprehend the dragon's strange thought processes.

"You're right, Elddreki, I didn't specifically want you to say anything earlier. But now that I know he's been following us, and that you were aware of it and I wasn't, I wish you had told me earlier, so that we could *both* have been aware."

"Fair enough," said Elddreki after a moment's thoughtful silence. "That makes sense. I'm a little surprised that you didn't know. He followed you to our meeting place the night you left Montego, and he hasn't been too far behind ever since, at least until we crossed the river. He wasn't exactly stealthy."

Kincaid had been watching this casual exchange with a dazed expression, but it turned rueful at Elddreki's slight on his tracking skills.

"Maybe not to you," said Jocelyn, softening the dragon's insult. "But he was stealthy enough that I had no idea. I suppose humans have weak hearing as well as weak eyesight."

"Indeed," agreed Elddreki amicably, apparently not catching the dry note in Jocelyn's voice. "But this is interesting information, Jocelyn, that you would like me to tell you anything that I know and you don't. I must confess that it is a daunting request, because there are a great many things that I know and you don't."

"I'm sure there are," said Jocelyn quickly. "And I certainly don't want you to attempt to tell me all of them. Just—just the ones that are relevant to our quest, perhaps."

"Hm," said Elddreki thoughtfully. "It sounds like a reasonable request, but I suspect that our estimation of what is relevant to our quest may differ." He paused, but Jocelyn remained silent, thinking that it was all too likely. "For example," Elddreki continued, "I would not have thought that this young man's pursuit was of particular relevance. If I thought he had the capacity to impede our efforts, I would not have allowed him to follow us."

"I have no desire to impede you, mighty beast," said Kincaid quickly, but he stopped at Jocelyn's poorly stifled snort of laughter.

"Sorry," she said quickly. "But you sounded like a quester. You can just call him Elddreki." She looked up at the dragon. "Can't he?"

"Certainly." Elddreki inclined his head in Kincaid's direction. "And what shall I call you? Jocelyn has informed me that she would prefer to be called by her name rather than the greeting more traditional to dragonkind."

"He kept calling me 'daughter of kings' every five seconds," Jocelyn muttered in response to Kincaid's inquiring look. His grin told her that he knew her well enough already to have a pretty good idea of how she would feel about that.

"Do you share the same preference?" the dragon was continuing.

"Yes," responded the Valorian. "My name is Kincaid, and I would be honored for you to use it."

The dragon again inclined his head graciously. "Very well, Kincaid. I believe you were speaking."

"Thank you," said Kincaid quickly. "I only wanted to say that I didn't follow you in order to cause you any mischief. But I saw Jocelyn leave Montego, and I wanted to ensure that she was safe."

"He's telling the truth," said Jocelyn quickly. "He came to my rescue in that town over there." She indicated with a tilt of her head. "I'm afraid I ran into some trouble trying to barter for food, and if Kincaid hadn't showed up, well...I'm not sure I would be here to meet you."

"Of course he's telling the truth," said Elddreki, sounding

surprised. "It's evident. Can you truly not tell when someone's lying, even another human?"

"Uh…" Jocelyn wasn't sure how to respond. As was so often the case, Elddreki had shown the most interest in the part of Jocelyn's speech that she had considered to be of least importance. "Not always."

"Incredible," mused Elddreki. "That must be why humans lie to one another so often. You can get away with it. I knew, of course, that humans can't tell whether dragons are telling the truth." He chuckled softly, talking as if to himself. "Your poor father certainly believed my deception when I told him that he must forfeit his life to save your mother. It was fascinating to watch his responses."

Jocelyn knew the story well, and wasn't interested in distractions, but Kincaid looked intrigued.

"Can dragons tell if another dragon is lying to them?" he asked, his curious tone very similar to the one Jocelyn had come to expect from Elddreki.

"Dragons do not lie to each other," said Elddreki simply. He turned to Jocelyn, apparently done for the moment with that train of thought. "But did you say that you ran into trouble in the town? That without Kincaid's intervention, you would not have been here to greet me?"

Jocelyn nodded, and Elddreki frowned.

"Previous conversation between us leads me to suspect that you mean more than your words imply. Are you saying that you would have been detained in the village, or that you would be dead?"

Jocelyn shrugged, uncomfortable. "I would at least have been detained. It's quite likely that I would be dead."

Elddreki let out a long exhale, but when he spoke his voice held frustration rather than concern. "How absurd it is! You are more frail than I would ever have imagined. How are you to fulfill your promise to aid me in my quest if you're liable to die any time you get lost in the mountains, or have to swim any great distance, or even are left to interact with your kind without my presence? How did you survive from your birth until the present time?"

Jocelyn resisted the urge to again rub her eyes. "Well, I'm a princess, so I've been pretty carefully looked after. But honestly, I don't think I've ever come close to dying before the last few days. It's not as frequent an occurrence as you think." She sighed. "But perhaps I am woefully incapable. It is a bit humiliating that I ran into trouble the moment I was left alone."

"Of course you're not incapable!" interjected Kincaid, speaking to Jocelyn but still looking at Elddreki. At the dragon's last speech, his expression of awe had rapidly disappeared, and now he simply looked unimpressed. "Anyone would be at risk wandering around this part of the kingdom alone, let alone a woman and a foreigner." His eyes narrowed slightly as he regarded the dragon. "It should have been obvious that it was irresponsible to send Jocelyn into town by herself late at night."

"Don't be silly," said Jocelyn hastily. "It's my own fault I ran into trouble. I'm very grateful to you for helping me out of the mess I got into, and now I'll be wiser next time. No harm done."

"Irresponsible?" repeated Elddreki, disregarding Jocelyn's speech. She was relieved to see that although he was clearly intrigued, he didn't look offended. "Do you think I should be responsible for Jocelyn? Why? Because we're traveling together, and I'm stronger and infinitely more capable?"

"Well..." Kincaid looked a little taken aback at this phrasing of the matter. "Yes, I suppose."

"So much for me not being incapable," muttered Jocelyn, but no one seemed to be listening to her.

"What an interesting perspective," Elddreki mused. "I wonder if that's what was behind his comments also."

"Whose comments?" Jocelyn frowned, but Elddreki was once again looking at Kincaid, his head tilted to the side in a familiar gesture.

"But you intervened on her behalf? You evidently felt responsible, but why?" He thought for a moment. "Jocelyn and I were just speaking about the protective instincts humans feel for their young. She said her parents feel protective toward her because they see her as little more than a child. I see that you're older than Jocelyn. Is that why you felt an instinct to protect her? Are you old enough to be her father? I wouldn't have thought so, but I may be mistaken."

"What?" said Kincaid, clearly startled. "Of course I'm not old enough to be her father! I'm only twenty-one! And Jocelyn is most certainly not a child."

"Then why did you intervene?"

"Well, I..." Kincaid seemed nonplussed, and Jocelyn sympathized with him. It was surprisingly difficult to explain to the dragon things that would be inherently obvious to any human. "I didn't want harm to come to her. It's just the right thing...the chivalrous thing to do. I think any basically decent man would do the same."

"Any man?" Elddreki repeated, frowning. "You're saying human men feel protective toward human women? I have observed that, but I thought it was generally only when—"

"I think we've had enough discussion about the workings of the human mind for one night," Jocelyn interrupted firmly. She had a feeling she knew where the conversation was going, and she didn't think either human would welcome its direction. Poor Kincaid was already beginning to look uncomfortable. "We were just about to leave, actually. We think it might not be a good idea to sleep so close to the town."

Elddreki looked around. "But this seems a pleasant place to rest. Why would it not be a good idea to sleep here?"

"Well, like I said," Jocelyn explained patiently, "I ran into some trouble in that village. Some of the men might...bother us...if we stay so nearby."

"Do you think so?" asked Elddreki skeptically, settling himself into a comfortable position on the pebble-strewn bank of the river, the tip of his tail dangling into the water. "I shouldn't imagine they would bother us."

Jocelyn sighed. She was tempted to point out that while it might not bother a dragon, it would bother her very much if a horde of angry and drunken villagers descended on her while she slept, bent on stripping her person of anything of value. And she had little reason to feel confident that Elddreki would take it on himself to protect her. Maybe if she explicitly asked him.

"It is a fairly exposed location," Elddreki mused, and for a moment Jocelyn was hopeful that he would agree to move. But his next words dispelled the illusion. "I don't think it's likely to rain, but it would be unpleasant if it did."

"Your scales don't keep out the rain?" Kincaid asked curiously, apparently distracted from the question of their security.

"They do," Elddreki said comfortably. "But the constant noise of the raindrops on my scales is irritating." He squinted at the sky. "Best to play it safe." With that, he opened his mouth, his jaws moving strangely as he released a huff of smoke. It formed a perfect ring, expanding as it stretched out from him. Jocelyn watched in amazement as the smoke ring settled in a perimeter around the three companions, retaining a solidity that shouldn't have been possible for smoke.

"Will it protect us?" she asked.

Elddreki nodded serenely. "It will keep out the rain."

Jocelyn and Kincaid exchanged a look. "But what about, you know...attackers?" the Valorian prompted.

Elddreki tilted his head. "You mean human attackers? It

won't have any effect on them. What need would a dragon have for such protection?"

Kincaid opened his mouth, presumably to remind Elddreki that not all members of their party were dragons, but Jocelyn shook her head slightly.

She suspected that there was little to be gained by pushing the point. Elddreki was curled up like a cat, ready for sleep, and clearly considered the matter settled. He was so large that he was only partially concealed by the rocky outcrop behind which they had taken refuge.

She risked a glance at Kincaid, and saw that the Valorian was watching Elddreki as well, his forehead once again creased with concern. His eyes flicked to Jocelyn.

"Well, if you're determined to sleep here, perhaps I'll stand guard for a while," he said. He had clearly reached the same conclusion she had earlier, about the uncertain chance of Elddreki stepping in during a crisis.

"Nonsense," she said quickly. "If you've been following us since Montego, you must be as tired as I am. You need to sleep as well."

Elddreki had closed his eyes, but at this exchange he opened one again. "You intend to remain with us through the night?" he asked, directing the question to Kincaid. "Are you requesting to stay with us as we travel and join our quest?"

"Oh." Kincaid hesitated, clearly thrown by the question. It was obvious to Jocelyn that he had just assumed that having caught up and revealed himself to them, he would continue on in their journey. His gaze again flicked to her. "Yes, I suppose I am."

"Well, then." Elddreki shifted, his scales rustling as he snaked his neck toward Kincaid. He remained reclined, but he still had no difficulty bringing his reptilian head to the level of Kincaid's face. The young human stood still as a stone while the dragon leaned alarmingly close. Elddreki pulled in a long slow inhale, during the course of which his head passed down and back up Kincaid's body twice. Then he pulled his head back and gave a tight nod, apparently pleased with the result of this examination.

"Yes," he said placidly. "You may join us, young wanderer."

"Thank you," said Kincaid, after a moment's expectant silence.

"And you should not stand guard. Jocelyn is right that you are tired, and should sleep. Otherwise you may delay us in our travels tomorrow. And while there is no urgency to our errand, Jocelyn is in a hurry, as was her father before her. And most humans, it seems." Elddreki voiced the last comment musingly, apparently as an afterthought, before laying his head back down on his front feet, which were crossed.

Jocelyn uttered a faint splutter of protest at what she considered a very unfair accusation, but she didn't bother to argue with the dragon. What was the point? Instead she turned to Kincaid, who was grinning at her with a knowing sparkle in his eye.

"So it seems you passed the test," she said quietly, giving a small smile of response in spite of herself.

"Apparently," said Kincaid cheerfully, also keeping his voice low.

It was probably silly, Jocelyn reflected, given Elddreki's comments about the superior hearing of dragons. But she continued to speak in a whisper. It made the conversation feel more personal somehow.

"Don't think you can get away with ignoring his instructions, though. You need to sleep, same as the rest of us."

Kincaid frowned thoughtfully as he glanced toward the dragon. "But what if some men do come looking for us?"

Jocelyn shrugged. "We'll stay close to Elddreki, obviously."

She glanced up at the smoke still hovering around them, and shot Kincaid a grin. "Within his useless ring of non-protection."

But Kincaid didn't chuckle. "Unless he takes off again." His whisper had become a mutter.

"I don't think he'll do that," she said reassuringly. "Not without telling us."

Kincaid didn't respond, but he did begin to ready himself for sleep. As casually as he moved, Jocelyn didn't miss the fact that he waited until she had settled for the night before lying down himself, or that he placed himself between her and the village, so that she found herself safely ensconced between Elddreki and Kincaid. The thought warmed her as much as a campfire would have done. She was still feeling its glow when a whisper came drifting through the darkness.

"Goodnight, daughter of kings."

With her back safely to the Valorian, Jocelyn allowed herself a secret smile.

"Goodnight, young wanderer."

CHAPTER ELEVEN

The expected attack came about an hour before dawn.

Although Elddreki had seemed to fall instantly into sleep upon closing his eyes, and Kincaid's deep breathing suggested he wasn't far behind, Jocelyn had lain awake for some time. She had passed probably the most eventful day of her life, and her mind kept jumping erratically from one dramatic incident to another.

And then there was the issue of Kincaid.

She had evaded him in Montego because he was alarmingly perceptive. She knew he'd probably followed her because he was determined to uncover the secret behind her strange behavior. The trouble was that even as her head told her Kincaid was a threat, her heart couldn't deny his appeal. She'd been attracted to him on first meeting. How much more so after he'd come heroically to her rescue! But for all he made her feel safe, his nearness actually put her—and by extension Eamon—in greater danger than ever.

Nevertheless, it was the attraction as much as the risk that made it hard to sleep. Her eyes might be fixed on the heaving flanks of the dragon in front of her, watching the way the moonlight edged his scales in silver, but the steady breathing of the very human man behind her drew her attention much more potently.

As Kyona's only princess, she was probably the most closely chaperoned girl in her kingdom. She hadn't slept in the same room as a male since childhood, and even then it was only ever Eamon, or Lucy's brothers. The presence of Elddreki kept the current sleeping arrangements from feeling intimate, but it was still both alarming and exciting.

With this bewildering cycle of thoughts, Jocelyn was sure she would never be able to drift into sleep. Her first realization of her error was when she was startled awake by a hand over her mouth.

The instinct to cry out was quickly stifled as she recognized Kincaid in the semi-darkness. He held a finger to his lips and waited for her to nod before releasing her. Her skin tingled strangely where his hand had rested.

Glancing over, she saw Elddreki still sleeping, but now she was awake, she could hear what had roused Kincaid. The sound of voices, and shuffling feet, apparently trying to be stealthy. Kincaid drew his sword slowly and silently, and Jocelyn retrieved her dagger as well.

Kincaid positioned himself just behind the rocky outcrop, and Jocelyn had to admire his accuracy in judging the moment the approaching men would round the corner. He sprang into action a second before the first villager appeared, and the man's startled oath was cut off as the hilt of Kincaid's sword caught him neatly under the chin, knocking him senseless.

The next man rushed forward with a shout. He clearly hadn't even noticed the ring of smoke still lingering around them, let alone been obstructed by it. He was brandishing a jagged and lethal-looking knife, but Kincaid flicked it from the villager's hand easily with his own blade. Jocelyn couldn't help but be impressed as she watched Kincaid in action. He moved with a deliberate calm, his actions graceful and controlled.

But in another moment the rest of the group had appeared around the outcrop, and her admiration turned to alarm. There were so many of them—Kincaid couldn't take them all on alone. She turned to rouse Elddreki, only to discover that there was no need. The dragon had finally been woken by the sounds of conflict.

He pushed himself slowly but fluidly to his feet, and even in the darkness, the movement drew the attention of every one of the villagers who remained conscious. Startled screams split the air, and all sounds of fighting stopped.

"Is that—?!"

"It's a dragon!"

"Do we kill it?"

Jocelyn rolled her eyes at that last one. Was the man still drunk from the evening's revels, or just stupid?

Elddreki seemed oblivious to the reaction he was creating. He stretched in an unhurried way, reaching his neck up to its full height and extending his head before giving it a rapid shake, like a dog flicking off water. He then did the same rattling shake of his scaled body that Jocelyn had seen him do once before, lifting his wings slightly as the ripple passed over his midsection. Finally he opened his cavernous jaws wide in a yawn, giving his head one final small shake for good measure. Then he turned his attention to the group of frozen humans standing in the chill pre-dawn light, staring at him in unmasked terror, and widened his eyes slightly, as if asking what they were waiting for.

In a movement so synchronized it would have been impressive if intentional, all the villagers—except two who were unconscious at Kincaid's feet—threw down their weapons and fled back the way they had come, some of them squealing like pigs as they ran.

"There, I said they wouldn't bother us," said Elddreki serenely, surveying the men over the top of the rocks which now hid them from his companions' view.

Kincaid paused for the briefest of moments in the act of putting away his sword, his eyes meeting Jocelyn's with a rueful look. He was still breathing hard from the exertion of fighting their attackers.

Jocelyn couldn't help but reflect that if Elddreki had been awake from the beginning, Kincaid wouldn't have needed to fight at all. And if he had time to wake her, surely he had time to wake the dragon. He must have chosen not to. But she shook the thought away, remembering her nighttime musings. It was foolish to think—and even more foolish to hope—that Kincaid wanted to impress her.

The dragon was looking around curiously, still blinking away sleep. "It's not dawn yet. Do you want to start so early?"

"I don't think I'll be going back to sleep," said Kincaid dryly, and Jocelyn nodded agreement.

Kincaid shot her a quick look, but she didn't meet his eyes this time. Her gaze fell instead on one of the men who was still out cold in the dew-dampened grass, and she realized with a jolt that she recognized him. He was the man who had grabbed her outside the tavern. Kincaid must still have been watching her, because her involuntary shiver brought his attention to the man. Jocelyn saw his expression darken as he also identified him.

"I should run him through right there," he said sternly. He didn't seem to see Jocelyn shaking her head, his eyes moving instead to the dragon. "Unless you want to eat him, Elddreki."

"Dragons don't eat humans, young Kincaid," said Elddreki placidly.

Kincaid chuckled. "I know. I was joking." His eyes came to rest on Jocelyn, who was still shaking her head. "I was joking on both counts," he clarified. "As much as he might deserve it, I wouldn't kill an unconscious man."

Jocelyn nodded, relieved, and shouldered her pack. Kincaid frowned at her, obviously having noticed her silence, but didn't comment.

"Well, let's get moving then," said Elddreki cheerfully. "We should easily reach Dragoncave today, even moving at your pace."

Jocelyn just rolled her eyes again. It was a new day, and she was resolved not to be as careless with her speech as she had been the night before. She had probably just gotten lucky with how little Kincaid had been affected. She could not afford for him to dig too deeply.

"Dragoncave?" Kincaid asked when they were moving, the first hints of dawn beginning to touch the horizon. "Is that where we're going?"

His eyes were on Jocelyn, but it was Elddreki who answered. "Yes, or at least that's what the locals call the place. Have you heard of it?"

Kincaid shook his head. "No, I haven't. But it's not surprising. I'm from Bryford, and I haven't spent much time up this way."

"Well, I'm not actually sure of the true name of the location," admitted Elddreki cheerfully. "Just that it is known colloquially as Dragoncave. Jocelyn has agreed to enter the cave for me. She will attempt to discover any clue it might contain as to the movements of a group of dragons who left Vasilisa long ago, and who I believe may have traveled to Valoria."

"You think there are dragons in Valoria?"

"Perhaps," said Elddreki, his tone as placid as always. "I hope we will know more after Jocelyn enters the cave."

Kincaid frowned. "Why does it have to be Jocelyn?"

He glanced over at her, and his frown deepened at the sight of her passive countenance. She supposed that after their easy conversation the night before, it must be strange to see her so unresponsive.

"Because she is petite," answered Elddreki, apparently not bothered by Jocelyn's silence.

"So am I, compared with a dragon," said Kincaid dryly.

"True," Elddreki agreed.

"Is it dangerous?" Kincaid persisted. "I could enter the cave instead of Jocelyn."

Jocelyn frowned at him, and he raised his eyebrows, as if daring her to vocalize any objections. She didn't.

"If you want to enter the cave, it is your own affair," said Elddreki, a hint of sternness entering his tone. "But Jocelyn has agreed to assist me. Is a promise worth so little to humans?" He transferred his gaze to Jocelyn, as if she had been the one to suggest that she stay out of the cave. "First your father and now Kincaid. No one seems to consider it important that you keep your word."

"I do," said Jocelyn hastily, then wished she hadn't spoken. She could feel the swirl of power that accompanied her declaration, and Kincaid had looked up eagerly in response to the first words she had spoken that day. She didn't dare dig deeper into Elddreki's comment about her father.

But Elddreki at least seemed satisfied by her contribution. "I am glad to hear it. I would think less of you if you tried to go back on your offer to search Dragoncave for me."

Jocelyn reflected to herself that "offer" was not quite how she would have phrased it, but it made no difference.

"So what will we be looking for in this cave?" Kincaid asked, edging closer to Jocelyn as they walked.

Jocelyn refused to meet his eyes, instead looking expectantly at Elddreki. It was a moment before the dragon noticed her gaze, but when he did, he compliantly took up the conversation.

"Any sign that dragons might have been there. Dragon runes,

markings, a lingering feeling of magic. Jocelyn should be able to sense it."

Jocelyn shot Elddreki a warning look, afraid that he was about to say something about her strange power, but she didn't need to worry.

"Jocelyn's heritage as part of the Kyonan royal family gives her a connection to dragon magic that on its own would be enough to allow her to detect its presence," Elddreki continued. "But even without it, she would probably sense the signature of power. She has mountain blood in her." The dragon turned his head toward Kincaid. "As do you, young Kincaid. Do you not?"

"I do," said Kincaid, surprised at the dragon's perception.

Jocelyn turned startled eyes on him, and he shrugged.

"I'm from Bryford, remember? The city is a day's walk from Montego. The mountains might technically be within Kyona, but mountain folk who want to leave the mountains for city life usually make for Bryford rather than Kynton. I'm not saying it happens a lot, but people do sometimes leave the mountains. There are plenty of people in Bryford with mountain blood. In my family it's generations back, I believe, but it's there. I think that's why they allowed me to stay in Montego as long as they did."

He flashed a grin. "Although after I ran off in the night, abducting the princess in the process, I'm not sure whether I'll be welcome back again."

Jocelyn's steps faltered, her mouth hanging open in surprise. Kincaid chuckled at her expression.

"I'm joking, Jocelyn, relax. Although I imagine some people will place that construction on our joint disappearance. Had the possibility not occurred to you?"

Jocelyn shook her head, swallowing uncomfortably.

"I'm sure it'll all get straightened out," said Kincaid easily. He certainly didn't seem to be a worrier. "I imagine rumor will spread very quickly about the pair of humans traveling with a dragon, after our little altercation with those villagers this morning."

Jocelyn glanced back toward the town. They had given it a wide berth, but had now rejoined the river and were continuing north. She had half expected an angry mob to appear from the village, pitchforks in hand, ready to hunt down the beast. But it seemed they had opted to hide from the dragon, which she reflected was the first sign of wisdom she had seen from the aggressive villagers.

"I never asked you," said Kincaid, startling her with how close he was. Their arms were almost touching as they walked, and although he spoke lightly, there was a keenness in his glance that told her he was once again trying to figure her out. "How did you sleep last night?"

Jocelyn shrugged, and gave a little half smile. She could see Kincaid's curiosity warring with frustration at her prolonged silence. Perhaps she should speak occasionally, just to keep his suspicions in check.

"Fine. You?"

The burst of power was small but potent. For a moment Kincaid's expression shifted. He didn't look confused exactly, more like he was recalculating.

"Uh...you know, I hadn't really thought about it. I slept well enough, I think. Until the little visit from our friends."

Jocelyn nodded, and the silence stretched awkwardly. She chanced a glance sideways and saw that Kincaid looked as ill-at-ease as she felt. A familiar ache spread through her, the old grief at the distance her powers placed between her and everyone else.

But now it was laced with a small but invigorating shot of anger. Why had Kincaid followed her? She had been able to speak openly with Elddreki. She had felt free, for the first time in a long time. And now she was back to being silent and isolated. Sullen. Empty-headed. That's how Kincaid would see her. And she couldn't even correct the impression, because the alternative—Kincaid figuring out the secret behind her silence—was far too dangerous.

Knowing it was unreasonable to blame Kincaid, but preferring the anger to the grief, she strode forward more vigorously, placing herself alongside Elddreki and putting some distance between her and the overly observant Valorian.

If he thought he could figure her out so easily, he would soon learn his mistake. She wasn't a puzzle for him to solve, and he had no right to weasel his way into her adventure. However good he might be at searching, she would be better at hiding. She had to be.

CHAPTER TWELVE

"Well, you weren't wrong about one thing, Elddreki. You won't fit."

Jocelyn smiled at Kincaid's understatement. He had taken the words right out of her mouth. Where she was holding them firmly in check.

She sighed, and Kincaid's eyes flicked quickly to her. His expression—that mix of frustration and curiosity—was already familiar. For all she was trying to keep her thoughts to herself, he seemed to have a way of knowing when she particularly wanted to speak. And he was clearly becoming more desperately curious by the hour to know why she didn't.

Shaking the thought off, she returned her attention to the sight before her. She had expected Dragoncave to be part of a small mountain range, given how close they were to the Kyonan mountains. But there were no mountains in this part of Valoria. Dragoncave was only a stone's throw from the river, but it stood all alone, an enormous rocky dome rising gently up out of the flat scrubby grassland around it. It wasn't difficult to imagine how the anomalous formation had captured the interest of the locals and become the focus of folklore.

The mound was large, although Jocelyn suspected the bulk of the cave was underground, making its size impossible to guess. But however big the cavern itself might prove to be, the only opening they had been able to find was anything but. If Jocelyn hadn't known it was a cave, she would have thought it was just a rocky hill, and wouldn't have dreamed there was anything underneath it. But on closer inspection, a slit had been found at ground level, barely big enough for a human to squeeze through, if that human was willing to crawl on his belly.

Jocelyn was fairly sure she would make it. She glanced up at Kincaid, taking in his broad shoulders. The weather was warm, and he had rolled up the sleeves of his light tunic, so his muscled arms were clearly visible. It was a good thing his was a lean strength, she reflected, rather than the stocky build of some of the knights who had come to Kynton for a tournament a couple of years before.

She and Luciana had giggled over the more handsome ones at every opportunity. But even then she had been able to see from the direction of Lucy's eyes that her friend found the lithe form of the then far-from-muscled Eamon more appealing. Jocelyn had rolled her eyes at the time, but on reflection she had to agree—she also found the understated strength of a slim build much more attractive than she had ever thought the bulky muscles of the tournament's victor.

Kincaid was studying the entrance to the cave, a look of calculation on his own face. But he seemed to suddenly feel her scrutiny, and he glanced over too quickly for Jocelyn to avert her gaze. He raised an eyebrow, and she felt herself flushing at being caught staring at his muscles.

"You won't have any difficulty," said Kincaid humorously. "Elddreki phrased it perfectly when he said you're petite." He frowned. "Although I still think you should stay out here and let me go into the cave."

Jocelyn scowled, turning her body pointedly back toward the opening.

Not that she was eager to crawl through the hole, exactly. The darkness beyond the thin entrance seemed more black than should be possible on such a sunny day. It yawned menacingly, and she felt claustrophobic just looking at it.

But that was beside the point. This was her task, and Kincaid needed to stop trying to interfere. She looked up to find Elddreki watching her expectantly. With a curt nod she started toward the opening.

"Whoa, hold on!" Kincaid reached out and grabbed her arm, pulling her to a stop. She glared at him, and he quickly let go.

Jocelyn once again started toward the opening, but Kincaid was in front of her instantly.

"Just wait a moment, Jocelyn. I'm not trying to stop you from going in, I swear. Just listen."

She stopped, letting out a sigh. She raised her eyebrows impatiently.

"I don't think we're ready to go straight in. We don't have any way to make light once we're in there, for one thing." He turned to Elddreki. "Plus, I've been thinking as we walked about what you said about dragon runes. If we find some in there, we won't know what they mean." He looked back at Jocelyn. "Unless you're going to tell me you know how to read dragon runes."

Jocelyn shook her head, conceding the point reluctantly.

"That's what I thought," said Kincaid. "But if we have the right supplies, we can make a copy and bring it out for Elddreki to read." He gestured to the east. "I think we need to visit the town first."

"Certainly, if you would like to," said Elddreki placidly. "I'm in no hurry, as you know."

Jocelyn frowned at the dragon, and Kincaid pushed on winningly.

"Come on Jocelyn, you know I'm right. It will be a good chance to find out what, if anything, the locals know about any connection between the cave and dragons." When she still hesitated, he added with a grin, "What if I promise to do all the talking?"

Jocelyn shot him a sharp look, and he raised his eyebrows challengingly. She felt a cold rush go over her. Just how much had he figured out? Flustered, she gave a curt nod, doing what she had done all too often before—agreeing because arguing would be too difficult without speech.

"If you don't mind," Kincaid said, turning to Elddreki. "I think it might be best if you stay out here." He was still grinning. "It's not that I don't want your company, but it will be difficult for us to buy supplies from salespeople who are hiding in their homes, with the doors barred and the windows shuttered."

Elddreki chuckled. "I can see how that would be difficult. I don't mind staying here. I will investigate the exterior of the cave, and see if I find anything else of interest."

"Good plan," said Kincaid politely, but the dragon had already turned away to begin his explorations, sniffing at the opening like a dog on a scent.

It only took about fifteen minutes to reach the town, and they walked in unbroken silence. Perhaps Kincaid had finally accepted the futility of trying to get Jocelyn to speak.

This town was the first they had passed since the village near which they had slept. The memory of her trip into that hamlet was fresh in Jocelyn's mind, but she felt no fear as she entered this town beside Kincaid, by the light of a hot afternoon sun. Still, this town seemed no more prosperous than the last one.

Thanks to the time of day, they were more fortunate in finding market stalls. Jocelyn trailed behind Kincaid, letting him do the talking as he gathered the supplies he thought would help them in the cave. A rope was easy to acquire, as was charcoal, although Jocelyn couldn't imagine what Kincaid wanted with that item. They had to traipse all over the town before Kincaid was able to find parchment. He grimaced at Jocelyn after the purchase was made, clearly aware he had paid far too much for it, but it couldn't be helped in such a remote location.

Jocelyn had been feeling gradually more uncomfortable as Kincaid spent his own money on items which were as much for her use as his. She wished she had something to contribute, but no coins had magically appeared in her pack since the day before. She did consider offering her bracelet, but she wasn't given the opportunity. Kincaid looked up from the purchase of a pair of oil lamps to see her playing with it, and once again demonstrated his uncanny ability to guess what she was thinking. He reached over quickly, placing his hand over her wrist, as if securing the bracelet in place.

"No," he said, his voice soft. "Keep it. I have enough coins."

Jocelyn felt her heartbeat pick up a little at the unexpected contact, but she met his look evenly, her forehead creased. It didn't seem right to let him pay, but she decided not to argue with him.

She recanted on this decision a short time later, however, when she realized Kincaid was bartering with an eagle-eyed woman for a dress. Jocelyn had been looking away, distracted by the wrestle of a nearby boy with his trio of goats. But her attention returned abruptly to the conversation when the woman seized her arms and held them out, assessing her size in a shrill voice.

Jocelyn shook her head frantically, her cheeks flaming. Neither Kincaid nor the woman paid her any heed. She grabbed Kincaid's arm.

"No," she said firmly, sucking in a breath at the surge of power that left her with the word.

Kincaid opened his mouth to argue, but paused, looking in

surprise at the woman. She had been loud and articulate in promoting the sale a moment before, but she now hesitated, looking uncertain.

"Perhaps you had better not buy the dress," she said, her tone as confused as her expression. "If the lady doesn't like the idea."

Kincaid blinked, looking more surprised than ever as his gaze traveled between Jocelyn and the local woman. "Of course I should buy it," he said.

"No," said Jocelyn again, tugging on his arm until he stepped away a little, so the woman couldn't hear them. He was frowning at her, and she could feel her cheeks still blazing. "You can't buy me clothes, Kincaid."

"Yes I can," he said stubbornly.

Jocelyn sighed, exasperated, and ran a hand over her face. Why did he have to make it so difficult? She didn't want to be forced to use more words, but she couldn't let him buy her a dress.

"I really don't mind, Jocelyn," he said, his voice softer. "And you can't keep wandering through the North Wilds wearing that." He gestured at her dress with his head. "You're attracting too much attention."

She followed his gaze, her forehead creasing as she looked at her gown. He was right—although it was far simpler than her elaborate court clothes, it was still much too costly for the setting. She was fully aware of the many pairs of eyes following her through town. Kincaid's tunic and leggings, while of good quality, were much less decorative and much more practical.

"If it makes you feel better, you can pay me back later," said Kincaid, as she hesitated.

Jocelyn gave in with another sigh, but the troubled expression didn't leave her face, and she remained at a distance, more embarrassed than ever, while Kincaid negotiated the deal.

They were finally heading out of town when they were stopped by a middle-aged man.

"Looking for a place to stay, travelers?"

The man spoke pleasantly, but his eyes lingered on Jocelyn in a way she didn't like. Neither did Kincaid, judging by his half-step forward, and the way he angled his body so she was partially behind him.

"No, thank you," he said, his voice polite but firm. "We're on our way out of town."

"Oh, surely not leaving in such a hurry!" said the man jovially. "I run an inn, you know. Small place, but very pleasant. You must stop for the night, really you must."

"No thank you," Kincaid repeated, starting to walk again. The man stepped into their path, clearly not the type to give up easily.

"But it's not safe to sleep out in the open, not in this part of the kingdom. And Thalia is the only town for miles."

Jocelyn started visibly at the name, and Kincaid hesitated, looking to her.

The local man pushed on eagerly. "You want to stay, don't you sweetheart?" he said to Jocelyn. Kincaid shifted at her side, and she could feel his disapproval at the inn-keeper's familiarity. The man turned to him at once. "You may be willing to take your chances sleeping out in the wilds, but you can see that your, uh...sister...?"

He trailed off hopefully, looking to Kincaid for clarification.

"My wife," said Kincaid shortly. Jocelyn was able to keep her start of surprise internal this time, but only just.

"Ah, of course, just so," said the man, his tone faintly disappointed. "Well, your wife clearly doesn't want to take her chances out—"

"What was that word you said before?" Kincaid interrupted,

clearly trying to identify the cause of Jocelyn's reaction. "Tha-something?"

"Thalia?" repeated the man, distracted for a moment from his attempt to sell them lodgings.

"Yes, that. What does it mean?"

"It's the name of the town you're standing in," said the man blankly. "I don't know that it has a meaning, as such."

Jocelyn stepped forward, a hundred questions buzzing through her mind. "Has the town always been called that?" she asked, wincing slightly at the way her power wrapped itself around her listener. His was clearly not the strongest of minds.

"Uh…" Predictably, the man looked confused. "I think so. That is, I don't know."

Jocelyn sighed, wishing she could somehow communicate her questions straight into Kincaid's mind so he could conduct the inquiries. Then they might actually get somewhere. She was just pondering the best words to try again when a cackle sounded from behind her.

"Of course it's always been called that." The croakiness of the voice was enough to tell Jocelyn the speaker was old, but she turned to look anyway. The woman hobbling past was stooped with age, but her eyes were bright with interest as she stopped and looked at the travelers. "And this town's been 'ere more'n two hundred years."

The inn-keeper—if he really was an inn-keeper—gave a barely perceptible sigh.

"Mother Gloria. Afternoon."

"Yes, yes." The woman waved a wrinkled hand at him dismissively, her eyes still on Jocelyn and Kincaid. "I seen you both in the markets. Buyin' oil lamps an' ropes an' such. Thinkin' of exploring Dragoncave, are ya?"

The man turned back to them, suddenly resuming his inter-est. "Ah, questers! Well, well, it's a while since we had any up this way. I can sell you some excellent dragon products." He smiled conspiratorially at Jocelyn. "Powdered dragon scales will make the hair grow twice as fast and thick you know. All the noble girls in the court at Bryford swear by it. It'll make this lovely golden hair shine like the sun."

He reached out a hand toward Jocelyn's braid, evidently intending to take it between his fingers, but at Kincaid's aggressive glare he seemed to think better of it. He dropped his hand and transferred his attention to the young man instead.

"Or perhaps you'd be more interested in a dragon tooth? If you wear it around your neck, you will be victorious in all your conflicts, you know." He leaned close, dropping his voice impressively. "I have one for sale, very rare. It's a tricky business harvesting dragon products, very dangerous, so they don't come cheap. I collected the tooth from a dragon myself."

Jocelyn snorted. She couldn't help herself. The man's gaze flicked to her, irritated.

"Ar, can't you see they're not so green to swallow that nonsense?" said Mother Gloria impatiently. "You never seen a dragon anymore'n I have. If they're questers, they should know perfectly well that the mountains aren't passable this far north." She gave them a pitying look. "If you want to look for the famous Kyonan dragons, you have to start from Montego, hasn't anyone told you that?"

"We're not questers," said Kincaid shortly. "And we're not interested in dragon products."

"Then why're you goin' to Dragoncave?" Mother Gloria insisted. "And why're you askin' about the history of this town?"

Kincaid frowned, looking between the two locals. To Jocelyn's immense relief, he voiced her own question.

"What does the history of this town have to do with dragons?"

Mother Gloria snorted. "Well, this town's only here because

of Dragoncave, ain't it? And how much more connected with dragons can you get than that?"

"What do you mean?" asked Kincaid, exchanging a look with Jocelyn. "Is there really some history of dragons at Dragoncave?"

The old woman shuffled closer, clearly only too ready to abandon whatever her original task had been and spin a yarn. The inn-keeper gave a tiny sigh and drifted away.

"Oh, there were dragons there once, no question. But it was long and long and long ago. Too far back to count. There's a magic in those walls, though, and it lingers still."

She leaned in impressively, but Jocelyn felt anything but impressed. She didn't believe this woman had ever wriggled her way inside the cave any more than she believed anyone in this town would be able to sense magic if it slapped them in the face.

"The dragons were here long before the town, and the cave was here long before the dragons," Mother Gloria was continuing, but Kincaid cut her off, sounding just as skeptical as Jocelyn felt.

"If the dragons were here and gone long before the town, then how is the town only here because of them?"

Mother Gloria frowned, annoyed by the interruption. "I'm gettin' to it," she growled, her voice losing some of its mystical storytelling tone. "Someone came lookin' for dragons, and found the cave. It was one of the royals, generations way back. She was—"

"She?" interrupted Kincaid, raising an eyebrow.

"Yes, she," snapped the old woman. "You think only men go questing for things?"

Jocelyn chuckled, shooting Kincaid a smug look when he glanced at her. He rolled his eyes, a faint smile on his face.

"She was one of our royals, but she didn't come from here," Mother Gloria continued. "She was a princess from a foreign land, and she—"

"From Kyona?" asked Kincaid, flicking another quick look at Jocelyn.

"Will you stop interrupting?" snapped Mother Gloria, her chest heaving with indignation. "No, she wasn't from *Kyona*." Her tone clearly expressed her disgust at such a tame suggestion. "She was from some far exotic land, where the people had magic. She could sense magic on the wind, and follow it like a hound follows a scent. She was looking for dragons—desperate to find them she was—and the magic brought her to this place. She had others travelin' with her, and they made a little camp here. Some of 'em liked this place, and stayed on when the princess returned to Bryford. It became a town, and she named it—"

"Thalia," finished Kincaid, his gaze questioning as he looked at Jocelyn.

She nodded slowly, indicating he had asked the right questions to reach the information she wanted. It was strange how quickly he'd fallen into the role, almost like Eamon was here. She glanced up at Kincaid, remembering how casually he had pretended she was his wife. He was still watching her intently, and she looked away again quickly. Not quite like Eamon was here.

"I wonder if she found what she was looking for," Kincaid mused. "The foreign princess."

"Ask the cave and find out," said Mother Gloria, with another cackle.

"What do you mean?" Kincaid sounded wary.

She grinned. "I told you, she was magic. She came from a race of magic storytellers, and they say she poured her stories into the cave. If you have the magic, you can ask the cave to tell you, and her stories will come out. It's part of the power of her kingdom, where—"

"Kyona," said Jocelyn, and both of her companions looked at her in surprise. "Her kingdom was Kyona."

"Eh?" asked Mother Gloria, already looking slightly confused. "No, I told you, she was from some far distant—"

"She was from Kyona." Jocelyn's voice was firm, and her power was tangible. At least it was tangible to her, apparently the second princess from this magical kingdom of legend to pass through the tiny town.

"She was...that is..." Mother Gloria frowned, looking more uncertain than ever. "Mayhap she was from Kyona...I thought... but now that you say it..."

Jocelyn tuned the woman out, well used to the verbal dithering with which her firm statements tended to be met. But she realized a moment too late that Kincaid was paying close attention, his shrewd gaze passing between the two women. She met his eye involuntarily. She was sure he was remembering how vehemently the woman had insisted a moment ago that the foreign princess was not from Kyona.

She cleared her throat, tilting her head toward the path out of town in a silent suggestion that they get going. The afternoon was wearing on, and she felt vaguely uneasy about the unceremonious disappearance of the inn-keeper earlier. If he was coming back, she'd rather be gone before he arrived.

Kincaid nodded, his expression thoughtful and his gaze still uncomfortably piercing. Mother Gloria still seemed very confused, but as they turned to leave, she came out of her stupor enough to hold out a hand, palm cupped suggestively. With a sigh, Kincaid pressed a small coin into it in payment for the tale, and then held his own hand out to Jocelyn.

Surprised, she took it, and the two of them hurried toward the edge of town. Kincaid's hand was warm and strong, his clasp somehow reassuring after the calculating look he had been giving her. At least whatever speculations he had about her weren't making him draw back. Jocelyn found it hard to focus on the path, her mind distracted by the unexpected contact, and for a few moments Kincaid was as silent as she was.

"I'm sorry if it was too big a presumption," he said suddenly. "Saying you were my wife."

Jocelyn looked up quickly, and found Kincaid regarding her steadily, his face showing none of the embarrassment she felt.

"I could see he was sizing you up, and I thought it was better to play it safe. Like I told you, this isn't a good area. It's bad enough for a beautiful young woman to be wandering around. Better not to make it known you're unclaimed into the bargain."

Jocelyn felt heat rising up her neck at the implication that Kincaid thought she was beautiful, but at the word "unclaimed", she raised an eyebrow, pulling her hand out of his.

He just grinned at her, unrepentant. "You know what I mean." She didn't reply, and his expression turned serious. "I'm afraid around here that's how people would see it. I thought it was better to 'claim' you, so to speak. Just temporarily," he added hastily, when her expression didn't soften. "And just as a pretense." He hesitated, seeming less sure of himself the longer she drew out the moment. "I hope you don't mind."

Jocelyn finally released him from her glare, a small smile tugging up the corner of her mouth. It was cruel, perhaps, but it had been fun to watch him squirm, just a little. He was always so sure of himself. It would be so satisfying to tease him, just good naturedly, if only she could let her tongue have free rein.

Kincaid chuckled, his spirits instantly restored. "Phew, you were making me sweat. You really have that haughty princess glare perfected, you know." He grinned at her. "But I didn't think you'd really be so stiff as to be offended."

He was looking at her, his eyes full of laughter, his vigilance relaxed. Jocelyn glanced at him a moment too late. He clearly saw her eyes widen as her gaze slid over his shoulder, but he had only half turned, his hand flying toward his hilt, when he was swarmed. Several pairs of hands grabbed him, and his sword was wrested from his grip before it was fully unsheathed. Jocelyn started toward him with a gasp, but before she could reach for her dagger, she was seized from behind, her arms snapped against her back in a vise-like grip.

She looked around frantically, but there was no source of help. There were only men, burly and leering, too many for Kincaid to fight off, even if his arms were free.

They were in trouble.

CHAPTER THIRTEEN

"Well, well, well. If it isn't the travelers."

The inn-keeper strolled forward into the space between the two captives, who had been dragged backward, away from each other. Kincaid, struggling wildly, snarled at the man, who smiled pleasantly back.

"It was very rude of you to prefer the open moor to my inn, you know." His eyes passed over Kincaid's livid face and settled on Jocelyn, trying fruitlessly to free her arms from the grip of the man holding her. "Especially when your lovely wife was so obviously reluctant to brave the dangers of the wilds." He smiled mockingly at her. "You were right to be concerned, my dear. There are dangerous men about."

Jocelyn narrowed her eyes, ignoring the guffaws that greeted this speech.

"I should apologize for suggesting you needed powdered dragon scales for your hair, though," the man persisted. He spoke to Jocelyn, but his eyes kept flicking to Kincaid, clearly baiting him. He reached out and ran his hand slowly and deliberately down her hair, from the crown of her head to the tip of her braid. It was like he was patting a dog. "It's already perfection."

"Don't touch her," choked Kincaid, and Jocelyn was startled by the fury on his face.

"Oh, my interest is purely mercenary," the inn-keeper assured him, still holding the end of Jocelyn's braid as if it was a leash. "You'd be surprised at the price this braid could fetch, if you know the right buyers." He smiled. "Which I do."

"Look at this, boss," grunted one of the men standing near Kincaid. He held out Kincaid's sword, and the inn-keeper gave a low whistle.

"That is a very nice sword, young man. Now *that* will fetch a very pretty price."

"The only function that sword will serve you will be to run you through, when it's back in my hands," Kincaid growled.

"Tut tut," chuckled the inn-keeper, an amused smile on his face. "That's no way to speak to the man who has you in his power."

Power. The word jolted Jocelyn's mind out of its immobility. She needed to use her power, and quickly. Kincaid had murder written across his face, and things were going to escalate rapidly. But what to say? What words would do the job most effectively while still being subtle? She swallowed nervously, her throat suddenly dry. She had never tried to use her words on this many people at once.

"Did you really expect no one to notice how much money you just threw around the market?" the ringleader was continuing. "And you can clearly afford to buy your wife expensive finery. Selfishness is a terrible fault, you know. Wealth like that should be shared. Now, where were we?" He turned back to Jocelyn.

Kincaid had been glaring at a man who was rifling through

the contents of his pack, but Jocelyn saw his attention snap quickly back to her at the inn-keeper's next words.

"You are very pretty, my dear, so don't be too disheartened. Even without your hair, and your fine dress," he grasped her skirt with a lazy hand and lifted the fabric so that her hem rose a few inches above the ground, "you will still turn heads."

Kincaid let out another snarl, struggling furiously against the men who held him. But he was securely restrained. Jocelyn ignored the flurry of movement, settling on what to say. She raised her eyes. If she could make them think the two of them weren't traveling alone…

But the inn-keeper wasn't looking at her, smiling pityingly upon Kincaid's impotent fury.

"It's no use getting angry now, my friend. If you wanted to keep her, you should have taken better care of her." He winked at Jocelyn. "That's why you shouldn't go for such young men, my dear. They make big promises, but they're nothing more than a puff of wind." He threw an arm around her shoulder, and she turned her head to avoid his reeking breath as he spoke into her ear. "Older, more mature men, like me, are a much better bet."

"Take your hands off her, or I will kill you." Kincaid had also stopped struggling, and his voice was steady, but its deadly calm sent a shiver down Jocelyn's spine.

The man just chuckled. "I can see why you value her. She's nice to look at, sure, but you've also got her very well trained. It's rare these days to see a girl so good at shutting up and letting the men do the talking."

A fury as violent as any Kincaid had shown welled up inside Jocelyn, and suddenly she forgot about being subtle. All the frustration of her restricted life bubbled to the surface, personified in this loathsome, offensive man. In that moment she wanted nothing more than to make him pay. She cast aside her carefully prepared speech, giving free rein to both her words and her anger. It was amazing how easily it came—the words and the power—when she didn't think, just spoke.

"You're bold to claim leadership of the group, being the size you are."

"What did you say?" The leader turned to her, his brows drawing together.

Jocelyn shrugged, nodding her head toward one of the men who held Kincaid. "Well, he's much bigger than you, for instance. I can only assume you were very cunning to find a way to defeat him when he challenged you for leadership of the gang."

A rustling went around the group, eyes flicking from the leader to the man Jocelyn had identified. The inn-keeper looked uneasy and confused.

"He has challenged you for leadership I assume?" Jocelyn went on, raising an eyebrow. The usual release of prolonged speech was swallowed in the anger still simmering just below her calm front. All the power she had held inside by continually refraining from speech all day was clamoring for release, giving extra emphasis to her words.

Kincaid had gone very still, and she could feel his eyes on her, but she didn't dare meet his gaze. She looked around the rest of the circle instead, her eyes lingering on the burliest individuals in the circle.

"There are at least half a dozen men here who I would have thought could best you." She could see her words sinking in, the idea of a challenge taking root, and she returned her gaze to the leader, feigning astonishment. "Are you saying none of these men have vied for control? They must have absolute faith in you as their leader."

This time the rustling was louder, many men shifting their feet and narrowing their eyes at the man in the middle of the circle. It didn't take much perception to see that they were all questioning their so-called trust in their leader. The first man she had nodded to released Kincaid, stepping forward.

"I *should* be leader," he said, his voice gruff and menacing. "I could beat you with my hands tied behind my back."

There were still three men holding Kincaid, but one of them let go with one hand, waving it dismissively toward the speaker. "You? I'd have you beggin' for your ma in minutes if you had the stones to fight me."

"I'll fight you any day you like," snapped the first challenger, turning to him. The second man let go of Kincaid completely, and Jocelyn met her companion's eyes at last. He was watching her with his mouth open, but at her significant look he gave himself a little shake, ready to take advantage of the diversion.

"Enough, both of you," said the leader, in a voice that lacked conviction. He still looked extremely unnerved.

"You're not the boss of me," grunted one of the challengers. "At least, you shouldn't be."

"Neither should you!" scoffed the man holding Jocelyn, releasing her to join the argument. She began to move toward Kincaid, her steps unhurried. He continued to stand still, not resisting the hold of the remaining two men on his arms. His restraint was rewarded a moment later, as they both joined the fight beginning to escalate in the middle of the circle, apparently forgetting about their captive.

By that time Jocelyn had reached him, and had begun to surreptitiously repack their purchases into Kincaid's pack, which lay abandoned on the ground nearby. As soon as he was released, Kincaid stepped quickly toward her. The altercation was growing in volume, as half the group seemed to be insisting they should be in charge, and all of them agreeing their original leader shouldn't. The man was attempting to back away, his expression alarmed as he argued with them. Jocelyn could see the doubt and confusion on his face, as if even he wasn't convinced he should be boss.

She was watching the chaos, her task momentarily forgotten, when the first blade was drawn. In a flash, jagged steel could be seen in all directions.

"Time to go," said Kincaid grimly, his voice unexpectedly close behind her.

He relieved her of his pack, slinging it onto his back before she'd fully turned around. Without warning he lunged past her toward the gang member who still held his sword, his fist striking the side of the man's head with enough force to knock him to the ground. Kincaid had his sword in one hand in a flash, and before she well knew what was happening, he had Jocelyn's hand in the other, and they were running out of town.

The sounds of violence followed them, and Jocelyn didn't need to look back to know the argument had become bloody. No one was pursuing them, but they still ran until Jocelyn's breathing was ragged. As soon as the town was out of sight, Kincaid pulled Jocelyn to a halt, even though Dragoncave was still some distance away. She let go of his hand, putting her own on her heaving chest as she tried to catch her breath.

"Are you all right?" Kincaid spoke quietly, but Jocelyn could hear the tightness in his voice. He was barely puffing, irritatingly unaffected by their sprint.

She nodded without meeting his eyes, running her hands down her arms and wincing as she passed over the spot where she had been held. She wouldn't be surprised if she had hand-shaped bruises there the next day.

"They hurt you." It wasn't a question, and Kincaid's voice was as hard as iron. Jocelyn remembered the fire in his eyes when the ringleader had run a hand over her hair, and she could feel her heart beating faster in her throat.

"I'm fine," she said quickly, her voice barely more than a whisper. She still hadn't looked him in the eye.

"You're not," said Kincaid shortly. He stepped toward her, then back again. Then he turned on his heel and strode several paces away, before turning and retracing his steps. His hands were balled into fists.

"I'm so sorry Jocelyn. I shouldn't have let my guard down—they should never have been able to sneak up on us like that."

"It wasn't your fault," said Jocelyn quietly, her breathing finally starting to return to normal. Not much power left her at the words—she seemed to have used it up in her attack on the gang.

"You saved us." Kincaid sounded awed, and Jocelyn looked up at last to find him watching her in amazement.

She shrugged and looked away, uncomfortable. But her head snapped back up as Kincaid continued.

"You saved us with your words."

Jocelyn opened her mouth and closed it again. She was still shaking from their near miss, and her thoughts were in too much of a jumble to know how to avert his suspicions. But it seemed they were beyond that possibility.

"Your words have power. Magic. When you speak, you have magic."

Again, it wasn't a question, and Jocelyn felt the color drain from her face. She stumbled back a step, putting her hands up in front of her in an involuntary gesture of defense.

Kincaid strode forward instantly, closing the distance between them again and grasping her wrists.

"Jocelyn, no! You have nothing to fear from me. I'll take your secret to the grave if that's what you want. I told you once before that I don't mean you any harm, and I meant it. I'm just trying to understand. I'm just trying to help you."

Jocelyn swallowed, tears pricking her eyes in spite of herself.

She wanted to trust him, she really did. But she had never told anyone about her power before, not even Lucy, not even her parents. Could she really tell this man she'd only known for a few days?

Would Eamon ever forgive her if she did?

"Jocelyn?" Kincaid pushed gently. He was still holding her wrists, and he turned his hands under hers, bringing them together so that her palms were pressed flat against one another, his own larger hands cupped around them.

She met his eyes, searching their depths for any gleam of calculation, or even for a hint of the satisfaction that comes from solving a puzzle or getting the better of someone. But there was nothing but kindness and concern. He truly didn't mean her any harm. She had to believe that.

"Yes," she said at last, her voice surprisingly steady. "My words have power. Unnatural power." Her shoulders slumped in defeat as she spoke, but inside, it felt more like a bird had been released from a cage. She could almost see it winging away into the sky.

"But—" Kincaid's hands tightened around hers, as if worried that if he let go the mystery would slip back out of reach. "How is such a thing possible?"

"I don't know," said Jocelyn softly. "I've always been this way."

He stared at her in amazement, and Jocelyn felt her face grow hot under his scrutiny. She had imagined the shock, the horror, perhaps the calculation, she would see on the faces of the court if her secret ever came out. But Kincaid's expression was nothing like what she had pictured. He looked amazed, certainly, but he didn't look disapproving. On the contrary, he was looking at her as though she was a priceless treasure.

"I had my suspicions," Kincaid said, still holding her eyes with his. "I knew there was something strange about your silence. I could tell it wasn't natural to you, that you were forcing it for some reason. But it wasn't until Elddreki started talking about how mountain blood gives the ability to sense magic that I had my first inkling about why it felt unusual when you spoke. And then your performances back there in the town…"

"Stupid interfering dragon," Jocelyn muttered, and Kincaid gave a delighted laugh. She looked up, surprised at the disproportionate reaction. He was grinning at her affectionately.

"You're saying things like that in your head constantly, aren't you?"

Jocelyn smiled reluctantly. "Yes, I suppose I am."

Kincaid laughed again, sounding eager, and more than a little pleased with himself. "I can tell. You have this look about you when you hold in a clever comment. Like you're bursting at the seams."

"I'm not sure what was clever about that comment," said Jocelyn dryly, but Kincaid just laughed again.

"Like that." He smiled at her with such open friendliness that she couldn't help but be buoyed. "Your silence was killing me, Jocelyn. This is much better. I like it when you talk."

She arched an eyebrow. "You like feeling uncomfortable?"

He paused, looking confused. "Of course I don't like feeling uncomfortable. Who would? But why would you ask that?"

She shrugged and attempted to draw her hands back, but Kincaid held on firmly. "No, don't dodge the question. Why would I be uncomfortable?"

Jocelyn sighed. "Most people feel uncomfortable around me, especially when I speak. I suppose it's only natural. No one likes to feel confused."

Kincaid frowned. "I don't feel uncomfortable around you," he said frankly. "And I don't feel confused."

"Your expression says otherwise," Jocelyn quipped, and Kincaid laughed again.

"Well, I am confused right now, but purely because of that suggestion."

"Don't you feel anything when I speak?" Jocelyn asked him curiously. "You must, if you figured out that your mountain blood was letting you sense the power."

"I do, sometimes," said Kincaid slowly, releasing her hands at last as he thought the question over. She returned them quickly to her sides, but they suddenly felt awkward there, like she didn't know what to do with them. "Sometimes much more strongly than others," Kincaid was continuing. "But it doesn't feel uncomfortable."

"How does it feel?" Jocelyn persisted.

Kincaid hesitated for a moment, then flashed her a grin which was more self-conscious than usual. "It feels exciting, actually."

"Oh." Jocelyn wasn't at all sure what to make of this information, and it was suddenly difficult to meet his eye.

"Why do you force yourself to be silent?" Kincaid asked unexpectedly.

"Because..." Jocelyn hesitated, confused. Hadn't they just covered this? "Because my words have power. I can't control when it comes, or how much impact it has. The only way to be sure it's not happening is to avoid speaking altogether."

"But why don't you want it to happen?" said Kincaid matter-of-factly. "Why wouldn't you want to use your...ability? You used it to great effect back there." He nodded his head over her shoulder, back toward the town.

"That was a life and death situation," said Jocelyn quickly, and a shadow passed over Kincaid's eyes at the truth of the statement. "But generally it's better for everyone involved if I keep my mouth shut. I mean, you saw what happened back there! Things got very ugly very quickly when I opened my mouth."

"You saved us," said Kincaid firmly. "However out of control the situation became, those men deserved it."

"Maybe," said Jocelyn with a shrug, "but I don't want to be the one to decide what people deserve. Of course I'm glad we got out safely, but do you think I like the idea that I probably just killed someone?"

Her voice cracked slightly at the end of this speech, and Kincaid's eyes softened. He reached out and placed a hand on her shoulder.

"Jocelyn, you didn't kill anyone. You didn't force those men to turn on each other."

"Didn't I?" asked Jocelyn dully. "I planted the seed in their minds, and I did it on purpose." She took a deep breath, trying to steady the sudden shaking in her hands. "I didn't have to do it, either. There were other ways to convince them to let us go, and I didn't initially plan to incite violence. But I got so angry at the way that man spoke about me—"

"I'm not surprised," said Kincaid grimly, his hand tightening on her shoulder. "I was furious too. When he touched you, I wanted to kill him myself." He gave her a twisted smile. "If you're inclined to blame yourself just for putting him in a tight spot, you can take comfort from the fact that I would have run him through myself if I had half the chance."

Jocelyn gave a half-hearted smile. "Say what you like, but your every move radiates honor. If you'd fought him, I'm sure it would have been a fair fight. What I did isn't like that." She shook her head. "My power isn't a good thing, Kincaid. It's dangerous."

He was silent for a moment, watching her with such a serious expression that she lowered her gaze. "So is my sword," he said at last. "But that doesn't make it evil. I control it, I choose how to wield it. It's only as good or evil as I am." He moved his hand from her shoulder to her chin, gently forcing her to look up at him. "And you're not evil, Jocelyn. You're just not."

She blinked rapidly, trying to prevent the tears from coming. "You don't understand, Kincaid," she whispered. "You said it yourself—you control your sword. But I can't control this." She gestured helplessly toward her throat. "I don't have to intend any harm for my words to do terrible damage."

Kincaid raised one shoulder, unconvinced. "I just don't believe that it justifies you closing yourself away, turning yourself into a statue." He gestured between them. "We're having a conversation right now, and it's not doing any harm that I can see."

"And I'm glad, but I don't know why," said Jocelyn desperately. "Some people are affected more than others, especially if they're not very strong-minded to begin with. And sometimes it just comes out stronger than other times, but I can't predict it." Kincaid opened his mouth, but she cut him off, wanting him to take her seriously, but at the same time afraid for him to know the worst of her.

"You don't understand, Kincaid. I've done terrible things." She took a deep breath. "I had a favorite merchant in the markets in Kynton when I was younger. He would always give me things for free, just little baubles, you know, and I used to hang around his stall whenever I was allowed to explore the square on market days. I brought him and his family to the edge of ruin with a thoughtless remark about his trade practices. He altered his entire approach, and it almost destroyed his business. That was years ago, and he still hasn't regained the success he had before I wreaked havoc on his life."

"You can't blame yourself for that," said Kincaid stubbornly. "If he was so weak-minded as to take business advice from a child—"

"But he wasn't weak-minded!" Jocelyn protested, a lump

rising to her throat at the memory of the disaster. "And he didn't know he was taking business advice from me any more than I knew I was giving it! I doubt he ever even connected his decision with my words. But the seed was planted, and he acted accordingly. My best guess is that my words had such effect on him because he knew me, and trusted me, and was predisposed to think well of me. Which makes the betrayal so much worse!"

"For it to be a betrayal, you would have had to intend him harm," said Kincaid firmly, but Jocelyn wasn't finished.

"That's not even the worst of it!" she choked out, her voice rising. "About a year ago, a lord in my father's court made me angry, and I made a snide comment about him, intended as a jest, to my brother. I didn't mean anyone else to hear, but another one of the nobles did, and it all spiraled out of control. It ended with the man being accused of treason, and he would likely have been hanged if Eamon hadn't stepped in and managed to manipulate the situation."

Tears were flowing down Jocelyn's cheeks now, the horror of that memory as fresh as if it had been the day before. "He wasn't guilty of anything but offending me, and he almost paid with his life. And no one but Eamon ever even found out what I did. I couldn't tell anyone about my role in it without revealing my secret, but even if I could, I don't think I would have. I was too ashamed, too horrified by what I had done."

There was a long moment of silence after her tale. She didn't dare to meet Kincaid's eyes, instead wiping the tears from her face with the back of her hand, suddenly self-conscious.

"I'm sorry," said Kincaid at last. "I'm sorry you've carried the burden of this secret and this fear for so long. And I understand why you feel that it's too dangerous to speak, even if I don't entirely agree. But please, Jocelyn." His voice was so earnest that she couldn't help but look up. He was watching her seriously.

"Please don't swallow your words when you're with me. I

hate to think how lonely your life has been, and I want you to be free when we're together, I truly do." He gave a crooked smile. "Otherwise I can't help but think I've ruined your peace by inviting myself on this quest. Because I'm guessing Elddreki isn't affected."

"He's not," Jocelyn acknowledged quietly. "He can tell there's power in my words—he says it's dragon magic, although even he can't explain how it got there—but it has no impact on him."

Kincaid nodded. "So you'll talk freely when I'm around?" he prompted.

Jocelyn hesitated. "I don't want to hurt you," she whispered.

"You won't," said Kincaid firmly.

"You can't know that."

He gave her an understanding smile. "I'm not afraid of you, Princess Jocelyn of the House of Dragonfriend." He chuckled. "Perhaps I should be, but I'm not."

"I'm afraid of you," Jocelyn whispered, only half intending him to hear. For a moment Kincaid looked startled, and a little hurt, but his expression cleared as he took her meaning.

"You don't need to be. I told you, I'll keep your secret." She kept her eyes down, but she could feel his gaze on her. "You've held this on your own for too long, Jocelyn. It's a good thing that I know now."

She wasn't looking at him, so she didn't have any warning before he took her by the shoulders, the warmth of his hands seeming to sear through the fabric of her conspicuous, costly dress as he pulled her closer.

"It really is, Jocelyn. Trust me."

She tried to look up, but his chest was somehow impossibly close all of a sudden. The physical and emotional exertions of the day were starting to take a toll, and she felt overwhelmed by her weariness. The temptation to lay her head against him was momentarily irresistible, and she gave in to it before she knew what she was doing. Kincaid took the gesture in stride, putting a comforting arm around her back. She remembered thinking that Eamon wouldn't want his sister crying on his shoulder. Well, she wasn't crying, so perhaps that was why Kincaid didn't seem to mind.

"You promised that if we went into town, you would do all the talking," she said, her voice coming out muffled.

Kincaid chuckled and released her, and Jocelyn stepped back quickly, trying to regain her composure.

"Good thing I didn't keep that promise, or we'd probably be locked in a wood cellar somewhere."

"You might be," said Jocelyn dryly. "I'd be off having my head shaved." She ran a hand down her braid, reassuring herself that it was all still there. Kincaid smiled knowingly at the gesture, and she dropped her hand quickly.

"He was right that your hair is perfect as it is."

"Are you sure?" Jocelyn asked lightly. "I was thinking of asking Elddreki if he could spare some scales for me to crush into powder, just in case."

Kincaid laughed again. "Speaking of Elddreki..." He inclined his head questioningly, and Jocelyn nodded.

With a last glance in the direction of the town, the two of them began to walk again.

CHAPTER FOURTEEN

Elddreki was not difficult to find.

He was sitting on the very top of Dragoncave, his tail curled around his legs and his head tilted toward the mountains across the river, where the Dragon Realm was concealed from human eyes. He was clearly waiting for them, but nothing in his posture suggested impatience. He was so still that from a distance, Jocelyn could almost believe he was just a statue of a dragon. But as they drew closer, he turned toward them, the late afternoon sunshine glinting off his scales in green and blue and purple. She had thought the mound that concealed Dragoncave was large, but with Elddreki perched on top, it looked smaller, somehow.

"Are you really the smallest dragon in your colony?" she asked when they were close enough for speech.

Elddreki looked down at her.

"Greetings, Jocelyn, Kincaid." There was a hint of reproach in his voice. Elddreki may have been willing to dispense with her title, but Jocelyn was learning that formalities were important to dragons. "I am indeed the smallest dragon in my colony. In fact, I am the youngest by quite a significant margin."

"The youngest?" repeated Kincaid curiously. "Does that relate to your size?"

"Of course," said Elddreki. "Do humans not grow larger as they get older?"

"Well, yes," Kincaid said. "But only to a certain point. Once we reach adulthood we sort of...stop growing."

"We actually get smaller sometimes, if we're really old," Jocelyn interjected helpfully.

"Smaller?" repeated Elddreki, amazed. "How odd." He looked between the two of them. "So you two, for example, will never be larger than you are now?"

"Nope," said Kincaid cheerfully. "This is as tall as I'll get." He shot Jocelyn a cheeky look. "And Jocelyn will always be petite."

She rolled her eyes, but her cheeks felt strangely warm.

"Well, dragons continue to grow indefinitely," said Elddreki. "As I am the youngest in my colony, I am smaller than my fellows. Our ruler, Qadir, is the oldest, and his size is immense, even in dragon terms."

"How old are you?" Kincaid's question seemed impertinent to Jocelyn, but Elddreki didn't seem to mind.

"Close to four hundred years, as a human would count," said Elddreki. "Much younger than most of the others in Vasilisa. I will continue to grow, of course, but so will the others, so I will always be the smallest of us."

"Unless new dragons come along," Jocelyn said encouragingly, but Elddreki shook his head sadly.

"There are no dragonlings in my colony's future, young Jocelyn."

"Can dragons see the future, then?" Kincaid asked, awed.

Elddreki looked amused for a moment, but then sadness descended on his face again. "No, Valorian, we cannot. But we can make predictions based on what we know, as any human can."

He peered down at the two companions below him, a slight frown crossing his features. "You look flushed, Jocelyn." His eyes passed to Kincaid. "And you are holding yourself unusually tightly."

"Am I?" asked Kincaid, rolling his shoulders as if to relieve the tension. "Well, it's probably because of what happened in the town. We uh..."

"Let me guess," Elddreki interrupted. "You ran into trouble?" He looked between them. "It is quite a habit, it seems. We must factor it into our plans, to allow for trouble every time you encounter other humans as we travel through this land."

"Nonsense," said Kincaid, sounding put out. "Valoria is actually a very pleasant kingdom." Jocelyn raised an eyebrow at him, and he looked pained. "It is, honestly," he said defensively. "You should see Bryford, where I'm from. It's a beautiful city, and the people are wonderful. It's just so isolated up here in the North Wilds, it's hard to get reliable law keepers who are willing to stay any length of time, and—"

"All right, we'll take your word for it," Jocelyn cut him off, amused. She supposed she would react similarly to a slight on Kyona.

"I won't," said Elddreki without heat. "I will make my own observations, and form my own conclusions."

Jocelyn giggled, and Kincaid shot her an unimpressed look.

"Did you achieve what you wished to achieve in the town, at least?" Elddreki continued. "Are you ready to attempt the cave?"

Kincaid hesitated, looking at Jocelyn. "It's been a big day, and it will be dark in a couple of hours. Perhaps we should wait until tomorrow."

Jocelyn shook her head. "No, let's do this. I suspect it will be dark inside the cave regardless of the time of day. And I'm not keen to linger near that town. I'd like to reach the supposedly pleasant rest of the kingdom."

"Before you go back to Kyona," said Kincaid sternly, "I will get you to acknowledge that Valoria is a wonderful kingdom. And that's a promise."

"Then it is a very hasty and foolish promise," observed Elddreki. "Since it is so utterly out of your control." He shook his vast head. "You humans really do make promises very lightly."

Kincaid looked rueful, but he didn't retract his promise. He knelt down on the scrubby ground, rummaging through his pack until he extracted the oil lamps he had bought in the town.

He filled them from a small jar of oil he had also purchased, then trimmed the wicks carefully with a knife, which was concealed in his boot, and which Jocelyn hadn't previously seen him use.

"I don't think a flame will survive the journey into the cave somehow, so I'll light them once we're in there if you don't object."

Jocelyn shook her head. "Whatever you think. I'm not really experienced in cave exploration."

Kincaid grinned. "Well, neither am I, to be honest."

"Not many dark and sinister caves in the Valorian capital city?" Jocelyn teased.

"About as many as in the Kyonan capital, I'm guessing."

Elddreki was looking between them carefully during this exchange. "Something is different between you," he said thoughtfully. "You're speaking more freely. There is a flavor of..." he thought for a moment, "release. And...affection? Or friendship, perhaps." He nodded, pleased with his conclusion.

"Very observant of you," acknowledged Kincaid, sounding amused. "Jocelyn was hardly speaking to me before. But now she can speak freely, because she told me about the power in her words. Or I figured it out, sort of."

"Didn't you know about it?" asked Elddreki. "It is most curious, is it not?"

"Most," agreed Kincaid. "Is it true you think it's dragon magic?"

"It is certainly dragon magic," said Elddreki. "Although how or why she can be a carrier of dragon magic, I have not yet figured out. Neither have I fully satisfied myself as to the nature of her power."

"You do know I'm right here, don't you?" Jocelyn asked the pair of them dryly.

"Sorry," said Kincaid, but his smile was unrepentant. "Have *you* figured out the nature of your power? How does it work? Do people just do whatever you tell them to?"

"Hardly," said Jocelyn grimly. "I wish it were that simple, and that predictable. Then I could prevent it when I didn't want to use it by simply not giving instructions." She frowned. "It's much more subtle than that. It's like planting seeds in the mind. And I've found the power of suggestion goes much further than plain statements. The trouble is it's dangerously easy to suggest an idea without meaning to, or even being aware you've done it."

She sighed. "I've given it a lot of thought over the years, as you can imagine, and I'm pretty sure I understand the basic gist of it. My power is confusion—I can confuse people with the seeds I plant. I can make them question what they thought before. Usually people won't question deeply held beliefs from my words, not unless they're particularly weak-minded. And exposure to me seems to decrease the potency of the power, fortunately. My parents, for example, are not usually affected. But still..."

She looked at Kincaid, sadness in her eyes. "You can see why I don't exactly see it as a good thing. Confusion isn't the nicest quality, is it? And far from ideal for someone at the center of court life, where decisions are made that affect the welfare of the whole kingdom. No kingdom wants a princess who spews chaos and confusion every time she opens her mouth. Kyona deserves better." She lowered her voice, no longer really speaking to her companions. "And I'm sure Valoria does, too."

A frown was creasing Kincaid's forehead, but he had no opportunity to speak, Elddreki beating him to it.

"Confusion? Do you think so? That's not how I would articulate it. I'm not entirely sure what it is, but I wouldn't have described it as either chaos or confusion."

"Don't you think I would be the most likely to know the nature of my own power?" asked Jocelyn, a little affronted.

"Certainly not," said Elddreki comfortably. "I would imagine I am more likely to know, being vastly superior to you in both intellect and knowledge."

Kincaid gave a choking cough which Jocelyn had no doubt concealed a laugh. She glared at the pair of them.

"That may be the case, but I apparently possess a quality you don't, namely that I'm petite. So let's get this over with." She craned her neck to look up at the dragon, who was still perched atop the mound. "Any further hints as to what we're looking for?"

Elddreki did a strange rippling shrug. "Not really, except I am now confident there is something to find."

"You are?" asked Jocelyn, startled.

Elddreki nodded. "I have examined the exterior in your absence, and my kind have certainly been here before. The signature is distant in time but distinct in nature."

"Really?" Jocelyn exchanged a look with Kincaid, and she could see her own excitement reflected on his face. She didn't doubt Elddreki's assessment—him being so vastly superior in intellect and all—and her enthusiasm for the task was significantly increased now she knew it wasn't a wild goose chase. She looked again at the narrow opening, momentarily dubious.

"But how would they have gotten in?"

"It has been a long time," said Elddreki. "I suspect the level of the ground has changed in the intervening centuries."

Jocelyn nodded. It was a reasonable explanation.

"Whatever you find inside," Elddreki continued, "dragons have certainly sat where I sit now. See for yourself."

With his usual casual grace, the dragon opened his jaws and released a white-hot plume of flame immediately down onto the rock below his talons. It spread out rapidly across the rocky mound, covering most of the surface. He sustained it for several long seconds, apparently oblivious to the involuntary cries of his companions, both of whom jumped back in alarm.

But when the stream ceased, Jocelyn gasped in amazement. She stepped forward, reaching out a cautious hand to touch the rock. It was cool under her fingers, despite being doused in the heat of Elddreki's fire. But that wasn't the phenomenon that captured her.

Strange markings had appeared on the rock, glowing with lingering light or heat or magic from the dragon flame. Where the contours of the rock had seemed unremarkable, Jocelyn suddenly saw patterns, even stories.

"These ridges were made by dragon talons," she said, running a hand along one of the glowing marks. She turned her attention to a small hollow. "And this was a launching point, where dragons pushed themselves off."

"How can you tell?" Kincaid asked, frowning as he joined her next to the mound.

"You don't see how it's lit up by Elddreki's magic?" she asked, turning to him in surprise.

"I can see the markings," said Kincaid. "But they don't look like runes or anything, just lines in the rock. How can you tell they were made by dragon talons?"

"I don't know," said Jocelyn, frowning herself now. "I just can."

"Interesting," Elddreki mused, drawing their attention back to him on his perch above them. "Maybe it is the dragon magic that lingers in you."

"Maybe," said Jocelyn uncomfortably. She glanced at Kincaid, who was watching her with a thoughtful expression. "If we're going into the cave, I think we should get on with it."

She walked purposefully toward the small opening, but Kincaid was ahead of her. She raised an eyebrow at him. "Shouldn't it be ladies first?"

He grinned. "But you're not a lady, are you? You're a princess."

"Kincaid—"

He shot her an impudent look. "I'm going in first, Jocelyn, and you're not going to change my mind about it." His grin widened. "Unless you manage to change it by using your power, that is."

She glared at him, but he was already at the fissure, dropping onto his belly. "I'll wriggle through, then you can push my pack in after me. I'll take one of these lamps though, so I can make some light and tell you if it's safe to follow."

"And I'll follow regardless of what you say," Jocelyn returned placidly.

Kincaid had been about to disappear into the hole, head first, but he turned around, his expression stern. "Don't be contrary, Jocelyn. It's not a becoming quality in a lady."

Jocelyn grinned, well aware he was teasing her. "But I'm not a lady, remember? I'm a princess." He turned back around, smiling, and she added, "And since we apparently have a flavor of friendship now, you can call me Joss. It's what my friends call me."

Kincaid paused for a moment, but he didn't turn around again. "Very well, Joss," he said, his voice coming out muffled since he had already started crawling into the darkness of the opening.

It was strange to watch him disappear inch by inch, legs, ankles, and eventually feet swallowed by the cave. Once he got his shoulders through—which took a little bit of wriggling—Jocelyn knew the rest of him would fit. It gave her a strange squirming feeling, to think of going face first into a dark hole. She would never have admitted it, but she was glad Kincaid was going first.

Nevertheless, she didn't wait for his call. As soon as he disappeared, she walked forward herself, dropping to her belly.

"I wish you success," said Elddreki placidly, as she poked her head into the hole. She couldn't see a thing.

"Thank you," she said, trying not to sound as nervous as she felt.

"I will most likely wait here until you return," Elddreki added, and Jocelyn paused. Most likely? But she didn't linger to question the dragon. She had a feeling the longer she stalled, the harder it would be to take the plunge.

With a deep breath, as though she really was plunging into water, she extended her arms into the black opening and began to pull herself forward along the ground, pushing Kincaid's pack in front of her. She fit through without difficulty, her much narrower shoulders presenting no barrier. For maybe thirty seconds her heart pounded uncomfortably in her throat as she inched through a narrow tunnel. But to her relief, the tunnel opened up quickly, and she felt the draft of a cavernous space.

She was still pulling herself through with her hands, so she could feel that the ground was sloping unevenly down from the opening, and she paused to prevent either the pack or herself from tumbling down. She could feel that no part of her body was outside now, but from her waist down she was still inside the tunnel.

Her body blocked any light that might have come from the opening, and it was utterly dark inside. For a moment her eyes searched the space fruitlessly, then she heard the sound of a flint, and a tiny spark momentarily appeared a little way below her.

"Kincaid?"

There was a pause.

"Jocelyn?" He sounded annoyed. "You were supposed to wait for my signal that it was safe."

"And you were supposed to be adventuring your way through Kyona, with no idea that either Elddreki or I exist."

Kincaid's only response was a grunt, before the sound of the flint resumed. After impressively few attempts, a small flame appeared, growing steadier by the second. Jocelyn blinked in the sudden illumination, faint as it was. The rough slope which stretched down below her was revealed, Kincaid crouching a few feet down it. She couldn't see very far beyond, but she received the impression of a very large space. She closed her eyes and took a deep breath, taking note of the tingling sensation, faint but familiar, that seemed to settle over her.

"I think I *can* sense some kind of magic in here," she said optimistically.

"Did you just try to smell magic, like Elddreki does?" asked Kincaid, a laugh in his voice. He seemed to be primarily made of laughter.

She glared at him. "Are you going to mock me, or are you going to help me out of this tunnel like a gentleman?"

"Who said I was a gentleman?" he grinned, but he set the lamp down carefully and scrambled up the slope all the same. He retrieved his pack from where she had pushed it, then took her hands and tugged gently until she had wriggled out onto her knees. She struggled to her feet while Kincaid removed the other lamp from his pack and lit it.

"Whoa."

Kincaid looked up at her words, following her glance around the cave. "Impressive, isn't it?"

"How big do you think it is?"

He handed her the second lamp, holding his own high. "I don't know, but much bigger than it looks from the outside. And much bigger than we can explore in the hour or so before it gets dark."

Jocelyn glanced back at the opening. Sunlight was only very dimly visible, and she gave an involuntary shudder.

"We'll be fine," said Kincaid reassuringly. "We'll stick together."

Jocelyn nodded gratefully, following him as he started to pick his way down the slope. "I'm glad you thought of getting the lamps," she said. "Or this would be completely pointless."

"Yes," Kincaid chuckled. "You were pretty ready to race right in."

"Well," said Jocelyn conversationally, "I was trying to get away from you as much as anything."

"Aren't princesses supposed to be gracious and kind?" asked Kincaid, his aggrieved tone not fooling Jocelyn for a moment.

She smiled. "Well, I don't mind your company in the least now that I can talk to you, if it makes you feel better."

"It does," said Kincaid with unexpected earnestness. "It makes me feel much better."

They had reached the bottom of the slope by this time, and the roof of the cavern towered above them, almost disappearing in the thin light of their little lamps. The cave floor stretched out in front of their feet, scattered with rocks, but mainly flat. They moved tentatively across the space, able to walk side by side now.

"It was funny what that woman said about the princess pouring her stories into the cave, and the cave holding them," said Kincaid, his voice echoing strangely in the empty space. "I suppose it's not surprising the story grew in the telling, but I must confess I never thought of Kyona as a far-off exotic land where the people have magic." He gave her a sideways glance. "With a few exceptions."

"It has grown in the telling, clearly," said Jocelyn, "but there's some truth in it. My father's line is a storytelling line. They—we—have an unnatural capacity to retain memories and details, and to pass stories on down the generations. It's a gift to our line from dragonkind. It's how my father knew the history of his bloodline, before he knew it *was* his bloodline, and was able to use that history to help him reclaim the throne. The stories had been handed down father to son for centuries. I grew up on them too, along with my father's own stories." She paused, a smile in her voice. "Which, I must say, rival any of his ancestors' stories, in my opinion."

"The stories about King Calinnae are incredible," said Kincaid eagerly. "Even I've grown up on them, although I suspect there's been a lot of embellishment. I doubt he really descended on the false king with an army of two score dragons at his back, for instance."

Jocelyn laughed, the sound leaping back at her from the distant walls and ceiling of the cave. "Definitely not. It was just one dragon. It was Elddreki, actually."

"Really?" Kincaid sounded intrigued. There was a moment of silence, then he pushed on. "Is it true he has a magic sword? Or is that another exaggeration?"

"No, that's true," said Jocelyn, hiding a smile. Kincaid sounded like an excited boy instead of the self-possessed man she was coming to know. "It belonged to his ancestor, King Cael, who was the last king before the throne was corrupted. The sword was kept in the Dragon Realm from the time of his death until my father took it back. It's steeped in dragon magic, and it has...unusual properties."

"Have you ever held it?"

"Yes," said Jocelyn, not quite able to hold back the indulgent smile this time. "But not nearly as often as Eamon has. He's tried to convince my father to let him train with it, but no luck so far."

"What did it feel like?" Kincaid asked curiously.

"Like..." Jocelyn hesitated. "Like instead of the power being in my words it was in my hands."

Kincaid was silent for a moment. "Eamon is your brother?" he asked at last, and Jocelyn nodded.

"My twin, actually."

"So he's the crown prince?"

"That's right."

"Is he affected by your power?"

There was a pause. "No." Jocelyn didn't elaborate, and Kincaid didn't press the point.

"So King Cael was the last king before the throne fell," he mused instead. "Is that the king Darius spoke of in his story, back in Montego? The one who married the daughter of the mountain chief?"

"That's right," said Jocelyn quietly. "Queen Jacqueline. She's the ancestor through whom I have mountain blood. And their daughter, the one who married the Valorian crown prince, was Princess Sarai. And unless I'm much mistaken, she's the one who came to this cave, searching for dragons, and named the town Thalia."

"How did you know to ask about it?" Kincaid probed. "That name didn't mean anything to me, but it obviously did to you."

Jocelyn sighed. It wasn't the nicest story. "Thalia was the name of Sarai's older sister, who died in childhood. She died protecting their brother, Jonathon, from an attempt on his life. He was the only son, and the heir. It was from that point that everything kind of started to fall apart actually." She looked at Kincaid. "Is Thalia a common name in Valoria?"

"No, not at all," he said. "In fact, I've never heard it before. I wouldn't have guessed it was a girl's name."

Jocelyn nodded. "It's not common in Kyona either. It fell out of favor after what happened to the princess with that name. It's been generations, but people still think of the name as cursed." She sighed. "Kyonans can be very superstitious about some things."

Kincaid smiled. "So can Valorians, don't worry. You should hear the easterners talk about wyverns."

"Wyverns?" Jocelyn repeated, and Kincaid rolled his eyes.

"Fearsome sea monsters. Purely mythical, of course, but you won't convince the easterners of that."

"Oh," said Jocelyn. "Well, in any event, the name Thalia is unusual enough that I thought instantly of the princess when I heard it." She frowned. "I wonder why Princess Sarai was looking for dragons after she came to live in Valoria?"

"Why don't you ask the walls and find out?" asked Kincaid humorously, and she shot him a look.

"You're hilarious."

He grinned, acknowledging at as a compliment. They had struck out into the middle of the open space, but Kincaid angled to the right, lifting his lamp high in front of him to illuminate the cave wall some distance ahead. Jocelyn copied him, the two thin beams of light leaping up the stone. Far above them, Jocelyn could see stalactites dangling from the ceiling of the cavern. The occasional drip of water ran down them to drop softly to the rocky floor below.

"Careful," said Kincaid, glancing back at her. "It's a little slippery here."

Jocelyn nodded, pushing ahead of him toward the wall. "I wonder if we really will find any dragon runes," she said. She looked up and out, into the dark space. "This place is huge. Definitely big enough for dragons to fit inside. I wonder if they found it, or if they made it somehow."

"Can dragons make land formations?" asked Kincaid, frowning.

Jocelyn shrugged. "Who knows? Some legends claim that the Kyonan mountains were flat grassland when dragons first came there, and that they drew the rocky slopes up from the ground over centuries. Mostly I think that's just myth, but..." She trailed off, looking around her. It was eerie in the cave, and the air seemed to tingle more strongly with magic now.

"But in here, anything seems possible," finished Kincaid, and he didn't seem to be laughing at her this time.

Jocelyn had reached the wall. She reached toward it, glancing back over her shoulder to give Kincaid a sly smile. "Exactly. And that being the case, I'll just ask the cave for any stories it might have to tell me, shall I?"

She had expected Kincaid to laugh, but his breath seemed to catch sharply in his throat for a moment, and he was looking at her with a strange expression. She had no time to ask what was on his mind, however, because at that moment her questing fingers found the stone of the cavern wall.

CHAPTER FIFTEEN

She noted that the wall was cool and unexpectedly smooth, but that was all she had time to take in before her senses spun wildly away from her. Her hand seemed fused to the rock, but her consciousness rushed alarmingly, as though she was being sucked into a whirlpool.

She opened her mouth to cry out to Kincaid, to ask him to catch her, to hold her back, to save her from being sucked away, but no sound came out. For a moment everything was confusion, then the chaos suddenly stilled, her every sense once again focused on the cool of the cavern wall.

Sarai leaned her head against the wall of the cave, the stone cool beneath her cheek. The emotions welling up inside her were too intense to contain, and she let out a small sob.

They had been here—she was sure of it. The same power she had felt in the mountains lingered here in this cave. It was dragon magic, without question. This place wasn't like the other spots she had explored, where local legend claimed some kind of magical history.

This place was real. The superstition around this cave had some basis in fact.

But the rush of elation was brief. She might be sure dragons had been here, but that didn't mean she would be able to convince anyone else of it. Her new father-in-law already thought her addled. She was sure he was regretting marrying his son and heir to the Kyonan princess.

Sarai choked on another sob. Well, she wished he'd thought of that earlier. She wished she'd been able to stay in Kyona. Better to share whatever fate had befallen her siblings after their father's murder than to be the last one left, far away and wondering what had become of everyone she cared about. No one in Valoria wanted her here, after all.

She pushed away from the wall, suddenly weary. She wasn't being fair to Germain, and she knew it. Her husband had been kind and respectful, and it wasn't his fault her heart was broken over what had happened in her homeland. If he wished he hadn't married her, he was far too well-bred to show any sign of it. But she didn't know him, not really. As Valoria's crown prince, he had many duties, and it felt like they'd barely seen each other in the months since their wedding.

He had been kind to allow her to come on this trip at all, she acknowledged to herself. His family clearly thought him foolish to indulge her mad hunt for dragons. They disapproved of her, every one of them. They thought she should be content to stay in Bryford, fulfilling her role as a member of the royal family, not off chasing a fantasy.

But they didn't understand. Dragons were real, she knew they were. And they had a friendship with her father's house—her house. If only she could find them, surely they would help Kyona. She had to believe Jonathon had survived the usurper's attack, that he was out there somewhere. If there was any chance he was, she had to find him somehow, to help him take the throne that was rightfully his.

Tears stung her eyes, tears for her family, for her kingdom, for the loss of a future that had seemed so sure and bright. She hated to think of her sisters, her little brother, dead or exiled. She could still feel Jonathon's arms around her as he had hugged her on the day of her wedding. She had been proud of her brother, of the man he had grown into. What had happened to the round-faced laughing child for whom any of his sisters would have willingly made the terrible sacrifice Thalia made? When had he turned into the serious and capable young man before her?

The thought that her father's line might end with his murder, that Jonathon might never be king, was more than she could bear.

She pounded a fist against the cave wall in frustration. It was all so futile. What could she do? Nothing. She couldn't find her sisters, she couldn't help Jonathon, she couldn't even find the dragons. Her shoulders slumped in defeat. Not that there had ever been much likelihood of that. It was always a slim chance that there really were dragons in Valoria. She knew where dragons were, of course. They were in the mountains. Kyona's mountains. Her eyes pricked.

Her mountains.

But Germain had been clear. Once news had reached Valoria of the events at Kynton, Germain's father, the king, had decreed that no one was to pass the border in either direction. And although Germain might be ready to let his Kyonan wife waste her time searching every corner of Valoria for any hint of dragons, he was adamant she was not to stray back into Kyona in her search. Even if he had been willing to defy his father's decree—which of course he wasn't—it was too dangerous, he said. Someone was trying to wipe her family out, and he had no intention of letting them get anywhere near her.

And although she had reflected at the time that some at the Valorian court might be delighted to be rid of the Kyonan alliance that now seemed more likely to be a liability than a strength, there had been no doubting the sincerity of Germain's determination to keep his new wife safe.

She felt a twinge of guilt at the memory of Germain's face as he *offered to accompany her to this place. He had looked almost hopeful, as though he had really wanted to come, instead of offering from politeness. She wondered if she had been cruel to decline his escort. She had accepted the official delegation, of course, including the squadron of guards who came to protect her. No member of the royal family—Sarai included—would expect to be allowed to wander over the kingdom alone. But none of those people took an active interest in what she was doing, and she preferred it that way. If Germain came, he might want to share in her search—really share in it—and that thought scared her.*

She sighed, loneliness welling up inside her at her isolation from everyone she had ever known. She had been willing enough to form the marriage alliance, as much as it grieved her to leave her homeland. But that had been before the coup. She had thought there would be regular communication between her and her family, frequent visits to Kyona. She had planned to host her sisters in her new home, hoping one of them might form an attachment to some Valorian noble, and come to live in Bryford with her.

But now her family house had been shattered, her kingdom desecrated, and the border closed. She was all alone, in a city where her welcome was now dubious at best. She had no one to turn to but a husband who was still little more than a stranger. But if she opened her heart to him, if she embraced him and by extension her new identity as a princess and future queen of Valoria, she was terrified she would lose who she was as a princess of Kyona. And she might be all that was left of her noble and ancient house.

Am I doing it all wrong? she asked herself, not for the first time. *Am I a failure as a wife? She wished desperately she could talk to her mother. She would have been able to help Sarai find the answers—she had always had such insight. But she was dead, gone before Sarai had been wed. And now her father was dead too, murdered by a member of his own court. And perhaps neither of them would have been able to advise her anyway, she thought dully. They had married for love, not for a political alliance.*

"Your Highness?"

The tentative voice of the guard startled her, and she wiped a surreptitious hand across her eyes before turning.

"Yes, I am here."

"Should—should we return to the surface, Your Highness?"

The guard sounded nervous, and Sarai felt a small prick of remorse. This place was eerie, there was no question, and none of her companions were enjoying the visit. The stirring of power that reminded her so strongly of the mountains—and that gave her a sense of comfort to undercut the dark and mysterious nature of the cave— was no benefit to anyone else. Even the Valorian royals wouldn't have felt it. They had no connection to the dragons like the Kyonan royals, and the Kyonan mountain folk, did.

"Yes," she said softly, running her hand one last time over the curious runes carved into the stone. She had no idea what they meant, and she wasn't sure whether to laugh or cry at her own folly. What was the point of coming here, of confirming that there really had been dragons in Valoria? What good did it do her, when she had no way of knowing where they were now? They were clearly long gone from this place.

And it was time for her to be gone, too. Germain had wanted her back within five days. Even if they started the ride back to Bryford immediately, they would still be cutting it close.

She turned away, taking in a deep breath, as if to fill her lungs one last time with that tingling power that made her heart ache with familiarity and longing. She would try to carry it with her as she returned to the solid, unimaginative life of the court at Bryford, where no one believed dragons were real, and there was no connection with the beasts' power.

Yes there is. The thought popped into Sarai's mind as she climbed, as though spoken by the cave itself.

She realized with a start that it was true. The court at Bryford did have a connection to dragons now—her. She supposed that from this time forward, the blood of Kyona's royal house would be mixed with that of Valoria's royal house, just as through her mother the blood of the mountain people had a place in Kyona's royal line.

It was a strange thought, but somehow it gave her comfort, like a tiny flicker of flame, which ever so slightly lightened the darkness of her loneliness.

~

"JOCELYN! *JOCELYN!*"

Jocelyn came back to reality with a gasp. The first thing she took in was the small tongue of fire sitting atop Kincaid's oil lamp, looking like the embodiment of Princess Sarai's thought. This irrelevant observation was quickly followed by the sensation of Kincaid's hand gripping her shoulder, as she recognized the alarm in his voice.

"Jocelyn!"

She pulled her hand from the wall, a shudder running through her. For a moment she stared unseeingly into Kincaid's face, still overwhelmed by the maelstrom of emotions she had just vicariously experienced. The all-consuming grief Princess Sarai had felt at the fate that had befallen her family, and her own powerlessness in the crisis, was almost more than she could take.

And Princess Sarai's loneliness and discomfort regarding her arranged marriage touched Jocelyn's own fears much too intimately. She didn't want to lose her identity as a Kyonan princess any more than Princess Sarai had wanted it, and for a moment she couldn't tear her mind from the icy thought of being married to a stranger. The idea had seemed unpleasant enough a week ago, but for some reason it now felt unbearable.

Without thinking about it, almost without realizing she was doing it, she buried her face in Kincaid's chest, her whole body shaking in the aftermath of the strange vision.

"Jocelyn!" Kincaid sounded almost as shaken as she felt. He still held the oil lamp aloft in one hand, but his free arm went around her immediately. "Are you all right? What happened? Did it hurt you somehow?"

"No," Jocelyn said, fully grasping for the first time that she was all but in Kincaid's arms. She stepped back quickly, taking deep breaths as she tried to calm her mind. "No, I'm not hurt. I just—I don't know exactly what happened. I think I just saw into Princess Sarai's memories somehow."

"What?" Kincaid sounded unnerved. "Are you...are you making a joke? Because of all that talk about the cave holding her stories?"

Jocelyn shook her head, another shiver running through her. "No, it's not a joke. Something just happened. Something unnatural. I've heard of such things, but I've never experienced anything like it."

"Neither have I," said Kincaid shakily. "You went all stiff and rigid, and you were unresponsive for ages. I thought you were having some kind of seizure."

"It was...indescribable," said Jocelyn. "It was like I was in her head." She stepped away from the wall. "You try."

Kincaid looked uncertain, but he stepped forward and laid his hand against the smooth rock of the cave wall.

"Well?"

He shook his head. "Nothing."

Jocelyn frowned. "But you have mountain blood in you. Elddreki said you do. Try again."

"Try what? What do I do?"

"Just...concentrate on Princess Sarai, on the story we heard." Jocelyn shrugged. "I don't know."

He turned back to the wall, his forehead creased in concentration. He closed his eyes and leaned in, and for a long moment Jocelyn held her breath.

"Did you feel anything?" she asked when he pulled away.

Kincaid nodded slowly, thoughtfully, his eyes on her rather than the wall. "I think I did, actually."

"Was it like you were in her head?" Jocelyn asked eagerly. "Like you were sharing her thoughts?"

Kincaid shook his head. "No, I wouldn't say that," he answered carefully. "It wasn't so much thoughts as...emotions. Just an impression. Grief, and loneliness, and a desperation to find something. It—"

"What?" prompted Jocelyn when he cut himself off.

"Well, it..." He looked apologetic. "It felt like you, actually."

Jocelyn looked away quickly, feeling uncomfortably exposed all of a sudden.

"But you heard her thoughts?" asked Kincaid, his tone more normal.

She nodded. "Strange that it was so much clearer for me. My mountain blood is also generations back."

"Not so strange," contradicted Kincaid. "The mountain folk aren't the only ones with a connection to dragon magic. You're also a Kyonan royal. Plus—"

"For now," muttered Jocelyn to herself, another shudder running through her as she remembered Princess Sarai's isolation and uncertainty.

"What?" Kincaid was frowning at her.

"Nothing," she said quickly. "What were you saying?"

He hesitated for a moment, still frowning, then continued. "I was saying that there's another fairly obvious reason why you might be more sensitive to the power in this cave."

"Which is...?"

He shrugged. "Well, you are magic, aren't you?"

"Oh, that." Jocelyn considered the point. The power swirling gently through the cave did feel familiar in signature, another indication that Elddreki's assessment of her power as dragon magic must be accurate. "You might be right."

"So what thoughts did you...overhear?" Kincaid asked.

She looked up. "I know now why she was looking for dragons, for one thing. It was after the Kyonan coup. Her father had been killed, and she was desperate to find out what happened to her siblings, and to help her brother reclaim the throne if he was still alive. She was convinced the dragons would help if she asked them. But she wasn't allowed to return to Kyona to try to make contact with the dragons in the mountains. So she was following any leads, any legends that suggested there might be dragons hidden in Valoria somewhere."

"Did she find any?" Kincaid asked eagerly.

Jocelyn shook her head, deflating. "I don't think so. She realized that dragons had been here, in this cave, once. But I don't think she left here with any clues about where they went next."

"Hm," said Kincaid, frowning. "Which means we probably won't either. Elddreki will be disappointed." He gave a weak chuckle, his normal good humor not quite fully restored after Jocelyn's strange vision. "Or at least, as disappointed as a creature who doesn't really understand emotion can be."

"Elddreki!" said Jocelyn suddenly, her face lighting up. "We have something Princess Sarai didn't have—an actual dragon with us!"

"How does that help?" asked Kincaid.

"The runes!" Jocelyn's excitement was starting to drive away the lingering feeling of eeriness from her vision. "There really are dragon runes here. Princess Sarai found them. But she had no way to know what they mean."

"And we do." Kincaid smiled at her. "Now we just have to find them."

"They're over here," said Jocelyn confidently, moving away from the wall, back toward the open space. Against the far wall."

"How do you know?"

She shrugged. "I just do."

She led the way across the space, Kincaid following behind. She walked with a spring in her step, enjoying being the one with the answers for a change.

"I think I'm getting used to this cave," she said brightly. "It's not so bad once you adjust to the—urrghh!"

"What happened?" asked Kincaid, clearly trying not laugh at Jocelyn's look of horrified disgust. She was shining her lamp frantically around her feet, looking for any sign of movement in the darkness. But whatever she had felt had disappeared into the gloom outside the small circle of her lamplight.

"Something slithered over my foot," she said with a shudder. "Are there—do you think there are snakes in this cave?"

"Quite likely," said Kincaid, not quite managing to keep the amusement out of his voice. "But don't worry. They're more afraid of you than you are of them."

"No they're not," said Jocelyn emphatically.

"Really, they are," said Kincaid earnestly, seeing the look on Jocelyn's face as she scoured the darkness. "They—"

"It might be true that they're more afraid of us than *you* are of them," Jocelyn cut him off dryly, and he chuckled.

"Don't worry, Joss," he said, and a curiously pleasant rush passed over Jocelyn at his use of her nickname. "There are no poisonous snakes in this part of the country. I know they're not the most appealing creatures, but they won't hurt you."

"If you say so," she said dubiously, casting one last uneasy glance around the cavern floor before continuing on her way. It took several minutes to cross the cave to the spot where Princess Sarai had been standing in the vision Jocelyn had seen. But once there, they had no difficulty finding what they were looking for.

"It's amazing," Jocelyn breathed, running her fingers along the elegant runes. She could feel magic pulsing out of them, as if responsive to her touch. "I've never seen figures like these before."

"Me neither," said Kincaid, leaning close to look. "They're nothing like our letters, are they?"

"Not at all," Jocelyn agreed. "They look more like pictures than words. But not any pictures I can recognize." But even as she said it, she gave a small jump. She had been tracing the shape of one of the runes, a curved, fluid arc, with her thumb. Although she could make no sense of the scratches, she formed a distinct impression of water. Kincaid looked at her questioningly, but she just shrugged, not sure if her assessment was correct.

"They're beautiful," she breathed. She leaned back to look up the wall. "But there are so many of them, and they go so high. We'll never be able to recreate them all for Elddreki."

"I'm not so sure," said Kincaid, his forehead creased in concentration as he also ran a hand over the runes. "I think it might be the same few repeated over and over."

Jocelyn stepped back from the wall, trying to get a sense of the big picture. "I think you're right. Well, that makes things considerably easier. Hold still."

She stepped toward Kincaid and began to rummage in his pack, which was slung over his shoulder. She had to stand on tiptoe to reach into it, and she felt around for a while before she found what she was looking for.

"Here."

She held out the roll of parchment he had bought at such an exorbitant price, and Kincaid took it automatically, his eyes still on the wall. After another forage, Jocelyn located the charcoal. She took the parchment back from Kincaid and stretched it out on the floor of the cave, her lamp placed carefully next to it. She looked at the charcoal dubiously. It didn't seem a very effective tool for the job, but she supposed it would have to do. She set one rounded edge against the parchment, and looked up expectantly.

"Can you hold your lamp closer to the runes?"

"Huh?" asked Kincaid, coming out of his abstraction and turning to look at her, crouched on the cave floor. "What are you doing?"

"Trying to copy the runes," said Jocelyn impatiently. "If we want to get out of here before it's completely dark, we need to get moving."

"I think it's probably already dark, to be honest," said Kincaid. "And that's not how you use the charcoal." Once again he was trying not to smile, and once again he was failing. "Let me show you."

Jocelyn handed over the parchment and charcoal with the slightest of pouts. "Has anyone ever told you how maddening it is that you know everything?"

Kincaid grinned. "Frequently."

"Let me guess." Jocelyn smiled back in spite of herself. "Your little sister?"

"Guessed it in one."

Jocelyn had followed Kincaid to the wall, and held her lamp high for illumination. She watched in fascination as Kincaid laid the parchment flat against the stone, right on top of the runes. He held it in place with one hand and began to rub the charcoal onto the parchment with the other, pressing it down only gently. When he pulled it away and held it up for her inspection, he was grinning again, looking a little too pleased with himself.

"That's a very neat trick," said Jocelyn, impressed in spite of herself by the imprint of the runes now visible on the parchment. They showed white in a background of charcoal black.

"Thank you," said Kincaid, his modest tone unconvincing.

He glanced up at the wall and back down at his parchment. "Do you think I got all the runes on this page?"

Jocelyn studied the wall critically. "Yes, I think you did."

"Excellent," he said briskly, rolling up the parchment with a businesslike air and stowing it safely back in his pack. "Do you want to explore further before we go back out to Elddreki?"

"No," said Jocelyn promptly, thinking of the snake. "I think we've done what we came to do."

"Then let's get going."

They took up their lamps again and began to make their way back across the cavern floor, in what Jocelyn hoped was the right direction. They had only walked for a couple of minutes, however, when Kincaid's lamp began to flicker.

"Oh," he said, his tone unconcerned as he looked down at it. "I thought the oil would last longer."

Jocelyn had kept walking, and she was some distance ahead, but she paused, glancing back at him. The erratic leaping of the light made her slightly dizzy, and she suddenly realized her lamp was also flickering.

"Kincaid," she said quickly, staring down at it. Kincaid looked up and followed her gaze.

"Yes, we lit them at the same time." He seemed to realize she was anxious, because he added reassuringly, "Don't worry, Jocelyn, there's plenty more oil. I have the jar here in my pack. We'll just refill the lamps."

Jocelyn nodded, starting back toward him. But she had only taken a step when the lamps, which had both been flickering more and more wildly, suddenly died. They were plunged into total blackness, and Jocelyn stopped mid-stride, uncertain of her footing on the uneven ground.

"Kincaid?" she said, her hand groping pointlessly out into the darkness, even though she knew he was well out of reach. She knew she sounded breathless, but she couldn't help herself.

The darkness was sudden and absolute, and she found it extremely unnerving.

"I'm here," said Kincaid reassuringly. He didn't sound in the least alarmed, and Jocelyn's breathing slowed slightly. "It's all right. I'll refill the lamps, then I can light them again with my flint, like I did the first time."

Jocelyn nodded, then remembered he couldn't see her. "All right."

She could hear Kincaid rummaging in his pack. "Here we go—uh oh!"

CHAPTER SIXTEEN

"Uh oh?" repeated Jocelyn, foreboding creeping over her. "What does 'uh oh' mean?" Although from the smash which had accompanied his words, she was pretty sure she knew.

There was a moment of silence. "That was the jar of oil," said Kincaid apologetically.

"What does that mean?" Jocelyn's voice rose alarmingly in pitch with the question.

"Well, that...you know. That we have no more oil."

There was another moment of silence.

"So we can't make any more light?"

"That's right."

More silence, longer this time.

"Kincaid?"

"Yes, I'm here."

"What are we going to do?" Jocelyn looked around, willing her eyes to see something, anything, through the gloom. But the darkness was so solid it felt like she had a blindfold pressed over her eyes.

Kincaid sighed. "Well, like I said, I think it would be dark outside by now. Even if we could find our way back across the cave safely without our lamps, I don't think we'd find the opening without the sunlight coming through it."

"So...what? You're saying we have to spend the night in here?" Jocelyn made no attempt to hide the horror in her voice.

"Unfortunately, I think we do."

The silence was so long that this time Kincaid broke it.

"Jocelyn? Are you all right?"

Jocelyn cleared her throat before answering, but her voice still came out as a squeak. "I'll be honest, I'm not wild about the idea."

"I know," said Kincaid, his voice again apologetic. "It's not ideal. But," his tone brightened, "at least we have the food with us."

Jocelyn didn't answer immediately. Her breathing was speeding up without her permission, a feeling of claustrophobia surging over her.

"But—but how will we even know when it's morning? What if we can't find the opening, even tomorrow? What if not enough sunlight comes through to show it up? What if we're stuck in here forever?" Her voice was getting faster and faster as panic rose inside her.

"We won't be," said Kincaid, his voice smooth and confident.

Not for the first time, Jocelyn felt a wave of relief wash over her at how little the Valorian seemed to be affected by her words. Most people would have been thrown into utter chaos by her barely controlled speech, and then they really would be in trouble. Jocelyn heard a strange shuffling sound, and jumped in spite of herself.

"What was that?"

"It's me." Kincaid's questing hand brushed against her shoulder, and she realized he had been moving toward her by guess. His hand slid down to her elbow, and he gripped it bracingly.

"We're going to be fine, Joss. We'll camp here for the night, then in the morning we'll find our way back out through the opening. We'll be fine. I promise."

Jocelyn let out a shuddering exhale, attempting to release her tension. "But you make promises so lightly," she said, in a weak attempt at humor.

Kincaid's familiar chuckle wafted through the darkness. "Not this time."

"Do we just...stop right here?"

"As good a place as any," said Kincaid cheerfully. "The ground is pretty flat." He let go of her elbow, and she could feel rather than hear him crouching down to feel the space beneath their feet. "Yep, it's quite clear here."

Jocelyn lowered herself reluctantly to the floor. She went to arrange her skirts modestly, then realized no one could see her. "Well, that's one benefit of suffocating darkness, I suppose," she muttered, as she indulged in the rare comfort of sitting cross-legged.

"What was that?" Kincaid asked curiously.

"Nothing," said Jocelyn quickly. "I'm starving, should we eat?"

"Sure," said Kincaid easily, and Jocelyn heard the sounds of him pulling the food from his pack. She wasn't sure if he was genuinely as unconcerned by their plight as he sounded, or if he was putting on a bold front to help ease her anxiety. Either way, she was grateful.

It was the strangest meal she had ever eaten. There was nothing unusual about the food, of course, but eating in total darkness was unnerving. As nice as it was not to be self-conscious about whether she was eating in a ladylike manner, that luxury wasn't worth not knowing with certainty what she was putting in her mouth until it got there.

And she quickly discovered that vision wasn't necessary in

order to be self-conscious, anyway. The food was in Kincaid's pack, meaning he had to hand it to her item by item. And because of the absolute darkness, it was necessary for their hands to make contact every time in order for him to be sure she was receiving the food. The touch, which might have been unremarkable enough in daylight, or even under the light of the moon, assumed an undeniable intimacy in the total blackness.

When Kincaid took Jocelyn's hand in one of his, turning it so he could place a hunk of bread in her upturned palm, the spark that jumped between them felt so tangible Jocelyn was half surprised it didn't light the blackness. She was sure Kincaid felt it, too. The cheerful Valorian was uncharacteristically quiet throughout the meal.

She couldn't help but wonder if there was something unnatural about the darkness of the cave, because even by the time they finished eating, her eyes hadn't adjusted at all. She wondered if the moon was bright back out where Elddreki was —hopefully—waiting for them.

"It's probably still early." Kincaid's voice startled her out of her thoughts. They had been sitting in silence for several minutes. "But there's not a lot of entertainment available in a pitch black cave." He gave a small chuckle. "I suppose I could spin you a yarn, if you like."

Jocelyn laughed herself, the sound slightly uneasy. "It doesn't matter," she said quickly. "It might be early, but I'm tired enough to sleep for a week. It's been a big day." Her voice turned rueful. "I guess I should have listened when you suggested waiting until tomorrow to explore in here."

"I don't know," said Kincaid lightly. "This is certainly a memorable experience."

Jocelyn said nothing, unable to disagree with that.

"I'm afraid there isn't going to be anywhere very comfortable to sleep in here," said Kincaid, sounding apologetic.

Jocelyn smiled. "You sound like a very considerate host, Kincaid, but it's not exactly your cave, is it?"

She could hear his smile in his words. "Not exactly, but I'm the Valorian here. I'm supposed to be getting you to admit this kingdom is wonderful, remember?"

"Don't hold your breath," muttered Jocelyn. There was silence for a moment. "Did I offend you?" she asked tentatively.

Kincaid sighed. "No, I'm not offended. I'm reasonable enough to acknowledge you have good reason not to have a very high opinion of Valoria. Yet." He added the last word in a firm tone.

Jocelyn didn't reply. She didn't want to say as much to Kincaid, but when she had spoken, her thoughts had not been on her own unsavory experiences in the kingdom, but on Princess Sarai's fate in marrying a stranger. And through that marriage losing her identity as a princess of Kyona to become a princess of Valoria. A fate Jocelyn seemed all too likely to share.

"Well, I'm getting quite used to sleeping on hard, uncomfortable ground," she said eventually, speaking lightly. "So I daresay I'll struggle through."

"You are a remarkable princess," said Kincaid, matching her tone. "I doubt one in a hundred would take our various adventures as much in their stride as you have." Jocelyn could hear him shuffling around in the darkness, but she had no idea what he was doing. "You said the first night I joined you, before Elddreki came back, that it was because of your mother that you weren't—how did you put it? 'An ordinary princess'. What did you mean by that? I assume you weren't talking about the power in your words?"

"No, I wasn't," acknowledged Jocelyn. "I was talking about the reason I carry a dagger on my person at all times."

"At all times?" Kincaid asked, clearly surprised. "I thought it was just because you were traveling." He paused. "And even that was unusual. And impressive."

"I wear it even at home," Jocelyn said. "And I've been trained in how to use it. Not extensively, but the basics." She grimaced into the darkness. "I'm afraid I'm not very proficient. Some people—like Eamon—just have a natural aptitude for these things. I'm not one of those people." She shrugged a shoulder that no one could see. "But still, I can use a dagger, and a sword, and a bow well enough to not kill anyone by accident."

"Is that a normal part of a princess's education in Kyona?" asked Kincaid, sounding fascinated.

"It is now," chuckled Jocelyn. There was an expectant silence, and she sighed. "You said you grew up on stories of my father's exploits, so I guess you know that we're not...you know... real royals."

"What?" Kincaid's frown was evident in his tone. "Of course you're real royals."

"Well, I suppose we are now. But my father, as royal as his blood might be, was raised in a small village on the coast, by a boat builder and his wife. He wasn't trained in court life until after he became king." She sighed again. "And it didn't make his road easy when he first assumed the throne. He's well-respected now, but he's had to fight for it in a way most kings never would."

"Then the respect is surely all the more deserved," said Kincaid reasonably.

"Yes, it is," Jocelyn agreed. "My father is an excellent king, and an even more excellent man. He just doesn't always do things in the traditional royal way."

"I suspect that's a good thing," responded Kincaid, "if it means he allowed his daughter to be trained to defend herself. Surely a prince would always be well-trained in such an area. I don't know why anyone thinks it's a good thing for princesses to be more vulnerable."

Jocelyn chuckled. "Nevertheless, I can assure you that a lot of people in the Kyonan court *did* think it was a good idea for me to be more vulnerable. Or at least, they thought it was a bad idea —and an outrageous scandal—for me to be trained in swordsmanship." Her voice turned dry. "I just wish I was more skilled at it, to prove them all wrong. But unfortunately, I never excelled."

For a moment she was distracted, brooding over the daydreams she used to entertain of silencing such critics as Sir Sanctimonious with her superior skills. It was so ironic, she thought for the hundredth time. Lucy's mother had also insisted that her daughter learn to defend herself. And despite having the aptitude Jocelyn lacked, Lucy didn't seem to enjoy training. She had been eager enough when they were younger, but in recent years, her parents practically had to force her to train. Still, she was a very competent fighter. Jocelyn smiled to herself. Pointless, really, since it was impossible to imagine sweet, kindhearted Lucy raising a weapon against anyone.

But she was straying from the point. She shook the thought off and continued.

"My father supported it, but it was actually my mother's idea. She always carries a weapon herself, ever since she was abducted, not long before my parents' marriage. She was taken by Father's enemies in an attempt to manipulate him. She wasn't armed when the men came for her, and she hasn't made the same mistake since. I don't mean to suggest my father required any convincing, but it was Mother who insisted her daughter be taught to defend herself, as well as her son. I guess..." she hesitated. "I guess you've heard of my mother, too."

"Of course," said Kincaid, sounding surprised. "Queen Elnora is almost as famous as King Calinnae."

"I can imagine," muttered Jocelyn.

"What does that mean?"

"Nothing," Jocelyn said hastily.

"No." The frown was back in Kincaid's voice as he pursued the point. It wasn't the first time Jocelyn had experienced his unnerving determination to find the thought behind her words. "Not 'nothing'. What did you mean?"

Jocelyn sighed. "Don't get me wrong, I think the world of my mother. But...if some people still mutter about my father not being raised royal, you can imagine how they feel about my mother."

"Oh," said Kincaid in sudden understanding. "You mean because she was a commoner by blood as well as by upbringing?"

"Not just a commoner," said Jocelyn dryly. "She was—by her own description in private conversation—a street rat. She grew up in the slums of Alezae, at least until she joined a street gang."

"Yes, I've heard all that," said Kincaid. "It's an amazing story, isn't it?" He paused. "My sister thinks it's terribly romantic." He chuckled darkly. "I think she imagines it would be a delightful adventure to grow up in a street gang."

"Well, it wouldn't," said Jocelyn bluntly. "And you can tell her to grow up. Fourteen is too old to be so foolish." Her words were met by ringing silence, and even she winced as she realized how harsh she had been. "I'm sorry," she amended quickly. "That was unkind. And unnecessary. But my mother has been very honest with Eamon and me in telling us about her childhood. And it was anything but romantic."

She let out a big breath. "Her lot was hard enough, barely escaping being sold into slavery in the South Lands. But my Aunt Constance, who *was* sold into slavery, has told us enough to know that hers was much worse." Her voice dropped, and she could hear the pain in her words, their power reaching out and wrapping around the very stones of the cavern. "Kyona has some dark pages in its history."

"I know," said Kincaid softly. "And what I said was foolish. I'm the one who should be sorry."

"No, you shouldn't," said Jocelyn sharply. She suspected that a moment ago, Kincaid had known as well as she did that he wasn't in the wrong, and her heart seized strangely at the fear that she had unintentionally influenced him with her unnatural words.

She breathed in slowly, trying to tamp down her unreasonable reaction. "What have you heard about my mother?" she asked. "What do they call her?" She gave an unconvincing chuckle. "The Peasant Queen? Kyona's Vagabond Royal?"

"What?" Kincaid sounded startled. "Of course not. I've never heard anyone in Valoria speak disrespectfully of your mother."

Jocelyn's skepticism must have been audible, because Kincaid pushed on.

"It's true. I told you, people think the story of her marriage to your father is very romantic. But the people here also have a very high respect for both your parents. I was only a baby at the time, of course, but before your father took the throne, Kyona was known as a dark place. Valorians didn't like to go there, and the superstitious were even starting to talk of curses. People were genuinely afraid, even in our kingdom. It was a type of darkness that people feared would creep across the border and infect us too. Well, you must know all this. The previous king, the current king's father, was on the point of marching on Kyona in war in an attempt to stop the disastrous trajectory of the false king's rule."

"Yes," Jocelyn acknowledged. "I do know that."

"But now," Kincaid continued, his voice earnest, "Kyona is a prosperous and respected kingdom, at peace with itself and everyone else. No one hesitates to do trade with you, and people travel back and forth across the border with absolute freedom. Your father—both your parents—have turned the kingdom around. Kyona is the strongest kingdom in the North Lands."

"Is that really how Valorians see us?" Jocelyn asked in surprise.

"Of course."

"That's heartening," she said. But she shook her head. "Not entirely accurate though, unfortunately."

"What do you mean?"

"Well, I suppose we're as prosperous as ever. But lately, we're not completely at peace with ourselves." Kincaid was again expectantly silent, and she sighed. "There's trouble brewing. It has everyone on edge. You know about the history with Balenol, don't you?"

"How they took lots of Kyonans as slaves, going back generations, and how they were all freed and brought home after your father took the throne?"

"That's right," said Jocelyn. "And they've been living prosperously back in Kyona ever since, on the whole. But lately someone's been stirring up trouble against them. Well—" she hesitated, "that's what I think, anyway. Someone must be behind it. It doesn't feel right that the source of the sudden prejudice is so difficult to locate. But in any event, the conflict is escalating between the freedmen—that's what we call them—and this new faction of people who resent them."

"That is strange, and...troubling," said Kincaid thoughtfully.

"What?" Jocelyn had the sense there was more behind Kincaid's words.

"Well, it's just that..." Kincaid hesitated. "As I said, I'm familiar with the basic story of the freedmen. Everyone is. And it hasn't generally been the subject of much interest in Valoria, since it doesn't affect us very directly. But lately..."

"Lately what?" asked Jocelyn sharply as he trailed off.

"Lately there's been a lot of talk about it. About them."

"What kind of talk?"

"Well…" Kincaid sounded thoughtful again. "I guess you could say prejudice. People complaining about them, worrying that the rest of Kyona is going to realize they're a burden, and when they find they're not welcome, they're going to come into Valoria and be a burden here."

"What?" demanded Jocelyn. "That makes no sense! Why would they come to Valoria? Most of them spent half their lives in captivity, dreaming of nothing but Kyona! Plus, they're not a burden. They're hardworking, normal citizens. Honestly, you wouldn't know that they're freedmen—there was nothing to distinguish them from anyone else, until this prejudice arose." She paused. "Except for the marks on the first generation freedmen, I suppose."

"Marks?"

"Their slave marks. The Balenans used to brand their slaves as soon as they were on the ships, then go over it with ink once they arrived in Balenol. I've seen the mark lots of times. It's a bit of a badge of honor now. It's two links of a chain, trailing up the arm."

"Oh." Kincaid was silent for a moment. "The Balenans must have been horrible."

"Yes," Jocelyn agreed. "Well, not all of them," she amended, thinking of Aunt Scarlett, and by extension Lucy and the boys.

Kincaid sighed, clearly lost in his own thoughts. "You're not wrong that the prejudice makes no sense, in Valoria at least. I thought it was strange from the moment I started hearing it. I don't know why people would become concerned all of a sudden about something that doesn't affect us."

"It is strange," Jocelyn agreed. "But it also proves my point, a little. You weren't being entirely honest that everyone sees Kyona as strong." She gave a sad laugh. "Why would they? Not with a half-breed royal family."

"Half-breed?" repeated Kincaid, and to Jocelyn's surprise he sounded angry. "That's a horrible way to speak of yourself, and I'd better not hear you doing it again in front of me, ever."

Jocelyn was silent, somehow feeling both chastened and stubborn. Kincaid seemed to sense she was not fully convinced.

"Jocelyn," he said, and his questing hand suddenly found one of hers, where it rested on the cavern's floor. She sucked in an involuntary breath at the contact. "Kyona is strong, and everyone knows it. Your mother's unusual background is not a liability. It's a strength. Even the *Valorian* commoners have an illogical level of affection for her. She's...a heroine. And your father is a legend personified. I mean," he sounded exasperated, "Kyona's royal house is known as the House of Dragonfriend!"

He let go of her hand, and she could imagine him gesturing toward the outside of the cave. "And with good reason, since the daughter of that house is roaming the countryside with the first dragon anyone's seen in two decades! Trust me when I say no kingdom in its right mind would mess with Kyona. Why do you think Valoria is seeking a marriage alliance?"

Jocelyn had been deep in contemplation of Kincaid's words, but his last question startled a sharp gasp out of her.

"What?" asked Kincaid, uneasily. "Should...should I not have said that?"

"No, I...I suppose there's no reason you shouldn't. It's just..." Jocelyn swallowed. "Does everyone in the kingdom know why I was invited to visit Bryford?"

"Of course not," said Kincaid, his tone unconvincing. "I'm sure not *everyone* knows."

Jocelyn groaned and put her head in her hands. So either she fulfilled everyone's expectations and married the Valorian prince, or she suffered the humiliation of two kingdoms knowing she had been found wanting. She wasn't sure what would be worse.

"What's the story, anyway?" asked Kincaid. He was clearly attempting to speak delicately, but Jocelyn didn't need sight to detect his curiosity. "Are you—are you truly promised to Crown Prince Ormond?"

"Of course not," she said quickly. "I'm not promised to anyone. I was just invited to come and meet the prince, and the king and queen, of course. There was no formal offer, and no obligation. At least," she added grimly, "my mother assured me that there was no obligation. But for reasons already discussed, she might not be the most accurate judge of the subtleties of these things." She sighed. "I should have listened to my father. He wasn't at all convinced about this trip. But then again," her tone brightened, "perhaps they'll think I'm so odd after my disappearance that they'll rescind the invitation."

"Don't you want to marry Prince Ormond?" asked Kincaid, his tone a little too nonchalant.

She shrugged, again forgetting he couldn't see. "I don't know. I've never met the man." She tilted her head. "What's he like?"

"I don't know," Kincaid echoed her, sounding uncomfortable. "I've never heard anything bad of him."

"Have you seen him? What does he look like?"

"Yes, I've seen him," said Kincaid, not very enthusiastically. "He's...tall. And has pale hair. Closely cropped."

"The haircut of princes," said Jocelyn, amused.

"What?"

"Nothing, it just sounded like you were describing my brother." She wrinkled her nose at the idea of marrying someone who looked like her twin. The thought was not appealing.

"Oh." Kincaid apparently had nothing more to say about Crown Prince Ormond.

"Is it true he's twenty-five?" Jocelyn pressed curiously, impatient of Kincaid's reticence.

Kincaid thought for a moment. "Twenty-six, I think," he answered. Jocelyn was silent. "Too old?" Kincaid suggested. Was it Jocelyn's imagination that he sounded faintly hopeful?

She sighed. "Not really, I suppose. I mean, I'm almost eighteen." She laughed self-consciously, the sound feeling unnatural as it came out. "It sounds a little old to me, but of course it could be worse. I've heard of much more uneven marriage alliances."

There was a long pause, and when Kincaid spoke, Jocelyn thought his voice sounded harder than usual. "That's why Darius told that story your first night in Montego, isn't it? The one about the Kyonan princess who traveled to Valoria to marry the crown prince, all those generations ago? He was drawing a parallel with your situation."

"I think so," said Jocelyn with a shrug.

"Hm."

"Hm?" Jocelyn prodded.

"I was just wondering if that's why you seem to feel such a connection to this Princess Sarai." Jocelyn didn't answer, and after a moment Kincaid let out a breath. "Well, you said you were tired, and here I am keeping you awake talking." His tone was light, but it rang a little false to Jocelyn. "I've laid out my traveling cloak for you, but even so, like I said, I'm afraid it won't be very comfortable."

"What?" protested Jocelyn, startled by the change in direction. "I'm not taking your traveling cloak."

"Of course you are," said Kincaid firmly. "What kind of a host would I be if I let a visiting princess sleep on the hard stone?"

"I thought we established that you're not the host of this cave," Jocelyn shot back. "What about you?"

"I'll be fine," said Kincaid dismissively. "Don't be stubborn."

"I'll be as stubborn as I like," said Jocelyn. "I insist that you take it."

"Well I insist that you do."

"Kincaid," said Jocelyn, unimpressed. "Don't make me use my dragon magic to convince you."

Kincaid laughed at that, the tone instantly lightening. For some reason it seemed like far too long since he had laughed. His chuckle died away, and there was a moment of silence. Then he spoke, and the mood suddenly leaped right back up to tense again.

"We could share it. It's large."

Jocelyn swallowed, her throat suddenly dry. Every rule of etiquette she had ever been taught was screaming in her head, but she felt herself teetering. Then she thought of the snake, and she knew the battle was lost.

"Yes, all right."

She felt her way over to where Kincaid had laid the cloak. It was thicker than she expected, delightfully soft under her fingers compared with the hard cold stone. She settled herself as close to the edge as possible. She could tell Kincaid was doing the same on the other edge of it, and after a moment they were both still. He was right, it was large—no part of them was touching.

"I know it's not exactly...standard behavior, but I don't have any, you know, dishonorable intentions." Kincaid's voice emerged unexpectedly from the darkness.

"I know."

There was a moment's awkward silence, then Jocelyn sighed. "We're stuck in a pitch black cave, Kincaid, we may as well make the best of it."

He chuckled. "That's what I figured."

"I wonder what Elddreki will make of our absence."

"Not much, I'm guessing," said Kincaid dryly. His tone

turned cheerful. "At least that's one benefit of traveling with a dragon—you know he won't be worried about you if you get delayed."

"Is that a benefit, though?" Jocelyn asked humorously. "I mean, if it was just the two of us traveling together, and one of us disappeared for hours longer than expected, the other one would know to come looking for them, to make sure they weren't in trouble. But I suspect we'd have to be missing for a year before Elddreki would think to start searching."

"If it was just the two of us traveling together," returned Kincaid, "I expect I would have a very uncomfortable conversation with your royal father in my future, with a lot of explaining to do."

Jocelyn was unable to think of a reply to this very accurate observation, and there was a long moment of silence.

"I'm teasing you," Kincaid said eventually.

Another moment of silence.

"I know."

The silence stretched out long enough for Kincaid's breathing to start to slow. But as tired as she was, Jocelyn had never felt further from sleep.

"Kincaid?"

"Yes?" Kincaid's voice came out of the darkness, reassuringly close.

"Do you really think we'll be able to find the opening once the sun comes up?"

"Yes, I really do." His voice was confident, and Jocelyn felt heartened.

The cave went quiet again, the only sound an occasional drip of water in the distance. It might have been her imagination, but Jocelyn thought she heard a faint rustling away somewhere to her right. She didn't even realize she was wriggling closer to Kincaid until her arm made contact with his.

"Jocelyn?" He sounded startled. "Are you all right?"

"Yes," she said quickly. "Sorry." She hesitated for a moment, then confessed sheepishly, "I was thinking of the snake."

"Oh."

Kincaid paused, then Jocelyn felt his arm move next to hers, and the next thing she knew, he had extended it fully to the side, in a silent invitation for her to shuffle closer. She did so, feeling a strange and heady emotion that was equal parts exhilaration and nervousness. Her sight was as blank as ever, but in her mind's eye she could see the disapproving glare of every tutor and chaperone and lady's maid she had ever had. A part of her mind tried to tell her that she would have to look Kincaid in the face again in the morning, but she ignored it.

"Nothing will harm you while you're in here, Jocelyn. I swear it."

Jocelyn wasn't at all sure how Kincaid could swear any such thing, but she felt comforted all the same.

They both fell silent, and remained that way so long that even Jocelyn's mind began to feel fuzzy with sleep. The darkness was as impenetrable as ever, and she felt a curious sensation of security, in spite of everything. She wondered if Kincaid had fallen asleep. She hesitated for a moment, but her fogginess combined with the concealing dark to make her bold.

"Kincaid?"

"Yes, I'm here." His voice was soft, but alert.

"I know that when you insisted on coming into the cave, I acted like I didn't need your help. But I'm glad you're here."

Kincaid didn't respond, and the drawn-out silence made Jocelyn feel less fuzzy and more self-conscious.

"Even if you're right that my father would probably have you hanged if he ever found out about this," she added, trying to lighten the mood.

Kincaid gave a weak chuckle, followed by another long silence.

"You are joking, right?"

She smiled under cover of the darkness. "Of course I am."

Well, she was mostly joking. Kyona's king wasn't exactly quick to execute people, but she suspected her father would have some kind of heart failure if he could see her current situation. And the dark and sinister cave in which she was potentially trapped would barely factor when compared with the attractive young man lying beside her in the darkness.

And he wouldn't be wrong that Kincaid was a threat, although not in the way an overprotective father might fear. Jocelyn was confident she had spoken the truth when she said Kincaid's every move radiated honor. But the more time they spent together, the more emotions the Valorian seemed to stir up inside the normally reserved princess. Emotions she was afraid to examine too closely.

Jocelyn shook her musings off. In the morning she would remember that she was supposed to be a closely guarded, well brought up princess, who was half promised in marriage to a foreign prince, and in any event not free to form an attachment with a free-spirited wanderer, however handsome and engaging he might be.

But tonight...tonight, she would forget about all of it. She felt sleep tugging at her at last. Tonight, she would just be Jocelyn.

CHAPTER SEVENTEEN

arai looked up into her father's face, noting with pride how regal and commanding he looked in his ceremonial garb. She hoped all the Valorian guests were impressed. She hoped Crown Prince Germain would feel glad to be making a marriage alliance with such a strong and noble kingdom.

Her heart raced nervously at the thought of the man who, within minutes, would be her husband. What was he like? She cast her mind back over the several polite conversations they had shared during the state visit preceding this wedding. None of them had revealed much about him as a person.

"You are beautiful, Sarai," her father said softly, such love shining in his eyes that Sarai's heart felt ready to burst with mingled joy and sadness. She couldn't imagine she would find any love with the serious, respectful Prince Germain or his family that could rival the love of her own family.

"I wish your mother could be here."

"Oh, Father," said Sarai. "I wish that, too. It doesn't feel right without her."

King Cael smiled sadly, looking suddenly older. "She would have been very proud of you." He squeezed her arm. "I am proud of you as well. We will miss you terribly."

She gave him an impulsive embrace, after looking around quickly to make sure no one would see the unladylike display of emotion. "I will miss you all as well, Father. More than I can tell."

Sarai tried to hold herself tall during the ceremonial approach to the throne, hoping none of the keen eyes trained on her could see how tightly she was clinging to her father's arm.

She knew Prince Germain was standing just in front of the throne, but she couldn't bring herself to meet his eyes as she walked the length of the long hall. It was lined with suits of armor instead of the vibrant tapestries in her father's throne room. It seemed cold and serious to Sarai.

When her father passed her hand to the Valorian prince in a symbolic gesture, she had to force herself not to follow him with her eyes as he walked to his seat. Instead, she took a deep breath and met her betrothed's gaze at last. He gave her a small smile, his expression kind but still somehow serious. She returned the smile tightly, trying not to focus on the unfamiliar feel of his hand in hers. It was warmer than her father's hand had been, and although Prince Germain clasped her firmly, she felt adrift, alone, without anchor.

Involuntarily, her eyes flicked to her father, and her brother standing next to him. They were both smiling at her, looking proud, and clearly satisfied with the alliance. She straightened her back and returned the pressure of Prince Germain's hand as they turned to the master of ceremonies.

She was a princess of Kyona. She would make her kingdom—and her family—proud.

Sarai frowned as she leaned against the windowpane, disoriented by the rushing in her ears. She looked out at the prospect, admiring the royal garden in spite of herself. Bryford was a beautiful city, there was no denying it. The sound of happy laughter drifted in to her from *a nearby courtyard, where women were gathered to chat as they washed clothes.*

Why had she come to this room again? She had been thinking about her wedding, but she couldn't remember why. How many months had it been? Five? Six?

"Sarai?"

She turned at the sound of her husband's voice, noting vaguely that he sounded different from usual—uncertain.

"Sire."

"Please, Sarai." He sounded pained. "Call me Germain."

"Of course," she said stupidly. He had told her that before, many times. Why was it so hard to remember where she was?

"Sarai, we have received some...news. From Kynton."

Kynton? She turned fully from the window, her interest captured. "From my family? Is Parmida going to accept our invitation to stay for the season?"

"No, Sarai," said Germain, and he looked uncharacteristically unsure of himself. He stepped forward and took her hands in his. She stared down at them, unnerved by the unusual display. Something was wrong. Why was it so hard to focus? The room was spinning strangely.

"Sarai, it's...it's the very worst news. I'm so sorry."

"What do you mean?" she asked, her heartbeat picking up. She forced an artificial laugh. "It can't be the very worst news. Not unless you're going to tell me that my whole family died in a terrible accident."

Germain bowed his head for a moment, and Sarai's heart seemed to stop beating. Surely that wasn't what he was saying. Her husband brought his eyes up resolutely to meet hers, and the expression she saw there filled her with terror like she had never known.

"I wish there was a way, any way, to tell you gently," he said, his voice soft but steady, "but I think the only way is to be direct. I don't

know if your whole family has died. But your father certainly has, and your sister Parmida. The others are...unaccounted for."

"I don't...understand," Sarai whispered, the rushing in her ears intensifying.

"The details are still unclear," said Germain softly, and some detached part of her mind registered the anguish in his voice and the kindness in his eyes. But she was in no state to appreciate such things. "But it appears that your father was killed in a revolt, led by one of the nobles, who is now claiming the throne."

"One...one of the nobles is claiming the throne?" Sarai repeated, dumbfounded. It was some kind of terrible mistake, it had to be. "That's impossible. Surely Jonathon—"

"Jonathon is nowhere to be found," interrupted Germain gently. "Whether he was also killed, or whether he has escaped, no one seems to know. Avalyn also has disappeared. But the noble is indeed sitting on the throne. Our spies confirm it."

"No," Sarai whispered. "It—it can't be true."

"It is true," Germain said, his voice strong even as his eyes brimmed with compassion. "I'm sorry, Sarai. I'm so desperately sorry."

He opened his arms to her, as if expecting her to fall into them, but she stepped backward. "I must go to them. I must find Jonathon, and Avalyn. I must help them—"

"No." Germain's voice was firm, and he gripped one of her shoulders. "You cannot go to Kyona, Sarai, it's much too dangerous. Father has closed the border. No one is to come or go."

"You cannot cut me off from my home," Sarai choked, aghast. "You cannot separate me from my family!"

"Sarai." Germain's voice was again gentle. "Your family are not there for you to rejoin."

"But you said no one can come or go—surely if Avalyn, or Jonathon, come to me for sanctuary, surely you will not turn them away!"

"Of course not!" said Germain quickly. "If we received a message *from either of them, even the slightest hint that they were still—that they wished for refuge here, we would welcome them. But we have received no such communication."*

Sarai's head was reeling. She gripped a nearby chair back for support, unable to grasp the magnitude of the catastrophe that had befallen her, that had befallen her family, her kingdom.

"Sarai," said Germain, again taking a step toward her.

She looked up at him numbly, and was startled to see tears standing in his eyes. She never would have imagined her serious, impenetrable husband capable of crying. She took a deep breath, trying to pull herself together. She was a princess of Kyona, and it was for that reason Germain had married her. She had her pride, and she would—she must—show him that she was as strong as a princess was expected to be. Even if it was a facade.

"I wish to be alone, please," she said, her voice coming out surprisingly even.

"Sarai, are...are you sure?" He sounded distressed, but she didn't dare to meet his eyes. The storm was coming, she could feel it moments away, and this grief was much too intimate to allow anyone to witness it.

"I am sure," she said, still not looking at him.

Germain hesitated for a long moment, but when she remained unmoving, he let go of her hands and stepped back. "I will of course respect your wishes," he said, with a formal bow. His voice softened. "But should you wish for company, for anything at all, I will be here."

She nodded tightly, averting her face as he walked from the room, shutting the door carefully behind him. She made herself count to one hundred before she moved, giving him time to pass out of hearing range. Then she collapsed onto the floor, her face pressed into the cold unfeeling stone as she sobbed long and hysterically, her heart breaking into a thousand pieces.

She was utterly alone.

"Sarai?"

"Oh, Germain, were you speaking to me?" Sarai turned to her husband, distracted.

Had she just been remembering that terrible day in the tower room? Why was she thinking of that now? It had been months. She felt confused, and it took her a moment to identify her current surroundings. She was in the castle courtyard, her hand on her mare, ready to mount and commence her ride.

She stroked the beautiful bay's mane as she looked up at Germain. She was more glad than ever that she had been allowed to bring her own horse with her from Kyona when they married. The beast would be her only friend from home ever to join her in Bryford.

"I was just asking..." Germain hesitated. "Are you sure you wish to go so soon after returning from your last trip? This Dragoncave place sounds far away. It will take you days to get there."

"I'm sure," she said firmly. She paused, casting her eyes down. "You are good to release me. I know some do not approve of my search, and I don't wish to cause you—"

"It's not that," Germain interrupted. He hesitated again, then reached out a hand to tuck a stray strand of hair behind her ears. Sarai stilled in surprise at the unexpected touch. "It's just that I will miss you," he said. "And your grief is still so fresh, Sarai. I cannot help but wonder if it's wise for you to be alone so much."

"I won't be alone," she said hastily, hoping he wouldn't notice she hadn't said she would miss him too. For a moment she wondered if he really would miss her, but she couldn't imagine why he would. They spent little enough time together even when she was in Bryford. "There's a whole delegation with me."

"I know, but—" Germain looked uncharacteristically conscious. "I don't mean literally alone. I suppose I mean...not with me."

"Oh." Sarai couldn't think of any further response.

"I could..." Germain looked down, then back up at her face. "I could come with you, if you would like it."

"But what of your duties?" asked Sarai, surprised. "Aren't you *expected with the Thoranian ambassador this afternoon, and the delegate from the eastern district tomorrow?"*

It was Germain's turn to look surprised. "You know my schedule better than I do, it seems," he said with a touch of humor.

"Of course." Sarai spoke with dignity. "I am your wife, and it's my responsibility to ensure nothing hinders you in your royal functions. I have calculated the time I will be absent. It will be no more than a week, and I don't believe I will be needed in any of your duties during that time."

"That's not what I'm worried about," said Germain softly. "I'm concerned for you."

"You are kind," said Sarai colorlessly, "and you have made your wishes clear as to my safety. You have my word I will not attempt to cross into Kyona. Surely you don't doubt it."

"Of course I don't," said Germain quickly. "I just meant—"

"Then you know I will be safe, Germain," Sarai interrupted. "I'm grateful for the offer, but there's no need for you to abandon your responsibilities in order to accompany me."

He frowned. "You are my responsibility."

"I know," said Sarai, looking up. "And after this trip, I will try not to be such a burdensome one."

He was still frowning, and for a moment he didn't speak. "Five days," he said at last, his voice curt. "I want you to return within five days."

"Very well," she agreed, turning to mount her horse at last. She looked down at him, her expression softening for a moment. "And thank you."

JOCELYN WOKE WITH A START, her mind racing frantically rather than groggy with sleep as it should have been. For a moment her eyes darted around erratically, trying to reclaim awareness. She felt confused, overwhelmed by emotions that were not her own, and yet were far too familiar for comfort. She half expected to see Germain standing nearby, and she spoke firmly to her overstimulated mind, reminding herself that she wasn't Sarai, she was Jocelyn.

Jocelyn, Jocelyn, Jocelyn.

All of a sudden she became aware of her own body, and it was all she could do not to scramble to her feet. She remembered now—she had fallen asleep irresponsibly, scandalously close to Kincaid, her arm pressed against his side, reassured by his presence and his confident certainty that they were safe.

That had been most improper.

But it was nothing to how she found herself now. Kincaid was right where he had been, but she had obviously shifted in her sleep, turning onto her side. Her head was cushioned on his shoulder, and she was—she winced as she thought it, but there was really no other word for it—snuggled up against him.

She sat up quickly, fervently grateful that he was still fast asleep, and not able to witness her humiliatingly loose behavior. Just as she had known but tried to deny the night before, she now had to look him in the face in the light of day.

The light of day!

"Kincaid!" she cried, forgetting her embarrassment in the sudden surge of excitement. "Look!"

"What? What is it?"

Kincaid passed from deep slumber to alert wakefulness in an impressively short space of time. Jocelyn had already leaped to her feet, and he followed her, his sword drawn in the same fluid motion that had propelled him from the cavern floor.

"It's light!" she said gleefully, gesturing around. "We can see!"

"So we can," he said, a smile growing on his face. He looked up at the cavern ceiling. "That's incredible."

Following his gaze, Jocelyn had to agree. She had thought

that at best the morning might bring a dim glow from the direction of the fissure through which they had entered. Instead, sunlight slanted in from the roof of the cave, high above them, not in one or two places, but in dozens. It seemed there were lots of long narrow slits occurring in the cavern roof, angled almost horizontally, and the whole space was illuminated with the soft light of morning.

It looked huge and intriguing, but no longer sinister. Stalactites and stalagmites sprouted everywhere, and Jocelyn could even see one or two pretty looking pools gathered in spots where the moisture dripped down from the ceiling above.

"Those fissures are all facing east," said Kincaid after a moment. "They would hardly let any light in during the afternoon or evening." He grinned at her. "Good thing we didn't oversleep."

"You were right," said Jocelyn, looking around in amazement. "We should definitely have waited until morning to explore."

"No." She glanced at Kincaid in surprise as he spoke the word, but looked away again quickly at the intensity in his gaze. "I'm glad we didn't."

He rolled his shoulders, wincing slightly.

"What is it?" Jocelyn asked quickly. "What's wrong?"

"Nothing," said Kincaid, sounding surprised at her tone. "Just a bit stiff is all." He rubbed one shoulder in particular, as if it was sore. From his look of confusion, Jocelyn could tell he was trying to figure out why that one spot was so much more uncomfortable than everywhere else. She turned away, her cheeks flaming.

"So." The intensity was gone, Kincaid's voice now bright and natural. "Since it's so light, do you want to explore more after all?"

"Definitely not," said Jocelyn quickly. "Let's get out of here."

He grinned. "Worried about snakes?"

"Yes, definitely," she said with a shudder. "Always." She looked around. The air still tingled with power, and the cave retained a measure of eeriness even in the daylight. "But it's not just that. I slept...restlessly."

"You did?" Kincaid sounded surprised. "I slept surprisingly solidly. I didn't hear or feel you stir."

Jocelyn's cheeks had cooled, but she felt heat rising back up them at this casual reference to their sleeping arrangement. "I don't mean that I woke up," she said hastily. "I had...strange dreams."

"Strange how?" Kincaid looked wary, and Jocelyn felt her curiosity flare as she wondered what was in his mind. But she didn't ask.

"Princess Sarai's stories, or memories, or whatever they are," she said instead. "I dreamed about them. It was like I was reviewing her memories, but all in a jumble, one rushing into the other. I saw her wedding day, then the day she found out about what happened to her family."

She paused, a shiver passing through her as she remembered the agony that had ripped Sarai apart as she wept all alone on the floor of the tower room. For a moment Jocelyn was distracted, thinking how she would feel if her own family were murdered. She shook the thought off resolutely.

"Then I saw her saying goodbye to her husband to come here, to look for Dragoncave. There was no more. I guess at the time she was here, when she left her stories behind, there was nothing further to add."

"It's a strange phenomenon," said Kincaid, frowning at Jocelyn. "I'm not entirely sure how I feel about it."

"Neither am I," said Jocelyn with feeling. She saw Kincaid's frown of concern, and continued pleadingly, "But I can't help it. I'm not trying to be weird and magical."

"Of course you're not," said Kincaid with a laugh. He examined her face, and a crease appeared between his eyebrows. "I didn't mean I'm unnerved by you, Joss. It just strikes me that you have enough grief, and loneliness, and...well...confusion in your life already. I don't like the idea of you being forced to experience someone else's as well."

Jocelyn glanced at his expression and turned away quickly. It wasn't the first time Kincaid had shown concern for her. But after their strange and intimate interactions the night before, there was a new warmth in his eyes as they rested on her face, and she wasn't sure how she felt about it.

Scratch that. She knew exactly how she felt about it, but she wasn't at all sure what to do with the information. As she had promised herself the night before, with the advent of morning, she had remembered in full force who she was and why she had come to Valoria in the first place.

She gave a tight smile. "I can handle it."

"I'm sure you can."

As they readied themselves to leave, Jocelyn glanced back toward the wall of dragon runes. They looked even more impressive in the daylight, stretching further up the wall than she'd realized. She hoped they had copied all of them on Kincaid's parchment. Her eyes were attracted by something on the cavern floor, and she smiled. The broken jar, still lying in a patch of slick oil, looked so innocent and unimportant now. It was strange to think what a panic it had thrown her into the night before.

Still, despite the extra light, Jocelyn felt immensely relieved when they located the opening without difficulty.

"This time, I insist," she said, scrambling up the slope ahead of Kincaid. "Ladies first. You're not leaving me alone in here with the snakes and the magical memories."

Kincaid didn't argue, his soft chuckle wafting through the air behind her. But he kept pace with her, and stopped her before she could begin crawling through the hole.

"Jocelyn." He hesitated, and Jocelyn tilted her head inquiringly.

"What is it?"

Kincaid was looking at the fissure, but not as if he really saw it. "Before we leave the cave, I just...I just wanted to thank you."

"Thank me for what?" asked Jocelyn, bewildered.

"For trusting me." Kincaid still wasn't looking her in the eye, and at first Jocelyn thought he was talking about the way they had arranged themselves for sleep. Before she could get too self-conscious, however, he looked up at last, and his steady gaze captured her.

"When it was dark, you were afraid," he said, and she made no attempt to disagree. "I told you we would be safe, and you trusted me. It felt—" He looked down again. "I was glad I could help you in that way."

Jocelyn blinked. It was a strange thing to thank her for, but she thought she understood. She felt it too. Things would be different once they exited this unnaturally isolated place, and Kincaid evidently wanted to acknowledge the shift that had happened in their relationship. But she couldn't afford to acknowledge it. Not now the inhibition-destroying darkness had fled, and all the consequences were once again staring her in the face.

"You don't need to thank me for anything, Kincaid," she said lightly, and she didn't miss the shadow of disappointment that crossed his face. "If you want to say something of that nature, you *could* say sorry for dropping the oil in the first place."

She had spoken jestingly, but Kincaid didn't match her tone.

"I could," he agreed quietly. "But it wouldn't be very honest, because I'm not sorry it happened."

CHAPTER EIGHTEEN

Jocelyn's chest tightened at the look Kincaid was giving her. Unable to think of a reply, she turned quickly to the fissure and dropped onto her knees. Kincaid's words seemed to chase her through the narrow space, and it was with relief that she greeted the burst of fresh air that met her as soon as her head emerged into the daylight.

She wriggled all the way out and leaped to her feet. She spun in a slow circle, her heart lifting at the sight of the open country, the river with the mountain range behind it, even the unwelcoming town of Thalia not far away.

A soft breeze tugged at her braid, the strands starting to come adrift after her various adventures. She pulled her hair fully free, combing her fingers through it, and laughed with delight at the feeling of freedom.

"Greetings, Jocelyn." Elddreki's voice sounded indulgent, and Jocelyn looked up to see him still on top of the mound, watching her twirl. She wondered if he'd been there all night. "You seem happy this morning."

"Greetings, Elddreki. I'm *very* happy to make it out of that cave in one piece," agreed Jocelyn with a grin.

"Was there something dangerous in there after all, then?" asked Elddreki, descending the slope in an unhurried way.

"Nothing more dangerous than my clumsiness." Kincaid's voice made Jocelyn turn—she hadn't realized he was so close behind her. His head had emerged from the fissure, but the rest of him was still inside.

She reflected to herself that his appeal was much more dangerous than his clumsiness, but she pushed the thought away, refusing to brood in the sparkling light of this glorious summer morning.

She stepped away from Elddreki, who was now on the ground beside her, and tripped back over to the Valorian, laughing at how absurd he looked. He was trying to wriggle free, but due to his size it wasn't as easy for him as it had been for her.

"Let me help," she offered, holding out her hands. He eyed them dubiously, and she grinned. "Trying to decide between whether to have the assistance or whether to have your dignity?" she guessed.

"Something like that." His voice was rueful.

"Well, your dignity is not very intact either way," she assured him with a laugh. "So you may as well let me tug you through." She seized his hands and did so, with more enthusiasm than skill. When he fully emerged and stood up, he was so covered in dirt that she had to step back, coughing, as he brushed himself off.

He gave her a pointed look when she continued to snicker. "Mock me all you like, but have you looked at your own clothes lately, Your Highness?"

She glanced quickly down at herself and grimaced at the state of her costly dress. It was ruined beyond repair, no doubt about it. So much dirt clung to it that it was hard to tell what its original color had been, and the fabric had been ripped in numerous places by her shuffle into and around the cave.

"Ready to thank me for buying you new clothes after all?" asked Kincaid, much too smug.

"Never," said Jocelyn impudently, even as she held out a hand. Kincaid grinned as he fished around in his pack before producing the simple garment he had purchased in Thalia the day before.

Jocelyn walked all the way around Dragoncave before changing, positioning herself on the very opposite side of the mound from her companions. She stripped off the old dress quickly, looking longingly at the sparkling water of the Great River as she did so. It would be glorious to bathe, even in cold river water, but she wasn't going to risk being interrupted in the process. Plus, the water was flowing very quickly here, and she wasn't sure it would be safe.

So she brushed herself off as well as she could, splashing river water on her face and washing her arms up to the elbow. Then she hurried into the dress Kincaid had bought her. It was a good fit, for which she was fairly certain she could thank the saleswoman rather than the purchaser. It was much simpler than anything she had ever worn, the coarse fabric scratching at her skin. But as she turned this way and that, she decided she was pleased with the effect.

The reddish brown was a natural color, not often found in the decadent fabrics of court. But Jocelyn thought it suited her well. The skirt was full enough not to restrict movement, but nothing like the voluminous folds of even her most practical gown at home. It was hard to tell without a looking glass, of course, but she had the impression that it gave her whole figure a much slimmer line.

And it wasn't entirely without embellishment. There was simple embroidery around the hem, cuffs, and neckline, and the lacing on the front of the bodice was a pretty golden color.

She walked back around the mound with a spring in her

step, enjoying how much easier it was to move in this practical garment. She found Elddreki and Kincaid deep in conversation, right where she had left them. Kincaid's eyes flicked to her as soon as she came into view.

"There you are," he said, his voice teasing. "You took so long I thought you'd fallen into the river."

Jocelyn scowled at him. She had tried to be quick, but she was used to having a lady's maid to help her dress. "You try lacing up this bodice, then we'll talk."

She regretted the words as soon as they left her mouth. Kincaid remained awkwardly silent, looking like he wasn't entirely sure where to look.

"It's a nice dress, though," she hurried on. "Thank you." She looked Kincaid over properly and realized he had changed his tunic while she was gone. His pants were still pretty dusty, but it was a definite improvement.

"Kincaid was just telling me about the power in the cave, and its curious effect on you," said Elddreki. "Most interesting."

"Did you tell him about the runes?" asked Jocelyn eagerly.

"I was just getting to that." Kincaid hurried to retrieve the parchment, looking like he was glad to have something to do. He stretched it out carefully while Jocelyn described to Elddreki what they had seen.

The dragon curved his long neck downward, lowering his enormous head toward the parchment with more eagerness than Jocelyn had ever seen him display. He didn't immediately read the runes, closing his eyes and inhaling deeply, as if his breath could lift the meaning off the page and take it directly into his mind.

"Hm," he said, opening his eyes. The snakelike orbs blinked once, scanning the markings at last. "You were right that the same runes are repeated more than once, even in this small space."

"What does it say?" asked Kincaid, looking excited.

Elddreki shook his head slowly, still studying the parchment. "It is not as simple as translating it into the language of men, a rune for a word. That is not how dragon runes work." He was silent another moment, then he gave a satisfied nod. "But I take the meaning, I think."

"Well?" Jocelyn prompted impatiently, when Elddreki fell silent.

"Water," said Elddreki, and Jocelyn stilled in surprise, remembering the impression she had formed when she first touched the runes. "But not just water," Elddreki was continuing. "The sea. The vastness of the ocean. Salt and waves and foam. The dragons who came to this cave were dreaming of the sea when they inscribed these runes."

"The sea?" Jocelyn repeated, and Elddreki nodded serenely.

"It is a common dream. Most of us who live in Vasilisa have never experienced the sea, but we see it often in our mind's eye. Many have a great curiosity to see it in its entirety."

"So you think the dragons probably left Valoria?" asked Jocelyn, disappointed. "That they traveled to the sea and went somewhere beyond?"

"I didn't say that," said Elddreki. "I said that they were dreaming of the sea, not that they went beyond it. I can't be certain of course, but my best guess would be that the dragons who left these runes traveled on from here toward the sea. Perhaps they found a place to settle near its waters. We should start there."

"Start...where?" asked Jocelyn dubiously.

"At the ocean," said Elddreki, his voice matter-of-fact.

Jocelyn frowned at Kincaid, and he raised in inquiring eyebrow.

"I'm just trying to picture the map of the North Lands in my father's castle," she explained. "You'd know better than I would, but my memory is that Valoria—"

"Has a lot of coastline, yes, it does," acknowledged Kincaid. "Starting at 'the ocean' is a bit of a daunting task."

"Well, there's no hurry, as I keep reminding you," said Elddreki.

"There might not be any hurry for you," said Jocelyn, exasperated, "but every day I spend out here is a day that's borrowed from the state visit I'm supposed to be making at Bryford." She looked over at Kincaid. "And Kincaid isn't supposed to be here at all. I doubt he can spend a decade on this quest."

"Probably not, no," said Kincaid apologetically.

"Well, that's no issue," said Elddreki. "Kincaid needn't be here if he doesn't wish to be. He can leave at any time, with no loss of honor."

"I'm not going anywhere until the quest is done," said Kincaid firmly.

Elddreki swung his head around, his eyes staring unblinkingly into Kincaid's. "Is that a promise, young Valorian?"

Kincaid met his gaze for a long moment, then lowered his eyes with a sigh. When he spoke, his words were directed at the dragon, but his eyes were on Jocelyn. "No. But it's my intention."

"Intentions change," said Elddreki dismissively. "Especially human intentions." He smiled at Kincaid, however, as if to soften his words. "But you are welcome to travel with us for as long as you choose. You have proven to be of great use on this quest."

"I have?" asked Kincaid, looking gratified but skeptical.

"Certainly," said Elddreki. "You seem dedicated to keeping Jocelyn alive, and given the frailty of humankind, that is a great encouragement to me. I desire her assistance in my efforts, and unlike you, she is under an obligation." He looked thoughtful for a moment. "I wonder if I should have mentioned your presence to her father. Would it perhaps have encouraged him also?"

"You've spoken to my father?" Jocelyn asked quickly. "When? While we were in the cave?" *Practically embracing in the dark*, she added silently. She had to exercise great restraint to prevent herself from looking over her shoulder nervously. She half expected her father to descend that very moment, sweeping her off to lock her away somewhere where she would never be allowed to speak to another male again.

"No, not last night," said Elddreki calmly. "The night before. It was his call that took my attention when you were about to enter the first village we came to. I thought it would be best to return to the mountains while I communicated with him. That's why I sent you on into the town alone."

"Not the best of ideas," muttered Kincaid, but Jocelyn ignored him.

"But that was ages ago!" she protested. "In human terms, at least," she added hastily, forestalling Elddreki's inevitable interruption. "Why didn't you mention it before now? For example some time yesterday, when we were walking in silence half the day?"

Elddreki did his rippling shrug. "You seemed disinclined to engage in conversation."

Jocelyn barely refrained from rolling her eyes. "Well, what did he say? Was he worried? Did you set his mind at ease?"

"He said a great many things," said Elddreki calmly. "And he was certainly worried. It seems you did not exaggerate when you described the effect your disappearance would create. He was reassured, however, to discover you were with me."

Elddreki tilted his head to the side in a pensive posture, giving a guttural chuckle. "Actually there is a certain irony in that thought. He was indeed greatly reassured in the belief that I knew where you were, and that you were safe. But as later information revealed, at that moment I did not know precisely where you were, and you were not in fact safe."

Jocelyn glanced involuntarily at Kincaid, and saw that her human companion clearly didn't find this observation as humorous as her dragon companion.

"What did he say when you told him I was fulfilling his promise to assist you?"

Elddreki frowned slightly. "His reaction was curious. I would describe him as astonished. If he remembered our agreement at all—which I am not certain he did—he certainly didn't seem to recognize the inevitability of me interpreting your trip through the mountains as an offer to commence the quest. And he was... I would have to say distressed...to discover you were now shouldering the burden of his promise."

Jocelyn sighed. "Yes, I can imagine. I doubt he thinks I'm capable of anything of the kind."

Kincaid frowned at her. "More likely he's just concerned about your safety, like any father would be."

She shrugged. "That too, of course."

Jocelyn turned her attention back to the dragon. "Did he say what he was going to do about the Valorian royals?"

"He did not," said Elddreki. "I mentioned you were hopeful he might communicate with them regarding your change in plan, so I imagine he will do so." For a moment they were all silent, then Elddreki spoke again. "I must say, given how lightly he has apparently held his own promise, I was surprised that he seemed almost to expect a promise from me. Or at least, he seemed to expect me to take responsibility for your safety." He brought his unblinking gaze to bear on Jocelyn. "Do you have such an expectation, Jocelyn?"

Jocelyn saw Kincaid shift in her peripherals, but she didn't look over at him. She thought for a moment about her answer. "No," she said quietly. "I don't have that expectation. I hope to survive this quest, of course, and I hope that if we are attacked you will assist me if you can. But I don't think I can expect you to make a promise to that effect."

Elddreki nodded, apparently well satisfied with this answer. But the strength of Kincaid's gaze brought Jocelyn's attention to him at last. She saw that he was much less pleased, his forehead creased in a frown.

"Well," said the dragon, straightening up again. "I did not make any promises. But I did tell him that should our quest go so well as to finish while the Kyonan delegation is still at Bryford, I would be glad to see you to the city, where you could rejoin them."

"Thank you." Jocelyn nodded briskly. She could feel Kincaid's eyes still on her, and she thought it was time to turn the conversation. "Now the real question is, where do we go next?" She held up a hand as Elddreki opened his mouth. "And don't say the coast. That's not specific enough."

"Well, where is the closest coast?" asked Elddreki reasonably. "Perhaps we can start there."

"No," said Kincaid unexpectedly. Both of the others turned to him, and he looked suddenly uncomfortable. "I mean, I know it's not for me to decide, but I don't think that's the best idea. The closest coast would be due south, but to get there we'd have to go through—"

"Bryford," finished Jocelyn in sudden understanding. "Yes, let's not go there." She frowned. "If I'm honest, I don't love the plan of wandering the coast aimlessly." She looked at Kincaid apologetically. "I have an idea, but you're not going to like it."

"What is it?" he asked warily.

"Well, Princess Sarai found this place by following local legends," Jocelyn started. "And it wasn't the first place she explored. She followed up all the superstitious stories she heard about magic, just in case one of them was true. And one of them was—Dragoncave really does have dragon history."

"What's your point?" asked Kincaid blankly.

"Just that maybe we should do the same. Follow up legends, I mean."

"That sounds like a sensible idea to me," interjected Elddreki. "That is precisely how I became interested in Dragoncave, after all."

"Exactly," said Jocelyn, encouraged. She turned to Kincaid. "If you don't want to head for the southern coast—and neither do I—then maybe we should try the eastern coast. You know, where the easterners live. The ones who believe in—"

Kincaid cut her off with a groan. "Wyverns. You're talking about the myths of wyverns." He shook his head. "They're not real, Joss. It would be a wild goose chase."

"Well, that's what I thought about this place," argued Jocelyn. "But I was wrong."

Kincaid groaned again. "Why did I have to tell you about those myths?" he grumbled.

"What are wyverns?" asked Elddreki. "I am unfamiliar with this word."

Kincaid sighed. "They're legendary sea monsters. Some of the people living on Valoria's eastern coast believe they inhabit the waters around Wyvern Islands, off the coast. They say the wyverns bring down ships that stray too close to their waters, and that they're the reason it's impossible to make landfall on the islands. It's a myth to explain the impassibility of very treacherous waters."

"Hm," said Elddreki thoughtfully. "Do not be too hasty to discount myths, Kincaid. Have not dragons been considered mythical for much of your human history? And yet here I am."

"That's what I thought!" said Jocelyn triumphantly. "It can't hurt to check it out. I mean, if we're headed for a random coast anyway, why not make it that one?"

"Because," said Kincaid, exasperated, "that's about the furthest we could go to reach coastline. Besides, even if they were real, what would be the use in finding wyverns? Aren't we supposed to be looking for dragons?"

"We know legends grow in the telling," said Jocelyn quickly. "What I'm wondering is whether the stories of wyverns could have grown from sightings of actual dragons, long ago."

Kincaid frowned. "You think the dragons who came to the cave, the ones who were dreaming of the ocean, might have settled in the east and become known as wyverns?"

Jocelyn shrugged. "It's not completely impossible."

Kincaid raised an eyebrow. "The standard is not high, apparently."

"You know what I mean," said Jocelyn, laughing in spite of herself.

"I like your plan, Jocelyn," said Elddreki approvingly.

"Thank you." She glanced at Kincaid, trying not to smirk. He couldn't fight her proposal now the dragon had endorsed it.

"Fine," he said with a sigh as he slung his pack over his shoulder. "We can look for unicorns on the way."

Jocelyn grinned at his sarcastic tone, but apparently it was lost on Elddreki.

"Unicorns?" he asked curiously. "What are they?"

"Another type of mythical creature," said Kincaid shortly. "Not real. They're like horses, but they have a horn in the middle of their heads, and they're...I don't know...magical."

"Ah yes," said Elddreki, sounding pleased. "The magic-carrying horned horses. Yes, I remember those."

Kincaid, ever ready for action, had already taken a step eastward, but he stopped dead at Elddreki's words.

"What? They're—they're not real."

"No, of course not," said Elddreki soothingly, apparently

noticing Kincaid's uneasy expression. "They haven't been around for hundreds of years. We made sure to get the last of them. But dragons have excellent memory, you know. I can recall them with perfect clarity."

CHAPTER NINETEEN

Elddreki had been squinting eastward as he spoke, as if trying to spy the far distant coast, and it took him several moments to realize both humans were staring at him in shock, mouths hanging open.

"You remember them?" Jocelyn repeated faintly. "You're saying unicorns were real, and you've seen them within your lifetime?"

"That's right," said Elddreki, faintly surprised. "Was I unclear?"

"But surely that's impossible," protested Jocelyn. "I thought dragons were the only source of magic."

"That's right," Elddreki repeated. He cocked his head slightly as he looked at her. "That's why you are such a mystery."

"Then how can there have been unicorns, or magical horses as you called them?" Kincaid cut in.

"I didn't call them magical horses," Elddreki corrected him. "I called them *magic-carrying* horses. It's a significant difference."

"Well, it's one you're going to have to explain if you want us to have any hope of understanding you," said Jocelyn frankly.

"I am very happy to do so," said Elddreki. "But perhaps I

should explain while we travel, now that we have settled on our direction. I suspect we cannot stay in this location for much longer without sustaining another visit from the people of the nearby town."

"Another visit?" asked Jocelyn quickly. "Has there been one already?"

"Indeed." Elddreki inclined his head. "While you were in the cave. The villagers who came seemed surprised to discover me here."

Jocelyn snorted at the measured comment, but Kincaid was looking dark again.

"The gang came looking for us," he said, his eyes flicking to Jocelyn.

"Gang?" repeated Elddreki. "I don't think so. And I don't think they were looking for you. From the items they were carrying I would guess their purpose was to collect water from the river."

"What happened when they saw you?" asked Jocelyn, trying not to laugh at the image of a group of girls traipsing down to the river for the daily water collection and encountering an actual dragon sitting casually by. She could picture just the look of detached curiosity Elddreki would have worn as he watched them.

"Well," said Elddreki placidly, "they did not seem to me to be of very noble bearing, so I decided I did not wish to converse with them. They returned rapidly to the village, without collecting water."

Even Kincaid chuckled this time, clearly imagining the scene as well. "You're going to set Valoria on fire with this quest of yours, Elddreki."

"Of course I'm not," said Elddreki, taken aback. "Not unless offered extreme provocation."

"What?" Kincaid looked alarmed as he clarified. "No, I spoke figuratively. The countryside will be ablaze with rumors within days."

"Oh, I see," said Elddreki comfortably. "Yes, my presence will probably make quite a stir."

Jocelyn saw that Kincaid was distracted, still watching Elddreki with a worried look in his eye, so she took control of the conversation.

"Well, let's get moving then, before the townsfolk come out to look, or send a messenger to bring the king's guards down on us or something."

Just the thought made her glance uneasily south, toward the distant Bryford. She had been nervous enough about the idea of meeting Valoria's king and queen when invited to their castle, surrounded by an official delegation. The idea of meeting them while roaming the countryside with a dragon and a handsome vagabond, herself dressed as a peasant, was nothing short of terrifying.

"Well, if we're going all the way to the east," Kincaid said, pulling himself from his abstraction, "then we need horses." He looked at Jocelyn. "I assume you can ride?"

"Of course I can," she said indignantly. "I'm a princess of Kyona."

He grinned. "You did that beautifully. You should practice that haughty lift of your chin for when you make it to the Valorian court, in case anyone slights your fair kingdom."

"Which it sounds like they might, if even Valoria is caught up in this prejudice against the freedmen," said Jocelyn with a frown.

The more she thought about her conversation with Kincaid the night before, the more sinister it seemed that the seemingly unnatural conflict had spread beyond Kyona's border. In fact, Kincaid had given her a lot to think about. His description of how her parents, and by extension their kingdom, were seen outside Kyona was as astounding to her as it was encouraging.

"Anyway, about the horses," said Kincaid quickly, "we'll have to buy some."

"That's a good idea," said Elddreki, sounding pleased. "If you ride instead of walking, I might be able to fly every once in a while, instead of crawling along the ground all the time."

"But I'm guessing it won't be easy to find horses for sale around here," said Jocelyn skeptically. "And what are we going to buy them with? Surely you didn't bring that much money with you when you left Bryford."

"No, I didn't," said Kincaid cheerfully. "But there are other ways."

Jocelyn frowned. "We've been over this, Kincaid. I can't let you keep paying for everything. It's not right."

"I thought you would feel that way," said Kincaid seriously. "Which is why I thought perhaps we could sell your hair to get enough money for the horses. Since we know it can fetch a tidy sum around here, if we find the right buyer."

Jocelyn froze, her mouth opening and closing several times, although nothing came out. Kincaid and Elddreki were both looking at her expectantly, and she reminded herself she had been the one to insist she should contribute. Her hair would grow back...eventually. She swallowed hard, steeling herself before speaking, but her voice still sounded small.

"I suppose that's only fair."

Kincaid's look of expectation vanished, and he roared with laughter. "I was joking, Joss! I wish you could see your face!"

Jocelyn scowled, her cheeks burning up. Elddreki was looking between them, seeming surprised that the suggestion had been false, but ready to share in Kincaid's mirth. He gave a small chuckle.

"Your expression was indeed entertaining."

Jocelyn expanded her glare to include the dragon as well. "Well, I don't see why it's so hilarious. We don't have much else of value to barter. Maybe I will sell my hair."

"No you won't," Kincaid contradicted, still smiling with amusement. "I won't let you." He stepped forward, reaching out and twining a strand of her golden hair around his fingers. "It looks nice released from its braid."

Jocelyn swallowed and didn't answer. Her mind flew to the way the gang leader in Thalia had touched her hair when he spoke of selling it. It was very very different when Kincaid did it.

"So will you buy horses in this town here?" asked Elddreki curiously, breaking the moment. Kincaid stepped back and gave the dragon a friendly smile.

"I'm not sure this town is prosperous enough to have decent horses for sale." He grimaced. "Plus I think we may have worn out our welcome."

He exchanged a look with Jocelyn, and she wrapped her arms around herself involuntarily, rubbing the spots on her arms where she had been restrained. In everything that happened since, she had forgotten about her fear that she might have caused the gang leader to be killed. Perhaps it was cowardly, but she found she had no desire to find out.

"Yes, let's wait until the next town. I don't mind walking for another day."

"Well then," said Kincaid, as cheerful as ever. "I suppose we head due east and see what we find."

They set out immediately, Kincaid in the lead. Elddreki followed him in his usual unhurried way, loping along on all fours. Given how long he had waited to explore Dragoncave, he showed a surprising lack of sentiment in leaving the place. Jocelyn hadn't heard of it a few days ago, but she felt like her world had turned upside down in the short time since arriving there. She lingered behind for a moment, running her hand along the outside of the mound. She felt a faint pulse of emotion, as though Princess Sarai's grief and powerlessness were reaching out to her one last time, begging not to be forgotten.

Jocelyn gave a small shiver and hurried after the others. As Kincaid had said, her own life held more than enough loneliness without taking on someone else's. And she felt powerless enough as it was, despite the power in her words. She didn't need a reminder of how dependent a princess's fate was on the decisions of others.

Heading east took them back past Thalia again. Kincaid was still in the lead, and he angled around the village, remaining a stone's throw away from the outlying buildings. Jocelyn was walking next to Elddreki in companionable silence, some paces behind the Valorian.

From behind, Jocelyn could see that although Kincaid walked with an apparently casual step, and appeared unaware of the nearby buildings, his hand rested on the hilt of his sword as he strolled past. She was the closest to Thalia, and she looked toward it curiously, wondering what had made some of Princess Sarai's original companions decide to come back and live here.

"There it is!"

The sudden shout and the succeeding whistling sound were the only warning Jocelyn received before searing pain sliced across her upper arm. She cried out involuntarily, her hand reaching up to grip the place. It came away red, and Jocelyn stared at it for a moment, confused.

"JOCELYN!"

She looked up at Kincaid's roar, distracted by the strange whistling that was still happening all around her. The Valorian was charging toward her, and it was only as she saw a flash of steel go past in the space between them that her mind suddenly made sense of what was happening.

"Kincaid!" she gasped, realizing he was putting himself in greater danger with every step he took toward her. "Stop!"

But he kept coming, reaching her in less than a moment, dodging through the hail of arrows that continued to fly around them. Even as he came alongside her, he lifted his pack like a shield, holding it between her and the attacking villagers. A second later there was a sudden thunk, and his arm shuddered under the impact of an arrow burying itself into the pack. Jocelyn stared at the steel tip protruding from the burlap, arrested in its course toward her chest, then up at Kincaid. His eyes were wide as they also traveled from the arrow to her face.

"Get behind me!" cried Elddreki, and both of them started, shaken from their stupor. The dragon had reared up on his hind legs, and they threw themselves forward, ducking around behind him.

Jocelyn had been so thrown by the unexpected attack that she hadn't stopped to think why it would be happening. But as she threw herself behind Elddreki, she realized the dragon was the target, and it all made sense. The girls who had seen him by the river had carried the tale home, and the town had been ready in case the beast should try to attack. The arrows continued to fly toward him, and although the townspeople didn't seem to be very good marksmen, he was a big enough target that some of them were hitting the dragon.

The occasional dinging sound, like rain falling on glass, was the only obvious impact of these successful hits. Well, that and Elddreki's growing irritation. It was clear he wasn't hurt by the arrows that were bouncing off his scales and dropping to the grass, but he was certainly starting to become annoyed.

He let out a roar, and Jocelyn heard answering screams from the direction of the town. She was crouched behind Elddreki, Kincaid having wrapped himself protectively around her, but she leaned sideways to look. The archers had been hiding inside or behind buildings, but she thought she saw some people fleeing further into the town.

After a moment's pause, however, the arrows continued, fewer in number but still steady. The fools were apparently too panicked to grasp the futility of shooting arrows at a creature of Elddreki's nature.

Elddreki reared even higher, spreading his wings on either side of him. This time, when he let out another roar, a flicker of flame leaped from his mouth. More screams sounded from the village, and Jocelyn saw with wide eyes that the fire had come dangerously close to the thatched roof of the closest building.

"Stop, Elddreki!" she shouted. "They don't understand! Don't burn their town down!"

Elddreki paused, turning his vast form carefully, so that he was still placed between the humans and the town, but was now looking down at them. The occasional ping told Jocelyn that the villagers were now shooting at his back.

Elddreki looked down at her, his reptilian forehead creased strangely.

"Are you all right, Jocelyn?" he asked, his gaze taking in her ripped sleeve and bleeding arm.

"I'm fine," she said quickly. "It's just a graze. Please. Don't destroy their homes because of a scratch."

Elddreki considered her for a moment, then gave a curt nod. He ignored the ongoing rain of arrows, bending down toward her. Before Jocelyn knew what was happening, he had grasped her in his taloned front feet, one wrapped around her knees, and one around her shoulders, and shot up into the air.

"Wait!" she screamed, hearing Kincaid's startled shout, already faint and far below them. "Go back! You can't leave Kincaid there!"

Elddreki seemed to hear her, because his rapid ascension checked slightly. He angled down, flying more slowly, and in moments reached the ground. Jocelyn leaped up as soon as he released her, looking around wildly. They were east of Thalia, and already far enough away that the town looked like a toy village.

"Kincaid!" she gasped, the color draining from her face at the thought of how they had left him in the midst of that deadly hail, his shield suddenly gone. She stumbled a few steps toward the town, but before her panic could rise too much, her questing eyes caught sight of a tall figure in the distance, sprinting toward them.

She breathed a sigh of relief, her knees suddenly so weak she could barely stand. She felt the presence of the dragon right behind her, and leaned back, letting his giant flank support her weight. The scales were surprisingly comfortable, and both warmth and magic seemed to seep out of him and settle over her reassuringly.

It took several minutes for Kincaid to reach them, but when he was within hailing distance Jocelyn pushed forward from the dragon and ran the last few steps to meet him.

"Jocelyn!"

Kincaid looked as relieved as she felt at their reunion. He pulled her into his arms and held her there for the space of one heartbeat. Then he stepped back, holding her firmly by her uninjured arm and searching her face.

"Are you all right?"

"You ran into a deadly stream of arrows to shield me," she said shakily. "You shouldn't have done that."

Kincaid ignored her words, his eyes sliding to her arm. "How badly were you hit?"

"Hardly at all," she said quickly, once again touching the spot. It was barely bleeding now.

Kincaid touched her shoulder gently, looking more closely at the wound. "You're right," he said with relief. "It's shallow."

He pulled off his pack, and Jocelyn shuddered at the sight of the hole now ripped into the coarse fabric. Kincaid pulled out a tunic and used his teeth to rip off a strip. He wound it deftly around his hand as he pulled a water skin out as well.

"Sit," he said, and Jocelyn obeyed without thinking about it. Kincaid crouched beside her, unstopping the water skin. He poured the clear liquid over the slice in her arm, and she winced in spite of herself.

"Sorry," he said quickly, but she shook her head.

"No, I'm sorry. We shouldn't have left you behind like that! I was terrified you'd be shot without Elddreki there to cover you."

Kincaid smiled, but the expression was strained. "No, they stopped shooting as soon as he was gone. I was never the target. But when I saw the speed he was moving, I thought I'd never be able to reach you. I thought I'd lose you."

He stopped speaking for a moment, blowing gently on her arm to dry it, and a tingle raced over Jocelyn's skin.

"Thank you," she said quietly, and Kincaid's eyes snapped to hers. "For saving my life."

Kincaid didn't answer for a moment, his eyes boring into hers. Then he dropped his gaze back to his work, his voice light. "That's what I'm here for, isn't it?"

Jocelyn felt a surge of disappointment, and wondered if that was how he had felt that morning when she had turned off his earnest words with a joke.

Kincaid bound the wound efficiently with the strip of fabric and stood up, looking to the dragon.

"Thank you, Elddreki," he said. "For shielding us. And for taking Jocelyn to safety."

Elddreki was silent, and Jocelyn looked up at him as she struggled to her feet. The dragon had watched the entire interaction between the two humans in passive silence, and there was an unreadable expression on his face.

Kincaid began to repack his things, not seeming to notice the dragon's more-than-usually strange behavior. "We should keep moving. I don't think it's a good idea to linger near that town." He looked at Jocelyn, his face softening. "But what about your arm? You should probably be resting."

She shook her head quickly. "I'm fine. I can barely feel it now." The shaking in her limbs had also started to recede, as their conversation distracted her from her most recent near-fatal experience.

Kincaid looked unconvinced, but he didn't argue. The three of them began to walk, Kincaid taking care this time to walk alongside Jocelyn, so she was in between the other two. Both of her companions kept shooting furtive looks at her at regular intervals. She sighed, less than impressed.

"I'm fine, honestly. Stop looking at me like I'm about to pass out."

"I wasn't concerned about your injury," said Elddreki, sounding more like his normal self. "It is slight, as Kincaid said. I was reflecting on what a strange phenomenon you are."

Jocelyn gave Kincaid a rueful look. He smiled sympathetically, but the gesture didn't quite reach his eyes. He still looked stressed.

They walked for most of the day, conversation limited. Despite her strong words, Jocelyn felt tired, and falling back into her habitual silence was easiest. Even Kincaid wasn't as cheerful as usual.

As for Elddreki, the dragon watched Jocelyn unashamedly as she walked, his expression still difficult to read.

They had headed out into open country after the attack, and they still hadn't encountered a town by the time the light began to fade. They stopped in a copse of scrubby trees, Kincaid collecting enough fallen branches to sustain a decent fire. It wasn't exactly cold, but Jocelyn was still grateful to draw close to the flames, naturally supplied by Elddreki. She had been feeling uncomfortable all day with the dragon's scrutiny, and the odd shiver still ran down her frame.

Kincaid sat close beside her on the ground as they shared a simple meal. She thought Elddreki would curl up for sleep, but instead he sat upright across the fire from them, his posture similar to a cat, but his size requiring them to crane their necks when he unexpectedly opened conversation.

"I have been thinking about this morning's events," he said, his voice thoughtful. "The experience was...strange. I think I am starting to understand."

"Understand what?" asked Jocelyn with a frown.

Elddreki turned his gaze onto her, and stared at her unblinkingly. The effect of his snakelike orbs was hypnotic in the flickering light of the fire, and she tugged at her sleeve nervously.

"This protective instinct," he said. "That parents feel for their young, and men for women, according to Kincaid." The dragon's eyes flicked to the Valorian as he said his name, but the next moment they were back on Jocelyn. "My reaction to that attack was strong, disproportionate. I knew they could not harm me, but I was angry you were caught in the path of the arrows, and concerned you would be hurt."

"Uh, thank you," said Jocelyn lamely, after a moment of silence.

"I have never before experienced vicarious concern of such potency," said Elddreki. "It is unexpected. It seems I am becoming fond of you."

Jocelyn exchanged a look with Kincaid, completely at a loss as to how to respond to this bizarre declaration. Elddreki didn't look fond. He was looking at her as though she were a fascinating—but dangerous—anomaly. Kincaid looked as unnerved as she felt.

"I caught a glimpse, for just a moment, of why I might wish

to take responsibility for your well-being," the dragon was continuing. "Of why your father, or even Kincaid, might expect me to." He frowned. "It is how I imagine I might feel toward a dragonling, if ever I were to meet one."

"Well, I...I appreciate it," said Jocelyn, finally. She cast around for something polite to say. "I'm sure you would make a good dragon father."

Elddreki sighed, a faint smell of smoke leaking out from his recent flames. "Impossible, I am afraid," he said heavily. He was still looking at her with uncomfortable intensity. "It is not good for me to become fond of you, Jocelyn. It is not good for me to see you as under my protection, as though we were family."

"Why not?" asked Kincaid, sounding defensive. "If you ask me, I think that's how you should have seen her from the moment you asked her to join your quest."

Elddreki turned to the young man, his expression sad. "But I did not ask you, and I would not be likely to do so, being aware of how little you know of the matter." He said the words matter-of-factly, without heat. "To answer your question, it is not good because Jocelyn will be dead and gone in the blink of my eye."

Kincaid shifted slightly toward Jocelyn, the protective gesture seeming unconscious. "No she won't," he said firmly. "She's not as frail as you think."

Jocelyn looked at him, surprised and gratified, but she spoke to Elddreki. "I think I know what you mean," she said kindly. "I was almost killed back there." She shuddered as she remembered the arrow that had come so close to claiming her life. "And even if I live to be a hundred, it will be over quickly for you. I can understand why it would be painful to care too much about humans when you know you're just going to watch them all die."

Elddreki returned her gaze steadily. "Your words reveal your kind heart, Jocelyn, but you are mistaken. You do not understand the matter any more than Kincaid does. It is not that dragons shy away from friendship with humans to avoid the pain of loss. Pain is a part of life, and must be accepted. But for immortal creatures to become attached to mortal creatures is dangerous. It can lead to actions—choices—with catastrophic consequences."

Jocelyn frowned. "I think that's another thing you need to explain if you want us to understand it." She smiled, trying to lighten the mood. "Because don't think we've forgotten about the unicorns. You promised to tell us about them while we traveled."

Elddreki smiled as well, stretching his tail out before curling it back around his feet. "You are mistaken again. I did not promise. But I did suggest it." He sighed. "And it is part of the same tale, in a sense. I am willing to tell you, but you must understand it is not a tale to be bandied about."

"We understand," said Jocelyn solemnly. She turned to Kincaid. "Don't we?"

"Yes, all right," he said, still eyeing the dragon dubiously.

Elddreki didn't respond, his eyes fixed on Jocelyn. "Do you remember, Jocelyn, that you asked me whether dragons can die?"

"I do," she said humorously. "As I recall, you gave a characteristically vague answer."

Kincaid chuckled, and even Elddreki smiled. "I said," he corrected, "that it is almost impossible for me to die. And I spoke the truth. But it is not the case for all dragons." He paused. "At least, it wasn't formerly. Whether it is the case for all dragons now depends on whether there are other dragons still living, beyond Vasilisa."

"What do you mean?" asked Jocelyn, confused.

Elddreki shook his wings out slightly, and his voice was

solemn. "How much has your father told you about dragon lore, Jocelyn?"

"Uh." Jocelyn hesitated. "Not much."

Elddreki nodded. "I suspect even he does not know what I am about to tell you. Do not treat my confidence lightly." He didn't wait for a reply. "It is true I am immortal, in that time will not enfeeble me."

The dragon paused, and the leaping light of the flames lent an eerie quality to his reptilian face. The moment was surreal, as dreamlike as the trance which had called Jocelyn from her bed in Montego and into this fantastical quest. She tried to grasp that the beast before her had not only lived for centuries before her birth, but would continue on for indefinite generations after her death. It was an impossible concept to comprehend.

"I have no expectation of death," Elddreki continued, the firelight glinting strangely on the glassy surface of his eyes. "But when dragonlings are born, they have no such certainty."

CHAPTER TWENTY

Jocelyn looked at Kincaid and saw that he also was surprised by this information, but neither of them interrupted.

"Dragons are born strong, certainly, and dragonlings are not prone to injury or death," Elddreki said. "But they are not born with the certainty of immortality. It is a choice."

"You can choose not to live forever?" Kincaid sounded startled. "Why would anyone choose to die?"

"Would you choose to live forever if you could?" Elddreki asked unexpectedly, turning his penetrating gaze on Kincaid.

"I don't know," said Kincaid, uncomfortably. "I suppose so."

"At what cost?" Elddreki probed.

"There's a cost?" Jocelyn asked, feeling vaguely uneasy. She hugged her knees to her chest, wishing the warmth of the fire could reach all the way around to her back.

"There is," said Elddreki, his eyes returning to the flames. "Or at least, an exchange. Dragons choose between two possibilities, and they are not as simple as life or death. A dragon may choose to be immortal, unaffected by the passage of time, outside the circle of generations. Or, a dragon may choose to participate in that cycle. To pass his, or her, seed and power to another generation. In a sense you could say that either way dragons choose for their lives to continue forever, but in two very different forms."

Jocelyn frowned. "You're saying immortal dragons can't have children, or rather dragonlings?"

"In simple terms, yes," said Elddreki. He looked again at Kincaid. "Would you still choose to live forever under such terms, young man?"

Jocelyn looked curiously to Kincaid for his answer. His eyes flicked to her and away before he spoke, but he hesitated only a moment.

"No, I wouldn't."

"So quick to answer," said Elddreki, clearly surprised. "Are you answering on the whim of the moment, or are you certain of your opinion?"

Kincaid stared into the fire, his eyes unseeing. "I'm certain," he said steadily.

"Why?" asked Elddreki, looking fascinated.

Kincaid shrugged. "I'm not sure how to explain it," he said. "But the desire to pass my bloodline, my name, my heritage, on to another generation is deep within me. So deep I don't know how to extricate it. If I was prevented from doing so for some reason out of my control, it would be hard, but I would accept it. I would have to. But if I could and chose not to, for the benefit of my own unnaturally prolonged life, I think I would regret it for the whole length of that life."

There was a long moment of silence as the dragon processed Kincaid's words. Jocelyn was distracted herself, picturing Kincaid with a child on his shoulders, a boy with his bouncing auburn waves, perhaps, or a girl with his clear brown eyes. She had no doubt he would make a good father one day. She chanced a glance at Elddreki, and his expression was impossible to read.

"What about you, daughter of kings?" asked Elddreki, reverting to his original form of address in his distraction. "Do you feel the same way?"

Jocelyn thought about it for a moment. She thought about her little cousins on her mother's side, remembering her delight when they had each been born, although she had been only a child herself. She remembered pinching the babies' sweet little cheeks. She tried to imagine a Kynton where no one died, but no new little people ever appeared. The thought was tragic.

"Yes," she said at last. "I think I do." She smiled at the dragon. "You said it yourself, I'm defined by who I am as a daughter of kings. If they hadn't chosen to have children, there would be no me. Besides, history is important to humans. I want to be part of history, not watching it from an elevated but removed position."

"Hm." Elddreki was again deep in thought, his tail twitching in an apparently unconscious rhythm. "Humans are curious creatures. You are so frequently foolish beyond belief, but at times you have a wisdom that baffles even me."

"So what happens to dragons who choose not to be immortal?" asked Kincaid. "Do they die as soon as they have a dragonling?"

Elddreki shook his vast head. "It is not so simple. Dragons who choose mortality will die even if they do not end up having dragonlings. They have a lifespan, long compared to a human, but still only two, perhaps three centuries. It is not always predictable, but there is reason to think that their decline is hastened by each dragonling's arrival."

"Why?" asked Jocelyn.

Elddreki gave her a long look. "As I said, we do not know for certain. But dragons are creatures of magic, Jocelyn. We are born with a certain amount of power. A dragon like me, who has chosen not to pass that power on to another generation, retains that power indefinitely. In fact, if anything, it seems to grow and build with time. One could argue that for a new dragon to be born, the power that will reside within him must come from somewhere. Our best understanding is that it comes from his parents. They give it as a gift, and it passes from them irrevocably."

Jocelyn frowned. "But if your power grows with time, why can't theirs just...replenish after they have a dragonling?"

Elddreki did his strange rippling shrug. "Even dragons do not have all the answers, Jocelyn, despite what you might think. All we know for certain is that dragons who have chosen mortality will die, sooner or later. My best guess is that a dragon's choice to procreate rather than to be immortal is a choice to allow his power to leave him, and that in a sense this process begins immediately. The power once ignited in the dragonling could grow indefinitely, if that dragonling becomes immortal. But it cannot be reignited in the parent."

Jocelyn thought this over. "How does it work?"

Elddreki looked at her, surprised. "The procreation of dragonlings? In much the same way as the formation of humans, as I understand. Do you really wish me to explain it to you?"

"No, no," said Jocelyn hastily, her cheeks flushing. Kincaid had been seized by a sudden coughing fit. She could feel the grin he was trying to hide, and she resolutely refused to look at him. "I mean how does the decision work. Do you decide at a certain age? Is there a ceremony? Who...receives the decision?"

"Ah, I understand what you mean," said Elddreki. "There is no ceremony, and there is no set age. The question is always there in your mind, from earliest memory. At some point it begins to tug at you more insistently, until it consumes much of your thoughts. The decision is not made all at once. It grows gradually as an inkling, until it is a certainty. Then one day you simply realize your decision is made, and there is no going back."

"And you chose to be immortal," interjected Kincaid.

Elddreki nodded. "I did."

"Why?"

Elddreki was silent for a moment. "I am not sure how to answer that, Kincaid," he said at last. "There were many thoughts in my mind as I considered the matter. But I will say that the fact that everyone else in my colony had chosen such influenced me."

"Do you regret it?" Jocelyn asked curiously.

Elddreki looked at her with eyes that seemed ancient and sad. "That question is more complicated than you realize, and I will not even attempt to answer it."

"Everyone in your colony chose immortality over having offspring," repeated Kincaid slowly.

"Over many generations," Elddreki clarified. "Those who had chosen to have offspring obviously died. Those of their offspring who chose to have offspring themselves eventually died too. More and more of the dragons being born chose to be immortal instead, until eventually there were no more dragonlings being born to make the decision. I was the last. My parents have long since gone on."

"That's why you're looking for more dragons," said Jocelyn softly. "You want to see if the dragons who left Vasilisa all those centuries ago ended up in the same state, or if their colony—assuming there is a colony somewhere—still has dragons who are choosing to give life to new generations."

"That's right," said Elddreki. He took a deep breath. "Vasilisa is a wondrous place. Every dragon there is both good and wise. But there is no change, nothing new. Only further building on an old foundation. I think many of us see the wisdom of having at least some dragons choose dragonlings over immortality, so that new generations can come. The trouble is, none of those who are in Vasilisa now wished to make the sacrifice of their own lives to that end."

He sighed. "I considered it, I really did. But a dragon must pair with another dragon who has made the same choice. Otherwise the union will be barren and full of grief. One dragon will live indefinitely, to experience eternal loss, and the other will face the bitterness of death without the comfort of passing on power to the next generation. And had I chosen differently, I would have been gambling on the chance of finding other dragons out there somewhere."

"I see," said Jocelyn softly, suddenly full of sympathy for the dragon, so powerful, and yet as little in control of his destiny as she was, it seemed.

"But what does all this have to do with the unicorns?" Kincaid cut in, a little insensitively, Jocelyn thought.

"Well," said Elddreki, "the unicorns, as you call them, are part of the story of why dragons left Vasilisa in the first place."

"I thought you said you don't speak of why they left," said Jocelyn.

Elddreki turned his gaze on her for a moment. "I did say that," he acknowledged. "But you confound me, Jocelyn. I think to understand the enigma of your power, I may need to examine a part of dragon history we usually prefer not to recall."

Jocelyn just frowned, waiting.

"I told you dragons are born with a certain amount of power," said Elddreki. "And it stays with us indefinitely if we make the choice I made. I also told you it is *almost* impossible for me to die. Meaning, of course—"

"That it is possible," interrupted Kincaid.

Elddreki inclined his head in assent.

"How?" asked Jocelyn, adding hastily, "Not that I want to do you any harm, obviously."

Elddreki gave a rattling laugh. "You cannot do me a mischief, Jocelyn, even if you wanted to. No one could. Only I could choose to die."

"But..." Jocelyn frowned. "I thought you said your choice was irrevocably made."

"Oh, it is," said Elddreki. "I no longer have the power to decide to have offspring and so to die. But I could, at least in theory, choose to pass my power on in another way. But it is not to be done. It is an abomination."

"What is this other way?" asked Kincaid, clearly intrigued.

Elddreki paused for a moment, as if considering whether to answer the question. He twisted his neck where he sat, looking back in the direction of the distant Kyonan mountain range. At last he let out a huff, the exhale sending the flames in front of him dancing dangerously close to his human listeners, who both leaned back quickly.

"It is not easy to explain," he said. "Perhaps it will help if I show you."

"Show us how?" Kincaid started, but Elddreki was already opening his jaws. A small stream of fire came out, nothing like the white-hot torrent that had deluged the top of Dragoncave.

Jocelyn frowned in concentration as the dragon sustained the flame, trying to test the air around her. She closed her eyes for a moment, and it was easier to concentrate on the familiar but much more potent sensation. Elddreki was releasing magic with his flame, steady and intricate.

Kincaid's gasp pulled her eyes open again, and she drew in a sharp breath herself. The fire had changed. It was no longer simply orange and yellow. Other colors streaked through it, and the flickering tongues were forming themselves into shapes.

"As I said," Elddreki continued, and although he was no

longer breathing fire, the magic continued to pour from him in a constant stream. "Dragons are creatures of power."

As he spoke, the flames seemed to become miniature dragons, different in color and size, but each glowing with an identical light. These small spots of radiance were not simply glints of firelight—they were something more.

"Our magic is our lifeblood," the dragon added, and the glow seemed to spread like veins throughout the tiny, moving figures. "We cannot live without it. Without it we are not...dragons. We simply cease to be—perhaps not all at once, but inevitably."

Jocelyn watched, mesmerized, as the light died out of one of the flame dragons, and the flickering image returned to nothing more than a tongue of fire.

"But the power doesn't disappear on its own," Elddreki went on. "It must be passed. A dragon who is not capable of passing his power to another generation of dragons, but who wished to forfeit that power and free himself to die, would have to pass it to someone."

In her peripheral vision, Jocelyn could see Elddreki look up at her, but she kept her eyes on the fire, fascinated by the sight of one of the mini flame dragons breathing a stream of actual fire onto a clearly formed sword of flame that had appeared alongside it.

"We can pour magic into objects," Elddreki was explaining, "like the sword your father carries. But that is a passive process on the part of the receiving object. It does not drain our power."

Jocelyn saw that, as Elddreki described, the dragon who was breathing onto the sword retained its inner glow, the light inside it not dimmed at all.

"For the power to properly leave us, there must be a recipient."

"You can pass your magic to another creature?" Kincaid

asked. His eyes flicked to Jocelyn, and his voice sounded strange. "You can give someone magical ability?"

"Yes," said Elddreki. "Or at least, so I understand. I do not know how it is done, precisely. It is not something we are taught how to do—as I said, it is an abomination."

"Has it ever been done?" Kincaid asked. Jocelyn pulled her eyes from the fire at last, looking up at the dragon.

Elddreki lowered his head, his expression somber. "Yes. There was a time, a terrible time of great suffering, many centuries ago, when there was war between dragons."

Jocelyn followed the dragon's gaze back toward the flames, and saw that the tiny figures, now multiplied, had burst into a frenzy of activity. They dove on each other, shooting flames from their mouths, gripping one another with their talons as they rolled and wrestled in the air. Each of them still glowed with that bright and inexplicable light from within. One threw another down mid-flight, the defeated dragon landing hard on a mountainside that was somehow recognizable as jagged rock, despite being made from flame.

She could sense Kincaid's fascination beside her as he watched the battle being waged, but she turned her face away from the warmth with a shudder. It was a terrible sight.

"I can see you share my distaste for the story," said Elddreki, his voice pulling Jocelyn's eyes back to him. "It brings me no pleasure to dwell on violence and conflict. It is why I have not been following the situation in Kyona as closely as some of my kin."

"What do you mean?" Jocelyn asked sharply. "You're saying there's violence in Kyona?"

Elddreki did his rippling shrug. "There is conflict, and it is growing. That usually means violence is not far behind." He sighed, his head tilting slightly to the side as he watched the flames. "Still, I cannot deny that I take some interest, given my friendship with your father. And his young friend who accompanied him into the mountains, who is perhaps even more heavily affected by what is happening."

Jocelyn followed the dragon's line of sight and started in surprise when she recognized the human figure now flickering in the flames as Uncle Jonan. He was deep in conversation with another man she didn't recognize, and he looked uncharacteristically serious. The image leaped and jumped, showing them a series of unintelligible interactions between unknown people, the only consistent feature the tension and anger on face after face. The overview was clear—conflict was spreading unchecked across her homeland, just as Elddreki had said.

Jocelyn shook her head. Not unchecked. Her father was actively trying to intervene in the issues arising around the freedmen. And even though the king didn't know it, he had an unimaginably powerful tool at his disposal with Eamon helping him. She sighed. She wished she could be the one still in Kynton, helping to find a real solution. It galled her that the best way she could contribute was to remove herself from the kingdom altogether. Especially when every time she thought of Lucy and everyone else at the settlement, she itched to be at home, fighting for the well-being of her own kingdom, not wandering Valoria on someone else's quest.

"So what happened in the dragon battle?" Kincaid prompted Elddreki, not as easily distracted by the reminder of the trouble brewing in Kyona.

"It is a long and grievous history," said Elddreki, his voice ancient and sad, "and I will not attempt to unfold all its pages for you. Suffice it to say, the conflict had its beginnings when immortal dragons paired with those who had chosen mortality. The grief of these unions was immense, and grief turned to anger. In the course of those wars, the terrible ability to forfeit magic to another was discovered. Some gave magic to other dragons, creating beasts with twice the power of a normal one of our kind."

As he spoke, the images of Kyonans disappeared, and a pair of dragons took their places. One of the dragons opened its jaws wide, and somehow—it was impossible to tell how—its light passed into its companion. The glow of the second dragon became so bright Jocelyn could hardly look at it as it turned and fell upon a third dragon with an irresistible ferocity. But her eyes were drawn to the first dragon, which had lost its glow altogether. Just like the dragon at the start of Elddreki's little drama, this dragon's shape slowly flickered, becoming less distinct until it was nothing more than dancing flame.

"Are they still out there?" asked Kincaid, looking as awed as Jocelyn felt at the concept of a double-strength dragon. "Wouldn't they live forever?"

"They are not," said Elddreki. "They should have lived forever, those of them who were immortal, but receiving a dragon's lifeblood, which is not your own, warps the receiver as well as the giver. Neither party survived the encounter, at least not indefinitely."

Elddreki rolled his shoulders stiffly, as though the narrative caused him physical pain, but he continued. The shapes in the flame changed again, the struggles of battle disappearing, leaving only a few dragons circling the campfire slowly.

"In the aftermath of the war, many dragons were left desolate. Those who had chosen offspring had only to wait until their time, but those who had chosen immortality had an endless time ahead in which to grieve their losses. Some could not face such a fate. There were those who chose to put a limit to their lifespans by forfeiting their magic to whatever creatures they could find."

A small horse suddenly cantered across a plain of fire, one of the dragons swooping low to approach it. The dragon breathed on the horse, which began to glow strangely.

"The creatures carried that magic, with strange and sometimes startling results. The dragons then expired, and died."

Again Jocelyn's eyes were drawn to the dragon who had forfeited its power. Somehow the sight of its glow disappearing, and its shape fading away entirely, was even worse this time.

Elddreki frowned. "Leaving the rest of the colony to deal with the consequences. It was after that point some of the dragons left, striking out from Vasilisa without any intention of ever returning."

Just as he described, a series of mini dragons took wing, pushing out of the circle of the fire. Their tiny forms started off into the night, still aflame despite having left the campfire. Jocelyn watched them until they faded.

"What were the strange and startling results?" asked Kincaid slowly.

But Jocelyn thought she knew. "You're saying that unicorns were horses who received dragon magic from a dragon who wished to die?"

"That's right," nodded Elddreki, and his human companions exchanged looks of astonishment. "Horses were not the only ones, of course." He returned his gaze to the fire, and his companions followed suit. The horse had now sprouted a horn, and it threw its head forcefully as it galloped across the space. Other creatures joined it, prowling and sniffing.

"Wolves roamed the mountains at that time, and they were a popular choice. It is said that some dragons even traveled to the sea, wishing to fulfill the common dream of which I spoke earlier before forfeiting their lives. There they found fish big and strong enough to receive their magic. The dragons all returned to the mountains to die, but they left behind their abominations in the deep. They were particularly difficult to track down."

"You mean...you mean *mermaids*?" Jocelyn gasped, watching the giant fish flopping around in the flames.

"And werewolves?" Kincaid added, his attention clearly drawn to the other creatures.

Elddreki shrugged. "I don't know these words. All I know is it was an almighty mess. The consequences of these creatures roaming the land, carrying borrowed dragon magic, were far-reaching. The dragons who remained had to hunt them all down and destroy them."

The creatures all faded, their unnatural glow—and their forms—disappearing into a normal campfire. The evening was mild, but Jocelyn had started to feel very cold. She rubbed her arms nervously, and Kincaid looked at her, concern in his face.

"Is your arm hurting? Do you want me to rebind it?"

"No, I'm fine," said Jocelyn quickly, dropping her hands.

"So," she said, trying to get Kincaid's attention off her and back onto the dragon. "I thought you said these events happened many centuries ago, but you said you remember the unicorns yourself."

"Ah yes," said Elddreki, sounding reminiscent. "The magic-carrying horses were peculiar. The effect of the dragon magic on various species was different, and not predictable. No one knows why the horses invariably turned white and grew a horn from their heads, for example. And the wolves were absolutely savage, regardless of the temperament of the dragon who gave them his power. Fortunately any such wolves who reproduced sired normal wolf offspring, so the task of wiping out the warped creatures was finite. But the horses..." he shook his head, "...the horses had the peculiar quality that their offspring would inherit the borrowed power, although it grew weaker with each reproduction. Still, it took generation upon generation to fully wipe them out. The last of them were found in the time of my youth."

Jocelyn glanced up at the dragon's face and saw that he looked sad. "They were beautiful creatures," he said softly. "It grieved me that they had to be destroyed." He shook his head, and his voice grew stronger. "But it had to be so."

"Why did the horses pass their power to their offspring when the wolves didn't?" Kincaid asked, frowning. "And why did the power get weaker with each generation, when in dragons that doesn't happen?"

Elddreki sighed, once again stirring the flames. "I cannot answer that. It is one of the many things we do not know. Magic is unpredictable. It can be safely carried by dragons, and safely passed from a sire to a dragonling. But other, lesser, creatures should not bear it." He paused, his eyes flicking to Jocelyn. "Or so we have always thought." His gaze returned to the fire. "In other creatures its effects do not necessarily follow any pattern we know. Whether—and how—the magic passes from one creature to its offspring is just one example of its unpredictability."

"Did any dragon ever forfeit power to a human?" asked Kincaid curiously, and Jocelyn drew her knees up more tightly against her.

Elddreki looked at Kincaid in astonishment. "A human? Of course not! No dragon would be that foolish, not even one in the grips of despair."

Jocelyn rubbed her arms once more, and Kincaid glanced over at her again, his expression inquiring. She ignored him. "I'm tired," she said. "Thank you for telling us that story, Elddreki. I will keep your confidence."

The dragon nodded. "You look tired, young human. We can speak more tomorrow."

Jocelyn nodded, turning her back on both her companions and the fire as she settled for sleep.

.   .   .

JOCELYN ROSE WITH THE DAWN, more than ready to continue their journey. She had slept poorly, her dreams plagued by the images from Elddreki's magic flames. The tiny fire dragons had chased her endlessly, all while an unnatural glow grew inside her, threatening to burst into flames that would consume her from within.

There was very little conversation as they ate a simple morning meal and prepared themselves to travel eastward. By the time the sun had fully cleared the horizon, they were walking toward it through gently sloping grassland, the landscape becoming less scrubby and more cultivated with each passing minute.

Elddreki glided above them at first, but after about an hour, he landed alongside Jocelyn, falling into a loping gait that matched their human pace.

"So now I have answered your questions," he said, as though seamlessly continuing their conversation from the evening before, "it is your turn to answer some of mine."

"What do you want to know?" asked Jocelyn warily.

"I wish to know more about your origins," the dragon said. "It is time I explored further into this power of yours."

Jocelyn swallowed. After the evening's stories, and her unnerving dreams, she was less eager than ever to talk about her unnatural ability. "I don't know its origins," she said quickly.

"When did you first become aware of it?" Elddreki insisted.

"I don't know," said Jocelyn again, with a shrug. "Before my earliest memory, I think. It took a long time to figure out what it was, but it's just...always been there."

"So you are confident you had it from birth?"

"Yes."

"Hm." Elddreki looked ahead again, walking for a moment in silence. "You have a brother, yes?"

Jocelyn acknowledged it, feeling apprehensive. It was one

thing to tell Kincaid and Elddreki about her power, but to betray Eamon's secret as well was unthinkable.

"You said he's your twin, right?" interjected Kincaid unexpectedly.

Jocelyn nodded, her mouth clamped firmly shut.

"And what is his power?" asked Elddreki placidly.

"What do you mean?" squeaked Jocelyn, knowing her surprise was unconvincing. "I never said he has power."

Elddreki turned an astonished gaze upon her. "You're saying that although he is your twin, born of the same parents in the same pregnancy, you have power and he does not?"

Jocelyn squirmed under that unblinking gaze, knowing she would never be able to successfully deceive the dragon.

"I didn't say that either, but...please, Elddreki," she tried. "I don't want to betray—"

"Nonsense," the dragon cut her off dismissively. "Neither Kincaid nor I mean your brother any harm, do we Kincaid?"

"Of course not," said Kincaid. "And I think we'd both already figured out that Eamon must have power, anyway." He grinned at her discomfort. "So what is it? I'm hoping for physical destruction instead of mental confusion. Do things break when he touches them? Or is it in his words, too?"

"What a terrible thing to hope!" Jocelyn glared. "Are you an enemy of Kyona that you like the idea of the heir being cursed with the power of destruction? It's bad enough to have a princess who sows confusion. Not to mention how terrible that would be for poor Eamon."

Kincaid was frowning now, but Elddreki cut in before he could speak. "Your power is not confusion, Jocelyn. I have already identified that, remember?"

Jocelyn sighed, deciding not to argue with the dragon. "We've had lots of theories over the years, trying to figure out how they work. But one thing we know for sure. We are two sides of a coin, our powers equal and opposite. And Eamon's power isn't bad like mine. It's good."

"Your power isn't bad," said Kincaid stubbornly, but Jocelyn ignored the interruption.

"He can control it much more than I can, as well, and his hasn't been growing stronger the way mine has. At one stage we thought it was comfort and discomfort. Just as people tend to be uncomfortable around me, Eamon puts people at their ease, without trying to."

She smiled fondly as she thought of her absent brother. Although come to think of it, she had been missing him less than she had expected to, since being able to talk freely with both Kincaid and Elddreki.

"He can also undo the damage I so often create. He knows me better than anyone, and he can always tell when I want to say something, but it will be too dangerous. He says it for me, and it's much better received."

She chuckled. "No one would guess it, not even my parents, but I've made some very popular and effective suggestions on state matters, via Eamon." She shook her head, getting back to the main point. "But discomfort and comfort are not the right concepts. We've given it a lot of thought, and experimented a great deal, and we've concluded that if—" she looked at Elddreki, "—I said *if*—mine is confusion, his is certainty."

She looked around at Kincaid in satisfaction. "Much better than destruction, right? Who wouldn't want a crown prince who creates certainty and confidence every time he opens his mouth?"

But Kincaid looked far from impressed. "He sounds awful," he said shortly. "I dislike him already."

Jocelyn's smile disappeared, her mouth falling open in astonishment. But her shock quickly turned to anger. "How dare you criticize him?" she demanded. "You don't even know him. He's not awful."

Kincaid shrugged one shoulder, not looking in the least repentant. "He sounds boring and pompous," he said. "Like he thinks he's always right."

Jocelyn stopped walking, barely refraining from stamping her foot like a petulant child. "He's nothing like that. And I won't let you speak about him that way. He's my closest ally—my only friend half the time."

"And whose fault is that?" asked Kincaid, his eyebrows raised. He had stopped walking too. "It sounds like he won't let you have your own voice, so it's no surprise if you struggle to form other friendships."

Jocelyn rolled her eyes. "You sound like my mother."

"Thank you," said Kincaid, with stiff dignity. "From all I know, Queen Elnora is a wise and intelligent person."

For a moment Jocelyn just stared at him, in all his haughty dignity. Then the humor of the situation suddenly struck her, and she burst out laughing. Kincaid slowly unbent, looking at her with an endearing mixture of amusement and irritation.

"The idea of you being delighted to be compared to my mother," she gasped, and Kincaid grinned sheepishly.

Jocelyn wiped her eyes, growing serious. "But honestly," she gestured to herself, "none of this is Eamon's fault. He didn't choose it any more than I did. And he doesn't tell me not to speak. He thinks I hold myself in far too much, but it's not his decision to make—it's mine. He just covers for me, because I ask him to."

"If you say so," said Kincaid, still doubtful. "But I don't think he's done you any favors by helping you muzzle yourself."

"No," mused Elddreki unexpectedly. "Confusion and certainty don't sound right to me at all." The dragon had watched their little spat in a detached way, his mind clearly somewhere else.

Jocelyn let out a huff, impatient with Elddreki's contradiction of the conclusion she and Eamon had reached from meticulous exploration of their powers. "Well, what do you think it is then?"

"I'm still trying to ascertain that," said Elddreki vaguely. He tilted his head to the side. "Tell me about your conception and birth."

Kincaid again choked, and Jocelyn spluttered in protest. "I can't do that! You'd have to ask my parents." She wrinkled her nose. "Although I very much hope you won't."

"Your parents have never spoken to you about your birth?" Elddreki pressed.

"Oh, that." Jocelyn considered the point. "Well, yes they have, actually." She looked up to see the dragon watching her expectantly. "Well, I'm a twin, like I told you," she said with a shrug. "So it was always going to be a complicated birth. But we both arrived safely, and my mother was all right."

She grimaced. "Although from what she says it wasn't the smoothest delivery. She said she felt like we were running circles inside her, like we were jostling for position as to who would come out first." She smiled humorously. "My father always says that's why they called me Jocelyn, but I'm *fairly* sure he's joking."

"And who was born first?" asked Elddreki, watching her keenly.

"Eamon," said Jocelyn. "By eight minutes."

"Interesting," breathed Elddreki. "That is telling, I think."

"What do you mean?" Jocelyn frowned.

Instead of answering, Elddreki posed another question. "Do you remember I told you your power felt familiar to me?"

Jocelyn nodded. "That was why you were confident it was dragon magic."

"Not just dragon magic," Elddreki said. "It feels like *my* magic. Not entirely of course. It is your own. But, still...I can sense my signature mixed in with everything else."

"What does that mean?" asked Kincaid, stepping closer to Jocelyn. But the dragon wasn't looking at him.

"Do you truly not know why I am interested to discover that your brother was born first and you second?" he asked Jocelyn, and she nodded. "Hm. I wonder if your father doesn't know this part of his history, or if he chose not to tell you in case you didn't like the information."

"I can't answer that," said Jocelyn shortly, "but if you think you're getting away this time with saying that if he hasn't told me, you're not going to—"

"I wasn't going to say that," Elddreki cut her off with a chuckle. "Do you know that the dragons have gifted your house with certain protections?"

Jocelyn nodded. "Yes. The storytelling, the unnaturally good memory, the unbroken line, even through the generations of the throne's corruption."

"The unbroken line, indeed," said Elddreki. "The bloodline has passed father to son, without fail, for many generations. It is part of that story that, in Kyona's royal bloodline, once a son is born, there are no more children."

"What do you mean?" Jocelyn frowned. "I know my father had no siblings, but that hasn't always been the case. Didn't King Cael and Queen Jacqueline have five children?"

"Indeed." Elddreki inclined his head. "But the only son was the fifth child. Once an heir was born, no more children were given to the king and queen. The same has been true since then." His eyes bored into Jocelyn's. "Until now."

Jocelyn stared back, her mind reeling.

"That's surprising," said Kincaid. "I would have thought most rulers would want to have more sons, to secure the succession in case something happened to the first one. You're saying no Kyonan monarch has thought that way?"

"It is not a matter of choice," said Elddreki. "It is not that they do not want to have more children. It is just that they... don't."

Jocelyn swallowed. "Until me."

"Until you," Elddreki agreed.

She turned away, trying to master the rush of emotion threatening to overpower her. She could feel Kincaid's eyes on her, and she stared frantically at the landscape around them, desperate to turn his attention away.

"Look," she said, gesturing to the east. Her throat felt dry, and the word came out as a rasp. "There's another town up ahead. We can look for horses."

"Oh good!" Kincaid was instantly distracted, sounding eager as he followed her gaze toward the huddle of buildings just visible in the distance. "Hopefully they won't be horned, magic-carrying abominations," he joked.

Jocelyn tried to laugh, but she choked on the sound. There was a creek running nearby, and she waved desperately toward it. "I'd better freshen up first," she managed to say. "There's still some dried blood on me from yesterday."

Then she fled.

CHAPTER TWENTY-ONE

"Jocelyn!"

She heard Kincaid's bewildered shout behind her, but she ignored it, racing toward the stream as if she could outrun the tears beginning to spill down her cheeks. She dropped to her knees beside the running water, plunging her hands into its flow and rubbing them frantically, trying to wash away the bloodstains still clinging to her skin.

She was a stain. A stain on the dragons. A stain on her royal house. A small sob escaped her.

"Jocelyn."

She jumped at Kincaid's soft voice, so close behind her. She hadn't even realized he had followed. She swiped quickly at her eyes, but he was on his knees beside her in a moment, his hands capturing hers in a firm but gentle clasp.

"What is it, Jocelyn? What's wrong? Don't say it's your injury, because I won't believe you."

"*I'm* what's wrong," she said unsteadily, the kindness in Kincaid's voice making her emotions even harder to hold in. "Everything about me, from my birth onward. You heard what Elddreki said! I'm an abomination!"

"You are *not* an abomination," said Kincaid firmly. "Don't you ever say that again!"

"But I am!" A tear escaped in spite of Jocelyn's best efforts. Kincaid's thumb was suddenly there, wiping it away, but she couldn't meet his eyes. "I don't know why Elddreki isn't more concerned about...what I am, but if the other dragons found out about me, they'd hunt me down and destroy me!" She pulled her hands from his. "And they wouldn't be wrong."

"Jocelyn, what are you talking about?" Kincaid sounded thoroughly alarmed now.

"You know what I'm talking about," she said dully. "My power isn't natural. Only dragons are supposed to have magic. Elddreki said it warps the receiver as well as the giver." She drew a shuddering breath. "At least, because there were two of us, I seem to have somehow taken all the bad. Maybe Eamon has escaped being warped."

"Jocelyn, stop it."

She looked up, startled by the anger in Kincaid's voice.

"Stop talking like that, like there's something wrong with you, like you're evil. You're letting your imagination run wild."

"You don't understand, Kincaid," she said quietly. "For some reason I can't explain, you're barely affected by my power. But this person," she gestured between them, indicating the ease of their conversation, "this isn't who I am. This isn't what my life is really like. I hardly open my mouth outside my own family, and usually when I do, something bad happens. Most of the court in Kynton think poorly of me, and half of them are so uncomfortable in my presence they can barely meet my eyes."

"Then they're all imbeciles," said Kincaid, with feeling. "No wonder you were willing to brave a loveless marriage with Prince Ormond in order to get away."

Jocelyn gave a hollow laugh. "Don't be ridiculous," she said. "I didn't want to get away. You think I want to leave Kyona? I love

Kyona. I agreed to leave because of the crisis with the freedmen."

"What do you mean?" asked Kincaid, frowning. "How does the crisis endanger you?"

"It doesn't endanger me," said Jocelyn in exasperation. "I endanger it. The kingdom is suddenly ill at ease, and no one understands why. I thought if I stayed at Kynton, where all the negotiations are going to happen, and all the decisions are going to be made, the risk of me making a bad situation worse would be too high."

"You exiled yourself in some kind of attempt to protect your kingdom?" Kincaid's voice vibrated with anger, and on reflection, Jocelyn couldn't blame him.

She released a long breath, her shoulders slumping. "In a manner of speaking. But I'm realizing now how unfair that is to Valoria. I shouldn't inflict myself on the court at Bryford just to protect the court at Kynton."

"Jocelyn, that is the stupidest thing I have ever heard," said Kincaid. She looked up quickly at him, and saw that there was steel in his eyes to match that in his voice.

"It's not," she said quietly. "I've been doing damage to Kyona's royal house for as long as I've been alive. You heard Elddreki. I shouldn't even exist. I wasn't supposed to be born." She held up a hand to forestall him as he opened his mouth. "It might seem foolish to you, but it's not. Kyona's royal bloodline is steeped in traditions, many of them magical. The one Elddreki just described about royal children is just an example. But that particular one, like many others, has survived for countless generations, even through a two hundred year exile from the throne! And then I come along and destroy it."

Kincaid was staring at her like she was crazy, and it was beginning to irk her.

"Why are you looking at me like that?" she snapped. "You heard Elddreki, the same as I did."

"Yes, I heard everything Elddreki said," Kincaid agreed. "And I don't know where you're getting all of this. He never said you're an abomination."

"That's true, I didn't." Elddreki's voice made both humans jump. Jocelyn looked over her shoulder, wondering how a creature so large could be so stealthy. Elddreki was sitting quite at his ease, making her wonder how long he had been there, silently observing her vulnerable moment.

"Not in as many words," she acknowledged. "But you said creatures who end up with dragon magic create an almighty mess. That sounds a lot like me. You also said they had to be destroyed."

"So they did, and we destroyed them," said Elddreki placidly. "They are all gone now. You are not one of them. As I told you, no dragon would give power to a human."

"But Elddreki..." Jocelyn forced herself to say the words, "*you used your power on a human. You used it on my mother.*"

"Indeed," affirmed Elddreki.

Kincaid shot Jocelyn a questioning look, and she remembered he didn't know the story. As briefly as possible, she explained how her mother had sustained an injury that should have been fatal when she fell from a great height in the mountains, and how Elddreki had used his magic to heal her. At least, he had done so after making her father believe he would have to exchange his own life for the healing to take place, as some kind of grueling dragon test of his character.

"That's right," said Elddreki placidly, having listened to her tale in silence. "But what I did was a simple use of my magic. I didn't pour it into her. At least," he paused, looking at Jocelyn intently, "I didn't intend to." His eyes glazed over for a moment, but then he shook his head.

"No. I have considered the possibility already, and there is no way I forfeited my power to your mother. I didn't lose any of my capacity—I merely used the effects of my magic to right the damage in her body. Besides," he swung his head around, turning the full beam of his gaze on Jocelyn, "I told you when we first met, your power doesn't hang about you, carried on your person like a cloak. It emanates from you. Any dragon would be able to recognize that you are not one of the creatures created by the forfeiting of power. Your magic is not borrowed—it is a part of you."

Jocelyn rocked back on her heels, thinking over the dragon's words. "But you said it feels like your signature. Doesn't that mean I've borrowed it from you somehow? From when you healed my mother?"

"I said I could sense my signature mixed in," Elddreki corrected. "You really must stop misquoting me. I believe my use of my magic to heal your mother is a critical part of the mystery behind you and your brother being born with dragon magic within you. But it is only one factor. The very fact of both your parents' entrance into the Dragon Realm—an incredibly rare occurrence for any human—may have just as significant a part to play."

Jocelyn considered this for a moment. Then she craned her neck, looking full into the beast's face. "Do you really believe my power isn't warped?"

He frowned at her. "Of course. You are not an abomination, Jocelyn. That is a strange and illogical interpretation of my words."

"As I said," Kincaid cut in, with a touch of humor. "And I never heard Elddreki say anything about you destroying ancient royal traditions, either."

"He said—"

"I know what he said," Kincaid cut her off. "I was standing

right next to you. He said it's always been the case that no more children come after the heir is born, until your appearance. Now something new is happening, something different. He never said anything about chaos or destruction or loss."

"But it is a loss," said Jocelyn dully.

Kincaid shrugged. "Most gains come with some kind of loss. Traditions change, Jocelyn, even ancient ones. Everything must change with time. Imagine how boring and predictable and *stuck* a kingdom would be without change."

"You say that because you're Valorian," said Jocelyn with a sigh. "Kyona has had as much change as a kingdom can handle, and more, these last few decades. My father's dramatic ascent to the throne might be an exciting story to you, but it's a reality for Kyona. Of course I'm glad he restored the crown, but the ramifications of such a sudden shift are huge. We're still feeling them now."

"And the kingdom wouldn't still be feeling the ramifications if the false king remained on the throne?" Kincaid challenged. "Your reactions make no sense to me, Jocelyn. Why do you hear mention of change and choose to interpret it as destruction? Couldn't it just as easily be interpreted as the creation of something new?"

Jocelyn couldn't think of a response, but she was saved the necessity. Elddreki was doing something strange, and both humans stopped their conversation to look up at him. He drew a deep breath, then let it out in a slow rumbling rattle, starting deep in his core and ending with the tiniest flicker of flame coming out of his nostrils.

"Remarkable," he said, apparently to himself. He glanced down to see the two of them, kneeling on the grass by the river, staring up at him blankly. His eyes focused on Kincaid.

"You have impressed me, Valorian," he said. "For one so

foolish and hotheaded, you see to the heart of the matter in a way I would not have expected."

"Thank...you?" Kincaid's lilt turned the hesitant words into a question. He looked as confused as Jocelyn felt.

"Change," said Elddreki simply. Jocelyn and Kincaid glanced at each other, brows furrowed.

"What?"

"Change," the dragon repeated.

Jocelyn looked down at her dress, brand new the day before, but already ripped and stained with blood. Was he telling her to change her clothes? It would be the first time the creature had ever shown an interest in such a detail.

"Change what?" she asked warily.

"Change is your power." Elddreki spoke confidently, clearly sure of his conclusion. "I suddenly understood when I heard Kincaid's reflections. He is quite right. What I said about the effect of your birth need not have been interpreted as destruction. Just as your power need not be seen as evil. It is a change, certainly, and a dramatic one. But change in itself is neither good nor bad. And I believe Kincaid is right that change is necessary. If I did not believe that, I wouldn't have left my own home to search for another colony of my kind, in the hope someone else chose differently from us, and new dragons are still being born somewhere out there."

He narrowed his eyes, leaning closer to Jocelyn. As comfortable as she had become with the fearsome beast, his proximity still made her nervous. Or perhaps it was the intensity in his gaze.

"Dragons do not change easily, especially those of us who have chosen immortality. Nor do we feel emotions keenly the way humans do. But I felt anger on your behalf yesterday. It is almost as though your power of change is starting to have its impact even on me."

"But..." Jocelyn was dumbfounded. "I didn't use my words—"

"Your power is not in your words," said Elddreki, shaking his head. "It is in you. Your words appear to be the primary vessel for its use, that's all. But that doesn't necessarily mean it's limited to your speech."

"Like the dance in Montego," said Kincaid suddenly. "You weren't speaking then, and you definitely let out a surge of power. Even I felt it, although I didn't understand what was going on at the time."

"Yes, it felt like my words in action form," acknowledged Jocelyn. "It terrified me. Nothing like it had ever happened before. Just like my words confuse people's thoughts, my dance confused everyone's movements."

"Not confused, *changed*," said Kincaid, sounding excited. "They'd probably been doing that dance the same way for a hundred years, but when you joined the dance, it changed." He thought for a moment. "That's why you're good at changing people's minds. And it's why the power of suggestion is better than telling someone outright what to do. Change comes slowly, and subtly, not all at once."

Jocelyn was silent, trying to wrap her mind around the idea of her power as change rather than confusion. It was a fascinating and terrifying thought, the idea that she had been wrong in her understanding of it for so long. She wasn't entirely sure that it was better, really, but it was still overwhelming to try to re-learn her own essence. Still, the dragon's words felt right somehow, as though she had been looking out of a dirty window, and he had wiped it clean. She saw the same things as before, but much more clearly.

It made sense. Her parents' ascension to Kyona's throne had been a dramatic event, and it had heralded great change for

Kyona. Even the nature of her parents' relationship was a matter of momentous change.

"I wonder what your brother's power is," Elddreki mused. "Without witnessing it myself, it would be difficult to form a conclusion."

"Boringness?" suggested Kincaid, shooting Jocelyn an impudent look. "Uptightness?"

Jocelyn ignored him. She thought about it for a moment, picturing change on one side of the coin, and the steadiness and security that hung about Eamon on the other side.

"Stability," she said, and as she said the word she knew it was true. "If mine is change, his is stability."

Again, it made sense that her parents' union, somehow laced with magic, would produce such a combination. Their appearance had brought change, certainly. But by the same token, the restoration of Kyona's ancient royal house, and the wisdom of her father's rule, had given the kingdom stability.

"Two sides of the same coin, indeed," said Elddreki gravely. "And certainly neither evil in itself. A kingdom with both of those qualities would surely prosper."

Jocelyn didn't respond, deep in thought. Could it be true? Was it possible her power was no more dangerous, no more harmful than Eamon's, if understood in the right light? It was a tantalizing thought, but she brushed it aside. It didn't tally with her experiences, with a lifetime of bitter lessons.

She pushed herself to her feet, and Kincaid copied the motion. "Well, it's given me a lot to think about, that's for certain," she said matter-of-factly. "I'm not sure what the impact of the difference will be, but I suppose time will tell." She dusted off her hands in a businesslike manner. "I'm sorry I fell apart. I'm all right now. We should continue into the town if we want to buy those horses."

Kincaid was watching her in silence, his forehead creased.

She could tell he wasn't convinced her internal crisis was over, but she didn't intend to give him the opportunity to question her further. She turned to the dragon.

"Will you stay out of the town again?"

Elddreki sighed. "I suppose so. I would like to visit a human town—I am curious as to your way of life. But it seems likely my presence will hinder rather than help."

"Probably true, I'm afraid," acknowledged Jocelyn with a smile.

"The question of buying the horses was never decided, incidentally," the dragon went on. "If not Jocelyn's hair, what will you barter?"

Kincaid came out of his abstraction, smiling in amusement at the curiosity on Elddreki's face.

"I have a few things," he said, with a lighthearted shrug. "My knife is worth a fair bit. I could give that up without too much disadvantage, as long as I still have my sword."

"My bracelet!" cried Jocelyn, belatedly remembering this article. "We'll barter my bracelet! You shouldn't give up your knife."

Kincaid shook his head. "No, Joss, keep your bracelet."

Jocelyn frowned. He was infuriatingly stubborn. And the worst of it was his manner as he said it made it clear he was confident of winning the argument. He was clearly far too used to getting his own way. She wondered what it would take to change his mind.

Change his mind. The thought tickled at her as they walked, daring her to explore it. Would she be able to change his mind if she tried? If her power really was change, would understanding that make it easier to control it?

They parted ways with the dragon not far beyond the creek. He said he would wait for them there, and wished them success on what he placidly called their "horse quest". Both humans admirably kept their gravity as they thanked him.

The two of them walked quickly as they continued on toward the town. Jocelyn kept shooting sideways glances at Kincaid as she mulled over what words to use, and eventually he noticed.

"What is it, Joss?"

"Nothing," she said quickly. "I'm just not happy about the idea of you selling your knife and me keeping my bracelet."

Kincaid grinned maddeningly. "I'm sure you're not, but you won't win this one, Jocelyn, so just let it go."

She narrowed her eyes, focusing on her words. "It's just that a knife is much more practical than a bracelet, Kincaid."

"True," he said easily. "But like I said, I'd still have my sword."

Jocelyn frowned. She had felt her power leave her, but it had been barely a trickle, and there had been no obvious effect. She focused on the power itself this time, rather than the words, teasing it out of herself, casting it in Kincaid's direction.

"It would be so unfortunate if we ran into trouble again, and you were prevented from coming to my aid this time because you'd lost your knife."

This time she felt the power reaching out much more tangibly, and a flicker crossed Kincaid's face.

"That would be unfortunate," he agreed slowly. "That would be awful." His face was creased in a look of calculation, but all of a sudden his features changed, astonishment leaping across them, and he came to a sudden halt.

"You were just doing it, weren't you?" he accused. "Trying to use your power to change my mind!"

Jocelyn ducked her head, ashamed. He had caught her out so quickly. "I was," she admitted, bracing herself for his reaction.

He had every right to be angry, after she had bemoaned at length how dangerous her power was.

But anger seemed to be the furthest thing from Kincaid's mind.

"That was incredible!" he said, delighted. "I could really feel it, even though I didn't recognize what it was at the time." He beamed at her. "That was brilliant."

She laughed in spite of herself. He was looking at her as though she had just performed an impressive juggling act while balancing on her hands.

"Not really," she said. "It didn't work, did it? I didn't change your mind." She cocked an eyebrow. "Or did I?"

Kincaid's grin was broader than ever. "Of course not. You're not bartering your bracelet, Jocelyn, just forget about it."

"Hm." She decided not to argue the point at that moment. She looked at him curiously. "What did it feel like?"

Kincaid thought it over, starting to walk again. "It just seemed all of a sudden that I should reconsider my position, that maybe what I'd thought was true wasn't so certain after all."

"Hm," said Jocelyn again. "Which would make most people uncomfortable, wouldn't it? People don't like change." She thought about her own feelings regarding the drastic changes that might be coming to her life if she went through with this marriage alliance, and deflated slightly. "And I don't blame them." She looked over at Kincaid. "But not you."

"Not me what?"

"Change doesn't make you uncomfortable. You said once," she colored slightly, "that talking to me didn't feel uncomfortable, it felt exciting. You find change exciting."

Kincaid considered it. "I suppose I do."

Jocelyn nodded, satisfied. "And you don't become confused or uncomfortable just because your views are challenged. You don't even become resentful of the person who made you question what you thought before. Trust me when I say that's unusual." She gave him an appraising glance. "It's a sign of a strong character, I think."

"Thank you," said Kincaid. He was clearly trying to speak modestly, but he looked very pleased with himself. He flashed her a sudden, devastatingly appealing grin. "So I can withstand you, O Mighty One."

She chuckled. "We'll see."

"But this is great," Kincaid enthused, still bizarrely delighted about her attempt to manipulate him. "It's an excellent idea."

"What is?" asked Jocelyn warily.

"You trying to train with your power. You can practice on me!"

"No." Jocelyn spoke flatly. "Absolutely not."

"Why not, Joss?" Kincaid protested. "Elddreki is out, because he's not affected by your power, at least not in the normal way. Who else is there but me?"

"I'm not going to intentionally try to mess with your mind on a regular basis, Kincaid," said Jocelyn firmly. "I shouldn't have done it at all. It was very wrong of me."

Kincaid waved her apology aside with a casual hand. "Nonsense! You need to stop being afraid of it, Jocelyn. It's an incredible tool, and you don't use it nearly enough. Besides, it would benefit everyone, especially you, if you could control it better."

Jocelyn wavered. The idea of being able to more reliably control her power was appealing, she couldn't deny it. But one look at Kincaid's eager, trusting face was enough to bring back all her doubts.

"No, Kincaid," she said. "I already told you I don't want to hurt you."

"And I already told you that you won't," said Kincaid, unconcerned. "You said it yourself, I'm barely affected by it. Besides, I trust you. Even if you find a way to make it impact me more, I'm not afraid you'll do anything nefarious to me."

"Not on purpose," said Jocelyn desperately.

"It will be fine, Joss," said Kincaid in that same tone of authority.

Jocelyn narrowed her eyes at his assumption of control, again focusing her mind. "I would hate for you to become less confident if I somehow changed your nature by accident."

Kincaid's expression stilled as he thought about this possibility, then all of a sudden he shook his head like a dog shaking off water.

"You little sneak!" he laughed, his delighted tone at odds with his words. "You were doing it again!"

Jocelyn grinned guiltily, unable to help herself. It was so bizarre, but so freeing, that Kincaid could tell she was trying to influence him but was still so pleased about it.

"You won't do me any harm, Jocelyn," he said seriously, "because I know what you're doing. It's not like the times you've accidentally influenced people who didn't even realize your words were what changed their minds."

Jocelyn hesitated, thinking it over. "Perhaps it is worth trying to get better at controlling it. Then I might be able to avoid using it altogether."

Kincaid rolled his eyes at how she intended to use the proposed training, but he didn't argue.

"So it's settled."

Jocelyn still felt uneasy, but they had just reached the first buildings, and she fell silent. She drew unconsciously closer to Kincaid, who shot her a reassuring smile that didn't quite match the keen alertness of his eyes as they swept the area. She swallowed, trying not to think about her experiences in the last two towns.

But she needn't have worried. She wouldn't have described

the place as pleasant, but the people's demeanor wasn't as hostile as in Thalia. It was a reasonably sized town, but even so, they were lucky to find horses available for sale. They weren't the fastest looking steeds, but they would certainly be better than walking all the way to the eastern coast.

As before, Kincaid took charge of the negotiations. Jocelyn felt guiltier than ever when she saw the knife up close. It was a beautiful weapon, the hilt intricately engraved, and the design elaborate. But Kincaid seemed to take its loss lightly.

In the end he had to trade his traveling cloak as well as his knife, which he did cheerfully enough. He waved off Jocelyn's protests, saying he could pick up a simpler, less costly cloak as they headed into the colder eastern region. Finally, when he threw in the extra parchment, which they hadn't used, and the two oil lamps, the seller was satisfied.

"Hopefully we don't find ourselves stranded in any more pitch black caves," Kincaid muttered humorously as the man placed the lamps in his own bag. Kincaid had leaned so close that his breath tickled Jocelyn's ear as he spoke, and she felt a pleasant shiver dancing over her skin at the reminder of the cave.

"You got cheated, didn't you?" she muttered accusingly, trying to turn the topic. "That dagger looked very costly."

Kincaid shrugged in acknowledgment, smiling slightly. "We need the horses more, Joss."

"But how much was it worth? It looked like a family heirloom!"

"It wasn't an heirloom," said Kincaid. "It's fine." He saw that she was raising an eyebrow at him. "It was a present from my parents," he admitted, relenting. "But it doesn't matter."

"Won't they be angry that you got rid of it?" asked Jocelyn anxiously.

He shrugged again, his voice and expression cheerful. "Hopefully not."

He turned back to the local man, who was waving an underling forward. The urchin led the horses toward their new owners, and Jocelyn was immediately distracted from their conversation.

She stepped up to one of them, a chestnut mare, and began to stroke her mane, crooning softly to her. The horse flicked her ears responsively, nuzzling Jocelyn's hand. Jocelyn leaned into the creature. She had always loved horses.

She looked up to see Kincaid watching her, his hand on the bridle of the other horse, and an affectionate smile on his face. She cleared her throat quickly, suddenly self-conscious.

"Should we go?"

Kincaid nodded, still smiling faintly, and they began to head out of town. They hadn't gone far, however, when Jocelyn detected the intangible but undeniable buzz that always heralded the arrival of news. A pair of small boys ran past them, talking eagerly to each other, their words indistinguishable.

Jocelyn and Kincaid exchanged looks.

"Did you hear?"

They both jumped at the eager voice immediately to their left, but a quick glance showed the woman wasn't speaking to them. Her friend was leaning in, ready for a gossip, but the volume of the speaker made the gesture unnecessary.

"The chandler's son just came back from Thalia, and he claims there was a *dragon* there yesterday! An actual dragon!!"

The second woman gasped dramatically, her hand flying to her ample bosom. "Was anyone eaten?"

"He claims no one was hurt," said the first woman, sounding faintly disappointed. "Apparently the beast was traveling with two humans, so maybe it's not dangerous. They came east when they left!"

The listener's eyes flicked to Jocelyn and Kincaid, standing nearby and clearly listening in.

"Did he say anything about these humans traveling with the creature?" she asked her friend.

"Time to go, I think," muttered Kincaid, and Jocelyn nodded fervently. They walked their horses out of town as quickly as possible, and mounted up as soon as they were clear of the buildings.

Jocelyn reveled in her first ride in days. She leaned close along the horse's neck and urged the mare forward, glad she had released her hair from its braid. She had always felt at her most free when on horseback—there was no other feeling quite like having the wind tugging at her hair as it streamed out behind her, unrestrained.

She and her mare overtook Kincaid on his bay, and he hastened to urge his own mount on in pursuit. Jocelyn glanced back, grinning slyly as she pushed her horse to a gallop. His eyes were on her, and they were shining with the same unfettered delight she felt. She saw that he had an excellent seat. If possible, he looked stronger and more confident on horseback than he did on his own two feet.

Predictably, Elddreki was not difficult to locate, curled up by the stream in a restful posture. He raised his head at their approach, his eyes assessing the new additions to their party with his usual bright curiosity.

Kincaid had been gaining on Jocelyn, and at the last moment he raced ahead of her, reaching the dragon first. She pulled up just behind him, laughing.

"I'll get you next time!" she called, and he grinned.

"We'll see."

Elddreki pushed himself languidly to his feet, smiling indulgently on their flushed and happy faces. Jocelyn's mount, which had been sidling nervously ever since reaching the beast, suddenly reared. She gasped, barely managing to keep her seat as she brought the animal back under control. Kincaid had his horse alongside hers in a flash, but she shook her head, indicating for him to stay out of the way. The mare was still dancing anxiously on the spot, but Jocelyn kept an iron hand on the reins, speaking soothingly as she calmed her.

She felt a flash of exasperation as Elddreki leaned closer, sure the dragon would throw her horse into a panic again. But when Elddreki spoke, in words Jocelyn didn't understand, the animal calmed slightly. Elddreki took a deep breath, exhaling it in a gentle, unnaturally warm wind that seemed to wrap itself around the horse. Focusing on the sensation, Jocelyn recognized with interest the signature of Elddreki's magic. The power settled over the horse like an invisible blanket, and the mare stilled altogether. The two humans watched in amazement as the horse stepped lightly forward, nuzzling against Elddreki's flank.

The dragon received the gesture of affection with his usual unruffled calm.

"She just needed to be reassured as to the nature of the beast she's dealing with," he explained. "Horses are very intelligent creatures." He looked down at the mare fondly. "I like horses. I can understand why the bereft dragons thought them gentle enough creatures to receive forfeited magic." He sighed. "Although it was still very wrong of them, of course."

"You're a good horsewoman," Kincaid commented to Jocelyn, admiration in his gaze. "You ride well, and you handled that crisis expertly."

"Thank you," said Jocelyn, her tone unconvincingly modest. She shot him a grin. "That *is* a normal part of a princess's education."

CHAPTER TWENTY-TWO

It was delightful, after days of trekking on foot, to move eastward at the rapid pace their new horses allowed. Even the inevitable aches of hours of riding couldn't dim Jocelyn's pleasure. They stopped to rest as regularly as horses or humans required, but they didn't enter another town again all that day. Elddreki had shown no visible reaction to the news that word of him had begun to spread, but Jocelyn felt eager to put some distance between them and the rumors if possible.

The scrubby grassland near the river had long since given way to more cultivated land, although towns were still few and far between. The summer sun was pleasantly warm, and the countryside was beautiful. Jocelyn could almost imagine herself in Kyona.

When darkness fell, they had a quick debate about whether to pay for lodgings somewhere. But as Kincaid was unwilling to let Jocelyn barter her bracelet, and Jocelyn was unwilling to let him pay for her lodgings, they reached an impasse.

Really, Jocelyn thought when they settled for sleep, it would have been a waste of their resources. Sleeping on the ground wasn't exactly luxurious, but the springy turf of the copse of trees where they stopped was more comfortable than either the cave or the riverbank had been. And as much as she knew a chaperone would disapprove, it didn't feel improper having Kincaid so close, not with Elddreki there. On the contrary, it felt comforting and reassuring.

Over the next week, the arrangement became quite familiar, and never once did Jocelyn feel afraid in the nighttime hours. In line with his new and apparently unnatural instinct of protection, Elddreki formed the habit of sleeping curled in an arc, his mighty tail stretched around to complete the circle of safety in which the two humans slept. The three of them often chatted easily as they slipped toward slumber, and Jocelyn couldn't help but compare the strange but comfortable camaraderie of the group with the inevitable pompous formality of the state visit she was supposed to be paying at that moment.

They continued to move rapidly through pleasant Valorian farmland, but Jocelyn's hope of outrunning rumors of their presence was soon shown to be foolish. They may have left the gossiping townsfolk of Thalia far behind, but the countryside became increasingly more populated as they moved away from the North Wilds. Elddreki always stayed out of the way on the occasions when they went into towns in order to restock on food. But the rest of the time he stayed close by, and his vast reptilian form could hardly fail to attract notice as he glided along above them, or ambled casually on the ground beside them.

After a few days Jocelyn almost stopped noticing the inevitable screams of terror that emerged any time Elddreki flew over a settlement, and had ceased to feel sorry for the lone goatherds they regularly saw fleeing from the travelers' approach. They would get over it soon enough, when they realized the beast was gone and they hadn't been eaten. They would probably relive the moment with excitement for the rest of their lives, the story growing with each retelling at the local tavern. Kincaid hadn't been wrong that Elddreki would metaphorically set the countryside on fire. Jocelyn had no doubt Valorians far and wide would be discussing the journey of the dragon for decades to come.

And she had no fear of being attacked again. The almost universal reaction to the dragon's appearance was to run and hide. And when it was clear the travelers were just passing through, no one seemed inclined to pursue them. A few bolder Valorians approached them for a closer look when they were resting, always with endearingly futile attempts at stealth, but no one actually tried to speak with them. And it seemed likely now that if any foolhardy local did attempt to do the group harm, Elddreki would protect his human companions.

"Do you think word has reached Bryford by now about Elddreki being in Valoria?" Jocelyn asked Kincaid on one occasion, as they passed a farmer's cottage and she watched a mother pulling a small child indoors with a frantic scream.

"Probably," said Kincaid cheerfully. They had slowed to a trot, but Elddreki was still flying, moving in large circles so as not to get too far ahead.

"Do you think the king will send a squadron of guards to try to...I don't know...deal with him?"

"Who knows?" said Kincaid, unconcerned. He grinned. "It would be quite entertaining if he did, don't you think?"

"Maybe for you," said Jocelyn dryly.

"What do you mean?"

She raised her eyebrows, surprised by Kincaid's tone. "Just that I don't particularly want to run into the king right now." She gestured down at her disheveled appearance. She was still wearing the red-brown dress, and it wasn't altogether clean. Her wound was hardly troubling her anymore, and no longer needed to be bandaged, but the gaping hole in her sleeve remained. "Not the best first impression."

"Oh, I see what you mean," said Kincaid, following her gesture with his eyes and nodding in agreement, not very chivalrously. "But surely the king wouldn't come himself."

"Hopefully not." Jocelyn was silent for a moment, her thoughts straying toward the distant Bryford. "Prince Ormond wouldn't be sent on such a mission, would he?" she asked nervously.

Kincaid glanced over at her quickly. "I don't know," he said apologetically. "It's not impossible."

Jocelyn gave a small groan, and Kincaid looked like he was trying to hide a smile.

"What else can you tell me about him?" she asked. "You said he's tall and fair. Is he handsome?"

Kincaid's smile instantly disappeared, and he shifted uncomfortably on his horse. "I don't know," he said. "I don't think my opinion on the topic would be very authoritative."

"Well, what do girls say when he rides past?" asked Jocelyn impatiently. "Does your sister think he's handsome?"

Kincaid paused, considering it. "I honestly don't know," he said. He saw Jocelyn's skepticism, and added, "Maybe fourteen is too young to swoon over a prince."

"Hm." Jocelyn thought of her own fourteen-year-old self—not to mention Lucy at that age—and pursed her lips skeptically. "Well, what do older girls say? Do *they* swoon over him?"

Kincaid sighed. "Yes, I suppose they do. But it's probably just because he's the prince. I don't think he's all that handsome, really."

Jocelyn raised her eyebrows. "I thought you didn't have an opinion."

Kincaid shrugged one shoulder, looking slightly petulant. Jocelyn looked down to hide her smile, choosing not to explore why she felt so pleased that Kincaid resented the absent Prince Ormond.

"I wonder what his personality is like," she mused. "Probably old and boring."

Kincaid let out a sudden snort of laughter, his mood instantly lifting. "What did you say?"

Jocelyn grinned back at him. "It's what my best friend said, or her little brother first I suppose." She sighed, deflating slightly. "All too likely, I'm guessing, him being crown prince and all. Old and boring and serious."

Kincaid looked amused. "Is that what Eamon is like? He's crown prince."

Jocelyn chuckled. "That's what Lucy said. No, he's not like that at all, thankfully. But like I've said before, my family are not your typical royals."

"Is Lucy your best friend?" asked Kincaid curiously, and Jocelyn nodded. "Tell me about her," Kincaid persisted. "I told you enough stories yesterday about my sister, and about Henrik." He named his own best friend. "It's your turn."

"Well..." Jocelyn paused, wondering how to sum up sixteen years of friendship in a few sentences. "Luciana is the best. We were destined to be friends, because our fathers are very close childhood friends themselves. So much so that I call her parents aunt and uncle, although there's no actual relation. Uncle Jonan and my father grew up like brothers, before Father knew he was royal. Lucy is a year younger than I am, and we've been close since before I can remember. But it's not just because of the family connection," she hastened to add. "I'm sure we'd be friends under any circumstances. She's sweet, and kind, and funny, and the most trusting person you'll ever meet."

She smiled. "She's also an extremely skilled fighter, like her mother, but not by choice."

"Not by choice?" Kincaid repeated, confused, and Jocelyn's smile grew.

"Her parents make her train, and she always showed a much greater aptitude than I ever did. But she doesn't want to. She doesn't like the idea of hurting anyone. She's got her mother's gentle nature. Lately it's become an absolute battle to get her to spar with me." Jocelyn's tone turned dry. "You'd think she would enjoy it, since she always beats me, every single time." She shook her head. "But she quite likes her throwing knives. She's trained most with them, and they're probably her best weapon." Jocelyn rolled her eyes. "I'm pretty sure it's just because she could practice on a target, without running the risk of hurting anyone by accident."

"She sounds great," said Kincaid. "I would like to meet her one day."

"She's also stunningly, stunningly beautiful," said Jocelyn, her tone slightly flatter. *And come to think of it, I don't particularly want you to meet her.* She didn't speak the last words aloud, ashamed of them even in her own head.

"Does she look like you?" asked Kincaid, his expression innocent.

Jocelyn chuckled. "Not at all. We're opposites in terms of appearance. She's dark, I'm light. I've often thought it ironic, because our personalities are the opposite way around."

"Your personality isn't dark, Joss," scolded Kincaid, with a frown. "So this Luciana has dark hair?" He leaned over in his saddle, flicking her braid impudently. "That's certainly the opposite to you."

She swatted his hand away, although she was secretly pleased. "Yes, she does, but it's also her skin." She chuckled to herself. "She's an exotic beauty, you see. She's half Balenan."

"Really?" Kincaid sounded startled, and Jocelyn looked at him, her eyebrows raised. "I don't have anything against Balenans," he clarified quickly. "I'm just surprised the royal family is so close with a half-Balenan family. I thought relations between Kyona and Balenol were still pretty frosty, what with the whole, you know..."

"Centuries of exploitation and slavery?" Jocelyn finished for him.

"Well, yes."

"You're not wrong," Jocelyn admitted. "Things will probably always be tense. But none of that is Lucy's fault."

"Of course not," Kincaid agreed hastily. He looked at her curiously. "So if her father grew up with your father in Kyona, does that mean it's her mother who's Balenan?"

"That's right. Aunt Scarlett." Jocelyn's eyes misted over for a moment. "She's amazing. One of my favorite people. And she's even more stunningly beautiful than Luciana." She looked over at Kincaid, who was watching her impatiently, clearly interested less in Aunt Scarlett's appearance and more in the story behind the Balenan's presence in Kyona.

Jocelyn sighed. "She met Uncle Jonan when he went to Balenol, not long after my father took the throne," she said. "That was when the slave trade was still flourishing. In fact," she paused, "they were the ones who stopped the slave trade." She could see Kincaid was intrigued, and she pushed on.

"Aunt Scarlett was a Balenan noblewoman, an influential one—she's a cousin of their royal family, and she grew up at the castle. Plus, her father was the Overseer of Slaves, but she was against the trade. She had this secret double life, like a spy in the Balenan court, even though she was my age. She started a resistance with renegade slaves who lived in the jungle, and they did everything they could to undermine the trade."

She snuck a look at Kincaid and thought he looked impressed.

"But the slaves who they liberated couldn't cross the sea back to Kyona because there was a curse," she continued. She glanced up at Elddreki, circling overhead. "A curse created by dragon magic."

"I've heard about that," said Kincaid, sounding awed. "I thought the stories had been hugely exaggerated, but maybe I was wrong."

Jocelyn shrugged. "I wouldn't be surprised if they'd grown, but the truth was pretty incredible, so maybe not. Uncle Jonan and Aunt Scarlett figured it out and broke the curse, then the freed slaves could all come back. Plus the Balenans found out about the friendship between the Kyonan royals and the dragons, and they released the rest of the slaves, too."

"The freedmen," Kincaid said, and she nodded. "And your Uncle Jonan and Aunt Scarlett obviously decided to stay in Kyona?"

Jocelyn chuckled darkly. "I don't think they would have been very welcome back in Balenol, to be honest. They went for a visit a year or so after they were married, and it was...eventful. They never went back. Lucy and her brothers—she has three younger brothers—have never even been there. Besides, there was no real reason for them to want to settle in Balenol once all the slaves came back to Kyona. Aunt Scarlett might be Balenan, and Uncle Jonan might never have been a slave, but the freedmen are their people, really."

"Are there many other Balenans in Kyona?" Kincaid asked curiously.

"Not many," said Jocelyn. "What about in Valoria?"

Kincaid shook his head. "Very few. We do more trade with Thorania than with Balenol." He frowned thoughtfully. "There was some Balenan diplomat or other who spent some time in Bryford recently. I remember seeing him around, riding about with the royals. I can't remember why he was here."

Jocelyn frowned. "That's peculiar. I wonder if he really was an official diplomat. No such person has come to Kynton recently. Like I said, Aunt Scarlett is related to the royal family, and I would have thought if they were sending a delegation they would at least have sent them to pay their respects…but then maybe the delegates refused to come to Kyona."

"Surely they couldn't refuse if they were officially sent," Kincaid protested.

Jocelyn shrugged. "Most Balenans are extremely prejudiced against Kyonans from what I've heard. Some of them think of us as little more than animals. Not many would choose to come to our kingdom, even to visit."

Kincaid raised his eyebrows. "You say that pretty calmly. I'd be angry if my people were seen that way by another kingdom."

Jocelyn shrugged again. "It's not a new discovery. And even though I know some Balenans think that way, the only ones I really know are Lucy's family, who are such wonderful people. They live only a few hours' ride from Kynton, and I'm as comfortable in their home as I am in my own." She sighed. "More, sometimes."

"And the members of your father's court really don't object to that level of intimacy between them and your family?"

Jocelyn chuckled. "If they do object, they keep it to themselves." Kincaid gave her a questioning look, and she smiled fondly. "My father is an even tempered man, but there are lines you don't cross with him, and the whole court knows it. No one would criticize Uncle Jonan or his family in front of my father any more than they would dare to make a disparaging remark about my mother's common blood in his presence."

Kincaid smiled responsively. "I like the sound of King Calinnae," he said warmly. He looked sideways at her. "I'm guessing he's a protective father, especially of you."

Jocelyn sighed, deflating. "Yes, he certainly is. And you've got it exactly right when you say especially of me. I don't think he has a very high opinion of my capability, and even though I know why he has that impression, and that it's not his fault, it's still hard to take sometimes."

"That's not what I meant, Jocelyn," said Kincaid, irritated. "Why do you always do that?"

"Do what?"

"I don't know how to explain it," said Kincaid, his tone frustrated. "You interpret everything in a certain light, as if you're some kind of problem." Jocelyn was silent, unsure how to respond, and when he spoke again, his voice was softer. "All I meant was that you must be your father's most precious treasure. Isn't it common for fathers to be especially protective of their daughters?"

"Yes, I suppose it is," said Jocelyn lightly.

"And I like that he's not uptight, like your brother is."

"Eamon is not—" Jocelyn started to protest, but she cut herself off, rolling her eyes, when she saw Kincaid's cheeky grin. Of course he was baiting her.

"But seriously," Kincaid continued. "It shows great strength of character that your father isn't deterred by prejudice from letting you grow up basically as siblings with Lucy and her family. What?" He frowned at Jocelyn's barely stifled choke of laughter. "What did I say that was funny?"

"Not quite like siblings," Jocelyn giggled. "Maybe like cousins. But even that..." She grinned. "I'm just trying to imagine Eamon's reaction to someone calling Lucy his sister."

"Why would that—oh!" Kincaid's frown smoothed into a look of surprise. "It's like that, is it?"

"Of course it is," said Jocelyn, smiling indulgently. "Didn't I tell you she's the sweetest person in the kingdom, not to mention stunningly beautiful?" She gave him a cheeky grin. "Sorry to tell you she's already spoken for. I know you were very eager to meet her."

Kincaid rolled his eyes. "I'll struggle on somehow." He gave her a curious look. "Is she really spoken for? By your brother?"

"Not officially," Jocelyn said hastily. "But the feeling is definitely mutual. No one who knows either of them well has any doubt as to the outcome. They're childhood sweethearts, I guess. It's adorable, really." She sighed. "Or it would be if it wasn't my brother and my best friend." She wrinkled her nose. "The way she looks at him sometimes. You want to talk about girls swooning over princes..." She shook her head. "But of course I would feel that way, because he's my brother. I don't actually dislike it. They're very well-suited I think."

"Do...do your parents know about it?" Kincaid asked hesitantly.

"Of course," said Jocelyn, surprised. "I told you anyone close to them is fully aware of which way the wind is blowing. My parents love Luciana."

Kincaid was silent for a moment, his expression hard to read. "What?"

"It's just...do you really think they'll be allowed to marry? Wouldn't that mean she would be queen one day?"

"Yes, that's right," said Jocelyn slowly, starting to understand the direction of Kincaid's thoughts. "She'll make an excellent queen."

"I don't mean any slight on your friend," said Kincaid quickly. "But with everything we've just been discussing regarding tensions between Kyona and Balenol—not to mention the current prejudice around the freedmen—do you really think Eamon will be allowed to choose her? The next heir to the throne would have Balenan blood, and might not even look Kyonan. Would the court stand for it?"

Jocelyn was silent for a long moment. "They'll just have to accept it," she said, her teeth gritted. It wasn't like she hadn't thought of this issue before. She had, many times. And she was as determined as she had always been that she wasn't going to let people like Sir Sanctimonious get their way, not with Eamon's happiness on the line.

"Don't think I don't admire your fighting spirit," said Kincaid gently. "But is that really how these things work? That they'll just have to accept it?"

Jocelyn deflated slightly. "No, it's not really how it works."

"So how can they be together?" Kincaid pressed.

"They can be together." Jocelyn squared her shoulders. "We'll just have to appease the more fastidious courtiers some… some other way."

"Some other way?"

She could feel Kincaid's eyes boring into her, and she kept her face straight ahead, refusing to meet his gaze. But his sudden intake of breath told her he knew what she was leaving unsaid.

"Some other way like your marriage to Valoria's crown prince, you mean," he said quietly. She didn't respond, aware he was still staring at her. "Even though you don't want to marry Prince Ormond. You don't even want to leave Kyona. You think if you sacrifice your happiness, you can help secure your brother's."

The silence stretched uncomfortably, and Jocelyn felt compelled to speak. "Who says I'd be sacrificing my happiness?" She spoke lightly. "Apparently Prince Ormond is tall and fair and the ladies swoon over him."

There was no answering chuckle. "Would you really do it for such a reason as that?" Kincaid asked quietly, and she knew he wasn't talking about Prince Ormond's looks.

Jocelyn didn't hesitate. "Of course." Her voice became harder. "I won't let people's prejudice separate Eamon and Lucy. I *won't*."

She gave a mirthless laugh. "Besides, marriage alliances are what princesses are for. Haven't you been paying any attention to Princess Sarai's story?"

Kincaid didn't respond, and Jocelyn pushed her horse forward into a canter. The sound of the other horse's hooves faded, and she snuck a look back. Kincaid was right where she'd left him, staring after her with an unreadable expression in his eyes, and his hand clenched into a fist on the reins.

She looked quickly ahead again. She had begun to accept long before now that she had little choice but to go through with the marriage alliance. It wasn't a new idea.

But just how much of a mess was she going to leave behind when she did?

CHAPTER TWENTY-THREE

"Concentrate, Jocelyn! You're not focusing."

Jocelyn groaned. "You concentrate for a while. You've had me at this for an hour, and my head feels like a sack of potatoes."

"I once saw a human whose head was completely bald, and it looked like a potato," interjected Elddreki conversationally.

Jocelyn shot the dragon a look. "You're not helping, Elddreki."

"Of course I am helping. Kincaid and I are both helping you in your attempt to train your power, and you do not appear to me to be very grateful for our assistance."

Jocelyn sighed, rubbing the back of her neck and shifting her feet on the tussock of grass where she stood. "Has anyone ever told you that you're right frustratingly often?"

Elddreki looked surprised. "Of course I am right. But why would that be frustrating?"

Kincaid chuckled. "I think she was trying to apologize."

Elddreki looked at Jocelyn in bewilderment. "That is the strangest apology I have ever heard."

Jocelyn grimaced in acknowledgment, her eyes cast down at

the dry golden grass of summer, whipping gently at her skirts in the breeze. "Yes it was. But Kincaid was right. I am grateful you want to help me. But it's a waste of time. We're not getting anywhere."

"I wouldn't say that," said Elddreki. "We can learn as much from your failures as from your successes, if we're paying attention. More, perhaps."

"Then we should be learning enough to fill a library."

"Enough chatting," said Kincaid curtly. He nodded imperiously at Jocelyn. "Try again."

She narrowed her eyes at him, her irritation returning. "Winter is so much more pleasant than summer," she said halfheartedly, her tone devoid of emotion. "Think of cozy evenings around a roaring fire."

"Jocelyn." Kincaid was unimpressed.

"Did it work?" she asked unenthusiastically. She knew the answer. She had not felt any power leave her. "Did I change your mind?"

"Of course not. You're not even trying."

"I've *been* trying, every day! And it's pointless. It's as unpredictable as ever."

This wasn't strictly true. Understanding her power as change had helped her to be more aware of when her words were and weren't having the desired effect. But that early breakthrough felt like forever ago. Whether it was because Kincaid was becoming immune from exposure to her, or because she was getting worse in her attempts, she was succeeding less and less in impacting his opinions.

She rubbed the back of her neck again, glancing over at the horses, who were grazing unconcernedly nearby. In the days since they had acquired their steeds, she had begun to dread stopping for the midday meal. It wasn't the food she disliked, just what inevitably followed. The soreness in her muscles from so many hours in the saddle was nothing to the aching in her head.

"Do we really have to do this every day? Can't we just keep riding? We could probably be at the coast by now."

"No," said Kincaid firmly. "This training is just as important as Elddreki's quest."

Jocelyn glanced at the dragon, expecting him to disagree, but he was silent. His eyes were on her, and he seemed deep in thought.

"Try again, Jocelyn," he said, and somehow the command didn't irk her as much coming from the dragon.

She sighed, thinking for a moment as she turned to face Kincaid again. He raised his eyebrows expectantly.

"As a child I hated the cold weather," she said, focusing her thoughts on the idea of changing Kincaid's mind about his preferred time of year. "Because it was dark for so much longer each day. Now I don't mind it. I suppose I simply had to outgrow my childish fears."

Again, she felt nothing. Well, nothing but irritation as Kincaid snorted at her weak attempt.

"I can sense the potential of your power," Elddreki mused. "But there's something blocking it. It's like you're at war with yourself."

"No, I'm at war with Kincaid," Jocelyn muttered. Kincaid grinned at that, but Jocelyn wasn't in the mood to be mollified by humor.

"Come on, Joss," said Kincaid, looking at her indulgently. "Did you really think you were going to change my mind by shaming me into thinking that if I don't like winter better it means I'm afraid of the dark?"

"There's nothing wrong with disliking the dark," snapped Jocelyn, stung. She was certain he was thinking of her panic in the cave. "It's the normal reaction of any responsible, level-headed person."

Kincaid raised an eyebrow, clearly starting to get annoyed himself. "So you think I'm irresponsible, do you?"

"Not at all," said Jocelyn, crushingly polite. "I'm sure whatever responsibilities you left in order to join us will wait patiently and not suffer for your absence. After all, who would expect you to think about such things when presented with the opportunity to chase after a dragon adventure and ingratiate yourself with an unguarded princess?"

As soon as the words left her mouth, she regretted them, and not just because they were unkind and unfair. The surge of power, which she had not intended to access, was much stronger than anything Kincaid had been exposed to before, with the exception of the dance in Montego.

He had frozen at her words, and he now stood staring at her, his mouth slightly open. He didn't wear the look of confusion she had so often seen on her listeners' faces, but there was no doubt he had been affected. He looked unsettled, almost like he was in pain.

"Kincaid—"

"I *am* irresponsible," he cut her off, his voice hardly above a whisper. "More than you even realize. And I have taken advantage of your vulnerability. I even pretended I didn't know who you were."

"Kincaid, no," said Jocelyn, tears starting to her eyes.

She took a step toward him, her hand outstretched, but he stepped back, the movement seeming involuntary. She dropped her hand, turning her face away in an attempt to hide the tears welling up. She had known this was a terrible idea. She had said it all along.

"Excellent," said Elddreki brightly, apparently oblivious to the anguish of his human companions. "We are getting some-where. Now we just need to understand why the dam burst."

Kincaid blinked unsteadily, focusing on the dragon with an apparent effort. "What do you mean?" he asked. His gaze returned to Jocelyn, who quickly averted her face again. But not before she saw the sudden understanding leap into his eyes.

"That was it, wasn't it?" he said, sounding dazed. "You used your power. That's why your comment had such a big impact on me."

"Not on purpose," she whispered. "I'm so sorry, Kincaid."

"You don't need to apologize," he said, his voice still not quite steady. "I'm the one who told you to practice on me." He took a deep breath, making a heroic attempt to return to his normal tone. "Elddreki's right, it's a good thing you were able to access your power that time."

"No," Jocelyn choked out. "It's not a good thing, because I didn't mean to access it. I wasn't even thinking about it. This is what I've been telling you all along. It's unpredictable, and dangerous. If I could choose when to use it or not use it, I wouldn't have spent most of my life keeping my words to myself."

"So you really weren't trying to experiment with your power when you said that?" Kincaid asked. Jocelyn shook her head, not quite able to read his tone. Kincaid tried to chuckle, but it was a woeful sound. "So you genuinely do think I'm irresponsible, then?"

"No!" said Jocelyn, looking up quickly. "No, Kincaid, truly I don't. I spoke in anger, and I know it was unfair. I may not have been able to control my power, but I can control my words, and I should never have said that."

"You weren't wrong," said Kincaid ruefully. "I was running away from my responsibilities when I decided to spend the summer wandering Kyona."

"Don't let my power get in your head, Kincaid," said Jocelyn earnestly. "I said I'm sorry, and I meant it. I don't think you're irresponsible, honestly."

"But do you..." Kincaid suddenly seemed unable to meet her eyes. "Do you truly think I've been taking advantage of your isolation...that I've been trying to...to ingratiate myself with you because you're royalty?"

"Of course not!" said Jocelyn, tears once again pricking her eyes.

"Good," said Kincaid, looking up at her again, his expression difficult to read. "Because I haven't been. At least," he chuckled grimly, still looking a little off balance, "I don't think I have."

"Of course you haven't," said Jocelyn firmly.

Kincaid took another deep breath, looking like he was emerging from a deep sleep. "It's a strange feeling," he said, almost to himself. "I've never felt it with that intensity before. It really does get inside your head." He blinked rapidly, then shook his head, his expression determined.

"Well, let's go again. I couldn't recognize your power while it was happening that time, but I think I can capture the feeling now it's over. I'm hoping next time I'll be able to feel it in the moment. That will help you identify it, and maybe help me withstand it."

He looked up at Jocelyn, his expression expectant, and raised an eyebrow at the look on her face. "What?"

"Go again?" she repeated incredulously. "Are you mad? We're not doing that again. Not ever."

"Nonsense, Joss," said Kincaid briskly. "How can you make progress if we don't build on what we just learned?"

"He's right," said Elddreki placidly. "If we stop now, when you have finally released your power with real potency, we will be losing a valuable opportunity to identify the nature of the blockage I mentioned, which you seem to have burst through for a moment."

"No," said Jocelyn firmly, keeping her words few.

"But Joss—"

"I said no."

"I'm fine, Jocelyn, honestly," Kincaid pushed. "I don't mind you trying again on me. We might be right on the edge of figuring something out. I can handle it."

Jocelyn didn't respond, her mouth clamped firmly shut. She began to gather the remains of their meal, repacking them into the damaged rucksack lying nearby.

"Jocelyn, what are you doing?" Kincaid sounded uneasy. She remained silent, beginning to untie her horse from the branch of a nearby tree.

"Jocelyn, stop." Kincaid seized her arm, startling her with his nearness. "I know that look. Don't you dare clam up again."

She turned to look at him, fire in her eyes, but her mouth still uncompromisingly closed.

"You can't go back to bottling it all up, Joss," he said, his expression strangely fearful. "Not after how free you've been. You'll go mad, or I will."

"No more training."

She spoke clearly and distinctly, and she knew he understood the alternatives she was offering without the need for further explanation. Which was good, because she could feel her power swirling so unsteadily within her that even those three words felt like a risk.

Kincaid met her eyes for a long moment, his expression keen and searching, then he nodded. "All right. No more training."

Elddreki gave a small humph of resignation, but Jocelyn ignored him. She let out a long breath, her shoulders relaxing, and she instantly felt the power ebb away within her. Kincaid's expression softened.

"I pushed you too hard," he said gently. "I'm sorry."

"I told you it was a bad idea," she whispered, the anguish of her recent slip creeping into her voice.

Kincaid shook his head. "I'm not going to press you to try again, but I still don't think it was a bad idea. I really can handle it. I'm not afraid for you to take the risk on me."

"It's not just you who would suffer," said Jocelyn, still whispering. "You should have seen the way you looked at me." She stopped, taking a deep shuddering breath. "I've spent my whole life afraid that if I really let myself out, everyone I know, everyone I care about, would look at me just like that. I can't bear it if you—" She cut herself off, not wanting to look too closely at the depth of agony she had felt when Kincaid had pulled away from her.

Suddenly Kincaid's hand was on her face, compelling her to look up at him. His eyes were searching hers, filled with remorse and understanding. Without warning, he pulled her against him, and she pressed her face into his chest. One of his strong arms went around her, holding her firmly, making her feel safe and secure in a way she hadn't since childhood.

"I'm sorry, Jocelyn. I should have listened to you instead of pushing you to do something you weren't comfortable doing. I was trying to help you, but I can see I was wrong to push so hard." He pulled back, holding her by one shoulder as he again looked into her eyes. "I just wanted so much for you to figure out how to control it, so you could see you don't need to be afraid of it."

Jocelyn smiled half-heartedly. Even after what had just happened, Kincaid seemed determined to be blind. But nothing could have more clearly confirmed to Jocelyn that her power *was* something to be afraid of.

"It's all right," she said aloud. "I know you were trying to help."

And she did know it. She bore Kincaid no ill will for the inevitable disaster his training exercise had turned into. But she was determined to be firmer this time. She would not be trying to use her power on him again.

They rode in silence for an hour or two, Elddreki most unusually choosing to join them on the ground, even though they were cantering. He had to maintain a slow run to keep up with the horses, and he placed himself alongside Jocelyn's mare. She tried to tolerate his constant searching looks and experimental sniffs patiently. It was clear he was trying to figure her out while the moment was fresh, still reluctant to waste the opportunity afforded by her loss of control.

It had been only the day before that Jocelyn had told Kincaid about Eamon and Lucy, but already the landscape had changed significantly. It was beginning to look rugged again, but it had none of the menacing quality of the North Wilds.

The grass was mostly dry in the summer sun, the golden blanket punctuated here and there by patches of green grass or dense clumps of small trees, their leaves already brown, although autumn was far away. The ground was uneven, boulders protruding from the turf every so often. The ground sloped steadily upward, and to the north Jocelyn could see a line of low-lying mountains marching east to west, the golden-brown of their slopes giving way halfway up to streaks of white snow against gray rock, even in the summer. And in fact it was starting to feel less like summer, the air growing colder the further they traveled and the more elevated the ground became.

They were coming into the eastern district at last.

The afternoon was well-advanced when they slowed to a walk to get a better look at what was ahead. It didn't look like a town to Jocelyn, but there was clearly some kind of gathering going on. She squinted as they approached it, taking in the wooden stalls, rough material stretched over the tops for protection against the weather.

"It must be a market day!" said Kincaid brightly. "That's lucky. We need more food, and I've been thinking we should get traveling cloaks, just simple ones, before we go too much further east. It's going to be cold by the coast."

"Do you have any coins left?" asked Jocelyn skeptically.

"A couple that I saved for emergencies," said Kincaid, as cheerful as ever. "And now that it's getting colder, I think we can manage without the second water skin. That will get us a bit of food, at least."

They had turned toward the market, and Jocelyn suddenly remembered Elddreki. She looked over at the dragon quickly. "Should you—?"

But it was too late. The familiar sound of a startled cry told them someone had already spotted the dragon. Jocelyn sighed, bracing herself for the inevitable disbanding of the market, and the loss of any opportunity to buy supplies.

But the chaos never came. They were very close now, and they could hear the startled gasps and the cries of astonishment rising up on all sides. Everywhere Jocelyn looked, she saw faces full of shock, and quite a few showing terror as well. But no one was running, no one was hiding. People certainly drew nervously away from the creature, but when Elddreki halted a stone's throw from the market and sat back on his haunches, clearly intending to watch from there, people started to move again. Jocelyn had the distinct impression that there was no longer much trading happening, excited conversation and furtive glances having taken its place.

Kincaid had clearly noticed the restrained reaction as well, because he was looking about them with his eyebrows raised.

"We really are in the east," he muttered to himself as they

dismounted, tying their horses to a wooden bar set up for the purpose, right next to a watering trough.

For a little while they just wandered through the market, enjoying the break from the saddle. It was nice, Jocelyn reflected, stealing a glance up at Kincaid walking beside her. It was pleasant to be natural and unassuming, no fanfare and no titles. Just strolling along with this man she had somehow come to trust as implicitly as she trusted her own family, looking to any onlookers like a normal young couple here to explore the market.

Kincaid seemed to feel her gaze, and he looked down at her suddenly, smiling in a friendly way.

"It feels a bit different from the North Wilds, doesn't it?"

Jocelyn laughed. "Just a bit." It was an understatement. She felt no fear in this marketplace. The difference in tone from the towns in the North Wilds could not have been greater.

"A beautiful young woman like you could probably even wander around without having her hair stolen right off her head."

Kincaid spoke jokingly, but Jocelyn felt her cheeks flushing, and she looked down at the ground, trying to hide her pleasure.

"Why do you get that look whenever I say you're beautiful?" Kincaid asked. Jocelyn felt her color deepen, but there was no self-consciousness in Kincaid's voice. "You look surprised, but surely you can't be. You must know you're beautiful. I mean," he glanced around and lowered his voice, "you're a princess. It's not likely you'd go unnoticed. Surely people say you're beautiful all the time."

Jocelyn laughed awkwardly but didn't answer, embarrassed at being asked to admit such a thing.

"Well?" Kincaid pressed, raising his eyebrows. "Don't they?"

She rubbed self-consciously at the back of her neck. "Yes," she acknowledged at last. "People do say I'm beautiful. But..."

"But what?" Kincaid persisted when she trailed off.

Jocelyn laughed again at the ridiculous conversation. "But 'but'," she said. "It's not, 'the princess is beautiful'. It's, 'the princess is beautiful, *but*'. But she's sullen, but she's always sulking, but she has nothing to say for herself, but there's nothing in that pretty head."

Kincaid had stopped walking, his eyes narrowed, and Jocelyn came to a halt as well, looking at him questioningly.

"The Kyonan court sounds like it collectively needs a good hard slap," he said shortly. He glared at her for a moment, and she stared back, unsure how to respond to his irritation.

Then all of a sudden his expression softened, and he stepped forward, closing the distance between them. Jocelyn's heart seemed to sputter, then it picked up at double speed when he reached up and placed his thumb gently on her cheek, his hand curling around the back of her head.

"Let me correct the mistake," he said, his voice much too intense for the public setting. "You are not beautiful *but*—you're beautiful *and*. Beautiful and intelligent, beautiful and kind, beautiful and selfless, beautiful and witty."

Jocelyn swallowed, unable to find a single word. No one had ever looked at her the way Kincaid was looking at her now. She had not thought it possible that anyone would look at her that way if they knew her secret. But Kincaid knew, and it had never even bothered him.

"A gift for your pretty sweetheart?"

The merchant's wheedling voice cut in on their moment, reminding Jocelyn of their surroundings. She stepped back quickly, giving a nervous chuckle. Kincaid dropped his hand, looking with disfavor at the man, and the vibrant green scarf he was holding out winningly.

"That's all wrong for her," he said irritably. "It's much too strong a color." He turned to see Jocelyn raising an amused eyebrow at him. "What?"

She chuckled, shaking her head as she turned away. "I must meet this sister of yours."

"I would like you to."

Kincaid spoke lightly enough, but Jocelyn resolutely avoided looking at him as they struck back off into the markets. It was straying into dangerous waters to talk about the future with Kincaid. It was well and truly time to turn the conversation to less personal matters.

"I see your dress is torn, miss. Can I interest you in a lovely new gown?"

Jocelyn turned to look at the speaker, taking in the deep blue dress he was fanning out suggestively.

"No thank you," she said politely. To her relief, her power was barely a trickle.

"It's an unusual design, isn't it?" interjected Kincaid doubtfully. Jocelyn wondered if he was being diplomatic or was just out of his depth. In her opinion, the dress was hideously ugly.

"It may not be common in Bryford," said the merchant quickly, "but this fashion is very popular in Kyona. It's what all the girls wear in Kynton."

Kincaid shot a humorous look at Jocelyn.

"I'm from Kynton," she said, amused. "And that isn't."

"You're Kyonan?" the man asked, looking at her carefully.

"That's right. What of it?" Kincaid frowned as he spoke, obviously not impressed with the man's tone. But the merchant ignored him, his eyes still trained on Jocelyn.

"Are you a real Kyonan, or one of these freedmen?" He said the last word with a slight sneer, and Jocelyn's mouth fell open.

"I beg your pardon?" Her tone was dangerous, and she felt her power swirl inside her.

"I think you heard me," the man said coldly.

Kincaid took a half step forward, but Jocelyn stopped him with a hand, her eyes narrowed as they rested on the merchant.

"I don't know how to answer your question, *sir*," it was her turn to sneer, "because I don't know the difference between those two types of Kyonans."

She felt the power thrumming in her words, and the man's forehead creased slightly in confusion. She didn't wait for more, pushing back into the crowd. She could feel Kincaid close behind her, but she didn't look at him. She was breathing hard, her mind ablaze with indignation. So the prejudice really *had* spread to Valoria. She knew it had been irresponsible to use her power, but she found herself hoping savagely that the man spent the rest of the afternoon confused and disoriented.

When Kincaid caught up with her he looked like he wanted to speak, but she indicated with a shrug of her shoulder that she didn't wish to discuss the incident. She had been enjoying the cheerful atmosphere of the market, and she didn't want to taint the day with depressing talk. Obliging as always, Kincaid refrained from bringing it up.

Jocelyn had wondered hopefully if Elddreki's presence would make the locals inclined to give them a good deal, but it seemed that a merchant was a merchant, no matter what mythical impossibilities might be occurring. Any sensible trader would be able to tell they were travelers coming from some distance, and in sore need of the goods they were bargaining for.

It quickly became evident they wouldn't get as much food as Kincaid had hoped for the items they had to barter, and traveling cloaks were no longer a realistic option. Jocelyn frowned. This was absurd. Kincaid was too stubborn for his own good. They needed food, that much wasn't optional. And traveling cloaks would make the journey so much more comfortable. Kincaid had more or less said it himself—she wasn't just a pretty face, to be pandered to.

She became impatient with standing around waiting while Kincaid argued with a shrewd-faced man about the worth of the water skin. She wandered away, looking appraisingly at the various goods for sale.

"Kincaid," she said, wandering back over to him. "I think I saw some traveling cloaks further down. I'm going to go have a look."

"All right," he said vaguely, his attention still on his debate with the merchant. He was still distracted when she returned, and he failed to notice the bundle in her arms or the flush of triumph on her face.

"Come on," he grumbled, shooting a disgruntled look at the merchant. "That's as much as we'll get, so we may as well be on our way."

"Fine with me," Jocelyn agreed amicably. She shoved her burden into the saddlebags strapped onto her mare, giving Kincaid a bright smile as he held out his hands, ready to help throw her into the saddle.

"You're in a good mood," he observed, eyebrows raised.

She shrugged, a smile still tugging at her lips. "It's a beautiful day."

They rode for a few more hours, Elddreki finally giving up on examining Jocelyn and resuming his position in the sky. Kincaid's mood lifted as they rode away from the uncooperative marketplace, and he taught her a Valorian folk song, about a goatherd who dreamed of being king.

"Should we look for a place to stop?" Jocelyn asked, as the first streaks of orange began to appear in the sky. She didn't want to admit how weary she was, but she was surprised they were still riding. Kincaid usually suggested making camp much earlier, and the horses were clearly weary as well, after climbing the steadily ascending ground all day.

"Let's go just a bit further," her companion said. "I think we're almost there."

"Almost whe—oh!"

They had reached the crest of a small slope, and Jocelyn's eyes widened at the sight before her. The water was dark, almost black in the failing light, but it still sparkled invitingly, looking impossibly still and peaceful.

"What is it?"

"It's called Loch Arine," said Kincaid eagerly. "It's just like people describe it. I've never been here before, but I've always wanted to see it."

"Is it a lake?"

"Not exactly," he explained. "It looks like a lake, but it's actually an inlet. It's connected to the sea by an underground chasm." He pointed to the other side of the body of water, and Jocelyn saw a small town perched on the far bank. "The chasm runs under that town, there. Arinton." He grinned at Jocelyn. "Arinton is the heart of the eastern district. This is where you'll find your wyvern-believers."

"It's beautiful," said Jocelyn. As they descended the small slope and their vantage point changed, the water began to reflect the colorful streaks appearing in the sky.

"It is," Kincaid agreed cheerfully. "And even better, it means we're almost at the coast."

Jocelyn raised her eyebrows at him. "Since when are you in such a rush to get there? I thought you weren't expecting to find any truth to the wyvern legends."

"It's not that I'm in a rush to get there." Kincaid was silent for a moment, not quite meeting her eye. "Actually, I've been thinking about what you said. About me being irresponsible."

"Kincaid—"

"No, don't apologize," he interrupted quickly. "There was truth in it. I didn't give enough thought to my family, or my responsibility to them, when I left Bryford. I've already been away too long."

Jocelyn lowered her gaze, wishing she wasn't suddenly finding it so hard to breathe at the thought of Kincaid leaving. But of course he had a home, a family, a life back in Bryford, completely unconnected to their surreal and unsustainable wanderings across the countryside. The thought made her feel unutterably lonely.

"I'm not about to abandon you," he hastened to add, perhaps picking up on her mood. "I want to see the quest through. But I guess I'm thinking it's a good thing to be finally getting somewhere."

She nodded curtly, not trusting her voice. It was awful to think it had been her, in a moment of selfish anger, who had planted the seed in Kincaid's mind that would make him realize he should walk away.

"It's quite amazing, really," Kincaid was musing, his eyes unfocused, "how deeply your words took root. Even knowing the impact came from your power, I can't shake the thought."

Jocelyn shrugged miserably. "Change is like that, I think. It's powerful, and its ripples are not always predictable. You can't just undo it. I told you how powerful—and how dangerous—my words can be. But I don't think you ever really believed me."

Kincaid looked over at her, his expression surprised. "I don't mean it as a bad thing, Jocelyn. Was it a bad thing if you changed that merchant's mind about his prejudice against the freedmen? What you said about me was the same. It wasn't exactly comfortable to have you point it out, but it was something I needed to hear. It was a change that needed to happen inside me. I'm not sorry it did."

Jocelyn stared at him in amazement.

"What?" he asked.

She shook her head. "I wish I could embrace change as well as you do."

"You can," said Kincaid encouragingly. "You just need some practice." He gestured around. "For example, living in Valoria wouldn't be such a bad change, would it? I know you love Kyona, but that doesn't mean you can't like it here, too."

Jocelyn grinned. "If you're trying to trick me into saying—what was it?—'Valoria is a wonderful kingdom', you'll have to try a bit harder than that."

Kincaid chuckled. "I'll convince you yet."

"We'll see."

They made camp alongside the water, Elddreki landing softly beside them.

"I'm sorry the fare isn't better," said Kincaid regretfully, laying out some less-than-appetizing food. He grimaced. "And it's going to be cold tonight without cloaks."

"Well, perhaps I can help with that," said Jocelyn brightly, pulling the bundle from her saddlebags with a mischievous grin. She unrolled it onto the grass next to Kincaid, revealing a substantial array of food, a water skin to replace the one Kincaid had bartered, and two hardy cloaks.

"How did you—?" Kincaid's startled exclamation quickly gave way to a growl. He reached out with lightning speed to grip her arm, yanking the sleeve up to reveal her unadorned wrist. "Jocelyn, you didn't!" he cried, sounding genuinely distressed. "Why?"

"Because we needed the supplies," she said sternly. "And because you were being ridiculous." She considered the point. "And," she added, "because I wanted to win a round for once."

"You shouldn't have done that," Kincaid scolded. "It was totally unnecessary."

"No," Jocelyn corrected. "It was totally unnecessary for you to pay for everything."

"Jocelyn..." Kincaid hesitated, then grimaced. "I didn't want to say it, because it's not very becoming of me to boast about it, but my family is quite wealthy. It's really no problem for me to supply us with a bit of food."

Jocelyn gave him a look. "Yes, I'd figured that much out, thank you Kincaid. I'm not a complete imbecile. But your family's wealth is back in Bryford, and we needed food and traveling cloaks here, now."

Kincaid was silent for a moment, still frowning unhappily at her. "I wanted you to keep it."

"Why does it matter so much to you?" Jocelyn insisted. "It's not a big deal."

"I don't know, I just...I didn't want you to have to give it up. You're always trying to make a sacrifice of yourself."

Jocelyn rolled her eyes. "It was a bracelet, Kincaid. Are you going to keep complaining, or are you going to eat the food?"

"Well." Kincaid's smile was already creeping back as he eyed some dried meat. "If those are my only options..."

CHAPTER TWENTY-FOUR

Jocelyn's first thought on waking was that she was very glad to have purchased the traveling cloaks. Even with hers wrapped tightly around her, the chill of the morning air seemed to have seeped into her bones.

She sat up slowly, trying to shake off the fog of sleep. She couldn't remember anything distinct, but she was certain she had been dreaming of Princess Sarai. She sighed. She had enough troubles of her own, without borrowing any from the long-dead royal.

She glanced over at Kincaid, still deeply asleep on the other side of the circle created by Elddreki's body. He looked peaceful, but there was something about his posture, perhaps the way his hand rested on his sword next to him, that suggested that he would be ready to spring into action the moment he was roused.

His auburn hair had flopped over his forehead, partially covering one eye, and she resisted the temptation to smooth it back. He lay on top of his traveling cloak, one corner of it folded up over his legs, his lean but muscular arms exposed to the cold and, she admitted to herself, to her clandestine scrutiny. She turned away from him with a sigh. He was as devastatingly attractive—and as off limits to her—as ever.

Her gaze traveled out over Loch Arine, and she pushed up onto her knees, captivated by the beautiful sight. The water was a steely gray in the early morning, still and flat and impossibly deep. She hadn't noticed it the night before, but dense clumps of bushes grew close to the water in many places, laden with flowers of a deep yellow. The pleasant color stood out strongly against the slate of the water.

The loch was an elongated shape, stretching west to east. They were at its northwestern tip, and it was no great distance to the southern bank. But she thought it would take an hour or two to ride the length of the inlet to reach Arinton on the eastern tip.

And then, the sea.

She smiled at the thought. She had been to Kyona's coast on a number of occasions, including visiting the seaside towns where each of her parents had grown up. But she had a feeling the coastline in this cold and rugged eastern region would be wilder, more impressive.

She turned to glance at Elddreki and jumped dramatically. The dragon was still curled up in his usual sleeping position, but his eyes were wide open and fixed on her in unabashed observation.

"Elddreki!" hissed Jocelyn, putting a hand to her heart. "You startled me."

"How peculiar," said Elddreki. "I neither moved nor spoke."

Jocelyn disregarded the comment. "How long have you been watching me?" she asked accusingly.

"Quite some time," said Elddreki, his tone conversational. "Since before you awoke." He tilted his head to the side. "Is that unnerving?"

"Yes," said Jocelyn shortly. "And not very polite."

"But you were just watching Kincaid while he slept," Elddreki pointed out.

Jocelyn colored. The observation was so unanswerable she made no attempt to answer it.

"You have a curious look in your eyes when you watch him," mused Elddreki. Jocelyn squirmed in place, not at all pleased with the direction the conversation was taking. She chanced a glance at Kincaid, but fortunately he seemed to still be fast asleep.

"Something emanates from you when you interact with Kincaid, sometimes," Elddreki persisted. "Something that I sense from you often, in fact. It reminds me of your power, and yet it is not a natural part of your power, I think."

Jocelyn frowned. "Is it confusion?" she asked, remembering her previous characterization of her power.

"No," said Elddreki pensively. "It is not confusion."

Jocelyn had no further suggestions, and they fell silent. After a couple of minutes, Jocelyn grew used to Elddreki's unwavering scrutiny, and stopped feeling self-conscious.

"Do you remember when you showed us the story in the fire?" she asked suddenly, and the dragon tilted his head toward her. "When you told us about the dragon war?"

"Of course."

"You didn't just show us dragon history," she said. "You showed us glimpses of what was happening in Kyona. I even saw Uncle Jonan." She paused, but Elddreki remained silent. "Was that something you'd witnessed in the past? Or was it happening at the time you showed us?"

"At the time," Elddreki answered. "I projected images from my farsight."

"Farsight?" Jocelyn frowned. "What's that?"

"You are not familiar with it?" asked Elddreki. "I suppose,

then, it is not an aspect of dragon magic that was transferred to you."

"It's hard for me to comment on that," said Jocelyn dryly, "since I still have no idea what it is."

"Farsight is an ability common to all dragons," explained Elddreki. "We can see things from afar, follow events not within our physical range of sight."

"You mean," Jocelyn frowned, "you can see anything, anywhere?"

Elddreki chuckled. "It's not quite as open as that. Distance is relevant. Only the most powerful dragons can see what occurs across the sea, for example. And we don't see just anything. Over our lifetimes, we form connections with places, or in the case of a few of us, with people. It is much easier to use farsight on those places or people. And, to put it in simple terms, the more we cultivate those connections, the more we see. For example, I saw what your father's friend was doing in his forest home on that other occasion, because I have taken an interest in him since we met in the mountains. But I have followed your parents' lives much more closely, so should I choose to watch them, I can see more clearly."

"Is that how my father communicated with you, just after we crossed the border?" Jocelyn asked, fascinated.

"No," said Elddreki. "Farsight does not involve two-way communication. Your father is not aware of it when I watch him from afar. He used a different means of contacting me."

"You still don't intend to tell me what that is, do you?" Jocelyn asked, resigned.

"I do not."

There was a moment of silence. "So...so if you wanted to, could you see what my parents are doing right now?"

"Certainly."

Jocelyn shifted, opening her mouth and then closing it again.

"Do you wish me to?" Elddreki asked, watching her with a familiar lively interest in his eyes. "You have my magic in your blood—perhaps you could even share the vision."

Jocelyn turned to him, wide eyed. "Is that possible?"

Elddreki's scales rippled in a shrug. "Not that I am aware of, but I would have said the same about you before I met you."

She hesitated for a moment. Part of her wasn't sure she wanted to know how her parents were reacting to her disappearance, but she told herself that was cowardly. "Yes. I would like to try."

"Place your hand on my scales, near my core." The dragon shuffled forward until he was within her reach. He didn't get up, just shifted his limbs in what should have been an awkward wriggle. But somehow he made the movement graceful.

Jocelyn wasn't really sure what he meant by his core, but she reached a tentative hand toward the region of his heart. Despite the chill of the morning, his scales felt warm under her palm.

Immediately, her vision rippled and blurred. She shut her eyes, overwhelmed by the onslaught of familiar images. She could feel her body still seated on the hard ground, but her mind was no longer there. It was in her father's private suite, watching her mother approach, yawning at the early hour.

The king sat at an elegant writing desk by the window. The vista below him stretched south, toward the rest of the kingdom, and Jocelyn had often heard her mother describe it as his "thinking spot".

"And what are we thinking about now?" the queen said, as if echoing her far-off daughter's thoughts. She reached her husband, wrapping her arms around him from behind and resting her head on his shoulder. "Or, I'd hazard a guess, worrying more than thinking."

The king let out a long sigh, looking more vulnerable than Jocelyn had ever seen him as he leaned his head against his wife's. She felt a twinge of guilt at spying on her parents like this, but it was too fascinating an opportunity to pass up.

"I was worrying," he admitted. "About Jo, and the others. I don't think a diplomatic solution will be easy to find, somehow. There's something I'm missing, and until I can figure out where all this came from, I don't think I'll be able to resolve it. And you know the nature of these things. Every day it doesn't get fixed is a day it gets worse."

"I wish I had the answer," said the queen softly. "Are you worried Jo will do something reckless in response to the escalation?"

"Only if provoked," said the king dryly. "Which means, yes, I am worried."

"Oh, Cal." It was her mother's turn to sound vulnerable and lost, most unlike the strong and collected queen Jocelyn usually saw. "I thought we'd gotten past all this prejudice. We weathered it so well. So many people said you were too young, too inexperienced when the slaves came back, that you wouldn't be able to handle the inevitable upheaval. But I thought we'd proved them wrong."

"So did I," said Jocelyn's father heavily. "What does Constance say?"

The queen frowned thoughtfully at the mention of her older sister. "She doesn't understand where it's coming from any more than we do." She sighed. "She tries to hold it in when she's talking to me, but she's angry, Cal. I can tell. Jo isn't the only one who's in danger of being pushed over the edge into rash retaliation."

Jocelyn leaned forward unconsciously, as if she would be able to hear better that way. Retaliation for what? What was the latest escalation? Of course her parents didn't say, presumably both well aware of developments. It was maddening to be cut off, so far from the crisis looming in her own kingdom.

"Yes, well, people tend to become less reasonable when those they care about are threatened," said King Calinnae wearily. "And I have to say, I sympathize."

His wife shook her head, the hint of a smile on her face as she ran her thumb down the king's temple. "I thought you were wearing your worried father face, not your burdened king one. You were really thinking about Jocelyn, weren't you?"

The daughter in question started at the mention of her name, feeling more uncomfortable than ever to be listening unobserved. But she made no effort to pull away.

"Do you really think she's with Elddreki?" her father asked anxiously.

"If Elddreki said she is, I'm sure he was telling the truth," said the queen simply.

"I hope so," the king answered, sounding rueful. "It wouldn't be the first time he'd intentionally deceived me, would it?"

His wife shook her head. "This is different, Cal. He was testing you last time, and he revealed the truth almost immediately."

Jocelyn's father sighed. "I suppose that's true. It's not that I mistrust Elddreki's intentions...it's just always hard to know with dragons. Their purposes don't always align with ours." He drummed his fingers absently on the desk in front of him. "Do you think she's all right? Honestly, Elnora, twenty-three hours out of the day, I'm this close to just leaving our bickering populace to their own devices and riding to Valoria to find her. It terrifies me to think of her wandering the countryside somewhere."

"What about the other hour?" his wife quipped.

The king shrugged. "Even kings have to sleep sometime I

suppose. If I'd imagined for a second something like this would happen, I would never have let her go at all."

His wife sighed. "Actually, I think 'something like this' is exactly what you imagined, and is why you didn't want to let her go." She straightened, giving her husband's shoulders a reassuring squeeze. "I'm worried about her too, Cal, but it's hard to imagine her coming to any serious harm while she's under the protection of a dragon."

Jocelyn grimaced. Hopefully her parents never found out how loosely Elddreki had recognized that protection at the start of their journey.

A sharp knock at the door made Jocelyn turn her head, forgetting for a moment that she wasn't physically in the room with her parents. At the king's curt order, a page boy entered, looking apologetic.

"I have a message from the steward, Your Majesty. He says at least a dozen more people have sought audiences with you, claiming grievances against freedmen."

Jocelyn could only imagine the sinking in her father's heart at the prospect, but it didn't show on his face. He began to respond to the page's message, but another curt knock cut across his words.

The new arrival was an errand boy, one Jocelyn had seen running messages between the barracks and the castle on a number of occasions.

"I'm sorry to intrude, Your Majesty, but it's an urgent message from the captain of your guard. He's just received word of two more attacks."

"Where?" asked the king, standing up at once.

"One was a small skirmish in Pravat, no bloodshed, but the soldiers had to step in to break up the riot. The other was in Kerr. A group of freedmen were traveling through, and a fight broke out. They fought back, and there were deaths on both sides."

Jocelyn's father ran a hand through his hair, exchanging a look with his wife before he turned back to the errand boy. "Tell the captain I will see him immediately."

Jocelyn pulled her hand away from Elddreki's flank, not wishing to see any more. She was horrified at how much the problem seemed to have escalated in her absence, and a rush of anger passed over her at her own uselessness. If only her power was beneficial, like Eamon's, she could be there helping, instead of far away and no good to anyone. Even if she could just be without her power, then at least she could have stayed and contributed to the negotiations in the normal way.

"Did you see what you wanted to see?" the dragon asked placidly, not seeming to grasp the distressing nature of the information they had overheard.

"I wouldn't exactly say that," said Jocelyn. Her flare of anger had subsided, leaving her feeling cold and guilty for the worry she was bringing on her parents in the midst of all this chaos. She shook herself slightly, trying to remember her manners. "But thank you for sharing your sight with me. I don't think I would want to have that ability normally, but it was certainly fascinating."

"Why wouldn't you want it?" Elddreki asked curiously, but Jocelyn just shook her head. She didn't think she would be able to explain the complexities of her feelings regarding magical eavesdropping to the unemotional dragon.

Her companion accepted her refusal to answer without comment, and they sat for another minute in silence. Kincaid stirred, but didn't open his eyes, simply rolling onto his side and continuing to sleep.

"Elddreki?" Jocelyn's eyes were on the water, her thoughts

swirling around in her head, centered on the familiar theme of her power.

"Yes, Jocelyn?" The dragon's voice was calm, and his orb-like eyes didn't shift from her countenance.

"You said, didn't you, that dragons aren't taught how to forfeit your power, that you don't actually know how it's done?"

"I did say that," Elddreki acknowledged. "It is the truth."

There was another long moment of silence. Kincaid was still on his side, his back to Jocelyn, unmoving and silent.

"So you don't have any idea how it works? Not even a guess?"

Elddreki gave her a penetrating look. "Why would you ask me such a thing, Jocelyn?"

Jocelyn didn't answer immediately. The topic had been sitting uncomfortably in the back of her mind since her disastrous final session of training with Kincaid. His words the night before, when he confessed that her suggestion was still impacting him powerfully, had brought it more sharply to the front.

"When you spoke about the unicorns, and those other animals, it sounded to me like you were saying that only dragons should have magic. That anything else is unnatural."

She waited for Elddreki to confirm or deny her interpretation of his words, but he remained silent.

"But I have magic."

"Hm," said Elddreki, lifting his head and extending his neck toward her.

"Hm?"

"You have it now, swirling about you," explained the dragon.

Jocelyn frowned in confusion. "Magic, you mean?"

Elddreki shook his head slowly from side to side. "No, I am not speaking of your power. I am speaking of that quality I mentioned before, the one that emanates from you so often."

"Oh." Jocelyn wasn't sure how to respond. She tried to

examine herself, to identify what Elddreki was talking about. She felt hyped up, on edge about the question she wanted to ask.

"But you were saying something," Elddreki prompted her. "If I understood you correctly, you were saying you formed the impression it was unnatural for any creature but a dragon to have magic, and then you commented that you have magic."

"That's right," said Jocelyn, shifting nervously.

"What is the thought behind your words, Jocelyn?" asked Elddreki, patiently.

Jocelyn took a deep breath. "If it's unnatural for me to have power, if I was never supposed to have it..."

She trailed off, nervous about articulating her thought. Elddreki waited silently, as patient as ever, not prodding her to speak.

"I know it would be wrong for you to do it," she tried again. "But if I were to learn how to do it—if I were to forfeit my power—would it really be such an abomination?"

"Yes."

She knew without looking around that the answer hadn't come from Elddreki. The voice was too impassioned, the emotion too strong. Plus, she would know it anywhere.

She turned with a huff of annoyance. Kincaid had pushed himself to a sitting position, and he was frowning at her.

"Good morning to you, too," she said lightly, but Kincaid was not to be distracted.

"It would be the worst kind of abomination, Jocelyn, you know it would. How could you consider that, even for a moment?"

She glared back. "I wasn't asking you." She turned her attention back to Elddreki, her eyebrows raised in a question.

He regarded her in silence for a long moment before replying. "On this occasion, Jocelyn, Kincaid is right," he said at last.

Her shoulders slumped, disheartened but not surprised. She hadn't really expected Elddreki to condone the idea.

"But why? I shouldn't have the magic in the first place."

"So you have said, more than once," Elddreki said in his usual measured way. "But it is not clear to me how you have reached that conclusion." He tilted his head to the side, studying her carefully. "You were born with your power, Jocelyn. You didn't steal it, or even borrow it. It is part of you."

Jocelyn turned away, her throat tight. "So I will never be free of it," she said, her words little more than a whisper.

"No," Elddreki agreed calmly. "You will carry it to your grave. Whether it will continue beyond your lifetime—whether you will pass it to your offspring—I cannot predict. As I told you and Kincaid previously, that process seems to change depending on the creature."

Jocelyn turned quickly to face him, a startled gasp escaping her before she could stop it. She stared at him wildly, saying nothing. Her power might pass to her children? The thought had never even occurred to her, even during the earlier conversation around the fire. Would she taint Valoria's royal line if she married Prince Ormond? Was there no escape from this nightmare, even after she died?

"Intriguing," said Elddreki quietly, sniffing gently at Jocelyn's face, his snout now so close to her, his breath ruffled her hair. "That substance, whatever it is, is pouring from you in torrents now." After another moment of observation, the dragon pulled his head back slightly, his voice even.

"Discard the idea of forfeiting your power, Jocelyn. It is not an option you should even consider. And there is not a dragon in the world who would tell you how to do it, even if they knew." He glanced at his other human companion, who was still frowning at Jocelyn. "If you wish to remove yourself from the mastery you seem to feel your magic has over you, then you should follow Kincaid's advice and train with it, learn to control it." Elddreki cocked his head to the side, as if a thought had just occurred to him. "Or I suppose you could end your life. That is always an option for humans, is it not? You would just need to ensure you died childless."

"That is *not* a helpful suggestion, Elddreki," Kincaid snapped, angrier than Jocelyn had ever heard him with the dragon.

"Hm." Elddreki turned his head—and his discomfiting scrutiny—onto Kincaid for a moment. "You had it too just then. It doesn't hang about you the way it does about Jocelyn, but you had it for a moment, when you spoke."

"Had what?" Kincaid said harshly, still scowling.

"The quality that is not part of Jocelyn's power, but that entangles itself with her power almost every time she uses it," the dragon explained patiently. "I think it is the blockage that is preventing her from learning to control it."

Kincaid didn't respond. His eyes remained on Jocelyn, and he was clearly uninterested in Elddreki's theories. After a moment the dragon pushed himself fluidly to his feet, shaking out his wings in a sudden motion that almost knocked Jocelyn and Kincaid flat with the wind it created.

"I would be pleased to begin our travels for the day," he said cheerfully, as though Jocelyn wasn't close to tears and Kincaid wasn't glowering at her. "I confess, I am almost impatient. We are so close to the sea, and I have longed to see it these two hundred years or more."

Without waiting for a response, he ambled down toward the loch, leaving the two humans alone.

Jocelyn could feel Kincaid's eyes on her, and she could sense his continued displeasure, but she refused to meet his gaze. She kept her eyes on Elddreki, who had dipped his head into the water and was drinking deeply.

"What were you thinking, Jocelyn?"

Jocelyn frowned at Kincaid's tone. He had no right to dictate, or to criticize, her actions.

"My thoughts are my own business, Kincaid. That's why they're thoughts instead of words."

"Jocelyn." His hand shot out and grasped her arm, his grip uncomfortably tight. "Tell me you're not thinking about it."

Jocelyn turned to him, startled by the sudden movement. She met his gaze at last and saw something more than anger there. She didn't know whether to laugh or cry.

"Relax, Kincaid," she said dully. "I'm not going to take my own life. I would never do such a thing." He relaxed slightly, the fear in his eyes ebbing away, and Jocelyn felt her anger mounting. "Honestly, I'm offended you would think even for a moment that I might."

Kincaid let go of her, shrugging. "Is it so unreasonable for me to think it? You were apparently ready to forfeit your power."

"That's completely different," Jocelyn argued. She looked away from him again, her voice dropping to a mutter. "I still don't see why it would be so bad."

"Of course it would be bad!" Kincaid protested. "You'd be losing a part of yourself. A crucial, central, precious part."

"It's not precious to me," said Jocelyn stubbornly. "Think how much safer Kyona would be without it. And if that doesn't matter to you, think how much safer *Valoria* would be." Her voice cracked. "The Valorian royals don't even have the slightest idea of the danger I pose to them."

"Nonsense," said Kincaid briskly. "For such an intelligent person, you say some incredibly stupid things." Jocelyn scowled, but he pushed on, unrepentant. "Forget about it, Joss. If you claim you'd never end your life, then you shouldn't consider forfeiting your power. You heard Elddreki—the dragons who forfeited their power died."

"But they were dragons," said Jocelyn quickly. "They died because magic is their lifeblood—they can't and shouldn't survive without it. Whereas I shouldn't even have it. I would probably be fine if I forfeited mine," she added optimistically.

"Probably?" Kincaid was less impressed than ever. "That's quite a gamble to take with your life." His voice turned hard. "I would never let you do it, not in ten centuries."

Jocelyn raised an eyebrow. "Who says you could stop me? What would it have to do with you?"

"Jocelyn." The fear was back in Kincaid's eyes, but the determination was stronger. "I wouldn't care what I had to do, or how interfering you thought I was being. I wouldn't let you do it." He gave her a look. "Besides, who would you forfeit it to? Elddreki said it warps the receiver as well as the giver."

Jocelyn shrugged. "Maybe I'd give it to you, to punish you for being such a busybody." Kincaid just rolled his eyes, and her tone became more serious. "I thought if I gave it to a dragon, it might not warp anyone. Dragons are the ones who are supposed to have magic."

"Elddreki said it himself, Jocelyn," said Kincaid. "You didn't steal your magic. *You* are supposed to have it."

Jocelyn just shrugged again. "It doesn't matter anyway. I don't know how to do it, and you heard Elddreki. No dragon is going to teach me."

She turned to greet Elddreki, who was returning from the loch, and Kincaid let the matter drop. They packed up camp quickly, all of them eager to be on their way.

"So you're finally starting to experience impatience, Elddreki," Kincaid joked as he threw Jocelyn into the saddle. She was still avoiding his gaze. "You're almost human, in fact."

Elddreki smiled in detached acknowledgment of the absurdity of Kincaid's jest.

"Will it bother you to move at our pace all the way along the loch, though?" Kincaid asked, genuine curiosity in his voice. "Wouldn't you rather fly ahead and get to the sea more quickly?"

"Of course not," said Elddreki placidly. "You are my companions on this quest. It has always been my intention to stay with you as we travel."

"Except for when you sent Jocelyn into a dangerous town alone at night," muttered Kincaid, and Jocelyn rolled her eyes.

"Are you *never* going to let that go?" she shot at Kincaid, before turning to the dragon, who was ambling beside the trotting horses. She gave him a considering look. "But can't dragons fly extremely quickly? My father told me that when you came to his aid, the day he reclaimed the throne, you must have traveled from the mountains to Kynton in a matter of minutes."

"That is correct," said Elddreki comfortably. "We can fly at such a speed as to be almost invisible to humans, if we were to wish it."

"That's ironic," chuckled Kincaid, and even Jocelyn smiled at the contradiction.

"Why?" asked Elddreki.

"Well," Jocelyn started, then paused. If dragons were so wise, why were things that were so obvious to humans so confusing to Elddreki? "It's just humorous to us, I guess, that immortal dragons, who have all the time in the world, and are never in a hurry to do anything or get anywhere, can move at lightning speed if they choose. But humans, who according to you are always in a hurry, are restricted to a pretty slow pace, all things considered."

Elddreki cocked his head to one side, considering her words. "Yes," he said at last. "I can see the humor in that."

"If you can fly so fast you're barely visible," Kincaid cut in, "and if you can sense where dragons have been, couldn't you have done this quest yourself, any time you like? Why did you need Jocelyn's help? You could've flown all over Valoria in a matter of days, sniffing around for dragons. You could have completed the quest much more quickly."

Elddreki gave an indulgent chuckle, the sound guttural and strange. "Humans," he said to himself. "So wise at times, but so foolish."

The dragon fell silent, and it seemed he didn't intend to give any further answer. Jocelyn and Kincaid exchanged a long-suffering look, and the Valorian sighed.

"Why am I so foolish, Elddreki?" he prompted.

"Hm?" Elddreki looked over at him, his expression vague. "Oh. You are foolish because you assume the speed at which I complete my quest is somehow an indication of its success. I do not believe there is any particular link between the two features."

Jocelyn couldn't quite resist sending a smirk Kincaid's way. There was no denying it was satisfying when the dragon put the confident young Valorian in his place. But Elddreki's next words wiped the smile away instantly.

"If I had not waited, but had attempted the quest on my own, I would not have met Jocelyn, for example. And that would be a loss indeed. Her powers are fascinating, and my attempt to unlock their mystery has engrossed my mind quite as much as my own search. I could be mistaken, but I have the sense that she is instrumental, I could say crucial, to the heart of my quest. Perhaps it is because her power is change, but there is a flavor about her—as though her very existence might change everything."

Jocelyn looked up into the beast's eyes. She was unnerved, to say the least, by this calmly delivered assessment. It was no surprise to find the dragon staring at her unblinkingly. Her eyes slid involuntarily over to Kincaid. He was watching her with equal focus, his expression hard to read.

"I couldn't agree more," he said unexpectedly, his voice quiet and intense.

Jocelyn swallowed uncomfortably, tearing her gaze from his with an effort. "The two of you sound like superstitious old housewives," she said lightly. Neither of her companions responded, and she could still feel both pairs of eyes trained on her.

"If we want to get to Arinton this week, we'd better pick up the pace." This time she didn't wait for a reply, just spurred her horse forward into a canter.

For several hours, they rode in silence along the loch, Elddreki remaining on the ground with them. The ground sloped up, and soon they were riding some distance above the water's edge. A rocky cliff dropped down on their right into the water below, the yellow flowers somehow clinging onto life in its cracks. On the far bank, Jocelyn could see that the ground sloped more gently down to the edge of the loch, covered with summer grass and the occasional patch of dense vegetation. The sky was clear, and the climbing sun made the water sparkle and dance, steely gray turning to a deep, mesmerizing blue. It reminded Jocelyn of the royal color of Kyona, strong and timeless and comforting.

The further they traveled, the more clearly they could see the town of Arinton, growing as they approached it. Its gray stone buildings were perched right on the water's edge, at the base of a small hill that rose gently up to hide the sea Jocelyn knew would be found beyond. It was picturesque, the foliage growing more thickly around it, with trees right up to the water's edge. Sound carried through the still air, and they could hear the happy noises of village life well before they reached the first stone house.

"What are you thinking?"

Kincaid's quiet voice startled Jocelyn. She had slowed to a trot as the town grew close, but she hadn't realized Kincaid had drawn his horse so close alongside hers. She turned to see him looking at her, his earlier look of intensity gone, and the normal friendly smile in his eyes.

She smiled back. "I was thinking it's beautiful." She swept out an arm, encompassing the loch, the countryside, and the town. "All of it."

Kincaid's eyes crinkled with his grin. "Is that a confession? Have I fulfilled my promise?"

She chuckled. "Not quite. Some beautiful countryside, friendly markets, and a picturesque town on an unusual deep sea inlet don't make Valoria a wonderful kingdom."

"Whew." Kincaid's face fell comically. "It takes a lot to impress you, clearly."

"Of course," she said archly. "And don't think I've forgotten the North Wilds."

"I don't know," said Kincaid. His words were light, but some of the intensity was back in his eyes, and Jocelyn felt suddenly wary. "Not all of the North Wilds was bad. I was very taken with Dragoncave, myself."

His eyes were still on her, and with annoyance Jocelyn felt her face heating. Her skin felt the ghost of a memory, her arms pressed against his side, her head cushioned on his shoulder.

"You *must* be somehow changing my nature," said Elddreki brightly, making Jocelyn jump. The dragon had appeared on her other side, in his usual impossibly stealthy way. "Not only did I feel a flicker of impatience this morning, but now I almost feel excitement."

His eyes were trained on the town ahead, and following his gaze, Jocelyn saw tiny forms racing between buildings. She had been distracted by the conversation with Kincaid, but she realized now that startled cries were carrying across the clear day. The dragon had obviously been spotted.

"It is entertaining," Elddreki commented. "The humans we

encounter always react so strongly to my presence. No one seems surprised to see you, Jocelyn, but if they only knew it, you are much more rare than I am."

Jocelyn squirmed uncomfortably, conscious of Kincaid's eyes still on her. "So you're excited to see the sea, Elddreki?" she tried.

"Not just the sea," Elddreki corrected. "Also the dragons."

"So you really think we'll find dragons here?" Kincaid asked curiously. "I mean, it was just a hunch, wasn't it?"

"It is no longer just a hunch," said Elddreki. "I think we are very likely to find dragons. When I drank from the loch this morning, I could detect a lingering taste of their magic. Whether that is simply because they once visited this place, or because the water of the loch connects to the sea where they are still to be found, remains to be seen."

It took Elddreki a moment to realize that both humans were staring at him. He tilted his head questioningly.

"You sensed dragon magic at the loch?" Kincaid asked. "Why didn't you tell us?"

"What do you mean?" asked Elddreki. "I just did tell you."

Jocelyn smiled, shaking her head slightly at Kincaid. She was becoming less and less surprised by the dragon's peculiar ways.

But Kincaid wasn't looking at her or at the dragon, his eyes directed ahead and a faint crease on his forehead. He suddenly reached over and put his hand on her mare's rein, pulling both horses to a stop. Following his gaze, she saw why.

The companions had almost reached Arinton, and word of the dragon's approach had clearly spread rapidly. This time there was no running, no hiding. A group of grim-faced towns-folk had assembled, forming an organized guard, their arms folded and their eyes on Elddreki. The message was clear without the need for words.

The way was barred.

CHAPTER TWENTY-FIVE

Kincaid drew his horse even closer to Jocelyn's, his hand still on her reins.

"It's fine, Kincaid," she whispered, and he shot her a sharp look. She nodded toward the townspeople. "No weapons. Look."

He followed her gaze, and his grip slackened as he seemed to realize she was right. Whether it was because they didn't have bows and arrows, or because they understood the invulnerability of dragons better than the residents of Thalia had, the people of Arinton were making no attempt to defend their town with force. They simply stood, silent and expectant, watching Elddreki with unwavering focus.

A glance at Elddreki showed him sitting back on his haunches, his head angled ever so slightly to the side as he took in the human barrier in front of him. Suddenly a ripple seemed to pass through the crowd. The clump of people parted, and a middle-aged man with short grizzled hair and a thick beard strode through. He had clearly hurried to get there, but his steps were stately and confident.

He reached the front of the crowd and bowed low. Elddreki,

to whom the gesture was clearly directed, acknowledged the bow with a gracious nod of his head.

"Mighty Dragon," the man said, his voice deep and pleasant. "We are honored at your presence. We hope you come to us in peace."

"I do," said Elddreki solemnly.

The man straightened from the bow, and there was a collective release in tension from the group. Some of them uncrossed their arms, and a few pairs of eyes flicked curiously toward Kincaid and Jocelyn before returning quickly to the dragon. Jocelyn thought Kincaid seemed ill-at-ease, fidgeting a little on his horse and shooting surreptitious looks at her, although she couldn't imagine why. Honestly, he was almost as overprotective as her father sometimes. It was as clear as day these people meant them no harm.

"Then you are very welcome, Sire," the man was continuing.

"Thank you," said Elddreki with great dignity.

The humor of the situation suddenly struck Jocelyn, and she raised a hand quickly to her face to stifle a giggle. Kincaid looked at her, raising an inquiring eyebrow.

"He's just very regal, isn't he?" she whispered, tilting her head toward Elddreki. "It's so much like my father being received in some outlying town in Kyona."

He chuckled. "Welcome to the eastern district. Anything mythical is royalty."

She raised an eyebrow. "You're still saying it mockingly. You do realize you're here with a dragon, right? The easterners are at the very least right about him being real."

Kincaid just grimaced, his eyes scanning the crowd, still not looking entirely comfortable.

"I apologize that you have not been more properly received," the spokesman was saying. "A message has been sent to the manor, but the lord who oversees these lands is most unfortunately in Bryford at present. I am the mayor," the man bowed low again, "and I am honored to make you welcome in his lordship's absence. It will take a matter of days for a messenger to reach and recall his lordship, but..."

"This is ridiculous," Kincaid muttered. "We're not interested in pomp and ceremony. We just want to find the dragons."

Jocelyn shot him a quelling look. Kincaid might think it was stupid, but she understood the importance of respecting the customs of these people. No one would benefit from them alienating the locals.

"It is not necessary to summon the lord of the manor," Elddreki was responding calmly. "My companions and I do not intend to stay long on your lands."

The mayor's eyes flicked to Kincaid and Jocelyn, curiosity behind his measured speech. "Of course. We would be honored to assist you—and your companions—in any way within our power."

Elddreki turned to the two of them, seeming to invite them to speak. Jocelyn cleared her throat and urged her horse forward a couple of steps.

"Thank you for your welcome, sir. Are you well versed in the history of these parts?"

He gave a slight bow. "I am indeed, ma'am."

She nodded. "We would be grateful to have speech with you. We wish to know more of your legends about the great sea beasts, the wyverns."

A ripple of excitement passed through the townsfolk. Jocelyn remembered how the mountain people could sense magic, and for a moment she wondered uneasily whether the group was responding to her power rather than her words. But the word "wyvern" was spreading out in increasingly audible whispers. She felt rather than heard Kincaid's sigh, but she ignored him.

"I would be delighted to oblige you, dragon companion," said the mayor. "Allow us first to provide you with food, and accommodation. You must be weary after your travels, and we would be honored to host you as our guests for as long as you wish to stay."

"Thank you, Sir Mayor, but that will not be necessary," interjected Kincaid unexpectedly. "We do not wish to linger. We must be on our way. If you will kindly consent to answer our questions, that will be more than sufficient hospitality."

Jocelyn shot him a look of surprise. She had been inclined to accept the offer. The idea of freshening up was very appealing after so long sleeping in the open. She had been careful not to complain, wanting to live up to Kincaid's early description of her as a remarkable princess. But her time in Valoria had certainly given her a deep appreciation for her luxurious suite in the castle at Kynton.

"As you wish," said the mayor with another partial bow. He glanced up at Elddreki, clearly trying to assess the practicalities. "We do not have a building suitable for the purpose here in Arinton, but if you will accompany me to our central courtyard, I will endeavor to answer your questions." He nodded to some of the townspeople. "If you will dismount, your horses will be cared for while we speak."

Jocelyn slid from her mare immediately. She raised an eyebrow at Kincaid, still in the saddle, and after a moment's hesitation, he followed her to the ground. She shook her head at him. Was he really in such a hurry to ride on? It was clear he didn't much like Arinton, but she had rarely been more taken with a place. The horses were led away, and Elddreki moved to stand immediately behind his human companions, his vast shadow falling over them.

At a gesture from the mayor, a clean and well-dressed young man stepped forward and offered his arm to Jocelyn.

"I would be honored to escort you, ma'am," he said, smiling personably at her.

Kincaid shifted slightly on Jocelyn's other side, his scowl visible even in her peripherals. She ignored him, smiling up at the local. He was dark-haired and broad-shouldered, and quite handsome, she thought.

"Thank you," she said softly, accepting the offered arm. She supposed it was primarily due to her connection with Elddreki, but she still felt a prickle of satisfaction to think she was considered worthy of such courtesy, even when no one knew she was royalty.

The mayor turned, and the crowd parted for him. The travelers followed as he made his way up the broad dirt street, Elddreki bringing up the rear, with a gaggle of curious onlookers trailing well behind.

"Did I detect an accent when you spoke before?" Jocelyn's escort asked her in a friendly way. "Are you from Kyona?"

She smiled up at him. He was tall, and she had to angle her head. "Yes, I am."

"How exciting," he said enthusiastically. "I would like to go there someday. My name is Eric," he volunteered. "The mayor is my father. What's your name?"

Jocelyn hesitated, not wanting to lie about her name, but concerned someone might guess who she was, now they knew she was Kyonan. Perhaps news of the visiting Kyonan princess had spread this far east.

"I'm Joss," she compromised. She saw Kincaid's slight twitch, but she resolutely ignored him.

"Welcome to Valoria, Joss," said Eric brightly. He was looking at her in open admiration, and her spirits got another lift.

"Thank you."

"She hasn't just arrived in Valoria," said Kincaid shortly. "It's a bit late to welcome her."

Jocelyn shot him a reproving look, but he showed no sign of repentance.

"Well, welcome to Arinton, then," said Eric easily. "It must be incredible to travel with a dragon!"

Jocelyn smiled encouragingly, keeping her words to herself just in case, but quite happy to listen to him talk. He didn't seem in the least deterred by her silence, continuing a stream of friendly chatter all the way through the town. She looked around as they walked, admiring the picturesque nature of Arinton.

The stone buildings looked like they had been there for centuries, and the steadily rising slope meant that any time she glanced back, she was rewarded with a spectacular view of Loch Arine. The water stretched westward, back the way they had come, and she was struck again with the beauty of the countryside out this way. Arinton was clearly a contented place. Faces were light, and even the presence of a dragon seemed to have inspired more excitement than fear.

"You'd be very welcome here, even without your dragon companion, you know," Eric was saying. He gave her a rueful smile. "The truth is, most Valorians are a little suspicious of us easterners. They think we're foolish, believing in wyverns and such. So we don't get a lot of visitors, especially not pretty young ones."

Kincaid grunted, but Jocelyn had no intention of letting him dampen her moment. Eric was smiling winningly down at her, and she looked up with a grin.

"You're flattering me."

She felt a flicker of power, and for a moment Eric looked confused, but then he shook his head, and the expression cleared. "No I'm not," he said earnestly. "Not at all." His smile was more gallant than ever, his tone just the right level of light playfulness to be appropriate to their slight acquaintance. "I think you're the prettiest visitor we've ever had."

Jocelyn felt herself warming to the young man. He was clearly not weak-minded, in any event.

Kincaid wasn't having the same reaction, judging by his derisive snort. Eric turned toward him, frowning for the first time.

"That's not very chivalrous," he scolded, apparently under the impression that Kincaid was disputing his conclusion. "If you can't be civil to a lady, you should keep your thoughts to yourself."

Kincaid opened his mouth, looking outraged, but Jocelyn cut him off with a grin. "That's right, Kincaid. Try to be civil." She gave him a pointed look, and he subsided, although he still looked mutinous.

They had reached Arinton's central square by this time, and Jocelyn ignored both men in order to admire it. It was larger than she had expected, and very well situated. The steeply sloping path up which they had just walked ran out from the square in a direct line, affording an excellent view of the water below. A large fountain stood in the middle of the square, water spewing from the mouth of a stone creature that looked like a cross between a dragon and an enormous eel. A wyvern, Jocelyn could only imagine. People had clearly scurried ahead of them, and chairs had been set up next to the fountain.

Eric gallantly showed Jocelyn to a chair, then sat down next to her, leaving Kincaid standing by a chair on his other side. Kincaid stood for a moment, looking far from impressed, then pointedly walked around to Jocelyn's other side, drawing up an empty chair next to her. She rolled her eyes at him, but didn't comment. She had to keep reminding herself not to speak now they were back in civilization. She had gotten too used to the freedom, traveling through the wilderness with only Elddreki and Kincaid for company.

The air was chilly, even though the sun was shining, and she drew her traveling cloak close around her.

"You're cold," said Eric quickly. "And no wonder, with only that thin cloak." He clucked his tongue. "And your sleeve is ripped, as well! I hope there wasn't an accident."

Jocelyn hesitated, not wanting to launch into a story that would require excessive speech.

"She was shot with an arrow," said Kincaid shortly. "In the North Wilds. They were aiming at our dragon friend." His eyes strayed to Elddreki as he spoke. The dragon was sitting on his haunches, facing the semi-circle of chairs as if he was preparing to be examined.

"You took her to the North Wilds?" Eric sounded horrified, and Kincaid's look of irritation deepened.

"*I* didn't take her there—"

But Eric wasn't listening to him, his attention back on Jocelyn, his expression still horrified. "And you were shot with an arrow?"

"I'm fine," she said quickly, then clamped her mouth shut at the small swirl of power.

"Well, I can help with the cold, anyway," said Eric, pushing himself to his feet. "I'll be right back."

"Is he going to stick to us like bog stench the entire time we're here?" grumbled Kincaid, as soon as Eric was out of earshot.

"Be nice," Jocelyn scolded. "He said the mayor is his father. I'm sure he's been assigned to entertain us while we're in town."

"Us?" said Kincaid dryly, and Jocelyn grinned.

"Well, no. Me, most likely." She shrugged cheerfully. "Men usually have to fend for themselves, don't they? It's just ladies who get escorts." She shot him a cheeky grin. "Particularly the pretty young ones, apparently."

Kincaid snorted again. "I didn't think you were so susceptible to flattery."

Jocelyn frowned at his condescending tone. "Why do you have to be such a spoilsport, Kincaid?" she demanded. "There's no harm in Eric. Is it really news to you that girls like being told they're pretty? You said it yourself at the market—everyone who's ever told me I'm beautiful only said it because I'm a princess. Can you blame me for wanting to know what impression I make when no one knows who I am?"

"That's not at all what I said!" Kincaid protested, but Eric chose that moment to return with a thick blanket, and Jocelyn didn't respond. Kincaid made no attempt to continue the argument in the presence of the local man, just watched with a disgruntled expression while Eric solicitously wrapped the blanket around Jocelyn's shoulders.

Kincaid's tunic was as light and thin as Jocelyn's dress, but for some reason Eric hadn't brought a blanket for him.

"Visitors." The mayor's clear voice called their attention to him. It seemed whatever important people had to be included in this event had been gathered. "You are most welcome to Arinton."

Jocelyn inclined her head graciously as the mayor looked over at them. With a small sigh, Kincaid gave a curt nod. He was still fidgeting uncomfortably.

The mayor's eyes settled on Jocelyn. "You said you wished to know more of our legends about the wyverns."

Jocelyn nodded, feeling nervous. She was still on edge from the altercation with Kincaid, and she was painfully aware of the power inside her, clamoring for release.

"What is it you wish to know?" the mayor prodded.

Jocelyn hesitated, not trusting herself to speak. She cast an appealing glance at Kincaid, and saw that he was watching her, his arms crossed and his expression grim. As the silence stretched out, he raised his eyebrows expectantly. She widened her eyes in a silent entreaty, asking for his help. It was clear he understood her, but his expression remained unyielding.

She looked around the square and saw that every eye was on her. Eric smiled encouragingly, perhaps thinking she was nervous to address such a crowd, but she didn't return the gesture. She felt panic rising inside her, and with it an increase in the potency of her unreleased power. In desperation, she met Elddreki's eyes, hoping he wasn't as stubborn as Kincaid.

The dragon tilted his head to the side, holding her gaze for a long moment. Then, with a barely perceptible nod, he came to her rescue.

"What is the origin of the legend?"

At Elddreki's words, the attention of the mayor, and everyone else in the square, transferred to the dragon. Jocelyn breathed a sigh of relief. She could feel Kincaid's disapproval, but she refused to look at him.

"Our ancestors saw wyverns from the very time of Arinton's settlement," the mayor said simply, in answer to Elddreki's question. "They have been seen but rarely in recent times, but we do not doubt their continued presence in the waters surrounding the islands."

"You speak of Wyvern Islands?" Elddreki asked, clearly remembering Kincaid's explanation of the eastern legends. "You believe the wyverns to dwell in the ocean?"

"Indeed, Mighty Dragon," said the mayor, inclining his head. "Although, according to our oldest records, Arinton's early inhabitants caught glimpses of them in the loch on occasion. They were believed to have traveled through the underground channel that connects Loch Arine to the sea."

"Hm." Elddreki's gaze strayed to the fountain in the middle of the square, and Jocelyn's followed. "Is that effigy intended as a depiction of a wyvern?" the dragon asked.

"It is, Sire," acknowledged the mayor. "Although the beasts have never been seen with sufficient clarity to be sure of its accuracy. They are usually spotted from a distance."

"That's not what my ma says," called a voice from the crowd, unexpectedly. The mayor frowned at the speaker, a young boy, but didn't contradict him.

"It is true that one of our residents claimed to have a sighting less than a year ago. She was on a boat on the loch, and she said a wyvern broke the water only a stone's throw from her. The only part of it to emerge was its head." The mayor hesitated. "Apparently the beast spoke to her."

The mayor spoke mildly, but for all his insistence that wyverns were real, Jocelyn could tell he wasn't entirely convinced this woman had told the truth.

"And what did the creature say?" Elddreki asked curiously.

The mayor hesitated again, and the boy hastened to fill the gap. "The wyvern offered me ma long life and great power! It said it could grant her greatest wish!"

"Hm," said Elddreki again. Glancing at Kincaid, Jocelyn saw him roll his eyes, and she had to agree. It sounded like a tall tale to her, too.

"And what did your mother say?" Kincaid interjected dryly.

The boy transferred his attention to Kincaid before answering. "She didn't say nothin' as such," he said proudly. "She screamed loud as she could an' paddled for shore." He grinned as he spoke, clearly delighted at being the center of attention.

"I'm sure," said Kincaid flatly. He looked around. "Can we ask her more about what she saw? Where is she?"

"Nah, she's gone," said the boy matter-of-factly, and Jocelyn gasped.

"She died?" She had spoken before she could stop herself, and she winced slightly at the burst of power. She was sure

Kincaid felt it too. She could feel his eyes on her, and she pulled Eric's blanket tighter around herself.

"What?" said the boy, startled. "Course she didn't die. At least," his expression became alarmed. "I don't think she did." He brought his gaze back up to Jocelyn with an effort. "I just meant she left Arinton for a bit. Thought people outside Arinton would have to believe about the wyverns once one had come so close. There are them who'll pay handsomely to hear from someone who's actually spoken with a wyvern." He frowned, still looking unsettled as he muttered to himself. "But we haven't heard from her in a while."

Jocelyn opened her mouth, then closed it again, miserable. It was clear she had planted the idea of his mother's death in the poor child's mind, but she knew trying to fix it would just make it worse.

"Yes, well, thank you Alec," said the mayor repressively. He turned to Elddreki again, reclaiming control of the conversation. "I know of no other legends of wyverns speaking to humans, but the sightings are well recorded. The rest of Valoria might scorn us for it—" Jocelyn noticed Eric directing a less than friendly look toward Kincaid, who shifted uncomfortably in his seat. "But no one in Arinton doubts they are out there," the mayor finished.

Elddreki was silent for a moment, pondering, and the whole square seemed to hold its breath. "Can you sense magic from the beasts?" he asked at last.

"Sense...magic?" the mayor repeated, sounding confused. "I don't know...that is, there are certainly signs of their presence. Like the impenetrable waters surrounding the islands. Regardless of wind or current, no vessel can get within two leagues of the rocks."

Elddreki's eyes strayed to Jocelyn and Kincaid, and she nodded in silent agreement. If the wyverns *were* dragons, it seemed Valoria's eastern people did not share the ability of Kyona's mountain people. They might be staunch believers, but it was more a matter of tradition than experience. They couldn't actually sense the dragons' power. Jocelyn let out a breath she hadn't realized she'd been holding. No one was likely to notice her power, then.

Elddreki pushed himself fluidly to his feet, and the onlookers drew back in a synchronized movement. The dragon walked a few paces toward the fountain, twisting his neck this way and that in order to examine the statue from every angle.

"Hm," he said again, sitting back on his haunches. "It does look similar enough to be credible." He turned his gaze unexpectedly on his human companions. "What do you think?"

Jocelyn shrugged one shoulder, not wanting to speak again. Kincaid frowned at her, then followed Elddreki's example and studied the statue for a moment.

"It's possible," he said curtly.

"What's possible?" asked the mayor, bewildered.

"I am searching for my lost kin," answered Elddreki placidly. "We suspect the wyverns you speak of may actually be a colony of dragons. We have come to this place in order to investigate."

There was a moment of stunned silence, then whispered conversations broke out all throughout the square.

"Impossible," said one man gruffly. "Preposterous."

Jocelyn hid a smile. She had anticipated that the locals would not like the suggestion that their legends were wrong, even if it meant a colony of dragons lived on their doorstep.

"Perhaps," said Elddreki calmly, his unblinking gaze trained on the speaker. "We will find out soon enough. We will travel to the islands and see for ourselves."

A frenzy of excited conversation broke out in response to this pronouncement, and Jocelyn found her attention being claimed by Eric.

"Is it true?" he asked eagerly. "Do you really think there might be dragons on Wyvern Islands?"

Jocelyn just shrugged, smiling in a friendly way at his enthusiasm.

"And you're going to try to go there?" Eric added, a look of concern creasing his forehead for a moment. "It's very dangerous. No one ever gets through. Aren't you worried you'll be drowned?"

Jocelyn just smiled again, giving a very pointed look in Elddreki's direction. Eric seemed to understand her point—she was quite adept at non-verbal communication after all—but Kincaid was apparently unsatisfied.

"What was that, sorry, *Joss*?" he asked blandly. "I didn't quite catch what you said."

Jocelyn and Eric both turned and glared at him, albeit for different reasons.

"Don't worry, Joss," said Eric. "I don't like speaking in front of crowds either." He clearly thought Kincaid was mocking her for her earlier unwillingness to address the group. Eric smiled. "My father is a natural, being the mayor and all, but I don't like the sound of my own voice quite as much as some people."

"That's hard to believe," muttered Kincaid, but they both ignored him.

"There's nothing wrong with not having a lot to say all the time," Eric pushed on, smiling kindly at Jocelyn. "I like that you're quiet and reserved, instead of chattering away constantly. It makes you graceful, and dignified."

Jocelyn kept her head down, not trusting herself to respond. She knew Eric meant well, but she didn't find this compliment quite as flattering as his previous ones. She tried not to look at Kincaid, but her eyes were drawn to his face without her permission. His gaze slid from Eric to her, his eyes blazing.

She looked away quickly. He had always had a way of making her feel exposed.

"Well," Eric was saying, "if you really are going to attempt to reach the islands tomorrow, you'll need a good night's rest. My father has had them prepare the best rooms for you at the inn, and I'd be very happy to show you—"

"No," interrupted Kincaid, not very politely. "We already told you, we're just passing through. We don't need lodgings for the night."

"Thank you," contradicted Jocelyn over the top of him, her attention on Eric. "I would be grateful." The local man turned a look on Kincaid that was undeniably smug, then bowed himself off to check the rooms were ready for them.

"Eric is right," said Jocelyn shortly, after he had disappeared from sight. "You could learn to be a little more chivalrous."

"I thought we were all in a hurry to—"

"I'm not talking about that," Jocelyn cut him off. "I'm talking about earlier. You knew I was asking for your help, and you refused to speak for me."

Kincaid was silent for a moment, his penetrating gaze on her face. "It's not helping you if I speak for you, Jocelyn," he said at last. "I don't want to take away your voice. I don't believe that's helping anyone."

"Tell that to the boy who'll now lie awake all night worrying his mother is dead," said Jocelyn dully.

"That wasn't your fault," said Kincaid, with his usual stubbornness. "If his mother is too busy running around like a traveling minstrel, trying to make a few coins off her sensational story, to send word home to her family that she's in one piece—"

"Enough, Kincaid," said Jocelyn wearily. "The more you try to blame everyone else, the more I'm going to blame myself. Haven't you figured that out by now?"

Kincaid was silent again. "Jocelyn," he said finally. "I know your power scares you. And I know nothing I say will change that. But the solution isn't for you to silence yourself forever, to pretend to be the demure, reserved, delicate little flower people like Eric admire." Jocelyn rolled her eyes at the way Kincaid said the other man's name, like it was an insult. "The solution is to—"

"Don't tell me to train, to practice," Jocelyn interrupted, wearier than ever. "We tried that, remember? And it didn't end well. I hurt you, like I knew I would."

"No you didn't," said Kincaid firmly, but Jocelyn wasn't to be deterred.

"Then I hurt myself." She turned away, not wanting him to see her face. "What I said to you is the reason you're in such a hurry to get to the islands, so you can finish the quest and leave. Even people who aren't afraid of my power will inevitably be driven away by it."

"Jocelyn." Kincaid said her name like a caress, and it was almost unbearable. She kept her face resolutely averted. "Jocelyn, I'm not in a hurry to leave you. Surely you know that. Surely you know—"

"The rooms are all ready." Eric's cheerful voice cut across the building intensity of the moment, and Jocelyn turned toward him with relief.

"Thank you."

Kincaid said nothing, looking anything but thankful for the interruption.

"Let me show you to your rooms," said Eric brightly. "My home is right next to the inn, so if you need anything at all, I would be happy to help."

"I bet you would," muttered Kincaid, looking at the young man with disfavor. He transferred his gaze to Jocelyn, and she could tell he was going to argue the issue of lodgings further.

"Kincaid." She laid a hand on his arm, and his muscles

jumped slightly under her touch. She met his eyes. "I'm tired. I want to rest."

His expression softened, and after a moment of hesitation, he gave a small nod.

"Thank you," she breathed, the words barely audible. It was true—she felt unutterably weary all of a sudden. The square was still abuzz with activity, a number of people looking like they were trying to work up the courage to approach Elddreki, but she allowed Eric to lead her away. She felt like she could sleep for two days.

Kincaid was apparently not as tired as she was, because he made no move to follow them. She couldn't resist sneaking a glance back at him, and was not surprised that he was watching her as well, that same look of blazing intensity on his face. Their eyes met, and she could have sworn she could read their message without the need for words.

She might have claimed he was in a hurry to leave, but once again, she was the one walking away.

CHAPTER TWENTY-SIX

The next day dawned clear but cold, and not just because Jocelyn was up before the sun. It wasn't that she had any cause for complaint. Her room had been comfortable, her bed luxurious after traveling rough. But she had slept poorly nonetheless.

She had a niggling feeling it had less to do with the furniture than the absence of a certain Valorian's steady breathing and reassuring presence. She shuddered at the thought of what any member of her family would say if they could read her mind in that moment. But it wasn't just Kincaid, she reasoned with herself. She had also felt the absence of Elddreki, the dragon's steady flow of magic as familiar a part of her sleep now as the warmth that seemed to permanently emanate from his scaled hide.

Whatever the cause, the fact remained. Somehow, despite the thick blankets and the homelike furnishings, the room at the inn had felt cold and unwelcoming by comparison. And as soon as the first streaks of light became visible on the eastern horizon, Jocelyn was packed and ready to go. She let herself out of her room, making her way quietly down to the inn's dining parlor.

She had expected the room to be empty, so she was surprised to see Kincaid there, as if waiting for her.

"Good morning," he said brightly, leaping to his feet. "You're ready early."

"Not as early as you, apparently," she said, raising an eyebrow.

Kincaid just shrugged, his expression cheerful. "I didn't sleep very well, to be honest."

"Me neither," said Jocelyn with a sigh. She grinned. "I guess we're just too used to sleeping rough."

"Yes," said Kincaid amicably. "Maybe that's it."

They hurried through a simple breakfast, Kincaid maintaining a light flow of cheerful conversation. Perhaps he was trying to make up for his surliness at their previous meal, the evening before. He had been less than impressed to discover that the room prepared for him was as far as possible from Jocelyn's, and had muttered all kinds of unfounded insinuations about Eric's intentions. Jocelyn, who doubted Eric had even had any say in the location of their rooms, had retired to bed early, sick of his griping.

The inn was situated just off the town square, and the first thing Jocelyn saw upon emerging from the building was Elddreki's massive form, curled up around one side of the fountain in his habitual sleeping posture.

The second was Eric, hovering not far from the entrance.

Jocelyn could feel Kincaid's cheerfulness instantly evaporate, and she sighed. She had nothing against the mayor's son, but she had a feeling the sooner they were rid of him, the more pleasant their journey would be.

"Joss," Eric greeted, with his usual smile. He gave Kincaid a nod. "I didn't expect to see you up and about so early."

"And yet, you're here," said Kincaid, his face deadpan.

Eric shrugged. "I'm an early riser." He took in their traveling cloaks, and the packs slung over their shoulders, and his face fell slightly. "You're not leaving already, are you?"

Jocelyn opened her mouth to reply, but Kincaid cut her off. "Yes, immediately. We've already delayed too long, and we need to be on our way."

"I thought you were refusing to speak for me," Jocelyn muttered, quietly enough that Eric couldn't hear. A slight twitch of the lips was the only indication that Kincaid could. "My friend here is in a hurry to return to his home in Bryford," she said at a normal volume, ignoring Kincaid's sudden frown.

"He's going to leave you with just the dragon?" asked Eric, startled.

"Of course not," snapped Kincaid. "I'm not going anywhere until our search is complete."

"Oh," said Eric, his eyes still on Jocelyn. "So will you go to Bryford as well, once you've found the answers you're looking for?"

"Uh..." Jocelyn hesitated, exchanging a look with Kincaid. He looked as off balance as she felt at being suddenly asked to comment on their future beyond the quest. Not *their* future, she scolded herself. Just *the* future.

"You'd be welcome to return as a guest to Arinton," said Eric quickly. "For as long as you like."

"Thank you," said Jocelyn hastily. "But I'm expected in Bryford." Power leaked out with the words, but she judged that speaking was a smaller risk than letting Kincaid say whatever he had been going to say in response to Eric's offer.

"Well," said Eric, "my father wanted to speak with you before you leave." He looked dubiously at Elddreki, still fast asleep. "Should we wake your...other companion?"

"Kincaid can wake him," said Jocelyn firmly.

She could sense Kincaid wasn't thrilled about being sent out of earshot, but she refused to meet his eye, and after a moment he strode off.

The truth was she needed a minute. Somehow she had not fully grasped before now the significance of the fact that both she and Kincaid were ultimately bound for Bryford. But Eric's casual question had turned her thoughts to the future in a new way. And she wasn't sure how to deal with the realization that if she married Prince Ormond, Kincaid would be living right there, in the city where she and her husband would get married, raise their children, grow old.

They could hardly avoid ever seeing each other, in passing at the very least. Would she feel his disapproving eyes on her at every public function, as she swallowed the Jocelyn he had come to know and kept her words inside so as to protect her new kingdom? He had said his family was wealthy. Were they influential enough to interact personally with the royals? Would the two of them be forced to meet publicly, obliged to pretend they were nothing to each other, perhaps that they didn't even know each other?

She watched Kincaid's confident form as he approached the sleeping dragon. Was the same thought occurring to him?

"I'm sorry you're leaving so soon." Eric's friendly voice cut across her thoughts, and she turned gratefully toward him, glad of the distraction. "You haven't had time to really appreciate the east yet."

Jocelyn smiled vaguely, and as usual he seemed to need no other encouragement to keep talking.

"But now Arinton is attracting more foreign visitors, maybe my father will be more open to the idea of me traveling. You never know, I might look you up in Kyona one day."

"More foreign visitors?" Jocelyn repeated, distracted. "I thought you said I was the only one."

"No one as pleasant as you," said Eric quickly, the swirl of power that left her having an unhelpful effect. "It's impressive to come all the way from the South Lands, of course, but I'd much rather host you." He smiled, a little flirtatiously, but Jocelyn frowned.

"Who came from the South Lands?"

"No one of importance," said Eric hastily, the seed Jocelyn had unintentionally planted clearly continuing to grow. "Some man, no one who holds a candle to you."

Jocelyn restrained a sigh, frustrated. As well as being dangerous, her power could sometimes be very counterproductive. Eric was so fixated on the idea of reassuring her as to her appeal, that any question she asked would probably lead to the same answer.

She abandoned the topic, but she felt dissatisfied. It struck her as odd that someone would come all the way from the South Lands to visit this remote spot. And was she jumping to conclusions to think that if Eric was responding to her power, it must mean she had changed his mind about the content of what he said? Had he previously thought the visitor *was* someone of importance, and was only reevaluating that now, when his head was filled with the pleasant pastime of flirting with a pretty stranger?

She shook off the thought. There was no point speculating. If Kincaid wasn't still talking to Elddreki, he would be able to probe deeper into the question. But then, she reflected with some irritation, he would probably refuse to do it, claiming it would be taking away her voice.

"...must be an anxious time for you, being from Kyona and all," Eric was saying when she tuned back in. "I hope Valoria can be a haven for you."

Jocelyn blinked, confused. Why was it an anxious time?

"I'm talking about all the problems these freedmen are causing," Eric explained, seeing her blank look. "It's such a pity." He frowned. "And I was quite surprised when I heard about it, actu ally. I wouldn't have thought they would be seeking to cause trouble, after so many years of peaceful living. If I didn't know for certain they're the ones in the wrong, I would think they'd been misrepresented."

Jocelyn stared, her mouth hanging open in unladylike shock. News of the freedmen—*prejudice* against the freedmen—had spread even to this remote corner of Valoria? She could hardly believe it. And what possible reason could Eric have for thinking he knew *for certain* that the freedmen were in the wrong?

She was still trying to decide whether it was worth risking speech in order to dig deeper when they were interrupted, and the moment was lost.

"All right, let's get this over with."

Jocelyn turned to see Kincaid, Elddreki now towering behind him. Kincaid looked faintly disgruntled as he spoke, but his expression changed instantly when he took in the look on her face.

Eric started to lead them toward the other side of the square, but Kincaid fell back a step, holding Jocelyn back with a hand on her arm.

"What is it?" he asked quickly. "Did he say something impertinent to you?"

"What? No, of course not," said Jocelyn, impatient of Kincaid's sour attitude toward Eric. "But he said something troubling." She recounted Eric's comments about the freedmen as they walked, and Kincaid's frown grew.

"That is strange," he agreed. "But likely he's just sharing the same prejudice we've come across before." His eyes flicked forward to Eric's back. "He's just the kind of person to claim he knows better than everyone what's true and what isn't."

Jocelyn frowned. She didn't see any benefit in pressing the point, but she was fairly certain it wasn't just Eric who was affected by prejudice. By her estimation, Eric didn't seem at all that kind of person. And he had seemed regretful about his poor opinion of the freedmen. He must have some external source for his belief.

But there was no further opportunity to ask Eric for clarification, even if she had been willing. The mayor's farewell was formal and drawn out, and by the time they were released, the sun had well and truly risen. They were sent off with three times the provisions they had come with, and their horses had been well fed and re-shod.

"It pays to travel with a dragon, apparently," Jocelyn whispered to Kincaid as some friendly townspeople loaded the supplies into their saddlebags.

Kincaid grunted. "If only the people at that market had responded this way, you could have kept your bracelet."

"For goodness' sake, Kincaid," hissed Jocelyn, exasperated. "Enough about the stupid bracelet."

They didn't mount their horses immediately, opting to walk through the town on foot. Someone helpfully led the horses along ahead of them while they walked toward the far edge of Arinton, which sat atop the hill. Gulls squawked overhead, and the salty smell of the ocean increased as they climbed. Jocelyn felt her excitement mounting, and each time she glanced at Elddreki, his gaze was trained unblinkingly ahead. She tried to imagine waiting two hundred years to see something, and could only admire his restraint.

They collected an unofficial honor guard as they went, children running alongside them, and a number of adults following, looking almost as eager. They had nearly reached the top of the street, and the far end of the town, when Eric came jogging up, out of breath.

"There you are!" he said, smiling at Jocelyn. "I got held up, and I was worried I would miss you." He gave her a wistful look. "I wish I could come with you, but my father won't hear of it. I'd love to see your reaction to Basal Headlands. They're beautiful, and unlike anywhere else you'll ever see, I imagine."

Kincaid was eyeing the young man with disfavor, clearly unimpressed with the very idea of him following them out of Arinton.

"What are Basal Headlands?" Jocelyn asked quickly, forestalling any rudeness.

"It's the rock formation on the coast, directly across from Wyvern Islands," explained Eric eagerly. "The rocks form these columns in all different heights. They sort of rise up in mounds, and you can walk across them. It's a bit like walking through a stone honeycomb. I used to play on them as a child, but it's quite dangerous. It can be very slippery when the waves crash over them."

"Sounds fun," said Jocelyn amicably.

"It's beautiful," said Eric. "And very rare. There's no formation like it anywhere else in Valoria, at least. Legends say wyverns weren't always confined to the water, but they used to be able to sun themselves on land, like seals. It was said the pattern in the rocks was caused by wyvern tracks when they first left the mainlands to reach the islands." He flashed her a grin. "But I guess we all know that's just an old wives' tale, really."

Kincaid raised an eyebrow. "Huh. So you people don't just believe every fool legend you hear, after all?"

Jocelyn frowned at him, and Eric's normally friendly countenance was darkened by a scowl. They had reached the edge of town, almost at the crest of the hill, and they had all stopped walking.

"I suppose it's what I would expect from a Bryford boy, but you're pretty skeptical for someone who's traveling with an actual dragon."

Kincaid narrowed his eyes. Jocelyn suspected he was more offended by being labeled a "boy" than any of the rest of it, but she didn't give him a chance to retaliate. Clearly she couldn't leave it to him to make the appropriate speeches of farewell. She would have to risk the words.

"Thank you," she said, offering her hand to Eric. "For making us so welcome, and taking such good care of us while we were here."

She felt power swirling gently out from her, and for a moment Eric's forehead creased as if in calculation.

"I don't feel I made you nearly welcome enough," he said slowly. He took her offered hand, and Kincaid shifted beside her. Eric ignored him, looking deeply into Jocelyn's eyes for a moment, still seeming slightly confused, then pressed his lips against the back of her hand. It was a normal, perfectly respectful gesture of farewell, but Jocelyn could feel the tension radiating off Kincaid in waves as Eric's lips lingered just a moment longer than necessary.

Jocelyn felt her cheeks go slightly pink as Eric again met her eyes, still a little dazed from the unintentional effect of her power.

"Perhaps I could see you as far as—" he began, but Kincaid had apparently heard enough.

"No thanks, that's not necessary," he said brusquely. "We'll be fine."

He reached over and grasped Jocelyn's hand, pulling it from Eric's grip, where it was still resting. He continued to clasp it tightly as he pulled her up the hill toward their horses. Kincaid seemed as full of nervous energy as Jocelyn felt, and they were almost running by the time they reached their mounts.

If Jocelyn's cheeks had been pink before, they must be crimson now. Kincaid was still holding her hand, and it wasn't the way she and Lucy had held hands as children. His strong, capable fingers were intertwined with hers. The slight tingle she had felt in the spot where Eric had kissed her was instantly eclipsed by the heat exploding in every point where their hands were touching. In fact, it took her about three seconds to forget Eric even existed.

Kincaid threw her into the saddle with more enthusiasm than usual, and she let out a sudden laugh. She felt like a princess in a story, being spirited away by a handsome knight from a fearsome beast, or perhaps a tyrannical father. Kincaid raised his eyebrows questioningly, but she didn't articulate the thought.

She was glad to be back in the saddle, and her heart felt light as they urged their horses forward. A moment before they crested the hill, Jocelyn felt both her hair and her skirts whip violently around her as a sudden rush of mighty wind told her Elddreki had just taken to the skies.

She was looking up at his vast reptilian form, circling above them, when they reached the top of the hill. A moment later, she brought her gaze down, and sucked in an involuntary breath.

The sea.

It was as beautiful as she had known it would be. Stretching east as far as the eye could see, the rising sun sparkling on the endless expanse. Perhaps the dragon magic that was inexplicably woven into her makeup gave her a share in the beasts' longing for the ocean, because she could feel its call as surely as Elddreki had. Her heart sang at the sight before her, and she laughed aloud for no other reason than sheer joy.

Just as she had guessed, the shoreline here was rugged and wild, no less beautiful than it was treacherous. Cliffs stretched along toward the north, but immediately in front of them the ground sloped steeply down to the rock formation Eric had mentioned. The waves crashed against the strange stone columns rather than hurling themselves at the cliffs, and Jocelyn could see that Basal Headlands was indeed a slippery and dangerous patch of ground.

But Eric was right. It was also unique, breathtaking in its natural beauty. Jocelyn had no difficulty imagining how legends of magic would grow up around this place. Looking further out, she saw the shape of Wyvern Islands, looming on the horizon, jagged and unapproachable. Were there dragons waiting for them there? Would Elddreki find the dragonlings he sought? Would these dragons maybe even have the answers Jocelyn so desperately wanted regarding her own power?

As she gazed at the islands, Jocelyn felt a strange tingling sensation, one she couldn't immediately identify. Was it magic? No, she realized with surprise. It was belonging. It was something she had never expected to feel for any place outside her beloved Kyona, but it was unmistakably there. Perhaps it was because she now knew for certain the power within her was dragon magic, but Jocelyn felt an inexplicable connection with the place.

She spurred her horse down the hill, toward Basal Headlands. She could sense Kincaid close behind, but she didn't wait for him. In minutes she reached the bottom of the slope, and she threw herself from the saddle. She scrambled up onto the rock columns, her heart as light as a child's as she skipped from surface to surface.

"Careful!" called Kincaid, a laugh in his voice. She turned to look at him, laughing as well.

"It's beautiful!"

"It is," he agreed, smiling in amusement. "You look like you belong here."

A shadow passing overhead made them both look up, and a moment later Elddreki had landed beside them, perched precariously on the uneven surface.

"Well?" Jocelyn demanded, grinning up at the dragon. "What do you think of the sea?"

Elddreki drew a deep breath before answering, his eyes closed and his expression serene.

"Transcendent," he said simply, and Jocelyn and Kincaid exchanged grins. A joyful mood seemed to have gripped them all. "Are you ready to travel to the islands?" Elddreki asked, and Jocelyn nodded, her expression solemn but her eyes still dancing.

"Will you carry me there?" she asked. "Like you carried me over the river? You did say you would like to take me on a true flight sometime."

Elddreki smiled. "I did indeed. I would be glad to carry you across the ocean, Jocelyn, daughter of kings." He turned to Kincaid. "I will come back for you, Kincaid, and carry you across the water also, if you wish it."

"Hang on," said Kincaid quickly. "Maybe I'd better go first. We don't know what we'll find over there."

"Which is precisely why we're going over there to explore," said Jocelyn lightly.

"Yes, I know that," Kincaid said, impatient. "I just don't like the idea of you going first. The whole area is supposed to be treacherous and impassable, remember? What if you can't get through? And even if you do make it to the islands, Elddreki would have to leave you there, alone, in order to come back for me."

"True," said Jocelyn, her expression cheeky. "But if you went first, you'd have to leave me here, alone. Eric might come looking for me and spirit me away to keep house for him and raise his wyvern-believing, eastern children."

Kincaid shot her a look, unimpressed, but she just grinned at him.

"The decision is not in your hands, Kincaid," said Elddreki placidly. "I did not offer to take you first."

"That's put you in your place," chuckled Jocelyn, still inexplicably gleeful. "You don't have to stand around waiting for us. You can take the horses back to Arinton while we're gone. It was unnecessary to bring them on such a short trip."

Kincaid didn't look happy, but he didn't argue the point further. He stepped back to watch, his arms folded and his forehead slightly creased. Jocelyn chuckled at his expression, then tripped lightly up to him, skipping over the honeycomb-like rock.

"Aren't you going to take your leave of me?" she asked brightly. "In case I'm swallowed by the ocean, or eaten by the wyverns, and never return?"

Kincaid didn't look like he found her joke very funny, but she swept him her best court curtsy anyway. She extended her hand as she rose, as she had done to Eric, but more formally.

Kincaid uncrossed his arms and took it as if by instinct, holding it lightly for a moment, his eyes burning into hers. Then he bowed over it as magnificently as any of her father's courtiers had ever done, and pressed his lips to her skin. The touch was light, but he lingered even longer than Eric had, and when he finally raised his head and their eyes again locked, Jocelyn felt strangely breathless.

"Be safe," he said, his voice low and intense.

She turned quickly away, shaking off the sudden tension of the moment, and leaped lightly onto the top of a nearby mound. She balanced on the highest column, her arms spread like wings and her face turned toward the distant islands.

"I'm ready, Elddreki," she said cheerfully. "I want to fly."

Whatever she had claimed, she wasn't entirely ready for the suddenness with which the dragon responded. Before she even realized he had moved, Elddreki's talons had curled around her shoulders and she was lifting into the air.

"Careful of her injured arm!"

Kincaid's shout was already faint, lost on the wind. Jocelyn knew it wasn't a good idea, but she looked down anyway. Kincaid was barely visible, an ant on the intricate stone pattern of Basal Headlands. The rock formation was beautiful from a bird's eye view, but it didn't hold her attention for long.

Her eyes were drawn irresistibly eastward, toward the rocky shapes protruding from the water, looming larger by the second.

Wyvern Islands at last.

CHAPTER TWENTY-SEVEN

Elddreki traveled over the water at an impossible speed. Jocelyn's stomach seemed to have gone missing, but she wasn't sure if that was because of the flight or because of her nerves about reaching the islands. The sensation was as exhilarating as it was terrifying, the water flying past below them more quickly than any river had ever run, and the islands approaching at a breathtaking rate. She felt secure, clasped firmly in Elddreki's talons, but it was still unnerving the way her legs dangled beneath her, with nothing between her feet and the ocean surface, far far below.

Within minutes, she could see the rocky slopes of the closest island, details starting to emerge. She suddenly felt a surge of power, seeming to emanate from the very air around her. She drew in a sharp breath, but the sensation was as brief as it was intense, and there was no check in Elddreki's flight. Testing the air around her, Jocelyn realized it hummed with power, similar to the Kyonan mountains.

Her excitement grew. Had they just passed through the magic barrier that kept humans from approaching the dragons' realm? She knew a moment of concern for Kincaid. He wasn't weirdly magical like she was. Would he be able to pass through it unscathed?

Elddreki had almost reached the island toward which they had been flying, but he suddenly swerved to the right, making for a different one, further south. Jocelyn focused her mind for a moment, and she thought she understood why. The power she felt in the air was not emanating from the first island. Elddreki was following its trail.

She barely had time to note that the new island was the largest she could see when Elddreki's mighty back feet touched land. He released her, and she stumbled forward a step, rolling her shoulders. They had landed on a large plateau, halfway up a barren rocky slope.

"I can feel it," she said eagerly to her dragon companion. "There are dragons here!"

"Indeed," Elddreki responded mildly.

His eyes were not on her, and the subsequent rush of wind told Jocelyn why. She followed his gaze to see two dragons alighting, only feet from them. She swallowed hard and stumbled backward, stopping only when she felt her back hit Elddreki's warm, solid scales.

For a long moment no one spoke. The dragons watched the newcomers unblinkingly, their expressions impossible to read. Although they were intimidating enough, Jocelyn noticed they were both smaller than Elddreki, presumably making him the oldest present. It must be a strange experience for him, she realized. One was close to him in size, but the other was noticeably smaller, with scales of a bright yellow-orange.

Finally the larger of the two spoke, his eyes trained on Elddreki. Jocelyn realized he must be speaking in dragon-tongue, because the sounds were incomprehensible to her. Elddreki responded, and the gaze of all three dragons flicked to Jocelyn. She resisted the urge to tug nervously at her skirts.

"Very well," said the first dragon, inclining his head. "We will speak in the language of men, for the sake of your companion."

There was a moment of silence before Jocelyn realized the creatures were all still looking at her, expectantly.

"Thank you," she squeaked out, and the attention returned to Elddreki.

"Who are you?" asked the smaller dragon, curiously, and something about her voice told Jocelyn she was female. "We have never had a dragon from outside visit this realm."

"And we have certainly never had a human within our lands," said the other dragon, disapproval clear in his voice. Jocelyn drew closer to Elddreki, and was reassured by the pulse of magic he projected over her. The female dragon watched her, tilting her head, and Jocelyn was sure she had sensed the interaction.

"I am Elddreki," Elddreki said. "I am a dragon of Vasilisa, and I have come in search of your colony. Many years have I wondered whether those who left Vasilisa long ago might be found by one willing to leave the mountains to search for them. And my companion is Jocelyn."

"If you come in peace, we will not turn one of our kind away," said the male dragon, inclining his head. "But you take a liberty bringing a human here."

"I am aware," responded Elddreki. "But she is my companion on this quest, she and another. They have assisted me in my search. She is a daughter of the kings of Kyona. There is a friendship spanning many generations between Vasilisa and her royal house."

"Indeed?" The dragon showed the first hint of interest in Jocelyn. "Our elders have seen something of this from afar, I believe." He gave her a penetrating look. "Are you the princess of Kyona who has married the Valorian prince, and seeks our presence across the land?"

"No," said Jocelyn, stunned. "I think you mean Princess Sarai. She was the sister of my distant father, but she passed to her ancestors generations ago."

"Ah," said the dragon, losing interest. "I forget how quickly human generations pass."

"But there is something unusual about you," interjected the younger dragon, curiously. "Especially when you speak. You have a signature of your own, not unlike that of Elddreki." She gave Jocelyn a long sniff. "Yes, a strong signature."

"The human has magic?" demanded the male dragon, drawing back in evident horror. "Is it as we feared? Is she—"

"Peace," interrupted the female. "She is no abomination." She sniffed at Jocelyn again. "She is something...entirely new."

The larger dragon frowned at Jocelyn, apparently still suspicious, but he seemed to accept the truth of his companion's words.

"She is indeed something new," Elddreki said. "She was born with her power, and she understands its origins no more than you do. We have examined it on our journey, and I believe she possesses the power of change."

"Change," mused the yellow dragon. "Yes, I believe you are right. What a noble and fearsome power."

Jocelyn just blinked, completely taken aback at this characterization of her magic.

"You said you have another human companion," said the male dragon. "Where is this other?"

"He is back on the mainland, awaiting my return. If you will permit, I will bring him here to join us."

The dragon frowned thoughtfully. "Is he also a member of the royal house with which Vasilisa claims friendship?"

"No," acknowledged Elddreki. "But he is of noble bearing."

Jocelyn waited, holding her breath.

"Of course you must bring him," the younger dragon said brightly. "I will stay with this young maiden while you are gone."

Again, the other dragon didn't look altogether pleased, but he didn't protest. Elddreki met Jocelyn's eyes for a brief moment, then, with his usual startling rapidity, launched into the air. Within moments he was out of sight.

Jocelyn turned to the two remaining dragons, swallowing nervously. They were both watching her unblinkingly.

"I am Raqisa," said the female dragon in a friendly way. She leaned down and once again inhaled deeply. "I have never met a human before. You are most fascinating, Jocelyn."

Jocelyn hesitated, unsure how to respond to this declaration. Should she say thank you again?

"How did you come to be part of Elddreki's quest?" Raqisa pushed on.

"He rendered my father a service, before I was born," Jocelyn answered. "My father promised to assist Elddreki in return, and I joined his quest in order to fulfill that promise."

Both dragons nodded, apparently accepting the explanation as normal.

"And how did you come to carry the power of change?" Raqisa asked.

Jocelyn hesitated. "That's harder to answer," she said. "I don't know. I was born with it, but I have always known it wasn't natural. I thought the power was confusion until Elddreki identified it as change." She shrugged. "Elddreki thinks I was born with it because both of my parents entered the Dragon Realm in their youth, and Elddreki even used his magic to heal my mother of a near-fatal injury."

"How interesting," said Raqisa. "So it is rare then for humans to enter the other Dragon Realm, the one in which Vasilisa is situated?"

"Very rare," Jocelyn confirmed. "When my parents, and their

friend, entered it about twenty years ago, it was the first time anyone had done so in centuries."

"I wonder then what the impact will be of you entering our Dragon Realm," said Raqisa thoughtfully. Jocelyn cringed. The last thing she needed was for her power to increase.

She was saved the necessity of responding, because Raqisa seemed as inquisitive as Elddreki, and she wasted no time in asking more questions.

"How did you find us?"

"We visited a place in Valoria's west," Jocelyn answered, glancing out across the water. How long would it take Elddreki to retrieve Kincaid? Would they pass through the barrier safely? "It's near the Kyonan mountains, where Vasilisa is, and the locals call it Dragoncave. Elddreki suspected the dragons who left Vasilisa all those centuries ago might have passed through there, and he was right. We sensed their lingering magic, and we found dragon runes pointing to the sea. So we followed the legends here."

"You can sense dragon magic?" the older dragon asked suspiciously.

Jocelyn nodded. "That's not because of my power though, or not just because of it. Even Kincaid—our other companion— can sense it a little. We both have mountain blood in us." She looked at the dragons appraisingly. "If you're both younger than Elddreki, I suppose you weren't born yet when the dragons left the mountains."

"That's right," said Raqisa brightly. "We were both born here." She cocked her head to the side. "How did you know we were younger? Our size or our color?"

"Color?" repeated Jocelyn, confused. "Your color changes when you get older?"

"It darkens," Raqisa explained. "We all start bright, but we get darker as we age. Our elders are so dark they're almost black."

A sudden rushing sound drew everyone's attention, and Jocelyn looked eagerly toward the sea. The familiar shape of Elddreki looked strange and lopsided, burdened as he was with the human form dangling below him. A moment later they alighted, and Jocelyn drew an unconscious breath of relief.

Kincaid looked extremely windswept, his eyes slightly wider than usual, and Jocelyn remembered it was the first time he had been carried by the dragon. But he didn't miss a beat, stumbling toward her the moment his feet touched the ground and putting out a hand to touch her shoulder, as if reassuring himself that she was in one piece.

"I'm all right," she said quietly. "You?"

He nodded, his gaze flicking to the two unfamiliar dragons who were silently watching this exchange.

"Greetings," Kincaid said, his voice impressively even. "I am Kincaid."

"Welcome, Kincaid," said Raqisa, her eyes flicking between the two humans curiously. "I am Raqisa. Now you are all present, I think we should take you further in, and bring this matter before our elders."

"Raqisa," said the other dragon warningly.

Raqisa flicked her tail impatiently. A chunk of rock the size of Jocelyn's torso broke off at the impact, crashing down the cliff face into the ocean far below.

"I'm not suggesting we take the humans into the heart of the realm, obviously. Just the outer circle. They can wait for Elddreki there." She smiled at Elddreki. "He will wish to meet with our elders, I am sure."

"I would be honored to do so," said Elddreki gravely.

"Then let us be off." Raqisa lunged with the paradoxical swiftness of dragonkind, seizing Jocelyn by the shoulders before she knew what was happening. Her breath left her in a rush, and she was conscious of a startled cry from Kincaid. But her attention was fully captured by the sight below her, as Raqisa bore her upward, scaling the rocky mountainside within seconds.

When they reached the top, Jocelyn let out an involuntary gasp. From the outside the island had looked like a mountain of barren rock, but once they reached the summit, a whole new landscape was revealed. The rocky slope she had seen formed only the outer ring, within which a green and pleasant haven was found. Jocelyn could see an inner circle, deeper toward the center of the mountain. She saw with fascination that the ring of rock encasing this inner circle seemed to be covered with crystals, the pale cylinders sprouting from the slope at frequent intervals, glinting in the sunlight. But Raqisa descended rapidly before she could get more than a glimpse.

Jocelyn found her feet hitting soft grass this time, and a moment later Elddreki landed beside her, bearing the other human. Kincaid was at her side within moments of being released, his face tight and annoyed.

"I wish everyone would stop doing that," he muttered. "The next dragon to whisk you away without warning is going to get an earful from me."

Jocelyn just chuckled, her gaze on Raqisa. She might be smaller than Elddreki, but her talons were just as long and her teeth looked just as sharp. It was hard to imagine Kincaid giving her an earful, somehow. Raqisa had been speaking with the other dragon, but she swung her mighty head around suddenly, as if aware of Jocelyn's gaze.

"You take Elddreki," she said, her words addressed to the dragon but her eyes on the humans. "I will stay with these two. I am eager to investigate the maiden, to learn more of her strange power."

CHAPTER TWENTY-EIGHT

At the dragon's words, Kincaid drew even closer to Jocelyn, in an apparently unconscious gesture of protection.

"It's all right," she said, speaking softly as Elddreki and the other dragon took off. "I don't think she means us any harm."

Kincaid met Jocelyn's eyes silently, his expression slightly troubled. Then he moved suddenly, and she was startled to feel his hand in hers again, their fingers intertwined once more. She made no attempt to disentangle herself. Clearly he had been serious about not wanting to be separated again, and she found she didn't mind.

"You are a pair?" Raqisa asked curiously, her snakelike eyes flicking to their joined hands and back to their faces.

"A pair?" asked Kincaid warily.

"Humans pair together as dragons do, I believe?" Raqisa said. "Mortal and mortal together?"

"Oh," said Kincaid, looking like he was trying to avoid meeting Jocelyn's eye. "No, we're merely...friends."

Raqisa looked between them, the smile that stretched her reptilian mouth somehow making her eyes glitter.

"Has your dragon companion not told you that our kind has a way of knowing when humans are not being truthful?"

Jocelyn felt her face heating, and tried to withdraw her hand, but Kincaid held fast. He was still not looking at her, but a quick glance showed his expression to be unyielding.

"I will not press you," said Raqisa indulgently. "It is no concern of mine." She turned her penetrating gaze on Jocelyn. "Your magic is of much more interest to me."

Jocelyn fidgeted for a moment, staring into Raqisa's orbs as if hypnotized. Then all of a sudden the absurdity of it hit her, and she had to hold back a chuckle. Here she was, against all the odds having found a second Dragon Realm, and apparently the most fascinating creature within it was her.

"I'm curious about you, too," she said. "Are you immortal, like Elddreki?"

Raqisa shook her head, her expression impossible to read. "I am not. I chose differently from your dragon companion."

"So have you paired?" Jocelyn pressed curiously. "Do you have dragonlings?"

"Not yet," said Raqisa.

She sounded relaxed, in no hurry, like she had no doubt she would. Jocelyn wondered whether Elddreki would have chosen differently if he had been born into a colony with lots of potential mortal dragons to pair with.

Raqisa leaned close to Jocelyn, inhaling deeply. She drew back, shaking her head slowly in evident amazement.

"You are incredible, Jocelyn," she said. "So many layers. Are all humans this fascinating?"

"No," answered Kincaid unexpectedly. "Jocelyn is a rarity."

Jocelyn let out a long breath, uncomfortable under the scrutiny. A rarity, was she? Another word for an anomaly. Another word, one could argue, for an abomination.

"What do you mean by layers?" Kincaid asked, frowning at the dragon.

"Well," said Raqisa, still examining Jocelyn, "she has the power of change, as Elddreki said. It is potent, and unmistakable. But there is other magic about her as well." She tilted her head to the side. "For example, a storytelling gift, subtle in style, but magical in origin."

"Yes," Jocelyn acknowledged, surprised. "My bloodline was gifted by the dragons of Vasilisa, centuries ago."

Raqisa nodded. "The gift has not lost its potency." She smiled at Jocelyn. "And it is more than just storytelling, I think. Humans are not known for their strong memories, are they? But you have something even dragons do not have—ancestral memories."

"I do?" Jocelyn blinked.

"The ability to see into the past, in the right circumstances," Raqisa explained. "Your connection with the past is strong, much stronger than I would expect in a human of such a short lifespan. The princess you spoke of earlier, for example, who sought our kind across the land, but failed to find us. When you said she passed to her ancestors, the emotion that swirled around you was strong, too strong for someone who died long before you were born. You feel a connection to her."

"I suppose I do," Jocelyn acknowledged slowly. "Our paths are aligned, to an extent. And that's not even counting the fact that we both came looking for your colony." Jocelyn sighed.

"What is the thought behind the sigh, young one?" asked Raqisa, the question reminding Jocelyn of Elddreki.

Jocelyn gave a rueful smile. "I was just scolding myself. Princess Sarai searched for dragons and didn't find you. She was probably devastated by her failure all her life. And here I am, having found you with relative ease, and I'm almost wishing I hadn't."

Raqisa flicked her tail, her expression intent. "You wish you hadn't found us?"

"Not exactly that," said Jocelyn hastily. "I just...I'm not sure I'm ready to be done with the quest." Kincaid's hand felt warm and firm in hers, and she tried not to think about how it would be when neither he nor Elddreki was part of her daily life. But she thought about it anyway, because she knew exactly how it would be. Lonely.

"I think I understand what you mean," said Raqisa calmly. "A quest is a sort of companion, one you may miss."

Jocelyn nodded, relieved. "Yes, exactly." Her voice turned thoughtful. "I wonder if Princess Sarai felt lonely once she gave up on her search. Lonelier than she was already," she added ruefully.

"Why don't you access her memories and see?" asked Raqisa matter-of-factly.

"I—I can't," said Jocelyn, startled. "At least, I don't think I can. She wasn't my ancestor, anyway."

"But you do have a connection to her," said Raqisa.

"And you've seen her memories before," interjected Kincaid.

"But...I wouldn't know how," Jocelyn objected. *And I'm not sure I want to share any further in her loneliness*, she added silently.

Perhaps she should have added that last part aloud, because Raqisa was not to be deterred. "Maybe your magic isn't sufficient on its own," she said brightly. "I might be able to help."

She opened her fearsome mouth wide, and Jocelyn drew back instinctively. But it wasn't fire that issued from the cavernous opening, it was magic, so potent it was almost tangible. It settled over Jocelyn like a blanket, and she felt her mind growing fuzzy. She turned to Kincaid, alarm in her eyes as she gripped his hand harder, willing it to be an anchor holding her to reality. But even as his eyes met hers, she could feel herself slipping away...

Sᴀʀᴀɪ ꜰᴇʟᴛ listless as she wandered the halls, taking no cheer from the afternoon sunshine streaming pleasantly through the castle's windows. She had known that it was a slim chance she would find anything of use at Dragoncave, so she had no real reason to be disappointed. But she felt rudderless without any more legends of magic to follow up. She had been back for two weeks, and she didn't know what to hope for now. The future stretched blankly in front of her, full of duty and grief and loneliness.

She wondered fleetingly what Germain was doing right now, surprising herself with the thought. It was rare for her to see him between the midday and evening meals, so there was no reason for her to notice his absence today.

The sounds of sparring reached her through an open window further along the corridor, and she drifted toward it idly. She knew the training yard was right below this wing of the castle, but she had never actually visited it. She stopped at a window set in the wall, just before the corridor turned a corner, running along another side of the courtyard below.

Men were training down on the ground, some sparring with long wooden poles, some practicing with swords, some fighting with their fists. Shouts and grunts and laughter drifted up to her. It wasn't as though she had any desire to join the men in their activity, but somehow their camaraderie only increased her loneliness.

Sarai leaned on the windowsill, trying to get a better look. The men were mostly shirtless, so it was difficult to properly identify their uniforms, but she thought they were members of the royal guard. For several minutes she watched, curious, as two of them battled with the long poles. They were clearly well-matched, the bout going on for longer than the others around them, a few other guards stopping to look on.

One guard eventually emerged the victor, and Sarai's eyes

wandered over the courtyard, looking for another match to observe. The clang of metal drew her attention to two swordsmen, both shirtless, fighting in one corner of the yard. She realized with a start of surprise that one of them was Germain just a moment before she heard the words.

"Prince Germain is so handsome, isn't he?"

Sarai didn't immediately recognize the voice, but to one who had grown up in a royal court, the simpering tone of a love-struck noble mooning over her prince was impossible to mistake. She glanced up surreptitiously and saw two young women, both members of her father-in-law's court, watching the training yard from one of the windows on the other wing of the corridor. They clearly hadn't seen her, and she breathed a sigh of relief.

"He's devastatingly handsome," the second young woman agreed, with a giggle.

Sarai returned her gaze to her husband, watching him critically. He was handsome, she realized with a hint of surprise. Tall, dark-haired like her, broad-shouldered. With his shirt off, she—and apparently half the ladies of the court—could see the muscles standing out in his back and in his broad, strong chest as he sparred. The power in his arms was evident in the way he pressed his opponent, and he was clearly extremely skilled at sword fighting.

Sarai felt just the tiniest flicker of smugness as she listened to the two young women sigh over the man who was their prince, but her husband. She scolded herself for the petty reaction. Prince Germain wasn't hers in heart any more than she was his. He had married her for the political benefit it would bring his kingdom to be allied with hers, and she could hardly claim any personal triumph in that.

She didn't think less of him for it, of course—it was what a dutiful prince who cared about his kingdom should do. It was just that it said nothing at all of his heart. And that was an accurate summary of Germain, she thought. A strong sense of duty, with not much emotion. Not for the first time, she was glad of it. If he had been a man of strong emotion, he would surely be disappointed with her. She had been emotionless enough about their marriage before her family was murdered. It was hard to imagine now that her heart would ever be open enough to truly love anyone.

"It's such a pity he's shackled to that Kyonan imposter."

The words shocked Sarai out of her reverie. She stilled completely, her hands fused to the windowsill. Her eyes were still on her husband, sparring below, but her ears strained without her permission to hear the conversation happening ten feet away.

"It's a waste is what it is. The king threw poor Prince Germain away on her."

The second speaker clucked her tongue. "It's not His Majesty's fault—how could he predict Kyona would fall apart, and the alliance would prove so worthless now that King Cael's house no longer holds the throne?"

"He couldn't, of course," sighed her companion. "But it's still such a waste of Prince Germain." She snickered. "She's not even that pretty."

Sarai felt her face burning, but she didn't move.

"Hmph." The first girl sounded unimpressed. "My brother and his friends seem to think she is. I don't know what they're seeing myself." She sniffed, but a moment later her voice turned smug. "Even my brother says he wouldn't want to be married to her, though. She's as cold as the Kyonan mountains. They call her an ice sculpture. A beautiful ice sculpture, but still...It can't be very pleasant for poor Prince Germain. I've certainly never seen him show any warmth toward her."

"Neither have I," said the other noblewoman. "If you ask me, he doesn't even like her. My father says this marriage alliance might be the biggest mistake Valoria has ever made. Poor Prince Germain." Her voice turned caressing as she said the name, and Sarai's hands clenched involuntarily on the windowsill. "He must regret it as much as we do." The girl sniggered unpleasantly. "Maybe when she's next off questing for mythical creatures, she'll fall off that precious

Kyonan mare of hers and get trampled, and Prince Germain will be free."

Sarai's gaze was still locked on Germain, who had just bested his adversary. She was surprised to feel tears standing in her eyes. She wouldn't have thought such paltry attacks had the power to wound her.

Her husband shook hands with the defeated guard, then wiped his face with a cloth. Before he could recommence his training, a page ran up to him. He leaned toward the boy, inclining his head, then gave a curt nod and handed his weapon off to a nearby squire.

"It looks like the prince is being called away," sighed one of the gossiping noblewomen. "No point tarrying to watch any longer."

Sarai remained rooted to the spot as their voices faded away. Once they had left, she leaned her head against the windowsill, trying to calm her breathing. She had known how the court whispered about her, but it was somehow much more painful to hear it with her own ears. She wished fleetingly that Parmida was there to pour out her troubles to. Her younger sister would have her back no matter what happened. She would tell her to ignore the petty noble girls who were just sour about not snagging the crown prince themselves.

Then she remembered afresh that Parmida was dead, murdered. A stab of pain shot through her, and she reminded herself dully that there was no one to listen to her troubles. She was all alone.

And yet, her gaze lingered on Prince Germain as he re-donned his tunic in Valoria's royal purple. She didn't move from the window until he was out of sight, and her eyes followed him all the way out of the training yard.

She was so disheartened by the overheard conversation, that for the first time since arriving in Valoria, she contemplated feigning illness in order to avoid the evening meal. But she told herself sternly that whether or not she felt lonely and miserable, she was still a princess, with all a princess's duties.

And when she arrived for the meal, her heart lifted. It seemed her *discipline was to be rewarded, and she would not have to face the two girls, and the countless other nobles who whispered about her behind their hands. There was no formal court spread. Prince Germain's sister, some five years older than him, had that moment arrived with her family from her husband's estate in the countryside. It seemed the royal family was to indulge in the rare comfort of an intimate family meal.*

Not that Sarai felt much intimacy with anyone present, of course. Germain's other sister, also older than him, had recently married a noble who spent most of his time in Bryford. But regular meals together had done nothing to form any understanding between Sarai and either the husband or the wife. Perhaps she was too sensitive, but she felt disapproval behind their cold politeness every time they spoke to her. And Germain's younger brother spoke to her as little as possible.

Still, it was infinitely better than another evening meal under the malicious scrutiny of the court. And in fact, the royal family seemed more relaxed and pleasant this evening than she had ever seen them. The visiting sister was obviously a favorite with everyone, and she had brought her two young children. Sarai had never seen Valoria's stately queen look so warm—the softness in her eyes as they rested on her grandchildren was startling. In the absence of anyone but the family and the servants, the children romped and played with astonishing freedom, and even the austere king didn't check them.

Germain was detained by something—Sarai had no more idea what it might be than anyone else present—and he was the last to arrive. He greeted his wife with respectful punctiliousness, kissing the back of her hand and inquiring after her health in the accepted mode. She found it strangely hard to meet his eyes after her clandestine observation of him earlier that day. Her gaze was drawn to his chest, and although it was now covered in formal garb, she could imagine the way his muscles rippled underneath.

He seemed to sense her hesitation, and she thought there was curiosity in his eyes when she finally met them. But she greeted him calmly, and after another moment he turned away to welcome his sister, embracing her warmly and exclaiming over how long it had been since her last visit. Sarai watched in amusement, and some surprise, as "Uncle Germain" was mobbed by the children, receiving their raptures with smiling good humor.

The evening was unseasonably chilly, and after the meal a fire was lit in the large fireplace. Sarai had expected the children would be sent to bed with their nursemaid immediately following the meal, if not before it, so she was amazed to see them clamoring for Germain's attention, demanding a story. She was even more amazed when he gave in readily, allowing himself to be pulled closer to the fire.

Sarai tried to attend to the conversation around her, but she couldn't tear her gaze from the scene by the fireplace. She was fascinated by the sight of her reserved husband, his normally inexpressive face alight as he told the children a fable about a mountain-dwelling goatherd who tamed a wild wolf, only to discover the wolf was an enchanted king. Germain looked so different, allowing one of the children to ride on his back as he pretended to be the wolf, growling and chuckling by turns.

It was a pleasant picture, and one she had certainly never seen before. Sarai found herself wondering if he was like this whenever his niece and nephew were present. Would he tell stories like that, and play so freely, with their children one day?

Her cheeks flushed at the thought, and at that moment Germain seemed to become suddenly aware of her eyes on him. He looked up quickly, and their gazes locked. Sarai could feel that her cheeks were still warm, but she didn't look away. Germain had a questioning look on his face, and she gave him the smallest of smiles. She thought his expression softened slightly, but a second later his attention was forcefully claimed by his nephew, and the moment passed.

When the children were finally shooed out of the room by their nursemaid, Germain came over to Sarai.

"How was my performance as the wolf?"

Sarai looked up in surprise at the uncharacteristic note of humor in his voice. The smile was still in Germain's eyes, and it softened his normally serious face. She cast her eyes down, smiling faintly herself.

"I was surprised to hear you telling that story. It was my favorite fable as a child."

"It was mine, as well," said Germain, sounding surprised himself. He sat down beside her, his body angled toward her and his air more relaxed than she had ever seen it.

"Truly?" asked Sarai, feeling strangely pleased. "I didn't know it was even told in Valoria."

"Oh yes," said Germain. "The mountains may be Kyona's, but we feel their fascination as well. We have many stories about the mountains."

Sarai smiled, but the gesture didn't quite reach her eyes this time. The mention of her homeland had sent her thoughts spinning in a familiar, and heart-wrenching, direction.

The silence stretched out for a moment, then Germain spoke, his tone tentative. "Would you like to stroll through the gardens with me?"

Sarai looked up, surprised yet again.

"I have been wanting to speak with you about something," Germain added quickly, as if an explanation was needed for why he wanted to enjoy a relaxed walk with his wife. Which, by Sarai's experience of marriage so far, it was.

"Very well," she agreed, rising from her seat.

Germain offered her his arm, and she took it almost shyly. As they walked toward the gardens, their steps unhurried, her thoughts circled back to that afternoon, how she had been struck by how handsome he was. His arm was strong under her hand, and she thought suddenly of the way his muscles had bunched as he fought the guard in the training yard. He had looked so powerful, dangerous even. But with those same arms he had wrestled his nephew playfully, and embraced his sister with the warmth of real affection.

Sarai wondered what it would be like if he were to greet her with such genuine gladness after they had been apart. She thought about how she had felt when she watched him by the fire, telling the old tale to his young listeners with unashamed enthusiasm. She thought of the softness on his face when their eyes had locked, and her own inevitable reflections that they might share just such a scene one day, but with their own children.

She felt a curious emotion, so out of place in her life these last months that it took a long moment to identify it. Happiness. It was a flicker of happiness, if not for the present, at least imagined for the future. The thought made her mind whirl confusingly. Could it be possible to actually be happy in her life here, with Germain?

No. She shook the idea off. Unthinkable to be happy in Valoria, when she was forever barred from her own beloved kingdom. Unthinkable to be happy anywhere or with anyone after what had happened to her family. She felt guilty for even considering putting aside her grief.

"What did you want to speak to me about?"

They had reached the gardens, lit by many bright lanterns, and had been walking through them in silence. The perfume of late-blooming flowers drifted through the air.

Germain hesitated for a moment too long, and Sarai began to feel nervous. She remembered the words of the women that afternoon. Was Germain going to reproach her for the unprofitable alliance their marriage had turned out to be? He behaved always with respectful restraint, but after all these months, could he no longer hold his peace? Was he going to admit he regretted their marriage?

"I wished to speak to you about your search," he said at last, his voice even. "Your search for dragons."

Sarai stilled, turning to look up at him with hard eyes. "What of it, Sire?"

Germain sighed, looking frustrated at the form of address, but he didn't correct her. Other people were enjoying the gardens, chatter and the occasional laugh reaching out to the royal couple through the still night air, and Germain spoke quietly.

"I do not begrudge you your search, Sarai, but I am not comfortable to have you away from Bryford so often. And I did not fully understand before you left on your last journey just how close the cave was to the border."

"I apologize, Sire," said Sarai colorlessly. Of course he disapproved. Of course he didn't understand. She had never expected him to. "It was not my intention to deceive you."

"I know it wasn't," said Germain calmly. "And you have returned safely, for which I am very glad. But I would like you to stop these trips. I want you to stay here, where you're safe, and where the court can see you growing into your role as my wife, and their future queen."

Sarai withdrew her hand from his arm and stepped back. The implication was clear, and even in her irritation she felt a prickle of shame at the realization that he didn't think she was adequately fulfilling her duties.

"I will of course do as you wish," she said, her tone more emotionless than ever. "You need not have mentioned it, because I did not intend any further trips. There are no more locations to visit. There is no more reason to hope."

Her voice caught ever so slightly on the last word, and Germain stepped forward, his voice growing softer.

"Sarai—"

"I will certainly stay in Bryford," she continued. "And I can only express my regret that I have been remiss in my duties. I will endeavor not to give you cause for complaint again."

"I did not mean to complain, Sarai," said Germain, sounding frustrated. "And I didn't say you have been remiss in your duties. I wish only to support you as you settle into your life here."

"You are good, Sire," Sarai said, inclining her head formally. "I *find that the night is colder than I anticipated, and I am tired. I think I will withdraw."*

Germain met her eyes for a moment, his expression hard and searching. Then he stepped back, kissing her hand in a formal gesture of release.

Sarai retreated quickly, but she didn't withdraw to her suite. She wandered the gardens aimlessly, breathing in the scent of the flowers and trying to calm the torrent of emotion roiling inside her. Germain's politely phrased reproach, and the disappointment in her that surely lay behind it, stung all the more bitterly because of the warmth that had preceded it. For a moment Sarai had almost dared to hope that she would not always be lonely and disliked.

She found a bench, partially concealed behind an arbor laden with blooms. She had been sitting there only a few minutes when she was startled by a greeting.

"Sarai. May I join you?"

She looked up in surprise to see Germain's visiting sister.

"Please," Sarai invited, gesturing toward the bench. She would have preferred to be alone, but she could hardly say as much.

"I am sorry I have not had the opportunity to get to know you better," said Sarai's sister-in-law, settling herself on the bench. "It must be lonely for you here in Bryford, so far from your former home."

Sarai's eyes pricked with unexpected tears. It was such a simple thing, but it touched her more than she could say to have someone acknowledge her crippling loneliness, instead of expecting her to occupy herself happily with Bryford's court life.

"Yes," she said softly.

Before her companion could reply, both ladies' attention was caught by a musical voice issuing from the next row of flowers.

"Your Highness! What an unexpected pleasure to meet you here. Is it not a delight to stroll among these beautiful blooms?"

Germain's answering voice was more moderated, and Sarai couldn't make out his words. Her heart thumped strangely—she hadn't realized he was still walking in the garden, and had certainly not been aware he was so close by.

As the young woman continued to simper, Sarai realized suddenly that she recognized the voice. It was the noblewoman who had expressed the hope that afternoon that the Kyonan princess might be trampled by her horse. Except now that she was talking to the prince instead of about him, her voice sounded much more pleasant and much less snide.

Sarai shifted slightly to the side so she could see the pair, although they would be unlikely to see her, hidden by the arbor as she was. She noted with a curious pang that the woman was beautiful. Her fair hair and angelic face made Sarai feel dark and dull in comparison.

"She, for example, has probably not been making a great effort to make you feel welcome."

Germain's sister spoke as though their conversation hadn't been interrupted, gesturing toward her brother and his companion with her head.

Sarai answered only with a grim smile.

"Lady Marietta," said her companion, speaking softly. "She is the oldest daughter of one of our best families, and unless I'm much mistaken, she's been determined to catch Germain since she was about fourteen."

Sarai said nothing, still watching the other conversation. Germain spoke quietly, his smile polite, but Lady Marietta gushed sycophantically, her voice much too loud. She was laughing unnaturally often, casting her gaze downward only to look up demurely at the prince through her lashes. Sarai narrowed her own eyes at the display.

"Be on your guard with her," Germain's sister cautioned. "I truly think she'd do you a mischief if she could." She glanced over and seemed to take in Sarai's expression. "Not that Germain would let anyone do you a mischief, I'm sure," she added quickly.

"No, he is very good in his concern for my safety," agreed Sarai.

She was thinking of his command that she go on no more searches, and her face and voice were expressionless.

"Of course he is. You're his wife. He will protect you and care for you for the rest of his life."

"I don't think Lady Marietta is quite so convinced of that," said Sarai dryly, her eyes on the fair-haired beauty who was still flirting shamelessly with the prince. As she watched, Lady Marietta laid a playful hand on Germain's arm, just where Sarai's hand had rested a short time before.

A spark of intense emotion flared up inside Sarai, overwhelming her with its potency. That was her *husband Lady Marietta was trying to captivate. Hers! Not even the fact that Germain withdrew his arm as soon as he could politely do so appeased her. She shook her head to clear it, knowing she was being foolish. Germain was an honorable man, however warm and engaging Lady Marietta might be able to make herself. And Sarai had no justification for feeling jealous if Germain didn't have her heart.*

But justification or not, heat seemed to rush through her body as the pair continued to converse. Germain said something in his deep steady voice, the words indistinguishable. Lady Marietta laughed, a tinkling, musical sound, and Germain smiled in response, his features once again softened by the pleasant expression.

Sarai glanced sideways to see that her sister-in-law was also watching the duo, a slight frown on her face.

"Shall we join them?" the Valorian princess suggested. "I daresay Germain would be pleased to escort you inside if you are ready to leave the gardens. And I think Lady Marietta at least would benefit from a reminder of your—"

Existence? *Sarai thought.*

"—presence," the older princess finished. She looked expectantly at Sarai.

But the Kyonan shook her head. "Certainly not," she said with dignity. "There is no occasion for me to interfere. It would be very wrong of me to expect to dictate to my husband how he should conduct himself."

Germain's sister was silent, but her forehead was creased, as though Sarai's answer troubled her. But Sarai had no intention of inserting herself into the situation like a jealous shrew. She might have lost her home and her family, but she still had her pride.

She told herself there was as little sense in her unexpected feeling of possessiveness over her husband as there was in her momentary vision of finding happiness here, with him.

But still...she continued to watch Germain until he extricated himself from the conversation and left the garden a short time later. And even then, Sarai's eyes followed him until he disappeared from sight, for the second time that day.

CHAPTER TWENTY-NINE

Jocelyn gasped, stumbling backward as she returned to the present. The first thing she became aware of was Kincaid's hand, still grasping hers firmly, and she yanked away.

"Why did you do that?" she shot at Raqisa, her chest heaving. "I didn't ask you to do that!"

The dragon drew back, her expression surprised.

"I thought you would welcome the chance to share in the past."

"Well, I didn't," said Jocelyn shortly. She knew she was falling far short of the level of civility she should give a dragon, but she wasn't enough in control of herself to behave more politely.

Fortunately Raqisa didn't seem inclined to take offense. "I fear I have overwhelmed you," she said mildly. "I will join Elddreki in his meeting with our elders, and give you some space."

And accompanied only by a short gust of wind, the dragon was gone.

"Jocelyn?" said Kincaid hesitantly, after a moment of silence.

"Are you all right?" She didn't answer, and he pushed on, his tone tentative. "That was strong that time. Even I felt it, a little."

Jocelyn looked up at him in surprise. "You heard her thoughts?"

He shook his head. "No, it was just the emotions, like in the cave. I guess I don't have the storytelling gift, but I was still affected by Raqisa's magic. I felt...loneliness, again. But also something different. Jealousy." He looked at his feet. "Possessiveness."

Again Jocelyn didn't respond. She had put the future from her mind in the excitement of their arrival at Wyvern Islands, but this glimpse into the past had brought it forcefully back to her thoughts. She looked away from Kincaid, shivering at the new fear that raced over her. Had Princess Sarai's fate been even worse than Jocelyn had imagined? Had she come to care for her husband in spite of herself?

Jocelyn had thought the idea of a marriage without love bad enough. But what if she were to marry Prince Ormond, and then over time come to love him, knowing full well he didn't love her in return? That he had married her purely for political reasons? The thought was horrifying.

But she shook it off. No, the softening she had witnessed in Princess Sarai's memories was surely a natural and necessary part of a husband and wife learning to live with one another, that was all. She had seen into Princess Sarai's mind and knew with perfect clarity what her thoughts and emotions had been upon her marriage, and in its early months. She couldn't believe the Kyonan princess had ever come to genuinely love her Valorian husband.

"You look tired," said Kincaid gently, when the silence continued to stretch out. "I'm sorry you were forced to relive something you didn't want to see."

Jocelyn sighed. "It wasn't as terrible as all that, it just took me off guard. I'm confused enough in my own skin most of the time. I don't need to muddy the waters by parading around in someone else's head."

Kincaid smiled sympathetically. "It seems like Elddreki might be gone a while. We may as well make ourselves comfortable."

He led the way over to a large boulder, and Jocelyn followed mechanically, seating herself on the grass and leaning back against the rock. The return of all her thoughts and fears about the future made it increasingly difficult to be comfortable around Kincaid.

Perhaps the Valorian sensed it, because he put a bit of distance between them when settling himself on the grass. After a minute he laid back on the turf, his eyes on the sky. They stayed that way for some time, in companionable silence. Jocelyn sat with her knees drawn up to her chest, her thoughts straying to Elddreki. How was he faring with the elders of this dragon colony? Hopefully he was safe. She shuddered to think how vulnerable she and Kincaid would be if anything happened to Elddreki.

"Whoa!"

The exclamation was startled out of her as something nosed her knee. Deep in her abstraction, she hadn't noticed anything approaching. Kincaid was up in a flash at the sound, his hand on his sword. But he stopped dead, staring at the sight before them in as much amazement as Jocelyn felt.

"A dragonling!" he breathed, and Jocelyn nodded, her eyes glowing.

"It must be." She reached out a tentative hand to stroke the miniature dragon's snout, and it purred contentedly. "Hey, there, little one. Easy!" she laughed, as the dragonling hiccuped, a tiny spurt of flame shooting out of its mouth and extinguishing in the air. She met Kincaid's eyes, and they shared a smile in acknowledgment of the wonder of the moment.

The dragonling was more startlingly beautiful than anything Jocelyn had ever seen. It was also adorable, gamboling and frisking around like an oversized puppy. Quite oversized, since it was larger than a full grown mastiff. In shape it was much like Elddreki, down to the bearded ridge around its temple and the triangular plates running the length of its back and tail. But the proportions were off—its scales were too big for its body, but its wings were tiny against its flanks, and its talons were positively cute.

But none of that was the most striking feature of the dragonling. It seemed Raqisa had spoken the truth when she said dragons start bright. This one's scales were magenta, and it was so vivid in color it was blinding. Jocelyn could imagine the color dimming to a dull burgundy over time, but for now it was breathtaking.

"Look, more!"

Kincaid's voice drew her attention away from the playful creature in front of her, and she laughed with delight. A group of several dragonlings was racing toward them, bumping each other with their awkward gait, clearly eager to join the fun. They converged on the humans, their scales a riot of green and orange and blue. Jocelyn glanced around but couldn't see any adult dragons in sight. It seemed the young ones had a lot of license to roam.

She chuckled as she patted them, small snouts tugging at her dress and sniffing at her hair.

"What are you laughing about?" Kincaid asked, looking down at her in amusement.

She grinned up at him. "I'm just thinking that Elddreki must have been a very cute little dragonling, with his green and purple and blue."

Kincaid grinned appreciatively. "Be sure to tell him that when he comes back."

Perhaps liking the sound of his voice, the dragonlings suddenly transferred their attention to Kincaid. As one, they abandoned Jocelyn and loped toward her companion, frolicking around his legs and vying for his favor.

"Hey!" he protested as they began to yank at his pants, but there was a laugh in his voice. Jocelyn couldn't help laughing herself as more than one of the dragonlings started to tug on his clothes, clearly inviting him to come and play.

They were strong in spite of their cuteness, and Kincaid shot Jocelyn a look of humorous helplessness as he was dragged in the direction of a small clump of trees.

"Save me, Princess!" he cried with a grin. "I'm being carried off by a horde of angry beasts."

Jocelyn just chuckled, not bothering to respond. She would have had to shout to do so, the dragonlings were buffeting Kincaid along so quickly. She grinned as the group reached the trees, most of the dragonlings releasing their prisoner to let out some energy by weaving enthusiastically between the trunks, checking to see if their new playmate was watching. One or two stayed with Kincaid, pulling him to the ground in their eagerness to play.

Jocelyn didn't have even a second's warning of what was coming. One moment she was chuckling lightheartedly, watching Kincaid as he wrestled with the dragonlings, for all the world like he was playing with energetic children, or overenthusiastic puppies. The next the sunlight was blocked by a vast shadow, and she was staring up in alarm at the sight of an unfamiliar dragon, wings spread impressively as he came to land immediately in front of her.

"What are you doing in our realm, human?" the dragon demanded without preamble. "How do you come to be here?"

"I, uh, I came with another dragon," she gasped, her voice coming out a squeak. "He—"

But her sentence was destined to remain unfinished. Fear had spiraled through her at the dragon's tone, and she felt her power jolting out uncontrollably as she spoke. The dragon had obviously noticed it, and he cut her off with a hiss that smelled like smoke.

"You have magic!" he declared, his horror evident in his face. "The abomination we have feared has come upon us!"

"No," Jocelyn gasped, her vision swimming strangely. "No, I —I didn't steal my power. I'm not an abomination. I'm—I'm supposed to have it."

But even she was unconvinced by her words, and the dragon clearly knew it. His horror melted away for a moment, replaced by a deep and inexpressible sadness.

"Dragons can tell when a human is not being honest," he said, his voice almost gentle. Jocelyn swallowed nervously, her gaze flicking to Kincaid. He was struggling to his feet, his eyes on the dragon and his expression wary.

"It is a grief," the dragon continued, and indeed Jocelyn saw no anger in his eyes, only sadness. "But you must be destroyed."

Without further discussion, the dragon opened his mouth, drawing a deep rattling breath. Jocelyn fumbled blindly away, her back hitting the boulder and trapping her in place.

"NO!"

Kincaid's roar cut across the scene, but the dragon paid it no attention. Jocelyn could already feel the warm air from his mouth, the prelude to a much hotter sequel. In her peripheral vision she could see Kincaid sprinting toward them, but it was useless. He would never reach them in time, and even if he did, all it would achieve would be for him to die in the flames as well. Elddreki might be able to shield her, but he was nowhere to be found.

All this passed through her thoughts in a second, but then her mind was strangely blank. She felt hypnotized as she stared into the dragon's jaws, not able to summon up a single emotion. There were no regrets, no reminiscences, no final reflections. Just the childish hope that it wouldn't hurt too terribly.

"JOCELYN!"

Kincaid's desperate shout, closer now, would be the last sound she heard. She could actually see the flames building within the creature's throat, their heat reaching across the space to sear her skin.

Then, just as the heat became too intense to bear, another shadow darkened the sky. Raqisa dropped to the ground like a stone between Jocelyn and the other dragon. The flames spewed from her attacker's mouth, too advanced to be withdrawn. They caught Raqisa full on the chest, tongues of fire licking around the edges of her massive body and leaping toward Jocelyn in small spurts. The hem of her dress caught alight, and she beat it out with her hand, her mind still strangely detached.

"Raqisa," the new dragon said sharply. "Do not interfere. The abomination must be destroyed, you know it is so."

"This human is not an abomination," said Raqisa impatiently, and Jocelyn was relieved that she sounded none the worse for the blast of dragon fire. "Take the time to examine her signature, and you will see for yourself."

"I have taken time," said the dragon harshly. "I was sent to investigate and have this minute returned. I discovered that our brethren did indeed offer his power to *humans*, and I return to find one here, in our realm, carrying magic! And you tell me it is no abomination?"

"She is not the result of a travesty," Raqisa said. "She was born with her power. And she is a guest here. She and her companion were brought here by a dragon of Vasilisa."

"Vasilisa?" repeated the male dragon in astonishment.

Jocelyn was almost completely blocked in by Raqisa's body, but she leaned slightly to the side to see the new dragon's reaction. He was a vibrant green and, she realized, no larger than Raqisa. Another young dragon.

"Come," said Raqisa persuasively. "Come to the elders and tell them what you have learned, and they will tell you what we have discovered this day also."

The dragon hesitated for only a moment, his eyes on Jocelyn, before giving a curt nod. Raqisa crouched, ready to take off, but turned her gaze on Jocelyn first.

"Are you all right, young maiden?"

Jocelyn gave a shaky nod, not able to master her voice.

"Good. Stay here."

Then Jocelyn blinked, and the two dragons were gone, the sudden breeze that ruffled her braid the only reminder of their presence. That and the singed hem of her dress.

For a moment she stared stupidly, dazzled by the sunlight. Then Kincaid was there, his way cleared by the exodus of the beasts, and she was on her feet and in his arms before she knew which way was up.

"Jocelyn," he whispered. "Jocelyn." His arms were as tight as iron around her, and she buried her face in his shoulder, tremors rocking her whole body. He didn't ask if she was all right, just repeated her name over and over, his arms seeming to tighten every time he said it.

"I told him I wasn't an abomination," she whispered, her voice so muffled by his shirt that she wondered if he could even hear. "But he could tell I didn't believe it."

He didn't respond, just pressed his cheek against the top of her head. "Jocelyn," he said again, his voice strangled. "I thought...I thought—"

"I know," she whispered, and he fell silent.

She realized after a moment that he was shaking as violently as she was. With her face in his shoulder, her ear was against his chest, and she could hear the frantic rhythm of his heart. She had the feeling she wasn't the only one who had just experienced the most terrifying moment of her life. For an indeterminate amount of time, he held her, neither speaking, both taking deep gulping breaths in an attempt to calm their racing hearts.

It was hard to judge the passage of time, but all of a sudden Jocelyn realized Kincaid's head was no longer resting on hers. She lifted her own face from his shoulder, but made no attempt to pull out of his arms. She closed her eyes and drew a deep breath, noting that her heart had slowed at last.

Then Kincaid pressed his lips against her forehead, right on the hairline, and it picked back up again.

One arm was still tight around her, but his other hand had strayed upward, cupping her neck. He kissed her not as a declaration, but as though he hardly knew he was doing it, as though it was the most natural expression of his relief at her narrow escape. She leaned into him, the action equally unconscious.

Then Kincaid's lips moved, and he kissed her temple, again without fanfare, as though it was the most natural thing in the world. Then his lips trailed down her face, along her cheekbone, as though it was even more natural for them to travel there. Jocelyn could barely breathe as his head dipped lower. She was afraid to move, afraid to break the spell. For the space of one frenzied heartbeat, his lips were at the corner of her mouth, their breath mingling.

Then he was kissing her, not in unconscious relief, but fully, intentionally, his lips tugging desperately at hers. And she abandoned herself to the sensation, pretending for one glorious moment that she was free to give her heart to this incredible man who she knew without doubt would give his life for her.

She slid her hands around his back and up over his shoulders, standing on her toes to better reach him as she kissed him more and more deeply. Her emotions were too varied and intense to name, and though she spoke no words she could feel her power swirling dizzyingly out and around her. But somehow she knew Kincaid wasn't affected—he was within the bubble, part of it.

She felt a tugging at the back of her head, and she realized Kincaid was pulling her hair loose from its braid. It flowed suddenly around her shoulders, as free as she was still pretending to be. She felt a heady sense of reckless release as he tangled his hands in it, his fingers warm against her scalp, drawing her face even closer to his, all without breaking their embrace. She hoped he would never break it.

"Is that what kissing looks like?"

The voice, its tone of bright curiosity all too familiar, caused both humans to jump back as though burned by dragon fire.

"Elddreki!" Jocelyn gasped, her cheeks flaming as she patted her disheveled hair nervously.

"It is a very strange type of interaction, isn't it?" Elddreki continued, his head tilted to the side as usual. "Dragons do not do that."

Kincaid was breathing as hard as Jocelyn as he gave a laugh that was half groan. He hadn't quite regained his usual self-possession, and he was looking at the dragon with an endearing mix of irritation and amusement.

"Raqisa told me that Jocelyn had run into trouble, yet again, so I came to ensure all was well."

"Yes, I'm fine," said Jocelyn, not quite meeting anyone's eye. Her lips burned and tingled so fiercely from Kincaid's touch that the memory of the attacking dragon's heat seemed weak by comparison.

"So I see." Elddreki looked doubtfully between them. "Does this mean you two will wed?"

"Elddreki!" gasped Jocelyn, looking anywhere but at Kincaid.

The dragon frowned at her. "I am not well versed in these matters, but I have some sense that in addition to protecting your safety, your father might have expected me to safeguard your honor as well."

"Elddreki," said Kincaid repressively. He was definitely still both irritated and amused. "Please stop talking, and go away."

Elddreki looked extremely taken aback by this blunt command. "Why?"

"Because," said Kincaid humorously, turning to face Jocelyn. "Most men prefer to speak for themselves when they're trying to propose marriage to a woman."

Jocelyn's eyes flew to his, her heart somersaulting strangely. The warmth in his gaze made her heart swell, but that only increased the agony a moment later, as it inevitably shattered.

"Kincaid," she said, putting out a hand in a clear gesture of restraint.

The flame in his eyes was immediately replaced by anxiety, and he reached out quickly to clasp both of her hands in his.

"What is it, Jocelyn? Why are you looking at me like that?"

She shrugged helplessly, her heart breaking a little more at the fear in his gaze. She was paying for her moment of abandon now. They both were. She couldn't blame him for assuming she would give a different answer, not when she had responded so passionately to his kiss.

"You know why I came to Valoria, Kincaid."

"The marriage alliance?" The color drained from his face as he said the words, his voice barely above a whisper. "You're still planning to go through with it, after...after everything? I thought you said you weren't promised to him!"

"I know what I said," she whispered. "But Kyona needs this. Eamon needs this."

"No." Kincaid sounded appalled, and his grip on her hands tightened convulsively.

"It won't be so bad," Jocelyn said, trying and failing to speak lightly. "You were right, Kincaid, I'll admit it. Valoria really is a wonderful kingdom. I think I could learn to be happy here. I can thank you for that. I couldn't imagine feeling that way when I first arrived, but you've made me see the beauty of this place and its people. You've made me realize that marrying Prince Ormond and becoming Valorian won't be so terrible."

"If my contribution has been to reconcile you to the idea of marrying another man," Kincaid said, his voice unsteady, "then I am my own worst enemy." His hands were still tight on hers. "Jocelyn, you can't marry Prince Ormond. You *can't*."

She met his eyes then, her expression uncertain. "If you're thinking of what Elddreki said about my power passing to my children, I've given it some thought, and I think it will be all right. There were two of us born with the power. I'm only one half of a whole, and I don't think that's enough to pass it on. I don't think I'll taint Valoria's royal bloodline."

"*Taint* it?" Kincaid repeated, his eyes wild. If Jocelyn had thought his grip on her hands was tight before, it had become a vise when she mentioned having children with Prince Ormond. "You can't think that's what I'm concerned about." Kincaid's eyes searched hers, almost frantically. "Jocelyn, I don't want you to marry Prince Ormond because I want you to marry *me*. And I hope our children *will* inherit your incredible gift. I can't think of anything better."

"Kincaid, stop," Jocelyn whispered. The vision of the future conjured up by Kincaid's words was unbearable, and tears were starting to her eyes. "I can't. You know I can't."

"I don't know anything of the kind," he contradicted with his familiar, beloved stubbornness. His eyes were still searching her face, and his voice softened. "Is it your parents, Jocelyn? Will they disapprove of you rejecting Prince Ormond?"

"No," she said, a hysterical sound escaping her, somewhere

between a laugh and a sob. "No, they would move the whole kingdom to let me marry as I chose, provided they thought well of you as a person, and thought you'd make me happy."

"Jocelyn," Kincaid whispered, pressing his forehead against hers. "I will do everything in my power to make you happy. I will love you for the rest of my life."

"Kincaid, *stop*," Jocelyn sobbed, pulling away. "Don't you understand? The fact that my parents won't be willing to put the kingdom before my own selfish desires is why I have to be! Kyona can't handle more controversy, more...more *change*. My father's unconventional choice of wife is still a source of tension in the court, even now. And Eamon's marriage, when it comes, will cause more than enough contention. We're still reeling from the upheavals of the last twenty years, and if I made it worse I would never forgive myself. People would say my parents had no control over either of their children, that they'd driven the monarchy into the ground."

She took a deep breath. "I don't expect you to understand, but I love Kyona, Kincaid. I *want* to do my duty as a princess. All I've ever been is a burden and a danger, and this is one way— maybe the *only* way—I can bring real benefit."

"You think I don't understand?" said Kincaid passionately. "You think you have to be a princess to understand duty? What you're talking about isn't duty! You're talking about letting the prejudices and the expectations of the feeble-minded rule your life. *Ruin* your life! You have a power within you that as far as we know is unprecedented in the history of humankind! How can you say the only way you can benefit your kingdom is to marry into Valoria's succession like a good little princess and satisfy a few stiff-rumped courtiers?"

"My power is *change*, Kincaid," Jocelyn cried. "It's the last thing that will help Kyona. Kyona needs stability—it needs Eamon."

"If I hear one more mention of that selfish, entitled brother of yours—" Kincaid began, his eyes flashing dangerously, but Jocelyn cut him off.

"Don't blame this on Eamon." She spoke wearily, no room left in her heart for anger. "If our positions were reversed, he'd probably be the one trying to give up what he wants for my sake. But our positions aren't reversed, and this is my choice, not his."

There was a long moment of silence, during which Kincaid watched her, his gaze as unblinking as a dragon's.

"You're right," he said at last, his voice quiet. "You're the one holding back. This is your choice, not your family's. And if I thought you were making it out of love for your brother, or your kingdom, maybe I'd feel better about it." He gave a twisted smile. "Probably not much better. But it doesn't matter anyway, because I don't think you're making it out of love. I think you're making it out of fear."

His voice grew even softer, and the tenderness in his face brought tears back into Jocelyn's eyes. "And seeing you afraid is what I've hated most of all since I met you, what I've tried most to free you from." He touched a hand gently to her cheek. "But I don't think it's something I can do for you."

"Kincaid," Jocelyn whispered, tears welling over. "I said I didn't want to hurt you."

He wiped a tear from her cheek with his thumb, with the saddest smile she had ever seen. "And I said you wouldn't. It's good for me to admit I'm wrong sometimes, I guess."

He turned away, his attention transferring to Elddreki, and Jocelyn started. She had forgotten the dragon was there, a silent observer of this most intimate, most devastating of moments.

"Elddreki," Kincaid was saying. "Given recent events, I would be more comfortable if you would stay with Jocelyn, to ensure no other dragons get the wrong idea about her power. But do you think Raqisa would be willing to take me back to the mainland?"

"I will ask," said Elddreki. He took off with a flap of his wings and a gust that tangled in Jocelyn's hair, still loose from Kincaid's embrace.

"Wait." She stumbled toward him. "You're leaving?"

Kincaid met her eyes with evident difficulty. "We finished our quest. We found the dragons." He gave a crooked, unconvincing smile. "You even admitted I was right about Valoria. I'll readily acknowledge I was wrong about the eastern people's superstitions. Now it's well past time I should be back home. Elddreki will keep you safe. He even said he would take you to Bryford when you're ready."

"But..." Jocelyn's mind was swirling frantically, panic threatening to claim her. Was that it, then? She had turned him down, and now he was just going to walk out of her life forever? "Will I ever see you again?"

"Yes," Kincaid said quickly, taking a step back toward her. "Of course you will." His eyes blazed into hers, and she lowered her gaze. "I'm not giving up," he said, his voice low and passionate. "I can't. But I'm not going to press you, either." She chanced a glance up and saw that he was once again smiling crookedly. "I can't force you to choose me. And even if I could, I wouldn't want to. You wouldn't really be choosing me then, would you?"

A shadow overhead made them both look up. Elddreki was returning, Raqisa in his wake. Kincaid suddenly stepped close, pressing his lips to Jocelyn's forehead again.

"But I wish you would choose me," he whispered, his lips so close to her ear that a shiver went through her. "I wish it desperately."

Then the dragons landed, and he stepped back, leaving Jocelyn feeling more cold and alone than she had in all her life.

"Thank you for everything," Kincaid said to Elddreki. "I'm

glad you found what you were looking for. And please—please —keep her safe." The request was murmured almost too quietly for her to hear. Then Kincaid walked calmly over to Raqisa, without another backward look.

Wait! Jocelyn wanted to cry. *Come back! I've changed my mind!* But she hadn't changed her mind, and she didn't call out, just watched him sling his pack over his shoulder, and nod toward the yellow dragon. A moment later, Raqisa had seized him by the shoulders and the two of them were rising, so rapidly Jocelyn couldn't even tell whether Kincaid looked back at her. In seconds they were a dot in the sky, disappearing west toward the mainland.

Jocelyn was left blinking, reeling, anchorless. Was it only a few minutes ago she and Kincaid had been kissing with passionate abandon on this very spot? Was it only a few minutes before that she had been seconds from fiery death? She had felt numb then, too numb for fear. But there was no numbness now, and the agony of the moment wrestled with her fear for the future in their attempts to rip her apart.

Heedless of Elddreki's presence, she sank to her knees right there on the grass, letting the tears come in a silent torrent.

"Well," the dragon interrupted her breakdown unexpectedly, "that was excellent!"

CHAPTER THIRTY

Jocelyn raised her eyes, stunned, her tears arrested mid-sob.

"W-What?"

"That was extremely helpful to witness," Elddreki explained brightly. "I think I've figured it out."

Jocelyn blinked stupidly. "Figured what out?"

"Your blockage," said Elddreki patiently. "The force that wrestles with your power whenever it leaves you, and prevents you from learning to control it."

Is it heartbreak? Jocelyn wanted to ask. *If not, I don't really want to talk about it right now.* Although, on reflection, she didn't want to talk about her heart, either. She wished Elddreki would go away, but she suspected there was little chance of that. With a supreme effort, she pushed herself to her feet, trying to put her agony of soul to one side.

"So what do you think it is?"

"Fear," said Elddreki. "You are held back by fear, just as Kincaid said."

Jocelyn shrugged. It wasn't exactly news. "Did you really

only just figure out I'm afraid of my power?" she asked dully. "It's quite a rational response, I think."

"Of course I knew you were afraid of your power," said Elddreki calmly. "That fact was evident almost from the moment I met you. But it is more than that. We already understood that you are afraid of the immediate effects of your power, of the damage you might accidentally do. But that isn't the blockage. The problem is much deeper."

He paused for a moment, thinking, and Jocelyn waited passively. It was hard to muster much interest even in such a crucial matter when she still felt like her whole world was in embers.

"It's all wrapped up in mortality, I think," Elddreki said pensively. "Fear for the future is not common in dragons, or at least, not in the dragons of my colony, who cannot die. In humans, however, it is extremely common, at least by my observation." He brought his gaze back to Jocelyn.

"You, for example, have it in an almost overwhelming quantity. I told you before that the quality I was trying to identify would sometimes swirl around you when you looked at Kincaid. I didn't think of it as fear, because you didn't seem afraid of him in an immediate sense. But perhaps as affection for him grew in your heart, it increased your fear for the future because somewhere deep in your consciousness you anticipated the interaction I just witnessed. An interaction that seems to have brought you great distress."

Jocelyn blinked sluggishly. It was all true, of course, but it was surreal to hear such crushing matters of her heart stated so unemotionally.

"So," her voice sounded unfamiliar in her ears, "I can't control my power because I have too much fear for the future?" It didn't altogether make sense to her, but she supposed she was in no position to question Elddreki's superior wisdom. Especially while she still felt like she had been metaphorically held under a jet of flame.

"No, no," said Elddreki. "I didn't say that. Just that it's all wrapped up in your fear for the future. No, I think your issue is that you are afraid of change. Very deeply afraid of it."

Jocelyn frowned, trying to make sense of it. "A lot of people are afraid of change, Elddreki. Maybe even most humans. Kincaid," it was hard to even say his name, "is unusual in how easily he embraces it."

"I can imagine a lot of other people are afraid of change," Elddreki acknowledged patiently. "But those people weren't born with the magic of change within them, inextricably woven into who they are. The effect in your case is that you are afraid of yourself, essentially. You are at war with yourself, unable to hold your power in because it is too strong, but unable to fully release it because you fear and mistrust it."

Jocelyn didn't know how to respond. She couldn't deny that for most of her life she had wrestled with herself, particularly in regard to her power.

"And you don't just mistrust its effects, you mistrust its essence," Elddreki was continuing. "You see it as inherently evil." The dragon shook his head. "Kincaid pointed out once before that when confronted with change, you see only the bad, only the destruction. It is as though you are incapable of recognizing its potential. And in the same way you are unable to see what Kincaid could immediately see—your power is just as valuable as it is dangerous. Its potential for good is at least as strong as its potential for destruction. Especially if you learn to control it. Because you have a true heart, Jocelyn. You are a safe custodian of such a power, if you could wield it without hindrance."

Tears started back to Jocelyn's eyes at this compliment, which she couldn't help but feel was undeserved. If her heart was really true, would she have denied it like she just had? Would she have put Kincaid through the agony she had seen in his eyes?

But Elddreki wasn't finished. "All of this I had begun to understand as we traveled together. But I didn't fully identify the problem until I witnessed you rejecting happiness, denying your own nature, simply because you are afraid of the change it will bring to your kingdom. You assume the change will be negative, because you are unable to recognize its potential to be anything else."

The dragon gave her a penetrating look. "You are even, I suspect, a little afraid of the change it would bring to your life. I imagine you and Kincaid would be very happy together, and it's not clear to me why you would be afraid to embrace a future with him. But if your fear and dislike of change is so deep, perhaps there doesn't need to be a logical reason."

"Maybe you're right," said Jocelyn wearily. "But I don't see how it helps me. I don't know how to overcome my fear any more than the next person."

Elddreki gave a guttural chuckle, his scales rustling as he shook out his shoulders. "I must confess, my intention in sharing my thoughts was not to help you. I am merely trying to unravel the fascinating riddle you present." He looked at her thoughtfully. "Not that I would be reluctant to help you, of course, if I could. It has not escaped my notice that you are in some distress. What would you like me to do?"

"Nothing," said Jocelyn dully. "There's nothing you can do. Unless you can turn back time and prevent me from ever meeting Kincaid."

"Is that what you want?" Elddreki demanded. "Dragons do not change the past, Jocelyn, although you would not be the first of your line to ask us to do so." Jocelyn looked up curiously, but Elddreki had moved on. "But there are other ways. Perhaps I can use my magic to clear your memories." He nodded decisively. "I can do so now, and you will have no recollection of Kincaid at all."

He opened wide his mouth, and Jocelyn could feel the magic growing inside him as surely as the flames had grown within the other dragon.

"What?!" she cried, putting her hands out defensively as she stumbled away from him.

A dozen memories flashed through her mind at once—the curiosity in Kincaid's warm brown eyes as he regarded her by the fire in Montego, his blazing fury when he had been powerless to protect her from the gang in Thalia, the exhilarating feel of him beside her in the darkness of the cave, the sincerity in his voice at the markets when he told her she was beautiful. His absurd, wonderful, inexplicable insistence that her power was nothing to be feared, that she wasn't dangerous. The way he had lingered over her hand as he kissed it before she left the mainland, a few short hours ago.

And more potent than all of them combined, the memory of Kincaid's lips on hers, his breath unsteady and his fingers tangled through her hair, leaped to the front of her mind. It screamed for her attention, refusing to be discarded.

"No!" she cried, and her power catapulted out from her with the word, its trajectory feeling more targeted than it ever had. "Elddreki, don't you dare!"

"No?" Elddreki paused, closing his mouth and cocking his head to the side. "You don't wish for me to remove your recollections of our former companion?"

Jocelyn glared at the dragon, ignoring the pang that shot through her at the word "former". "Of course I don't! That's an outrageous suggestion!"

"But it is clear his effect on you has been substantial," argued Elddreki. "Can you deny he has changed you?"

"No," Jocelyn choked out. "I don't deny it. But that doesn't mean I want to forget him!"

"Even though the change is permanent?" Elddreki probed. "Even though it is a change you did not plan, a change that is painful?"

"Yes, even so, I don't—wait a minute." Jocelyn frowned, the sparkle in Elddreki's eyes tipping her off as much as his repeated use of the word *change*. "Elddreki..." she said suspiciously. "*Can* you even use your magic to remove memories?"

Elddreki didn't answer, his eyes continuing to twinkle.

"Elddreki!" Jocelyn's mouth dropped open in indignation. "Are you...are you tricking me? Are you manipulating my emotions and playing on my heartbreak in order to make a point?"

On a human, Elddreki's smile would be called a grin. "Humans are so dramatic in their reactions to such things," he said unrepentantly. "The temptation is almost irresistible."

Jocelyn glowered at him, her chest heaving with indignation and her heart still racing in response to the recent scare.

"But in all seriousness," Elddreki said, his voice suddenly earnest. "I said I want to help you, and I do. Can you not see the point I was trying to make?"

Jocelyn frowned at him, but inside she acknowledged it. Kincaid was as dramatic a change as she had ever encountered. And even though it might lead to devastating loss, she still wouldn't undo it if she could. She wouldn't choose to go back to who she was before she'd met him. She wouldn't choose to be unchanged. In spite of everything, she didn't truly believe that particular change was bad.

"Believe me, Jocelyn, change is necessary." Elddreki's tone had become heavy. "Coming from a colony which has chosen to close itself to change for all eternity, I can say that with authority."

Jocelyn met his eyes, her own heart touched by the sadness she saw there.

"I don't think any other dragon in Vasilisa would admit it to you," Elddreki went on, his voice unusually quiet. "But as foolish and as fragile as you humans are, we envy you. We envy your place in the cycle of generations. We even envy the knowledge you gain when you cross the threshold of death. It is a question that will never be answered for us."

He looked away from her. "You asked me once if I regret my choice, and I did not answer you. But seeing this place, witnessing the life of this colony, seeing the dragonlings..." He looked back at her, and his gaze was too intense for her to handle. "I do regret it. Do not spurn the gift of change you have within you, Jocelyn. To do so is to dishonor those who have it not. I cannot change, but if I could, I would do so without hesitation."

Jocelyn was silent, unable to think of a single thing to say. After a moment, Elddreki bent his neck, lowering his head until it was right before hers.

"Your power is a gift, Jocelyn." She could feel the magic coming out of his mouth, intermingling with the words. A delicious fuzziness began to steal through her, dulling her senses and making her feel weightless. "Do not be afraid of it. Do not distrust yourself. Your kingdom doesn't just need stability, it needs change. You need change."

And with those final words, Jocelyn felt herself sink into the welcome embrace of unconsciousness.

JOCELYN WOKE SLOWLY, her senses returning in a gentle progression. She couldn't remember the last time she had slept so deeply and dreamlessly, and it took her a moment to remember where she was. She became aware that she was lying on her traveling cloak on soft ground, the clear light of morning shining on the branches above her. Beyond the trees, she caught a glimpse of a rocky slope, and it all came rushing back.

Wyvern Islands! The second dragon colony!

She sat up quickly, trying to remember how she had come to be sleeping in a copse of trees. She frowned in concentration. Elddreki had been speaking to her, and he had breathed his magic over her, making her...what? Fall asleep? She remembered his offer to take away her memories, and her heart seized in sudden alarm.

She cast around in her mind, searching for the memory of Kincaid's kiss, then let out a relieved breath. It was still there. Still agonizing. Still indescribably precious.

She was still changed.

She sat up, stretching her stiff limbs as she thought over all the dragon had said. He had certainly made a compelling case for the value of change. Could he be right? Could it be that if she stopped letting her fear rule her, if she started seeing change as something that was necessary, even good, she could learn to control her power? Could choose to use it or not use it as the occasion merited? To make it predictable in both potency and effect?

That would be nice.

She pushed herself to her feet, looking around. She didn't think she was in the copse of trees where Kincaid had played with the dragonlings. This grove was bigger.

"Good morning, young princess!"

The bright voice made Jocelyn turn. Whether Raqisa had been there the whole time or had just landed, Jocelyn couldn't say. Dragons were so unnervingly stealthy.

"Good morning," she responded, smoothing her hair self-consciously. "Did I sleep through the whole afternoon and night?"

"You did indeed," Raqisa affirmed. "You were weary in more ways than one, I think."

Jocelyn acknowledged it with a nod. She looked uncertainly up at the beast. Raqisa was watching her silently. "You...you took my...my companion back to the mainland, didn't you?"

"I did."

"Did he...was he...did he arrive safely?"

Raqisa smiled. "Why do you not ask the question you wish to ask, Jocelyn?"

Jocelyn let out a breath. Irritatingly perceptive mythical monsters. "Did he say anything when you parted?" she asked. She colored slightly. "Anything about...me?"

"He thanked me most earnestly for preserving your life yesterday when you almost perished in flame," said Raqisa conversationally. "A curious courtesy for him to perform if you are not a pair."

Raqisa's words reminded Jocelyn suddenly of her own omission. "I didn't even thank you!" she said quickly. "I'm more grateful than I can say."

Raqisa inclined her head graciously. "I would have been frustrated indeed had you been destroyed before I could fully investigate your unusual properties."

Jocelyn tried not to roll her eyes. She had almost forgotten how cavalier Elddreki had been about her safety before he had changed into a faintly emotional dragon. She frowned to herself. Had she really changed him—a dragon—simply by virtue of her presence? It seemed her power was strong indeed.

"Elddreki said he can't change, even if he wanted to," she said suddenly. "But you can, can't you? You age in a way he doesn't. You can bear dragonlings, you can...well, die."

"I can," Raqisa acknowledged when Jocelyn fell silent.

"Are you afraid to die, eventually?" she asked curiously.

"I am not."

"Why not?" Jocelyn persisted.

Raqisa thought about her answer before speaking, shaking out her shoulders with a rustling ripple that passed all the way down her back to the tip of her tail.

"I had a choice, Jocelyn. I could have chosen not to die, which is a privilege most creatures do not have. I did not make the decision lightly. I would not have chosen as I did had I not felt confident that what I was gaining in the exchange was worth losing what I was sacrificing."

Jocelyn looked into the distance. Kincaid had said something similar once, that most gains involve some loss. Would the gain of Kincaid be worth the sacrifice it would involve for Kyona? She shook her head. How could she choose to sacrifice on someone else's behalf? A whole kingdom of someones.

"Elddreki has told me that his colony consists entirely of immortal dragons," Raqisa continued. "We are not the opposite here. We have not all chosen mortality. There are many dragons here who have chosen not to die. The one who was with me when I greeted you is just such a one. And our elders are immortal. Some of them are almost as old as the dragon-ruler of Elddreki's colony in Vasilisa. I see the effect of their unchanging years, and I am glad we have them. But I do not envy them."

Jocelyn looked up at Raqisa in fascination. "So you really think it's better, the way it is in this colony? Better to have change, even though it means death?"

"Of course," said Raqisa calmly. "Even Elddreki agrees."

"Yes," said Jocelyn absently, remembering Elddreki's confession of regret. He said he would change if he could, but he was incapable of it. She frowned. But he also claimed she had changed him, even if only subtly.

"Speaking of Elddreki," Raqisa said, her head tilted to the side, "I think I can sense his signature approaching." She gave a guttural chuckle, the sound too deep to be feminine. "But it is difficult to be certain with you so close by, confusing the scent." She gave Jocelyn a curious sniff. "It is an incredible anomaly, the way you carry his signature within your own. It reminds me of the interconnected magic of a dragonling and his sire. It is like you are kin, but how can a dragon and a human be kin?"

Jocelyn listened only vaguely, her mind pursuing a different track. "So you can sense my power, right?"

"Of course."

"And you could recognize it as change?"

"That's right. It would perhaps have taken me longer to identify it on my own, but when Elddreki named it, the essence became clear."

"But does it affect you?" Jocelyn pushed. "Do you experience any change?"

"Me?" asked Raqisa, surprised. "Of course not. I imagine your power would only impact other humans."

Jocelyn was silent for a moment, deep in thought. "Elddreki said my power isn't in my words, it's in me. My words are just one of the main ways I let it out. Do you think that's true?"

"It sounds reasonable."

Jocelyn looked up at the yellow dragon. "Can you use your magic on me again? So I can watch? Not to submerge me in memories of the past again," she added hastily. She had no desire to get lost in Princess Sarai's troubles at the moment. "Some other magic."

Raqisa looked surprised, but she didn't object. "What would you like me to do?"

Jocelyn cast her mind around for something simple, something not too intrusive. The morning air was chill, and her traveling cloak was still on the ground instead of around her shoulders. The traveling cloak she had bought with her bracelet. Kincaid had been so cross at the discovery. For all his talk of gain requiring loss, Kincaid hadn't even wanted her to lose something as unimportant as jewelry. No wonder she had seen nothing short of horror in his eyes when she said she intended to sacrifice her heart for the marriage alliance.

Stop, she commanded herself sternly. No good would come of brooding.

"It's cold," she said to Raqisa, her voice firm. "Elddreki always seems to emanate warmth. Can you use magic to warm me up?"

"Certainly."

Raqisa opened her mouth, only a fraction, and Jocelyn tried to focus her attention on it. She realized she was unconsciously watching for fire, as had built in the other dragon's mouth, and she closed her eyes. It was easier to focus on the magic without sight, sometimes. She could feel Raqisa's power now—it felt different from Elddreki's, or Eamon's, or her own. She almost thought she was starting to recognize its signature.

It didn't leak out of Raqisa as Jocelyn's power had so often leaked, or shoot out in unstable bursts. She could sense the way Raqisa gathered its strength, containing it until it was ready. Then she cast it out from her, almost like the fishermen Jocelyn had seen casting out their nets when she visited her father's hometown on the coast.

Jocelyn felt it settle over her, molding to her shape for a moment, then seeping into her skin. She had been so focused on the magic she wasn't paying attention to the physical sensation, but she suddenly realized she was delightfully warm.

"Thank you," she said, referring both to the warmth and the demonstration. She hesitated. "Do you mind if I try?"

Raqisa chuckled. "I do not mind in the least, young maiden. But you do not have fire inside you, and I do not think you will be able to warm me."

"No, no, I'll try something different," said Jocelyn absently.

But what to try? Her power was change, apparently, but it

was a bit ambitious to try to actually change anything about the dragon. What was she good at?

Making people uncomfortable, she thought ruefully, but that seemed a poor repayment for Raqisa warming her up. She sighed. Little as she might like it, change was her only area. Changing people's minds usually, rather than their nature. She glanced up at the dragon. On the off chance that it worked, she should try to make it a good change.

"If you're not afraid of dying, what are you afraid of?" she asked.

Raqisa considered the point. "Sometimes I fear discovery by humans. I fear the loss of our isolation here."

Jocelyn considered Raqisa's words, tilting her head to the side in an unconsciously dragon-like gesture. It wasn't difficult to think of the words to use. That part she had been doing all her life. She focused instead on trying to harness her power.

"That would certainly be a change," Jocelyn acknowledged. As soon as the words emerged, her power wanted to catapult out as well. But she thought of how Raqisa had crafted her magic before releasing it, and she concentrated her mind on holding it in. *Not forever*, she promised silently. *I'm not trying to hold it back altogether. Just until it's ready.* She felt her power swirl within her, potent and familiar and unexpectedly accessible.

"But does that mean it would be bad?"

She cast the net out as she spoke, trying to copy the way Raqisa had done it. She realized the truth of her own suggestion even as she made it. Raqisa was assuming interactions with humans would be a bad change, but there was just as much reason to think of it as a good change. Elddreki had been traveling with humans all this time, and she was fairly certain he was glad of it.

She remembered Elddreki had said her power wasn't actually in her words, and she continued to send it out even after she had finished speaking. She was amazed at the quantity. It seemed to just keep coming.

Eventually it stopped, and Jocelyn opened her eyes. Raqisa was watching her carefully, the expression on her reptilian face difficult to make out.

"You are right, Jocelyn," the dragon breathed. "Your implication is clear, and sound. My fear is based on an assumption. Isolation from humans may not be necessary simply because it is what we have always done." The dragon shook her head slowly. "It is more than just the logic of your argument. I can hardly credit my own senses, but I believe your power did just affect me. Minimally, but even so."

"Yes," Jocelyn agreed, feeling awed—and a little frightened—at her success. "Even so."

"Well done, Jocelyn." The new voice made Jocelyn jump. "You are learning at last."

CHAPTER THIRTY-ONE

"Elddreki!" Jocelyn gasped, turning around. "How long have you been there?"

"Long enough to be pleased you are taking my advice," said Elddreki approvingly. "You wish to learn how to control your power."

It wasn't a question, but Jocelyn confirmed it with a nod anyway. "For a moment I really convinced myself that using my power was a good thing, and it was incredible how easily I could draw on it."

"That's how it should always have been," Elddreki affirmed. "That's probably how it is for your brother."

"Yes," mused Jocelyn. "He's never had any reason to fear or mistrust stability, has he? And if holding it in has only made it more unstable and unpredictable, that's probably why mine has seemed to be getting stronger and his hasn't."

She frowned thoughtfully. "But I don't think it's true he can access it so intentionally. He didn't even agree with me that our power was magic. I don't think he can recognize its form and its potential the way I've been learning to do. He's never been directly exposed to dragon magic like I have since I met you." She felt a stirring of excitement as she imagined telling her twin all she had learned. "But maybe I can teach him!"

"I'm sure you can," smiled Raqisa. "Although you might want to practice more yourself first."

"Yes," agreed Jocelyn, surprising herself with her eagerness. "And this is the perfect place to practice, because I don't think I can really do a dragon any harm, do you?"

Elddreki shook his head indulgently. "You are making progress Jocelyn, but you still see your power as primarily a danger. You will not do us any harm. You may even do us some good, who knows?" He looked at Raqisa. "I am speaking based on an assumption that we will be welcome to stay, but perhaps that is hasty."

Jocelyn stifled a chuckle at the idea of Elddreki being hasty about anything.

"You are certainly welcome to stay," said Raqisa. "Both of you. For as long as you choose."

Jocelyn had been about to comment, regretfully, that she should probably think about rejoining her delegation in Bryford soon, but Elddreki spoke before she could.

"It is gracious of you to say so, Raqisa, since my presence may be a source of grief."

Raqisa inclined her head in acknowledgment, but Jocelyn frowned.

"Why would your presence be a source of grief?"

"Raqisa and I would be glad to pair," said Elddreki matter-of-factly. "But my choice has made that impossible."

"You could just as accurately say my choice has made that impossible," interjected Raqisa serenely.

Jocelyn stared between them, her eyebrows raised. She was as astonished by the total absence of self-consciousness on the part of either dragon as she was by the declaration itself.

"But..." she felt her own cheeks heating in vicarious embarrassment. "You know that so soon after meeting?"

Elddreki looked surprised. "Dragons generally recognize their pair instantly," he said. "Does it take humans so long?"

"Uh..."

Jocelyn tried not to think about Kincaid, and failed instantly. It seemed impossible that a few weeks ago she hadn't even met him yet. She remembered their first conversation, his unsettling attractiveness, the way his gaze had seemed to see straight into her. She hadn't felt for him then what she did now, of course. But had it really taken that long, in the scheme of things?

"Not always," she admitted uncomfortably. "But it's not generally instant." She looked between the dragons in wonder for another moment, then gave a sudden chuckle. "Another contradiction, like your impossible speed. You have all the time in the world to find a pair, but you know the instant you lay eyes on them."

"Not all dragons have all the time in the world," said Elddreki sadly, his eyes resting on Raqisa. "But I take your point, and I suppose there is a certain humor." But Jocelyn could see no humor in his face, only the same sadness she had seen the day before, when he told her he regretted his choice. Her heart twisted on his behalf. Who would have imagined Elddreki was suffering his own dragon version of heartbreak? The thought was bizarre.

"And you definitely can't pair?" she asked tentatively.

"Certainly not," said both dragons, in a unified tone of stern disapproval.

"I have already told you, Jocelyn," Elddreki continued. "Unions between mortal and immortal dragons lead only to great grief and destruction. It is as unthinkable to make such a choice as it is to create an abomination. No dragon would do it, not for any consideration."

"Alas, if only that were true," said Raqisa sadly. Both her dragon and human listeners turned to her, and this time Elddreki looked as astonished as Jocelyn.

"What do you mean?" he asked warily.

Raqisa looked back at him with eyes that seemed ancient, for all her relative youth. "You come from a colony of immortals, Elddreki," she said. "You are the youngest and probably considered the least wise. But here you are older than half of our colony. Many of the dragons on these islands do not have a fraction of the wisdom or the experience you have come to think universal in dragons."

"You say that unions between mortals and immortals are sanctioned here?" Elddreki demanded in astonishment.

"Of course not," said Raqisa quickly. "We are taught the dangers as you have been. It is forbidden, as is the abomination of which you speak. But occasionally there is a dragon who questions the wisdom of the restriction."

Her eyes clouded over for a moment, and it was clearly with great effort that she continued.

"There were two such dragons within my lifetime. One had only just made his choice of immortality when the other emerged from the confines of youth. Filled with the idea of nurturing a generation of dragonlings as she had herself been nurtured, she rushed toward her decision, not taking the proper time to let it craft itself within her being." Raqisa's voice was so filled with grief Jocelyn felt a sudden inexplicable desire to cry. "Then they met, and recognized one another," the dragon finished. "The result was devastation."

"But surely they knew they could not pair," protested Elddreki. "Surely they knew they must let their paths diverge, and wait patiently, and that in time each had great likelihood of recognizing another."

Raqisa turned a sad smile on him. "Patience is another of those traits not universal to dragons, my friend. They were both young, very young, and they did not follow the course of wisdom. They knew they ought not to pair, so they did so in secret."

"What happened?" Jocelyn asked, equal parts fascinated and unnerved. It was so contrary to everything she thought she knew of dragons to hear of them behaving like, well, human teenagers.

"The pair once made could not be unmade," Raqisa said simply. "The elders were grieved, but they did not attempt to separate the two. They knew they must let the tragedy run its course, and deal with the consequences when they came. We are doing so now."

Jocelyn glanced at Elddreki. He looked horrified, but she was still in the dark. "What do you mean?"

Raqisa sighed. "In time, she passed into death, the vision of dragonlings that led her to make her initial choice never realized. And he lingered." Raqisa frowned. "He lingers still. It must be so, whatever has been reported. I cannot believe he would forfeit his power, young though he still is. He may have played with the idea in his darker moments, but he knows as well as we all do how evil such a course would be."

"Where is he now?" Elddreki asked sharply.

Raqisa gave a rippling shrug. "We do not know. He left to nurse his grief in privacy, and has not returned to the Dragon Realm for some time. But he must be lying low, wherever he is. There have not been sufficient reports of a dragon roaming the land to suggest he is showing himself abroad. At least," she gave Elddreki a pointed look, "until the very recent reports of a dragon traveling across Valoria."

But Elddreki ignored this reference to himself. "You do not speak the whole truth that is in your mind, Raqisa," he said firmly. "You speak as though you are trying to convince yourself, not us. What is it you are withholding?"

Raqisa shook out her shoulders uncomfortably. "You are right, Elddreki. I am troubled by what I have heard, and I do not wish to believe it." Her gaze transferred unexpectedly to Jocelyn. "The dragon who almost destroyed you yesterday had but just returned to our realm. Our elders had seen from afar certain rumors swirling among humans. They feared our missing dragon may be contemplating the worst of all crimes. Forfeiting his power to a human."

Elddreki drew in a sharp breath. "Surely no dragon would do so!"

"So I keep telling myself," said Raqisa heavily. "But as I have said, not all dragons are as wise or as restrained as those of Vasilisa. I cannot bring myself to believe he actually did so, but apparently the dragon who returned yesterday discovered that our kinsman has at least approached humans to discover if they would be willing."

Jocelyn gasped, the pieces suddenly falling into place. "The woman on the loch! The one who claimed a wyvern emerged from the water near her boat and offered to grant her greatest wish!"

Raqisa inclined her head. "We are aware of the superstitions of the people who live on the mainland near our islands. We do not begrudge them their legends of sea monsters, or particularly wish to correct their understanding."

Jocelyn and Elddreki exchanged a look, and Jocelyn was sure her companion was also remembering their public declaration in Arinton's central square. It might be a little late to keep the reality of wyverns a secret.

"But we believe a true encounter did occur," Raqisa was continuing. "The human in question did not accept the offer, of course. But you can understand why my kinsman was alarmed when he returned from his investigation to discover a human in our realm, one with magic."

Jocelyn nodded, shuddering at the memory of the heat that had licked her face as the dragon's deadly fire had built within his core.

"He thought this dragon, the one who's grieving and wishes to die, had forfeited his power to me."

"He did," Raqisa assented.

"He should not have been so hasty in acting on his suspicions," said Elddreki sternly. "He should have taken time to properly understand the situation." But his severe expression soon subsided, replaced with amusement. "How turbulent must be the life of this colony, with so many young and impetuous dragons. It sounds...exciting."

Jocelyn smiled, accepting without rancor the ease with which her supposed protector dismissed the attempt on her life.

"You know, Elddreki, if I really do carry your signature, then I think you probably have as big a part to play as my parents in the fact that my power is change." She shook her head at him. "My father told me you seemed different from the other dragons of Vasilisa, and I can see it's true. You obviously have some yearning for change within you that none of your fellows have. Has anyone else showed any interest in exploring beyond the mountains, or looking for another colony?"

Elddreki fixed Jocelyn with a long look, his head tilted to the side as usual.

"You make an interesting and perceptive observation, Jocelyn," he said, and she tried not to be offended at the patent surprise in his tone.

She turned back to Raqisa, who was watching Elddreki with a smile of her own. Looking more closely, Jocelyn could see the admiration in the younger dragon's gaze. She was clearly still very taken with the newcomer, despite knowing they couldn't have a future together.

Jocelyn knew the feeling.

"So would the human be like me then? If your missing dragon forfeited his power to them, I mean? Is that why the dragon yesterday thought that's what I was?"

Raqisa brought her gaze slowly back to Jocelyn's face. "I do not know," she said. "No one does, because no one has ever forfeited power to a human. Power was forfeited in the past, in our dark days, but always to less intelligent beasts. The idea of actually offering your power to a human, giving them the chance to choose what form it might take, is as novel as it is alarming. But I do not think the result would smell like you."

Jocelyn patted her hair uncomfortably. It had been days since she had properly bathed, and she wished dragons would fixate less on her smell. It was making her self-conscious.

"A dragon who was not paying attention might not recognize it immediately," Raqisa was continuing, "but I could tell as soon as I encountered you that your magic was woven through your core. You do not carry it like an artifact. A human who received forfeited power might reek of magic, but it would not be a part of him. Rather, he would be warped by it."

Jocelyn nodded, but Raqisa had one final comment to make.

"The warped magic would also be finite. Yours, however, will not run out as long as you are alive, perhaps even beyond. Your power is defined, restricted to one function. But within that function, I truly believe its potential is limitless."

RAQISA's startling pronouncement played over and over in Jocelyn's mind throughout the day. There wasn't much else to occupy her as she wandered through the outer circle of the Dragon Realm. The green grass and shady trees were pleasant, and dragonlings occasionally romped past, brightening the landscape. But Elddreki and Raqisa had returned to the inner circle of the island, where Jocelyn was not allowed, and where the adult dragons clearly spent most of their time. Jocelyn felt a little lonely, accustomed as she had been to her traveling companions. But she was also glad of the space to think. The last twenty-four hours had given her an overwhelming amount to think about.

I truly believe its potential is limitless.

The dragon's words exhilarated and terrified Jocelyn in equal measure. Could it be true? And if Elddreki and Kincaid were right that change was nothing to fear, and that by extension her power was at its core an instrument for good, what did that mean? Could she actually help solve Kyona's problems rather than making them worse? Could she change people's minds about the freedmen, for example?

Change. Change change change.

Her thoughts always circled back to the concept, trying to figure out if Elddreki's reflections on her deep dark fears were correct.

Do not spurn the gift of change...to do so is to dishonor those who have it not. I cannot change, but if I could, I would do so without hesitation.

Elddreki's earlier words haunted her memory, reproaching her even more now she understood the full impact of his regret. They combined with Raqisa's declaration to tickle an idea that had been slowly building in Jocelyn's mind. It was such an outrageous idea that at first she refused even to explore it. It was surely impossible.

But her mind kept coming back to it. She wanted so much to believe her power could be good. And she wanted to do something good with it. And the idea was so ridiculous it almost seemed like it would never have occurred to her if she didn't know, somewhere deep in her consciousness, that she was capable of it.

Elddreki was her kin, Raqisa had said, his signature mixed in with hers. Jocelyn's power was limitless, Raqisa had said. And there was something about Elddreki in his own right. Something no other dragon in Vasilisa had. Something that had driven him to seek out this colony.

But no. She was being fanciful.

She almost laughed aloud at the thought. If she was being fanciful, she was right on target. What could be more fanciful than being here, in a hitherto unsuspected second Dragon Realm? What could be more fanciful than a magic connection to the memories of a long-dead half-Kyonan half-Valorian princess who wasn't even her ancestor? What could be more fanciful than this entire quest?

But she could think of several very likely outcomes of making the attempt, none of them good, and the most probable being that she would make a fool of herself. She sighed. That shouldn't be too high a price to pay, if there was any chance of success.

She wasn't going to try. It would be crazy. But just in case, she practiced. All day she practiced, over and over. She practiced on the trees, on the rocks, on the dragonlings. Throwing out her net of power, pulling it back, throwing it out again. Telling herself over and over that change was good, change was necessary, change didn't have to mean fear. She was mentally weary by the time the sun began to set, but perhaps Raqisa was right, because her well of power didn't seem to have run dry.

She ate a simple, solitary meal, glad of the provisions from the kind people of Arinton, since she had seen nothing in the Dragon Realm fit for a human to eat. Then she waited for Elddreki, who had said he would return to speak with her before nightfall.

She wasn't surprised when Raqisa accompanied him. She had begun to grow quite fond of the yellow dragon. Not as fond as Elddreki, judging by the occasional wistfulness she saw in his face as he looked at Raqisa.

Good. He was halfway there all by himself, experiencing emotions and everything. Most unlike an immortal dragon.

"You look...excited," said Elddreki, after the appropriate greetings had been exchanged.

"I was going to say nervous," Raqisa offered.

Jocelyn nodded. "I'm both," she acknowledged. She turned to Elddreki. "I've been thinking about...well, everything. And I've been practicing. And I want to try something on you, if you're willing to take the chance."

"Certainly I am willing," said Elddreki, sounding indulgent.

"First I need to ask you something, and I need a very serious answer from you."

Elddreki sat back on his haunches, his eyes curious. "I will endeavor to answer most solemnly," he said, his voice grave.

Jocelyn took a deep breath. "Did you mean it when you said you regret your decision? That you would change it if you could?"

Elddreki's eyes flicked to Raqisa before he responded. "To give a solemn answer, yes. I did mean it, Jocelyn."

"Good," said Jocelyn, her heart beating a quick staccato. "Then hold still."

She didn't know whether or not Elddreki obeyed, because she squeezed her eyes shut immediately. She took a moment to breathe deeply, trying to focus her mind. There was no rush—Elddreki was never in a hurry.

Then she dug deep, deep within herself, drawing up every ounce of power she could find, gathering it in her core, sculpting it, crafting it, holding it back from releasing. She thought about Elddreki's bright and curious eyes, his recognition of his own signature within her magic, his insatiable interest in the humans who the rest of the dragons were happy to ignore, his steady growth of emotion toward her.

She thought about the longing in his voice when he spoke of dragonlings, the sadness in his eyes as they rested on Raqisa. He had said he couldn't change, but he had said she'd begun to change him. The power was well-formed within her now, clear in its purpose, needing no words, awaiting release. She remembered the certainty of Elddreki's declaration—*I cannot change, but if I could, I would do so without hesitation.*

Then she cast her power out, making the physical gesture with her hands, and audibly breathing the word "change" just in case either helped. She felt her hands touch Elddreki's scales, and she continued to pour out her power.

She tried to visualize it as limitless, and indeed it kept coming and coming. The place where she was touching Elddreki began to burn, and her hands felt scorched, but she didn't break contact. She could feel something shifting within him, feel it with an extra sense she couldn't possibly describe if someone asked. But it wasn't enough, it needed more force.

She reached deeper, putting every other consideration aside, reserving nothing for any other change, past, present, or future.

"Jocelyn." She heard the warning in Elddreki's voice, but it sounded like he was on the other end of a long tunnel. "Take care, Jocelyn."

She squeezed her eyes tighter, ignoring his words. More power, more change. Something was wavering, something was ready to break, to be destroyed, to be created and remolded and *changed.* She took a shuddering gasp and refocused, drawing on the magic that was woven through her, a part of her consciousness since she first had consciousness. It was still coming. It hadn't run out.

But all of a sudden, she knew that she had.

Just as she sensed some kind of flame roaring into life within the dragon under her hands, her palms feeling like they were immersed in the dragon fire that had nearly claimed her life the day before, she felt her mind suddenly give in, and she fell abruptly into blackness.

CHAPTER THIRTY-TWO

Jocelyn groaned as consciousness returned. Every inch of her ached, and she frowned, her eyes still closed, as she tried to remember who had beaten her and why. And what had happened to her hands? They stung as if she was grasping poisonous nettles.

She would have thought Kincaid would have stopped someone from beating her senseless, she thought, disgruntled. But no. Kincaid was gone, wasn't he? She couldn't remember the details at that moment, but she was aware of a huge hole, an aching sense of loss, in the place where he should have been.

Elddreki, then, she argued with herself. Wasn't the dragon supposed to be keeping her safe? Where was he when she was being subjected to whatever had caused this body-wide bruise?

Elddreki!

She gasped, her eyes flying open as she shot up into a sitting position. Her limbs ached at the sudden movement, but other than an involuntary wince, she ignored it. She was on a makeshift bed on the springy turf of a copse, perhaps the same one she had woken up in last time. But the coverings beneath her were thicker now, and she was surrounded by a positive bower of blooms. Their scent wafted pleasantly over her, although she had a vaguely uneasy sense that her position resembled nothing so much as a funeral display.

Everything came rushing back, and she winced again as she glanced down at her hands. The feeling of dragon flame had not been imagined, apparently. Her palms looked like they had suffered serious burns where they had been placed against Elddreki's flank. She frowned. Something was strange, though. The burns were not fresh. Had someone accelerated the healing using dragon magic? She flexed her fingers, grimacing. If so, could they do it again?

A sudden sound startled her, and she looked over to see a red and blue dragon, smaller even than Raqisa, loping through the trees toward her. The beast looked up and stopped abruptly at the sight of her, upright and awake. She opened her mouth to speak, but before she could do so, the dragon had taken to the air in a gust of wind that shook the trees.

Jocelyn blinked, disoriented.

She leaned forward with a groan, shaking out her stiff and aching limbs. Before she could push herself to her feet, she looked up, alerted by a rushing sound. Elddreki and Raqisa alighted together, their eyes unusually wide as they stared at her.

"Jocelyn. You have woken."

"Did it work?" Jocelyn asked eagerly, without preamble. She stared at Elddreki, trying to tell if he seemed different. "Did the change happen?"

"Yes," Raqisa answered, sounding awestruck. Jocelyn glanced at the yellow dragon and swallowed. It was unnerving to have a creature of such wisdom and power as a dragon look at her with that wonder in her eyes. "I can hardly believe my own words, but yes. It worked."

Jocelyn looked at Elddreki. He was the same, and yet different, and he was looking at her with an unfathomable expression.

"You're...you're mortal?" she whispered.

"I am," he said evenly.

"Are..." She swallowed again. "Are you glad?"

His reptilian face softened into a smile. "I am glad. More than that. I am grateful."

"As am I," said Raqisa softly. A look passed between the two dragons. There was nothing remotely romantic, or even emotional, about it, but somehow it felt too intimate for comfort, and Jocelyn looked away.

"There are no words to convey my astonishment, Jocelyn," Elddreki continued. "That such a thing should be possible...it would never have occurred to me. I still can hardly believe it." His eyes searched her form, concern lingering in their depths. "I know it was I who encouraged you to use your power without fear. But I didn't expect you to undertake such an ambitious task so quickly. I fear it was too great an exertion for you. You pushed yourself further than your human form could sustain. We feared you would not wake."

"I do feel pretty battered," Jocelyn admitted with a grimace. "How long was I unconscious?"

"No great span of time, all things considered," said Elddreki. He gave a grim chuckle. "Although already the passage of time is starting to take on a new meaning for me." He looked up and seemed to realize she was still waiting. "You have been unconscious for only a week."

"A week?!" Jocelyn shot to her feet, her mouth falling open. "I've been lying here for a week?!"

"Indeed," Raqisa acknowledged mildly. "How do you feel?"

Jocelyn took stock of herself, rolling her shoulders. "Hungry," she said, with the hint of a laugh. She looked around. "Is my pack still here somewhere? Some of the food will still be all right." She blinked rapidly, trying to clear her head. "I can't believe I've been out of it for a week."

"I'm afraid your pack fell victim to some overenthusiastic dragonlings," said Raqisa apologetically. "I don't think anything edible would have survived."

Jocelyn tried not to show her dismay. But now she'd articulated it, her hunger was overwhelming.

"Perhaps I can hunt for you back on the mainland," offered Elddreki. "And bring you food here." He gave her an appraising look. "To speak honestly, you still look much too weak to fend for yourself."

Jocelyn shook her head. "Actually, I think it's time for me to stop hiding away, especially if I've already lost a week." She looked up at her dragon companion. "Are you willing to help me fly again, Elddreki?"

"I am," he responded gravely. "To any place you can name. Where are we going?"

She took a deep breath, trying to calm her sudden nerves.

"Bryford."

It wasn't exactly comfortable being carried through the air in a dragon's talons, especially when every inch of Jocelyn still ached with the slightest movement. But nevertheless, the flight was absurdly, terrifyingly short. In less than an hour, they had covered a distance that would have taken days by horse, and Jocelyn could see the Valorian capital, drawing closer by the second on the plain below.

She swallowed nervously. Bryford at last.

It was certainly a beautiful city, at least from a bird's eye view. It sat right on the bank of the Great River, which formed the border between Valoria and Kyona. Immediately south of the city, the river cascaded down in a mighty waterfall, beautiful and dangerous and captivating. The late morning sunshine glinted off the dancing spray, making the falls seem alive.

Just across the river, the mountains loomed in an imposing barrier. Peering down from her vantage point in Elddreki's claws, Jocelyn could see the path she was supposed to have taken, winding down through the mountains from Montego, then making straight for Bryford, across a sturdy wooden bridge spanning the water some way upstream from the falls.

The city itself was gray stone, not unlike Kynton. It was perched at the top of the falls, its wall looking solid and strong. The castle was the clear feature, even from high above. It sat right at the center of the city, its turrets rising impressively, many brightly colored pennants waving merrily in the light breeze. Jocelyn wondered fleetingly whether Princess Sarai would have formed a better first impression of the city if she could have arrived by dragon.

Jocelyn barely had time to take it all in before Elddreki began to descend. Of course they bypassed the city's massive wooden gates, which opened onto the main highway, running south from the capital. Elddreki simply dropped in from above, completely unhindered by walls or sentries. In moments she could hear panicked screams issuing from the city. And in moments more, she found her feet hitting the stone flagway of the large courtyard from which the castle rose. She winced as the impact sent pain shooting up the aching muscles of her legs.

She shook out her skirts and smoothed her hair nervously, aware she must look as windswept as she felt. People had been milling around the courtyard when they approached, but upon the arrival of the dragon and his burden, everyone fled. The flag-stones were deserted, and Jocelyn could dimly hear the sounds of the dramatic tale spreading further throughout the city.

She hesitated, looking up at Elddreki. He was watching her expectantly, his head cocked to the side in a questioning gesture.

She felt foolish. She had thought only of getting to Bryford—she hadn't even questioned what she would do once she arrived. Should she stroll up to the front door of the castle and announce herself as the missing princess, come to stay after all? It would be helpful to know what, if anything, her father had told the Valorian royals about her change in plan.

Before she could decide what to do, she heard the stamp of approaching feet. A moment later a full troop of what appeared to be royal guards hurried into the courtyard in good order. They drew into formation, shields raised and swords out, with archers at the rear. Jocelyn drew back instinctively, leaning against Elddreki for protection. She saw a middle-aged guard give a curt nod, and following his gaze she saw archers positioned along the battlements of the castle. She swallowed.

The guards made no move to advance, just waited expectantly. Within minutes another troop arrived, forming up alongside the first. Jocelyn was blinking at the array of spears and swords before her, their metal glistening in the sunshine, when a ripple passed through the two groups. A tall middle-aged man strode forward from the troops, flanked by two burly guards. He wore no crown, but from his bearing and the behavior of the guards, Jocelyn had no doubt she was looking at King Malcolm.

She gulped. This was not quite how she had pictured her introduction to her potential future father-in-law.

"I am the king of this land," King Malcolm said, his voice steady and his eyes on Elddreki. "Do you come to us in peace, Mighty Beast?"

Elddreki inclined his head ever so slightly. "I come in peace, king of men. I come to deliver my companion safely to you, as she has fulfilled the quest she undertook in order to make good her father's promise to me. I believe you are expecting her."

The king's eyes moved calmly from the dragon to the young woman still cowering against his flanks. Jocelyn took a deep breath and stepped forward, trying to act like the princess she was raised to be.

"Greetings, Your Majesty," she said, sweeping as graceful a curtsy as she could manage in her simple skirts. The movement was painful, but she didn't show it on her face. "I am Princess Jocelyn of Kyona, and I am honored to meet you at last. I offer my apologies for the unexpected delay that prevented me from arriving with the rest of the delegation sent from Kynton by my father the king."

She resisted the urge to again smooth her hair, miserably conscious of how little she looked like a princess of Kyona, in her stained and rumpled peasant dress, ripped at the sleeve and singed at the hem. The peaceful haven of Wyvern Islands seemed far far away, and back in the world of men she felt almost as fearful as she ever had. Her power swirled alarmingly, and it was all she could do to hold it in. At least she had a better idea now of how to do that.

King Malcolm's keen eyes assessed Jocelyn with unnerving penetration. "Greetings, Princess Jocelyn," he said at last. "You are welcome here. As your noble companion has said, we are expecting you."

"Thank you, Sire," said Jocelyn formally, and the Valorian king's attention returned to Elddreki.

Jocelyn had to be impressed by his air of confidence under the circumstances. It was no surprise that he was much older than her own father, and not just because Prince Ormond was some nine years her senior. She knew her father had become king very young, and that her parents had been only a couple of years older than Jocelyn was now when she and Eamon were born. But somehow, seeing the stately silver-haired foreign king brought home to her in a new way just how inexperienced a king her father still was, relatively speaking.

"We would be honored to make you welcome, should you

wish to stay with your companion," King Malcolm was saying to Elddreki, but the dragon shook his head.

"Thank you, but I will not linger." He met Jocelyn's eyes, a gentle smile curving his reptilian mouth. "I find my time is suddenly more precious of late."

Jocelyn forgot about her audience for a moment, turning fully to face Elddreki. Tears suddenly pricked at her eyes at the realization that they were about to say goodbye. The friendship between her and the dragon was as unexpected as it was unusual, but she knew she would miss him terribly when he was gone.

"Will I see you again?" she asked.

"I do not know," Elddreki acknowledged. "I cannot see the future."

Jocelyn nodded, a lump in her throat. "Thank you," she said quietly. "For everything. I am more glad than I can say that our quest was successful."

"No indeed, daughter of kings," said Elddreki. "It is for me to thank you. For your assistance, and for the gift you have given me." He lowered his head until it was directly before hers. "You have much more than repaid my services to your father, and it is now I who stand in your debt. And so I shall tell your father if ever again we speak."

Jocelyn reached out and laid one blistered palm on the dragon's bearded head, closing her eyes for a moment as she breathed in the familiar signature of his magic.

"Goodbye, Elddreki."

"Goodbye, Jocelyn."

And with a mighty wind that caused the pennants to flutter wildly, he took to the air and disappeared, his imposing form headed eastward.

CHAPTER THIRTY-THREE

Jocelyn turned slowly. King Malcolm was watching her appraisingly, his expression uncommunicative. The guards had lowered their weapons, and many of them were staring at her in open astonishment.

Now that the dragon was gone, people had started to emerge from hiding all around the edges of the courtyard. Jocelyn could see them pointing into the sky, clutching each other, and just generally gossiping about the dramatic incident.

"There really *is* a dragon in Valoria! Did you see its claws?!"

"What did it want?"

"That's the Kyonan princess!"

"Are you sure?"

Jocelyn flushed involuntarily at the doubtful tone in which that last carrying whisper had been uttered.

"Let me once again welcome you, Princess Jocelyn Dragon-friend." King Malcolm's clear words rang across the space, and all other voices ceased. "You are clearly a daughter of your royal house." There was a note of humor in his voice, and she saw that he was smiling, although his face somehow still looked stern despite the expression.

"Thank you, Your Majesty," she said, holding her head high. She was representing her father's house, after all. If Princess Sarai could maintain her kingdom's honor in much more crushing circumstances, surely Jocelyn could too. But the silence stretched out uncomfortably, and the king's continued scrutiny made her feel young and vulnerable.

Perhaps he could see it, because all at once King Malcolm's countenance softened, and he beckoned to her. "Come, my dear. Your delegation will be overjoyed to learn of your arrival."

Jocelyn stumbled forward, the subsequent aching in her limbs eclipsed by her relief that the rest of the group from Kyona were still in Bryford. With any luck, she would be in her own royal clothes before she had to face the rest of King Malcolm's family.

But it seemed she had no luck. She had ascended the steps to the castle and was crossing the wide entrance hall in the king's wake, when the sound of running feet made her look up. A tall young man was racing down a corridor toward them, strapping a sword to his side as he came. He was fair-haired, with broad shoulders and thick muscles. His hair was cropped close and his face was attractive, although its expression at that moment was very serious. Jocelyn judged him to be in his mid-twenties, and she didn't need the familiarity with which he addressed the king to know who he was.

Prince Ormond.

Jocelyn held in a groan at the unlucky encounter. She had never felt more disheveled in her life, and she had a feeling it would be hard to undo the first impression she was about to make.

"Father," the prince was saying. "I came as soon as the report reached me. A dragon in the courtyard?"

"All is well, Ormond," said King Malcolm steadily. "The

dragon came peacefully, and has now departed. It seems it came only to deliver our guest."

He glanced over at Jocelyn, and she thought he looked slightly annoyed, as if he too had hoped she would freshen up before he introduced her to his son as a recommended bride. But none of that showed in his voice as he made the introduction.

"Ormond, you will welcome Her Royal Highness Princess Jocelyn of Kyona. Princess, allow me to introduce my son and heir, His Royal Highness Crown Prince Ormond."

Prince Ormond's gaze traveled to Jocelyn, whom he seemed to have only just noticed, and his eyes widened in shock as he took in her appearance. The expression was fleeting, quickly replaced by the well-trained politeness of a hosting prince. But Jocelyn had seen it, and she wished the floor would open and swallow her up.

"You are indeed welcome, Princess Jocelyn," said Prince Ormond formally. Even with the threat of the dragon over, his face retained its serious expression.

"Thank you, Your Highness," said Jocelyn, attempting to hide her wince as she curtsied again. "I am pleased to be here." Her power swirled from her alarmingly, and this time she did wince.

Before any of the royals could say another word, a middle-aged woman in a high-necked dress of severe cut strode purposefully into the entranceway.

"Your Highness," she said sternly. "You have arrived."

Jocelyn had never thought she would be glad to see the grim-faced lady-in-waiting who had been assigned as her chaperone on this trip, but in the circumstances it was all she could do to prevent herself from falling into the woman's arms. The older Kyonan might be severe, but her poise was admirable. No one would have suspected she saw anything amiss either in

Jocelyn's attire or the manner of her arrival as she swept the princess off to the suite long prepared for her. Jocelyn gladly allowed herself to be shepherded down the broad stone corridors, not even risking a glance back at Valoria's crown prince.

Once they were alone, her chaperone was not quite so restrained, but Jocelyn didn't begrudge the woman her scold. She knew she must have given them all a heart-stopping scare with her disappearance, and she was truly repentant. She endured the strictures in her habitual silence. She knew a moment of alarm when her burning cheeks almost betrayed her as the woman expounded on how fortunate she was that she had not run afoul of any men who might get the wrong impression of her, traveling about the kingdom in a peasant dress with only a dragon for escort.

More to the point, Jocelyn thought, she was extremely fortunate her chaperone had no idea of Kincaid's existence. The very thought of what the woman would say if she knew about their time in Dragoncave, or even worse, their passionate kiss on Wyvern Islands, made her shudder internally.

Of course she hadn't forgotten Kincaid. She had thought at first that he was probably still traveling back from the east, given he didn't have the advantage of flight. But then she remembered with a jolt that she'd lost a week to unconsciousness. The thought that he might be there, in the city somewhere, made her heart swell and ache at the same time.

But she pushed the thought to the side because she had plenty else to think about. It was surreal how seamlessly she was reintegrated into the Kyonan delegation. Her maids—including the poor girl whom she had abandoned in Montego, who now seemed to have a permanent look of alarm on her face—fussed over her endearingly. They washed her hair and dressed her in one of her own gowns, and she almost began to feel like a princess again.

She stood it for as long as she could, but when her stomach began to growl audibly, she dropped a hint to a serving girl that she would be grateful for some food. She didn't mention that she hadn't eaten in a week, of course. The girl told her she'd just missed the midday meal, but obligingly hurried away to procure something for her. Jocelyn felt cowardly for admitting it even to herself, but she was relieved to be able to eat in the privacy of her own room, rather than facing Prince Ormond again so soon.

A number of the diplomatic officials who had come with her from Kynton sought her out once she was presentable, to welcome her and express their relief at her safety, and other such wearying formalities. Jocelyn's hands were growing stiff from keeping them folded in her skirts, to hide the burns. None of the officials mentioned the dragon factor in her escapade. They acted like she had been detained in the mountains and had only now emerged. She smiled, nodded, and kept her mouth shut. It felt like nothing had changed. It was more surreal than she could describe.

Less absurd, but more nerve-wracking, was the visit from Queen Marguerite, to welcome her guest. She didn't shy away from the fact that Jocelyn had arrived in Bryford in the company of a dragon. It seemed Jocelyn's father had indeed told the Valorian king and queen that Jocelyn had been detained by a dragon ally from his past. Whether they had passed that on outside their family Jocelyn wasn't sure.

In any event, the queen asked some searching questions, and Jocelyn was unable to get away with swallowing her words like she had with the Kyonans. It took all her recent practice at controlling her power just to keep it inside. She was alarmed to find that the more she kept it in, the stronger it seemed to grow.

She remembered Kincaid's opinion of her suggestion that the only benefit of training with her power would be to avoid using it. She knew that was exactly what she was doing, and she felt like a failure. But the idea of embracing a magical power of change had seemed much more feasible and much less terrifying on a dragon-inhabited island in the middle of the ocean.

Back in the world of humans, Jocelyn felt jumpy and on edge. She knew now just how much her power was capable of, and she shuddered to think of what might happen to a human on the receiving end of the kind of force she had unleashed on Elddreki. Even she, on the giving end, had almost been killed by it.

But still, Queen Marguerite's eyes were kind, and she certainly leveled no reproach at Jocelyn, either for her tardiness or for her unconventional adventure.

"Will you...will you send word to my parents in Kynton, to let them know of my safe arrival?" Jocelyn asked softly, and the queen looked surprised.

"Word has already been sent, naturally. But they are not in Kynton."

"They're not?" Jocelyn asked, startled.

"They were called to Alezae to respond to a disturbance," said Queen Marguerite delicately. "They had requested us to inform them as soon as you arrived, so they kindly notified us of their removal from the capital."

"I see," said Jocelyn, frowning over the unexpected information. What did "a disturbance" mean?

"At all events, your arrival is timely, my dear," the queen said as she rose to leave. "We had been planning tonight's gala for months, and were not at all sure whether to continue with it in your absence. Now the question is pleasantly resolved."

"There's a gala tonight?" Jocelyn asked blankly. She was so dismayed by the idea of being paraded before the kingdom so soon that she forgot to regulate her power, and it leaked out a little. A flicker crossed the queen's face, but it was quickly smoothed out. She was not easily susceptible, then. That was a very good thing.

"Of course, Jocelyn. We know it is a great sacrifice for you to be our guest here on this day, instead of spending your eighteenth birthday with your twin, and your parents. We would be remiss as hosts if we didn't throw you a celebration."

For a moment Jocelyn just gaped at the older woman, her mouth hanging open in unladylike surprise.

"Today is my eighteenth birthday?"

Queen Marguerite had been standing, half turned to the door. But at Jocelyn's question, she resumed her seat, frowning. "You were not aware? I was certain I had the date correct."

"No, I'm sure you do," said Jocelyn quickly. "I just...had no way of knowing the date when I was traveling, and I hadn't realized..." She trailed off, knowing the excuse sounded lame. But she wasn't about to tell the queen, who might be her future mother-in-law, that she had no concept whatsoever of the date because she had spent the last week or so lying unconscious in a funereal bower on a secret dragon island as a result of overextending her innate magical power in order to give an immortal dragon mortality.

She had made a questionable enough first impression as it was.

"My dear," said Queen Marguerite hesitantly. "It has not escaped my notice that you have not been entirely forthright in what you have told me of your recent experiences." Jocelyn colored, thinking of the glaring omission from her story of any mention of Kincaid, and the queen hastened to reassure her. "I don't mean to press you. But...are you sure you're well? You don't look altogether robust."

Jocelyn smiled ruefully at this diplomatic phrasing. She had seen her reflection in the tall looking glass in the room. The fresh clothes were an improvement, but she still looked a little bit like how she felt—as though she had been caught in a stampede of wild elk. Before she could politely if dishonestly assure the queen she was well, the Valorian woman reached out and took her hand unexpectedly. Jocelyn couldn't restrain her wince, and Queen Marguerite's sudden intake of breath told Jocelyn that she'd seen the burns.

"What happened to you, my poor child?" Her forehead creased in concern. "I thought you said the dragons were friendly."

"They were," Jocelyn hastened to assure her. "These injuries were not the result of dragon fire. I was just...careless."

The queen looked unconvinced, but with the same forbearance she had so far shown, she didn't press Jocelyn for details, just promised to send a physician to examine the wounds.

As much as Jocelyn appreciated the gesture, between the physician and the preparations necessary for the evening's festivities, she didn't have a moment to catch her breath all afternoon.

"Oh Your Highness," one of her maids gushed, as she pinned Jocelyn's hair for the gala. "I'm so relieved you're here in time for tonight. You're going to blow them all away."

Jocelyn, sitting in front of the looking glass, met her own eyes ruefully. Somehow she doubted it. With her mouth firmly shut, there was going to be nothing to recommend her but her looks, and they weren't exactly at their best. There were hollows under her eyes, and her face was paler than normal. She was dressed in one of her best gowns, a sky blue creation with lace forming the slim-fitted bodice and cap sleeves, and a full skirt of silk flowing to her ankles, given shape by layer upon layer of tulle underneath.

Normally it suited her brilliantly, and it was still pretty enough. But her week of hibernation had hollowed out her already slim form, and nothing fit quite right.

"I probably shouldn't say it," giggled the maid, needing no encouragement from the princess, "because I know there's nothing official yet. But I think you'll be a little blown away yourself. Prince Ormond is so handsome."

Jocelyn smiled painfully, making no attempt to correct the girl's assumption that she had yet to lay eyes on the crown prince.

"And you'll have plenty of opportunity to see for yourself, Your Highness, because from what I can discover, you'll be seated next to him at the gala. *And* he's going to lead you out for the first dance, of course."

Of course. Jocelyn barely restrained a groan.

"There are lots of handsome men here in Bryford," the maid continued with another giggle. "Even that visiting noble is very handsome, even if he's a little old."

"I never thought I'd say it of a southerner," interjected the other maid. "But I agree, he is very handsome."

"A southerner?" Jocelyn looked up, frowning. "What southerner?"

"Some Balenan noble," said the first maid, narrowing her eyes in concentration as she wrestled with a wayward golden curl on top of Jocelyn's head. "He's a guest of the Valorian royal family, and I gather he's been here before."

Jocelyn's frown deepened. He must be the diplomat Kincaid had once mentioned. "But we've never had a Balenan noble visit Kynton," she said slowly. "Other than Aunt Scarlett's family."

The maid clucked her tongue sadly. "I expect Balenans are wanting to stay away from Kyona these days, and who can blame them? With these nasty freedmen causing such a ruckus, acting like they're so downtrodden."

Jocelyn turned in her seat, her mouth falling open in astonishment at the girl's tone. She had never heard her maid express any such opinion before.

"What are you talking about? The freedmen aren't the problem!"

"I can understand why you'd want to believe that, Your Highness," said the other maid sadly. "What with your friend's family being so close with so many of them. I used to think the same. But I'm afraid it just can't be denied. And it's no wonder if Balenans don't want to come while the freedmen are so uncontrolled, not after the way they wronged Balenol when they left all those years ago."

Jocelyn pushed herself to her feet, her chest heaving, and the maids both fell back a step in surprise.

"*They* wronged *Balenol*? What madness are you speaking? They were slaves in Balenol—*slaves!*"

The maids exchanged glances, their expressions of confusion identical. Jocelyn had made no attempt this time to restrain her power, and she could see them struggling to make sense of their own opinions.

"They were, weren't they?" said one of the maids, looking slightly dazed. "But I thought..." She shook her head in bewilderment. "You'll have to ask the Balenan nobleman to explain it all to you. He's sure to be at the gala tonight."

"You can believe I'll do exactly that," said Jocelyn sharply, all thought of keeping her mouth shut at the celebration forgotten.

CHAPTER THIRTY-FOUR

The royal ballroom of Valoria's castle was one of the most impressive things Jocelyn had ever seen, dragons excepted. She arrived feeling strangely edgy from her walk through the castle. It was surreal to recognize a place she had never been, but thanks to her time in Princess Sarai's head, she did.

The ballroom she hadn't seen before, however, and she had to admit she was enchanted by the sight. Thanks to the long summer days, light still streamed in through the many arched windows stretching almost to the ceiling. Thousands of candles already shone from elaborate chandeliers, ready for the sun to sink. The walls and ceiling were draped with huge swaths of fabric, in Valorian purple, and silver tassels and embroidery could be seen everywhere.

After so long roaming the countryside anonymously, it was strange to enter with all the fanfare of a princess. The long tables were already packed when she and her delegation arrived, those fortunate enough to have been invited for the meal having already taken their seats.

She was announced at the door, and everyone rose, with the

obvious exception of the king and queen. Prince Ormond approached with a stately stride, offering his arm to escort her to her seat beside him. Jocelyn took a steady breath before accepting it, determined to improve on the impression she had given last time.

"Thank you, Your Highness," she said, keeping her power firmly inside.

"Please," he said, "call me Ormond." His voice was pleasant enough, but the tone was so formal it didn't match the words. She dipped her head in acknowledgment.

"You look beautiful tonight, Princess Jocelyn," he said as he led her to her seat.

She glanced up quickly and caught the look in his eyes as they rested on her. He probably didn't intend her to see, but it was impossible to miss the relief. She sighed internally. She couldn't blame him for being glad she had the capacity to look like a princess instead of a peasant wench.

And there was undeniably admiration in his gaze, as well. She felt her cheeks warm slightly—she couldn't help but be pleased he thought she was beautiful. But the memory of his momentary shock at first sight of her intruded uncomfortably. She knew it wasn't Prince Ormond's fault—the expression had been involuntary, and his words and conduct since then had been irreproachable.

But try as she might to avoid it, the comparison with Kincaid was inevitable. The admiration in Prince Ormond's eyes was nothing to the way Kincaid had looked at her in the markets when he told her she was beautiful. And he had looked at her like that regardless of the peasant dress, and the unwashed hair, and the knowledge of her strange and dangerous power.

Stop thinking about Kincaid, she told herself, knowing full well that articulating it would only make her more certain to do so. Once she and the prince were seated, she cast her eyes around surreptitiously. Many people had been invited tonight, nobles and influential commoners alike, if her practiced eye was any judge. Was it completely foolish to think Kincaid might be here? Would it be better or worse if he was?

But she could see no sign of him, and she told herself it was for the best. She resolutely turned her attention to Prince Ormond, determined to get some sense of him as a person. He inquired politely after her health, his eyes lingering for the briefest of seconds on her now-bandaged hands, and she returned an impersonal answer.

"I'm sorry our first meeting was so haphazard," she said softly, as the soup was served. "I'm afraid it wasn't quite the arrival in Bryford I had pictured."

"Not at all," said Prince Ormond politely. "It was my honor to meet you, regardless of the circumstances. And we are all relieved you've arrived safely."

Disappointed in his formality, Jocelyn responded with a strained smile.

"I wish I'd been there!" interjected an eager new voice. Jocelyn turned in surprise to see an attractive young girl, a few years younger than her. She was seated next to the nobleman on Jocelyn's other side. "I can't think of anything more exciting that arriving with a dragon! You'll go down in Valorian history! Much better than arriving with some delegation."

The girl lowered her voice conspiratorially, the attempt fairly useless since she was leaning around the nobleman seated between them in order to speak to the visiting princess. "To be honest, your delegation's arrival was positively boring by comparison."

"Lavinia," said Prince Ormond repressively. She just smirked at him, and he didn't quite manage to restrain an eye roll. It was the most natural behavior Jocelyn had yet seen from him, and it warmed her to the serious young prince.

"Princess Jocelyn," he said in a voice of long-suffering, "allow me to introduce you to my sister, Princess Lavinia."

"You didn't do it properly," Princess Lavinia complained. "You should have called me Her Royal Highness Princess Lavinia, and you should have called her Her Royal Highness Princess Jocelyn of the House of Dragonfriend. I've been dying to hear someone say it all summer."

Jocelyn held out a restraining hand, laughing in spite of herself. "Please, I'm begging you—don't burden me down with all that! Call me Jocelyn."

The younger princess beamed at her. "And you can call me Lavinia, obviously."

"I'm very happy to meet you, Lavinia," said Jocelyn with a smile. She hadn't quite been able to bring herself to call Ormond by just his name yet, but with Lavinia it was easy.

"So the dragon," Lavinia said in a business-like tone. "What was it like?"

"He, not it," Jocelyn corrected automatically. "His name is Elddreki."

"Whoa," Lavinia said, her eyes as round as if Jocelyn had said something unbelievable. "So they really do talk?"

Jocelyn tried not to smile. "Of course they do."

"Lavinia," said Prince Ormond reproachfully. "Don't drown her with questions the moment she arrives. Princess Jocelyn may not want to talk about her...ordeal."

"It wasn't an ordeal," said Jocelyn, surprised. "And I don't mind talking about it."

Prince Ormond looked surprised but, unless Jocelyn was entirely mistaken, his polite front was concealing a curiosity as avid as his sister's. She hid a smile.

"So what did—oh, this is ridiculous," Lavinia complained, clearly tired of leaning halfway across the table to speak. "Lord Irwing, trade seats with me."

The nobleman sitting between Jocelyn and Lavinia continued to sip his soup, untroubled by the young princess's curt command.

"You know I can't do that, Your Highness. The queen would have my hide." His voice was indulgent, and Lavinia pouted slightly.

"Mother and her stupid rules. Why is it so important that we sit man, woman, man, woman?"

"Tradition is not stupid," said Ormond disapprovingly. He turned to Jocelyn. "You'll have to forgive my sister's...vivacity."

"Readily." Jocelyn extended her smile to include Lavinia. "Not that there's anything to forgive." She had taken an instant liking to the young princess, and she could certainly relate to her frustration at the restrictions of royal life. "We princesses need to stick together," she said humorously. "I've often wished for a sister to commiserate with."

Lavinia shot her brother a cheeky look as she responded. "Well, maybe you'll have one soon."

"Lavinia." Prince Ormond's voice was sharp. He looked more scandalized than embarrassed at his sister's allusion to their potential marriage. But Jocelyn's cheeks were heating, and she returned her attention to her soup.

Prince Ormond took charge of the conversation then, talking politely of the trade agreement being renegotiated between their kingdoms. Jocelyn supposed it was a count in his favor that he took it for granted that she would be educated and intelligent enough to share in the conversation, but it wasn't exactly a romantic topic.

Not that she wanted him to be romantic, she reminded herself hastily. The very thought of Prince Ormond trying to speak to her of romance was unsettling to say the least. How would she feel if he put an arm around her to comfort her, or touched her cheek with his thumb, as Kincaid had done more than once? An unpleasant jolt went through her at the thought, and she knew it was more horror than embarrassment. But she was thinking about Kincaid again. She needed to stop doing that.

She looked up at Prince Ormond, surreptitiously observing him as they chatted. He was handsome, she admitted to herself. Very much so. Kincaid's description had been right on target. Tall and fair and swoon worthy, in his way. At least, she might have thought so if her mind hadn't been filled with auburn hair and warm brown eyes. Unfortunately, from what she had seen so far, she thought her own speculative description had also been apt. Old and boring and serious.

She supposed old was a bit unfair. At twenty-six, he was nine years older than her—eight, she realized, remembering again with a start that it was her birthday—but he seemed youthful and strong. But he was certainly serious. And emotionless. She returned her attention to her food with an internal sigh. She was practiced at presenting an unemotional front to the world. She had become very good at it. But the idea of returning to that persona was anything but appealing.

Once the food was finished, King Malcolm rose from his seat to address the assembled guests. He spoke at length, welcoming Jocelyn formally and acknowledging her birthday as an event to be celebrated. It was embarrassing, but inevitable, and Jocelyn bore the scrutiny gracefully.

She hadn't previously been able to see anyone seated on the king's other side on the long table, but with the king on his feet, she had a clearer view. Glancing down the table's length, her attention was caught by a face that was darker than the others. Someone from the South Lands. It must be the Balenan diplomat who her maids claimed could explain to her why the freedmen were the problem in Kyona. She narrowed her eyes. He was seated only a few seats down from the queen, in a position of high honor. What were the Valorian royals thinking, welcoming him here?

When King Malcolm finished speaking, the gala began in earnest. The tables were cleared and pushed against the wall with impressive speed, only to be restocked with an array of food as impressive as the feast they had just consumed. Guests who were not invited for the meal began to arrive in droves, and soon the room felt crowded, large as it was.

"Thank you," breathed a voice at Jocelyn's side, and she turned in some amusement to see Lavinia hovering there, an expression of rapture on her face.

"For what?"

"For being a royal guest of sufficient importance that my parents think I should be here for this." Jocelyn raised a questioning eyebrow, and Lavinia grimaced. "They think I'm too young to be at galas. Usually I have to retire after the meal."

The words tickled something in Jocelyn's memory, even as she smiled sympathetically. "Well, I'm happy to help."

"My brother usually sneaks me some pastries when Mother isn't watching," Lavinia confided. "But tonight I'm actually in the room, and I intend to gorge on them until I'm sick."

Jocelyn couldn't help but laugh at Lavinia's grin. Privately she thought there was no surer way for the enthusiastic princess to solidify her parents' opinion that she was too young for such events, but she saw no reason to rain on Lavinia's parade. She found herself watching Ormond thoughtfully. She was surprised to hear he snuck his sister food in defiance of their mother's restrictions. It was the sort of thing she could picture Eamon doing. Perhaps she had been hasty in her assessment of Ormond.

He looked up from his conversation and caught her gaze. The next moment he was striding across the floor to her, and she realized with a rush of nerves that the musicians were striking up for the first dance.

Ormond claimed her hand with polite formality, and the next thing she knew he was sweeping her across the floor. The ten or so seconds before other couples began to join them felt like the longest of Jocelyn's life, but soon the room was filled with swirling couples, and she felt slightly less conspicuous.

Ormond danced skillfully, but his steps were too studied, too correct for grace. He held Jocelyn with his arms stiffly in the correct position, and she was glad for the distance between their bodies. She wondered how Kincaid would dance, sure her reflections in that situation would be quite different. She barely restrained a groan. He may as well be in the room for how much he was intruding on her thoughts.

At first they danced in silence, and Jocelyn was surprised when Ormond was the one to break it.

"I don't believe I've wished you happy birthday yet."

"Thank you," she said politely.

"You are very poised for your eighteen years."

Jocelyn smiled uncomfortably at the compliment and its unintentional reminder of the gulf in their ages. Could she really marry this man? Could she build a life here, at his side? Princess Sarai had done it, and many other princesses before and since. But Jocelyn felt cold all over at the idea of committing herself to such a bloodless alliance.

She snuck a curious look up at Ormond's face, wishing she could read his thoughts. What did he want? Did he have misgivings of his own about the idea of shackling himself to a stranger for life?

He looked down into her face suddenly, and she looked away, uncomfortable to be caught looking. Her eyes fell on the Balenan man she had seen earlier. He was in a corner, talking with some other men his age, looking on at the dancers with disinterest.

"Who's that?" she asked, tilting her head in the man's direction. "Is he Balenan?"

Ormond followed her gaze. "You mean Lord Randall. Yes, he's from Balenol. He's a guest of my parents."

"Is it unusual to receive guests from Balenol?" Jocelyn asked hesitantly.

"It is," Ormond acknowledged. His tone showed he was aware of the awkwardness of the topic. "Although perhaps not quite as unusual as it is in Kyona. Lord Randall is a senior member of the Balenan court, and he has spent time with us here before."

"I wonder what he wants," said Jocelyn, narrowing her eyes as she watched him. Her power leaked out unintentionally, and Prince Ormond stiffened slightly.

"I'm not sure what reason you would have to wonder about it," he said, a hint of reproach in his voice. "I find him to be a man of great good sense."

Jocelyn raised her eyebrows. "Have you spoken with him a great deal, then?"

"Naturally," said Ormond. "He has been most helpful in advising us as to the best approach to take regarding the aggression of the freedmen."

Jocelyn stopped short, right there on the dance floor. "The aggression of the freedmen?" she repeated blankly. Her tone grew dangerous. "What are you talking about?"

"I mean no disrespect to your kingdom, Jocelyn," said Ormond, his strong arms compelling her to move again, as the dance required. "All kingdoms have their areas of conflict and discontent. Our own northern region is called the North Wilds with good reason. There are lots of—"

"I know all about the North Wilds," she interrupted shortly.

"I don't want to talk about that. I want to know why you think the freedmen are being aggressive, and why you think there's any need for Valoria to take a stance on the matter at all."

"I didn't mean to suggest Valoria would interfere," Ormond assured her quickly. "I referred only to our approach to those embittered freedmen who attempt to cross our border."

"But this is nonsense," said Jocelyn, flicking a shoulder impatiently. Ormond's hands were uncomfortably tight given the dull ache still present in all of her muscles, and it was doing nothing to improve her mood. "This whole idea of freedmen trying to cross the border is ridiculous. Have any tried to do so?"

Ormond hesitated for a moment. "Not yet," he admitted. "But Lord Randall assures us it's only a matter of time before—"

"And you trust this Lord Randall?"

Ormond frowned slightly as she cut him off again, but he seemed surprised by the question.

"Of course. Implicitly."

She stared up into his eyes, confused as much as irritated. Ormond's expression softened.

"I can understand you feeling some prejudice against him, Jocelyn," he said. "Your country's history with Balenol is not exactly pleasant. And I'll admit that the first time Lord Randall came to us, I suspected him of having dishonest intentions. But that was before I spent time speaking with him. Having done so, I cannot doubt his sincerity. He wishes to see harmony restored between your kingdoms, and he is anxious to help Kyona address the threat the freedmen are posing. He said he feels some sense of responsibility, since it was from Balenol that the freedmen came."

"Does he?" said Jocelyn darkly. Whatever Ormond said, she couldn't imagine a scenario in which she would trust a word coming from the Balenan nobleman's mouth, if he was spreading such tales. She was surprised and a little disdainful to find Ormond so easily led. Not a good quality in a crown prince. Eamon wouldn't be so gullible.

"He does," Ormond affirmed, bizarrely eager to further Lord Randall's cause. "And I gather his time in Kyona has been very fruitful. I know you've been away, but he said the Kyonan royal family have been very receptive to his attempts to restore harmony."

"He's been in Kyona?" Jocelyn asked, stunned. "Speaking with my family?"

Ormond nodded. "He's only just returned, and I believe he means to go back almost immediately. He said Prince Eamon has been most enthusiastic to work with him to contain the freedmen."

"Contain them?" Jocelyn asked ominously.

"Contain the threat," Ormond amended hastily.

Jocelyn didn't respond, her mind reeling. How long had she been gone from home, and what in the kingdom had been happening in her absence? She didn't believe for a moment that Eamon would be won over by this nobleman like Ormond apparently had been.

She hesitated. Could Eamon have been taken in, blinded by his feelings for Lucy, and predisposed to think well of any Balenan as a result? But no, surely not. He knew as well as Jocelyn how grim their history with Balenol was. Eamon was no fool, and he would see through anyone talking about containing the freedmen in a heartbeat.

But she suddenly remembered that her parents were apparently not in Kynton, and she was uneasy. She didn't like the sound of Lord Randall returning to Kyona imminently. Some kind of trouble was brewing.

"You look troubled, Jocelyn," said Ormond, not unkindly. "You should speak with Lord Randall yourself. I'm sure he will set your mind at ease."

"If you'll introduce me, I'll do just that," said Jocelyn tightly, as the dance drew to a close.

Ormond obligingly led her over, and made the necessary introductions.

"Your Highness," said Lord Randall, his tone pleasant and polite. "I am honored to meet you."

Jocelyn inclined her head, her brow slightly furrowed. She was expecting duplicity and oiliness, but he certainly seemed sincere. She realized what she was thinking and gave herself a mental shake. He hadn't yet said anything of substance from which she could draw a conclusion about his sincerity.

"I was sorry to miss you, Princess, when I was recently in Kyona," Lord Randall continued. "Your brother received me most graciously. He is an excellent young man."

Jocelyn opened her mouth, then closed it. She felt extremely off-kilter. She had been determined to mistrust this man, and yet she found herself warming to him. He was even very handsome, she admitted to herself. His nose was crooked, but the poor man couldn't help that. Up close, she realized he was younger than she had expected. Probably not much above forty. His coloring and features were familiar, reminding her of her beloved Aunt Scarlett. Perhaps that was why she was so drawn to him in spite of herself.

"Yes," she said, dazed. "Eamon is a wonderful brother." Dimly she registered that Lord Randall had made no mention of her parents. Had they already been in Alezae by the time he reached Kynton? But it didn't matter. She simply couldn't suspect Lord Randall of intending Eamon any harm. She wasn't sure why it was, but somehow he simply reeked of trustworthiness.

The thought sparked something in her mind, but she couldn't grasp it, too distracted by the conversation.

"You must be very proud of him," Lord Randall was continuing, and she warmed to him a little more. After Kincaid's most unfair prejudice against her brother, it was heartening to have someone recognize Eamon's worth. Ormond was right. Lord Randal was a man of great good sense.

"He is young to have so much responsibility on his shoulders, but he is handling the discontent of the freedmen very maturely."

Jocelyn's eyes snapped up, feeling like she was coming out of a daze.

"Their discontent?" she said. "If they're discontented, it's only because of the sudden *unfounded* prejudice against them." In her agitation, she felt her control slip, and power swirled out from her, potent and uncultivated.

Lord Randall stilled, and for the briefest of moments Jocelyn caught a strange glitter in his eyes. She swallowed nervously, trying to read his expression. It was only a second before he pushed on smoothly.

"It does you credit, Princess, that you wish to think well of all your father's subjects. Alas that I should be the one to disillusion you."

Jocelyn felt rooted to the spot, barely able to follow the nobleman's smooth words. And it wasn't the fact that Lord Randall had clearly been unaffected by her power that troubled her. The fleeting look she had witnessed was imprinted in her mind, and she couldn't doubt its meaning. Somehow, impossibly, the Balenan had sensed her power.

CHAPTER THIRTY-FIVE

Jocelyn's mind reeled at the realization. How was such a thing possible? Only people with mountain blood in them, or descendants of Kyona's royal house, had the capacity to sense magic. And it was surely impossible that this Balenan man from across the seas could fit either category.

The slip had put Jocelyn's senses on high alert, and she found herself speaking in tight syllables, monitoring for any power that might make it past her defenses. She searched Lord Randall's eyes as he kept talking, looking for any sign that he was sensing something. Now she was looking closely, she realized with a jolt that the strange glitter was still present in his eyes. In fact, there was something very strange about them, something that she couldn't articulate, but that made her stomach coil sickeningly when she looked into them for too long. How had she not noticed it before?

She glanced at Ormond beside her. He was smiling comfortably, nodding along with Lord Randall's speech. Again she couldn't name it, but there was something about the look on Ormond's face that made her uneasy. Jocelyn returned her focus to Lord Randall, ignoring his words and trying to focus on whatever essence it was that had set her teeth on edge. There was definitely something, something not quite right. But she couldn't put her finger on it.

She responded mechanically to the nobleman's conversation, her face tight with the concentration of keeping her power locked away, giving him no more cause for suspicion. It was as she tested the air around her for any leakage that she felt it. Power, seeping into the space between them. As soon as she identified it, it was unmistakable. But it wasn't coming from her. She stared at the Balenan, and it was all she could do to keep her mouth from hanging open.

He had power? He had magic? Surely it was impossible.

But it wasn't impossible. It was happening, and it was happening right in front of her. She didn't think she would have identified it if she hadn't been through such a rigorous process of learning to recognize, harness, and manipulate her own power. But now she had no doubt.

Had she really thought this man trustworthy only a few minutes ago? With his glittering eyes and his smooth words hiding a strange power, he seemed like a wolf in a thin disguise. But as she tested the power flowing from him in a smooth and constant torrent she realized there was a sense of rightness about it, a sense of confidence in the man who was releasing it. It tugged at her mind, and when she didn't think too hard, all she wanted was to give in to it, to trust him. Only, now she had named it as what it was, the essence rang false. It was not true integrity—it was the appearance of integrity.

She took a quick step back, too shaken to fully hide her shock and consternation.

"Princess Jocelyn?" Ormond's voice was surprised and concerned. "Are you well?"

"I..." Jocelyn tore her gaze from Lord Randall with an effort.

He was watching her with slightly narrowed eyes. "Actually, I'm a little overtired after my travels," she managed. "Perhaps I should retire early after all."

"But..." Prince Ormond protested, and she was sure he was looking for a polite way to tell her she couldn't run out on her own gala.

But Jocelyn wasn't listening. She had already turned away and was hurrying for the large intricately carved doorway. She heard Lavinia call out to her as she passed, but she didn't stop. She needed space to think, and she wouldn't get it in the crowded ballroom. Neither the fact that she was behaving with less than the expected decorum nor the pain shooting through her aching body at the speed of her flight slowed her down for a moment.

Something was wrong, and although she didn't yet know what it was, she knew it took priority over making a good impression on the Valorian royals. She looked at the information she knew so far as she hurried back toward her suite.

There was a Balenan nobleman in Valoria, one who impossibly possessed some kind of magic. He was an enemy to the freedmen, and although he was making sure everyone knew it, no one was calling him out on it. He was apparently coming and going from Kynton at will. If he was to be believed, he was also charming her brother, and even more suspiciously, doing so in her parents' absence.

She didn't need to understand exactly what was happening in order for that information to make her extremely uneasy. She felt a shot of fear go through her heart at the thought of her brother. She didn't know when the feeling had become so strong, but she suddenly had the unshakable conviction that Eamon was in some kind of trouble.

Darkness had fallen some time before, and when she reached her suite, she was glad to find someone had come by and lit a number of candles in preparation for her return. For several frenzied minutes, she paced back and forth, trying to decide what to do. Should she return to Kyona immediately? Should she try to enlist the help of Prince Ormond and his family?

But that idea was unlikely to bear much fruit. Ormond had said himself that he trusted Lord Randall implicitly, and if his parents had accepted the nobleman as a guest on more than one occasion, they presumably trusted him too. They were probably all under the effect of his strange power. The thought made Jocelyn feel sick.

But not as sick as the realization of how close she had come to falling prey to it. Without her time with the dragons, she doubted she would ever have recognized what was happening.

If the Valorians couldn't help her, who could? She wished she had a way to communicate with Elddreki, but she didn't. Her thoughts flew to Kincaid, and the ache in her heart throbbed intensely, momentarily eclipsing her other thoughts. He would take her seriously, and he would want to help. But she had no idea where to find him, and even if she did, she couldn't ask more of him, not after she'd broken his heart. Plus, what could he do?

Fleetingly she considered taking the matter to one of the officials in the Kyonan delegation, but she was afraid to do it. Quite apart from the fact that it would knock any one of them flat to hear her expressing an opinion on matters of state, her maids had clearly demonstrated that Lord Randall had managed to infiltrate the delegation with his lies.

She let out a groan. There was no one to turn to. She was as alone as Princess Sarai. The thought of the other princess, and the permanence of her isolation, filled Jocelyn with a sudden terror. She had comforted herself with the reflection that their paths were not so similar, because there was no risk of a violent uprising cutting her off from her homeland if she married the present day Valorian prince. But now she wasn't so sure. Some kind of threat was looming over Kyona, undefined in nature, but clearly sinister.

She stopped pacing, drawing deep breaths to calm her racing heart. She wouldn't help Kyona by panicking. She needed to think. It wasn't too late. Princess Sarai didn't find out about the threat to her homeland until it was all over, but Jocelyn was one step ahead. There must be something she could do to thwart whatever was being planned. She was not doomed to isolation and grief like Princess Sarai.

Her breathing calmer, she glanced around the room, looking for inspiration. Her eyes fell on a large portrait above the mantel, and she approached it absently. The portrait showed a couple, the man seated and the woman standing just behind him, her hand on his shoulder. They both wore crowns, and the expressions on their faces were peaceful.

Jocelyn stared at the portrait, momentarily distracted from her anxiety. In the natural course of things she should not have recognized these faces from Valoria's past. But natural wasn't the best description of Jocelyn, and she did recognize them.

It was Prince Germain and Princess Sarai. She squinted at the crowns, and the sash the prince was wearing over his ceremonial garb. Or were they king and queen by this stage?

She reached out a hand, feeling like she had found an old friend. She touched her fingers to the skirts of the painted princess. She supposed she should have seen it coming, but when she felt her consciousness suddenly beginning to spin, her only thought was, *not again.*

Sarai handed her horse off to the groom and flung the skirt of her riding habit over her arm. The last thing she needed was to trip on the thing and fall flat as she made her way up the castle stairs. The morning was fresh, and she had been invigorated by her ride over the fields. And, she thought darkly, her mare had shown no sudden inclination to throw and trample her.

She scolded herself internally for the petty thought as she reached the castle's entrance. It had been weeks since the overheard insult, and she was disappointed in herself with how much her resentment over the incident was still lingering. Although if she was honest, Lady Marietta's words bothered her less than Germain's smile as he had spoken to the noblewoman in the gardens.

Sarai sighed, trying to put the incident from her mind. At least Germain's sister had continued to be kind to her, despite clearly disapproving of Sarai's passive response to Lady Marietta's unbecoming behavior. In fact, they had spent so much time together in the weeks of her visit, that Sarai's impromptu ride today felt almost lonely without her. The visiting family had departed only a few days earlier.

Sarai looked up as she crossed the broad entranceway. The morning sun streamed in through many windows, and she found herself admiring the castle's welcoming entrance before she realized she was doing it. It was a beautiful building, she could acknowledge that now. She still found herself comparing it to the castle at Kynton, but she was reasonable enough to recognize that it was well designed and flawlessly decorated. And no less filled with pleasant chatter and cheerful faces than her childhood home had been. She knew it was a testament in her family-in-law's favor that the castle's servants were contented as well as efficient.

She left the entranceway, continuing down a broad corridor. Her thoughts drawn to the servants, she noticed for the first time that there weren't many about. She looked around her, frowning. She had been too caught up in her thoughts before, but now she was paying attention, she recognized that indefinable quality to the air that said something was happening.

She picked up her pace slightly as she neared the large throne room, and she felt her heart skip a beat when she heard imperious voices issuing from within it. Was there some formal address occurring at that moment? She hurried on, dismayed. She had answered the impulse of the moment in going for her ride. She had not strictly cleared it with anyone. She tried to keep abreast of all official happenings at which she might be expected to be present, and would not have left if she had thought anything of importance was scheduled. But perhaps she had forgotten something.

She swallowed anxiously, remembering Germain's words in the garden about wanting the court to see her fulfilling her role, and her inference that he'd been unsatisfied with her fulfillment of that role so far. If there was a formal audience in the throne room, she should be present, standing at Germain's side, doing her part as a member of the royal family. She reached the doorway and hesitated, wondering if it would be a worse offense to enter in her riding habit, or to delay her arrival further by changing into court attire.

The door was open, a young servant standing at attention just outside, as was usual. He hesitated at her approach. She acknowledged him with a gracious nod before peeking into the room, hoping to get a sense of what was happening before committing herself.

She frowned in confusion at what she saw. It was not a formal audience, as the king was not present, but there could be no doubt the gathering was serious in nature. There were some dozen nobles present, their expressions ranging from grave to agitated. No one sat on the thrones, and she could see no sign of her husband, but Germain's younger brother stood on the dais at the end of the long room, his arms crossed and his forehead creased as he listened to one of the nobles. She had just started to withdraw, deciding that since Germain wasn't present, there could be no expectation of her attendance, when the nobleman's words penetrated to her consciousness.

"...must listen now to our concerns. Many of us have believed since

receiving news of the coup that the Kyonan princess is a liability Valoria can ill afford. Now I would say it is indisputable."

"That's right," another chipped in. "The border cannot stay closed forever. We must agree to trade and treat with Kyona's new king."

Sarai had been frozen in place at the realization that they were speaking of her, but a flash of anger passed through her at these words. Treat with Kyona's new king? "New king"? He was no king! He was a usurper, a murderer. She closed her eyes for a moment, her agony returning. If only she knew where Jonathon was! Surely he could not be dead. Surely the usurper would have advertised it if he was.

"Of course the crown will listen to whatever concerns you may have, but I think perhaps you exaggerate the risks, My Lords," said her brother-in-law mildly.

"I am afraid not, Your Highness," a third noble interjected, his voice oily. Sarai recognized him—Germain had told her once that he was the head of the king's intelligence network. "Our spies report not only that our...unfortunate alliance...has seriously damaged Valoria's image in the eyes of Kyona's new king, but that he actively resents the fact that we are harboring the princess."

"And why should we harbor her at cost to Valoria's interests?" another nobleman added gruffly. The noble in charge of intelligence shot him a look of irritation at the interruption, and continued, his tone still wheedling.

"All our sources are agreed that the Kyonan king remains determined to ensure the total destruction of the house of his predecessor, including the princess. Not only does that put Valoria at risk of war should he send men across the border to pursue her, but should she bear a son to the crown prince, even our own succession would be endangered by the Kyonan king's intentions."

There was a muttering hiss around the room, and Germain's brother unfolded his arms, looking shaken. Sarai felt shaken herself at the idea that her father's murderer might try to kill a future child of hers in his desire to wipe out all trace of King Cael's line. The thought had never occurred to her.

"We are fortunate indeed that she is not yet with child!" boomed the noble who had been speaking when Sarai first arrived. Sarai realized she recognized him, too. He was Lady Marietta's father, and probably the most influential nobleman in the court. "It is a gift, one we must not waste. We must take action now to remove this threat before it is too late."

Sarai's blood was pounding in her ears. She glanced at the servant standing alongside her, and he met her eyes involuntarily, looking as horrified as she felt at the predicament, and as unsure what to do. For a moment they stared at each other, then without a word the servant turned and fled. Sarai stared after him blankly, her own legs seeming strangely incapable of movement.

"My Lords!"

The startled cry brought her attention back to the throne room, and she realized with a jolt of horror that every eye within it was now trained on her. Someone had obviously noticed her presence, perhaps alerted by the servant's sudden movement.

For a moment she considered retreating as hastily as the servant had done, but only for a moment. She lifted her chin high, advancing into the room.

"My Lords, it appears my presence here has caused some concern," she said with as much dignity as she could muster.

"I think it would be a matter of concern for any court, Your Highness, to have a princess with no more conduct than to eavesdrop on conversations about matters of state."

Sarai had walked halfway down the room, but she stopped dead at the insult. It was as much the nobleman's tone as his words that felt like a slap in the face. She had not realized how completely she had lost the respect of the Valorian court.

"My Lord," said the prince, clearing his throat uncomfortably. His tone held a slight note of reproach, but it was a weak response to such open disrespect toward a member of the royal family.

Sarai mustered her courage and walked the rest of the hall's length. The suits of armor lining the throne room seemed more menacing than ever, and it was impossible not to recall her long walk down this same room on the occasion of her wedding. Little did she suspect then, as she leaned on her father's arm, how bitterly her new court would regret that day.

The nobleman gave the prince a half-bow. "I would not wish to speak out of turn, Your Highness, but my concern, and I believe that of every man in this room, is only for the welfare of our fair kingdom."

He turned to Sarai. "If you have been listening, Your Highness," the tone somehow made the title an insult this time, "you know you are a danger to Valoria. And in light of that, if you honored the vows you took upon your marriage and your inauguration as a princess of Valoria, you would neither resent nor resist our attempt to protect Valoria's interests."

Sarai felt the color drain from her face. "What attempt is that?"

The nobleman took a half step toward her, his voice low and aggressive. "You inserted yourself into our royal family through fraud. The offered alliance was nothing more than a worthless sham."

Sarai stared at the man, her shock leaving no room for anger. Was he a fool? Did he suppose she had known her royal house was about to be usurped, her family murdered? Or was he just seeking to win over his other listeners to his cause?

But glancing around, Sarai couldn't see that he had much need to convince anyone. Every noble in the room was looking at her with mistrust and dislike, and in some cases open anger. Those present were far from the whole court. She suspected the group consisted of those noblemen who were already embittered against her, and that they had gathered for the specific purpose of lobbying for her removal.

She swallowed involuntarily as she tried to imagine what form that removal might take. She had thought at one stage it would have been better to have been murdered in Kyona with her family than to be the only one left to mourn their deaths. But she found now, with a curious and out-of-place little lift of her heart, that she didn't want to die at all.

The nobleman took another step toward her, then another, and she fell back slightly.

"We cannot allow her to endanger our succession," one of the other nobles said, his voice tight. There were murmurs of agreement on all sides, and one or two others moved slightly toward her. Sarai cast her eyes around beseechingly, meeting her brother-in-law's gaze at last. He looked uncomfortable and uncertain, but he said nothing, did nothing to stop the attack that seemed to be building.

Lady Marietta's father had almost reached Sarai. She had no idea what his immediate intention was, but she found it didn't matter. She had lost all power of movement, and could do nothing but stare as he reached a hand toward her.

"We will not stand by and watch you ruin Valoria the way your father allowed Kyona to be ruined," he said firmly, his hand an inch from seizing her arm.

"STOP!"

The authoritative voice drew every eye to the doorway, and Sarai's limbs suddenly unlocked at the sight of her husband striding powerfully into the room. His chest was heaving, and he had clearly run there. She caught a glimpse of the servant boy hovering in the doorway and suddenly understood, with a rush of gratitude, the reason for his precipitate flight.

She stared at Germain, feeling as if she was seeing him for the first time. His bearing was more regal than she had ever seen it, and fury radiated from every line of his tall, strong form. She couldn't take her eyes off him, but he wasn't looking at her, his attention directed to the nobleman who still stood, frozen in momentary surprise, his hand outstretched toward her.

"If you dare to lay a finger on my wife, your future queen,"

Germain said, his voice vibrating with passion, "I will personally ensure you are hanged before another sunrise."

There was a collective intake of breath at the severity of the crown prince's reaction, and more than one noble drew back slightly. Lady Marietta's father was not among them.

Sarai herself drew a shuddering breath, feeling as though she had been under water and was only now able to fill her lungs. Germain's gaze flicked suddenly to her, his anger disappearing momentarily, but his eyes still blazing with intensity. She stumbled toward him, the movement involuntary, and he reached out with one of those powerful arms to draw her in until she was safely at his side. Then his attention turned to his brother, still standing on the dais, and his anger returned.

"Brother, have you taken leave of your senses to be condoning this outrageous conduct?"

The younger prince looked shaken, and his tone was half-ashamed, but he offered no apologies.

"Germain, I think you should hear what they have to say."

"I have no interest in listening to treasonous talk," snapped Germain, and Sarai could feel the tension radiating from him. The arm which was still around her shoulders was as hard as stone, his muscles quivering with the strain of containing his anger. Hardly aware of her actions, she leaned against him, and his arm tightened even further. It was all she could do to refrain from burying her face in his shoulder.

"Treason, Your Highness?" objected Lady Marietta's father, stepping forward quickly. Germain's eyes flew to him, disfavor in his face. "Never! Absolutely the reverse, I assure you. We wish only to protect Valoria, always. This woman—"

"You will address my wife in accordance with her status as your princess," interrupted Germain, his voice dangerously calm. He looked around the room, pausing slowly, deliberately, on every face present. "I will expect each one of you to answer to my father the king for your *conduct toward a member of his household. And I can only imagine that he will expect an explanation as to your disloyalty in meeting in his absence to discuss the security of our kingdom."*

There was now unease on every face, including that of the younger prince, who stepped off the dais and hurried toward the couple.

"Germain—" he began, but his brother cut him off.

"I will speak to you at a later time. At present I have a considerably higher priority than listening to anything you have to say." He released Sarai and turned to face her, holding out his arm. "Come, my love."

For a moment she stared up into his face, hardly able to master her thoughts enough to move. He had never called her that before, had never used that word. Even in the tension of the moment, she was captivated by the way it sounded on his lips, by the apparently unconscious softening of his voice as he said it.

She took the offered arm, and they exited the room together, their steps stately and slow, as though strolling casually through the gardens again. But Germain's chest was still heaving, and Sarai could feel the way the muscles in his arm jumped under her hand. She herself felt curiously numb. She barely noticed where he was leading her, only realizing as the door closed behind them that he had taken her to his own private suite.

He removed his arm as soon as they were inside, crossing the length of the room and back with short, agitated strides. He came to a stop just before her, still breathing hard.

"Are you all right?" he asked, his voice tight.

Sarai nodded, then found that she was shaking. "Thank you," she whispered. "For...for..."

"I don't want your thanks."

Germain's words were clipped, and Sarai stepped back slightly. She took a deep breath, trying to calm the spasms rocking her body, and to school her features into an expression befitting a princess.

Germain closed his eyes, looking pained. "I can't do this anymore," he whispered.

Sarai felt her heart drop into her stomach. What was he saying? Where would she go, how could she live, if he cast her off?

"Germain, I—I'm sorry," she said desperately, her voice unsteady.

"You're sorry?" he repeated, opening his eyes and staring at her so intently that she felt forced to lower her gaze.

"I am, truly. I...I know that our marriage has brought you nothing but trouble. I know the alliance is not the advantage you hoped. And," she swallowed, willing herself not to let the tears spill out, "I know it's my conduct in chasing all over the country as much as the disappointment of the alliance that has contributed to the court's disapproval of me."

"Sarai—" Germain cut himself off, taking a deep breath as though trying to master himself. "I don't want your apology any more than I want your thanks."

Sarai chanced a look up at him, and her heart faltered at the storm in his eyes. She opened her mouth, but there seemed to be nothing she could say. She flinched involuntarily as Germain took a sudden step toward her, then was taken by surprise when he seized her hands roughly.

"I want you," he said, his voice low and intense. "You torment me, Sarai." She raised her eyes to his, stunned at how his words vibrated with passion. Was this wild-eyed desperate man the reserved, unimpassioned prince she had married? He released one of her hands to lay his own on her cheek, and she stilled completely at the gentle touch.

"But how do I reach you?" he whispered, his eyes searching her face. "How do I get inside this wall?"

"Germain..." she whispered, then trailed off, unable to think of a single thing to say in her shock.

He suddenly laid his forehead against hers, and Sarai realized she was once again shaking violently.

"I have tried to be respectful," he said, his voice barely audible. "I *know you have been in terrible grief, and even before that, you were in an unfamiliar place, among unfamiliar people. I didn't want to press you to open your heart to me. I wanted to give you space, let you find your feet in your own way. But I probably went about it all wrong."* He took a deep breath. *"It doesn't come naturally to me, to express...affection, or emotion."* He gave a small groan and pulled away. *"I am probably the last man in the world to have success in breaking through the barrier around your heart."*

He wasn't meeting her eyes, but Sarai couldn't stop staring at him, dumbfounded. She was shaken to the core by this uncharacteristic outburst.

"I'm sorry," she whispered again. *"I didn't want to be cold, and I know I have been."* The tears were standing in her eyes. *"I know you deserve better—"*

"Sarai, stop," he groaned. *"You have nothing to apologize for. You cannot believe you share any blame for what has happened in Kyona, or for what you have endured. There has been nothing—nothing—in your conduct to justify the prejudice just displayed against you. I have feared something like this. Why do you think I wanted you here, visible, so the court couldn't make false accusations that you were somehow shirking your duty?"*

She could feel his keen gaze back on her, but it was Sarai's turn to lower her eyes. *"I was afraid, Germain,"* she whispered, and he took a small step back toward her. *"I know you don't want me to thank you, but when you walked into that room, I...I could not have been more grateful, or more relieved to see you, if you had pulled me from a burning building."*

"Sarai, you are my wife. I would not hesitate to run into a burning building for you," said Germain, and she couldn't doubt the sincerity in his voice.

"Do you think it's true?" she whispered. *"That the usurper might send someone to kill me? That he might even try to kill our children?"*

"I don't know if it's true he will try," said Germain. A flicker of

something had passed over his form when she mentioned their future children, but his voice was quite even. "But I know he will not succeed if he does. Valoria is strong, Sarai. You are a Valorian royal now, and so will our children be. Valoria will protect you. I will protect you with my last breath."

He reached out a hand, tilting her chin gently up, forcing her to meet his eyes. He searched her gaze silently for a long moment before speaking.

"Sarai..."

He released her suddenly, once again striding up the room. When he next spoke, he wasn't facing her, and she had to strain to hear him.

"You have acknowledged yourself that you have been distant," he said, his tone stilted. "And that emboldens me to ask..." He paused. "Perhaps I should not ask this. But back in Kyona did you...was there anyone..." He took a deep breath, then turned to face her, meeting her gaze with determination. "I know you made sacrifices to come here. I know you left your family, and your home, to come and be with me. But—if I can ask such an intrusive question—did you sacrifice your heart as well?"

Sarai had been frowning in confusion, but she suddenly took his meaning, and her expression cleared.

"No Germain," she said in her soft voice. "I made no sacrifice of that kind. There was never anyone else."

His whole figure seemed to lighten with relief, and his face was softer than ever as he strode back toward her. He took her hands in his again.

"Then surely," he said, his voice low, "surely there is some hope of me winning your heart."

She didn't know how to answer him. Her mind was reeling from his revelations. She had never imagined he was bottling up such emotions. How could she tell him whether there was hope of him winning her heart? It felt like an age since she had hope of any kind, and she had even begun to wonder whether she had a heart, ice sculpture that she was.

The remembered insult brought Lady Marietta to mind, and before she could lose her nerve, Sarai found herself returning the question. A week ago—an hour ago—she would never have imagined taking such a liberty, but everything felt changed now.

"And you?" Germain looked confused, so Sarai pushed on, her face coloring. "Did you sacrifice your heart to...to form our alliance?"

"Me? Of course not." Germain searched her face, as if desperate to read the thought behind her question. "Is that what has been in your mind? Has that thought been troubling you?"

Sarai couldn't quite meet his eye, but she found to her own astonishment that a small smile was curling her lips at his reply. "No, I haven't been troubled, exactly. I mean, I never assumed I had any right to your heart simply because our kingdoms wished for an alliance. I have wondered at times...I know there are many beautiful women in the court here, who are...more skilled at being agreeable than—"

"If I didn't know better," interrupted Germain, in grim amusement, "I would think you were speaking of Lady Marietta."

She raised her head quickly, a self-conscious look in her eyes. He scanned her face again, and she could see he knew he had guessed correctly.

"Her constant attempts to engage my attention have barely decreased since our marriage." His voice dropped as he studied her. "I have wondered why it didn't seem to bother you."

"It does bother me," she blurted out before she could stop herself. "But I felt I had no right to resent it. And I think I was too proud to admit it even to myself. But when she said that if only my horse would trample me, then you might be free, I realized that—"

"She said what?!" Germain's expression was thunderous.

"It was nothing, Germain," said Sarai quickly, wishing she hadn't let her tongue run away with her. "She spoke maliciously, yes, but it *was in jest, and to a friend. She didn't intend for me to hear. She didn't know I stood nearby, also watching you in the training yard."*

"You were watching me in the training yard?" Germain looked intrigued, instantly distracted from his anger. Sarai sighed. They were straying further from the point.

"Yes, I was, and I can't help but feel that if you don't want to be pursued by the ladies of the court, you shouldn't train half-dressed in public." She reached out to lightly touch his chest, and his muscles jumped beneath her fingers. She looked up to see him watching her with a smile that was a little too knowing. She stilled, captured by his gaze, and his expression softened.

"Oh Sarai. I'm sorry Lady Marietta's attentions have made you uncomfortable. It was unnecessary, I promise you. Long before I married you, I was perfectly able to recognize her interest for what it is—a coveting of my crown." He smiled. "A coveting of your crown, I should say. I do not find her flattery particularly agreeable. I suppose," he spoke dispassionately, "that she is beautiful. But myself," he reached out to twine a strand of her dark hair around his fingers, "I prefer a dark-haired kind of beauty."

Sarai's heart thumped unevenly in her chest, and she couldn't calm its beating any more than she could tear her eyes away from her husband's face. His hand traveled from her hair to her face, resting lightly on her cheek.

"I have never loved any woman but you, Sarai," he said, his voice again softening around the word until it was a caress.

For a moment Sarai could only blink, the declaration was so wholly unexpected. "You...love me?"

"Of course I do," said Germain sternly. "I have loved you since the moment I married you."

She lifted an eyebrow. "You didn't know me when you married me, Germain."

"I know," he acknowledged easily.

"Then how can you say you loved me?"

His eyes searched her face, his expression serious. "I loved you because I chose to love you. I was very willing to make this marriage alliance, Sarai. I wanted to do my duty to my kingdom. But like any man, I didn't want to spend my life in a loveless marriage. So I chose to love you. I decided before we even met that I would love you, and I committed myself to that love when we took our vows, as surely as I committed my kingdom to an alliance."

Sarai could barely draw breath. Was it truly that simple? Could she just choose to love him? Did she dare to take the risk?

"I hoped also that you would come to love me," Germain continued. "I didn't expect it to happen straight away, and when Kyona was attacked..." He trailed off, clearly not wanting to cause her pain.

Her eyes were on the ground, tears pooling in them yet again. "I have felt so alone, Germain."

"I know," he responded gently. "And it has broken my heart to see it. More than anything I wish to ease your loneliness. Do you think..." He hesitated. "Do you think there is any chance you could come to love me, with time? That you could come to trust me with your heart as well as your hand?"

The tears were running down her cheeks now, and still she couldn't look at him. "I think there is a chance, and that's what terrifies me," she whispered. "I have felt love trying to take root, in my heart, but I'm too afraid to let it grow. I'm too broken, too bruised from what I have lost. I don't think my heart is capable of loving, Germain. I'm too afraid to let it open again."

"Sarai." His voice was a whisper. "You are wrong to think yourself incapable of love. I don't expect you to be whole and undamaged after what you have suffered. I don't expect you to put aside your grief in order to love me."

He took a deep breath. "I love you Sarai, I truly do. And I don't want to wait respectfully anymore for a distant day when your heart will be healed enough for you to believe you're worthy of love. Because if you continue to wander like a ghost, lonely and without hope, that day will never come. Let me in now—let me share your grief, let me share your burdens. You will find they're half as heavy."

There was a long moment of silence, as Sarai continued to cry, and Germain continued to watch her. She could hardly believe her ears. She had thought she was alone, unseen and unknown. But he had seen everything, he knew everything, and he longed for her heart as desperately as she had longed for his, without being willing to admit it to herself.

"Whatever you decide, whether or not you can let me in," Germain continued, his voice steady, "know that I will love you for the rest of my life, as I swore to do."

She looked up at last, seeing him fully for the first time, and yet finding his face as familiar as her own. Had she been surprised a few weeks ago to realize he was handsome? He was the most magnificent thing she had ever seen. And he was hers, truly hers, all hers.

"Germain," she whispered, putting all the words she couldn't say into those two syllables.

It was enough.

His hand had still been on her cheek, but he slid it behind her neck, pulling her against him at last. His other arm wound around her waist as he bent his head to claim her lips. She leaned up into him, twining her arms around his neck and returning his kiss with a passion she had thought she'd never be able to unlock. Her cheeks were still wet with tears, but he didn't seem to mind as he kissed her hungrily, possessively, his hand straying to her cheek, her neck, to tangle through the dark waves of her hair.

She had been so afraid to let her heart be vulnerable—she had never imagined letting herself love him would feel so safe, so complete, so right.

After a long and blissful minute, they pulled back, and Germain again rested his forehead against hers.

"I didn't know you could kiss like that," Sarai said, her voice breathless. She could feel that her hair was a mess, and she flushed to think what her lady's maid would say at being called to rearrange it in the middle of the morning.

Germain chuckled, his own breathing unsteady. "In all honesty, neither did I." His arms tightened around her. "But you unlock me, Sarai."

She smiled, breathing in the smell of him, and reveling in her sudden lightheadedness.

"I shouldn't have sent you away that day—that terrible day in the tower room," she said suddenly, her voice soft. "I should have come to you when you held your arms out to me. I shouldn't have chosen to be alone when I didn't have to be."

He pulled back further, his eyes searching hers. "Do you mean that?" he asked.

"Yes," said Sarai. "I'm sorry I didn't let you in. Perhaps we could have had this conversation months ago."

Germain let out a long exhale. "Then perhaps you won't be angry when I make my confession."

"What confession?" asked Sarai, startled.

Germain's expression was an endearing mix of sheepish and proud. "I didn't leave. You sent me away, but I didn't go. I left the room, of course. I felt I couldn't refuse your request. But I couldn't bear to deliver such news to you and then leave you alone." He rubbed her cheek gently with his thumb. "I wept with you, Sarai, I just did it on the other side of the door."

She looked at him in wonder. In the worst moment of her life, when she had thought she was utterly alone in the world, he had been there. Even after she had unfeelingly sent him away when he tried to comfort her, still he had been there.

She had no words, but she didn't need them. She leaned toward him again, and in less than a heartbeat she was back in his arms, his lips once again pressed against hers. His arms were around her waist, those powerful muscles growing tighter, tighter, until she was sure he would never let go, that this moment would last forever.

Rap rap rap.

"Your Highness?"

The servant's muffled voice sounded nervous, even through the door, and Sarai remembered with faint surprise how angry Germain had been when they had entered this room.

"Your Highness, you're needed urgently."

Germain groaned, his arms tightening around Sarai for a moment as she tried to pull away.

"It's all right, Germain," she said with a smile, straightening his hair with a gentle hand. He closed his eyes at the contact, a smile on his own face. "Go. This can wait until later. We have time."

"Yes, we do." He opened his eyes again, and their intense gaze instantly captured hers. He lifted her hand to his mouth, as he had done so many times before, but this time he flipped it gently so that he pressed his kiss against her palm. A tingle seemed to leap from his lips, spreading through her whole body. "We have the rest of our lives."

CHAPTER THIRTY-SIX

Jocelyn gasped as she pulled away, her palm tingling as though it was her who had been kissed so tenderly. Her mind raced with thoughts and emotions, both foreign and familiar, and she pressed her hands to her flaming cheeks.

What a moment to witness! What a conversation to overhear, what an encounter to vicariously experience. It was too much, too intense.

She felt a curious mixture of joy and alarm at the discovery that Princess Sarai had found happiness with her husband after all. Joy for the long-dead Kyonan royal, alarm for herself and what it all might mean for her. She had felt like Princess Sarai was a friend, another Kyonan princess who could empathize, across the generations, with Jocelyn's own plight. But suddenly their paths seemed to diverge, with Princess Sarai's change in attitude.

Change.

Princess Sarai had been as afraid of change as Jocelyn was herself. But she had found a way to overcome that fear, and to embrace her new identity. Quite literally embrace. Jocelyn had just shared her thoughts with embarrassing intimacy, and she knew how genuine was the change in Princess Sarai's heart.

Jocelyn wanted to be inspired by the other princess's example, she truly did. She wanted to find it in herself to accept an alliance with Prince Ormond, to embrace a new role as a Valorian princess, to secure the advantages of such a connection for Kyona, and for Eamon. But somehow she felt further than ever from being able to do it.

She cast her eyes around the room, still trying to master the jumble of emotions produced by the strange vision. Her eyes fell on the bed, drawn to something sitting on the white pillow, glinting in the light of the candles.

She crossed the room in two strides, catching it into her hands with a gasp.

Her bracelet!

How was it possible? She examined it closely, but there could be no doubt. It was her own bracelet, the one she had bartered at the market day in the east, so much to Kincaid's disapproval. How had it come to be in her room?

Kincaid must be here. There was no other explanation. He must have redeemed it before returning to Bryford. She shook her head in amazement, picturing the merchant she had given it to, and the bustle and chaos of the market, all temporary stalls and shouting traders. What a task it must have been! What a foolish, wonderful, ridiculous way for Kincaid to waste his time and effort.

And he must be here somewhere, in Bryford, perhaps even in the castle. Her every nerve tingled at the thought of his nearness.

Jocelyn slipped the bracelet onto her wrist, clutching it like a lifeline as her heart soared, then plummeted, then soared again.

Because the bauble, as frivolous an item as it was, had brought a flash of clarity to Jocelyn's mind, and everything was suddenly unalterably clear. She was glad Princess Sarai had found happiness in her political marriage, but her path was not an example for Jocelyn to follow, because there was one very crucial difference.

There was no Kincaid in Princess Sarai's story.

She may not have come to her marriage with an open heart, but she had come to it unattached. If Jocelyn were to go through with her marriage alliance, the same would not be true. Perhaps a month ago, Jocelyn could have done what the other princess had done, could even have chosen to love Prince Ormond. But it was as impossible now as it was for her to sprout wings and fly over the mountains like Elddreki.

She had just been inside Princess Sarai's head, and as intense as the other Kyonan's emotions had been upon being kissed—truly kissed—by her husband, they were not stronger than Jocelyn's own feelings when Kincaid had taken her in his arms and claimed her lips with his. Heat rushed through Jocelyn even now at the memory.

His face swam before her sight, and her heartbeat picked up as she remembered the longing in his voice as he whispered how desperately he wished she would choose him. And of course she would choose him. How could she ever have considered any other choice?

He had been right, absolutely right, in his observation that it was not her family who held her back, but herself. She had spoken of duty, but she had merely been hiding behind it to avoid confronting her fear of change, of herself. What a sweet thought it was now to know that her parents wouldn't oppose her choice, would be ready to do whatever it took to overcome any hurdles between her and happiness. How foolish she had been to think she somehow needed to carry their burdens for them, to counteract their unconventional past by sacrificing her own future.

Her heart sang with her certainty, and she wanted nothing more than to dash from the room and go in search of him then and there. But where would she find him? Perhaps she should wait for him to come to her. He would come, she knew he would. He had said he wasn't giving up, and the bracelet was proof.

She knew a moment of dread at the thought of explaining to the Valorian king and queen that she was unwilling to enter into an alliance with Prince Ormond because she had fallen hopelessly in love with a handsome wanderer while on her dragon quest. Perhaps she should leave the explanations to her father. He had been clear that there was no obligation on her, that he could handle any tension that might arise should the Valorians seek an alliance she didn't want.

All of a sudden Jocelyn remembered Eamon and Lucy, and her happiness faltered for a moment. Her parents would stand by her, but her decision to spurn the offered alliance and marry someone without political connections would undoubtedly make the other couple's road even harder.

But she took a deep breath, pressing the thought into its proper size and shape within her mind. It was unfortunate, but not a reason to make both herself and Kincaid suffer the agony of separation. Eamon surely would not expect her to sacrifice her happiness for the possibility of making his more attainable. She would never ask it of him if their positions were reversed.

A knock on the door startled her from her thoughts, and she turned to see a tentative face peeking through.

"Princess Jocelyn? Are you all right?"

"Lavinia," said Jocelyn, trying to return to reality. "Yes, I'm fine. Come in."

Lavinia came all the way into the room and closed the door behind her, but she looked doubtful. "Are you sure you're all right? I hope you don't mind me following you, but you left in such a hurry, and you looked upset..."

Jocelyn pushed thoughts of her heart to the side with an effort, trying to smile naturally at the younger girl. "Of course I don't mind," she reassured her. "It was kind of you to check on me."

"Ormond didn't say anything enraging, did he?" asked Lavinia, and Jocelyn caught the note of real concern behind the joking words.

"Of course not," she soothed. "It's nothing to do with him, I just needed a moment to myself."

Lavinia settled herself on Jocelyn's bed, drawing her knees up with a fine disregard for her elaborate gown.

"Are you going to marry him?"

Jocelyn looked at her in surprise. The younger girl was meeting her gaze steadily. "No, I'm not."

Lavinia's face fell slightly. "I would like you as a sister, I think," she said, with a faint sigh. "I know he's a bit stiff and serious," she added hopefully, "but he's actually very nice. He has a kind heart under all that formality, and as much as he infuriates me on a daily basis, he'd never really hurt a fly. He positively reeks of honor."

Lavinia's words tugged at Jocelyn's mind, and she struggled to marshal her thoughts as she responded. "I don't doubt it. I'm sure he's an excellent man. It's nothing against him."

"Why then?" asked Lavinia, frowning.

"It's, well..." Jocelyn colored in spite of herself, and the younger girl pounced.

"You're in love with someone else!"

"Well, yes, I am," said Jocelyn, unable to help the grin that spread across her face as she admitted it out loud for the first time.

"Who is he?" Lavinia breathed, clearly eager for a cozy gossip, but Jocelyn didn't respond.

The latest vision of Princess Sarai's past, and her subsequent revelation about Kincaid, had distracted Jocelyn from her concerns, but they were returning to the fore now. The thought that had been dancing around the edges of her mind had suddenly taken shape.

Lavinia's comment about Ormond reeking of honor had tickled her memory because she had used that particular phrase in her own mind just a short time ago. Her first impression of Lord Randall had been that he reeked of trustworthiness. And it had caught in her mind even then. Where had she heard it before?

With a sudden intake of breath, Jocelyn felt Raqisa's words come back to her.

A human who received forfeited power might reek of magic, but it would not be a part of him. Rather, he would be warped by it.

Jocelyn remembered the strange and unnatural glitter in Lord Randall's eyes, and a growing sense of horror washed over her.

"Jocelyn?" Lavinia's voice was tentative, and she was clearly wondering why Jocelyn hadn't responded to her. "You *are* upset. Was it Lord Randall?" Jocelyn's eyes snapped to the other princess at the name. "I saw you were talking to him before you ran out. I know you don't have much reason to like Balenans, but he's different, trust me. He really is a good—"

"Lavinia," said Jocelyn earnestly, her thoughts too frenzied to fully hold in her power. The word "trust" had jolted her into speech. "Lord Randall is not what he pretends to be. I don't know exactly what he's up to yet, but he doesn't mean well by Kyona, and probably not by Valoria either."

"But..." Lavinia looked confused, and a little unsettled. Jocelyn suspected her opinion was being seriously challenged by Jocelyn's power, and she found she didn't mind. If she could change the Valorian girl's view of Lord Randall, it would be a very good thing.

"If you mean he's not genuinely interested in our kingdom like he claims, and is just trying to ingratiate himself with the court, I don't think that can be true. He's explored all over. He even went to the east the last time he was here, and he said he enjoyed it very much. Most Valorians don't even want to go there, so I don't think he was faking his interest."

"He went to the east?" Jocelyn asked sharply. "To Arinton?"

Lavinia nodded, looking confused and alarmed. Jocelyn drew a deep breath, shuddering on the exhale. Eric's visitor from the South Lands, Kincaid's diplomat, the unidentified human the dragon colony was concerned about. They were all the same person, and that person was standing in the ballroom just down the corridor.

Any lingering doubt was gone. Lord Randall had received, and been warped by, the forfeited power of the grief-stricken dragon who was still missing from Wyvern Islands. Jocelyn wondered, feeling a little ill, whether the dragon was actually dead yet, or was still slowly expiring somewhere. Would he find what he sought when he crossed the threshold of death?

She shook the thought off. She had much more pressing concerns. If Lord Randall had sought out the dragons to gain an unnatural power, then what was he planning to do with it? Why was he targeting the freedmen, and to what end?

She paused, frowning. How would he have known, though? How would he have thought to seek out the dragons? She knew stories of dragons and magic must have circulated wildly through Balenol after the dramatic events of Aunt Scarlett and Uncle Jonan's time there twenty years ago. But she had been under the impression when Elddreki told her and Kincaid the dragon lore that the ability to forfeit power was a closely guarded secret, one no other human would be trusted with.

All of a sudden she remembered the story from Arinton, of the woman who had been in a boat on the loch when a wyvern surfaced and offered to grant her greatest wish. She groaned. The woman's son had said his mother traveled far and wide, trying to sell her tale. And that had been months and months ago. Was it so impossible it had reached the South Lands? Had reached Lord Randall?

She remembered with a cold rush that Raqisa had said a human receiving forfeited power might actually be able to choose what form it would take. She didn't know what Lord Randall would choose, but she was sure it couldn't be anything good.

"Lavinia," she said suddenly. "Lord Randall is up to something." She cut the younger princess off as she tried to speak. "I know you all like him, but I'm telling you, something's not right about him. I need to get a message to my parents. I don't know what the disturbance is that took them to Alezae, but they need to get back to Kynton."

Lavinia still looked unconvinced, but to her credit she didn't hesitate. "What can I do to help?"

Jocelyn frowned thoughtfully for a moment. "Can you go back to the ballroom? Keep an eye on Lord Randall? I assume you have a royal courier service, where I can dispatch a message to Alezae?"

Lavinia nodded, giving Jocelyn directions. "I can't really believe he's so sinister," she said, hesitating at the door. "But it can't do any harm to keep an eye on him."

"Thank you Lavinia," said Jocelyn earnestly. She fiddled absent-mindedly with her bracelet as she followed Lavinia into the corridor. She wished very much that she knew where

Kincaid was. She could really use an ally, one who didn't need convincing. But there was no time to worry about it.

The girls parted ways within moments, their paths taking them in opposite directions. Jocelyn raced down the dimly lit corridors, hoping she was remembering Lavinia's instructions correctly. There was no one about, everyone still in the ballroom, celebrating her birthday. She wondered with a pang what Eamon was doing tonight. It was strange not to spend this most significant of birthdays with her twin. What, if anything, had Lord Randall done to Eamon?

She was so lost in her thoughts she didn't even hear the footsteps until they were upon her. Before she could cry out, one powerful arm was around her torso, trapping her own arms to her side, and a hand was clamped firmly over her mouth.

"Not running off to do me a mischief, are you, *Princess*?"

She couldn't see her captor, directly behind her. But she had no difficulty recognizing the voice, although the smooth sincerity was gone. How had she ever thought this man trustworthy, even for a moment?

"It was very considerate of you to lose your composure so dramatically, Your Highness," Lord Randall continued. "If you hadn't run from the room so precipitately, I might not have realized you were a threat."

Her angry retort died on her lips, the words muffled by the large shapely hand still covering her mouth. For such a slender man, he was surprisingly strong.

"Tut tut," said Lord Randall indulgently. "I don't think I'll be inviting you to speak, my dear. Not until I figure out precisely what power is in your words." He leaned over her shoulder, putting his face right next to her cheek and inhaling, so his breath tickled her ear uncomfortably. "It smells different from your brother's somehow."

Jocelyn froze, a shard of ice shooting through her heart. He knew about Eamon's power.

"Yes indeed," Lord Randall was continuing, "it seems it was well worth my effort to travel back here for your birthday gala in order to acquire the matching set. I was deeply disappointed when I arrived to discover you hadn't yet reached Bryford, but things have turned out for the best. It's most fortuitous you arrived in time for tonight's gala after all."

He gave a dark chuckle. "Almost as fortuitous as the discovery that the heir to the Kyonan throne is harboring illicit magic of his own. What a happy day that was. It's really going to be almost too easy to bring down your upstart little slave kingdom."

Jocelyn growled, longing to reach for her dagger. But her arms were still trapped. Lord Randall's grip was like a vise, and her battered muscles screamed in protest as he squeezed her more tightly.

"Well, well," he said lightly. "You may not turn out to be as useful as your brother is proving himself to be, but I'm sure we can find some way for you to contribute. It's a good thing you're in the habit of running away—I wouldn't be surprised if your hosts don't even suspect foul play."

Before Jocelyn could grasp his meaning, she felt Lord Randall gesture with his head, and three thickset men emerged from the shadows. One of them pulled a swath of fabric from his pocket, and Lord Randall removed his hand from Jocelyn's mouth. She pulled in a lungful of air, ready to scream with all her might, but she had no opportunity. Instantly the man covered her mouth and nose with the fabric, and her nostrils were filled with a foul and sickening smell.

She flailed desperately for a moment, trying frantically to draw in air. But within seconds she felt consciousness beginning to slip away.

CHAPTER THIRTY-SEVEN

Jocelyn's first awareness was of an aching pain in every muscle of her body. All the progress she had made since waking up in the bower on Wyvern Islands had been undone. Her palms stung furiously, and her limbs felt like they were being held down with weights. In addition, her head now felt like it had been pounded against a rock.

Whatever she was lying on was also much less comfortable than the springy ground of the copse, and there was a sharp pain in her wrists. She realized suddenly that her hands were bound behind her back, and she wriggled her shoulders uncomfortably. She drew a deep breath in through her nose, and immediately realized there was a gag shoved into her mouth. Instantly, she could think of nothing else. The fabric tasted foul, and it was all she could do not to choke on it.

Her eyes flew open, but there was little to see. Wherever she was, the light was dim. It seemed like some kind of vegetable cellar. She struggled to her knees, unable to hold in a sharp cry of pain at the movement.

The sound alerted someone, and within moments a heavy door scraped open, flooding the space with daylight. Jocelyn blinked rapidly, trying to get her bearings. Had she been unconscious all night?

"Good morning, my dear," said Lord Randall amicably. "I trust you slept well?"

Jocelyn just glared at him, and he chuckled.

"I'm glad to see you awake at last. I need to leave almost immediately, but I was so hoping to chat with you before I go." He considered her. "I think I can take the risk of your words." He walked over to her, his movements lazy, and untied the gag.

Jocelyn took a deep gasping breath, then spat on the floor, trying to rid herself of the awful taste.

"Goodness," said Lord Randall mildly. "That's not very proper behavior for a princess."

"How dare you?" Jocelyn hissed at him. "How dare you attack me, and keep me here? When my father gets hold of—"

"By the time your father is aware of your predicament," said Lord Randall calmly, "he will no longer have the power to do much of anything." He settled himself on an upturned barrel, and fixed her with a humorous look. "But never mind that. I'm desperately curious to know what tipped you off last night. Was it my magic you recognized, or my identity?"

"Your identity?" Jocelyn repeated, confused. She could feel power leaving her with her words, but it just seemed to bounce off the warped, unnatural man in front of her.

"So it was the magic, then," Lord Randall said. "That is more impressive, and more concerning. Let's hope there aren't too many others running around with secret magic who might recognize my...gift."

Jocelyn snorted at the word gift, but she didn't understand his other comment. How would she recognize his identity? She knew no one from the Balenan court, other than Aunt Scarlett. And the royal family, who were Aunt Scarlett's cousins on her mother's side.

She stared at Lord Randall, who was smiling serenely, and suddenly it hit her. Aunt Scarlett had other family, too. There was a reason his features had reminded her so much of Aunt Scarlett, beyond the race.

"Your name isn't Randall," she said slowly. "It's Wrendal, isn't it? Aunt Scarlett's name before she was married. I remember she had a brother called Scanlon. You're Lucy's uncle."

He raised a haughty eyebrow. "I know no such person, and I certainly wouldn't claim relationship with any mongrel brat of my harlot sister's." Jocelyn recoiled involuntarily from the poison in his words. "But yes, of course my name is Wrendal." He gave her a contemptuous look. "*Aunt* Scarlett, is it? My sister is a bigger fool even than I realized."

Jocelyn bristled in defense of her beloved second family. She cast around for something scathing to say, wanting to discomfit the despicable nobleman.

"That's why your nose is crooked, isn't it?" she asked innocently. "Uncle Jonan broke it when he punched you. I heard the whole story about how they thwarted your little military coup when they visited Balenol that one time."

Lord Randall—or rather Lord Wrendal—leaped to his feet. Jocelyn hadn't missed the way his face had twitched in fury at the mention of his brother-in-law's name. He crossed the cellar in two strides, seizing Jocelyn by the hair and dragging her up from the floor.

She cried out as pain shot through her, and Scanlon once again brought his face uncomfortably close to hers.

"Do not try my patience, you Kyonan filth. It would be delightfully easy to decide to simply end your life and be done with the inconvenience."

He threw her to the ground, and she landed in a crumpled heap, pain blossoming from every point of contact with the hard floor. Tears stung her eyes, but she blinked them back, refusing to give him the satisfaction.

For a moment he stood there, looking down at her, still breathing hard. Then he abruptly resumed his seat, his expression once again benign.

"But where were we?" he asked, and his polite tone made Jocelyn shudder more than his preceding anger. This man was clearly unbalanced, and she was in his power. "What can you tell me about your magic?" he asked calmly. "Or any insights you care to share regarding your brother's?"

She glared at him, still drawing deep gasping breaths. "How did you convince the dragon to forfeit his power to you?" she asked, instead of answering his question.

A look of shock flitted across Scanlon's face, but he recovered quickly. "It wasn't a matter of convincing," he said in amusement. "The stupid beast practically begged me to take it." Jocelyn felt ill at the thought of such a mighty creature brought so low. "I consider myself fortunate no one else saw the truth in the foolish stories being spread around, and beat me to Valoria to investigate." He smiled in a self-satisfied way. "But I had long been doing my own research on how I might turn the power of the dragons who supposedly haunt the North Lands to my own purposes."

He looked back at her. "Far from needing to convince the dragon, I was in a position to impose conditions of my own."

"What conditions?" asked Jocelyn uneasily, but Scanlon just gave her an unpleasant smile.

"I don't think that's something you need to know, my dear."

"And were you able to choose what form it would take?" Jocelyn pushed on recklessly. She had the sense he was about to leave, and she wanted to get as much information as she could while he was still talking.

He raised his eyebrows. "You seem to be singularly well-informed, Princess. Do I take it that your own magic was acquired in the same way?"

"Of course not," Jocelyn shot back in disgust. "Your power is a travesty of dragon magic, and mine is nothing like it. I am not an abomination." She spoke with conviction. Perhaps for the first time, she really believed the words.

Scanlon just chuckled at the epithet, not offended. "I chose its form, yes."

Jocelyn's mind was whirring. "So what, you asked him to make you some kind of silver-tongue, able to convince people you were right?" She frowned. "No, that's not it, is it? It's not in your words—you had me wanting to trust you when you'd barely opened your mouth."

"Very good, Princess," approved Scanlon lazily. "You and your brother are woefully limited, but my magic is not restricted to my words." He sighed. "But there were limitations, as it turns out. The dragon was not able to give me whatever I desired, without boundary. I thought long and hard about what to ask for. I was tempted to seek the might required to destroy Kyona from the outside. But I decided in the end it would be much more poetic to watch the kingdom tear itself apart from within. The presence of the escaped slaves was the perfect fracture point. It really only needed a little push. And it was a delightfully neat scheme, after all. Revenge against your upstart king, revenge against the slaves, revenge against the whole kingdom for the humiliation and ruin it has visited on Balenol."

Jocelyn frowned. "This isn't about Balenol," she said softly. "Your ego is too big for that. It's personal."

"You had better believe it's personal." Scanlon was once again on his feet, and Jocelyn cowered away in spite of herself. "Every day my sister spends as the wife of that dog is an offense. I will destroy them and their spawn and restore the honor to my noble house."

Again Jocelyn recoiled, her terror for Lucy and the rest of the family mingling with horror. Spit was flying from Scanlon's mouth, and he looked quite mad. Had he always been this way, or had the stolen dragon magic done this to him?

"But it's more than that," he raged. "Your father took everything from me when he liberated his precious slaves. And my revenge will be deliciously personal when he watches his own son lead the way to civil war."

"What have you done to Eamon?!" Jocelyn shouted, her power flaring uselessly from her with the words.

"Why, nothing," said Scanlon, in false surprise. "Just talked with him a little. We've become friends—we see quite eye to eye on a number of issues. And," Scanlon's eyes glinted maliciously, "he's been most helpful in convincing the rest of your father's court. I've barely needed to be involved."

Horror swirled inside Jocelyn, as strongly as her power. If Scanlon had identified Eamon's power, if he had found a way to manipulate Eamon into using it for the Balenan's purposes, the danger to Kyona was greater than she'd feared. Eamon had always been better at controlling his power than she had. On a good day, he could convince a room full of dissenters to fall into line with only a few well-chosen sentences.

"Eamon will never be taken in by you," she spat, wishing there was more conviction in her words.

Scanlon chuckled. "Ah, but I'm so sincere. You said this was personal, Princess, and you were quite right." His strangely glittering eyes grew dark. "I should have been the most influential nobleman in Balenol's court. My father was the Overseer of Slaves, as I would have been after him. My sister was supposed to marry our cousin and become queen. The house of Wrendal was well-respected and powerful."

He ground his teeth. "And it was all ripped away from me by a pack of filthy slaves. Thanks to my father being fool enough to get himself killed by Scarlett's pet Kyonan before he could see his plans through, he came out looking like an imbecile and a traitor. The soft-hearted fools in my country, including most of the royal family, were never going to trust me because of my relationship to him. And all the ones who should have been my allies didn't trust me because of my relationship to my sister, who betrayed her kingdom when she started her repulsive slave resistance."

"I'm guessing your own attempt to carry out a military coup didn't help, either," Jocelyn interjected scornfully.

Scanlon gave her a nasty smile. "Just another count against my sister and her mongrel. They'll pay in full, don't worry." He took a deep breath. "All of that is in the past now, because that pathetic dragon gave me what I most lacked."

"A heart?" said Jocelyn sarcastically, but he ignored her.

"Trust." He smiled angelically at her. "People tend to trust me, Princess. And you're right, it's not in my words, although they help. It's just my presence. That indefinable something about me."

An involuntary shiver ran down Jocelyn's spine at the memory of how even she had reacted that way to the nobleman on first meeting. But now she recognized his power for what it was, she knew she would never be deceived by it again. Everything about him felt unnatural and sinister, barely human.

"At what cost?" she whispered. "You got the magic you wanted, but it's warped you."

Scanlon just laughed lightly. "I'm not squeamish, Your Highness." He stood, stretching his limbs. "I think I'll leave you now. I'm expected in Kynton, you know."

"If you so much as—"

Her empty threats were cut off by the gag, which Scanlon shoved mercilessly back into her mouth. He tied the cloth around it even more tightly than before, and Jocelyn could barely keep from gagging on it.

"I wouldn't want you to have any unhelpful chats with my men in my absence," he explained cheerfully. He strolled to the door, pausing to make sure she was listening as he addressed someone on the other side. "Keep her here until I decide how best to put her to good account. Don't remove the gag, for any purpose." His eyes sparkled maliciously as they met hers. "I do hope you ate your fill at that lovely birthday feast of yours, my dear."

Then he was gone, and darkness descended once more.

For a moment Jocelyn remained on the floor, stunned and horrified. Then she pushed herself to her feet and hobbled toward the door. She could hear nothing, and it took only a minute to ascertain that there was no other route of escape from the room. Clenching her teeth against the pain, she wrestled with all her might against the bindings on her wrists, but it was futile.

She was a little ashamed of how quickly she gave up, but with every muscle on fire, it was so much easier to just slump on the floor, letting tears run silently down her face. She remembered with a sudden hysterical laugh that she had told Elddreki the night they'd met that she couldn't be less free if she was locked in a cage.

She had been wrong.

As wrong as the Valorians, and apparently Eamon, had been to trust Scanlon.

As wrong as she'd been not to use her power when she had the chance. Maybe she could have changed the Valorian royals' minds about their underhanded guest.

As wrong as Kincaid had been when he said she wouldn't hurt him. And now she might never get the chance to tell him she chose him after all.

The thought of Kincaid was too much, and for several minutes she wept openly, not caring if her guards heard her. But eventually she stilled. If they really weren't going to feed her, she had better conserve her energy. She rolled over, and felt her dagger in its place on her leg, uncomfortable beneath her.

They hadn't found it!

She shuddered in momentarily relief that no one had searched her that thoroughly while she was unconscious. But why would they? Princesses didn't carry weapons concealed under their ballgowns. She smiled grimly. Not ordinary princesses.

It took a while, and it hurt quite a lot, but she managed to contort her body into the right position to grasp hold of the blade. After a lot of fruitless effort, she was forced to conclude that due to the angle at which her hands were bound, she wouldn't be able to use the dagger to cut her bonds. At least not without slicing her hand off. She shuffled around so her back was to the wall, holding it loosely behind her. She had no idea if she would have an opportunity to use it, but she wanted to be prepared just in case.

The day crawled on interminably. As the effects of whatever drug Scanlon had used on her wore off, Jocelyn's head mercifully stopped pounding. But it was only a small improvement. Her thirst battled with the pain in her limbs for the position of her greatest discomfort, and the continued presence of the gag in her mouth was almost more than she could take. She had no way to tell the time, but it felt like endless hours had passed when she next heard a sound.

She had slumped against the wall in her exhaustion, but the sound of the heavy door opening caused her to scramble up into a proper sitting position, her knife clenched tightly in her hand.

"Ready for your meal, Your Royal Highness?"

The man who came in was burly and rough. She noted with

interest that he wasn't Balenan. His voice, heavy with mockery, betrayed him to be Valorian. Probably from the North Wilds, she thought wryly.

Her stomach had grumbled hopefully at the mention of a meal, but he had no food with him. He had a pitcher in his hand, however, and Jocelyn was more than ready to take what she could get.

"I'd bring you food, but how you'd eat it with that in your mouth I couldn't say," grinned the man, obviously delighted with her helplessness. "But I thought you might be thirsty."

Jocelyn glared at him, but she was in fact so thirsty that she didn't protest when he tipped the pitcher up and poured water into her face. She coughed and spluttered, but enough of the liquid made it past her gag to soothe her dry throat. The man guffawed at the sight, but she refused to let him rattle her. When he turned to leave, she struggled to her feet, grunting for his attention.

He turned around, raising an eyebrow at her. "Sad to see me leave, darlin'?" he asked with a jeer. "I'm not surprised." He sauntered back toward her, leaning into her face. "I do have a way with the ladies."

His breath was foul, and several teeth were missing. He ran a meaty hand down one of her arms, and if she hadn't wanted to gag before, she certainly would have now. But his proximity was exactly the opening she needed. In a flash, Jocelyn turned around, bringing her bound hands to the man, and plunged her dagger into his thigh.

He let out a scream of rage and pain, and Jocelyn didn't even pause to retrieve the blade. Forcing her flaming muscles to move, she ran for the open door, emerging into the glowing light of a summer twilight. She was surprised it was so late in the day, but she didn't pause to think about it. A swift glance back showed she had indeed been held in a vegetable cellar. It wasn't connected to any building, but not far away stood a simple farmhouse, to which it must belong.

Any hope she had that the owners of the farm might be unaware of the goings on in their yard, and might come to her aid, was dashed when three thickset men emerged from the building, alerted by their comrade's shout.

Jocelyn took off sprinting, moving as quickly as she could manage. She could only imagine what a picture she presented. Half drenched from the water, collapsed curls flying wildly, hands bound behind her back, glorious ballgown disheveled. But there was no one to observe the sight, no one to help her. She raced down a dirt track, the main road from which it ran visible a little way ahead.

A shout told her the men were gaining on her, and she pushed herself faster, her muscles screaming. She had almost reached the main road when, to her horror, a group of men hurried off it, starting up the dirt track to the farm. She skidded to a halt, and they froze at the sight of her.

"What's the prisoner doing out?" one of them roared, and any slim hope that they weren't part of the plot disappeared. She tried uselessly to dodge as they raced toward her. The two groups of men converged on her, rough arms seizing her shoulders. She bit back a scream as someone grabbed her burned hands and pain lanced through her body.

"Get her inside!" yelled one of the newcomers. "This is a disaster! The prince is coming, with his blasted knights."

"What?" yelped one of the men from the original group, his eyes going wide. "We need to get her out of sight, now!"

Jocelyn's heart soared and flopped at the same time. She struggled against her captors with all her might, determined to stall her removal as long as possible in the hope the rescue party would reach them before she was once again hidden away.

It was a relief that the Valorian royals had realized she'd

been taken and hadn't run away again. And of course she wanted Prince Ormond to get there in time. Of course she did. She had no desire to go back in that vegetable cellar. But still... the only thing more awful and humiliating than being outmaneuvered and captured by Lucy's evil uncle was being rescued from that uncle like a damsel in distress by none other than the handsome prince. The handsome prince whom she'd just decided to reject. She grimaced even as she wrestled with the men.

She heard the sound of pounding hooves a second before the men did. She turned her head hopefully toward it, but at that moment a cry of fury drew her attention back in the other direction.

The man she had stabbed was limping toward her, unaware of the approaching rescue, and clearly enraged beyond the point of reason. The other men shouted to him, but he ignored them, his eyes trained on Jocelyn.

"You little hussy," he growled as he got close. "You'll pay for that."

He raised his arm. Jocelyn, held by many captors, was powerless to evade his hand as he dealt her a ringing slap to her face. Her head snapped to the side. There was a tinny sound in her ears, but she was sure she could hear hoof beats somewhere behind it. All of a sudden, cries of terror went up all around her, and she found herself released as the men fled. She looked around, dazed, for the one who had slapped her, and stumbled back a step at the sight of his lifeless body stretched before her on the ground, an arrow through the heart.

She turned as if in a dream toward the hoof beats that were now upon her. She braced herself for the awkward explanations Prince Ormond was sure to require, but the sight before her shocked her out of all thought of speech.

Because it wasn't Prince Ormond who was leading the

knights, dressed in Valoria's royal purple and silver. It wasn't Prince Ormond who was stowing his bow and unsheathing his sword in one fluid motion, the wrath of an avenging god on his face.

It was Kincaid.

CHAPTER THIRTY-EIGHT

"Pursue them," Kincaid ordered curtly.

The knights behind him urged their mounts forward to chase down the fleeing men, with the exception of two who flanked their leader as he dismounted.

Kincaid reached Jocelyn in three quick strides. She could only stare at him as he cut her bonds efficiently with his sword, then ripped the gag from her mouth.

"Are you all right, Your Highness?" he asked tightly, his eyes scanning her body for signs of injury.

She just blinked. None of her training in poise and etiquette could prevent her from gaping open-mouthed.

"Your Highness?" interrupted one of the knights who had stayed. Jocelyn looked up at him, but he was clearly speaking to Kincaid. Her head swam, and for a moment she was unsure of her balance. "Would you like us to—"

"Secure the farmhouse, then go and assist the others," Kincaid interrupted curtly, his steadying hand grasping Jocelyn's arm as she swayed. "There is no threat to me. I will take Princess Jocelyn to the building to rest, and we will await the knights there."

"Very good, Your Highness."

The two knights spurred their horses toward the farmhouse. Kincaid and Jocelyn stood, not speaking, his hand still supporting her arm, while the men searched the building. When they announced it empty and secure, Kincaid dismissed them with a curt nod, and they remounted, taking off after the rest of the group.

Kincaid didn't speak a word, just led Jocelyn firmly toward the small building. She stumbled several times, sore and weary beyond belief, but his strong hand kept her from falling.

She felt like she was in a dream, confronted with this stern, unfamiliar Kincaid who had still not looked her in the eye. Could he really be a prince? The men had called him Your Highness, but she still wasn't sure she could believe it. Had she fallen asleep in the cellar, into a very strange, very realistic dream?

But the moment they passed through the doors into the farmhouse, away from any observing eyes, Kincaid's stiffness fell away. The door had barely closed behind them when he pulled her into his arms, drawing a deep shuddering breath.

"Jocelyn," he choked out. "Jocelyn, my darling. Tell me you're all right."

She melted against him, not caring about the ache in her muscles awoken by the tightness of his arms around her. She let out a strangled sob of joy and relief, and buried her face in his chest.

"Jocelyn," he said again, his voice a whisper. "I was so afraid we'd be too late. When that...that *animal* slapped you..." He growled. "That death was too good for him." He drew back, looking intently into her eyes. "Are you really all right? Where's Lord Randall? What happened?"

"Slow down," said Jocelyn faintly, extending a hand to stop

his flow of words. She didn't know if it was relief or fatigue, but she could barely stay on her feet.

Kincaid let out a sudden hiss, distracted from the conversation as he caught her hand in his. "What happened?" His eyes darkened. "What did they do to you?"

Jocelyn followed his gaze and grimaced. Her wrists were red and raw from the bindings, and the bandages had been pulled partially off her hands. The still-healing burns were clearly visible on her palms, and they stung even under Kincaid's gentle touch.

"They bound my wrists," she said matter-of-factly, "but the burns were my own doing."

"What do you mean?" Kincaid frowned.

"We can talk about that later," Jocelyn said sternly. "I think you have some explaining to do first, *Your Highness*."

"Oh." Kincaid looked sheepish. "That."

"Yes, that," said Jocelyn, taking a step back from him. "Kincaid, are you really a prince?"

He sighed. "Yes."

"Of Valoria?"

"Yes, obviously."

Jocelyn spread her hands out in appeal. "Why would you keep that from me?"

"You hid your identity in Montego," said Kincaid quickly, but his sheepish expression returned as Jocelyn raised an eyebrow. "I know, I should have told you later, once you admitted who you were. But the longer I went, the more impossible it seemed to bring it up. Besides, I liked being just Kincaid. I doubt you would have said or done half the things you did if you'd known who I was."

Jocelyn sighed, thinking of her nerves about impressing the Valorian royal family. "You're probably right."

"Did you really not know?"

"Of course I didn't!" protested Jocelyn. "I had no idea."

"Huh." Kincaid looked faintly amused. "Sometimes I wondered if you were just playing along. You really didn't know there's a second son in my family? A prince called Kincaid? I knew your name and your brother's name long before we ever met."

Jocelyn shrugged, embarrassed. "I can't say I took much interest in Valoria before the king and queen's—your parents'—invitation. I'm sure I'd heard the names sometime, but they didn't stick. Besides, that's no reason to assume you were the prince! Isn't Kincaid a common name in Valoria?"

"It is now," said Kincaid humorously. "For the last twenty-one years, to be precise. Doesn't it work the same way in Kyona?"

Jocelyn smiled. "Yes, it does." She had lost count of the number of times she had been presented with a baby or little girl named Jocelyn, with the expectation that she would be especially delighted to be the namesake of the random child. And sometimes it seemed like every second boy in the Kyonan countryside was called Eamon.

"So Ormond is your brother," Jocelyn said slowly.

"Yes," said Kincaid, sounding anxious. "And like I said, he's not especially handsome, is he?"

Jocelyn just smiled, not willing to grace the question with a response.

"How were you wandering around the mountains without a care in the world, Kincaid?" she asked instead. "No wonder I didn't guess you were a prince."

He sighed, running a hand through his auburn hair. It was windswept, as if he had ridden hard to find her. "It was a concession," he admitted. "An unusual one. I begged my parents to let me have one summer of freedom before I followed Ormond's example in settling down, and they agreed in light of the circumstances."

"What circumstances?"

He grimaced apologetically at her. "The horrifying prospect of an entire summer of mind numbing galas and formalities and speeches to honor our royal guest."

Jocelyn tried to look offended, but she couldn't hold the expression for long. A giggle escaped her, and Kincaid's familiar, impossibly attractive grin resurfaced.

"You looked so astonished when I rode up. Are you telling me you still didn't know? My family didn't mention me when you were with them in Bryford?"

She shrugged, amused by the note of outrage in his voice. "No one mentioned you. I wasn't there for very long, and I guess I didn't ask."

"Humph," Kincaid snorted, unimpressed. He sent her a wry glance. "The trials of being the spare instead of the heir, right? Expendable."

Jocelyn shook her head slowly, and not just because she seriously doubted anyone would consider Kincaid expendable. It was surreal to have Kincaid joking with her about how they were both the second-born in their kingdoms' royal families.

"I just can't get over the fact you're a prince," she said. "And that you didn't tell me."

"I truly did intend to tell you eventually," Kincaid assured her seriously. "I was just waiting for the right moment."

"And..." It was suddenly hard to meet his eyes. "And when I basically turned you down for not being a prince, that wasn't the right moment?"

Kincaid took one of her hands in his again, holding it gently, palm up, so as not to touch the burns. He traced a finger along the side of her hand, not meeting her gaze.

"Maybe I should have told you then. If you had said you wanted to be with me, but you didn't think your parents would approve of you marrying a vagabond, I would have told you in a heartbeat. But that's not what you said. You were the one who wasn't willing to marry me without the position." He looked up into her eyes, his smile twisting painfully. "Can you blame me for wanting you to choose me, for my own sake?"

"No," said Jocelyn quietly. "I don't blame you at all."

"Plus," Kincaid pushed on, "I was terrified it wouldn't be enough. I didn't understand your absurd self-imposed martyrdom at all. For all I knew, even knowing I was a prince, you might still have considered it your duty to marry the heir." He shuddered. "The very idea of you marrying Ormond, of seeing you at every meal, walking the same halls as you for the rest of my life, knowing you were only there because you were my brother's wife..."

He squeezed his eyes shut. "It's been ripping me apart, Jocelyn. I realized pretty early on that I didn't want you to marry Ormond. But it wasn't until that idiot Eric started fawning over you, and I found myself behaving like a jealous fool, that I realized just what flavor of hell my life would become if you did."

Jocelyn smiled, deciding not to comment on the unjust description of Eric. "Is that why you were such a bear the whole time we were in Arinton?"

"It was mostly that," Kincaid said. "Plus I was worried about being recognized from the moment they started talking about summoning the local lord. I got lucky that he was in Bryford at the time. He would certainly have known who I was."

Jocelyn gave him a look. "So you were actively trying to carry on the deception." He didn't try to deny it, and she rolled her eyes. But she wasn't mad, not really. She'd already forgiven him, and she had a feeling he knew it.

She reached out a tentative hand, tracing the silver embroidery on Kincaid's purple tunic. She could still hardly believe the sight of him. He was even more devastatingly handsome in his royal attire than he had been as a wanderer. The image of him descending at the head of his knights, sword drawn and eyes blazing, was possibly the most impressive thing she had ever seen.

"You look different like this," she said softly. She met his eyes, captured by the intensity of his gaze. "I like it."

"You look different, too," Kincaid said, his voice lower than before. He smiled as he looked her up and down. "You're glorious. I like the dress."

Jocelyn made a disbelieving noise. "I'm a mess."

Abruptly, Kincaid put an arm around her waist, drawing her in so his cheek rested against her head, his mouth close to her ear. "You're perfect."

She closed her eyes, letting herself get lost for a long moment in the feel of being so near him again.

"I'm sorry I missed your birthday," Kincaid said at last. His voice was still low and throaty, and his breath tickled her ear. "I wanted to be there."

"It doesn't matter." Jocelyn smiled as she drew back to show him her arm. "I got your birthday gift."

"You got it!" he cried joyfully, touching the bracelet with feather light fingers, to avoid her injured wrists. "I didn't think you'd had time."

"Kincaid, that was a very foolish thing for you to do," she said sternly. Then her face dimpled in a smile in spite of herself. "Foolish and delightful."

He chuckled. "I tracked it down as soon as I left the east. I didn't have much to barter, but it turns out identifying myself was more effective than gold." His eyes softened as he looked at her. "I kept it on me every minute, trying to think of how to win you over. I planned to give it to you in person, of course, and if I'd known you were going to be there for your birthday gala, I would have." He rolled his eyes. "Did you know they were going to have the party even if you weren't there yet? Ridiculous."

Jocelyn hid a smile. Kincaid's dislike of such events shouldn't surprise her, but she still found it amusing.

"But I was on patrol with my squadron when you arrived, and I didn't hear anything about it. We weren't due to return until late, and my parents were willing to let me get away with missing the gala, since you weren't expected to be there. But then one of the knights rode out to join us, having been delayed by a personal matter, and he told us about your dramatic arrival."

He flashed her a grin. "I like your style, by the way. I was very tempted to ride straight for Bryford, but the patrol wasn't complete, and that would mean leaving my squadron to finish it without me." He gave her a rueful look. "And I'm making an effort to be more responsible these days."

She gave him a smile that was more a grimace at the reminder of their disastrous training session.

"I intended to be back in time to claim the last dance at least," Kincaid said, again reaching out to touch the bracelet. "And to face whatever wrath you might unleash on me. I assumed my family would have alerted you to my existence and you would have put the pieces together by then."

"So how did the bracelet get to my room?" Jocelyn asked, confused.

Kincaid looked a little sheepish. "I couldn't leave my squadron, but I had a squire return to Bryford immediately with my token, under strict instructions to have a maid leave it in your room." His eyes met hers in appeal. "I just couldn't bear the idea of you sitting next to Ormond, dancing with him, looking to everyone like his chosen partner, without some reminder that I exist."

"You think I needed a reminder?" asked Jocelyn, amused. She touched his chin lightly, holding his gaze with her own. "You didn't need to be actually in the room for you to be all I could see wherever I looked." She looked down, her cheeks suddenly heating. "I didn't find the bracelet until after I left the gala. But it certainly did its job. One look at it, and I suddenly knew I couldn't do it. I couldn't marry Ormond, not when you were out there somewhere."

"Truly, Jocelyn?" Kincaid sounded amazed. "Do you mean that?"

She nodded, still not looking him in the eye. "I'd already chosen you, Kincaid, before I found out who you are. I just hadn't had the chance to tell you. That is," she looked up self-consciously, "if you still want me."

"If I still want you?" he repeated, incredulous. "If I still want you?" His arms tightened around her for a moment, his eyes blazing. Then all of a sudden his lips were on hers, answering her more effectively than words ever could. She clung to him, her exhaustion making her knees go weak like some simpering damsel.

Kincaid didn't seem to mind, just pulling her so tightly against his chest that she was lifted almost off her feet. She surrendered herself to the feeling, and soon his strong arms were all that was holding her up as she returned his kiss, tears of relief and release mingling with their embrace. Their kiss slowed, became gentler, but neither seemed quite willing to end it. Jocelyn slid her arms around his neck, playing idly with the soft hair at its nape.

Kincaid eventually pulled away, laying his cheek on her head again. "The knights are taking a long time," he said breathlessly. "I'm guessing Henrik is stalling them. I owe him one."

"Henrik is here?" Jocelyn asked lazily, her eyes closed as she leaned into him.

"He's one of the knights in my squadron."

"Oh." There was a moment of contented silence.

"Jocelyn," Kincaid whispered, and the intensity in his quiet voice sent a thrill through her. "Are you really all right?"

"Of course I am," she said, smiling into his tunic. "Now, anyway."

He let out a long breath. "It was torturing me, Jocelyn, the thought that you might marry Ormond anyway. But it was nothing to what I felt when I learned you were gone. Everyone seemed to think you'd just run off, because you'd looked upset when you left the gala. But I didn't believe it for a moment. I was frantic. It wasn't until late this morning that Lavvy told me what you'd said about Lord Randall, and how she hadn't been able to find him last night like you asked her to."

"Lavvy," said Jocelyn, with a laugh. "Of course. Lavinia is your sister. The one I've heard so much about." She laughed again at a sudden realization. "You're the one who sneaks her pastries when she's not allowed to stay for the galas!"

"Uh, yes, I do, sometimes," said Kincaid in bewilderment.

Jocelyn shook her head. "She mentioned it to me last night, and I thought she meant Ormond. It made me like him more."

Kincaid snorted. "Ormond sneaking Lavvy pastries? Not likely. He thinks Lavinia should be restrained half the time." He grinned. "And he's not altogether wrong. She's a handful, isn't she?"

"She is," Jocelyn chuckled. "But I like her." She grimaced. "She probably thinks I'm out of my mind, though. She came to see me after I left the gala, but I was in a daze. I'd just had another one of those strange visions about Princess Sarai, and then I saw your bracelet, and I—wait a minute!" she stared at him. "I've just realized. You're part of the Valorian royal family."

"Yes," said Kincaid cautiously.

Jocelyn laughed aloud. "Princess Sarai may not be my ancestor, but she's yours!"

"She is," said Kincaid, with a barely concealed grin. "I had a hard time pretending I didn't really know who you were talking about. I had to learn the names of every king and queen in our history as a child, and I knew perfectly well that King Germain's queen was a Kyonan princess named Sarai."

Jocelyn shook her head, trying and failing to look reproachful. "That's why you got a hint of her memories when we were in Dragoncave, and again on the island," she said. "Because her blood is in you." She laughed again at another realization. "So all that talk about having mountain blood in your family, generations back, was just a cover! Your ancestor with the mountain blood is the same as mine! Queen Jacqueline—King Cael's wife, and Princess Sarai's mother." She shook her head in amazement. "We're some kind of distant kin."

"I suppose we are," said Kincaid, looking slightly alarmed. "That doesn't count against me, does it?"

Jocelyn rolled her eyes. "Of course not. It was hundreds of years ago." She smiled up at him. "You don't have to win me over anymore, Kincaid. I'm already convinced." Her expression fell. "Although your family probably all think I'm out of my mind."

"Of course they don't!" Kincaid protested. He grinned. "Lavinia at least thinks you're great. I mean, I was ready to push her into the fishpond when she told me I would have liked you as a sister, but of course she didn't know any better." His expression grew serious. "She can be impossible sometimes, but she was nothing but helpful today. I'm forever grateful to her for being the only one to realize there might be a connection between your disappearance and your conversation with Lord Randall."

He frowned. "I don't think I've ever actually spoken to the man myself. One of the benefits of being the spare is you can get out of entertaining foreign diplomats if you're clever. But everyone else sure seems to think the world of him. But I knew if you thought he was up to something, he couldn't be all everyone thought he was. The trouble was that by then the trail wasn't fresh. All we knew was what direction he'd taken. I didn't even really know what I was looking for. I wouldn't have turned off the main road at this unremarkable farmhouse if there hadn't been such an obvious commotion."

Jocelyn shuddered at how close she had come to not being found. But there was a note of pride in her voice as she said, "I wasn't supposed to be in sight, obviously. They'd been holding me in the vegetable cellar all day, but I stabbed one of the men with my dagger, and started running."

Kincaid chuckled, his eyes warm with affection and amusement. "That's my girl."

She looked up at him, gratitude brimming in her own eyes. "I wouldn't have made it far without you, though."

His arms tightened around her again. "I would have turned the entire kingdom upside down to find you, Jocelyn. I would never have stopped looking." He scowled suddenly. "How dare they lock you in a cellar? Did they hurt you?"

She shrugged. "Not really. My wrists are sore, and my head ached from the drug they used to knock me out, but that's all." She considered for a moment. "Plus I'm hungry, of course. And my scalp is a little tender from being picked up by the hair."

"What?!" Kincaid's scowl had been getting progressively blacker as she spoke, and the last comment was too much for him. "I'll see them all hanged!"

"Honestly, it's the least of my concerns, Kincaid," said Jocelyn seriously. She rolled her shoulders stiffly. "I can't deny I'm sore all over, but that was already the case."

"What do you mean?" demanded Kincaid. "And what happened to your hands?"

"I did something, Kincaid," Jocelyn said, excitement tinging her words. "Something big. I did what you always said I should do."

"What did you do?" Kincaid sounded wary.

"I changed Elddreki," she said matter-of-factly. "Using my power, like you told me to."

"Changed him how?"

"He said he regretted his choice. He wanted to settle down and have a family of dragonlings with Raqisa, that yellow dragon, can you believe it? They were practically star-crossed lovers!" Jocelyn was becoming enthusiastic. "But they couldn't because she was mortal and he was immortal. So I changed him."

"You mean, you—"

"Made him mortal, yes."

For perhaps twenty seconds Kincaid just stared at her.

"You made an immortal dragon mortal using just your words?" he asked finally, his voice sounding strange.

Jocelyn shook her head. "It wasn't my words. It was my power. I've been learning how to use it, and it doesn't always have to be words." She paused, considering. "Although I suspect that will always be the way I find easiest. But I put my hands on him and just sort of...threw the magic."

"Jocelyn, that's...unbelievable," said Kincaid, his tone hushed. His eyes dropped to her hands, and he took one of them gently in his own. "And that's how your palms got burned."

She nodded. "I'm afraid I overextended myself a little, and I'm still paying for it. I'm not sure human bodies can handle that level of magic, really. I probably shouldn't try it again." She grimaced. "I was unconscious for a week—Elddreki and Raqisa were worried I wouldn't wake up. And I still feel a bit like I've been trampled by a cart horse. But like I said, that truly is the least of my worries right now."

Kincaid's expression was back to being horrified. "It's not the least of mine!" he protested. "Jocelyn, you could have died! It sounds like you almost did! That's not at all what I meant when I suggested you practice with your power. I meant try to change my mind about my favorite color, not kill yourself remolding mythical beasts!"

Jocelyn shrugged. "All's well that ends well," she said brightly.

"I can't believe you were unconscious for a week!" Kincaid still sounded horrified, and he clearly wasn't listening to her. "And I wasn't there! I should never have left."

"What would you have done?" Jocelyn asked, amused. "Entertain my unconscious body with fables?"

Kincaid gave her the ghost of a grin. "I would have woken the princess with true love's kiss, of course."

"I'm feeling quite sleepy now," she suggested innocently.

But before Kincaid could do more than lean toward her, the door behind him opened, and an attractive young man with a slim build and dark hair stepped through. He raised his eyebrows at the sight of Jocelyn in Kincaid's arms, and she flushed, stepping back.

There was lingering amusement in the knight's eyes as he swept her an elegant bow. "Princess Jocelyn of Kyona, I gather." His glance flicked to Kincaid. "Aren't you going to introduce me, Kincaid?"

Kincaid huffed, still looking put out about the interruption. "Jocelyn, this is Henrik."

"Ah." Jocelyn's face cleared, and she looked at the young man with increased interest. "So you're Henrik."

"Lord Henrik, Your Highness," he corrected, shooting a reproachful glance at his friend. "And I'm not sure whether to be flattered or alarmed that my fame has preceded me."

Jocelyn smiled, choosing not to enlighten him. From all Kincaid had told her, it wouldn't do the overconfident young man any harm to squirm a little.

Kincaid appeared to have already dismissed his friend from

his mind, turning back to Jocelyn. "What happened though, Jocelyn? After you left the gala last night."

"You haven't even asked her what happened yet?" protested Henrik. "What have you been doing all this time? There's only so long I can distract the whole squadron, you know."

Kincaid scowled at him. "We had a lot of catching up to do."

"Is that what you call it?" Henrik muttered, but Kincaid silenced him with a glare and turned back to Jocelyn.

"Was Lavinia right? Was it Lord Randall who took you?"

"Yes and no," said Jocelyn grimly. "His name isn't Randall, it's Wrendal. He's Lucy's uncle."

"Lucy's uncle?" Kincaid repeated, startled. "So you knew him already?"

"No," she said quickly. "I'd never seen him before last night. It's a long story, and I'll tell you," her gaze flicked momentarily to their audience of one, "later." Kincaid nodded, seeming to understand that she couldn't say what she needed to say in front of Henrik. "Suffice it to say, he's up to something, and it's not good."

"That much we'd figured out," said Kincaid darkly. He glanced at Henrik. "It's unfortunate he's not still here. Hopefully your story will be enough to convince my parents." He met Jocelyn's questioning look and grimaced. "This is my squadron, and they rode out on my command. But I'm afraid our little rescue mission wasn't exactly...sanctioned. No one else believed you hadn't left of your own free will. And everyone was offended by the very suggestion Lord Randall might have had a hand in it all."

Jocelyn nodded slowly, not surprised. Scanlon had invested some time into making a haven for himself in Bryford, it seemed. "So it was all you. You really did save my life," she said softly, meeting Kincaid's eyes. "Yet again."

His own eyes were warm as they looked at her, their expression saying all that was needed. "You must be exhausted," he said aloud. "And your injuries need attention. There'll be time enough for you to tell me the rest of the story when I have you safely back in Bryford."

"What?" said Jocelyn, startled. "I'm not going back to Bryford."

Kincaid frowned. "It will be all right, Joss, don't worry. My parents won't hold this against you, not once they understand you were abducted. And if you're worried about what they'll think about you and me, I don't think it will take much to convince them the alliance can just as easily be made through us as through you and Ormond."

"No, no, it's not that," said Jocelyn distractedly. "We don't have time to go back to Bryford. I've lingered too long as it is. Scanlon left this morning, and if I'm going to stop him, I need to go, now."

"Go where?" asked Kincaid, nonplussed.

"Kyona, of course," said Jocelyn. "I need to go home."

CHAPTER THIRTY-NINE

Jocelyn looked down at the vista below, her heart soaring for a moment in spite of her constant nagging fear that they might be too late.

Kyona.

It felt like a year she'd been gone. But there was no time to dwell on the homecoming, not if she was going to save Kyona, and Eamon, from whatever Scanlon had set in motion. Her horse fidgeted under her, seeming to feel her tension. Kynton was still so far away.

"We'll get there in time." Kincaid's confident voice reassured her, even though he couldn't possibly know for sure. "Don't worry."

She sighed. "I wonder if we should've gone through Montego after all. It was further south to the highway than I realized. We're backtracking so far."

"Don't second guess yourself now," said Kincaid firmly. "We would've reached the other side without horses if we'd gone through Montego. The southern highway was the smartest route, especially since Lord Wrendal's men had helpfully taken you halfway there."

"So helpful of them," she agreed dryly.

Kincaid glanced back over his shoulder, toward Bryford, out of sight beyond the mountains. "The rest of the knights have probably taken them back to the capital by now." He scowled. "I hope Father has them all flogged for what they did to you. At the very least."

"I'm fine, Kincaid," said Jocelyn impatiently. And she did feel better. She had been unimpressed at the time, but now she had to admit Kincaid had been right to insist she eat a proper meal from her captors' supplies before they left, and stop for a few hours of sleep along the road.

"You should've slept for longer," he said now. His eyes were worried as they rested on her. "You're still exhausted, don't try to deny it."

"I'm fine," she repeated dismissively. She turned her eyes southwest, toward Alezae. "Where's that squire?"

"I'm here, Your Highness." The boy's eager voice almost made her smile. She wished time permitted her to alert her parents to the crisis herself, but she didn't begrudge the squire his excitement about being chosen to carry the message. And there was no way she was going to sidetrack to Alezae. Scanlon already had too big a head start.

She pulled the sealed parchment from her saddlebag and handed it to him.

"Only to King Calinnae or Queen Elnora, understand?" Kincaid said sternly. "To no one else."

The boy nodded solemnly, tucking the letter inside his tunic. Then he peeled away, urging his mount to a gallop within seconds, and racing across the grassy terrain as if his life depended on it.

"He's a good kid," said Kincaid indulgently, a faint smile on his face as he watched the squire disappear. "He'll make a loyal knight."

Jocelyn hid a smile at his paternal tone, but Kincaid seemed to catch her amusement.

"It's kind of my province," he explained. "I'm involved in training the knights. I'm being trained myself, to take over as their commander one day."

"I'm sure you'll be excellent," said Jocelyn warmly.

"Enough of that." Henrik's unimpressed voice broke in on their moment as he pulled his horse up alongside Jocelyn's. "His ego doesn't need any help."

"Why are you here again, instead of taking the prisoners back to the castle with the rest of the knights?" asked Kincaid, irritated.

"Making sure you keep the line, of course," said Henrik innocently. "Now your dragon chaperone is gone, you need me around to protect the princess's reputation."

Jocelyn barely held back her snort. Somehow she didn't think anyone would consider the charming young man a suitable chaperone. But with the fate of her kingdom possibly at stake, that was the last of her concerns.

"We need to get moving," she said tersely. "It will take us days to get to Kynton."

In fact it took three days of very hard riding, by the end of which Jocelyn's nerves were frayed almost past endurance. Her ruined ballgown hung limply from her, and the supplies they had taken from Scanlon's men had almost run out, but neither of those things was what had her on edge. Even the night they spent at a less than reputable inn in Kerr, the most notorious of Kyona's cities—Kincaid's tension rising with every man who glanced too long at Jocelyn in her disheveled finery—hadn't been enough to distract her. Her mind kept running through all the possible catastrophes Scanlon could be inflicting on Eamon —or worse, inflicting on Kyona through Eamon—and she could hardly bear her own powerlessness.

To her relief, Kincaid, while astonished, hadn't hesitated to believe her account of what she had discovered about the Balenan nobleman. She was more grateful than she could say that Kincaid hadn't come much in Scanlon's way on the man's previous visit to Bryford. She thought it would have crushed her if Kincaid had been as convinced of the man's good intentions as everyone else, and as unwilling to give credit to her suspicions. But as it was, he was as horrified as she was to learn Scanlon had used forfeited dragon magic to charm the entire Valorian court, his own family included, and to spread lies and discontent regarding the freedmen.

"I knew it couldn't be coming from nowhere," Jocelyn muttered now, for at least the tenth time. "I knew someone had to be behind it. But I would never have guessed it was Aunt Scarlett's brother. I would never have believed he would dare to come to the North Lands himself. Let alone have the nerve to install himself in the castle at Bryford!"

"Speaking of castles," Kincaid said, nudging his horse up alongside hers. "Look."

She looked up, and her breath caught in her throat. They had just reached the top of a small rise, and suddenly Kynton was visible before them. The sight of her home city, the castle walls rising impressively, tall and strong and familiar, almost brought tears to her eyes.

"It's beautiful," said Kincaid, admiration clear in his voice. Jocelyn nodded, but didn't respond. This wasn't the time for sentiment.

"Come on," she said instead, spurring her horse into a canter.

They crossed the ground quickly now their destination was finally in sight. Jocelyn could tell the moment they passed through the city gates that something was wrong. There was a buzz of activity in the air, but it had a definite edge of tension to it, nothing like the happy buzz of a market bazaar, or a tournament.

A shout went up when she rode through the gates, and someone hurried forward from the guardhouse to intercept them. Jocelyn had clearly been recognized, and she pulled up impatiently. She remembered with grim humor how reluctant Kincaid had been about the idea of passing through Bryford when he was trying to keep his identity a secret.

"Your Highness!" the guard said, his wide eyes traveling from Jocelyn's tattered gown to her two companions. "Is all well?"

"Has a Balenan nobleman arrived to visit my brother at the castle?" Jocelyn asked, ignoring his question. She spoke curtly, keeping her power restrained within her with difficulty.

The man looked surprised at the authoritative question, but he replied without hesitation.

"Yes, he arrived late yesterday afternoon, Your Highness."

"We will go to the castle without delay," said Jocelyn, fear swirling within her.

"But, Your Highness, he's not—" The man's words were lost as Jocelyn spurred her horse forward. There was no time for explanations. She rode through the cobbled streets of Kynton at an unsafe speed, pedestrians shouting as they dove out of her way. Kincaid and Henrik followed close behind her.

When they reached the castle, she dismounted before her horse was fully stationary, sprinting up the castle steps without pausing to speak to the startled groom who ran forward to take her mount. The guards standing at attention at either side of the intricately carved wooden front doors were as astonished to see her as the gatekeeper had been.

"Your Highness!" Again, their eyes flicked to the two armed young men behind her, still dressed in the livery of Valoria's royal house.

"I need to speak to my brother," Jocelyn said without preamble.

"He's not here, Your Highness," one of the guards said.

"What do you mean?" she asked uneasily. "Where did he go?"

"I don't know, Your Highness."

Jocelyn growled with frustration. "Summon my father's steward," she said curtly. The guards exchanged a look, clearly thrown by her unusual conduct in issuing commands, but one of them nodded to a nearby page, who ran off.

Jocelyn strode into the entrance hall, the others behind her. As they crossed the wide space, four pages hurried past them, toward the door. They were dressed for travel and clutching parchments. Jocelyn frowned at them, her suspicions stirred.

"Wait," she said, grabbing the last one by the arm as he brushed past. He looked at her with wide, startled eyes, but when he took in her identity, he bobbed a quick bow. "What do you have there?" Jocelyn asked.

"The royal edict, Your Highness," he said nervously. "We're to take the news to each major city."

"Let me see it," she said, holding out an imperious hand. Her power leaked out slightly, and after only a moment of hesitation, the page handed it over.

Her eyes widened in horror, and her breath seemed caught in her throat as she quickly scanned the page.

"Stop the others," she shot at Kincaid and Henrik. "Bring them back immediately. Use force if you have to."

They didn't hesitate, both of them sprinting out of the entrance without a word. Jocelyn knew the risks she took in sending a prince and a knight of Valoria to forcefully stop the dissemination of a royal Kyonan edict, but the stakes were too high to worry about diplomacy.

"This is outrageous," she said to the page, her voice shaking.

She knew he had no role in the writing of the edict, but she couldn't keep the anger from her voice. She glanced down at the royal seal on the top of the parchment. "You're telling me my father approved this order?"

"No, Your Highness," said the page nervously. "The king and queen are in Alezae. It was Prince Eamon who issued the edict."

Jocelyn closed her eyes, horror overwhelming her. Of course her father would leave Eamon in charge in his absence. Why would he hesitate to entrust his royal signet ring to his only son? But even knowing of Scanlon's unnatural power, it was hard to accept Eamon could ever have been persuaded to approve such a travesty.

Sounds of a scuffle in the doorway drew her attention, and she strode forward to intercede on her companions' behalf. The guards were disputing their entry now they dragged unwilling royal pages behind them.

"Let them through," she said commandingly. "They're acting on my instructions."

The guards looked uncertain, but they let Kincaid and Henrik past. Jocelyn saw with relief that between them they had retrieved all three of the other pages.

"Is this all of you?" she asked the page whose parchment she still held. "Were there any others taking the edict throughout the kingdom?"

"Just us four, Your Highness," he said, his eyes still wide and confused. She breathed a sigh of relief and gratitude, the tension in her body loosening slightly. They had arrived not a moment too soon.

"Look at this." She thrust the parchment toward Kincaid, and he scanned it quickly, his eyes widening as he read. Henrik leaned forward to read over his shoulder.

"They were going to round up the freedmen?" Kincaid said

in a strange voice. "Put them in special camps? They were going to—"

"Brand them," Jocelyn finished, her voice hard. "All the second and third-generation freedmen were to be branded to identify them like their parents."

Kincaid looked up slowly, his eyes meeting Jocelyn's, and she knew she didn't need to explain to him what such an action would provoke across the kingdom. Scanlon had not exaggerated when he said he intended to start a civil war. And using Eamon to do it was the cruelest, cleverest stroke of all. There was no surer way to undermine the succession, to turn people against him.

And her father would never be persuaded, no matter how trustworthy the Balenan nobleman's illicit magic made him seem. She shuddered. They were one small step from a devastating fissure across the kingdom, half the people supporting her father and the other half his heir. She turned to the four pages, all watching her warily.

"This edict is a mistake. It was not my brother's intention, I guarantee it. There has been treasonous interference. You will not carry the news anywhere." She held out her hand. "All of you, give me the parchments."

"But..." The first page exchanged nervous glances with the others. "Your Highness, it's a royal edict, with the king's seal. It's our duty to deliver it as instructed."

Jocelyn barely restrained a grimace. He was right. She had no authority to revoke a royal edict, and the pages knew it as well as she did. She squared her shoulders with determination. Fortunately she had another source of authority at her disposal.

"Is my father, or mother, or brother here?" She didn't hesitate even for a moment as she threw her power out and over them.

"No, Your Highness," said the page, after again looking at his fellows uncertainly.

"Do you wish to explain to them, on their return, why you refused to obey the only member of the royal family present? Or do you think you outrank me?" She raised an eyebrow.

"Of course not, Your Highness," said one of the other pages, horrified.

"I tell you this edict is a trick by my father's enemies," she said with authority. She could almost feel the way her power accompanied her words into the minds of her hearers, breaking down their preconceptions, molding their opinions to match her own. It was a heady, dangerous feeling—and a drain on her already depleted resources—but she made no attempt to draw back. "You show your loyalty to the crown, to both my father and my brother, by giving me those parchments and returning to your normal duties."

Not one of the pages even hesitated this time. They all handed her the edicts, bowed respectfully, and wandered back into the castle, their steps slightly unsteady.

Jocelyn turned to the others, letting out a long breath of relief. Henrik was looking between the pages and the princess in astonishment, clearly surprised at their acquiescence. But Kincaid was looking straight at her, his expression fierce and his eyes blazing with such pride that a small flush rose to her cheeks.

"Well done, Jocelyn," he said quietly. Before she could respond, they were interrupted by a new arrival, as her father's steward came hurrying across the entryway.

"Princess Jocelyn," he exclaimed. "We were not expecting you." His eyes traveled from her disheveled dress to her companions. "I trust nothing is amiss in Valoria?"

"Not in Valoria, no," said Jocelyn grimly. "This is Prince Kincaid of Valoria, and Lord Henrik of the king's royal guard."

The steward bowed to Kincaid, looking startled and confused, but Jocelyn gave him no opportunity to ask any questions.

"I need to see my brother, immediately. The guards told me he isn't here. Do you know where he went?"

"Yes, Your Highness," said the steward uneasily. "He and his Balenan guest rode for Raldon less than an hour ago, with two squadrons."

"What?!" Jocelyn said, color draining from her face. "Why did they take squadrons?"

The steward swallowed nervously. "In case...in case there might be resistance, Your Highness. Raldon holds the largest, and most influential, gathering of the freedmen. It was decided it would be the best place to start the—"

Jocelyn cut him off with a hand. "Decided by whom? Was the court consulted?"

The steward nodded. "They have just now disbanded, Your Highness."

"Gather them again."

"The...the court, Your Highness?"

"Yes," said Jocelyn in a hard voice. "I want them assembled immediately. I will address them." She gave the man an appraising look. Clearly he had also been affected. "I wish you to attend also."

The steward hesitated another moment, but taking in the look in her eyes he scurried off to do as she bid. She strode for the council room, her steps impatient. They couldn't afford to spend a moment longer here than necessary, not if they were going to prevent bloodshed. They had taken two squadrons *in case* there might be resistance? Of course there would be resistance. She couldn't imagine a single former slave would allow their families to be branded without a fight.

And unless she was much mistaken, both Uncle Jonan and

Aunt Scarlett would die before they allowed their people to be rounded up and marked like livestock. Tears stung her eyes at the thought of what they would feel when they saw Eamon leading the group coming against them.

It was all she could do to stay in place as the courtiers began to file into the room, their faces showing either curiosity or indignation, depending on the person. She wanted to race straight for Raldon, but all that would achieve—even if she was successful—would be to stop the immediate conflict. If she wanted to stop the further-reaching damage threatening Kyona, she needed to fight the battle here first.

When everyone was assembled, she spoke. She had never addressed the court before, had rarely even spoken in front of most of them, but she pushed all nerves aside. Too much was at stake to think about herself.

"Have I been correctly informed that this court is aware of a squadron of guards having ridden from this castle, intent on violence toward some of my father's subjects?"

"Your Highness." Jocelyn had no difficulty recognizing the voice of Sir Sanctimonious, even before he rose to his feet. She narrowed her eyes at his indulgent tone. "This is hardly a matter for a princess. We are not accustomed to being—"

"Enough." Jocelyn cut him off mercilessly. "My parents and my brother are not at present in Kynton. I am the sole representative of the royal family, and as such it is my authority you will answer to."

Gone was the need to use subtle suggestions. Her power had never felt stronger, and she had never been more in control of it. She cast it effortlessly over her hearers, guiding their minds in the direction she chose. Confusion flickered in their eyes for only a moment before they began to nod. Whether or not her words were the truth, every person in the room believed them.

"The attack proposed against the freedmen is an act of treason, perpetrated by the Balenan nobleman who has been visiting this castle."

"Lord Randall is a good man," protested one of the nobles, and others nodded in agreement. "He is no enemy of our people. He wishes only to help Kyona successfully overcome the threat of the freedmen."

"The freedmen are not a threat," said Jocelyn, keeping her temper with an effort. "That man has imposed upon you all." She gestured to Kincaid. "This is His Royal Highness Prince Kincaid of Valoria. He can attest that the Balenan has been stirring up trouble in his kingdom, also. He has shown himself an enemy to both our kingdoms."

All eyes flicked to Kincaid, standing just behind Jocelyn with his arms crossed, and he nodded curtly. Everywhere brows were furrowed. Her power was having an effect, and people's certainty was wavering, but they weren't going to be so easily convinced on this point. Scanlon's power was strong, too, and he had cast it well. Jocelyn abandoned the topic, deciding to focus her efforts in a different direction.

"The squadrons that have ridden for Raldon are acting under false instructions. The edict to the rest of the kingdom has been revoked." She drew a breath, conveniently failing to mention she'd been the one to revoke it. "My brother has discovered the imposition, and has ridden after the troops to prevent the intended atrocity," she continued, with a total disregard for the truth.

She looked slowly and deliberately around the group, meeting their eyes unflinchingly. Many looked confused, but she could sense they were persuadable, now the barrier of Scanlon's power didn't stand in the way of the admittedly drastic change she was trying to make to their opinions.

"The freedmen are innocent in this conflict," she said, speaking clearly and confidently. "The source of the tension that has plagued us for months past is a misunderstanding, one we can overcome with time and patience."

She paused, measuring their responses with that extra sense that allowed her to monitor her power. Some part way in the back of her mind wondered if she would have mixed emotions about what she was doing once it was all over. She had never wielded her power in quite this way, and she was alarmed by its strength.

But she pushed such thoughts aside. This whole situation was as much her doing as Eamon's. The kingdom had been given her as well as her twin in their royal family. If she had just been willing to use her power in a more subtle way earlier, she might have been able to change the course of the freedman crisis—to cut it off before it properly began.

Once she would have been terrified at the very thought of what she was doing. But she realized now how right Kincaid had been that her power was not something to be afraid of. It was no more good or evil than his sword, and equally dependent on its wielder. Some part of her had always known that, and it wasn't really her power she had been afraid of, had distrusted. It was herself.

She shook off her doubts with a barely perceptible flick of her shoulders. No more.

"My companions and I will ride after Prince Eamon to assist him. In our absence, you will respect the wishes of the royal family that no measures of any kind be proposed against the freedmen, and there will be no dissemination of the revoked edict."

Her power was resting so heavily on the group now, she wondered people weren't suffocating from it. She could feel it continuing to flow out from her, and she felt slightly suffocated herself, her growing exhaustion making it hard to get enough breath to fill her lungs. She ignored the sensation, waiting until she was confident there was no sign of defiance in any eyes before she continued.

"A message has been sent to the king and queen to recall them to Kynton in light of the attempted attack. I trust Eamon and I will return soon, and I expect my parents to arrive at any time. You will answer to them for your conduct in my absence."

She didn't wait for a reply, just swept from the room, Kincaid and Henrik flanking her like bodyguards. That was more than enough diplomacy. It was time for action.

CHAPTER FORTY

Although they completed it in record time, the ride to Raldon had never felt longer. Jocelyn's heart was in her throat the whole way, trying not to think of all that could be happening at her second home. She even begrudged the minutes it had taken her to run to her own chambers and change her clothes. But as her horse galloped beneath her, she couldn't deny it was a relief to finally be out of the ruined ballgown.

They were nearing Raldon before she registered that Kincaid kept throwing concerned glances in her direction.

"What is it?" she asked, her voice curt.

"I'm concerned about you," he said frankly. "You're exhausted. That display with the court back there depleted you more than you want to admit."

"You're one to talk," said Jocelyn, raising her eyebrows.

Kincaid frowned, turning his attention forward again for a moment. He had refused to acknowledge it, but from how heavy-eyed and irritable he'd been the next morning, she was pretty sure he'd spent their night at the inn in Kerr standing guard outside the door of her room instead of sleeping in his own. He must still be feeling the effects of losing a night's sleep.

"Don't change the subject," he said briskly, turning back to her. "You need to be careful. Last time you overdid it with your power, you were unconscious for a week, remember?"

She met his eyes. "I'm going to do whatever it takes to save Kyona, Kincaid," she said evenly.

His eyes were troubled as they rested on hers, reading her determination. He turned away, but not before she caught the determination in his own gaze. She sighed. She was going to do whatever she had to in order to keep her kingdom safe, and he was going to do whatever he had to in order to keep her safe. She just hoped this day didn't end with the loss of anything either of them couldn't live without.

They heard the sounds of the chaos long before they reached the clearing, and when they finally burst through the trees, a scene of pandemonium unfolded before them.

Guards were everywhere, and Jocelyn's stomach turned at the sight of men dressed in the Kyonan royal livery that she had always associated with safety and strength rounding up children. Freedmen and other foresters alike were shouting, attempting to hold off the guards, many of them armed. The scene didn't seem to have descended to bloodshed yet, but it was surely only a matter of time.

She scanned the clearing frantically, looking for a familiar figure. All of a sudden she saw three, and her heart dropped into her stomach. She spurred her horse forward, dimly aware of Kincaid sticking close beside her.

"Stand down, Eamon." Uncle Jonan's clear voice carried across the clearing. Even from the other side of it, Jocelyn could see the angry glint in the older man's eyes.

"Tell your people to stop resisting the guards!" Eamon's voice was as familiar to Jocelyn as her own, and her heart twisted to hear it again after their separation. She could tell in an instant her twin wasn't angry like Uncle Jonan was. He spoke earnestly, pleadingly. "I don't want anyone to get hurt."

"What are you thinking, Eamon?" Aunt Scarlett was as angry as her husband, but there was also grief in her words. "How can you be supporting this? How could you do this to your own people?"

"It's for the best, Aunt Scarlett," said Eamon quickly, and it was clear he believed it. "This will help everyone know where they stand. This will help resolve the conflict."

Jocelyn had reached them by this time, and she threw herself from the saddle before her horse had fully stopped. She had looked around the clearing in vain as she rode across it—there was no sign of Scanlon, and his absence made her uneasy.

"Eamon!" she cried, seizing his arm and making him jump. "Eamon, stop!"

He turned to her in astonishment. "Joss?" For a moment he stared blankly, then he swept her into a hug, delighted amazement on his face. "Joss, you're here! You're all right! How is it possible?"

"Eamon, you have to stop this," she said frantically, pulling away and gesturing at the mayhem all around them. A number of younger freedmen had been successfully corralled and were being held in a large cart. "You can't let this happen. Call off the guards!"

"You don't understand, Jocelyn," said Eamon seriously. "I'm doing what's necessary to resolve this crisis. Everyone will thank us when it's over, and they see how well this worked."

The sincerity in his face brought tears to her eyes. Scanlon had smothered the prince with his power. She could feel it lingering on him even now, in the Balenan's absence. Apparently she wasn't the only one who had learned how to control her magic's potency.

But the sound of steel on steel pulled her out of her grief. Those whose children were being gathered for branding had reached their limit with peaceful resistance. They had to end this, and fast.

"Eamon, you've been deceived. You're not acting of your own free will, you have to listen to me!"

Eamon frowned at her. "Of course I am. This whole solution was my idea."

Jocelyn's stomach twisted. "Eamon," she said sharply. "It's a travesty. You can't think it's a good idea to round up the freedmen. To brand their children!"

"Listen to your sister, Eamon," said Aunt Scarlett firmly.

Eamon's glance flicked to the older woman, annoyed.

"I will die before I let you brand a single child," said Uncle Jonan fiercely.

He had his hand on the hilt of his sword, his eyes on Eamon, but Aunt Scarlett put a restraining hand on his arm, a warning light in her eye. Jocelyn drew a breath of relief. At least one of them was keeping her head enough to know that drawing steel on the crown prince was an action that couldn't be taken back, no matter how out of line Eamon was.

"No one needs to die," Eamon snapped, his accusing gaze on the older man. "I thought you said the mark was a badge of honor now. Why should the freedmen object to their children wearing it as they do?"

"You must see how different it is," Aunt Scarlett reasoned, but Jocelyn turned away. She could see guards drawing their weapons everywhere, and it was clear Eamon wasn't going to be convinced, not quickly enough to save lives.

She cast her eyes around, spotting a large severed stump nearby. She darted up onto it, projecting her voice and her power as strongly as she could.

"STOP!"

For a moment all activity in the clearing ceased, and all eyes turned to her. She scanned the crowd even as she spoke, looking anxiously for the Balenan lord. But he was nowhere to be seen.

"Everyone stop! The royal order is a mistake."

She looked around blindly, the drain of the power on her energy making her vision swim. Not that it mattered, because she barely used her eyesight as she instead tested the space with her extra sense, feeling the way her power was affecting the guards, changing their certainty of purpose. Men hesitated all around her, some of them starting to lower their weapons.

"Jocelyn! What are you doing?!"

She turned to look down at Eamon, standing just below her now, and she could barely stand the hurt and betrayal in his eyes.

"I'm trying to prevent a catastrophe, Eamon," she said pleadingly.

"You don't have all the facts," Eamon said, shaking his head. "Don't you think I know what I'm doing? Don't you trust me?"

He sounded genuinely hurt, and Jocelyn wanted to cry. "Of course I trust you, Eamon, but *you're* trusting the wrong person. It's *you* who doesn't have all the facts!"

"You're out of line, Jocelyn," said Eamon sternly. He turned to his waiting guards. "Proceed as instructed," he shouted, and Jocelyn could feel the certainty, the confidence, issuing from his voice. It was so potent that even she felt a strange urge to pick up a weapon and help the guards. She shook it off, but she could see that all across the clearing, the guards' confusion was disappearing, their expressions stabilizing as they turned back toward the resisting freedmen.

"But avoid bloodshed," Eamon reminded the guards in his clear, confident voice. "You see, Jocelyn," he said, still sounding hurt. "I'm doing the right thing by our people." His eyes hardened. "Unlike you."

He reached out and grabbed her arm, yanking her down from the stump unceremoniously. She let out an involuntary yelp of pain, her body still battered from previous events. Kincaid, who had stationed himself in front of the stump, let out a growl and started forward threateningly. Eamon shot him a look of confusion, but otherwise ignored the movement.

"How could you Jocelyn?" he hissed in an undertone. "How could you do such a thing?"

"How could *I*—" Jocelyn gasped, stung by the accusation in his voice, but her brother cut her off, still speaking in a barely audible hiss.

"You know how dangerous your power is. How could you unleash it like that on a crowd of people? Our own people? Since when are you so careless? Do you want to destroy Kyona?"

Tears sprang to Jocelyn's eyes, but she had no chance to respond. Kincaid appeared out of nowhere, a very ugly look on his face. It was clear he'd heard Eamon's reprimand, and her heart wrenched at the thought that Eamon's very uncharacteristic behavior was confirming all Kincaid's prejudices against her brother. Eamon was still holding Jocelyn's arm in a firm grip, and Kincaid grabbed Eamon's arm himself, yanking him free from his sister.

Eamon instantly turned, squaring up to the other young man aggressively. "Who do you think you are, Valorian? How dare you lay a hand on Kyona's crown prince?!"

"You think I'm impressed by your title?" sneered Kincaid.

"Enough, both of you," snapped Jocelyn, before things could escalate. Eamon's hand was twitching in a way that told her he was one more insult away from drawing his own sword. "Kincaid, you're not helping. Eamon, this is Prince Kincaid of Valoria. Don't do anything stupid."

Eamon looked between them, distracted for a moment. His glance fell on Henrik, who was standing nearby, looking unsure what to do. "Is that Prince Ormond, then?" he asked doubtfully.

Jocelyn followed his gaze and shook her head. "No, that's Kincaid's friend, Lord Henrik."

Eamon was still looking confused, his gaze flicking back to Kincaid. "But isn't he the wrong prince?"

"No," said Jocelyn, the tiniest hint of a smile tugging at her lips in spite of everything. "He's absolutely the right prince." Her eyes slid past her brother to see Uncle Jonan, having apparently abandoned diplomacy, running at a group of guards who were herding half a dozen children toward the cart. This was no time for storytelling.

"Eamon, you have to stop this!" she said urgently, even as Uncle Jonan fell on the men. To Jocelyn's relief, he hadn't drawn a weapon. Not that he needed one. He burst upon the group with ferocity, fists flying. In moments the guards were all unconscious on the ground, some of them having flown several feet before landing.

Jocelyn's eyes widened. She had heard Lucy talk about her father's magic artifact, and even now Jocelyn could see the apparently unremarkable gray rock thudding against Uncle Jonan's chest as he moved, suspended on a silver chain. But she had never seen it in action before. She was amazed at the familiar essence of dragon magic that surged out from the talisman as Uncle Jonan interposed himself between the children and more advancing guards. She didn't think she would have noticed the magic before, but she was so practiced at feeling for it now.

As she watched, Uncle Jonan gestured urgently to the children, and they ran toward a small building nearby. Jocelyn looked around frantically. The thought of Lucy had brought her friend forcibly to mind, and she searched the clearing in vain for her.

"Eamon," she started, hoping a new angle would get through to him, "how can you do this to Lucy? Do you think she deserves to be rounded up, to be *branded* just because of who her parents are?"

"Of course not!" Eamon looked shocked. "I would never suggest such a thing. Lucy isn't affected by this. She's not a freedman, and neither is Uncle Jonan, or Aunt Scarlett."

"Not affected?" Jocelyn repeated, futile tears again standing in her eyes. "Can't you see this will break her heart?"

For a moment Eamon looked uneasy, and Jocelyn pressed her advantage. "Eamon, you're being manipulated. Lord Wrendal—"

"Lord Randall is Kyona's closest ally," said Eamon, his expression hardening instantly. He seemed not to have noticed the difference in Jocelyn's pronunciation of the name. The Balenan had evidently not revealed his identity to Eamon. Perhaps that was why he was staying out of sight—he must know his sister, or her husband, would recognize him instantly.

Jocelyn's heart seized as she remembered what he had said about her second family. She had gotten the sense that it was just as important to him to see them all killed as it was to cause Kyona to turn on itself. She would have to abandon Eamon for the time being. She had felt Scanlon's power on him when he spoke in the nobleman's defense, and she knew he wouldn't be easily talked down on this point. She needed to warn the others while there was still time.

Ignoring Eamon's call for her to come back, she darted away through the mass of bodies, looking for Lucy, or any of her family. She spotted Aunt Scarlett through the melee, and made straight for her. Like many of the other residents of Raldon, she had her weapon in her hand. The fact that the clearing wasn't a total bloodbath was thanks only to the strictness with which the guards were following Eamon's command to avoid bloodshed. Jocelyn could only be grateful he retained enough of his normal mind to give such an order. She couldn't imagine it was part of Scanlon's instructions.

Jocelyn had to admire how skillfully Aunt Scarlett fought, her blade flashing as she incapacitated guard after guard without inflicting lasting injury on any of them. It had been a long time since she lived her double life, secretly leading Nohl's infamous slave resistance. But she had clearly kept her skills fresh in the intervening decades. The years seemed to fall away from her as she moved, and Jocelyn could almost see the older woman as a teenager, no older than she was herself.

She realized with a jolt that many of those fighting alongside Aunt Scarlett had fought with her then, as well. She strongly suspected it was only loyalty to their leader that had so far kept them from killing any of the guards. Jocelyn's heart wrenched. They had come here for peace and freedom, and now they were being treated like slaves once again.

She looked behind her, expecting to see Kincaid still close on her heels, but he wasn't there. After a moment she caught a glimpse of him through the crowd. He was still squaring up to Eamon, the two of them glaring at each other in a way that would have broken her heart if she had time for such things.

"Aunt Scarlett!" she cried as she drew close, unthinkingly distracting the older woman from her fight. Aunt Scarlett looked up at an inopportune moment, and the guard she was fighting made the most of her lapse, seizing her wrist and wrenching the blade from her hand. Before Jocelyn could even cry out, he had his arms wrapped around the slender Balenan woman, holding her in a vise-like grip.

Whether or not Aunt Scarlett could have extricated herself from the man's meaty arms, Jocelyn would never know. Because before she even made the attempt, Uncle Jonan came barreling out of nowhere, a roar of rage on his lips at the sight of the guard restraining his wife. Before the man had fully turned toward the sound, Uncle Jonan had seized him and thrown him bodily across the clearing. He hit a nearby tree with a sickening crunch, and slid limply to the ground.

The action was followed by a brief lull in their immediate surroundings. A number of guards were unconscious on the ground around them, but to Jocelyn's relief, none of them seemed to be dead. Further afield, the clearing was still mayhem. Jocelyn's throat tightened at the sight of the guards continuing to clash with Raldon's residents. This wasn't the fault of the guards. They were simply doing as their prince had instructed—and any who might have objected under normal circumstances were never going to do so under the influence of Eamon's misapplied power.

She turned back to Aunt Scarlett, who was assuring her husband impatiently that she was fine.

"Aunt Scarlett," Jocelyn started, thinking of her untimely interruption, "sorry for—"

Aunt Scarlett waved her apology away with a hand. "I don't know how you're here, Joss, but I'm certainly glad to see you. And glad you at least don't seem to be gripped by whatever madness has seized Eamon."

"It is a madness, of sorts," said Jocelyn quickly, jumping on the opportunity. "He doesn't realize it, but he's being manipulated. He's under the influence of a twisted version of dragon magic."

Both Uncle Jonan and Aunt Scarlett were watching her with creased brows, but neither protested. It was a testament both to their knowledge of Eamon as he normally was, and to their own unnatural experiences, that they didn't dismiss her claim out of hand.

"It's a long story, and there's no time to tell it now," Jocelyn pushed on. "But you're in danger, your family most of all." She looked around. "Where's Lucy?"

Lucy's parents exchanged uneasy looks.

"She and Matheus were out riding when the guards arrived," Aunt Scarlett said. "As far as I know, they still haven't returned. They would have no idea what's going on."

Jocelyn frowned, unsure whether to be relieved or anxious that Lucy and the oldest of her brothers were removed from the disastrous events at Raldon.

"Who's manipulating Eamon, Joss?" Uncle Jonan asked quickly. "Is it this Balenan nobleman we've been hearing about, the one who's apparently made himself quite at home in Kynton while your parents have been away?"

Aunt Scarlett was shaking her head. "I don't think he can really be a nobleman, whoever he is. I know I've been away from Balenol for a long time, but apparently he's at least as old as I am, so I would be sure to have come across him. I know every noble in the Balenan court. There's no Randall in Nohl."

"You know him all right," said Jocelyn grimly. "He's modified his name, presumably to avoid being connected with you. It's your brother."

"Scanlon?!" Aunt Scarlett said, over the top of Uncle Jonan's sharp intake of breath. Her eyes were wide and horrified. "Surely he wouldn't dare to come here!"

"He has dared," Jocelyn assured her. "I think there isn't much he wouldn't dare to do. He abducted me right out of the castle at Bryford and locked me in a cellar to try to stop me from intervening." She looked between the two adults, her expression serious. "And I wasn't speaking in metaphors when I said he's using warped dragon magic to control people, Eamon included. He wants to make Kyona turn on itself, in punishment for what Balenol suffered when the slaves left. But it's much more personal than that."

"This is about me," Aunt Scarlett whispered. Her eyes flew to her husband's, and Jocelyn was shaken by their expression. She'd never seen her adoptive aunt afraid before. "He's going to try to kill us." She clutched Uncle Jonan's arm. "He's going to try to kill our children, Jo. He thinks their very existence is an abomination—he basically told me so when we were in Balenol."

"He actually did tell me so," Jocelyn said grimly. "He called them your spawn, and he said only by destroying all of you would he restore the honor of his house."

There was a fire in Uncle Jonan's eyes that was just as deadly as dragon flame. "I will kill him with my bare hands before I let him lay a finger on any of our children," he said, his voice vibrating with fury. He met his wife's eyes. "Or on you." Jocelyn barely repressed a shudder at his expression. She didn't doubt either his sincerity or his capability. But it wasn't enough to silence the fear still swirling through her.

"That's all very well," she said shortly, "but that will be hard to achieve if we have no idea where he is. I was told he rode for Raldon with Eamon, but I can't see any sign of him."

Aunt Scarlett cast her eyes around quickly, as if expecting her brother to spring from behind a boulder. Her gaze alighted on a slim freedman, several years younger than her, who was standing just behind her. He had clearly been listening to their conversation, and he looked almost as furious as Uncle Jonan.

"Cody," she said abruptly. "Can you check on Miles and Benjamin?"

He nodded curtly. "I'm on it, Scar." He hurried away toward the nearby building where Uncle Jonan had previously sent the group of children he rescued from Eamon's guards.

Aunt Scarlett followed him with her eyes for a moment, before looking up at her husband. "We need to find Lucy and

Matheus," she said with determination. She turned back to Jocelyn. "And we need to end this."

Jocelyn nodded. Her very bones felt weary at the thought of what she had to do, but she didn't hesitate. "Leave Eamon to me." They both nodded, starting to turn away, but she reached out and grabbed Aunt Scarlett's arm. "And please believe me," she said pleadingly, her eyes passing between them, "this isn't Eamon. He doesn't know what he's doing."

Even in the midst of her fear for her children, Aunt Scarlett had compassion in her eyes as she nodded. Uncle Jonan's expression was steelier, and Jocelyn could see he wasn't quite so ready to forgive his best friend's son. But she had to believe she'd be able to make them understand once it was all over. Because there was no time to convince them now.

She fought her way back to where she had left Eamon and Kincaid, but there was no sign of either of them. She twisted around frantically, trying to spot her brother through the crowd of clashing people. She caught sight of him on the other side of the space, arguing with one of Aunt Scarlett's closest friends, a woman called Bonnie.

Like many others in Raldon, she had known Eamon since he was an infant, and it was clear she wasn't standing on ceremony with him. Even from a distance, Jocelyn could see the tightness in his jaw as the woman scolded him like a child, and she felt a thrill of fear. What would this unfamiliar version of Eamon do if pushed past his limit?

But before she could start toward them, she felt a hand grab her arm. She turned quickly, letting out a cry, but sagged in relief when she saw who it was.

"It's just me." Kincaid sounded apologetic. "I lost you for a moment."

"I have to get to Eamon," she said curtly, trying to ignore the way his eyes hardened at the name.

"I'll come with you," he said. It was clearly not a request.

But they had only taken a few steps toward her brother when two new figures burst into the clearing not far from where Eamon stood, leaping from their horses the moment they were free of the trees.

CHAPTER FORTY-ONE

"Lucy!" Jocelyn gasped, propelling herself forward more quickly. Lucy and Matheus stared around with wide eyes at the unprecedented assault on their home. Jocelyn was only halfway to them when her twin spotted the new arrivals, abandoning his argument with Bonnie mid-sentence to stride toward them.

"Lucy!" His familiar voice carried easily to Jocelyn's ears as she ran. "Thank goodness you're all right! Where have you been?"

He held out his arms, and Lucy fell into them for the briefest of moments before pulling back. It was the most open sign of affection Jocelyn had ever seen between them, and it made her wonder if more concrete promises had been exchanged than she was aware of.

"Eamon!" Lucy cried. "I heard the royal guard was attacking Raldon, but I could hardly believe it could be true!" She looked up into Eamon's eyes with evident relief. "But now you're here, it will be all right."

Jocelyn's heart clenched at the trust in her best friend's eyes, and it took all her strength not to turn away from the disillusionment about to unfold.

"They're not attacking, Lucy," said Eamon earnestly. "If everyone would calm down and stop acting like they're in some kind of war, everything would be fine. We're just trying to resolve the tension. It will help everyone to know where we all stand."

Lucy drew back, her horror evident in every line of her graceful form. "No." Her voice was a whisper, but Jocelyn had almost reached them now, and she could hear the words. "*You're* behind this?"

"Not you, too," said Eamon, clearly exasperated. "Why does everyone seem to think this is a catastrophe?" Neither he nor Lucy seemed to have noticed Jocelyn and Kincaid's approach.

"Someone said they were rounding everyone up, Eamon," protested Lucy. "That they're going to *brand* the children!"

"You make it sound so villainous," said Eamon, his tone impatient. "It's just a marker, to help identify everyone. I thought the freedmen were proud of who they are." He frowned at Lucy. "Why are you so worked up? Your family aren't even freedmen."

"Yes we are," she said, her voice furious despite the tears in her eyes. "They're our people." She held up her forearm, her hand clenched into a fist. "If you're going to brand anyone, I *insist* that I be first."

"Lucy," said Eamon, sounding uneasy. "Don't be difficult on this. I won't allow—"

But Lucy had suddenly seen their audience, and she cut Eamon off unceremoniously to turn to her friend.

"Joss!" She raced forward, as if to embrace her, then fell back a step. "Why are you here? We thought you were still in Valoria. There have been the wildest rumors about what you've been..." Her gaze flicked between the twins, the betrayal in her eyes wrenching Jocelyn's heart yet again. "Are you part of this, Joss? Are you—"

"No!" Jocelyn assured her. "Of course not. I'm trying to stop this." She dropped her voice. "And Eamon doesn't know what he's doing, Lucy. He's being manipulated by—"

"He seems to know exactly what he's doing to me," said Matheus in a hard voice, inserting himself into the situation. He was looking up at his former hero with an expression Jocelyn had never seen on his young face before.

"Of course I do," said Eamon shortly, glaring at Jocelyn. "Stop saying I'm being manipulated, Jocelyn."

"This is ridiculous," said Jocelyn, losing patience. Chaos still reigned all around them, and there was no more time for arguments. She stepped forward, startling Eamon when she placed a hand on his chest. Her shoulders were already sagging with exhaustion, but she wasn't going to be deterred by such a thought.

Apparently Kincaid was, however.

"Jocelyn!" His voice was sharp, and he grabbed her shoulder as he spoke. "You can't. He's too deep in it—it's too big a task, and you're already weak from everything else."

Before she could respond, a new voice cut across their conversation, relief vibrating from every syllable.

"Lucy, Matheus!" Uncle Jonan strode out of nowhere, seizing his two oldest children by one shoulder in each of his strong hands. "We were so worried he'd found you!"

"Father!" Lucy cried, melting against him much as she had done to Eamon a moment before. "What's happening?"

"You were worried who had found us?" asked Matheus, frowning.

Uncle Jonan's face and voice were grim. "Your mother's brother is behind this," he said. "Apparently he's using some kind of warped magic, but the main point is he wants to revenge himself on our family."

"Scanlon?" said Lucy and Matheus in unison, their expressions equally astonished. Lucy glanced at Jocelyn, who nodded seriously.

"Yes, he's here somewhere, although I don't know where he's hiding."

"What are you all talking about?" demanded Eamon, his expression confused. "Scanlon? Aunt Scarlett's brother? What does he have to do with anything?"

"He's Lord Randall, Eamon," said Jocelyn quickly. "He's been deceiving you." But she knew words were useless. A shutter had gone down over her brother's eyes the moment she said the nobleman's assumed name. Eamon was too far under the Balenan's magical influence to hear any criticism of him.

"That's nonsense, Joss," he said sternly. "Are you the one who's spread this wild story? Lord Randall isn't Scanlon, and he isn't after revenge."

Uncle Jonan was staring at Eamon, and Jocelyn felt a small bubble of hope inflating inside her at his expression, which was more thoughtful than angry. It seemed he could tell there was something unnatural about Eamon's response, his inability to even consider Jocelyn's words. Perhaps Uncle Jonan's experiences, not to mention his own magical talisman, had helped him to cultivate an ability to sense magic that his lineage had never given him. After all, he had entered the Dragon Realm with her parents, all those years ago.

After a moment Uncle Jonan shook his head. He clearly had a higher priority than figuring Eamon out, and Jocelyn didn't blame him.

"Lucy, Matheus, you need to get to safety. Miles and Benjy are in that building, with some of the other children. Cody is guarding the door, and you know he won't let anyone hurt you all. I need you to go in there and stay out of sight until we find Scanlon."

"No way," said Matheus flatly. "I'm not hiding away when Raldon is under attack." He drew a blade from his belt. "I'm going to help."

"Matheus," said Uncle Jonan sharply. "We're not going to argue about this. If you want to help, then help protect Lucy and your brothers."

"Your family is not in danger," said Eamon to Uncle Jonan, exasperated. "Do you think I would let anything happen to any of you?"

"Look around you, Eamon," said Uncle Jonan curtly. "Something is happening. I don't have time for your blindness." He turned to his fourteen-year-old son. "Or for your arguments." His face softened for a moment as he took in the belligerent stance of his oldest son. "It does you credit that you want to help, Matheus, but this isn't the moment. Your uncle is an evil, bloodthirsty lunatic, and he's determined to wipe our family out of existence. Unless we know you're all safe, your mother and I are doubly vulnerable."

"Why have you been teaching me to fight since I was Benjy's age if you don't want me to actually fight?" Matheus insisted, ignoring Eamon's sound of protest at Uncle Jonan's description of the man he knew as Lord Randall.

"Don't argue, Matheus," interjected Lucy unexpectedly. She threw a look at Eamon that was evidently intended to communicate disgust, but which, to Jocelyn at least, radiated heartbreak. She drew a blade of her own. "If Miles and Benjy are in danger, of course we'll keep them safe."

"Thank you, Lucy," said Uncle Jonan quickly, shepherding them both toward the building. Once satisfied they were doing as instructed, he turned back to the others.

"I don't know what's come over you," he said to Eamon,

before his gaze slid across to Kincaid, still hovering protectively next to Jocelyn. "And I don't know or care who you are." His eyes settled on Jocelyn. "But I can tell something unnatural is happening here. I haven't felt so much power in one place since…well, I won't go into that, but I will say this."

His gaze was still locked on Jocelyn. "Scarlett has often said that every time she speaks to you, it feels like you're holding back. I never really understood what she meant, but clearly I wasn't looking for the right signs. All I can say is, if you're still holding back, *don't*."

"I won't," Jocelyn promised him, her voice determined. Uncle Jonan nodded, and with a final glance toward his oldest children, who had just reached the building, he disappeared back into the melee.

Jocelyn followed his gaze. Lucy seemed to be all but dragging a protesting Matheus to the doorway. Jocelyn saw that Henrik had joined Cody in his defensive stance outside the building full of children. She was glad the Valorian knight had found something useful to do, but her heart sank as she saw the way his eyes were trained on Luciana. Even from across the clearing, she could see the blatant admiration on his face, and she had no doubt Eamon would see it too.

Sure enough, irritation seemed to radiate from Eamon, still standing beside her. Before she could say a word, he was striding off toward the building. She started after him, but Kincaid held her back with a hand on her arm.

"I know what you're intending to do Jocelyn, and it's too much. You're already dead on your feet."

"I have to, Kincaid," she said earnestly. "You heard Uncle Jonan. This isn't the time to hold back."

"That's all well and good for him to say, when he just sent his own children to safety!" Kincaid said waspishly. "What do you think *your* father would say if he was here?"

Jocelyn shuddered at the thought of her father witnessing any of what was happening in the clearing. "Let's be glad my father isn't here, and not just because he'd probably send me straight back to Kynton, surrounded by four squadrons of guards." Kincaid still looked unhappy, and she laid a hand on his arm.

"Kincaid, I know you want to protect me. But you're the one who told me there's much more I can do for my kingdom than marry a prince. You're the one who said my power is a gift." She met his eyes seriously. "I might be the only one who can stop this."

"Eamon could stop it, if he stopped being such a fool," snapped Kincaid.

Jocelyn shook her head, looking over at her twin. He had reached the building, and he seemed to be arguing with Luciana, digging himself in deeper by the second, most likely.

"He can't stop it, not by himself. Eamon needs me. I'm the other side of the coin, Kincaid. *Kyona* needs me right now. I thought stability was enough, that it was better than change. But bad things happen when there's no openness to change. Eamon can't do this without me. Scanlon has manipulated his mind too powerfully, and he needs my help to change it."

For a moment Kincaid was silent, watching her unhappily. "You're right," he said eventually. "I know you are. And it's not that I don't want you to use your power. I just wish so much didn't depend on you."

She smiled absently, too distracted to reassure him. "I'll be fine." She started across the clearing, shoving her way through the combatants, none of whom seemed to have the smallest interest in accosting her, fortunately.

She reached the others in moments, and without further ceremony, she grabbed Eamon's arm and swung him around to face her.

"What are you—?" His startled question broke off as she laid both her hands on his chest, squeezing her eyes shut in concentration.

It was both like and unlike her attempt to change Elddreki. There was no dragon fire within Eamon's core, and mercifully her healing palms encountered no new source of heat. But as before, her extra sense allowed her to find the structure she was trying to change. Elddreki's had been deep, deep within him, part of his very makeup. It had been the natural result of his decision.

But the blockage within Eamon was unnatural, ugly. The harder she pushed her mind into his, the more she could sense his own, familiar power. But there was a dark, warped power twisting around it, trying to graft itself onto the upright certainty that characterized her brother. She could sense the confidence within him, much as it had always been, but now it was all wrapped up in Scanlon's dark power. She could feel the way his certainty and the darker power were intertwined, like weeds choking a healthy plant.

But if she could change the essence of an immortal dragon, who had made his decision hundreds of years ago, then surely she could change the course of this recent twisting that had begun within her own brother.

Just the process of identifying the power within him had exhausted her scant resources, but she couldn't afford to stop now. Summoning all the energy she could find, she poured her own power into him, focusing all her effort on trying to untangle the two forces, to change the direction of Eamon's power, to return it to its original independent path.

She drew a shuddering breath, her head starting to swim as her mind tilted toward unconsciousness. Then she felt a steadying hand on her elbow, and without needing to open her eyes, she recognized Kincaid's presence. The knowledge that he was supporting her instead of trying to stop her buoyed her up, and she cast her net of power outward with renewed vigor. She could feel something inside Eamon starting to teeter, to weaken. With a gasp of triumph she homed in on the sensation.

"Jocelyn? What...what are you doing?"

Eamon sounded uncertain, more so than she had ever heard him. But he wasn't pushing her away, and that was good enough. Just as Jocelyn really started to believe the stranglehold would break, a surge of power rushed out of her brother. It felt so much like being slapped in the face that she actually fell back a step.

Her eyes flew open, to see the astonished faces of Lucy, Henrik, Cody, and Matheus in the doorway of the building, children clamoring for a view from behind them. Looking to the side, she saw Kincaid, still gripping her elbow, his expression questioning and anxious. But none of those people were who she was looking for. The power hadn't come from them any more than it had come from Eamon, although he seemed to be the medium.

"Jocelyn?" Kincaid asked, his voice low and worried. "Are you all right?"

"He's here," she gasped. "He's...I don't know how to describe it. It's like he knows what I'm trying to do, and he's fighting me."

"Who's fighting you?" Eamon sounded dazed, his expression bewildered. "What were you just doing to me?"

Jocelyn ignored him, speaking to Kincaid as she continued to scan the area. "I don't think he's far away."

"Jocelyn." Eamon's voice was stern. "I don't know what you're doing, but you need to help me stabilize this situation, not make it more volatile."

Jocelyn didn't bother to respond. She could feel Scanlon's power wrapping around Eamon's every word, sickly and strong and suffocating.

"I'll find him," said Kincaid grimly, also ignoring the Kyonan prince. He let go of Jocelyn's arm, and she swayed involuntarily, bringing him instantly back to her side.

"I'm fine," she said hastily. Kincaid looked unconvinced, but after a moment's hesitation he stepped away again, wending his way through the nearby crowd, his eyes scanning the sea of people. At a nod from the Valorian prince, Henrik joined him.

Jocelyn placed her hands back on Eamon's chest, meeting her twin's gaze. He looked unnerved by her strange behavior, but again he didn't push her away.

"Eamon," she said, casting her power out as she spoke. She was able to find the tangled mess inside him instantly this time, and she focused her waning strength on it. "Don't you trust me?"

He looked down into her eyes, confused and a little hurt. "Of course I trust you, Joss. But like I said, you don't have all the—"

"Because I trust you," she interrupted. "And this isn't you." She pushed at the twisted power inside him, trying to rip it away strand by strand. Her breath was coming in pants now, sweat running down her face, but she didn't let up. It was wavering— Eamon was wavering. His mind was becoming less stubbornly closed, more open to being changed.

"Jocelyn," he said unsteadily. "What did you say before? Why do you think I'm being manipulated?"

Tears ran down Jocelyn's cheeks, mingling with the beads of sweat. He sounded almost like himself again. But before she could answer, she was grabbed roughly from behind, strong hands yanking her away from her brother. Startled cries sounded on all sides, and she gave an involuntary yelp of pain at the force with which her arms were being gripped. Her whole form was sagging in weariness, and she longed merely to collapse, but she forced herself to keep going just a little longer, thrashing and kicking with all her limited might. It was futile— her captor continued to drag her inexorably away from her brother, and she didn't need Eamon's shocked voice to tell her who held her in his grip.

"Lord Randall! What are you doing? Let go of my sister!"

"It is noble of you to wish to shield her, Your Highness," said Scanlon, his voice sounding sincere and sorrowful. "But I must protect you, whatever your feelings. She is assaulting you with some kind of illicit magic, can you truly not feel it? I don't know how she comes to be in Kyona—when I left Valoria, she had been imprisoned for attempting to raise trouble there. And now she's brought her lies and discord here."

Jocelyn craned her neck in a fruitless attempt to look into the face of her accuser. She didn't know whether to be infuriated or contemptuous. Did he really think he could turn her twin against her so easily? Surely he knew not all siblings had as little love for each other as there was between him and his sister. Eamon would never be brought to doubt her.

But she looked back at Eamon's face, and her heart dropped into her stomach at the uncertainty there. Surely he wasn't going to turn on her!

"Lord Randall," said Eamon carefully. "I believe you must have been misinformed, or perhaps you've misunderstood."

Jocelyn breathed a sigh of relief. Eamon's uncertainty was not about her. It was about Scanlon—his initial shock at the nobleman's actions was being challenged by the trust he still held in the man. He was searching for an explanation that would fit with both his unshakable knowledge of his sister, and his unnatural determination to think well of the Balenan.

But Jocelyn had no intention of waiting around for Scanlon to figure that out and find just such an explanation. Scanlon had clearly realized she was using her power to try to free Eamon from his grip, and he seemed to think that by physically removing her, he could stop the process. But putting her hands against Eamon was just a way to focus her mind. She remembered what Elddreki had said. Her power wasn't in her touch any more than it was in her words. It was in her.

She ignored Scanlon, still oozing oily words to ensnare her brother, and again focused her energy on Eamon. Her shoulders sagged with the effort of pouring out more of her power, Scanlon's grip unintentionally helping her to stay on her feet. But Jocelyn could feel the loosening within Eamon of Scanlon's stranglehold. The process started by her initial efforts had only been expanded by Scanlon's conduct, and it was being strengthened by every ounce of power she focused into it. Eamon's own power was straining against the hold on it, reaching upward, trying to return to its upright path.

Her vision swam sickeningly, but she managed to drag her gaze up to her twin. His blue eyes, so different from the warm brown of Kincaid's, locked with hers, and she saw the moment it happened as surely as she felt it with her extra sense. The unnatural link tethering him to Scanlon snapped, and the choking tendrils fell away. The prince's mind changed course as rapidly as a sapling that had been bent down by a clinging creeper, and was suddenly released. His own familiar, potent certainty shot upright again, stretching eagerly toward the sun.

He gave a sharp and sudden inhale, and he had the look of a man emerging from deep water. He looked away from Jocelyn for a moment, taking in the scene of ongoing chaos in the clearing as if seeing it for the first time.

"What have I done?" he whispered, aghast, and even in the intensity of her relief, Jocelyn's heart broke a little at the anguish in his voice. For a moment he seemed to have forgotten about her predicament, his focus on the guards he had unleashed on the peaceful settlement.

"STOP!" he shouted commandingly.

His clear voice carried across the clearing, and everywhere, movement ceased. Guards lowered their weapons, looking to their prince uncertainly.

"Let them go!" Eamon commanded the group of guards who were watching those children already loaded into a cart. "Return them to their families *at once*! No one is to be rounded up—there has been a terrible mistake!" Jocelyn could feel the way his power laced his words, and the guards, so confused only a moment before, sprang into action in response to his certainty.

Scanlon gave a hiss of fury, reminding Eamon of his presence. The prince turned back toward the man who was still gripping Jocelyn by the shoulders. Eamon's eyes widened, then narrowed, and his sword was in his hand before Jocelyn could blink.

"Let go of my sister instantly, you snake!" he said, his voice ringing with power and certainty.

But Scanlon just laughed. "Your little act doesn't work on me, boy." Before Jocelyn knew what he was about, the Balenan had his own blade against her throat. "I should have killed your interfering little sister last time. Don't think I won't rectify my mistake if you give me the slightest provocation."

"It doesn't matter what you do to me, you cowardly dog," Jocelyn spat. "You'll never have power over him again. And you won't tear Kyona apart."

"You little hussy, how dare you speak to me like that?" Scanlon hissed. With one of his hands he kept his blade to Jocelyn's throat, but with the other he reached up and again seized her by the hair, yanking her head up so forcefully, she let out a scream of pain.

CHAPTER FORTY-TWO

Jocelyn's eyes were watering, and her vision still swam from her exertion, but she blinked rapidly at the roar of fury that answered her scream, trying to clear her sight enough to locate Kincaid. He was pushing his way through the now-milling crowd, his eyes on Scanlon, and his expression more enraged than she had ever seen it. In seconds he was alongside Eamon, his own sword drawn.

"Stop!" shouted Scanlon. "One more step, and I will slit her throat and drain every last drop of her worthless Kyonan blood." Kincaid and Eamon both paused, their expressions furious but afraid. "Won't that be a nice show for all these sweet little children?" Scanlon continued mockingly.

Following the direction of his gaze, Jocelyn saw that the children had emerged from the building now the fighting had stopped. She could see Benjy and Miles both watching her with wide, terrified eyes, one of Lucy's hands resting protectively on each of their shoulders. She couldn't bring herself to meet her best friend's eyes, too afraid of the goodbye she might see there. Matheus, meanwhile, had drawn his small blade and moved forward to stand alongside Eamon. He was glaring at his uncle with an expression of determination.

"Stay back, all of you," said Scanlon calmly. Across the other side of the clearing, Jocelyn caught a glimpse of movement, and realized Uncle Jonan and Aunt Scarlett were both rushing toward the action. She had no idea where they'd been—searching the forest for the missing Balenan most likely.

But Scanlon hadn't seen his sister or her husband. His eyes were still fixed on the three young figures before him, weapons drawn and expressions murderous.

"If you come any closer, or if you try to follow us, she dies," he said, and Jocelyn felt a chill go down her spine at the sincerity in his voice. He started to walk backward, dragging her with him. Jocelyn was so exhausted she could barely stay upright, and she stumbled as he pulled her. His blade nicked her neck, and she felt a dribble of warmth rolling down toward her chest.

Kincaid's growl ripped audibly across the space, and Jocelyn tried to keep her expression even, knowing any sign of distress from her would likely tip him over the edge. But every muscle in her body felt like it was on fire, and her scalp screamed in protest as Scanlon continued to pull her backward by the hair. It was all she could do to stay on her feet, and she couldn't help the small whimper that escaped her.

Involuntarily, her eyes flew to Kincaid's, and she could see the same terror there that she'd heard in his voice when she'd been moments from being engulfed by dragon fire. He had raced toward her then, though he must have known as well as she did how futile it was. Even now, as he took a step toward Scanlon, she remembered how she had thought that all he would achieve would be to die with her. She was suddenly filled with a terrifying certainty that he was going to throw his own life away in an attempt to save her.

"Kincaid, stay back!" she shouted, and Scanlon laughed unpleasantly in her ear.

"Wouldn't it comfort you to have your beloved join you in death, my dear?" he said, low enough only she could hear. "I can easily arrange for him to join you soon." His voice turned menacing. "You may think you've won, and I can't deny you've been more of a nuisance than I would have dreamed possible. But no matter. This little village is only the beginning. Already the edict has gone across the land. Kyona will tear itself apart, don't worry. And today, tomorrow, next year—it doesn't matter. I will destroy my traitor of a sister, and all of her half-breeds."

They had reached the trees now, and in moments Jocelyn would lose sight of Kincaid and Eamon. She looked desperately between them, trying to memorize their faces as tears welled up at her powerlessness. Even if she had energy to spare, she knew there was no point trying to influence Scanlon. He was immune to her power.

All of a sudden, just before the clearing disappeared, she felt the blade drop from her throat. Scanlon's form fell heavily to the forest floor behind her, and she swayed on the spot, unable to comprehend what was happening. With a shout, Kincaid raced forward, and she collapsed into his arms, no longer able to hold herself up. She felt unconsciousness tugging at her, but she forced it back with a supreme effort, determined to remain in the present.

"Jocelyn," Kincaid was whispering over and over, his hand running shakily down her hair. Her scalp was still tender, and she winced slightly, but she didn't tell him to stop. His touch was too comforting.

"Thank you," said Kincaid earnestly. "Thank you from the bottom of my heart. I'll never give you a hard time again."

Jocelyn turned her head slowly to see who he was talking to. Henrik was standing nearby, his sword in his hand and his expression grim. Jocelyn looked dazedly from him to the figure on the forest floor several times before she understood what had happened. She hadn't even realized the Valorian had been absent from the recent confrontation, but he must have circled behind, waiting for Scanlon to reach the trees.

"Thank you," she said as well, her voice coming out a whisper. Henrik nodded, his usually charming smile gone, and a serious expression on his face.

"I wasn't sure whether the Kyonans would want him alive for questioning, so I just knocked him out."

Jocelyn nodded vaguely, and Kincaid seemed to be barely listening. He was holding Jocelyn so tightly, she suspected he never intended to let her go again. She didn't mind.

"Joss." Her brother's shaken voice pulled her out of her semi-daze, her weary eyes searching for him. "Are you all right?"

"I'm fine," she said, trying to pull herself together. "Just exhausted."

"I'm so sorry, Jocelyn," Eamon said, his voice anguished. "I don't understand what happened. I wish I could say I didn't remember, or that I wasn't in control of my own actions. But I remember everything, and I know I was the one making those decisions. But I can't even recognize my own opinions. Things that make no sense at all now seemed perfectly clear and indisputable."

"It's all right, Eamon," she said softly. "I know how you must be feeling, but...but it's going to be all right."

"Joss!" Luciana brushed past Eamon, embracing her friend enthusiastically, if a little awkwardly, given Kincaid's arms were still around her. The Valorian made no move to let her go, so Lucy spoke around him.

"Are you all right? Oh, Joss, I thought he would kill you."

"Is that really our uncle?"

Jocelyn looked down at the new voice. Benjy had followed

his sister, Miles and Matheus not far behind, their parents still racing to catch up.

"Yes, Benjy, I think it is," said Lucy softly. "He looks like Mother, don't you think?"

"Of course not," said Benjy, with all a ten-year-old's disdain for the foolishness of grown ups. "He's a *man*."

Lucy rolled her eyes as Benjy stepped up to the inert form on the ground, leaning close to eye him appraisingly.

"His nose is crooked."

"I think that's my handiwork," said Uncle Jonan with a note of pride, arriving at last, Aunt Scarlett just behind him. "I guess I did break his nose that time."

"Don't stand so close, Benjy," said Aunt Scarlett sharply, a strange expression in her eyes as they rested on her brother's unconscious form. Jocelyn couldn't even imagine a world in which she and her brother had the kind of relationship Aunt Scarlett had with hers.

But the warning was too late. Just as Benjy looked up in response to his mother's voice, the still form of Scanlon suddenly burst into motion. Startled cries rang around the group, but everyone who had started forward suddenly stopped dead as the nobleman pressed the tip of his blade into Benjy's throat. Henrik had removed his sword, but Scanlon must have had a dagger hidden somewhere on his person.

Jocelyn felt Kincaid's arms, still encircling her, harden with fury. She felt numb with horror, and she was so weak she didn't think she could move her limbs even if she'd had any idea what to do with them. But her mind was sharp again, focused on the terrifying sight of Benjy's pale face, wide eyed with shock.

"Scanlon, stop!" Aunt Scarlett's anguished scream was worse than any sound Jocelyn had ever heard. "Let him go!"

"I don't think so, sister," said Scanlon, a very ugly look in his eye. "Ah, ah, ah," he tsked, his eyes sliding across to Uncle Jonan, who had taken a step forward. "Don't do anything rash, now, Kyonan. I know you were always...impulsive, but surely you've mellowed in your old age." Uncle Jonan paused, his eyes blazing with such fire that Jocelyn wondered Scanlon didn't quail before it.

But the nobleman seemed instead to be amused by the anguish of his sister and brother-in-law. He looked between them with a mocking smile. "Your youngest mongrel, is he?" he sneered, giving Benjy a little shake. His eyes settled on Aunt Scarlett. "Well, that's quite appropriate. I swore a long time ago that I would annihilate your brood of half-breeds, and it's not fair that the youngest always has to go last, is it Scarlett?"

Aunt Scarlett was trembling, her face drained of color, but Uncle Jonan was growing more furious by the second. Jocelyn could see his hand clenched on his sword, and knew he was longing to run the blade through the evil heart before him just as he had done many years ago to the former Lord Wrendal, when Aunt Scarlett's father had been about to kill his own daughter.

But a sword was no good if you couldn't get close enough to use it. Jocelyn reached her shaking arms up to Kincaid's back, patting blindly at the fabric of his tunic. But he was no longer wearing the bow he had used to kill the man who had slapped her.

"Benjy." Luciana's voice had only a slight quiver, and her expression was steady. Every eye flicked to her, but she kept her gaze trained on her youngest brother. "Benjy, just like Master Tanner."

The words made no sense to Jocelyn, but she saw the flicker of understanding that lit Benjy's eyes the moment before he moved. Then his skinny little arm flashed backward with surprising speed, his elbow connecting with his uncle's stomach.

The Balenan was taken completely by surprise, his grip loosening as he grunted in pain.

Benjy didn't waste the opening. He ducked down the moment Scanlon's blade wasn't flush against his throat, attempting to dart out of reach. But Scanlon was too quick. He reached out with lightning speed, gripping the boy by the arm.

"Not so fast, you little—"

The insult was destined to remain unfinished. Jocelyn saw a flash of silver pass through the air, then she found herself staring, dumbfounded, at the sight of Scanlon once again on the forest floor. This time his eyes were open and staring, and blood was pooling from the dagger buried in his heart.

Her eyes passed in shock to Lucy. Her friend was staring at the lifeless body of her uncle with an expression Jocelyn knew she would never forget. For a long moment she couldn't even grasp that the threat was over. The only thought in her head was that Lucy—who in spite of her natural skill, didn't even spar if she could avoid it—had just thrown a knife into someone's heart and killed him on the spot. And not just anyone—her own uncle.

All of this passed through Jocelyn's head in the space of a second. She became dimly aware of people rushing toward them from the main clearing. She thought she heard Cody's voice, and Bonnie's, but she couldn't tear her eyes from her best friend's face to look. Then, in the heartbeat before anyone moved, Uncle Jonan suddenly sprang into motion. Jocelyn expected him to embrace his daughter, but instead he stepped in front of her, sweeping her behind him with one strong arm.

Aunt Scarlett raced forward to embrace Benjy, who was staring from his uncle's body to his sister. Only his gaze now fell instead on his father. All of a sudden the space was filled with people, exclaiming and crying and shouting with relief. Many pairs of eyes shot from Scanlon's body to Uncle Jonan's tall, confident form, and suddenly Jocelyn understood.

Those of them who had been right there would always know, but to everyone else, it appeared as though it had been the older man who threw the knife, not the slim teenage girl. Her pale face and trembling form would be seen as a natural response just to witnessing the events that unfolded. No one need suspect she had actually killed the man herself.

People started shaking Uncle Jonan's arm, expressing their relief and congratulating him on having neutralized the threat. He never confirmed it, but he didn't protest, either. His steady gaze moved around the group who had actually witnessed the incident, wordlessly requesting their silence. Jocelyn nodded, tears in her eyes, and she felt Kincaid do the same, Henrik following suit.

She didn't think Eamon even saw Uncle Jonan's silent demand—his eyes were riveted on Lucy. Following his gaze, Jocelyn longed to run and put her arms around her friend, who seemed frozen to the spot. But Jocelyn's limbs were no longer following her commands. Kincaid's arms were still around her, and she leaned into him, letting him take most of her weight. She was just so very weary.

Benjy had squirmed away from Aunt Scarlett, recovering enough of his usual enthusiasm to caper around the space, preening in all the attention. Still, Jocelyn noticed he kept far away from his uncle's body. Aunt Scarlett turned quickly to her daughter, putting an arm around her shoulders and speaking quietly to her.

After a prolonged moment, Eamon tore his gaze from the two women with an effort, turning his eyes to his sister.

"Jocelyn," he said, his face drained of color. "Are you sure you're all right? I don't exactly know what you did to me, but it felt strong."

"I'm fine, Eamon," she assured him. "I just overdid it with my power a little. Normally it would be fine, but I still haven't recovered from something…enormous several days ago." Eamon's gaze flicked uncertainly between her and Kincaid, and she added quickly, "Kincaid knows all about my power, Eamon, it's all right. He figured it out, and he's been helping me learn to understand it, and to use it safely."

"I didn't know your power could run out," said Eamon softly, and Jocelyn shook her head.

"I'm not sure it can. It's not my power, it's me. I guess I have a limited amount of energy, and my body can only take so much." She smiled softly up at Kincaid. "Which is why Kincaid's basically holding me up." Kincaid's arms tightened around her slightly, his face expressing his relief that it was finally over.

Jocelyn pulled her gaze away, looking back toward her brother. Eamon still looked dubious, so she decided not to mention Kincaid knew all about his power, too.

"I've missed you," she said instead, giving him a small smile. She started to pull away from Kincaid, and he released her with reluctance. She stumbled the few steps to Eamon, and he extended his arms automatically to receive her. She leaned into him, giving him a quick and relieved squeeze.

"What have I done, Jocelyn?" he whispered, too low for Kincaid to hear. "What have I done to Kyona? And how will Father ever trust me again?"

"You didn't know, Eamon," she said earnestly, pulling back to look him in the eye. "Scanlon targeted you, specifically, because he wanted his revenge on Father to be personal. He came at you when you were alone—I suspect he was the one to call our parents away."

Eamon frowned. "They heard a report that the street gangs were operating again in Alezae. That children were going missing from the dockside district, just like they did when Mother was a child."

Jocelyn shook her head, an angry glint in her eye. "That sounds like Scanlon to me. It wouldn't have taken much research for him to discover that such a report would be guaranteed to take Father to Alezae immediately, and that Mother would insist on accompanying him." She looked at her brother, her eyes serious. "He orchestrated the whole thing, Eamon, I'm sure of it. And then he doused you with his power before you knew what was happening."

"And I was taken in, like a fool," said Eamon bitterly. He let go of her, covering his face in his hands, and she swayed slightly before regaining her balance. He lowered his hands, meeting her eyes. "Was there really some kind of dragon magic involved?"

Jocelyn nodded. "And ours is definitely dragon magic, too, Eamon. I met Elddreki—the dragon from Father's stories. We traveled together, and he knew instantly that I had some kind of dragon power in me."

Eamon shook his head slowly. "You were right," he said hollowly, but it was clear his mind was still caught up on Scanlon's betrayal. "And it makes sense, in a way." His voice was quiet, talking more to himself than his sister. "I think it was the very familiarity of him that drew me in. It felt like he was akin to me, somehow."

"But his was a warped power, Eamon, and ours isn't," said Jocelyn earnestly. She laid a hand on his arm. "Don't be too hard on yourself. His power was strong, and you were hardly the only one taken in by it. Most of the court at Bryford worship him."

"*You* saw straight through him," said Eamon, his voice full of bitter self-reproach.

"Not at first," she said quickly. "At first I wanted to trust him, too. But I've had so much practice lately at recognizing and controlling this type of power. Once I realized what it was, it was all I could see every time he opened his mouth. And then the rest of the pieces fell into place." She squeezed his arm. "There's a lot of information you don't have, Eamon. This isn't your fault."

He shook his head. "It's worse than you know, Joss." His voice was anguished. "I'm grateful—so grateful—for what you did here today. For me, and for Raldon. But it's not enough to prevent the disaster I've unleashed on our kingdom." He squeezed his eyes shut, as if it was difficult to confess it, even to his twin. "Before I rode for Raldon, I sent an edict out across the kingdom."

"No you didn't," said Jocelyn quickly. "I intercepted the pages, all of them, on the way out of the castle. The edict didn't go out."

"What?" Eamon's eyes flew open, their expression startled. Kincaid had approached, winding one supporting arm around Jocelyn's waist, but her brother ignored him, his eyes fixed on Jocelyn. "Are you sure?"

She nodded. "Very sure."

"But..." Eamon hesitated. "I used Father's signet ring. The edict was binding. How did you convince them to..." He trailed off, as if suddenly realizing the answer to his own question.

Jocelyn nodded, and he looked both impressed and a little alarmed. He let out a long breath. "That's an incredible relief." He eyed his sister appraisingly. "Again, I'm eternally grateful. But maybe you shouldn't make a habit of using your power to override royal edicts."

She chuckled. "I wasn't planning on it."

Eamon's face instantly became troubled again. "The situation is not as drastic as I thought, if the edict didn't go out. But it's still going to be a devastating rift. The court approved the order." His eyes met hers, again anguished. "They know I rode here, and what I was intending."

"I've spoken to the court," said Jocelyn matter-of-factly. "They know this was a plot by our enemies, and the edict has been revoked."

Eamon shook his head. "It's not that simple, Joss. They agreed to the proposal." Shame again marred his features. "I convinced them to agree, with my words."

"And I changed their minds with my words," said Jocelyn, a hint of amusement in her voice. "Although..." She cocked her head to one side. "The power isn't actually in our words, Eamon, it's in *us*." She felt a surge of energy returning at the thought of how much she could teach her twin. "I have so much to tell you, Eamon. You won't believe all the things I've learned. You won't believe where I've *been*." But a quick glance around reminded her it was hardly the time.

"But for the moment," she hurried on, "just trust me that the court has been...persuaded. They believe the whole proposal was a plot against us—which, let's be honest, it was—and you rode out to Raldon for the express purpose of stopping it."

Eamon looked astonished. "You really have been busy!" He shook his head, and Jocelyn's heart was wrenched by the shame still spread across his face. "You came to my rescue in the nick of time, Joss, and that version of events is more than I deserve."

"No it's not," she said firmly. "This was Scanlon's fault, Eamon, not yours. And we stopped him. There's no harm done."

But she knew the words weren't true, even as she said them. Her gaze was drawn to Lucy, who was still visibly shaken. The terrible burden Lucy would carry forever was probably the most heartbreaking consequence of the whole plot. Jocelyn realized Eamon's gaze was focused in the same direction, and she gave him a nudge.

"Go on."

He hesitated for a moment, looking at her with an expression she found difficult to read. Then he strode away toward Lucy, where she stood near the door of the small building.

Although Jocelyn was too far away to hear their words, there was no mistaking the apology in Eamon's eyes, or the pleading way he reached out a hand toward Lucy. And there was equally no mistaking the coldness with which she turned away. Jocelyn's heart twisted at Eamon's posture as Lucy walked away from him. She had never seen her twin look so lost.

"Will she forgive him, do you think?" Kincaid asked quietly, clearly having watched the interaction as well. "Given time?"

"I hope so," Jocelyn whispered.

"Joss." She turned quickly to see Uncle Jonan. He didn't appear to have witnessed the interaction between his daughter and Eamon, and his face was light with relief. "Thank you. I think it's safe to say you saved the day."

"You're exaggerating, Uncle Jo," said Jocelyn with a faint smile.

"Nonsense," he said brightly. He turned to Kincaid. "So who are you, then, with your arm around our Joss so shamelessly?"

The humor was clear in his words, and Kincaid grinned responsively. "I'm the charming prince, come to sweep the princess away, of course." He extended a hand toward Uncle Jonan. "I'm Kincaid, sir, and I'm honored to meet you."

Uncle Jonan ignored the hand, instead grasping Kincaid's arm in the traditional Kyonan greeting. But there was a slight frown on his face. "Kincaid, is it? Why is that name not familiar?"

"I'm the wrong prince," Kincaid admitted with a chuckle. "Everyone was expecting Jocelyn to get stuck with my older brother, Crown Prince Ormond. But he's such a dull dog I couldn't let her do it, not once I saw how much fire she has in her."

Uncle Jonan laughed aloud. "I like you," he announced. He grinned at Jocelyn. "So you fell for the wrong brother, did you, Joss? Well, well." He sounded indulgent. "I never take much interest in court intrigue when I can avoid it, but surely one prince is as good as another as far as all the sticklers are concerned." He glanced away from them around the clearing, and his expression grew serious for a moment. "I don't know what the court will make of all this. I don't even know how to explain it all to Cal when he gets back."

"Let me do that, Uncle Jonan," said Jocelyn quickly. "There's a lot I need to tell him and Mother. And I expect them in Kynton imminently. I sent a message to them in Alezae as soon as I crossed back into Kyona."

"Is that right?" Uncle Jonan looked thoughtful for a moment. "In that case, I think I'll head to Kynton as soon as this mess is cleared up." His gaze fell on Eamon. "I'm relieved your brother came out of whatever enchantment he was under. This will be hardest on him, I think."

"Yes," said Jocelyn softly.

Uncle Jonan seemed to catch the grief in her voice, because he turned back with a reassuring smile. "He's young, Joss, he'll get past this mistake." He chuckled. "He's certainly no more a fool than I was at his age."

"Be sure to tell him that," said Jocelyn dryly. "I'm sure it will make him feel much better."

CHAPTER FORTY-THREE

The ride back to Kynton was much slower, partly because Kincaid insisted Jocelyn ride in front of him on his horse rather than on her own. She didn't protest, only too ready to lean back against him and let him guide the horse. Her eyes were drooping so much that she thought she might have drifted off a few times, but Kincaid's strong arms kept her from falling.

The sense of security and belonging that washed over her as she leaned into his chest was almost as potent as dragon magic. She could hardly believe that not only was Kyona safe, but she had somehow gotten everything she wanted. The idea of waking up every day to the solid comfort of Kincaid's presence beside her made her feel almost giddy. She found her head resting against his shoulder, and she chuckled to herself at a sudden memory.

"What are you laughing about?" he asked quietly.

Jocelyn glanced around before answering, checking Eamon wasn't within hearing. He was riding a short way behind them, uncharacteristically subdued, Henrik beside him and his squadrons at his back.

"Do you remember that night in Dragoncave?"

"Do I remember it?" Kincaid sounded amused. Then his voice dropped, and his breath tickled her ear as he spoke. "I will never forget it, as long as I live." His tone sent a delicious shiver down her spine.

"It felt so scandalous," she said with a smile, "letting my arm touch your side like that. But I was mortified when I woke up. You were still asleep, so you never saw, but I had shuffled all the way over while I slept, and I had my arm halfway across you and my head on your shoulder." She snuggled it in as she spoke. "Much like this, actually."

"What?" Kincaid's arms tightened around her, and he sounded aggrieved. "I can't believe I missed it. I wish I'd woken up first."

"Not likely," said Jocelyn cheerfully. "I'm an early riser."

At that moment, the sound of thundering hooves reached them from ahead. They had almost made it to the capital, and Jocelyn sat up straighter, straining her eyes to see who was approaching from Kynton. A squadron came pounding into view, and she gave an inarticulate cry when she caught sight of the mounted figure at the front of the group.

"Is that King Calinnae?" Kincaid asked, and Jocelyn hid a smile at the slightly breathless edge to his voice. She wasn't sure if it was her father's legendary status or the fact that he had his arms wrapped around the man's daughter that made Kincaid seem nervous. Some combination of both, probably.

"Yes," she said, "that's Father." Her eyes flicked to the rider immediately beside him. "And Mother as well!" she cried joyfully. She leaned forward, and their horse seemed to respond to her enthusiasm, lengthening its stride and bearing them more swiftly to intercept the other party.

"Jocelyn!" her father cried, as soon as they were close

enough for speech. His expression was strained and anxious, but some of the tension left his face as his gaze passed from his daughter to his son and back again. "Eamon! Are you both all right?"

They all pulled up their mounts as they met in the middle, the squadrons moving seamlessly to form a loose ring around the royals and Henrik.

"We're all right, Father," Jocelyn said quickly. Her eyes passed to her mother, joy bubbling up within her at the reunion. "You got my message?"

"We did," said her mother, pulling her horse close enough to lean over and grasp Jocelyn's hand. "We left Alezae immediately."

"Is Scanlon here somewhere?" her father asked sharply. "Is everyone at Raldon safe?"

Jocelyn took a deep breath. "They're all safe. But Scanlon is dead. We have a lot to tell you." She glanced back at her brother, who had barely greeted their parents, his gaze on the ground. "But not here."

"Of course not," said the queen briskly. "We will return to the castle at once, and you can tell us all about it."

"I think Jocelyn should rest first, Your Majesties," said Kincaid firmly. "She's barely able to stay upright."

"Who are you?" asked the king, a bit aggressively, seeming to take in Kincaid's presence for the first time. His gaze flicked to Kincaid's arms, which were still stretched around Jocelyn's form in order to grasp the reins, and his eyes narrowed.

"Cal," reproved Queen Elnora, in an admonishing undertone. Jocelyn could feel Kincaid shifting nervously, and she could barely restrain a grin.

"This is Prince Kincaid," said Jocelyn quickly. "And that's Lord Henrik. They've been great friends to our kingdom today.

But I don't need to rest. I mean," she amended, "I do, but it can wait. There's so much I need to say first."

"We were told at the castle that someone had sent guards to Raldon, and that Eamon had gone to stop them, and you had followed, Jocelyn."

"That's just the story Joss spread, Father," said Eamon dully. "The truth is it's all my fault."

"No it isn't," said Jocelyn, frowning at him in spite of her relief that the seed she had planted with the court had grown so successfully.

The queen's eyes were passing between her children, her expression shrewd. "We can discuss it at home," she said firmly.

They traveled the remaining distance in silence, Kincaid suddenly holding his arms in a stiff and unnatural way, so there was as little contact as possible between him and his passenger. It was much less comfortable, but Jocelyn didn't complain. She remembered all too clearly how nervous she had felt about meeting the Valorian royals when she thought they might become her parents-in-law.

Which they would of course, she reminded herself with an internal laugh. Lavinia would get her for a sister after all. She wondered how Ormond would feel about having his prospective bride stolen away from him by his little brother. Perhaps his pride would be stung, but remembering his shocked expression when he first saw her, in all her traveling filth, she suspected that deep down he would be relieved.

She insisted on Kincaid accompanying her into her father's private receiving room, but Henrik very considerately excused himself. Jocelyn was glad. She liked the dashing knight—and she wouldn't be forgetting that he'd saved her life—but she didn't think she'd be able to speak freely to her parents in front of him.

Not that she was given much chance to speak at first, her father being unable to focus on anything but the presence of the unknown young man sitting so close beside his only daughter.

"So who are you?" he tried again the moment they were all alone in the room.

Kincaid stood, bowing very correctly to the king. "I am Prince Kincaid of Valoria, Your Majesty. And I'm honored to meet you."

"Welcome, Prince Kincaid," said the queen quickly, shooting a restraining look toward her husband. "You are the *younger* of the two Valorian princes, I believe?" Her gaze slid to her daughter, one eyebrow slightly raised. To her annoyance, Jocelyn felt herself flushing, and the sudden twinkle in her mother's eyes told her that the perceptive queen had already pieced together everything she needed to know.

"I am, Your Majesty," Kincaid confirmed.

"And how do you come to be traveling with Jocelyn?" the king asked, his tone making the question an accusation.

"He followed me when I went to meet Elddreki," Jocelyn answered for him. "After I accidentally broke the mountain people's ancient ancestral dance."

"You broke the...what?"

All three members of Jocelyn's family were staring at her with identical expressions of confusion. At least she had succeeded in distracting her father from probing too deeply into her very poorly chaperoned travels with Kincaid.

"To explain that, I need to go way further back," she said seriously. She locked eyes with her twin. "It's time, Eamon. It's way, way, way past time."

He held her gaze for a long moment before giving a tight nod. "I don't mind. It was at your request I always kept it to myself."

Jocelyn nodded. "I know. And I'm grateful you did, but I was wrong about needing to keep it so secret. I was wrong about almost everything."

"Needing to keep what a secret?" asked their mother sharply.

Jocelyn took a deep breath, looking between her parents. "There's something we should have told you a very long time ago." She glanced again at her brother. "Eamon and I were born with something...something we've never known how to explain. And I still wouldn't know if Elddreki hadn't helped me figure it out."

"So you really were with Elddreki all this time," said her father, shaking his head. "I hardly knew whether to believe it."

But her mother was not to be sidetracked. "What were you born with?" she asked. She had clearly grasped much more quickly than her husband the gravity of whatever revelation Jocelyn was about to make.

Without further encouragement, Jocelyn launched into the tale of her power, her caged existence before leaving Kynton, and her travels since she set out from home. She talked for a long time, and by the end her mind felt as weary as her body. But she persisted through her exhaustion, knowing she needed to get it all out. Eamon interjected a few times as she talked about their childhood, but he fell silent once she began her account of what had befallen her from the time she set foot in the mountains.

Her father's eyes were round with horror from the moment she described her first near miss in the town where Kincaid had caught up with her at last, and they didn't relax from then on. But Jocelyn did notice a softening in the glances the king kept throwing at Kincaid after she described him coming to her rescue. Wanting to encourage this friendlier attitude, she skated over certain parts of the story. She could feel Kincaid's eyes on her as she described Dragoncave, failing to mention that the two of them had been stranded in there overnight.

It was all she could do to keep a flush from her face, and she pushed on quickly to the part where Kincaid had run into a hail of deadly arrows to shield her with his pack. Her father looked ready to embrace the Valorian prince by this point, and she had a feeling the battle was half won. If she was changing his mind about Kincaid as much with her power as with her words, it wasn't intentional, and she found she didn't care.

Eamon's fascination with all Elddreki had revealed about the nature of their power pulled him temporarily from his dejection, and he asked a number of eager questions. Her parents were both absolutely astonished—and at least in her mother's case, more than a little amused—by her description of Elddreki's almost-tragic romance. But all of them were stunned into silence when she explained how she had used her power to change the dragon's very nature.

Her parents had been so captivated by her story they had almost seemed to move past their initial shock and distress at discovering their children had secret magic power they'd never told them about. But this revelation clearly brought it all back to the fore.

Jocelyn didn't linger over that part of the tale, uncomfortable with the looks on their faces. As soon as Scanlon entered her retelling, Eamon once again fell silent, his expression anguished. And her father became so furious at her account of her abduction and imprisonment by the Balenan lord that he seemed unable to take in anything else. But her mother continued to watch Jocelyn with an expression that told her the queen would not quickly forget the extent to which her daughter had withheld herself from her own parents. Jocelyn felt a surge of guilt at the sadness in her mother's eyes, but it was soon eclipsed by her anxiety for her brother as the story turned toward Scanlon's—and by extension Eamon's—actions in Kyona.

She was relieved that her parents accepted her story about Scanlon and his warped magic without question. Just like Uncle Jonan and Aunt Scarlett, they had enough out of the ordinary experiences of their own not to discount something just because it sounded far-fetched. And they knew their son well enough to find the idea that he would knowingly come up with such a scheme even more impossible to believe than a tale of magic.

But although they were quick to forgive Eamon, it was clear the young prince would not so easily forgive himself. Jocelyn's heart was heavy as she watched her brother's face. Lucy wasn't the only one who would carry the scars of this incident for a long time to come.

But still...Kyona was safe, Eamon's mind was his own again, Scanlon had gone where he couldn't hurt anyone ever again, and Kincaid was by her side. Considering all she had feared only a matter of hours before, it was hard not to feel elated.

"So I suppose you'll be returning to Bryford now," King Calinnae said suddenly to Kincaid. Jocelyn frowned at her father, but he wasn't looking at her, his eyes trained on the young Valorian prince. Clearly her story hadn't warmed him to Kincaid quite as completely as she'd hoped.

"Well, yes, Your Majesty," said Kincaid slowly. "I must do so soon, of course. But I would be very reluctant to leave without first..." He hesitated, glancing at Jocelyn then clearing his throat. All at once he broke into a sheepish grin.

"I think maybe I'll do best to just be upfront, Your Majesties. I know my parents implied in their invitation that they would be pleased for Jocelyn to form an attachment with my brother Ormond. But as you've heard, I met her first, quite by chance. And once I knew her, it took very little time for me to realize I would regret it forever if I didn't do my very best to convince her —and you—to take a different offer. If you're willing to enter discussions with my parents, I think you'll find they're more than open to the alliance our marriage would represent. And as for myself…" He looked at Jocelyn, and she felt heat rush through her at the warmth in his eyes. "I can promise I would treasure your daughter forever."

The queen was smiling warmly at him by the end of this speech, but King Calinnae just looked alarmed. And Eamon seemed as stunned as his father by this forthright declaration.

"I'm not sure you met entirely by chance," said Jocelyn's mother with a touch of humor.

"It truly wasn't by design that I met Jocelyn in Montego, Your Majesty," said Kincaid earnestly, but the queen just shook her head, a smile playing around her lips.

"Not by your design, maybe. But Elddreki told us once that chance is just the name humans give to any purpose they don't understand."

Kincaid chuckled. "That sounds like something he would say."

Jocelyn's father cleared his throat, his eyes still slightly narrowed as they rested on the Valorian prince. "You want to marry Jocelyn?" Apparently he was not in the mood to bond over tales of their shared dragon acquaintance.

"I do, Your Majesty," Kincaid said evenly.

"But she's only seventeen!" King Calinnae protested.

"Eighteen, Father," Jocelyn reminded him, a bit anxiously. His eyes flew to her.

"Is this what you want, Jocelyn?"

"It is," she said, coloring faintly. "Most definitely."

"But you promised to dislike everyone and everything in Valoria," her father protested.

Eamon gave a hastily choked snort of laughter, and Kincaid

looked startled by the king's announcement. But this lapse in formality told Jocelyn that her father had already accepted Kincaid, whether he realized it or not. She chuckled.

"I tried, Father, I really did. But Kincaid won me over in spite of myself." Her voice grew more serious. "When I left home, I didn't want to live in Valoria because it seemed like too big a change from everything I knew, and it frightened me. And then when I convinced myself it was my duty to marry Ormond no matter what I felt about it, I was just worrying about what the impact would be on Kyona if I made another unpolitical marriage."

She cast her mother an apologetic look. "I thought the kingdom couldn't handle the change it's seen, but it was me who couldn't handle change. I know you encouraged me to go away this summer because you wanted me to come out of myself. Well, I did, and it's mainly thanks to Kincaid. He's the one who could see from the start that my power wasn't something to be afraid of. He's the one who encouraged me to stop hiding, and the one who called me out on my fear."

"You don't have to convince me, Joss," the queen said quietly. "I could tell from the moment you greeted me that something was different, that you were free of your shackles." She nodded toward Kincaid. "And if this is the person responsible for it, he has my support."

Jocelyn's eyes were full of warmth as she looked at her mother, but she couldn't resist sending a grin Kincaid's way.

"We're clear, Kincaid. If Mother is convinced, there's no way Father can hold out much longer."

Her father sighed. "She's right, I'm afraid." He looked at his wife with an endearing mix of affection and exasperation. "No matter how stubborn I try to be, this one can always change my mind, no dragon magic required."

. . .

DESPITE HIS ADMISSION that he needed to return to Bryford imminently, it was several days before Kincaid actually allowed Henrik to pull him away. Not that Jocelyn was complaining about the delay. They had all agreed it would just be ridiculous at this point for her to attempt to resume her twice interrupted state visit to the Valorian capital, and consequently she would stay behind in Kynton when he left.

Kincaid hoped and expected to secure a formal invitation for all of the Kyonan royals in the near future, to negotiate the proposed marriage alliance in its new form. Jocelyn could hardly bear to let him go until then, because she knew it would be some time before her father would be free to leave Kynton again, after the recent upheavals. But she wanted to be there to help smooth over the near disaster that had visited them all.

After her prolonged tale, she had fallen into her own bed with exhausted relief and slept for the rest of the day and all through that night. Reunited with her comfortable suite, she had slept well every night and soon felt greatly restored. The day after her arrival, she had readily abandoned Kincaid for the entire morning when her mother sought her out for a private discussion. The two women had spent hours talking over the past, both recent and further back, with many tears and more than a little laughter.

Jocelyn had never felt so close to her mother, and she could only wonder at her own foolishness in thinking she had to withhold her secret even from her own parents. Of course it was easy to think that way now, when she knew how to control her power, and wasn't afraid it would burst destructively from her when she least expected it.

But other than that morning, Jocelyn had been shamelessly letting Kincaid monopolize her attention. On the morning of Kincaid's departure, she sought her brother out, feeling a bit guilty for having neglected him. It had been clear that Eamon was still struggling to come to terms with what he had been involved in.

"Are you going to come see Kincaid and Henrik off?" she asked, having found him skulking in a corridor with windows facing east, toward the Forest of Rune.

He drew his gaze from the distant trees with a sigh. "Yes, of course I am."

"Eamon." Jocelyn laid her hand on his arm.

She didn't need him to say it aloud to know what he was thinking about. Uncle Jonan had come to Kynton as promised the day after the incident at Raldon. He had spent a long time shut up in conversation with the king, and Jocelyn had been relieved that there seemed to be no loss of goodwill between them. Uncle Jonan had treated Jocelyn like a conquering hero, and had even greeted Eamon very kindly. But when Jocelyn had inquired after Lucy, expressing the wish that she'd come with her father, Uncle Jonan's eyes had flicked unmistakably to Eamon as he said that she'd been quite adamant that she didn't wish to visit the capital at the moment.

"She'll come around, Eamon," said Jocelyn softly now. "She saw you come out from under Scanlon's enchantment, like everyone else did. Just give her time."

He just nodded gloomily, but she could see in his eyes that he didn't believe her. And a worried part in the back of Jocelyn's mind wasn't sure she believed it herself. Not when she remembered the look in Lucy's eyes after she'd killed her uncle.

"There's something that worries me," she said absently, as her thoughts dwelt on the deceased Balenan. "Scanlon said he placed conditions on the dragon who forfeited its power to him. He made it sound like he bargained for more than just the power we know about. But he wouldn't tell me what he meant."

Eamon sighed. "He's dead now, Joss. It doesn't matter what else he bargained for. He can't make use of it anymore."

Jocelyn remained silent. She couldn't dismiss the nobleman's words quite so easily, but with no idea what had been behind them, she didn't see what she could do about it.

"Will you really be happy in Valoria, Joss?" Eamon asked suddenly. "You'll be so far away. I thought you didn't want to get married off to a Valorian prince."

Jocelyn smiled. "That was before I met Kincaid." She looked up to find Eamon frowning down at her, and she gave him a nudge. "It won't be so bad, Eamon. He's not the heir like Ormond is, so it will be much easier for us to visit Kyona regularly. We could probably spend every summer here if we wanted to. And you can come and visit us in Bryford." She shook her head, talking half to herself. "If Princess Sarai could be happy there, I certainly can."

Eamon put an arm around her shoulder. "I'm going to miss you, you know. I'll feel like half of a whole with you so far away." His voice was only half joking. "How will Kyona cope with all stability and no change?"

Jocelyn rolled her eyes. "You don't need me around to have change." She grinned. "But we certainly are a potent combination, aren't we?"

For a moment her eyes blurred, her thoughts drifting back to Princess Sarai. If she could embrace change after her harrowing experiences, Eamon surely could. Jocelyn closed her eyes, trying to recall all the details of the visions she'd seen. She was eager to search the records at Bryford for any mention of the princess's later life. Now she knew Princess Sarai had been happy in her new home instead of perpetually lonely, she no longer shied away from the thought of delving into her history. She would quite like to know more of how that previous royal couple had fared after their momentous decision to give their hearts to their marriage.

She remembered how Raqisa had seemed to think Jocelyn would be able to access Princess Sarai's memories at will. The dragon had suggested Jocelyn's power might not be enough on its own. Could she draw on Eamon's as well? The thought had barely occurred to her when her vision began to blur, and she felt herself dipping into the now-familiar mind. It wasn't as potent or as clear as before, but it was definitely there, and she found herself straining toward it.

"He's perfect, Sarai."

Sarai could hear the emotion in her husband's voice, and it brought the tears to her own eyes. She couldn't agree more. She looked down at her newborn son, her heart swelling with satisfaction. And not just because she had fulfilled her most important duty in the eyes of the court, and provided Valoria with an heir. More to the point, he was truly the most beautiful thing she had ever seen.

"He looks like you," said Sarai, smiling mistily at her husband. "I hope he'll be just like you, Germain."

Germain touched the infant's cheek, his fingers as light as a feather. "He has your eyes. He's perfect," he repeated.

"And now the succession is secure," Sarai said proudly.

"And now," Germain said, "Kyona's royal house is forever mingled with Valoria's." He pressed his lips to her forehead. "Your father's bloodline continues with you Sarai, and with this most perfect son of ours. And I am proud to be a part of it."

Sarai looked up at him, her heart in her eyes. "Just as I am proud to be a princess of Valoria."

JOCELYN INHALED SHARPLY as she returned to the corridor, Eamon's arm still around her shoulder. He didn't seem to have even noticed her moment of detachment, and she didn't tell him about it. But he was part of it, somehow. Stability and change, a potent combination. Princess Sarai's arrival in the Valorian court had certainly been a point of great change, for her new kingdom as well as for herself. But her legacy, as evidenced by Kincaid and all the rest of his family, was stability. She and Eamon would just have to each find ways to cultivate both strengths within their respective kingdoms.

Jocelyn might feel sad at the thought of one day moving away from her brother, but the wrench of parting from Kincaid, mere minutes later, was much more immediate and therefore much more acute. She made no protest as he pulled her behind his horse, making the most of the inadequate shield the animal provided between them and her watching family to press his lips briefly to hers.

"I will miss you every minute," he said sincerely, his eyes roaming over her face, as if trying to memorize her features.

Jocelyn looked up at him, trying herself to soak in every detail of his familiar, outrageously handsome face. Was it her imagination he had those same eyes, the eyes Princess Sarai had passed to her son?

"Why are you looking at me like that?" he asked, his smile coloring his voice.

She smiled back. "I was thinking about Princess Sarai," she said. "And I just realized something."

"What's that?"

She leaned up suddenly to plant a kiss on his cheek. "You have a little Kyona in you."

He grinned, wrapping his arms around her and trapping her in place. "It's my most attractive feature, some would argue."

She shook her head, smiling mischievously up at him. "No, it's not that."

"What is it, then?" he challenged.

"How much you love change, of course," she said innocently.

His arms tightened around her as he smiled down into her eyes. "I do," he said, his eyes twinkling but his words sincere. "I love her very much."

Thank you for reading *Legacy of the Curse*. I hope you enjoyed diving into the next generation of Kyonan adventurers. I would be so grateful if you would consider leaving a review on Amazon —it would really make a difference!

If you want to find out what becomes of Lucy and Eamon, as well as seeing the next adventure for Jocelyn and Kincaid, check out *Downfall of the Curse*, the fifth installment of the Kyona Chronicles, where more adventure, fantasy, mystery, and romance await.

Join up to my mailing list at deborahgracewhite.com to be kept up to date on new releases, specials, and giveaways, such as bonus chapters. You will also receive *Dragon's Sight*, an 8,000 word prequel to the series, told from Elddreki's perspective.

Again, thanks for entering the world of the Kyona Chronicles! I hope to see you back again.

ACKNOWLEDGMENTS

By the time I finished the first three installments of the Kyona Chronicles, there was no way I was closing the cover on this world without finding out what becomes of the next generation. Cal and Elnora's children grew up in court, not in obscurity, and I wanted to see how they faced the different set of challenges that would bring.

I couldn't have followed the story forward without the support of my incredible team. My fondest thanks to my husband Ray, the first to discover the stories with me, and my biggest encourager to keep going.

A massive thank you to my beta readers: Mum, Dad, Andrew, Adrian, Tamara, and Cherilyn. Thanks for investing so much time in my series! Again, extra thanks to Dad for developmental and copy editing, to Mum for line editing, and to Dad and Mel for assistance with publication and release.

Karri, the cover is perfect, as always. Rebecca, your map continues to make the world come alive.

To you, the reader, thank you for giving me the privilege of being an author.

And most importantly, to God, who gave us words, and teaches us that they have the power of life and death. Help me never to take that lightly.

ABOUT THE AUTHOR

I've been a reader since I can remember, growing up on a wide range of books, from classic literature to light-hearted romps. The love of reading has traveled with me unchanged across multiple continents, and carried me from my own childhood all the way to having children of my own.

But if reading is like looking through a window into a magical and beautiful world, beginning to write my own stories was like discovering that I could open that window and climb right out into fantasyland.

I cannot believe how privileged I am to actually be living that childhood dream and publishing my own novels. I do so from my hometown of Adelaide, Australia, where I live with my husband and our two, soon to be three, little munchkins.

I've never outgrown my love of young adult stories, and my first series, the Kyona Chronicles, is a young adult fantasy series of six installments.

Feel free to email me at deborah@deborahgracewhite.com

and introduce yourself! Or subscribe to my mailing list at deborahgracewhite.com for free giveaways, sales, and updates.